A native of Mississippi, Thomas Harris began his writing career covering crime in the United States and Mexico, and was a reporter and editor for the Associated Press in New York City. His first novel, *Black Sunday*, was published in 1975, followed by *Red Dragon* in 1981, *The Silence of the Lambs* in 1988 and *Hannibal* in 1999.

Also by Thomas Harris

BLACK SUNDAY

THE
HANNIBAL LECTER
OMNIBUS

THOMAS HARRIS

THE
HANNIBAL LECTER
OMNIBUS

Red Dragon

The Silence of the Lambs

Hannibal

William Heinemann: London

First published in the United Kingdom by
William Heinemann, 2001

1 3 5 7 9 10 8 6 4 2

The publishers thank the University of Toronto Press for permission to use
scholarly material from Anthony K. Cassell's *Dante's Fearful Art of Justice*
in Dr. Lecter's presentation to the Studiolo.

Red Dragon first published in the United Kingdom by
Bodley Head, 1982

The Silence of the Lambs first published in the United Kingdom by
William Heinemann, 1989

Hannibal first published in the United Kingdom by
William Heinemann, 1999

William Heinemann
The Random House Group Limited
20 Vauxhall Bridge Road, London, SW1V 2SA

Random House Australia (Pty) Limited
20 Alfred Street, Milsons Point, Sydney,
New South Wales 2061, Australia

Random House New Zealand Limited
18 Poland Road, Glenfield
Auckland 10, New Zealand

Random House (Pty) Limited
Endulini, 5a Jubilee Road, Parktown 2193, South Africa

The Random House Group Limited Reg. No. 954009

www.randomhouse.co.uk

A CIP catalogue record for this book
is available from the British Library

Papers used by Random House are natural, recyclable products made from
wood grown in sustainable forests. The manufacturing processes conform to
the environmental regulations of the country of origin

ISBN 0 434 00905 9

Typeset by Palimpsest Book Production Limited,
Polmont, Stirlingshire
Printed and bound in the UK by
Clays Ltd, St Ives plc

Foreword to a Fatal Interview

I WANT TO TELL you the circumstances in which I first encountered Hannibal Lecter, M.D.

In the fall of 1979, owing to an illness in my family, I returned home to the Mississippi Delta and remained there eighteen months. I was working on *Red Dragon*. My neighbor in the village of Rich kindly gave me the use of a shotgun house in the center of a vast cotton field, and there I worked, often at night.

To write a novel, you begin with what you can see and then you add what came before and what came after. Here in the village of Rich, Mississippi, working under difficult circumstances, I could see the investigator Will Graham in the home of the victim family, in the house where they all died, watching the dead family's home movies. I did not know at the time who was committing the crimes. I pushed to find out, to see what came before and what came after I went through the home, the crime scene, in the dark with Will and could see no more and no less than he could see.

Sometimes at night I would leave the lights on in my little house and walk across the flat fields. When I looked back from a distance, the house looked like a boat at sea, and all around me the vast Delta night.

I soon became acquainted with the semi-feral dogs who roamed free across the fields in what was more or less a pack. Some of them had casual arrangements with the families of farm workers, but much of the time they had to forage for themselves. In the hard winter months with the ground frozen and dry, I started giving them dog food and soon they were going through fifty pounds of dog food a week. They followed me around, and they were a lot of company—tall dogs, short ones, relatively friendly dogs and big rough dogs you could not touch. They walked with me in the fields at night and when I couldn't see them, I could hear them all around me, breathing and snuffling along in the dark. When I was working in the cabin, they waited on the front porch, and when the moon was full they would sing.

Standing baffled in the vast fields outside my cabin in the heart of the night, the sound of breathing all around me, my vision still clouded with the desk lamp, I tried to see what had happened at the crime scene. All that came to my dim sight were loomings, intimations, the occasional glow when a retina not human reflected the moon. There was no question that *something* had happened. You must understand that when you are writing a novel you are not making anything up. It's all there and you just have to find it.

Will Graham had to ask somebody, he needed some help and he knew it. He knew where he had to go, long before he let himself think about it. I knew Graham had been severely damaged in a previous case. I knew he was terribly reluctant to consult the best source he had. At the time, I myself was accruing painful memories every day, and in my evening's work I felt for Graham.

So it was with some trepidation that I accompanied him to the Baltimore State Hospital for the Criminally Insane, and there, maddeningly, before we could get down to business, we encountered the kind of fool you know from conducting your own daily business, Dr. Frederick Chilton, who delayed us for two or three interminable days.

I found that I could leave Chilton in the cabin with the lights on and look back at him from the dark, surrounded by my friends the dogs. I was invisible then, out there in the dark, the way I am invisible to my characters when I'm in a room with them and they are deciding their fates with little or no help from me.

Finished with the tedious Chilton at last, Graham and I went on to the Violent Ward and the steel door slammed shut behind us with a terrific noise.

Will Graham and I, approaching Dr. Lecter's cell. Graham was tense and I could smell fear on him. I thought Dr. Lecter was asleep and I jumped when he recognized Will Graham by scent without opening his eyes.

I was enjoying my usual immunity while working, my invisibility to Chilton and Graham and the staff, but I was not comfortable in the presence of Dr. Lecter, not sure at all that the doctor could not see me.

Like Graham, I found, and find, the scrutiny of Dr. Lecter uncomfortable, intrusive, like the humming in your thoughts when they X-ray your head. Graham's interview with Dr. Lecter went quickly, in real time at the speed of swordplay, me following it, my frantic notes spilling into the margin and over whatever surface was uppermost on my table. I was worn out when it was over—the incidental clashes and howls of an asylum rang on in my head, and on the front porch of my cabin in Rich thirteen dogs were singing, seated with their eyes closed, faces upturned to the full moon. Most of them crooned their single vowel between O and U, a few just hummed along.

I had to revisit Graham's interview with Dr. Lecter a hundred times to understand it and to get rid of the superfluous static, the jail noises, the screaming of the damned that had made some of the words hard to hear.

I still didn't know who was committing the crimes, but I knew for the first time that we would find out, and that we would arrive at him. I also knew the knowledge would be terribly, perhaps tragically, expensive to others in the book. And so it turned out.

Years later when I started *The Silence of the Lambs*, I did not know that Dr. Lecter would return. I had always liked the character of Dahlia Lyad in *Black Sunday* and wanted to do a novel with a strong woman as the central character. So I began with Clarice Starling and, not two pages into the novel, I found she had to go visit the doctor. I admired Clarice Starling enormously and I think I suffered some feelings of jealousy at the ease with which Dr. Lecter saw into her, when it was so difficult for me.

By the time I undertook to record the events in *Hannibal*, the doctor, to my surprise, had taken on a life of his own. You seemed to find him as oddly engaging as I did.

I dreaded doing *Hannibal*, dreaded the personal wear and tear, dreaded the choices I would have to watch, feared for Starling. In the end I let them go, as you must let characters go, let Dr. Lecter and Clarice Starling decide events according to their natures. There is a certain amount of courtesy involved.

As a sultan once said: I do not *keep* falcons—they live with me.

When in the winter of 1979 I entered the Baltimore State Hospital for the Criminally Insane and the great metal door crashed closed behind me, little did I know what waited at the end of the corridor; how seldom we recognize the sound when the bolt of our fate slides home.

T.H.
Miami, January 2000

Red Dragon

One can only see what one observes,
and one observes only things which are
already in the mind.
ALPHONSE BERTILLON

. . . For Mercy has a human heart,
Pity a human face,
And Love, the human form divine,
And Peace, the human dress.

   WILLIAM BLAKE, *Songs of Innocence*,
   ("The Divine Image")

Cruelty has a Human Heart,
And Jealousy a Human Face,
Terror the Human Form Divine,
And Secrecy the Human Dress.

The Human Dress is forged Iron,
The Human Form a fiery Forge,
The Human Face a Furnace seal'd,
The Human Heart its hungry Gorge.

   WILLIAM BLAKE, *Songs of Experience*,
   ("A Divine Image")★

★After Blake's death, this poem was found with prints from the plates
of *Songs of Experience*. It appears only in posthumous editions.

CHAPTER

1

WILL GRAHAM sat Crawford down at a picnic table between the house and the ocean and gave him a glass of iced tea.

Jack Crawford looked at the pleasant old house, salt-silvered wood in the clear light: "I should have caught you in Marathon when you got off work," he said. "You don't want to talk about it here."

"I don't want to talk about it anywhere, Jack. You've got to talk about it, so let's have it. Just don't get out any pictures. If you brought pictures, leave them in the briefcase—Molly and Willy will be back soon."

"How much do you know?"

"What was in the *Miami Herald* and the *Times*," Graham said. "Two families killed in their houses a month apart. Birmingham and Atlanta. The circumstances were similar."

"Not similar. The same."

"How many confessions so far?"

"Eighty-six when I called in this afternoon," Crawford said. "Cranks. None of them knew details. He smashes the mirrors and uses the pieces. None of them knew that."

"What else did you keep out of the papers?"

"He's blond, right-handed and really strong, wears a size 11 shoe. He can tie a bowline. The prints are all smooth gloves."

"You said that in public."

"He's not too comfortable with locks," Crawford said. "Used a glass-cutter and a suction-cup to get in the house last time. Oh, and his blood's AB positive."

"Somebody hurt him?"

"Not that we know of. We typed him from semen and saliva. He's a secretor." Crawford looked out at the flat sea. "Will, I want to ask you something. You saw this in the papers. The second one was all over the T.V. Did you ever think about giving me a call?"

"No."

"Why not?"

"There weren't many details at first on the one in Birmingham. It could have been anything—revenge, a relative."

"But after the second one, you knew what it was."

"Yeah. A psychopath. I didn't call you because I didn't want to. I know who you already have to work on this. You've got the best lab. You'd have Heimlich at Harvard, Bloom at the University of Chicago—"

"And I've got you down here fixing fucking boat motors."

"I don't think I'd be all that useful to you, Jack. I never think about it any more."

"Really? You caught two. The last two we had, you caught."

"How? By doing the same things you and the rest of them are doing."

"That's not entirely true, Will. It's the way you think."

"I think there's been a lot of bullshit about the way I think."

"You made some jumps you never explained."

"The evidence was there," Graham said.

"Sure. Sure there was. Plenty of it—afterwards. Before the collar there was so damn little we couldn't get probable cause to go in."

"You have the people you need, Jack. I don't think I'd be an improvement. I came down here to get away from that."

"I know it. You got hurt last time. Now you look all right."

"I'm all right. It's not getting cut. You've been cut."

"I've been cut, but not like that."

"It's not getting cut. I just decided to stop. I don't think I can explain it."

"If you couldn't look at it any more, God knows I'd understand that."

"No. You know—having to look. It's always bad but you get so you can function anyway, as long as they're dead. The hospital, interviews, that's worse. You have to shake it off and keep on thinking. I don't believe I could do it now. I could make myself look, but I'd shut down the thinking."

"These are all dead, Will," Crawford said as kindly as he could.

Jack Crawford heard the rhythm and syntax of his own speech in Graham's voice. He had heard Graham do that before, with other people. Often in intense conversation Graham took on the other person's speech patterns. At first, Crawford had thought he was doing it deliberately, that it was a gimmick to get the back-and-forth rhythm going.

Later Crawford realized that Graham did it involuntarily, that sometimes he tried to stop and couldn't.

Crawford dipped into his jacket pocket with two fingers. He flipped two photographs across the table, face up.

"All dead," he said.

Graham stared at him a moment before picking up the pictures.

They were only snapshots: a woman followed by three children and a duck carried picnic items up the bank of a pond. A family stood behind a cake.

After half a minute he put the photographs down again. He pushed them into a stack with his finger and looked far down the beach where the boy hunkered, examining something in the sand. The woman stood watching, hand on her hip, spent waves creaming around her ankles. She leaned inland to swing her wet hair off her shoulders.

Graham, ignoring his guest, watched Molly and the boy for as long as he had looked at the pictures.

Crawford was pleased. He kept the satisfaction out of his face with the same care he had used to choose the site of this conversation. He thought he had Graham. Let it cook.

Three remarkably ugly dogs wandered up and flopped to the ground around the table.

"My God," Crawford said.

"These are probably dogs," Graham explained. "People dump small ones here all the time. I can give away the cute ones. The rest stay around and get to be big ones."

"They're fat enough."

"Molly's a sucker for strays."

"You've got a nice life here, Will. Molly and the boy. How old is he?"

"Eleven."

"Good-looking kid. He's going to be taller than you."

Graham nodded. "His father was. I'm lucky here. I know that."

"I wanted to bring Phyllis down here. Florida. Get a place when I retire and stop living like a cave fish. She says all her friends are in Arlington."

"I meant to thank her for the books she brought me in the hospital, but I never did. Tell her for me."

"I'll tell her."

Two small bright birds lit on the table hoping to find jelly. Crawford watched them hop around until they flew away.

"Will, this freak seems to be in phase with the moon. He killed the Jacobi family in Birmingham on Saturday night, June 28th, full moon. He killed the Leeds in Atlanta night before last, July 26th. That's one day short of a lunar month. So if we're lucky we may have a little over three weeks before he does it again.

"I don't think you want to wait here in the Keys and read about the next one in your *Miami Herald*. Hell, I'm not the Pope, I'm not saying what you ought to do, but I want to ask you, do you respect my judgement, Will?"

"Yes."

"I think we have a better chance to get him fast if you help. Hell, Will, saddle up and help us. Go to Atlanta and Birmingham and look, then come on to Washington. Just T.D.Y."

Graham did not reply.

Crawford waited while five waves lapped the beach. Then he got up and slung his coat over his shoulder. "Let's talk after dinner."

"Stay and eat."

Crawford shook his head. "I'll come back later. There'll be messages at the Holiday Inn and I'll be a while on the phone. Tell Molly thanks, though."

Crawford's rented car raised thin dust that settled on the bushes outside the shell road.

Graham returned to the table. He was afraid that this was how he would remember the end of Sugarloaf Key—ice melting in two glasses and paper napkins fluttering off the redwood table in the breeze and Molly and Willy far down the beach.

Sunset on Sugarloaf, the herons still and the red sun swelling.

Will Graham and Molly Foster Graham sat on a bleached drift log, their faces orange in the sunset, backs in violet shadow. She picked up his hand.

"Crawford stopped by to see me at the shop before he came out here," she said. "He asked directions to the house. I tried to call you. You really ought to answer the phone once in a while. We saw the car when we got home and went round to the beach."

"What else did he ask you?"

"How you are."

"And you said?"

"I said you're fine and he should leave you the hell alone. What does he want you to do?"

"Look at evidence. I'm a forensic specialist, Molly. You've seen my diploma."

"You mended a crack in the ceiling paper with your diploma, I saw that." She straddled the log to face him. "If you missed your other life, what you used to do, I think you'd talk about it. You never do. You're open and calm and easy now . . . I love that."

"We have a good time, don't we?"

Her single styptic blink told him he should have said something better. Before he could fix it, she went on.

"What you did for Crawford was bad for you. He has a lot of other people—the whole damn government I guess—why can't he leave us alone?"

"Didn't Crawford tell you that? He was my supervisor the two times I left the F.B.I. Academy to go back to the field. Those two cases were the only ones like this he ever had, and Jack's been working a long time. Now he's got a new one. This kind of psychopath is very rare. He knows I've had . . . experience."

"Yes, you have," Molly said. His shirt was unbuttoned and she could see the looping scar across his stomach. It was finger-width and raised and it never tanned. It ran down from his left hip-bone and turned up to notch his rib-cage on the other side.

Dr. Hannibal Lecter did that with a linoleum knife. It happened a year before Molly met Graham and it very nearly killed him. Dr. Lecter, known in the tabloids as "Hannibal the Cannibal", was the second psychopath Graham had caught.

When he finally got out of hospital, Graham resigned from the Federal Bureau of Investigation, left Washington, and found a job as a diesel mechanic in the boat-yard at Marathon in the Florida Keys.

It was a trade he grew up with. He slept in a trailer at the boat-yard until Molly and her good ramshackle house on Sugarloaf Key.

Now he straddled the drift log and held both her hands. Her feet burrowed under his.

"All right, Molly. Crawford thinks I have a knack for the monsters. It's like a superstition with him."

"Do you believe it?"

Graham watched three pelicans fly in line across the tidal flats. "Molly, an intelligent psychopath—particularly a sadist—is hard to catch for several reasons. First, there's no traceable motive. So you can't go that way. And most of the time you won't have any help from informants. See, there's a lot more stooling than sleuthing behind most arrests, but in a case like this there won't *be* any informants. *He* may not even know that he's doing it. So you have to take whatever evidence you have and extrapolate. You try to reconstruct his thinking. You try to find patterns."

"And follow him and find him," Molly said. "I'm afraid if you go after this maniac, or whatever he is—I'm afraid he'll do you like the last one did. That's it. That's what scares me."

"He'll never see me or know my name, Molly. The police, they'll have to take him down if they can find him, not me. Crawford just wants another point of view."

She watched the red sun spread over the sea. High cirrus glowed above it.

Graham loved the way she turned her head, artlessly giving him her less perfect profile. He could see the pulse in her throat, and remembered suddenly and completely the taste of salt on her skin. He swallowed and said, "What the hell can I do?"

"What you've already decided. If you stay here and there's more killing, maybe it would sour this place for you. *High Noon* and all that crap. If it's that way, you weren't really asking."

"If I *were* asking, what would you say?"

"Stay here with me. Me. Me. Me. And Willy, I'd drag him in if it would do any good. I'm supposed to dry my eyes and wave my hanky. If things don't go so well, I'll have the satisfaction that you did the right thing. That'll last about as long as Taps. Then I can go home and switch one side of the blanket on."

"I'd be at the back of the pack."

"Never in your life. I'm selfish, huh?"

"I don't care."

"Neither do I. It's keen and sweet here. All the things that happened to you before make you know it. Value it, I mean."

He nodded.

"Don't want to lose it either way," she said.

"Nope. We won't either."

Darkness fell quickly and Jupiter appeared, low in the southwest.

They walked back to the house beside the rising gibbous moon. Far out past the tidal flats, bait fish leaped for their lives.

Crawford came back after dinner. He had taken off his coat and tie and rolled up his sleeves for the casual effect. Molly thought Crawford's thick pale forearms were repulsive. To her he looked like a damnably wise ape. She served him coffee under the porch fan and sat with him while Graham and Willy went out to feed dogs. She said nothing. Moths batted softly at the screens.

"He looks good, Molly," Crawford said. "You both do—skinny and brown."

"Whatever I say, you'll take him anyway, won't you?"

"Yeah. I have to. I have to do it. But I swear to God, Molly, I'll make it as easy on him as I can. He's changed. It's great you got married."

"He's better and better. He doesn't dream so often now. He was really obsessed with the dogs for a while. Now he just takes care of them; he doesn't talk about them all the time. You're his friend, Jack. Why can't you leave him alone?"

"Because it's his bad luck to be the best. Because he doesn't think like other people. Somehow he never got in a rut."

"He thinks you want him to look at evidence."

"I do want him to look at evidence. There's nobody better with evidence. But he has the other thing too. Imagination, projection, whatever. He doesn't like that part of it."

"You wouldn't like it either if you had it. Promise me something, Jack. Promise me you'll see to it he doesn't get too close. I think it would kill him to have to fight."

"He won't have to fight. I can promise you that."

When Graham finished with the dogs, Molly helped him pack.

WILL GRAHAM drove slowly past the house where the Charles Leeds family had lived and died. The windows were dark. One yard-light burned. He parked two blocks away and walked back through the warm night, carrying the Atlanta police detectives' report in a cardboard box.

Graham had insisted on coming alone. Anyone else in the house would distract him—that was the reason he gave Crawford. He had another, private reason: he was not sure how he would act. He didn't want a face aimed at him all the time.

He had been all right at the morgue.

The two-storey brick home was set back from the street on a wooded lot. Graham stood under the trees for a long time looking at it. He tried to be still inside. In his mind a silver pendulum swung in darkness. He waited until the pendulum was still.

A few neighbours drove by, looking at the house quickly and looking away. A murder house is ugly to the neighbours, like the face of someone who betrayed them. Only outsiders and children stare.

The shades were up. Graham was glad. That meant no relatives had been inside. Relatives always lower the shades.

He walked around the side of the house, moving carefully, not using his flashlight. He stopped twice to listen. The Atlanta police knew he was here, but the neighbours did not. They would be jumpy. They might shoot.

Looking in a rear window he could see all the way through to the light in the front yard, past silhouettes of furniture. The scent of Cape Jasmine was heavy in the air. A latticed porch ran across most of the back. On the porch door was the seal of the Atlanta Police Department. Graham removed the seal and went in.

The door from the porch into the kitchen was patched with plywood where the police had taken out the glass. By flashlight he unlocked it with the key the police had given him. He wanted to turn on lights. He wanted to put on his shiny badge and make some official noises to justify himself to the silent house where five people had died. He did none of that. He went into the dark kitchen and sat down at the breakfast table.

Two pilot-lights on the kitchen range glowed blue in the dark. He smelled furniture polish and apples.

The thermostat clicked and the air conditioning came on. Graham started at the noise, felt a trickle of fear. He was an old hand at fear. He could manage this one. He simply was afraid and he could go on anyway.

He could see and hear better afraid; he could not speak as concisely and fear sometimes made him rude. Here, there was nobody left to speak to, there was nobody to offend any more.

Madness came into this house through that door into this kitchen, moving on size 11 feet. Sitting in the dark he sensed madness like a bloodhound sniffs a shirt.

Graham had studied the detectives' report at Atlanta Homicide for most of the day and early evening. He remembered that the light on the vent-hood over the stove had been on when the police arrived. He turned it on now.

Two framed samplers hung on the wall beside the stove. One said, "Kissin' don't last, cookin' do." The other was "It's always to the kitchen that our friends best like to come, to hear the heartbeat of the house, take comfort in its hum."

Graham looked at his watch. 11.30 p.m. According to the pathologist the deaths occurred between 11 p.m. and 1 a.m.

First there was the entry. He thought about that . . .

The madman slipped the hook on the outside screen door. Stood in the darkness of the porch and took something from his pocket. A suction-cup, maybe the base of a pencil sharpener designed to stick to a desk-top.

Crouched against the wooden lower half of the kitchen door, the madman raised his head to peer through the glass. He put out his tongue and licked the cup, pressed it to the glass and flicked the lever to make it stick. A small glass-cutter was attached to the cup with string so that he could cut a circle.

Tiny squeal of the glass-cutter and one solid tap to break the glass. One hand to tap, one hand to hold the suction-cup. The glass must not fall. The loose piece of glass is slightly egg-shaped because the string wrapped around the shaft of the suction-cup as he cut. A little grating noise as he pulls the piece of glass back outside. He does not care that he leaves AB saliva on the glass.

His hand in the tight glove snakes in through the hole, finds the lock. The door opens silently. He is inside. In the light of the vent-hood he can see his body in this strange kitchen. It is pleasantly cool in the house.

Will Graham ate two Di-Gels. The crackle of the cellophane irritated him as he stuffed it in his pocket. He walked through the living-room, holding his flashlight well away from him by habit. Though he had studied the floor plan, he made one wrong turn before he found the stairs. They did not creak.

Now he stood in the doorway of the master bedroom. He could see faintly without the flashlight. A digital clock on a nightstand projected the time on the ceiling and an orange night light burned above the baseboard by the bathroom. The coppery smell of blood was strong.

Eyes accustomed to the dark could see well enough. The madman could distinguish Mr. Leeds from his wife. There was enough light for him to cross the room, grab Leeds's hair and cut his throat. What then? Back to the wall switch, a greeting to Mrs. Leeds and then the gunshot that disabled her?

Graham switched on the lights and bloodstains shouted at him from the walls, from the mattress and the floor. The very air had screams smeared on it. He flinched from the noise in this silent room full of dark stains drying.

Graham sat on the floor until his head was quiet. Still, still, be still.

The number and variety of the bloodstains had puzzled Atlanta detectives trying to reconstruct the crime. All the victims were found slain in their beds. This was not consistent with the locations of the stains.

At first they believed Charles Leeds was attacked in his daughter's room and his body dragged to the master bedroom. Closer examination of the splash patterns made them reconsider.

The killer's exact movements in the rooms were not yet determined.

Now, with the advantage of the autopsy and lab reports, Will Graham began to see how it had happened.

The intruder cut Charles Leeds's throat as he lay asleep beside his wife, went back to the wall switch and turned on the light—hairs and oil from Mr. Leeds's head were left on the switchplate by a smooth glove. He shot Mrs. Leeds as she was rising, then went toward the children's rooms.

Leeds rose with his cut throat and tried to protect the children, losing great gouts of blood and an unmistakable arterial spray as he tried to fight. He was shoved away, fell and died with his daughter in her room.

One of the two boys was shot in bed. The other boy was also found in bed, but he had dust balls in his hair. Police believed he was dragged out from under his bed to be shot.

When all of them were dead, except possibly Mrs. Leeds, the smashing of mirrors began, the selection of shards, the further attention to Mrs. Leeds.

Graham had full copies of all the autopsy protocols in his box. Here was the one on Mrs. Leeds. The bullet entered to the right of her navel and lodged in her lumbar spine, but she died of strangulation.

The increase in serotonin and free histamine levels in the gunshot wound indicated she had lived at least five minutes after she was shot. The histamine was much higher than the serotonin, so she had not lived more than fifteen minutes. Most of her other injuries were probably, but not conclusively, post-mortem.

If the other injuries were post-mortem, what was the killer doing in the interval while Mrs. Leeds waited to die, Graham wondered. Struggling with Leeds and killing the others, yes, but that would have taken less than a minute. Smashing the mirrors. But what else?

The Atlanta detectives were thorough. They had measured and photographed exhaustively, had vacuumed and grid-searched and taken the traps from the drains. Still, Graham looked for himself.

From the police photographs and taped outlines on the mattresses, Graham could see where the bodies had been found. The evidence— nitrate traces on bedclothes in the case of the gunshot wounds— indicated that they were found in positions approximating to those in which they died.

But the profusion of bloodstains and matted sliding marks on the hall carpet remained unexplained. One detective had theorized that some of the victims tried to crawl away from the killer. Graham did not believe it—clearly the killer moved them after they were dead and then put them back the way they were when he killed them.

What he did with Mrs. Leeds was obvious. But what about the others? He had not disfigured them further as he did Mrs. Leeds. The children each suffered a single gunshot wound in the head. Charles Leeds bled to death with aspirated blood contributing. The only additional mark on him was a superficial ligature mark around his chest, believed to be post-mortem. What did the killer do with them after they were dead?

From his box Graham took the police photographs, lab reports on the individual blood and organic stains in the rooms and standard comparison plates of blood drop trajectories.

He went over the upstairs rooms minutely, trying to match injuries to stains, trying to work backward. He plotted each splash on a measured field sketch of the master bedroom, using the standard comparison plates to estimate the direction and velocity of the bloodfall. In this way he hoped to learn the position the bodies were in at different times.

Here was a row of three bloodstains slanting up and around a corner of the bedroom wall. Here were three faint stains on the carpet beneath them. The wall above the headboard on Charles Leeds's side of the bed was bloodstained and there were swipes along the baseboards. Graham's field sketch began to look like a join-the-dots puzzle with no numbers. He stared at it, looked up at the room and back to the sketch until his head ached.

He went into the bathroom and took his last two Bufferin, scooping up water in his hand from the tap in the sink. He splashed water on his face and dried it with his shirt-tail. Water spilled on the floor. He had forgotten that the trap was gone from the drain. Otherwise the bathroom was undisturbed, except for the broken mirror and traces of the red fingerprint powder called Dragon's Blood. Tooth-brushes, facial cream, razor, were all in place.

The bathroom looked as though a family still used it. Mrs. Leeds's pantyhose hung on the towel racks where she had left them to dry. He saw that she cut the leg off a pair when it had a run so she could match two one-legged pairs, wear them at the same time and save money. Mrs. Leeds's small, homely economy pierced him. Molly did the same thing.

Graham climbed out a window on to the porch roof and sat on the gritty shingles. He hugged his knees, his damp shirt pressed cold across his back, and snorted the smell of slaughter out of his nose.

The lights of Atlanta rusted the night sky and the stars were hard to see. The night would be clear in the Keys. He could be watching shooting stars with Molly and Willy, listening for the whoosh they solemnly agreed a shooting star must make. The Delta Aquarid meteor shower was at its maximum and Willy was up for it.

He shivered and snorted again. He did not want to think of Molly now. To do so was tasteless as well as distracting.

Graham had a lot of trouble with taste. Often his thoughts were not tasty. There were no effective partitions in his mind. What he saw and learned touched everything else he knew. Some of the combinations were hard to live with. But he could not anticipate them, could not block and repress. His learned values of decency and propriety tagged along, shocked at his associations, appalled at his dreams; sorry that in the bone area of his skull there were no forts for what he loved. His associations came at the speed of light. His value judgements were at the pace of a responsive reading. They could never keep up and direct his thinking.

He viewed his own mentality as grotesque but useful, like a chair made of antlers. There was nothing he could do about it.

Graham turned off the lights in the Leeds house and went out through the kitchen. At the far end of the back porch, his flashlight revealed a bicycle and a wicker dog-bed. There was a doghouse in the backyard, a dog-bowl by the steps.

The evidence indicated the Leeds were surprised in their sleep.

Holding the flashlight between his chin and chest, he wrote a memo: *Jack—where was the dog?*

Graham drove back to his hotel. He had to concentrate on his driving, though there was little traffic at 4.30 a.m. His head still ached and he watched for an all-night pharmacy.

He found one on Peachtree. A slovenly rent-a-cop dozed near

the door. A pharmacist in a jacket dingy enough to highlight his dandruff sold Graham Bufferin. The glare in the place was painful. Graham disliked young pharmacists. They had a middle-of-the-litter look about them. They were often smug and he suspected that they were unpleasant at home.

"What else?" the pharmacist said, his fingers poised above the cash register keys. "What else?"

The Atlanta F.B.I. office had booked him into an absurd hotel near the city's new Peachtree Center. It had glass elevators shaped like milkweek-pods to let him know he was really in town now.

Graham rode up to his room with two conventioneers wearing name tags with the printed greeting "Hi!" They held on to the rail and looked over the lobby as they ascended.

"Looka yonder by the desk—that's Wilma and them just now coming in," the larger one said. "Goddamn, I'd love to tear off a piece of that."

"Fuck her till her nose bleeds," the other one said.

Fear and rut, and anger at the fear.

"Say, you know why a woman has legs?"

"Why?"

"So she won't leave a trail like a snail."

The elevator doors opened.

"Is this it? This is it," the larger one said. He lurched against the facing as he got off.

"This is the blind leading the blind," the other one said.

Graham put his cardboard box on the dresser in his room. Then he put it in a drawer where he could not see it. He had had enough of the wide-eyed dead. He wanted to call Molly, but it was too early.

A meeting was scheduled for 8 a.m. at the Atlanta Police Head-quarters. He'd have little enough to tell them.

He would try to sleep. His mind was a busy rooming house with arguments all around him and they were fighting somewhere down the hall. He was numb and empty and he drank two fingers of whisky from his bathroom glass before he lay down. The darkness pressed too closely on him. He turned on the bathroom light and went back to bed. He pretended Molly was in the bathroom brushing her hair.

Lines from the autopsy protocols sounded in his own voice, though he had never read them aloud . . . "the faeces were formed . . . a trace of talcum on the lower right leg. Fracture of the medial orbit wall owing to insertion of mirror shard . . ."

Graham tried to think about the beach at Sugarloaf Key, he tried to hear the waves. He pictured his work-bench in his mind and thought about the escapement for the water-clock he and Willy were building. He sang "Whiskey River" under his breath and tried to run "Black Mountain Rag" through his head from one end to the other. Molly's music. Doc Watson's guitar part was all right, but he always lost it in the fiddle break. Molly had tried to teach him clog dancing in the back yard and she was bouncing . . . and finally he dozed.

He woke in an hour, rigid and sweating, seeing the other pillow silhouetted against the bathroom light and it was Mrs. Leeds lying beside him bitten and torn, mirrored eyes and blood like the legs of spectacles over her temples and ears. He could not turn his head to face her. Brain screaming like a smoke alarm, he put his hand over there and touched dry cloth.

Having acted, he felt some immediate relief. He rose, his heart pounding, and put on a dry tee-shirt. He threw the wet one into the bathtub. He could not move over to the dry side of the bed. Instead he put a towel on the side where he had sweated and lay down on it, propped against the headboard with a stiff drink in his hand. He swallowed a third of it.

He reached for something to think about, anything. The pharmacy where he bought the Bufferin, then; perhaps because it was his only experience all day that was not related to death.

He could remember old drugstores with soda fountains. As a boy, he thought old drugstores had a slightly furtive air. When you went in, you always thought about buying rubbers whether you needed any or not. There were things on the shelves you shouldn't look at too long.

In the pharmacy where he bought the Bufferin, the contraceptives with their illustrated wrappings were in a lucite case on the wall behind the cash register, framed like art.

He preferred the drugstore and sundry of his childhood. Graham was nearly forty and just beginning to feel the tug of the way the world was then; it was a sea anchor streamed behind him in heavy weather.

He thought about Smoot. Old Smoot had been the soda jerk and manager for the pharmacist who owned the local drugstore when Graham was a child. Smoot, who drank on the job, forgot to unroll the awning and the sneakers melted in the window. Smoot forgot to unplug the coffee pot and the fire department was summoned. Smoot sold ice cream cones to children on credit.

His principal outrage was ordering fifty Cupie dolls from a detail man while the store owner was on vacation. On his return, the owner fired Smoot for a week. Then they held a Cupie doll sale. Fifty of the Cupie dolls were arranged in a semicircle in the front window so that they all stared at whoever was looking in.

They had wide eyes of cornflower blue. It was a striking display and Graham had looked at it for some time. He knew they were only Cupie dolls, but he could feel the focus of their attention. So many of them looking. A number of people stopped to look at them. Plaster dolls, all with the same silly spit curl, yet their concentrated gaze had made his face tingle.

Graham began to relax a little on the bed. Cupie dolls staring. He started to take a drink, gasped and choked it on to his chest. He fumbled for the bedside lamp and fetched his box from the dresser drawer. He took out the autopsy protocols of the three Leeds children and his measured field sketches of the master bedroom and spread them on the bed.

Here were the three bloodstains slanting up the corner, and here were the matching stains on the carpet. Here were the dimensions of the three children. Brother, sister, big brother. Match. Match. Match.

They had been in a row, seated along the wall facing the bed. An audience. A dead audience. And Leeds. Tied around the chest to the headboard. Composed to look as though he were sitting up in bed. Getting the ligature mark, staining the wall above the headboard.

What were they watching? Nothing, they were all dead. But their eyes were open. They were watching a performance starring the madman and the body of Mrs. Leeds, beside Mr. Leeds in the bed. An audience. The crazy could look around at their faces.

Graham wondered if he had lit a candle. The flickering light would simulate expression on their faces. No candle was found. Maybe he would think to do that next time . . .

This first small bond to the killer itched and stung like a leech. Graham bit the sheet, thinking.

Why did you move them again? Why didn't you leave them that way? Graham asked. There's something you don't want me to know about you. Why, there's something you're ashamed of. Or is it something you can't afford for me to know?

Did you open their eyes?

Mrs. Leeds was lovely, wasn't she? You turned on the light after you cut his throat so Mrs. Leeds could watch him flop, didn't you? It was maddening to have to wear gloves when you touched her, wasn't it?

There was talcum on her leg.

There was no talcum in the bathroom.

Someone else seemed to speak those two facts in a flat voice.

You took off your gloves, didn't you? The powder came out of a rubber glove as you pulled it off to touch her, DIDN'T IT, YOU SON OF A

BITCH. You touched her with your bare hands and then you put the gloves back on and you wiped her down. But while the gloves were off DID YOU OPEN THEIR EYES?

Jack Crawford answered his telephone on the fifth ring. He had answered the telephone in the night many times and he was not confused.

"Jack, this is Will."

"Yes, Will."

"Is Price still in Latent Prints?"

"Yeah. He doesn't go out much any more. He's working on the single-print index."

"I think he ought to come to Atlanta."

"Why? You said yourself the guy down here is good."

"He *is* good, but not as good as Price."

"What do you want him to do? Where would he look?"

"Mrs. Leeds's finger-nails and toe-nails. They're painted, it's a slick surface. And the corneas of all their eyes. I think he took his gloves off, Jack."

"Jesus, Price'll have to gun it," Crawford said. "The funeral's this afternoon."

3

"I THINK he had to touch her," Graham said in greeting.

Crawford handed him a Coke from the machine in Atlanta Police Headquarters. It was 7.50 a.m.

"Sure, he moved her around," Crawford said. "There were grip marks on her wrists and behind her knees. But every print in the place is from non-porous gloves. Don't worry, Price is here. Grouchy old bastard. He's on his way to the funeral home now. The morgue released the bodies last night, but the funeral home's not doing anything yet. You look bushed. Did you get any sleep?"

"Maybe an hour. I think he had to touch her with his hands."

"I hope you're right, but the Atlanta lab swears he wore, like, surgeon's gloves the whole time," Crawford said. "The mirror pieces had those smooth prints. Forefinger on the back of the piece wedged in the labia, smudged thumb on the front."

"He polished it after he placed it, so he could see his damn face in there probably," Graham said.

"The one in her mouth was obscured with blood. Same with the eyes. He never took the gloves off."

"Mrs. Leeds was a good-looking woman," Graham said. "You've

seen the family pictures, right? I'd want to touch her skin in an intimate situation, wouldn't you?"

"*Intimate?*" Distaste sounded in Crawford's voice before he could stop it. Suddenly he was busy rummaging in his pockets for change.

"Intimate—they had privacy. Everybody else was dead. He could have their eyes open or shut, however he liked."

"Any way he liked," Crawford said. "They tried her skin for prints of course. Nothing. They did get a hand spread off her neck."

"The report didn't say anything about dusting nails."

"I expect her finger-nails were smudged when they took scrapings. The scrapings were just where she cut her palms with them. She never scratched him."

"She had pretty feet," Graham said.

"Umm hmm. Let's head upstairs," Crawford said. "The troops are about to muster."

Jimmy Price had a lot of equipment—two heavy cases plus his camera bag and tripod. He made a clatter coming through the front door of the Lombard Funeral Home in Atlanta. He was a frail old man and his humour had not been improved by a long taxi ride from the airport in the morning rush.

An officious young fellow with styled hair hustled him into an office decorated in apricot and cream. The desk was bare except for a sculpture called "The Praying Hands".

Price was examining the fingertips of the Praying Hands when Mr. Lombard himself came in. Lombard checked Price's credentials with extreme care.

"Your Atlanta office or agency or whatever called me, of course, Mr. Price. But last night we had to get the police to remove an obnoxious fellow who was trying to take pictures for the *National Tattler*, so I'm being very careful. I'm sure you understand. Mr.

Price, the bodies were only released to us about 1 a.m. this morning and the funeral is this afternoon at five. We simply can't delay it."

"This won't take a lot of time," Price said. "I need one reasonably intelligent assistant, if you have one. Have you touched the bodies, Mr. Lombard?"

"No."

"Find out who has. I'll have to print them all."

The morning briefing of police detectives on the Leeds case was concerned mostly with teeth.

Atlanta Chief of Detectives R. J. (Buddy) Springfield, a burly man in shirtsleeves, stood by the door with Dr. Dominic Princi as the twenty-three detectives filed in.

"All right, boys, let's have the big grin as you come by," Springfield said. "Show Dr. Princi your teeth. That's right, let's see 'em all. Christ, Sparks, is that your tongue or are you swallowing a squirrel? Keep moving."

A large frontal view of a set of teeth, upper and lower, was tacked to the bulletin-board at the front of the squad room. It reminded Graham of the celluloid strip of printed teeth in a dime store jack o'lantern. He and Crawford sat down at the back of the room while the detectives took their places at schoolroom desks.

Atlanta Public Safety Commissioner Gilbert Lewis and his public relations officer sat apart from them in folding chairs. Lewis had to face a news conference in an hour.

Chief of Detectives Springfield took charge.

"All right. Let's cease fire with the bullshit. If you read up this morning, you saw zero progress.

"House-to-house interviews will continue for a radius of four additional blocks around the scene. R. & I. has loaned us two clerks to help cross-matching airline reservations and car rentals in Birmingham and Atlanta.

"Airport and hotel details will make the rounds again today. Yes, again to*day*. Catch every maid and attendant as well as the desk people. He had to clean up somewhere and he may have left a mess. If you find somebody who cleaned up a mess, roust out whoever's in the room, seal it and get on the horn to the laundry double-quick. This time we've got something for you to show around. Dr. Princi?"

Dr. Dominic Princi, chief medical examiner for Fulton County, walked to the front and stood under the drawing of the teeth. He held up a dental cast.

"Gentlemen, this is what the subject's teeth look like. The Smithsonian in Washington reconstructed them from the impressions we took of bite-marks on Mrs. Leeds and a clear bite-mark in a piece of cheese from the Leeds's refrigerator," Princi said.

"As you can see, he has pegged lateral incisors—the teeth here and here." Princi pointed to the cast in his hand, then to the chart above him. "The teeth are crooked in alignment and a corner is missing from this central incisor. The other incisor is grooved, here. It looks like a 'tailor's notch', the kind of wear you get biting thread."

"Snaggle-toothed son of a bitch," somebody mumbled.

"How do you know for sure it was the perpetrator that bit the cheese, Doc?" a tall detective in the front row asked.

Princi disliked being called "doc", but he swallowed it. "Saliva washes from the cheese and from the bite wounds matched for blood type," he said. "The victims' teeth and blood type didn't match."

"Fine, Doctor," Springfield said. "We'll pass out pictures of the teeth to show around."

"What about giving it to the papers?" the public relations officer, Simpkins, was speaking. "A 'have you seen these teeth?' sort of thing?"

"I see no objection to that," Springfield said. "What about it, Commissioner?"

Lewis nodded.

Simpkins was not through. "Dr. Princi, the press is going to ask why it took four days to get this dental representation you have here. And why it all had to be done in Washington."

Special Agent Crawford studied the button on his ballpoint pen.

Princi reddened but his voice was calm. "Bite-marks on flesh are distorted when a body is moved, Mr. Simpson—"

"Simpkins."

"Simpkins, then. We couldn't make this using only the bite-marks on the victims. That is the importance of the cheese. Cheese is relatively solid, but tricky to cast. You have to oil it first to keep the moisture out of the casting medium. Usually you get one shot at it. The Smithsonian has done it for the F.B.I. crime lab before. They're better equipped to do a face bow registration and they have an anatomical articulator. They have a consulting forensic odontologist. We do not. Anything else?"

"Would it be fair to say that the delay was caused by the F.B.I. lab and not here?"

Princi turned on him. "What it would be fair to say, Mr. Simpkins, is that a federal investigator, Special Agent Crawford, found the cheese in the refrigerator two days ago—after your people had been through the place. He expedited the lab work at my request. It would be fair to say I'm relieved that it wasn't one of you that bit the goddamned thing."

Commissioner Lewis broke in, his heavy voice booming in the squad room. "Nobody's questioning your judgement, Dr. Princi. Simpkins, the last thing we need is to start a pissing contest with the F.B.I. Let's get on with it."

"We're all after the same thing," Springfield said. "Jack, do you fellows want to add anything?"

Crawford took the floor. The faces he saw were not entirely friendly. He had to do something about that.

"I just want to clear the air, Chief. Years ago there was a lot of rivalry about who got the collar. Each side, federal and local, held out on the other. It made a gap that crooks slipped through. That's not Bureau policy now and it's not my policy. I don't give a damn who gets the collar. Neither does Investigator Graham. That's him sitting back there, if some of you are wondering. If the man who did this is run over by a garbage truck it would suit me just fine as long as it puts him off the street. I think you feel the same way."

Crawford looked over the detectives and hoped they were mollified. He hoped they wouldn't hoard leads. Commissioner Lewis was talking to him.

"Investigator Graham has worked on this kind of thing before."

"Yes, sir."

"Can you add anything, Mr. Graham, suggest anything?"

Crawford raised his eyebrows at Graham.

"Would you come up to the front?" Springfield said.

Graham wished he had been given the chance to talk to Springfield in private. He didn't want to go to the front. He went, though.

Rumpled and sunblasted, Graham didn't look like a federal investigator. Springfield thought he looked more like a housepainter who had put on a suit to appear in court.

The detectives shifted from one buttock to the other.

When Graham turned to face the room, the ice-blue eyes were startling in his brown face.

"Just a couple of things," he said. "We can't assume he's a former mental patient or somebody with a record of sex offences. There's a high probability that he doesn't have any kind of record. If he does, it's more likely to be breaking and entering than a minor sex offence.

"He may have a history of biting in lesser assaults—bar fights or child abuse. The biggest help we'll have on that will come from emergency room personnel and the child welfare people.

"Any bad bite they can remember is worth checking, regardless of who was bitten and how they said it happened. That's all I have."

The tall detective in the front row raised his hand and spoke at the same time.

"But he only bit women so far, right?"

"That's all we know about. He bites a lot though. Six bad ones in Mrs. Leeds, eight in Mrs. Jacobi. That's way above average."

"What's average?"

"In a sex murder, three. He likes to bite."

"Women."

"Most of the time in sex assaults the bite-mark has a livid spot in the centre, a suck-mark. These don't. Dr. Princi mentioned it in his autopsy report and I saw it at the morgue. No suck-marks. For him biting may be a fighting pattern as much as sexual behaviour."

"Pretty thin," the detective said.

"It's worth checking," Graham said. "Any bite is worth checking. People lie about how it happened. Parents of a bitten child will claim an animal did it and let the child take rabies shots to cover for a snapper in the family—you've all seen that. It's worth asking at the hospitals— who's been referred for rabies shots.

"That's all I have." Graham's thigh-muscles fluttered with fatigue when he sat down.

"It's worth asking, and we'll ask," Chief of Detectives Springfield said. "Now. The Safe and Loft Squad works the neighbourhood along with Larceny. Work the dog angle. You'll see the update and the picture in the file. Find out if any stranger was seen with the dog. Vice and Narcotics take the K-Y cowboys and the leather bars after you finish the day tour. Marcus and Whitman—heads up at the funeral. Do you have relatives, friends of the family, lined up to spot for you? Good. What about the photographer? All right. Turn in the funeral guest book to R. & I. They've got the one from Birmingham already. The rest of the assignments are on the sheet. Let's go."

"One other thing," Commissioner Lewis said. The detectives sank back in their seats. "I have heard officers in this command referring to the killer as the Tooth Fairy. I don't care what you call him among yourselves, I realize you have to call him something. But I had better not hear any police-officer refer to him as the Tooth Fairy in public. It sounds flippant. Neither will you use that name on any internal memoranda.

"That's all."

Crawford and Graham followed Springfield back to his office. The Chief of Detectives gave them coffee while Crawford checked in with the switchboard and jotted down his messages.

"I didn't get a chance to talk to you when you got here yesterday," Springfield said to Graham. "This place has been a fucking madhouse. It's Will, right? Did the boys give you everything you need?"

"Yeah, they were fine."

"We don't have shit and we know it," Springfield said. "Oh, we developed a walking picture from the footprints in the flower bed. He was walking around bushes and stuff so you can't tell much more than his shoe size, maybe his height. The left print's a little deeper, so he may have been carrying something. It's busy work. We did get a burglar, though, a couple of years ago, off a walking picture. Showed Parkinson's disease. Princi picked it up. No luck this time."

"You have a good crew," Graham said.

"They are. But this kind of thing is out of our usual line, thank God. Let me get it straight, do you fellows work together all the time—you and Jack and Dr. Bloom—or do you just get together for one of these?"

"Just for these," Graham said.

"Some reunion. The commissioner was saying you were the one who nailed Lecter three years ago."

"We were all there with the Maryland police," Graham said. "The Maryland State Troopers arrested him."

Springfield was bluff, not stupid. He could see that Graham was uncomfortable. He swivelled in his chair and picked up some notes.

"You asked about the dog. Here's the sheet on it. Last night a vet here called Leeds's brother. He had the dog. Leeds and his oldest boy brought it in to the vet the afternoon before they were killed. It had a puncture wound in the abdomen. The vet operated and it's all right. He thought it was shot at first, but he didn't find a bullet. He thinks it was stabbed with something like an ice-pick or an awl. We're asking the neighbours if they saw anybody fooling with the dog, and we're working the phones today checking local vets for other animal mutilations."

"Was the dog wearing a collar with the Leeds name on it?"

"No."

"Did the Jacobis in Birmingham have a dog?" Graham asked.

"We're supposed to be finding that out," Springfield said. "Hold on, let me see." He dialled an inside number. "Lt. Flatt is our liaison with Birmingham – yeah, Flatt. What about the Jacobis' dog? Uh huh . . . uh huh. Just a minute." He put his hand over the phone. "No dog. They found a little box in the downstairs bathroom with cat-droppings in it. They didn't find any cat. The neighbours are watching for it."

"Could you ask Birmingham to check around in the yard and behind any out-buildings," Graham asked. "If the cat was hurt the children might not have found it in time and they might have buried it. You know how cats do. They hide to die. Dogs come home. And would you ask if it's wearing a collar?"

"Tell them if they need a methane probe, we'll send one," Crawford said. "Save a lot of digging."

Springfield relayed the request. The telephone rang as soon as he'd hung it up. The call was for Jack Crawford. It was Jimmy Price at the Lombard Funeral Home. Crawford punched on from the other phone.

"Jack, I got a partial that's probably a thumb and a fragment of a palm."

"Jimmy, you're the light of my life."

"I know. The partial's a tented arch but it's smudged. I'll have to see what I can do with it when I get back. Came off the oldest kid's left eye. I never did that before. Never would have seen it, but it stood out against an eight-ball haemorrhage from the gunshot wound."

"Can you make an identification off it?"

"It's a very long shot, Jack. If he's in the single-print index, maybe, but that's like the Irish Sweepstakes, you know that. The palm came off the nail of Mrs. Leeds's left big toe. It's only good for comparison. We'll be lucky to get six points off it. The Assistant S.A.C. witnessed and so did Lombard. He's a notary. I've got pictures *in situ*. Will that do?"

"What about elimination prints on the funeral home employees?"

"I inked up Lombard and all his Merry Men, major case prints whether they said they had touched her or not. They're scrubbing their hands and bitching now. Let me go home, Jack. I want to work these up in my own dark-room. Who knows what's in the water here—turtles?—who knows?

"I can catch a plane to Washington in an hour and fax the prints down to you by early afternoon."

Crawford thought a moment. "Okay, Jimmy, but step on it. Copies to Atlanta and Birmingham P.D.'s and bureau offices."

"You got it. Now, something else we've got to get straight on your end."

Crawford rolled his eyes to the ceiling. "Gonna piss in my ear about the per diem, aren't you?"

"Right."

"Today, Jimmy my lad, nothing's too good for you."

Graham stared out the window while Crawford told them about the prints.

"That's by God remarkable," was all Springfield said.

Graham's face was blank, closed like a lifer's face, Springfield thought.

He watched Graham all the way to the door.

The public safety commissioner's news conference was breaking up in the foyer as Crawford left Springfield's office. The print reporters headed for the phones. Television reporters were doing "cut aways", standing alone before their cameras asking the best questions they had heard at the news conference and extending their microphones to thin air for a reply that would be spliced in later from film of the commissioner.

Crawford and Graham had started down the front steps when a small man darted ahead of them, spun and took a picture. His face popped up from behind his camera.

"Will Graham!" he said. "Remember me—Freddy Lounds? I covered the Lecter case for the *Tattler*. I did the paperback."

"I remember," Graham said. He and Crawford continued down the steps, Lounds walking sideways ahead of them.

"When did they call you in, Will? What have you got?"

"I won't talk to you, Lounds."

"How does this guy compare with Lecter? Does he do them—"

"Lounds." Graham's voice was loud and Crawford got in front of him fast. "Lounds, you write lying shit and the *National Tattler* is an asswipe. Keep away from me."

Crawford gripped Graham's arm. "Get away, Lounds. *Go on*. Will, let's get some breakfast. Come on, Will." They rounded the corner, walking swiftly.

"I'm sorry, Jack. I can't stand that bastard. When I was in the hospital he came in and . . ."

"I know it," Crawford said. "I reamed him out, much good it did." Crawford remembered the picture in the *National Tattler* at the end of the Lecter case. Lounds had come into the hospital room while Graham was asleep. He flipped back the sheet and shot a picture of Graham's temporary colostomy. The paper ran it retouched with a black square covering Graham's groin. The caption said "Crazy Guts Cop."

The diner was bright and clean. Graham's hands trembled and he slopped coffee in his saucer.

He saw Crawford's cigarette smoke bothering a couple in the next booth. The couple ate in peptic silence, their resentment hanging in the smoke.

Two women, apparently mother and daughter, argued at a table near the door. They spoke in low voices, anger ugly in their faces. Graham could feel their anger on his face and neck.

Crawford was griping about having to testify at a trial in Washington in the morning. He was afraid the trial could tie him up for several days. As he lit another cigarette he peered across the flame at Graham's hands and his colour.

"Atlanta and Birmingham can run the thumb-print against their known sex offenders," Crawford said. "So can we. And Price has dug a single print out of the files before. He'll programme the F I N D E R with it—we've come a long way with that just since you left."

"F I N D E R", the F.B.I.'s automated fingerprint reader and processor, might recognize the thumb-print on an incoming fingerprint card from some unrelated case.

"When we get him, that print and his teeth will put him away," Crawford said. "What we have to do, we have to figure on what he *could* be. We have to swing a wide loop. Indulge me, now. Say we've arrested a good suspect. You walk in and see him. What is there about him that doesn't surprise you?"

"I don't know, Jack. Goddammit, he's got no face for me. We could spend a lot of time looking for people we've invented. Have you talked to Bloom?"

"On the phone last night. Bloom doubts he's suicidal and so does Heimlich. Bloom was only here a couple of hours the first day, but he and Heimlich have the whole file. Bloom's examining Ph.D. candidates this week. He said tell you hello. Do you have his number in Chicago?"

"I have it."

Graham liked Dr. Alan Bloom, a small round man with sad eyes, a good forensic psychiatrist—maybe the best. Graham appreciated the fact that Dr. Bloom had never displayed professional interest in him. That was not always the case with psychiatrists.

"Bloom says he wouldn't be surprised if we heard from the Tooth Fairy. He might write us a note," Crawford said.

"On a bedroom wall."

"Bloom thinks he might be disfigured or he may believe he's disfigured. He told me not to give that a lot of weight. 'I won't set up a straw man to chase, Jack' is what he told me. 'That would be a distraction and would diffuse the effort.' Said they taught him to talk like that in graduate school."

"He's right," Graham said.

"You could tell something about him or you wouldn't have found that fingerprint," Crawford said.

"That was the evidence on the damn wall, Jack. Don't put this on me. Look, don't expect too much from me, all right?"

"Oh, we'll get him. You know we'll get him, don't you?"

"I know it. One way or the other."

"What's one way?"

"We'll find evidence we've overlooked."

"What's the other?"

"He'll do it and do it until one night he makes too much noise going in and the husband gets to a gun in time."

"No other possibilities?"

"You think I'm going to spot him across a crowded room? No, that's Ezio Pinza you're thinking about, does that. The Tooth Fairy will go on and on until we get smart or get lucky. He won't stop."

"Why?"

"Because he's got a genuine taste for it."

"See, you do know something about him," Crawford said.

Graham did not speak again until they were on the sidewalk. "Wait until the next full moon," he told Crawford. "Then tell me how much I know about him."

Graham went back to his hotel and slept for two and a half hours. He woke at noon, showered and ordered a pot of coffee and a sandwich. It was time to make a close study of the Jacobi file from Birmingham. He scrubbed his reading glasses with hotel soap and settled in by the window with the file. For the first few minutes he looked up at every sound, footsteps in the hall, the distant thud of the elevator door. Then he knew nothing but the file.

The waiter with the tray knocked and waited, knocked and waited. Finally he left the lunch on the floor outside the door and signed the bill himself.

4

HOYT LEWIS, meter reader for Georgia Power Company, parked his
truck under a big tree in the alley and settled back with his lunch-box.
It was no fun opening his lunch now that he packed it himself. No
little notes in there any more, no surprise Twinkie.

He was half-way through his sandwich when a loud voice at his
ear made him jump.

"I guess I used a thousand dollars' worth of electricity this month,
is that right?"

Lewis turned and saw at the truck window the red face of H. G.
Parsons. Parsons wore Bermuda shorts and carried a yard broom.

"I didn't understand what you said."

"I guess you'll say I used a thousand dollars' worth of electricity this
month. Did you hear me that time?"

"I don't know what you've used because I haven't read your meter
yet, Mr. Parsons. When I do read it, I'll put it down on this piece of
paper right here."

Parsons was bitter about the size of his bill. He had complained to
the power company that he was being prorated.

"I'm keeping up with what I use," Parsons said. "I'm going to the

Public Service Commission with it too."

"You want to read your meter with me? Let's go over there right now and—"

"I know how to read a meter. I guess you could read one too if it wasn't too much trouble."

"Just be quiet a minute, Parsons." Lewis got out of his truck. "Just be quiet a minute now, dammit. Last year you put a magnet on your meter. Your wife said you was in the hospital, so I just took it off and didn't say anything. When you poured molasses in it last winter, I reported it. I notice you paid up when we charged you for it.

"Your bill went up after you did all that wiring yourself. I've told you until I'm blue in the face: something in that house is draining off current. Do you hire an electrician to find it? No, you call down to the office and bitch about me. I've about got a bait of you." Lewis was pale with anger.

"I'll get to the bottom of this," Parsons said, retreating down the alley toward his yard. "They're checking up on you, *Mister* Lewis. I saw somebody reading your route ahead of you," he said across the fence. "Pretty soon you'll have to go to work like everybody else."

Lewis cranked his truck and drove down the alley. Now he would have to find another place to finish his lunch. He was sorry. The big shade tree had been a good lunch place for years.

It was directly behind Charles Leeds's house.

At 5.30 p.m. Hoyt Lewis drove in his own automobile to the Cloud Nine Lounge where he had several boilermakers to ease his mind.

When he called his estranged wife, all he could think of to say was "I wish you was still fixing my lunch."

"You ought to have thought about that, Mr. Smarty," she said and hung up.

He played a gloomy game of shuffle-board with some linemen

and a dispatcher from Georgia Power and looked over the crowd. Goddamned airline clerks had started coming in the Cloud Nine. All had the same little moustache and pinky ring. Pretty soon they'd be fixing the Cloud Nine English with a damned dart board. You can't depend on nothing.

"Hey, Hoyt. I'll match you for a bottle of beer." It was his supervisor, Billy Meeks.

"Say, Billy, I need to talk to you."

"What's up?"

"You know that old son of a bitch Parsons, that's all the time calling up?"

"Called me last week as a matter of fact," Meeks said. "What about him?"

"He said somebody was reading my route ahead of me, like maybe somebody thought I wasn't making the rounds. You don't think I'm reading meters at home, do you?"

"Nope."

"You don't think that, do you? I mean, if I'm on a man's shit-list I want him to come right out and say it."

"If you was on my shit-list, you think I'd be scared to say so to your face?"

"No."

"All right then. If anybody was checking your route, I'd know it. Your executives is always aware of a situation like that. Nobody's checking up on you, Hoyt. You can't pay any attention to Parsons, he's just old and contrary. He called me up last week and said, 'Congratulations on getting wise to that Hoyt Lewis.' I didn't pay him any mind."

"I wish we'd put the law on him about that meter," Lewis said. "I was just setting back there in the alley under a tree trying to eat my lunch today and he jumped me. What he needs is a good ass kicking."

"I used to set back there myself when I had the route," Meeks said. "Boy, I tell you one time I seen Mrs. Leeds—well, it don't seem right to talk about it now she's dead—but one or two times she was out there sunning herself in the backyard in her swimming-suit. Whooee. Had a cute little peter belly. That was a damn shame about them. She was a nice lady."

"Did they catch anybody yet?"

"Naw."

"Too bad he got the Leeds when old Parsons was right down the street convenient," Lewis observed.

"I'll tell you what, I don't let my old lady lay around out in the yard in no swimming-suit. She goes, 'Silly Billy, who's gonna see me?' I told her, I said you can't tell what kind of an insane bastard might jump over that hedge with his private out. Did the cops talk to you? Ask you had you seen anybody?"

"Yeah, I think they got everybody that has a route out there. Mailmen, everybody. I was working Laurelwood on the other side of Betty Jane Drive the whole week until today, though." Lewis picked at the label on his beer. "You say Parsons called you up last week?"

"Yep."

"Then he must have saw somebody reading his meter. He wouldn't have called in if he'd just made it up today to bother me. You say you didn't send nobody and it sure wasn't me he saw."

"Might have been Southeastern Bell checking something."

"Might have been."

"We don't share poles out there though."

"Reckon I ought to call the cops?"

"Wouldn't hurt nothing," Meeks said.

"Naw, it might do Parsons some good, talk with the law. Scare the shit out of him when they drive up, anyhow."

GRAHAM WENT back to the Leeds house in the late afternoon. He
entered through the front door and tried not to look at the ruin the
killer had left. So far he had seen files, a killing floor and meat—all
aftermath. He knew a fair amount about how they died. How they
had lived was on his mind today.

A survey, then. The garage contained a good ski-boat, well-used
and well-maintained, and a station-wagon. Golf clubs were there and
a trail-bike. The power tools were almost unused. Adult toys.

Graham took a wedge from the golf-bag and had to choke up on the
long shaft as he made a jerky swing. The bag puffed a smell of leather
at him as he leaned it back against the wall. Charles Leeds's things.

Graham pursued Charles Leeds through the house. His hunting
prints hung in the den. His set of the Great Books all in a row.
Sewanee annuals. H. Allen Smith and Perelman and Max Schulman
on the bookshelves. Vonnegut and Evelyn Waugh. C. S. Forester's
Beat to Quarters was open on a table.

In the den closet a good skeet-gun, a Nikon camera, a Bolex Super
Eight movie camera and projector.

Graham, who owned almost nothing except basic fishing equipment, a third-hand Volkswagen and two cases of Montrachet, felt a mild animosity toward the adult toys and wondered why.

Who was Leeds? A successful tax attorney, a Sewanee footballer, a rangy man who liked to laugh, a man who got up and fought with his throat cut.

Graham followed him through the house out of an odd sense of obligation. Learning about him first was a way of asking permission to look at his wife.

Graham felt that it was she who drew the monster, as surely as a singing cricket attracts death from the red-eyed fly.

Mrs. Leeds, then.

She had a small dressing-room upstairs. Graham managed to reach it without looking around the bedroom. The room was yellow and appeared undisturbed except for the smashed mirror above the dressing-table. A pair of L. L. Bean moccasins were on the floor in front of the closet as though she had just stepped out of them. Her dressing-gown appeared to have been flung on its peg and the closet revealed the mild disorder of a woman who has many other closets to organize.

Mrs. Leeds's diary was in a plum velvet box on the dressing-table. The key was taped to the lid along with a check tag from the police property room.

Graham sat on a spindly white chair and opened the diary at random:

December 23rd, Tuesday, Mama's house. The children are still asleep. When Mama glassed in the sun porch, I hated the way it changed the looks of the house, but it's very pleasant and I can sit here warm looking out at the snow. How many more Christmases can she manage a houseful of grandchildren? A lot I hope.

A hard drive yesterday up from Atlanta, snowing after Raleigh. We had to creep. I was tired anyway from getting everyone ready. Outside Chapel Hill, Charlie stopped the car and got out. He snapped some icicles off a branch to make me a martini. He came back to the car, long legs lifting high in the snow and there was snow in his hair and on his eyelashes and I remembered that I love him. It felt like something breaking with a little pain and spilling warm.

I hope the parka fits him. If he got me that tacky dinner ring I'll die. I could kick Madelyn's big cellulite behind for showing hers and carrying on. Four ridiculously big diamonds the colour of dirty ice. Icicle ice is so clear. The sun came through the car window and where the icicle was broken off it stuck up out of the glass and made a little prism. It made a spot of red and green on my hand holding the glass. I could feel the colour on my hand.

He asked me what I want for Christmas and I cupped my hands around his ear and whispered your big prick, silly, in as far as it will go.

The bald spot on the back of his head turned red. He's always afraid the children will hear. Men have no confidence in whispers.

The page was flecked with detectives' cigar ash.

Graham read on as the light faded, through the daughter's tonsil-lectomy, and a scare in June when Mrs. Leeds found a small lump in her breast. (*Dear God, the children are so small.*)

Three pages later the lump was a small benign cyst, easily removed.

Dr. Janovich turned me loose this afternoon. We left the hospital and drove to the pond. We hadn't been there in a long while. There never seems to be enough time. Charlie had two bottles of champagne on ice and we drank them and fed the ducks while the sun went down. He stood at the edge of the water with his back to me for a while and I think he cried a little.

Susan said she was afraid we were coming home from the hospital with another brother for her. Home!

Graham heard the telephone ring in the bedroom. A click and the hum of an answering machine. "Hello, this is Valerie Leeds. I'm sorry I can't come to the phone right now, but if you'll leave your name and number after the tone, we'll get back to you. Thank you."

Graham half expected to hear Crawford's voice after the beep, but there was only the dial tone. The caller had hung up.

He had heard her voice, now he wanted to see her. He went down to the den.

He had in his pocket a reel of Super Eight movie film belonging to Charles Leeds. Three weeks before his death, Leeds had left the film with a druggist who sent it away for processing. He never picked it up. Police found the receipt in Leeds's wallet and got the film from the druggist. Detectives viewed the home movie along with family snapshots developed at the same time and found nothing of interest.

Graham wanted to see the Leeds alive. At the police station, the detectives had offered Graham their projector. He wanted to watch the movie at the house. Reluctantly, they let him check it out of the property room.

Graham found the screen and projector in the den closet, set them up and sat down in Charles Leeds's big leather armchair to watch. He felt something tacky on the chair arm under his palm—a child's sticky fingerprint fuzzed with lint. Graham's hand smelled like candy.

It was a pleasant little silent movie, more imaginative than most. It opened with the dog, a grey Scottie, asleep on the den rug. The dog was disturbed momentarily by the movie-making and raised his head to look at the camera. Then he went to sleep again. A jumpy cut to the dog still asleep. Then the Scottie's ears perked up. He rose and barked and the camera followed him into the kitchen as he ran to the door and stood expectantly, shivering and wagging his stumpy tail.

Graham bit his lower lip and waited too. On the screen, the door opened and Mrs. Leeds came in carrying groceries. She blinked and laughed in surprise and touched her tousled hair with her free hand. Her lips moved as she walked out of the picture and the children came in behind her carrying smaller sacks. The girl was six, the boys eight and ten.

The younger boy, apparently a veteran of home movies, pointed to his ears and wiggled them. The camera position was fairly high. Leeds was 75 inches tall, according to the coroner's report.

Graham believed that this part of the movie must have been made in the early spring. The children wore windbreakers and Mrs. Leeds appeared pale. At the morgue she had a good tan and bathing-suit marks.

Brief scenes followed of the boys playing ping-pong in the basement and the girl Susan, wrapping a present in her room, tongue curled over her upper lip in concentration and a wisp of hair down over her forehead. She brushed her hair back with her plump hand, as her mother had done in the kitchen.

A subsequent scene showed Susan in a bubble bath, crouched like a small frog. She wore a large shower cap. The camera angle was lower and the focus uncertain, clearly the work of a brother. The scene ended with her shouting soundlessly at the camera and covering her six-year-old chest as her shower cap slipped down over her eyes.

Not to be outdone, Leeds had surprised Mrs. Leeds in the shower. The shower curtain bumped and bulged as the curtain does before a grade school theatrical. Mrs. Leeds's arm appeared around the curtain. In her hand was a large bath sponge. The scene closed with the lens obscured in soapsuds.

The film ended with a shot of Norman Vincent Peale speaking on television and a pan to Charles Leeds snoring in the chair where Graham now sat.

Graham stared at the blank square of light on the screen. He liked the Leeds. He was sorry that he had been to the morgue. He thought the madman who visited them might have liked them too. But the madman would like them better the way they were now.

Graham's head felt stuffed and stupid. He swam in the pool at his hotel until he was rubber-legged and came out of the water thinking of two things at once—a Tanqueray martini and the taste of Molly's mouth.

He made the martini himself in a plastic glass and telephoned Molly.

"Hello, hotshot."

"Hey, baby! Where are you?"

"In this damned hotel in Atlanta."

"Doing some good?"

"None you'd notice. I'm lonesome."

"Me too."

"Horny."

"Me too."

"Tell me about yourself."

"Well, I had a run-in with Mrs. Holper today. She wanted to return a dress with a huge big whisky stain on the seat. I mean, obviously she had worn it to the Jaycee thing."

"And what did *you* say?"

"I told her I didn't sell it to her like that."

"And what did *she* say?"

"She said she never had any trouble returning dresses before, which was one reason she shopped at my place rather than some others that she knew about."

"And then what did *you* say?"

"Oh, I said I was upset because Will talks like a jackass on the phone."

"I see."

"Willy's fine. He's covering some turtle eggs the dogs dug up. Tell me what you're doing."

"Reading reports. Eating junk food."

"Thinking a good bit, I expect."

"Yep."

"Can I help you?"

"I just don't have a lock on anything, Molly. There's not enough information. Well, there's a lot of information but I haven't done enough with it."

"Will you be in Atlanta for a while? I'm not bugging you about coming home, I just wonder."

"I don't know. I'll be here a few more days at least. I miss you."

"Want to talk about fucking?"

"I don't think I could stand it. I think maybe we'd better not do that."

"Do what?"

"Talk about fucking."

"Okay. You don't mind if I think about it though?"

"Absolutely not."

"We've got a new dog."

"Oh hell."

"Looks like a cross between a basset-hound and a Pekingese."

"Lovely."

"He's got big balls."

"Never mind about his balls."

"They almost drag the ground. He has to retract them when he runs."

"He can't do that."

"Yes he can. *You* don't know."

"Yes I do know."

"Can you retract yours?"

"I thought we were coming to that."

"Well?"

"If you must know, I retracted them once."

"When was that?"

"In my youth. I had to clear a barbed wire fence in a hurry."

"Why?"

"I was carrying this watermelon that I had not cultivated."

"You were fleeing? From whom?"

"A swineherd of my acquaintance. Alerted by his dogs, he burst from his dwelling in his B.V.D.s wearing a fowling piece.

Fortunately, he tripped over a butterbean trellis and gave me a running start."

"Did he shoot at you?"

"I thought so at the time, yes. But the reports I heard might have issued from my behind. I've never been entirely clear on that."

"Did you clear the fence?"

"Handily."

"A criminal mind, even at that age."

"I don't have a criminal mind."

"Of course you don't. I'm thinking about painting the kitchen. What colour do you like? Will? What colour do you like? Are you there?"

"Yeah, uh, yellow. Let's paint it yellow."

"Yellow is a bad colour for me. I'll look green at breakfast."

"Blue, then."

"Blue is cold."

"Well goddammit, paint it baby-shit-tan for all I care . . . No, look, I'll probably be home before long and we'll go to the paint store and get some chips and stuff, okay? And maybe some new handles and that."

"Let's do, let's get some handles. I don't know why I'm talking about this stuff. Look, I love you and I miss you and you're doing the right thing. It's costing you too, I know that. I'm here and I'll be here whenever you come home, or I'll meet you anywhere, any time. That's what."

"Dear Molly. Dear Molly. Go to bed now."

"All right."

"Good night."

Graham lay with his hands behind his head and conjured dinners with Molly. Stone crab and Sancerre, the salt breeze mixed with the wine.

But it was his curse to pick at conversations and he began to do it now. He had snapped at her after a harmless remark about his "criminal mind". Stupid.

Graham found Molly's interest in him largely inexplicable.

He called police headquarters and left word for Springfield that he wanted to start helping with the legwork in the morning. There was nothing else to do.

The gin helped him sleep.

6

FLIMSY COPIES of the notes on all calls about the Leeds case were placed on Buddy Springfield's desk. Tuesday morning at 7 a.m. when Springfield arrived at his office there were sixty-three of them. The top one was red-flagged.

It said Birmingham police had found a cat buried in a shoebox behind the Jacobis' garage. The cat had a flower between its paws and was wrapped in a dish-towel. The cat's name was printed on the lid in a childish hand. It wore no collar. A string tied in a granny knot held the lid on.

The Birmingham medical examiner said the cat was strangled. He had shaved it and found no puncture wound.

Springfield tapped the ear-piece of his glasses against his teeth.

They had found soft ground and dug it up with a shovel. Didn't need any damned methane probe. Still, Graham had been right.

The chief of detectives licked his thumb and started through the rest of the stack of flimsies. Most were reports of suspicious vehicles in the neighbourhood during the past week, vague descriptions giving only vehicle type or colour. Four anonymous telephone callers had told Atlanta residents "I'm gonna do you like the Leeds."

Hoyt Lewis's report was in the middle of the pile.

Springfield called the overnight watch commander.

"What about the meter reader's report on this Parsons? Number 48."

"We tried to check with the utilities last night, Chief, to see if they had anybody in that alley," the watch commander said. "They'll have to get back to us this morning."

"You have somebody get back to *them* now," Springfield said. "Check sanitation, the city manager, check for construction permits along the alley and catch me in my car."

He dialed Will Graham's number. "Will? Meet me in front of your hotel in ten minutes and let's take a little ride."

At 7.45 a.m. Springfield parked near the end of the alley. He and Graham walked abreast in wheel-tracks pressed in the gravel. Even this early the sun was hot.

"You need to get you a hat," Springfield said. His own snappy straw was tilted down over his eyes.

The chain-link fence at the rear of the Leeds property was covered with vines. They paused by the light meter on the pole.

"If he came down this way, he could see the whole back end of the house," Springfield said.

In only five days the Leeds property had begun to look neglected. The lawn was uneven and wild onions sprouted above the grass. Small branches had fallen in the yard. Graham wanted to pick them up. The house seemed asleep, the latticed porch striped and dappled with the long morning shadows of the trees. Standing with Springfield in the alley, Graham could see himself looking in the back window, opening the porch door. Oddly, his reconstruction of the entry by the killer seemed to elude him now, in the sunlight. He watched a child's swing move gently in the breeze.

"That looks like Parsons," Springfield said.

H. G. Parsons was out early, grubbing in a flower-bed in his backyard, two houses down. Springfield and Graham went to Parsons's back gate and stood beside his garbage cans. The lids were chained to the fence.

Springfield measured the height of the light meter with a tape.

He had notes on all the Leeds's neighbours. His notes said Parsons had taken early retirement from the post office at his supervisor's request. The supervisor had reported Parsons to be "increasingly absent-minded".

Springfield's notes contained gossip too. The neighbours said Parsons's wife stayed with her sister in Macon as much as she could and that his son never called him any more.

"Mr. Parsons. Mr. Parsons," Springfield called.

Parsons leaned his tilling fork against the house and came to the fence. He wore sandals and white socks. Dirt and grass had stained the toes of his socks. His face was shiny pink.

Arteriosclerosis, Graham thought. He's taken his pill.

"Yes?"

"Mr. Parsons, could we talk to you for a minute? We were hoping you could help us," Springfield said.

"Are you from the power company?"

"No, I'm Buddy Springfield from the Police Department."

"It's about the murder then. My wife and I were in Macon as I told the officer—"

"I know, Mr. Parsons. We wanted to ask about your light meter. Did—"

"If that . . . meter reader said I did anything improper, he's just—"

"No, no. Mr. Parsons, did you see a stranger reading your meter last week?"

"No."

"Are you sure? I believe you told Hoyt Lewis that someone else read your meter ahead of him."

"I did. And it's about time. I'm keeping up with this and the Public Service Commission will get a full report from me."

"Yes, sir. I'm sure they'll take care of it. Who did you see reading your meter?"

"It wasn't a stranger, it was somebody from Georgia Power."

"How do you know?"

"Well, he looked like a meter reader."

"What was he wearing?"

"What they all wear, I guess. What is it? A brown outfit and the cap."

"Did you see his face?"

"I can't remember if I did. I was looking out the kitchen window when I saw him. I wanted to talk to him, but I had to put on my robe and by the time I got outside, he was gone."

"Did he have a truck?"

"I don't remember seeing one. What's going on? Why do you want to know?"

"We're checking everybody who was in this neighbourhood last week. It's really important, Mr. Parsons. Try hard to remember."

"So it is about the murder. You haven't arrested anybody yet, have you?"

"No."

"I watched the street last night and *fifteen minutes* went by without a single squad car passing. It was horrible, what happened to the Leeds. My wife has been beside herself. I wonder who'll buy their house. I saw some Negroes looking at it the other day. You know, I had to speak to Leeds a few times about his children, but they were all right. Of course he wouldn't do anything I suggested about his lawn. The Department of Agriculture has some *excellent* pamphlets on the control of nuisance grasses. Finally I just put them in his mail-box. Honestly, when he mowed the wild onions were suffocating."

"Mr. Parsons, exactly when did you see this fellow in the alley?" Springfield asked.

"I'm not sure, I was trying to think."

"Do you recall the time of day? Morning? Noon? Afternoon?"

"I know the times of day, you don't have to name them. Afternoon, maybe. I don't remember."

Springfield rubbed the back of his neck. "Excuse me, Mr. Parsons, but I have to get this just right. Could we go in your kitchen and you show us just where you saw him from?"

"Let me see your credentials. Both of you."

In the house, silence, shiny surfaces and dead air. Neat. Neat. The desperate order of an ageing couple who see their lives begin to blur.

Graham wished he had stayed outside. He was sure the drawers held polished silver with egg between the tines.

Stop it and let's pump the old fart.

The window over the kitchen sink gave a good view of the backyard.

"There. Are you satisfied?" Parsons asked. "You *can* see out there from here. I never talked to him, I don't remember what he looked like. If that's all, I have a lot to do."

Graham spoke for the first time. "You said you went to get your robe and when you came back he was gone. You weren't dressed then?"

"No."

"In the middle of the afternoon? Were you not feeling well, Mr. Parsons?"

"What I do in my own house is my business. I can wear a kangaroo suit in here if I want to. Why aren't you out looking for the killer? Probably because it's cool in here."

"I understand you're retired, Mr. Parsons, so I guess it doesn't matter if you put on your clothes every day or not. A lot of days you just don't get dressed at all, am I right?"

Veins stood out in Parsons's temples. "Just because I'm retired doesn't mean I don't put my clothes on and get busy every day. I just got hot and I came in and took a shower. I was working. I was mulching and I had done a day's work by afternoon, which is more than you'll do today."

"You were what?"

"Mulching."

"What day did you mulch?"

"Thursday. It was last Thursday. They delivered it in the morning, a big load, and I had—I had it all spread by afternoon. You can ask at the Garden Centre how much it was."

"And you got hot and came in and took a shower. What were you doing in the kitchen?"

"Fixing a glass of iced tea."

"And you got out some ice? But the refrigerator is over there, away from the window."

Parsons looked from the window to the refrigerator, lost and confused. His eyes were dull like the eyes of a fish in the market towards the end of the day. Then they brightened in triumph. He went to the cabinet by the sink.

"I was right here, getting some Sweet 'N Low when I saw him. That's it. That's all. Now if you're through prying—"

"I think he saw Hoyt Lewis," Graham said.

"So do I," Springfield said.

"It was *not* Hoyt Lewis. It was *not*." Parsons's eyes were watering.

"How do you know?" Springfield said. "It might have been Hoyt Lewis and you just *thought*—"

"Lewis is brown from the sun. He's got old greasy hair and those peckerwood sideburns." Parsons's voice had risen and he was talking so fast it was hard to understand him. "That's how I knew. Of course it wasn't Lewis. This fellow was paler and his hair was blond. He turned to write on his clipboard and I could see under the back of his hat. Blond. Cut off square on the back of his neck."

Springfield stood absolutely still and when he spoke his voice was still sceptical. "What about his face?"

"I don't know. He may have had a moustache."

"Like Lewis?"

"Lewis doesn't have a moustache."

"Oh," Springfield said. "Was he at eye-level with the meter? Did he have to look up?"

"Eye-level, I guess."

"Would you know him if you saw him again?"

"No."

"What age was he?"

"Not old. I don't know."

"Did you see the Leeds's dog anywhere around him?"

"No."

"Look, Mr. Parsons, I can see I was wrong," Springfield said. "You're a real big help to us. If you don't mind, I'm going to send our artist out here and if you'd just let him sit right here at your kitchen table, maybe you could give him an idea of what this fellow looked like. It sure wasn't Lewis."

"I don't want my name in any newspapers."

"It won't be."

Parsons followed them outside.

"You've done a hell of a fine job on this yard, Mr. Parsons," Springfield said. "It ought to win some kind of a prize."

Parsons said nothing. His face was red and working, his eyes wet. He stood there in his baggy shorts and sandals and glared at them. As they left the yard he grabbed his fork and began to grub furiously in the ground, hacking blindly through the flowers, scattering mulch on the grass.

★   ★   ★

Springfield checked in on his car radio. None of the utilities or city agencies could account for the man in the alley on the day before the murders. Springfield reported Parsons's description and gave instructions for the artist. "Tell him to draw the pole and the meter first and go from there. He'll have to ease the witness along."

"Our artist doesn't much like to make house-calls," the chief of detectives told Graham as he slid the stripline Ford through the traffic. "He likes for the secretaries to see him work, with the witness standing on one foot and then the other looking over his shoulder. A police station is a damn poor place to question anybody that you don't need to scare. Soon as we get the picture, we'll door-to-door the neighbourhood with it.

"I feel like we just got a whiff, Will. Just faint, but a whiff, don't you? Look, we did it to the poor old devil and he came through, now let's do something with it."

"If the man in the alley is the one we want, it's the best news yet," Graham said. He was sick of himself.

"Right. It means he's not just getting off a bus and going whichever way his peter points. He's got a plan. He stayed in town overnight. He knows where he's going a day or two ahead. He's got some kind of an idea. Case the place, kill the pet, then the family. What the hell kind of an idea is that?" Springfield paused. "That's kind of your territory, isn't it?"

"It is, yes. If it's anybody's I suppose it's mine."

"I know you've seen this kind of thing before. You didn't like it the other day when I asked you about Lecter, but I need to talk to you about it."

"All right."

"He killed nine people, didn't he, in all?"

"Nine we know of. Two others didn't die."

"What happened to them?"

"One is on a respirator at a hospital in Baltimore. The other is in a private mental hospital in Denver."

"What made him do it, how was he crazy?"

Graham looked out the car window at the people on the sidewalk. His voice sounded detached, as though he were dictating a letter.

"He did it because he liked it. Still does. Dr. Lecter is not crazy, in any common way we think of being crazy. He did some hideous things because he enjoyed them. But he can function perfectly when he wants to."

"What did the psychologists call it—what was wrong with him?"

"They say he's a sociopath because they don't know what else to call him. He has some of the characteristics of what they call a sociopath. He has no remorse or guilt at all. And he had the first and worst sign— sadism to animals as a child."

Springfield grunted.

"But he doesn't have any of the other marks," Graham said. "He wasn't a drifter, he had no history of trouble with the law. He wasn't shallow and exploitive in small things, like most sociopaths are. He's not insensitive. They don't know what to call him. His electroencephalograms show some odd patterns, but they haven't been able to tell much from them."

"What would you call him?" Springfield asked.

Graham hesitated.

"Just to yourself, what do you call him?"

"He's a monster. I think of him as one of those pitiful things that are born in hospitals from time to time. They feed it, and keep it warm, but they don't put it on the machines and it dies. Lecter is the same way in his head, but he looks normal and nobody could tell."

"A couple of friends of mine in the chiefs' association are from Baltimore. I asked them how you spotted Lecter. They said they didn't know. How did you do it? What was the first indication, the first thing you felt?"

"It was a coincidence," Graham said. "The sixth victim was killed in his workshop. He had woodworking equipment and he kept his hunting stuff out there. He was laced to a pegboard where the tools hung and he was really torn up, cut and stabbed and he had arrows in him. The wounds reminded me of something. I couldn't think what it was."

"And you had to go on to the next ones."

"Yes. Lecter was very hot—he did the next three in nine days. But this sixth one, he had two old scars on his thigh. The pathologist checked with the local hospital and found he had fallen out of a tree-blind five years before while he was bow hunting and stuck an arrow through his leg.

"The doctor of record was a resident surgeon, but Lecter had treated him first – he was on duty in the emergency room. His name was on the admissions log. It had been a long time since the accident, but I thought Lecter might remember if anything had seemed fishy about the arrow wound, so I went to his office to see him. We were grabbing at anything then.

"He was practicing psychiatry by that time. He had a nice office. Antiques. He said he didn't remember much about the arrow wound, that one of the victim's hunting buddies had brought him in, and that was it.

"Something bothered me though. I thought it was something Lecter had said or something in the office. Crawford and I hashed it over. We checked the files and Lecter had no record. I wanted some time in his office by myself but we couldn't get a warrant. We had nothing to show. So I went back to see him.

"It was Sunday, he saw patients on Sunday. The building was empty except for a couple of people in his waiting-room. He saw me right away. We were talking and he was making this polite effort to help me and I looked up at some very old medical books on the shelf above his head. And I knew it was him.

"When I looked at him again maybe my face changed, I don't know. I knew it and *he knew* I knew it. I still couldn't think of the reason though. I didn't trust it. I had to figure it out. So I mumbled something and got out of there, into the hall. There was a pay phone in the hall. I didn't want to stir him up until I had some help. I was talking to the police switchboard when he came out of a service door behind me in his socks. I never heard him coming. I felt his breath was all and then—there was the rest of it."

"How did you know, though?"

"I think it was maybe a week later in the hospital I finally figured it out. It was *Wound Man*—an illustration they used in a lot of the early medical books like the ones Lecter had. It shows different kinds of battle injuries, all in one figure. I had seen it in a survey course a pathologist was teaching at G.W.U. The sixth victim's position and his injuries were a close match to *Wound Man*."

"*Wound Man*, you say? That's all you had?"

"Well, yeah. It was a coincidence that I had seen it. A piece of luck."

"That's some luck."

"If you don't believe me, what the fuck did you ask me for?"

"I didn't hear that."

"Good. I didn't mean to say it. That's the way it happened, though."

"Okay," Springfield said. "Okay. Thank you for telling me. I need to know things like that."

Parsons's description of the man in the alley and the information on the cat and the dog were possible indications of the killer's methods: it seemed likely that he scouted as a meter reader and felt compelled to hurt the victims' pets before he came to kill the family.

The immediate problem the police faced was whether or not to publicize their theory.

With the public aware of the danger signals and watching, police might get advance warning of the killer's next attack—but the killer probably followed the news too.

He might change his habits.

There was a strong feeling in the police department that the slender leads should be kept secret except for a special bulletin to veterinarians and animal shelters throughout the southeast asking for immediate reports on pet mutilations.

That meant not giving the public the best possible warning. It was a moral question and the police were not comfortable with it.

They consulted Dr. Alan Bloom in Chicago. Dr. Bloom said that if the killer read a warning in the newspaper, he would probably change his method of casing a house. Dr. Bloom doubted that the man could stop attacking the pets, regardless of the risk. The psychiatrist told the police that they should by no means assume they had 25 days to work—the period before the next full moon on August 25th.

On the morning of July 31st, three hours after Parsons gave his description, a decision was reached in a telephone conference among Birmingham and Atlanta police and Crawford in Washington: they would send the private bulletin to veterinarians, canvass for three days in the neighbourhoods with the artist's sketch, then release the information to the news media.

For those three days Graham and the Atlanta detectives pounded the sidewalks showing the sketch to householders in the area of the Leeds's home. There was only a suggestion of a face in the sketch, but they hoped to find someone who could improve it.

Graham's copy of the sketch grew soft around the edges from the sweat of his hands. Often it was difficult to get residents to answer the door. At night he lay in his room with powder on his heat rash, his mind circling the problem as though it were a hologram. He courted the feeling that precedes an idea. It would not come.

Meanwhile, there were four accidental injuries and one fatality in Atlanta as householders shot at relatives coming home late. Prowler calls multiplied and useless tips stacked up in the "In" baskets at police headquarters. Despair went around like the flu.

Crawford returned from Washington at the end of the third day and dropped in on Graham as he sat peeling off his wet socks.

"Hot work?"

"Grab a sketch in the morning and see," Graham said.

"No, it'll be on the news tonight. Did you walk all day?"

"I can't drive through their yards."

"I didn't think anything would come of this canvass," Crawford said.

"Well, what the hell did you expect me to do?"

"The best you can, that's all." Crawford rose to leave. "Busy work's been a narcotic for me sometimes, especially after I quit the booze. For you too, I think."

Graham was angry. Crawford was right, of course.

Graham was a natural procrastinator and he knew it. Long ago in school he made up for it with speed. He was not in school now.

There was something else he could do and he had known it for days. He could wait until he was driven to it by desperation in the last days before the full moon. Or he could do it now, while it might be of some use.

There was an opinion he wanted. A very strange view he needed to share; a mind-set he had to recover after his warm round years in the Keys.

The reasons clacked like roller-coaster cogs pulling up to the first long plunge and, at the top, unaware that he clutched his belly, Graham said it aloud.

"I have to see Lecter."

7

DR. FREDERICK CHILTON, chief of staff at the Chesapeake State Hospital for the Criminally Insane, came around his desk to shake Will Graham's hand.

"Dr. Bloom called me yesterday, Mr. Graham—or should I call you Dr. Graham?"

"I'm not a doctor."

"I was delighted to hear from Dr. Bloom, we've known each other for *years*. Take that chair."

"We appreciate your help, Dr. Chilton."

"Frankly, I sometimes feel like Lecter's secretary rather than his keeper," Chilton said. "The volume of his mail alone is a nuisance. I think among some researchers it's considered chic to correspond with him—I've seen his letters *framed* in psychology departments—and for a while it seemed that every Ph.D. candidate in the field wanted to interview him. Glad to co-operate with *you* of course, and Dr. Bloom."

"I need to see Dr. Lecter in as much privacy as possible," Graham said. "I may need to see him again or telephone him after today."

Chilton nodded. "To begin with, Dr. Lecter will stay in his room.

That is absolutely the only place where he is not put in restraints. One wall of his room is a double barrier which opens on the hall. I'll have a chair put there and screens if you like.

"I must ask you not to pass him any objects whatever, other than paper free of clips or staples. No ring-binders, pencils or pens. He has his own felt-tipped pens."

"I might have to show him some material that could stimulate him," Graham said.

"You can show him what you like as long as it's on soft paper. Pass him documents through the sliding food tray. Don't hand anything through the barrier and do not accept anything he might extend through the barrier. He can return papers in the food tray. I insist on that. Dr. Bloom and Mr. Crawford assured me that you would co-operate on procedure."

"I will," Graham said. He started to rise.

"I know you're anxious to get on with it, Mr. Graham, but I want to tell you something first. This will interest you.

"It may seem gratuitous to warn *you*, of all people, about Lecter. But he's very disarming. For a year after he was brought here he behaved perfectly and gave the appearance of co-operating with attempts at therapy. As a result—this was under the previous administrator— security around him was slightly relaxed.

"On the afternoon of July 8th, 1976, he complained of chest pain. His restraints were removed in the examining-room to make it easier to give him an electrocardiogram. One of his attendants left the room to smoke and the other turned away for a second. The nurse was very quick and strong. She managed to save one of her eyes.

"You may find this curious," Chilton took a strip of E K G tape from a drawer and unrolled it on his desk. He traced the spiky line with his forefinger. "Here, he's resting on the examining-table. Pulse 72. Here, he grabs the nurse's head and pulls her down on him. Here, he is subdued by the attendant. He didn't resist by the way, though the attendant dislocated his shoulder. Do you notice the strange thing? His pulse never got over 85. Even when he tore out her tongue."

Chilton could read nothing in Graham's face. He leaned back in his chair and steepled his fingers under his chin. His hands were dry and shiny.

"You know, when Lecter was first captured we thought he might provide us with a singular opportunity to study a pure sociopath," Chilton said. "It's so rare to get one alive. Lecter is so lucid, so perceptive; he's trained in psychiatry—and he's a mass murderer. He seemed to co-operate and we thought that he could be a window on this kind of aberration. We thought we'd be like Beaumont studying digestion through the opening in St. Martin's stomach.

"As it turned out, I don't think we're any closer to understanding him now than the day he came in. Have you ever talked to Lecter for any length of time?"

"No. I just saw him when . . . I saw him mainly in court. Dr. Bloom showed me his articles in the journals," Graham said.

"He's very familiar with *you*. He's given you a lot of thought."

"You had some sessions with him?"

"Yes. Twelve. He's impenetrable. Too sophisticated about the tests for them to register anything. Edwards, Fabre, even Dr. Bloom himself had a crack at him. I have their notes. He was an enigma to them too. It's impossible, of course, to tell what he's holding back or whether he understands more than he'll say. Oh, since his commitment he's done some brilliant pieces for the *American Journal of Psychiatry* and the *General Archives*. But they're always about problems he doesn't have. I think he's afraid that, if we 'solve' him, nobody will be interested in him any more and he'll be stuck in a back ward somewhere for the rest of his life."

Chilton paused. He had practised using his peripheral vision to watch his subjects in interviews. He believed that he could watch Graham this way undetected.

"The consensus around here is that the only person who has demonstrated any practical understanding of Hannibal Lecter is you, Mr. Graham. Can you tell me anything about him?"

"No."

"Some of the staff are curious about this: when you saw Dr. Lecter's murders, their 'style' so to speak, were you able perhaps to reconstruct his fantasies? And did that help you identify him?"

Graham did not answer.

"We're woefully short of material on that sort of thing. There's one single piece in the *Journal of Abnormal Psychology*. Would you mind talking with some of the staff—no, no, not this trip—Dr. Bloom was very severe with me on that point. We're to leave you alone. Next trip, perhaps."

Dr. Chilton had seen a lot of hostility. He was seeing some at the moment.

Graham stood up. "Thank you, Doctor. I want to see Lecter now."

The steel door of the maximum security section closed behind Graham. He heard the bolt slide home.

Graham knew that Lecter slept most of the morning. He looked down the corridor. At that angle he could not see into Lecter's cell, but he could tell that the lights inside were dimmed.

Graham wanted to see Dr. Lecter asleep. He wanted time to brace himself. If he felt Lecter's madness in his head, he had to contain it quickly, like a spill.

To cover the sound of his footsteps, he followed an orderly pushing a linen cart. Dr. Lecter is very difficult to slip up on.

Graham paused part way down the hall. Steel bars covered the entire front of the cell. Behind the bars, farther than arm's reach, was a stout nylon net stretched ceiling to floor and wall to wall. Through the barrier, Graham could see a table and chair bolted to the floor. The table was stacked with softcover books and correspondence. He walked up to the bars, put his hands on them, took his hands away.

Dr. Hannibal Lecter lay on his cot asleep. His head propped on a pillow against the wall. Alexandre Dumas's *Le Grand Dictionnaire de Cuisine* was open on his chest.

Graham had stared through the bars for about five seconds when Lecter opened his eyes and said, "That's the same atrocious aftershave you wore in court."

"I keep getting it for Christmas."

Dr. Lecter's eyes are maroon and they reflect the light redly in tiny points. Graham felt each hair bristle on his nape. He put his hand on the back of his neck.

"Christmas, yes," Lecter said. "Did you get my card?"

"I got it. Thank you."

Dr. Lecter's Christmas card had been forwarded to Graham from the F.B.I. crime laboratory in Washington. He took it into the backyard, burned it, and washed his hands before touching Molly.

Lecter rose and walked over to his table. He is a small, lithe man. Very neat. "Why don't you have a seat, Will? I think there are some folding chairs in a closet just down that way. At least, that's where it sounds like they come from."

"The orderly's bringing one."

Lecter stood until Graham was seated in the hall. "And how is Officer Stewart?" he asked.

"Stewart's fine." Officer Stewart left law enforcement after he saw Dr. Lecter's basement. He managed a motel now. Graham did not mention this. He didn't think Stewart would appreciate any mail from Lecter.

"Unfortunate that his emotional problems got the better of him. I thought he was a very promising young officer. Do you ever have any problems, Will?"

"No."

"Of course you don't."

Graham felt that Lecter was looking through to the back of his skull. His attention felt like a fly walking around in there.

"I'm glad you came. It's been what now, three years? My callers are all professional. Banal clinical psychiatrists and grasping second-rate *doctors* of psychology from silo colleges somewhere. Pencil-lickers trying to protect their tenure with pieces in the journals."

"Dr. Bloom showed me your article on surgical addiction in the *Journal of Clinical Psychiatry*."

"And?"

"Very interesting, even to a layman."

"A layman . . . layman, layman. Interesting term," Lecter said. "So many learned fellows going about. So many *experts* on government grants. And you say you're a layman. But it was you who caught me, wasn't it, Will? Do you know how you did it?"

"I'm sure you've read the transcript. It's all in there."

"No, it's not. Do you know how you did it, Will?"

"It's in the transcript. What does it matter now?"

"It doesn't matter to *me*, Will."

"I want you to help me, Dr. Lecter."

"Yes, I thought so."

"It's about Atlanta and Birmingham."

"Yes."

"You read about it, I'm sure."

"I've read the papers. I can't clip them. They won't let me have scissors, of course. Sometimes they threaten me with loss of books, you know. I wouldn't want them to think I was dwelling on anything morbid." He laughed. Dr. Lecter has small white teeth. "You want to know how he's choosing them, don't you?"

"I thought you would have some ideas. I'm asking you to tell me what they are."

"Why should I?"

Graham had anticipated the question. A reason to stop multiple murders would not occur readily to Dr. Lecter.

"There are things you don't have," Graham said. "Research materials, film-strips even. I'd speak to the chief of staff."

"Chilton. You must have seen him when you came in. Gruesome, isn't it? Tell me the truth, he fumbles at your head like a freshman pulling at a panty girdle, doesn't he? Watched you out of the corner of his eyes. Picked *that* up, didn't you? You may not believe this, but he actually tried to give *me* a Thematic Apperception Test. He was sitting there just like the Cheshire cat, waiting for Mf 13 to come up. Ha. Forgive me, I forget that you're not among the annointed. It's a card with a woman in bed and a man in the foreground. I was supposed to avoid a sexual interpretation. I laughed. He puffed up and told everybody I avoided prison with a Ganser syndrome— never mind, it's boring."

"You'd have access to the A.M.A. film-strip library."

"I don't think you'd get me the things I want."

"Try me."

"I have quite enough to read as it is."

"You'd get to see the file on this case. There's another reason."

"Pray."

"I thought you might be curious to find out if you're smarter than the person I'm looking for."

"Then, by implication, you think you are smarter than I am, since you caught me."

"No. I know I'm not smarter than you are."

"Then how did you catch me, Will?"

"You had disadvantages."

"What disadvantages?"

"Passion. And you're insane."

"You're very tan, Will."

Graham did not answer.

"Your hands are rough. They don't look like a cop's hands any more. That shaving lotion is something a child would select. It has a ship on the bottle, doesn't it?" Dr. Lecter seldom holds his head upright. He tilts it as he asks a question, as though he were screwing an augur of curiosity into your face. Another silence, and Lecter said, "Don't think you can persuade me with appeals to my intellectual vanity."

"I don't think I'll persuade you. You'll do it or you won't. Dr. Bloom is working on it anyway, and he's the most—"

"Do you have the file with you?"

"Yes."

"And pictures?"

"Yes."

"Let me have them and I might consider it."

"No."

"Do you dream much, Will?"

"Goodbye, Dr. Lecter."

"You haven't threatened to take away my books yet."

Graham walked away.

"Let me have the file, then. I'll tell you what I think."

Graham had to pack the abridged file tightly into the sliding tray. Lecter pulled it through.

"There's a summary on top. You can read that now," Graham said.

"Do you mind if I do it privately? Give me an hour."

Graham waited on a tired plastic couch in a grim lounge. Orderlies came in for coffee. He did not speak to them. He stared at small objects in the room and was glad they held still in his vision. He had to go to the rest-room twice. He was numb.

The turnkey admitted him to the maximum security section again.

Lecter sat at his table, his eyes filmed with thought. Graham knew he had spent most of the hour with the pictures.

"This is a very shy boy, Will. I'd love to meet him . . . Have you considered the possibility that he's disfigured? Or that he may believe he's disfigured?"

"The mirrors."

"Yes. You notice he smashes all the mirrors in the houses, not just enough to get the pieces he wants. He doesn't just put the shards in place for the damage they cause. They're set so he can see himself. In their eyes—Mrs. Jacobi and—what was the other name?"

"Mrs. Leeds."

"Yes."

"That's interesting," Graham said.

"It's not 'interesting'. You'd thought of that before."

"I had considered it."

"You just came here to look at me. Just to get the old scent again, didn't you? Why don't you just smell yourself?"

"I want your opinion."

"I don't have one right now."

"When you do have one, I'd like to hear it."

"May I keep the file?"

"I haven't decided yet," Graham said.

"Why are there no descriptions of the grounds? Here we have frontal views of the houses, floor plans, diagrams of the rooms where the deaths occurred, and little mention of the grounds. What were the yards like?"

"Big backyards, fenced, with some hedges. Why?"

"Because, my dear Will, if this pilgrim feels a special relationship with the moon, he might like to go outside and look at it. Before he tidies himself up, you understand? Have you seen blood in the moonlight, Will? It appears quite black. Of course, it keeps the distinctive sheen. If one were nude, say, it would be better to have outdoor privacy for that sort of thing. One must show some consideration for the neighbours, hmmmm?"

"You think the yard might be a factor when he selects victims?"

"Oh yes. And there will be more victims, of course. Let me keep the file, Will. I'll study it. When you get more files, I'd like to see them too. You can call me. On the rare occasions when my lawyer calls, they bring me a telephone. They used to patch him through on the intercom, but everyone listened of course. Would you like to give me your home number?"

"No."

"Do you know how you caught me, Will?"

"Goodbye, Dr. Lecter. You can leave messages for me at the number on the file." Graham walked away.

"Do you know how you caught me?"

Graham was out of Lecter's sight now and he walked faster toward the far steel door.

"The reason you caught me is that WE'RE JUST ALIKE," was the last thing Graham heard as the steel door closed behind him.

He was numb except for dreading the loss of numbness. Walking with his head down, speaking to no one, he could hear his blood like a hollow drumming of wings. It seemed a very short distance to the outside. This was only a building; there were only five doors between Lecter and the outside. He had the absurd feeling that Lecter had walked out with him. He stopped outside the entrance and looked around him, assuring himself that he was alone.

From a car across the street, his long lens propped on the window sill, Freddy Lounds got a nice profile shot of Graham in the doorway and the words in stone above him: "Chesapeake State Hospital for the Criminally Insane."

As it turned out, the *National Tattler* cropped the picture to just Graham's face and the last two words in the stone.

8

DR. HANNIBAL LECTER lay on his cot with the cell lights down after Graham left him. Several hours passed.

For a while he had textures; the weave of the pillowcase against his hands clasped behind his head, the smooth membrane that lined his cheek.

Then he had odours and let his mind play over them. Some were real, some were not. They had put Chlorox in the drains; semen. They were serving chili down the hall; sweat-stiffened khaki. Graham would not give him his home telephone number; the bitter green smell of cut cockleburr and sea-weed.

Lecter sat up. The man might have been civil. His thoughts had the warm brass smell of an electric clock.

Lecter blinked several times and his eyebrows rose. He turned up the lights and wrote a note to Chilton asking for a telephone call to his counsel.

Lecter was entitled by law to speak with his lawyer in privacy and he hadn't abused the right. Since Chilton would never allow him to go to the telephone, the telephone was brought to him.

Two guards brought it, unrolling a long cord from the telephone jack at their desk. One of the guards had the keys. The other held a can of Mace.

"Go to the back of the cell, Dr. Lecter. Face the wall. If you turn around or approach the barrier before you hear the lock snap, I'll Mace you in the face. Understand?"

"Yes indeed," Lecter said. "Thank you so much for bringing the telephone."

He had to reach through the nylon net to dial. Chicago Information gave him numbers for the University of Chicago Departments of Psychiatry and Dr. Alan Bloom's office number. He dialed the psychiatry department switchboard.

"I'm trying to reach Dr. Alan Bloom."

"I'm not sure he's in today, but I'll connect you."

"Just a second, I'm supposed to know his secretary's name and I'm embarrassed to say I've forgotten it."

"Linda King. Just a moment."

"Thank you."

The telephone rang eight times before it was picked up.

"Linda King's desk."

"Hi, Linda?"

"Linda doesn't come in on Saturday."

Dr. Lecter had counted on that. "Maybe you could help me, if you don't mind. This is Bob Greer at Blaine and Edwards Publishing Co. Dr. Bloom asked me to send a copy of the Overholser book, *The Psychiatrist and the Law*, to Will Graham and Linda was supposed to send me the address and phone number, but she never did."

"I'm just a graduate assistant, she'll be in on Mon—"

"I have to catch Federal Express with it in about five minutes and I hate to bother Dr. Bloom about it at home because he told Linda to send it and I don't want to get her in hot water. It's right there in her Rolodex or whatever. I'll dance at your wedding if you'll read it to me."

"She doesn't have a Rolodex."

"How about a Call Caddy with the slide on the side?"

"Yes."

"Be a darling and slide that rascal and I won't take up any more of your time."

"What was the name?"

"Graham. Will Graham."

"All right, his home number is 305 JL 5 7002."

"I'm supposed to mail it to his address."

"It doesn't give the address of his house."

"What does it have?"

"Federal Bureau of Investigation, Tenth and Pennsylvania, Washington, D.C. Oh, and Post Office Box 3680, Marathon, Florida."

"That's fine, you're an angel."

"You're welcome."

Lecter felt much better. He thought he might surprise Graham with a call sometime or, if the man couldn't be civil, he might have a hospital supply-house mail Graham a colostomy bag for old time's sake.

9

SEVEN HUNDRED miles to the southwest, in the cafeteria at Gateway Film Laboratory of St. Louis, Francis Dolarhyde was waiting for a hamburger. The entrées offered in the steam table were filmed over. He stood beside the cash register and sipped coffee from a paper cup.

A red-haired young woman wearing a laboratory smock came into the cafeteria and studied the candy machine. She looked at Francis Dolarhyde's back several times and pursed her lips. Finally she walked over to him and said, "Mr. D.?"

Dolarhyde turned. He always wore red goggles outside the darkroom. She kept her eyes on the nose-piece of the goggles.

"Will you sit down with me a minute? I want to tell you something."

"What can you tell me, Eileen?"

"That I'm really sorry. Bob was just really drunk and, you know, clowning around. He didn't mean anything. Please come sit down. Just for a minute. Will you do that?"

"Mmmmm hmmmm." Dolarhyde never said "yes", as he had trouble with the sibilant "s".

They sat. She twisted a napkin in her hands.

"Everybody was having a good time at the party and we were glad you came by," she said. "Real glad and surprised, too. You know how Bob is, he does voices all the time—he ought to be on the radio. He did two or three accents, telling jokes and all—he can talk just like a Negro. When he did that other voice he didn't mean to make you feel bad. He was too drunk to know who was there."

"They were all laughing and then they . . . didn't laugh." Dolarhyde never said "stopped" because of the fricative "s".

"That's when Bob realized what he had done."

"He went on though."

"I know it," she said, managing to look from her napkin to his goggles without lingering on the way. "I got on his case about it, too. He said he didn't mean anything, he just saw he was into it and tried to keep up the joke. You saw how red his face got."

"He invited me to . . . perform a duet with him."

"He hugged you and tried to put his arm around you. He wanted you to laugh it off, Mr. D."

"I've laughed it off, Eileen."

"Bob feels terrible."

"Well, I don't want him to feel terrible. I don't want that. Tell him for me. And it won't make it any different here at the plant. Golly, if I had talent like Bob I'd make jo—a joke all the time." Dolarhyde avoided plurals whenever he could. "We'll all get together before long and he'll know how I feel."

"Good, Mr. D. You know he's really, under all the fun, he's a sensitive guy."

"I'll bet. Tender, I imagine." Dolarhyde's voice was muffled by his hand. When seated, he always pressed the knuckle of his forefinger under his nose.

"Pardon?"

"I think you're good for him, Eileen."

"I think so, I really do. He's not drinking but just on week-ends. He just starts to relax and his wife calls the house. He makes faces while I talk to her, but I can tell he's upset after. A woman knows." She tapped Dolarhyde on the wrist and, despite the goggles, saw the touch register in his eyes. "Take it easy, Mr. D. I'm glad we had this talk."

"I am too, Eileen."

Dolarhyde watched her walk away. She had a suck-mark on the back of her knee. He thought, correctly, that Eileen did not appreciate him. No one did, actually.

The great dark-room was cool and smelled of chemicals. Working under the red safety lights, Francis Dolarhyde checked the developer in the A tank. Hundreds of feet of home movie from all over the country moved through the tank hourly. The temperature and freshness of the chemicals were critical. This was his responsibility along with all the other operations until the film had passed through the dryer. Many times a day he lifted samples of film from the tank and checked them frame by frame. The red-lit room was quiet. Dolarhyde discouraged chatter among his assistants and communicated with them largely in gestures.

When the evening shift ended, he remained alone in the dark-room to develop, dry and splice some film of his own.

Dolarhyde got home about 10 p.m. He lived alone in a big house his grandparents had left him. It stood at the end of a gravel drive that runs through an apple orchard north of St. Charles, Mo., across the Missouri River from St. Louis. The orchard's absentee owner did not take care of it. Dead and twisted trees stood among the green ones. Now, in early August, the smell of rotting apples hung over the orchard. There were many bees in the daytime. The nearest neighbour was a half-mile away.

Dolarhyde always made an inspection tour of the house as soon as he got home; there had been an abortive burglary attempt some years before. He flicked on the lights in each room and looked around. A visitor would not think he lived alone. His grandparents' clothes still hung in the closets, his grandmother's brushes were on her dresser with combings of hair in them. Her teeth were in a glass on the bedside table. The water had long since evaporated. His grandmother had been dead for ten years.

(The funeral director had asked him, "Mr. Dolarhyde, wouldn't you like to bring me your grandmother's teeth?" He replied, "Just drop the lid.")

Satisfied he was alone in the house, Dolarhyde went upstairs, took a long shower and washed his hair.

He put on a kimono of a synthetic material that felt like silk and lay down on his narrow bed in the room he had occupied since childhood. His grandmother's hair-dryer had a plastic cap and hose. He put on the cap and, while he dried, he thumbed through a new high-fashion magazine. The hatred and brutishness in some of the photographs was remarkable.

He began to feel excited. He swivelled the metal shade of his reading-lamp to light a print on the wall at the foot of the bed. It was William Blake's *The Great Red Dragon and the Woman Clothed with the Sun.*

The picture had stunned him the first time he saw it. Never before had he seen anything that approached his graphic thought. He felt that Blake must have peeked in his ear and seen the Red Dragon. For weeks Dolarhyde had worried that his thoughts might glow out of his ears, might be visible in the dark-room, might fog the film. He put cotton balls in his ears. Then, fearing that cotton was too flammable, he tried steel wool. That made his ears bleed. Finally he cut small pieces of asbestos cloth from an ironing-board cover and rolled them into little pills that would fit in his ears.

The Red Dragon was all he had for a long time. It was not all he had now. He felt the beginnings of an erection.

He had wanted to go through this slowly, but now he could not wait.

Dolarhyde closed the heavy draperies over windows in the downstairs parlour. He set up his screen and projector. His grandfather had put a La-Z-Boy recliner in the parlour over his grandmother's objections. (She had put a doily on the headrest.) Now Dolarhyde was glad. It was very comfortable. He draped a towel over the arm of the chair.

He turned out the lamps. Lying back in the dark room, he might have been anywhere. Over the ceiling fixture he had a good light-machine which rotated, making varicoloured dots of light crawl over the walls, the floor, his skin. He might have been reclining on the acceleration couch of a space vehicle, in a glass bubble out among the stars. When he closed his eyes he thought he could feel the points of light move over him and when he opened them, those might be the lights of cities above or beneath him. There was no more down or up. The light-machine turned faster as it got warm and the dots swarmed over him, flowed over furniture in angular streams, fell in meteor showers down the walls. He might have been a comet plunging through the Crab Nebula.

There was one place shielded from the light. He had placed a piece of cardboard near the machine and it cast a shadow over the movie screen.

Sometimes, in the future, he would smoke first to heighten the effect, but he did not need it now, this time.

He thumbed the drop switch at his side to start the projector. A white rectangle sprang on the screen, greyed and streaked as the leader moved past the lens, and then the grey Scottie perked up his ears and ran to the kitchen door, shivering and wagging his stump of a tail. A cut to the Scottie running beside a kerb, turning to snap at his side as he ran.

Now Mrs. Leeds came into the kitchen carrying groceries. She laughed and touched her hair. The children came in behind her.

A cut to a badly lit shot in Dolarhyde's own bedroom upstairs. He is standing nude before the print of *The Great Red Dragon and the Woman Clothed with the Sun*. He is wearing "combat glasses", the close-fitting wraparound plastic glasses favoured by hockey players. He has an erection which he improves with his hand.

The focus blurs as he approaches the camera with stylized movements, hand reaching to change the focus as his face fills the frame. The picture quivers and sharpens suddenly to a close-up of his mouth, his disfigured upper lip rolled back, tongue out through the teeth, one rolling eye still in the frame. The mouth fills the screen, writhing lips pulled back from jagged teeth and darkness as his mouth engulfs the lens.

The difficulty of the next part was evident.

A bouncing blur in a harsh movie light became a bed and Charles Leeds thrashing. Mrs. Leeds sitting up, shielding her eyes, turning to Leeds and putting her hands on him, rolling toward the edge of the bed, legs tangled in the covers, trying to rise. The camera jerked toward the ceiling, moulding whipping across the screen like a stave, and then the picture steadied, Mrs. Leeds back down on the mattress, a dark spot on her nightdress spreading and Leeds, hand to his neck and eyes wild rising. The screen went black for five beats, then the tic of a splice.

The camera was steady now, on a tripod. They were all dead now. Arranged. Two children seated against the wall facing the bed, one seated across the corner from them facing the camera. Mr. and Mrs. Leeds in bed with the covers over them. Mr. Leeds propped up against the headboard, the sheet covering the rope around his chest and his head lolled to the side.

Dolarhyde came into the picture from the left with the stylized movements of a Balinese dancer. Blood-smeared and naked except for his glasses and gloves, he mugged and capered among the dead.

He approached the far side of the bed, Mrs. Leeds's side, took the corner of the covers, whipped them off the bed and held the pose as though he had executed a veronica.

Now, watching in the parlour of his grandparents' house, Dolarhyde was covered with a sheen of sweat. His thick tongue ran out constantly, the scar on his upper lip wet and shiny and he moaned as he stimulated himself.

Even at the height of his pleasure he was sorry to see that in the film's ensuing scene he lost all his grace and elegance of motion, rooting pig-like with his bottom turned carelessly to the camera. There were no dramatic pauses, no sense of pace or climax, just brutish frenzy.

It was wonderful anyway. Watching the film was wonderful. But not as wonderful as the acts themselves.

Two major flaws, Dolarhyde felt, were that the film did not actually show the deaths of the Leeds, and his own poor performance toward the end. He seemed to lose all his values. That was not how the Red Dragon would do it.

Well. He had many films to make and, with experience, he hoped he could maintain some aesthetic distance, even in the most intimate moments.

He must bear down. This was his life's work, a magnificent thing. It would live forever.

He must press on soon. He must select his fellow performers. Already, he had copied several films of Fourth of July family outings. The end of summer always brought a rush of business at the film processing plant as vacation movies came in. Thanksgiving would bring another rush.

Families were mailing their applications to him every day.

CHAPTER

10

THE PLANE from Washington to Birmingham was half-empty. Graham took a window seat with no one beside him.

He declined the tired sandwich the stewardess offered and put his Jacobi file on the tray table. At the front he had listed the similarities between the Jacobis and the Leeds.

Both couples were in their late thirties, both had children—two boys and a girl. Edward Jacobi had another son, by a previous marriage, who was away at college when the family was killed.

Both parents in each case had college degrees and both families lived in two-storey houses in pleasant suburbs. Mrs. Jacobi and Mrs. Leeds were attractive women. The families had some of the same credit cards and they subscribed to some of the same popular magazines.

There the similarities ended. Charles Leeds was a tax attorney, while Edward Jacobi was an engineer and metallurgist. The Atlanta family were Presbyterian; the Jacobis were Catholic. The Leeds were lifelong Atlanta residents, while the Jacobis had lived in Birmingham only three months, transferred there from Detroit.

The word "random" sounded in Graham's head like a dripping

faucet. "Random selection of victims", "no apparent motive"—news-papers used those terms and detectives spat them out in anger and frustration in homicide squadrooms.

"Random" wasn't accurate though. Graham knew that mass mur-derers and serial killers do not select their victims at random.

The man who killed the Jacobis and the Leeds saw something in them that drew him and drove him to do it. He might have known them well—Graham hoped so – or he might not have known them at all. But Graham was sure the killer saw them at some time before he killed them. He chose them because *something* in them spoke to him, and the women were at the core of it. What was it?

There were some differences in the crimes.

Edward Jacobi was shot as he came down the stairs carrying a flashlight—probably he was awakened by a noise.

Mrs. Jacobi and her children were shot in the head, Mrs. Leeds in the abdomen. The weapon was a 9mm automatic pistol in all the shootings. Traces of steel wool from a home-made silencer were found in the wounds. The cartridge cases bore no fingerprints.

The knife had been used only on Charles Leeds. Dr. Princi believed it was thin-bladed and very keen, possibly a filleting knife.

The methods of entry were different too; a patio door pried open at the Jacobis', the glass-cutter at the Leeds's.

Photographs of the crime in Birmingham did not show the quantity of blood found at the Leeds's, but there were stains on the bedroom walls about two and one-half feet above the floor. So the killer had an audience in Birmingham too. The Birmingham police checked the bodies for fingerprints, including the fingernails, and found nothing. Burial for a summer month in Birmingham would destroy any prints like the one on the Leeds child.

In both places were the same blond hairs, same spit, same semen.

Graham propped photographs of the two smiling families against the seat-back in front of him and stared at them for a long time in the hanging quiet of the aeroplane.

What could have attracted the murderer specifically to *them*? Graham wanted very much to believe there was a common factor and that he would find it soon.

Otherwise he would have to enter more houses and see what the Tooth Fairy had left for him.

Graham got directions from the Birmingham field office and checked in with the police by telephone from the airport. The compact car he rented spat water from the air-conditioner vents on to his hands and arms.

His first stop was the Geehan Realty office on Dennison Avenue.

Geehan, tall and bald, made haste across his turquoise shag to greet Graham. His smile faded when Graham showed his identification and asked for the key to the Jacobi house.

"Will there be some cops in uniform out there today?" he asked, his hand on the top of his head.

"I don't know."

"I hope to God not, I've got a chance to show it twice this afternoon. It's a nice house. People see it and they forget this other. Last Thursday I had a couple from Duluth, substantial retired people hot on the Sun Belt. I had them down to the short rows—talking mortgages—I mean that man could have fronted a *third*, when the squad car rode up and in they came. Couple asked them questions and, boy, did they get some answers. These good officers gave 'em the whole tour—who was lying where. Then it was Goodbye, Geehan, much obliged for your trouble. I try to show 'em how safe we've fixed it but they don't listen. There they go, jake-legged through the gravel, climbing back in their Sedan DeVille."

"Have any single men asked to look at it?"

"They haven't asked me. It's a multiple listing. I don't think so though. Police wouldn't let us start painting until, I don't know, we just got finished inside last Tuesday. Took two coats of interior Latex, three in places. We're still working outside. It'll be a genuine show-place."

"How can you sell it before the estate's probated?"

"I can't *close* until probate, but that doesn't mean I can't be ready. People could move in on a memorandum of understanding. I need to do something. A business associate of mine is holding the paper and that interest just works all day and all night while you're asleep."

"Who is Mr. Jacobi's executor?"

"Byron Metcalf, firm of Metcalf and Barnes. How long you figure on being out there?"

"I don't know. Until I've finished."

"You can drop that key in the mail. You don't have to come back by."

Graham had the flat feeling of a cold trail as he drove out to the Jacobi house. It was barely within the city limits in an area newly annexed. He stopped beside the highway once to check his map before he found the turnoff on to an asphalt secondary road.

More than a month had passed since they were killed. What had he been doing then? Putting a pair of diesels in a 65-foot Rybovich hull, signalling to Ariaga in the crane to come down another half-inch. Molly came over in the late afternoon and he and Molly and Ariaga sat under an awning in the cockpit of the half-finished boat and ate the big prawns Molly brought and drank cold Dos Equis beer. Ariaga explained the best way to clean crayfish, drawing the tail fan in sawdust on the deck and the sunlight, broken on the water, played on the undersides of the wheeling gulls.

Water from the air-conditioning squirted on the front of Graham's shirt and he was in Birmingham now and there were no prawns or gulls. He was driving and pastures and wooded lots were on his right with goats and horses in them and on his left was Stonebridge, a long-established residential area with a few elegant homes and a number of rich people's houses.

He saw the realtor's sign a hundred yards before he reached it. The Jacobi house was the only one on the right side of the road. Sap from the pecan trees beside the drive had made the gravel sticky and it rattled inside the fenders of the car. A carpenter on a ladder was installing window guards. The workman raised a hand to Graham as he walked around the house.

A flagged patio at the side was shaded by a large oak tree. At night the tree would block out the floodlight in the side yard as well. This was where the Tooth Fairy had entered, through sliding glass doors. The doors had been replaced with new ones, the aluminium frames still bright and bearing the manufacturer's sticker. Covering the sliding doors was a new wrought-iron security gate. The basement door was new too—flush steel and secured by deadbolts. The components of a hot tub stood in crates on the flagstones.

Graham went inside. Bare floors and dead air. His footsteps echoed in the empty house.

The new mirrors in the bathrooms had never reflected the Jacobis' faces or the killer's. On each was a fuzzy white spot where the price had been torn off. A folded drop cloth lay in a corner of the master bedroom. Graham sat on it long enough for the sunlight through the bare windows to move one board-width across the floor.

There was nothing here. Nothing any more.

If he had come here immediately after the Jacobis were killed, would the Leeds still be alive? Graham wondered. He tested the weight of that burden.

It did not lift when he was out of the house and under the sky again.

Graham stood in the shade of a pecan tree, shoulders hunched, hands in his pockets, and looked down the long drive to the road that passed in front of the Jacobi house.

How had the Tooth Fairy come to the Jacobi house? He had to drive. Where did he park? The gravel driveway was too noisy for a midnight visit, Graham thought. The Birmingham police did not agree.

He walked down the drive to the roadside. The asphalt road was bordered with ditches as far as he could see. It might be possible to pull across the ditch and hide a vehicle in the brush on the Jacobis' side of the road if the ground were hard and dry.

Facing the Jacobi house across the road was the single entrance to Stonebridge. The sign said that Stonebridge had a private patrol service. A strange vehicle would be noticed there. So would a man walking late at night. Scratch parking in Stonebridge.

Graham went back into the house and was surprised to find a telephone working. He called the Weather Bureau and learned that three inches of rain fell on the day before the Jacobis were killed. The ditches were full, then. The Tooth Fairy did not hide his vehicle beside the asphalt road.

A horse in the pasture beside the yard kept pace with Graham as he walked along the whitewashed fence toward the rear of the property. He gave the horse a Life Saver and left him at the corner as he turned along the back fence behind the out-buildings.

He stopped when he saw the depression in the ground where the Jacobi children had buried their cat. Thinking about it in the Atlanta police station with Springfield, he had pictured the out-buildings as white. Actually they were dark green.

The children had wrapped the cat in a dish towel and buried it in a shoebox with a flower between its paws.

Graham rested his forearm on top of the fence and leaned his forehead against it.

A pet funeral, solemn rite of childhood. Parent going back into the house, ashamed to pray. The children looking at one another, discovering new nerves in the place loss pierces. One bows her head, then they all do, the shovel taller than any of them. Afterward a discussion of whether or not the cat is in Heaven with God and Jesus, and the children don't shout for a while.

A certainty came to Graham as he stood, sun hot on the back of his neck: as surely as the Tooth Fairy killed the cat, he had watched the children bury it. He had to see that if he possibly could.

He did not make two trips out here, one to kill the cat and the second for the Jacobis. He came and killed the cat and waited for the children to find it.

There was no way to determine exactly where the children found the cat. The police had located no one who spoke to the Jacobis after noon, ten hours or so before they died.

How had the Tooth Fairy come and where had he waited?

Behind the back fence the brush began, running head high for thirty yards to the trees. Graham dug his wrinkled map out of his back pocket and spread it on the fence. It showed an unbroken strip of woods a quarter-mile deep running across the back of the Jacobi property and continuing in both directions. Beyond the woods, bounding them on the south, was a section line road that paralleled the one in front of the Jacobi house.

Graham drove from the house back to the highway, measuring the distance on his odometer. He went south on the highway and turned on to the section line he had seen on the map. Measuring again, he drove slowly along it until the odometer showed him he was behind the Jacobi house on the other side of the woods.

Here the pavement ended at a low-income housing project so new it did not show on his map. He pulled into the parking lot. Most of the cars were old and sagging on their springs. Two were up on blocks.

Black children played basketball on the bare earth around a single netless goal. Graham sat on his fender to watch the game for a moment.

He wanted to take off his jacket, but he knew the .44 Special and the flat camera on his belt would attract attention. He always felt a curious embarrassment when people looked at his pistol.

There were eight players on the team wearing shirts. The skins had eleven, all playing at once. Refereeing was by acclamation.

A small skin, shoved down in the rebounding, stalked home mad. He came back fortified with a cookie and dived into the pack again.

The yelling and the thump of the ball lifted Graham's spirits.

One goal, one basketball. It struck him again how many *things* the Leeds had. The Jacobis too, according to the Birmingham police when they ruled out burglary. Boats and sporting equipment, camping equipment, cameras and guns and rods. It was another thing the families had in common.

And with the thought of the Leeds and the Jacobis alive came the thought of how they were afterward and Graham couldn't watch basketball anymore. He took a deep breath and headed for the dark woods across the road.

The underbrush, heavy at the edge of the pine woods, thinned when Graham reached the deep shade and he had easy going over the pine needles. The air was warm and still. Bluejays in the trees ahead announced his coming.

The ground sloped gently to a dry stream bed where a few cypresses grew and the tracks of racoons and field mice were pressed into the red clay. A number of human footprints marked the stream bed, some of them left by children. All were caved in and rounded, left several rains ago.

Past the stream bed the land rose again, changing to sandy loam that supported ferns beneath the pines. Graham worked his way uphill in the heat until he saw the light beneath the trees at the edge of the woods.

Between the trunks he could see the upper storey of the Jacobi house.

Undergrowth again, head high from the edge of the woods to the Jacobis' back fence. Graham worked his way through it and stood at the fence looking into the yard.

The Tooth Fairy could have parked at the housing development and come through the woods to the brush behind the house. He could have lured the cat into the brush and choked it, the body limp in one hand as he crawled on his knees and other hand to the fence. Graham could see the cat in the air, never twisting to land on its feet, but hitting on its back with a thump in the yard.

The Tooth Fairy did that in daylight—the children would not have found or buried the cat at night.

And he waited to see them find it.

Did he wait for the rest of the day in the heat of the underbrush? At the fence he would be visible through the rails. In order to see the yard from further back in the brush he would have to stand and face the windows of the house with the sun beating on him. Clearly he would go back to the trees. So did Graham.

The Birmingham police were not stupid. He could see where they had pushed through the brush, searching the area as a matter of course. But that was before the cat was found. They were looking for clues, dropped objects, tracks – not for a vantage point.

He went a few yards into the forest behind the Jacobi house and worked back and forth in the dappled shade. First he took the high ground that afforded a partial view of the yard and then worked his way down the tree line.

He had searched for more than an hour when a wink of light from the ground caught his eye. He lost it, found it again. It was a ring-pull tab from a soft drink can half-buried in the leaves beneath an elm tree, one of the few elms among the pines.

He spotted it from eight feet away and went no closer for five minutes while he scanned the ground around the tree. He squatted and brushed the leaves away ahead of him as he approached the tree, duck-walking in the path he made to avoid ruining any impressions. Working slowly, he cleared the leaves all around the trunk. No footprints had pressed through the mat of last year's leaves.

Near the aluminium tab he found a dried apple-core eaten thin by ants. Birds had pecked out the seeds. He studied the ground for ten more minutes. Finally, he sat on the ground, stretched out his aching legs and leaned back against the tree.

A cone of gnats swarmed in a column of sunlight. A caterpillar rippled along the underside of a leaf.

There was a wedge of red creek mud from the instep of a boot on the limb above his head.

Graham hung his coat on a branch and began to climb carefully on the opposite side of the tree, peering around the trunk at the limbs above the wedge of mud. At 30 feet he looked round the trunk and there was the Jacobi house 175 yards away. It looked different from this height, the roof colour dominant. He could see the backyard and the ground behind the out-buildings very well. A decent pair of field-glasses would pick up the expression on a face easily at this distance.

Graham could hear traffic in the distance and far away he heard a beagle on a case. A cicada started its numbing bandsaw buzz and drowned out the other sounds.

A thick limb just above him joined the trunk at a right angle to the Jacobi house. He pulled himself up until he could see and leaned round the trunk to look at it.

Close by his cheek a soft drink can was wedged between the limb and the trunk.

"I love it," Graham whispered into the bark. "Oh Sweet Jesus, yes. Come on, can."

Still, a child might have left it.

He climbed higher on his side of the tree, dicey work on small branches, and moved around until he could look down on the big limb.

A patch of outer bark on the upper side of the limb was shaved away leaving a field of green inner bark the size of a playing card. Centred in the green rectangle, carved through to the white wood, Graham saw this:

It was done carefully and cleanly with a very sharp knife. It was not the work of a child.

Graham photographed the mark, carefully bracketing his expossures.

The view from the big limb was good and it had been improved: the stub of a small branch jutted down from the limb above. It had been clipped off to clear the view. The fibres were compressed and the end slightly flattened in the cutting.

Graham looked for the severed branch. If it had been on the ground he would have seen it. There, tangled in the limbs below, brown withered leaves amid the green foliage.

The laboratory would need both sides of the cut in order to measure the pitch of the cutting edges. That meant coming back here with a saw. He made several photographs of the stub. All the while he mumbled to himself.

I think that after you killed the cat and threw it into the yard, my man, you climbed up here and waited. I think you watched the children and passed the time whittling and dreaming. When night came you saw them passing their bright windows and you watched the shades go down, and you saw the lights go out one by one. And after a while you climbed down and went in to them. Didn't you? It wouldn't be too hard

*a climb straight down from the big limb with a flashlight and the bright
moon rising.*

It was a hard enough climb for Graham. He stuck a twig into the
opening of the soft drink can, gently lifting it from the crotch of the
tree and descended, holding the twig in his teeth when he had to use
both hands.

Back at the housing project, Graham found that someone had
written "Levon is a doo-doo head" in the dust on the side of his car.
The height of the writing indicated that even the youngest residents
were well along in literacy.

He wondered if they had written on the Tooth Fairy's car.

Graham sat for a few minutes looking up at the rows of windows.
There appeared to be about a hundred units. It was possible that
someone might remember a white stranger in the parking lot late
at night. Even though a month had passed it was well worth trying.
To ask every resident, and get it done quickly, he would need the
help of the Birmingham police.

He fought the temptation to send the drink can straight to Jimmy
Price in Washington. He had to ask the Birmingham police for
manpower. It would be better to give them what he had. Dusting the
can would be a straightforward job. Trying for fingerprints edged by
acid sweat was another matter. Price could still do it after Birmingham
dusted, as long as the can wasn't handled with bare fingers. Better give
it to the police. He knew the F.B.I. Document section would fall on
the carving like a rabid mongoose. Pictures of that for everybody,
nothing lost there.

He called Birmingham Homicide from the Jacobi house. The
detectives arrived just as the realtor, Geehan, was ushering in his
prospective buyers.

11

EILEEN WAS reading a *National Tattler* article called "FILTH IN YOUR BREAD!" when Dolarhyde came into the cafeteria. She had eaten only the filling in her tuna-salad sandwich.

Behind the red goggles, Dolarhyde's eyes zigged down the front page of the *Tattler*. Cover lines in addition to "FILTH IN YOUR BREAD!" included "ELVIS AT SECRET RETREAT—EXCLUSIVE PIX!!", "STUNNING BREAKTHROUGH FOR CANCER VICTIMS" and the big banner headline "HANNIBAL THE CANNIBAL HELPS LAWMEN—COPS CONSULT FIEND IN 'TOOTH FAIRY' MURDERS."

He stood at the window absently stirring his coffee until he heard Eileen get up. She dumped her tray in the trash container and was about to throw in the *Tattler* when Dolarhyde touched her shoulder.

"May I have that paper, Eileen?"

"Sure, Mr. D. I just get it for the horoscopes."

Dolarhyde read it in his office with the door closed.

Freddy Lounds had two bylines in the same double-page centre spread. The main story was a breathless reconstruction of the Jacobi and Leeds murders. Since the police had not divulged many of the specifics, Lounds consulted his imagination for lurid details.

Dolarhyde found them banal.

The sidebar was more interesting.

Insane Fiend Consulted in Mass Murders by Cop He Tried to Kill
by
FREDDY LOUNDS

CHESAPEAKE, MD.—Federal manhunters, stymied in their search for the "Tooth Fairy", psychopathic slayer of entire families in Birmingham and Atlanta, have turned to the most savage killer in captivity for help.

Dr. Hannibal Lecter, whose unspeakable practices were reported in these pages three years ago, was consulted this week in his maximum-security asylum cell by ace investigator William (Will) Graham.

Graham suffered a near-fatal slashing at Lecter's hands when he unmasked the mass-murderer.

He was brought back from early retirement to spearhead the hunt for the "Tooth Fairy".

What went on in this bizarre meeting of two mortal enemies? What was Graham after?

"It takes one to catch one," a high federal official told this reporter. He was referring to Lecter, known as "Hannibal the Cannibal", who is both a psychiatrist and a mass-murderer.

OR WAS HE REFERRING TO GRAHAM???

The *Tattler* has learned that Graham, former instructor in forensics at the F.B.I. Academy in Quantico, Va., was once confined to a mental institution for a period of four weeks . . .

Federal officials refused to say why they placed a man with a history of mental instability at the forefront of a desperate manhunt.

The nature of Graham's mental problem was not revealed, but one former psychiatric worker called it "deep depression".

Garmon Evans, a paraprofessional formerly employed at Bethesda Naval Hospital, said Graham was admitted to the psychiatric wing soon after he killed Garrett Jacob Hobbs, the "Minnesota Shrike". Graham shot Hobbs to death in 1975, ending Hobbs's eight-month reign of terror in Minneapolis.

Evans said Graham was withdrawn and refused to eat or speak during the first weeks of his stay.

Graham has never been an F.B.I. agent. Veteran observers attribute this to the Bureau's strict screening procedures, designed to detect instability.

Federal sources would reveal only that Graham originally worked in the F.B.I. Crime Laboratory and was assigned teaching duties at the F.B.I. Academy after outstanding work both in the laboratory and in the field where he served as a "special investigator".

The *Tattler* learned that before his federal service, Graham was in the Homicide division of the New Orleans Police Department, a post he left to attend graduate school in forensics at George Washington University.

One New Orleans officer who served with Graham commented, "Well, you can call him retired, but the feds like to know he's around. It's like having a king snake under the house. They may not see him much, but it's nice to know he's there to eat the moccasins."

Dr. Lecter is confined for the rest of his life. If he is ever declared sane, he will have to stand trial on nine counts of first-degree murder.

Lecter's attorney says the mass-murderer spends his time writing useful articles for the scientific journals and has an "ongoing dialogue" by mail with some of the most respected figures in psychiatry.

Dolarhyde stopped reading and looked at the pictures. There were two of them above the sidebar. One showed Lecter pinned against the side of a state trooper's car. The other was the picture of Will Graham taken by Freddy Lounds outside the Chesapeake State Hospital. A small photograph of Lounds ran beside each of his bylines.

Dolarhyde looked at the pictures for a long time. He ran the tip of his forefinger over them slowly, back and forth, his touch exquisitely sensitive to the rough newsprint. Ink left a smudge on his fingertip. He wet the smudge with his tongue and wiped it off on a Kleenex. Then he cut out the sidebar and put it in his pocket.

On his way home from the plant, Dolarhyde bought toilet paper of the quick-dissolving kind used in boats and campers, and a nasal inhaler.

He felt good despite his hay fever—like many people who have undergone extensive rhinoplasty, Dolarhyde had no hair in his nose and hay fever plagued him. So did upper respiratory infections.

When a stalled truck held him up for ten minutes on the Missouri River bridge to St. Charles, he sat patiently. His black van was carpeted, cool and quiet. Handel's Water Music played on the stereo.

He rippled his fingers on the steering wheel in time with the music and dabbed at his nose.

Two women in a convertible were in the lane beside him. They wore shorts and blouses tied across the midriff. Dolarhyde looked down into the convertible from his van. They seemed tired and bored squinting into the lowering sun. The woman on the passenger side had her head against the seat back and her feet on the dash. Her slumped posture made two creases across her bare stomach. Dolarhyde could see a suck-mark on the inside of her thigh. She caught him looking, sat up and crossed her legs. He saw weary distaste in her face.

She said something to the woman at the wheel. Both looked straight ahead. He knew they were talking about him. He was *so* glad it did not make him angry. Few things made him angry any more. He knew that he was developing a becoming dignity.

The music was very pleasant.

The traffic in front of Dolarhyde began to move. The lane beside him was still stalled. He looked forward to getting home. He tapped the wheel in time with the music and rolled down the window with his other hand.

He hawked and spat a blob of green phlegm into the lap of the woman beside him, hitting her just beside the navel. Her curses sounded high and thin over the Handel as he drove away.

Dolarhyde's great ledger was at least a hundred years old. Bound in black leather with brass corners, it was so heavy that a sturdy machine-table supported it in the locked closet at the top of the stairs. From the moment he saw it at the bankruptcy sale of an old St. Louis printing company, Dolarhyde knew it should be his.

Now, bathed and in his kimono, he unlocked the closet and rolled it out. When the book was centred beneath the painting of the Great Red Dragon, he settled himself in a chair and opened it. The smell of foxed paper rose to his face.

Across the first page, in large letters he had illuminated himself, were the words from Revelation: "And There Came a Great Red Dragon Also . . ."

The first item in the book was the only one not neatly mounted. Loose between the pages was a yellowed photograph of Dolarhyde as a small child with his grandmother on the steps of the big house. He is holding Grandmother's skirt. Her arms are folded and her back is straight.

Dolarhyde turned past it. He ignored it as though it had been left there by mistake.

There were many clippings in the ledger, the earliest ones about the disappearances of elderly women in St. Louis and Toledo. Pages between the clippings were covered with Dolarhyde's writing—black ink in a fine copperplate script not unlike William Blake's own handwriting.

Fastened in the margins, ragged bites of scalp trailed their tails of hair like comets pressed in God's scrapbook.

The Jacobi clippings from Birmingham were there along with film cartridges and slides set in pockets glued to the pages.

So were stories on the Leeds, with film beside them.

The term "Tooth Fairy" had not appeared in the press until Atlanta. The name was marked out in all the Leeds stories.

Now Dolarhyde did the same with his *Tattler* clipping, obliterating "Tooth Fairy" with angry slashes of a red marker pen.

He turned to a new, blank page in his ledger and trimmed the *Tattler* clipping to fit. Should Graham's picture go in? The words "Criminally Insane" carved in the stone above Graham offended Dolarhyde. He hated the sight of any place of confinement. Graham's face was closed to him. He set it aside for the time being.

But Lecter . . . Lecter. This was not a good picture of the doctor. Dolarhyde had a better one which he fetched from a box in his closet. It was published upon Lecter's committal and showed the fine eyes. Still, it was not satisfactory. In Dolarhyde's mind, Lecter's likeness should be the dark portrait of a Renaissance prince. For Lecter, alone among all men, might have the sensitivity and experience to understand the glory, the majesty of Dolarhyde's Becoming.

Dolarhyde felt that Lecter knew the unreality of the people who die to help you in these things—understood that they are not flesh, but light and air and colour and quick sounds quickly ended when you change them. Like balloons of colour bursting. That they are more important for the changing, more important than the lives they scrabble after, pleading.

Dolarhyde bore screams as a sculptor bears dust from the beaten stone.

Lecter was capable of understanding that blood and breath were only elements undergoing change to fuel his Radiance. Just as the source of light is burning.

He would like to meet Lecter, talk and share with him, rejoice with him in their shared vision, be recognized by him as John the Baptist recognized the One who came after, sit on him as the Dragon sat on 666 in Blake's Revelation series, and film his death as, dying, he melded with the strength of the Dragon.

Dolarhyde pulled on a new pair of rubber gloves and went to his desk. He unrolled and discarded the outer layer of the toilet paper he had bought. Then he unrolled a strip of seven sheets and tore it off.

Printing carefully on the tissue with his left hand, he wrote a letter to Lecter.

Speech is never a reliable indicator of how a person writes; you never know. Dolarhyde's speech was bent and pruned by disabilities real and imagined, and the difference between his speech and his writing was startling. Still, he found he could not say the most important things he felt.

He wanted to hear from Lecter. He needed a personal response before he could tell Dr. Lecter the important things.

How could he manage that? He rummaged through his box of Lecter clippings, read them all again.

Finally a simple way occurred to him and he wrote again.

The letter seemed too diffident and shy when he read it over. He had signed it "Avid Fan."

He brooded over the signature for several minutes.

"Avid Fan" indeed. His chin rose an imperious fraction.

He put his gloved thumb in his mouth, removed his dentures and placed them on the blotter.

The upper plate was unusual. The teeth were normal, straight and white, but the pink acrylic upper part was a tortuous shape cast to fit the twists and fissures of his gums. Attached to the plate was a soft plastic prosthesis with an obturator on top which helped him close off his soft palate in speech.

He took a small case from his desk. It held another set of teeth. The upper casting was the same, but there was no prosthesis. The crooked teeth had dark stains between them and gave off a faint stench.

They were identical to Grandmother's teeth in the bedside glass downstairs.

Dolarhyde's nostrils flared at the odour. He opened his sunken smile and put them in place and wet them with his tongue.

He folded the letter across the signature and bit down hard on it. When he opened the letter again the signature was enclosed in an oval bite-mark; his notary seal, an imprimatur flecked with old blood.

12

ATTORNEY BYRON Metcalf took off his tie at five o'clock, made himself a drink and put his feet up on his desk.

"Sure you won't have one?"

"Another time." Graham, picking the cockleburrs off his cuffs, was grateful for the air-conditioning.

"I didn't know the Jacobis very well," Metcalf said. "They'd only been here three months. My wife and I were there for drinks a couple of times. Ed Jacobi came to me for a new will soon after he was transferred here, that's how I met him."

"But you're his executor."

"Yes. His wife was listed first as executor, then me as alternate in case she was deceased or infirm. He has a brother in Philadelphia but I gather they weren't close."

"You were an assistant district attorney."

"Yeah, 1968 to '72. I ran for D.A. in '72. It was close, but I lost. I'm not sorry now."

"How do you see what happened here, Mr. Metcalf?"

"The first thing I thought about was Joseph Yablonski, the labour leader?"

Graham nodded.

"A crime with a motive, power in that case, disguised as an insane attack. We went over Ed Jacobi's papers with a fine tooth-comb—Jerry Estridge from the D.A.'s office and I.

"Nothing. Nobody stood to make much money off Ed Jacobi's death. He made a big salary and he had some patents paying off; but he spent it about as fast as it came in. Everything was to go to the wife, with a little land in California entailed to the kids and their descendants. He had a small spendthrift trust set up for the surviving son. It'll pay his way through three more years of college. I'm sure he'll still be a freshman by then."

"Niles Jacobi."

"Yeah. The kid gave Ed a big pain in the ass. He lived with his mother in California. Went to Chino for theft. I gather his mother's a flake. Ed went out there to see about him last year. Brought him back to Birmingham and put him in school at Bardwell Community College. Tried to keep him at home, but he dumped on the other kids and made it unpleasant for everybody. Mrs. Jacobi put up with it for a while, but finally they moved him to a dorm."

"Where was he?"

"On the night of June 28th?" Metcalf's eyes were hooded as he looked at Graham. "The police wondered about that and so did I. He went to a movie and then back to school. It's verified. Besides, he has Type O blood. Mr. Graham, I have to pick up my wife in half an hour. We can talk tomorrow if you like. Tell me how I can help you."

"I'd like to see the Jacobis' personal effects. Diaries, pictures, whatever."

"There's not much of that—they lost about everything in a fire in Detroit before they moved down here. Nothing suspicious, Ed was welding in the basement and the sparks got into some paint he had stored down there and the house went up.

"There's some personal correspondence. I have it in the lock boxes with the small valuables. I don't remember any diaries. Everything else is in storage. Niles may have some pictures, but I doubt it. Tell you what—I'm going to court at 9.30 in the morning, but I could get you into the bank to look at the stuff and come back by for you afterward."

"Fine," Graham said. "One other thing, I could use copies of everything to do with the probate: claims against the estate, any contest of the will, correspondence. I'd like to have all the paper."

"The Atlanta D.A.'s office asked me for that already. They're comparing with the Leeds estate in Atlanta, I know," Metcalf said.

"Still, I'd like copies for myself."

"Okay, copies to you. You don't really think it's money, though, do you?"

"No. I just keep hoping the same name will come up here and in Atlanta."

"So do I."

Student housing at Bardwell Community College was four small dormitory buildings set round a littered quadrangle of beaten earth. A stereo war was in progress when Graham got there.

Opposing sets of speakers on the motel-style balconies blared at each other across the quad. It was Kiss versus the 1812 Overture. A water balloon arched high in the air and burst on the ground ten feet from Graham.

He ducked under a clothes-line and stepped over a bicycle to get through the sitting-room of the suite Niles Jacobi shared. The door to Jacobi's bedroom was ajar and music blasted through the crack. Graham knocked.

No response.

He pushed open the door. A tall boy with a spotty face sat on one of the twin beds sucking on a four-foot bong pipe. A girl in dungarees lay on the other bed.

The boy's head jerked around to face Graham. He was struggling to think.

"I'm looking for Niles Jacobi."

The boy appeared stupified. Graham switched off the stereo.

"I'm looking for Niles Jacobi."

"Just some stuff for my asthma, man. Don't you ever knock?"

"Where's Niles Jacobi?"

"Fuck if I know. What do you want him for?"

Graham showed him the tin. "Try real hard to remember."

"Oh shit," the girl said.

"Narc, goddammit. I ain't worth it, look let's talk about this a minute, man."

"Let's talk about where Jacobi is."

"I think I can find out for you," the girl said.

Graham waited while she asked in the other rooms. Everywhere she went, commodes flushed.

There were few traces of Niles Jacobi in the room—one photograph of the Jacobi family lay on a dresser. Graham lifted a glass of melting ice off it and wiped away the wet ring with his sleeve.

The girl returned. "Try the Hateful Snake," she said.

The Hateful Snake bar was in a storefront with the windows painted dark green. The vehicles parked outside were an odd assortment, big trucks looking bob-tailed without their trailers, compact cars, a lilac convertible, old Dodges and Chevrolets crippled with high rear-ends for the drag strip look, four full-dress Harley-Davidsons.

An air-conditioner, mounted in the transom over the door, dripped steadily on to the sidewalk.

Graham ducked around the dribble and went inside.

The place was crowded and smelled of disinfectant and stale Canoe. The bartender, a husky woman in overalls, reached over heads at the service bar to hand Graham his Coke. She was the only woman there.

Niles Jacobi, dark and razor-thin, was at the jukebox. He put the money in the machine but the man beside him pushed the buttons.

Jacobi looked like a dissolute schoolboy, but the one selecting the music did not.

Jacobi's companion was a strange mixture; he had a boyish face on a knobby, muscular body. He wore a tee-shirt and jeans, worn white over the objects in his pockets. His arms were knotty with muscle and he had large, ugly hands. One professional tattoo on his left forearm said "Born to Fuck". A crude, jailhouse tattoo on his other arm said "Randy". His short jail haircut had grown out unevenly. As he reached for a button on the lighted jukebox, Graham saw a small shaved patch on his forearm.

Graham felt a cold place in his stomach.

He followed Niles Jacobi and "Randy" through the crowd to the back of the room. They sat in a booth.

Graham stopped two feet from the table.

"Niles, my name is Will Graham. I need to talk with you for a few minutes."

Randy looked up with a bright false smile. One of his front teeth was dead. "Do I know you?"

"No. Niles, I want to talk to you."

Niles arched a quizzical eyebrow. Graham wondered what had happened to him in Chino.

"We were having a private conversation here. Butt out," Randy said.

Graham looked thoughtfully at the marred muscular forearms, the dot of adhesive in the crook of the elbow, the shaved patch where Randy had rested the edge of his knife. Knife fighter's mange.

I'm afraid of Randy. Fire or fall back.

"Did you hear me?" Randy said. "Butt out."

Graham unbuttoned his jacket and put his identification on the table.

"Sit still, Randy. If you try to get up you're gonna have two navels."

"I'm sorry, sir." Instant inmate sincerity.

"Randy, I want you to do something for me. I want you to reach in your left back pocket. Just use two fingers. You'll find a five-inch knife in there with a Flicket clamped to the blade. Put it on the table . . . Thank you."

Graham dropped the knife into his pocket. It felt greasy.

"Now, in your other pocket is your wallet. Get it out. You sold some blood today, didn't you?"

"So what?"

"So hand me the slip they gave you, the one you show next time at the blood bank. Spread it out on the table."

Randy had Type O blood. Scratch Randy.

"How long have you been out of jail?"

"Three weeks."

"Who's your parole officer?"

"I'm not on parole."

"That's probably a lie." Graham wanted to roust Randy. He could get him for carrying a knife over the legal length. Being in a place with a liquor licence was a parole violation. Graham knew he was angry at Randy because he had feared him.

"Randy."

"Yeah."

"Get out."

★   ★   ★

"I don't know what I can tell you, I didn't know my father very well," Niles Jacobi said as Graham drove him to the school. "He left Mother when I was three and I didn't see him after that—Mother wouldn't *have* it."

"He came to see you last spring."

"Yes."

"At Chino."

"You know about that."

"I'm just trying to get it straight. What happened?"

"Well, there he was in Visitors, uptight and trying not to look around—so many people treat it like the *zoo*. I'd heard a lot about him from Mother, but he didn't look so bad. He was just a man standing there in a tacky sportcoat."

"What did he say?"

"Well, I *expected* him either to jump right in my shit or to be real guilty, that's the way it goes mostly in Visitors. But he just asked me if I thought I could go to school. He said he'd go custody if I'd go to school. And try. 'You have to help *yourself* a little. Try and help yourself and I'll see you get in school,' and like that."

"How long before you got out?"

"Two weeks."

"Niles, did you ever talk about your family while you were in Chino? To your cellmates or anybody?"

Niles Jacobi looked at Graham quickly. "Oh. Oh, I see. No. Not about my *father*. I hadn't *thought* about him in years, why would I talk about him?"

"How about here? Did you ever take any of your friends over to your parents' house?"

"*Parent*, not parents. She was not my mother."

"Did you ever take anybody over there? School friends or . . ."

"Or rough trade, Officer Graham?"

"That's right."

"No."

"Never?"

"Not once."

"Did he ever mention any kind of threat, was he ever disturbed about anything in the last month or two before it happened?"

"He was disturbed the last time I talked to him, but it was just my grades. I had a lot of cuts. He bought me two alarm clocks. There wasn't anything else that I know of."

"Do you have any personal papers of his, correspondence, photographs, anything?"

"No."

"You have a picture of the family. It's on the dresser in your room. Near the bong."

"That's not my bong. I wouldn't put that filthy thing in my mouth."

"I need the picture. I'll have it copied and send it back to you. What else do you have?"

Jacobi shook a cigarette out of his pack and patted his pockets for matches. "That's all. I can't imagine why they gave *that* to me. My father smiling at *Mrs.* Jacobi and all the little Munchkins. You can have it. He never looked like that to me."

Graham needed to know the Jacobis. Their new acquaintances in Birmingham were little help.

Byron Metcalf gave him the run of the lock boxes. He read the thin stack of letters, mostly business, and poked through the jewellery and the silver.

For three hot days he worked in the warehouse where the Jacobis' household goods were stored. Metcalf helped him at night. Every crate on every pallet was opened and the contents examined. Police photographs helped Graham see where things had been in the house.

Most of the furnishings were new, bought with the insurance from the Detroit fire. The Jacobis hardly had time to leave their marks on their possessions.

One item, a bedside table with traces of fingerprint powder still on it, held Graham's attention. In the centre of the table top was a blob of green wax.

For the second time he wondered if the killer liked candlelight.

The Birmingham forensics unit was good about sharing.

The blurred print of the end of a nose was the best Birmingham and Jimmy Price in Washington could do with the soft drink can from the tree.

The F.B.I. laboratory's Firearms and Toolmarks section reported on the severed branch. The blades that clipped it were thick, with a shallow pitch: it had been done with a bolt-cutter.

Document Section had referred the mark cut in the bark to the Asian Studies department at Langley.

Graham sat on a packing-case at the warehouse and read the long report. Asian Studies advised that the mark was a Chinese character which meant "You hit it" or "You hit it on the head"—an expression sometimes used in gambling. It was considered a "positive" or "lucky" sign. The character also appeared on a Mah-Jongg piece, the Asian scholars said. It marked the Red Dragon.

13

CRAWFORD AT F.B.I. headquarters in Washington was on the telephone with Graham at the Birmingham airport when his secretary leaned into the office and flagged his attention.

"Dr. Chilton at Chesapeake hospital on 2706. He says it's urgent."

Crawford nodded. "Hang on, Will." He punched the telephone. "Crawford."

"Frederick Chilton, Mr. Crawford, at the—"

"Yes, Doctor."

"I have a note here, or two pieces of a note, that appears to be from the man who killed those people in Atlanta and—"

"Where did you get it?"

"From Hannibal Lecter's cell. It's written on toilet tissue, of all things, and it has teeth marks pressed in it."

"Can you read it to me without handling it any more?"

Straining to sound calm, Chilton read it:

My Dear Dr. Lecter,

I wanted to tell you I'm delighted that you have taken an interest in me. And when I learned of your vast correspondence

I thought *Dare I?* Of course I do. I don't believe you'd tell them who I am, even if you knew. Besides, what particular body I currently occupy is trivia.

The important thing is what I am *Becoming*. I know that you alone can understand this. I have some things I'd love to show you. Someday, perhaps, if circumstances permit. I hope we can correspond—(Mr. Crawford, there's a hole torn and punched out. Then it says:) I have admired you for *years* and have a complete collection of your press notices. Actually, I think of them as unfair reviews. As unfair as mine. They like to sling demeaning nicknames, don't they? The *Tooth Fairy*. What could be more inappropriate? It would shame me for you to see that if I didn't know you had suffered the same distortions in the press.

Investigator Graham interests me. Odd-looking for a flatfoot, isn't he? Not very handsome, but purposeful-looking. You should have taught him not to meddle.

Forgive the stationery. I chose it because it will dissolve very quickly if you should have to swallow it.

(There's a piece missing here, Mr. Crawford. I'll read the bottom part.)

If I hear from you, next time I might send you something wet. Until then I remain your

Avid Fan

Silence after Chilton finished reading. "Are you there?"

"Yes. Does Lecter know you have the note?"

"Not yet. This morning he was moved to a holding-cell while his quarters were cleaned. Instead of using a proper rag, the cleaning man was pulling handfuls of toilet paper off the roll to wipe round the sink. He found the note wound up in the roll and brought it to me. They bring me anything they find hidden."

"Where's Lecter now?"

"Still in the holding-cell."

"Can he see his quarters at all from there?"

"Let me think . . . No, no he can't."

"Wait a second, Doctor." Crawford put Chilton on hold. He stared at the two winking buttons on his telephone for several seconds without seeing them. Crawford, fisher of men, was watching his cork move against the current. He got Graham again.

"Will—a note, maybe from the Tooth Fairy, hidden in Lecter's cell at Chesapeake. Sounds like a fan letter. He wants Lecter's approval, he's curious about you. He's asking questions."

"How was Lecter supposed to answer?"

"Don't know yet. Part's torn out, part's scratched out. Looks like there's a chance of correspondence as long as Lecter's not aware that we know. I want the note for the lab and I want to toss his cell, but it'll be risky. If Lecter gets wise, who knows how he could warn the bastard? We need the link but we need the note too."

Crawford told Graham where Lecter was held, how the note was found. "It's eighty miles over to Chesapeake. I can't wait for you, buddy. What do you think?"

"Ten people dead in a month—we can't play a long mail game. I say go for it."

"I am," Crawford said.

"See you in two hours."

Crawford hailed his secretary. "Sarah, order a helicopter. I want the whole thing smoking and I don't care whose it is—ours, D.C.P.D. or Marines. I'll be on the roof in five minutes. Call Documents, tell them to have a document case up there. Tell Herbert to scramble a search team. On the roof. Five minutes."

He picked up Chilton's line.

"Dr. Chilton, we have to search Lecter's cell without his knowledge and we need your help. Have you mentioned this to anybody else?"

"No."

"Where's the cleaning man who found the note?"

"He's here in my office."

"Keep him there please and tell him to keep quiet. How long has Lecter been out of his cell?"

"About half an hour."

"Is that unusually long?"

"No, not yet. But it takes only about a half-hour to clean it. Soon he'll begin to wonder what's wrong."

"Okay, do this for me: call your building superintendent or engineer, whoever's in charge. Tell him to shut off the water in the building and to pull the circuit breakers on Lecter's hall. Have the super walk down the hall past the holding-cell carrying tools. He'll be in a hurry; pissed off, too busy to answer any questions—got it? Tell him he'll get an explanation from me. Have the garbage pick-up cancelled for today if they haven't already come. Don't touch the note, okay? We're coming."

Crawford called the Section Chief, Scientific Analysis. "Brian, I have a note coming in on the fly, possibly from the Tooth Fairy. Number one priority. It has to go back where it came from within the hour and unmarked. It'll go to Hair and Fibre, Latent Prints and Documents, then to you, so co-ordinate with them, will you? Yes. I'll walk it through. I'll deliver it to you myself."

It was warm—the federally-mandated 80°—in the elevator when Crawford came down from the roof with the note, his hair blown silly by the helicopter blast. He was mopping his face by the time he reached the Hair and Fibre section of the laboratory.

Hair and Fibre is a small section, calm and busy. The common room is stacked with boxes of evidence sent by police departments all over the country; swatches of tape that have sealed mouths and bound wrists, torn and stained clothing, deathbed sheets.

Crawford spotted Beverly Katz through the window of an examining room as he weaved his way between the boxes. She had a pair of child's coveralls suspended from a hanger over a table covered with white paper. Working under bright lights in the draught-free room, she brushed the overalls with a metal spatula, carefully working with the wale and across it, with the nap and against it. A sprinkle of dirt and sand fell to the paper. With it, falling through the still air more slowly than sand but faster than lint, came a tightly-coiled hair. She cocked her head and looked at it with her bright robin's eye.

Crawford could see her lips moving. He knew what she was saying. "Gotcha."

That's what she always said.

Crawford pecked on the glass and she came out fast, stripping off her white gloves.

"It hasn't been printed yet, right?"

"No."

"I'm set up in the next examining room." She put on a fresh pair of white gloves while Crawford opened the document case.

The note, in two pieces, was contained gently between two sheets of plastic film. Beverley Katz saw the tooth impressions and glanced up at Crawford, not wasting time with the question.

He nodded: the impressions matched the clear overlay of the killer's bite he had carried with him to Chesapeake.

Crawford watched through the window as she lifted the note on a slender dowel and hung it over white paper. She looked it over with a powerful glass, then fanned it gently. She tapped the dowel with the edge of a spatula and went over the paper beneath it with a magnifying glass.

Crawford looked at his watch.

Katz flipped the note over another dowel to get the reverse side up. She removed one tiny object from its surface with tweezers almost as fine as a hair.

She photographed the torn ends of the notes under high magnification and returned it to its case. She put a clean pair of white gloves in the case with it. The white gloves—the signal not to touch—would always be beside the evidence until it was checked for fingerprints.

"That's it," she said, handing the case back to Crawford. "One hair, maybe a thirty-second of an inch. A couple of blue grains. I'll work it up. What else have you got?"

Crawford gave her three marked envelopes. "Hair from Lecter's comb. Whiskers from an electric razor they let him use. This is hair from the cleaning man. Gotta go."

"See you later," Katz said. "Love *your* hair."

Jimmy Price in Latent Prints winced at the sight of the porous toilet paper. He squinted fiercely over the shoulder of his technician operating the helium cadmium laser as they tried to find a fingerprint and make it fluoresce. Glowing smudges appeared on the paper, perspiration stains, nothing.

Crawford started to ask him a question, thought better of it, waited with the blue light reflecting off his half-glasses.

"We know three guys handled this without gloves, right?" Price said.

"Yeah, the clean-up man, Lecter and Chilton."

"The fellow scrubbing sinks had probably washed the oil off his fingers. But the others—this stuff is terrible." Price held the paper to the light, forceps steady in his mottled old hand. "I could fume it, Jack, but I couldn't guarantee the iodine stains would fade out in the time you've got."

"Ninhydrin? Boost it with heat?" Ordinarily, Crawford would not have ventured a technical suggestion to Price but he was floundering for anything. He expected a huffy reply, but the old man sounded rueful and sad.

"No. We couldn't wash it after. I can't get you a print off this, Jack. There isn't one."

"Fuck," Crawford said.

The old man turned away. Crawford put his hand on Price's bony shoulder. "Hell, Jimmy. If there was one you'd have found it."

Price didn't answer. He was unpacking a pair of hands that had arrived for another matter. Dry ice smoked in his wastebasket. Crawford dropped the white gloves into the smoke.

Disappointment growling in his stomach, Crawford hurried on to Documents where Lloyd Bowman was waiting. Bowman had been called out of court and the abrupt shear in his concentration left him blinking like a man just wakened.

"I congratulate you on your hairstyle. A brave departure," Bowman said, his hands quick and careful as he transferred the note to his work surface. "How long do I have?"

"Twenty minutes max."

Two pieces of the note seemed to glow under Bowman's lights. His blotter showed dark green through a jagged oblong hole in the upper piece.

"The main thing, the first thing, is how Lecter was to reply," Crawford said when Bowman had finished reading.

"Instructions for answering were probably in the part torn out." Bowman worked steadily with his lights and filters and copy camera as he talked. "Here in the top piece he says 'I hope we can correspond—' and then the hole begins. Lecter scratched over that with a felt-tip pen and then folded it and pinched most of it out."

"He doesn't have anything to cut with."

Bowman photographed the tooth impressions and the back of the note under extremely oblique light, his shadow leaping from wall to wall as he moved the light through 360 degrees around the paper and his hands made phantom folding motions in the air.

"Now we can mash just a little." Bowman put the note between two panes of glass to flatten the jagged edges of the hole. The tatters were smeared with vermillion ink. He was chanting under his breath. On the third repetition Crawford made out what he was saying. "You're so sly, but so am I."

Bowman switched filters on his small television camera and focused it on the note. He darkened the room until there was only the dull red glow of a lamp and the blue-green of his monitor screen.

The words "I hope we can correspond" and the jagged hole appeared enlarged on the screen. The ink smear was gone and on the tattered edges appeared fragments of writing.

"Aniline dyes in coloured inks are transparent to infra-red," Bowman said. "These could be the tips of Ts here and here. On the end is the tail of what could be an M or N, or possibly an R." Bowman took a photograph and turned the lights on. "Jack, there are just two common ways of carrying on a communication that's one-way blind— the phone and publication. Could Lecter take a fast phone call?"

"He can take calls, but it's slow and they have to come in through the hospital switchboard."

"Publication is the only safe way then."

"We know this sweetheart reads the *Tattler*. The stuff about Graham and Lecter was in the *Tattler*. I don't know of any other paper that carried it."

"Three Ts and an R in *Tattler*. Personal column, you think? It's a place to look."

Crawford checked with the F.B.I. library, then telephoned instructions to the Chicago field office.

Bowman handed him the case as he finished.

"The *Tattler* comes out this evening," Crawford said. "It's printed in Chicago on Mondays and Thursdays. We'll get proofs of the classified pages."

"I'll have some more stuff, minor, I think," Bowman said.

"Anything useful, fire it straight to Chicago. Fill me in when I get back from the asylum," Crawford said on his way out the door.

14

THE TURNSTILE at Washington's Metro Central spat Graham's fare-card back to him and he came out into the hot afternoon carrying his flight bag.

The J. Edgar Hoover Building looked like a great concrete cage above the heat shimmer on Tenth Street. The F.B.I.'s move to the new headquarters had been underway when Graham left Washington. He had never worked there.

Crawford met him at the escort desk off the underground driveway to augment Graham's hastily-issued credentials with his own. Graham looked tired and he was impatient with the signing in. Crawford wondered how he felt, knowing that the killer was thinking about him.

Graham was issued a magnetically encoded tag like the one on Crawford's waistcoat. He plugged it into the gate and passed into the long white corridors. Crawford carried his flight bag.

"I forgot to tell Sarah to send a car for you."

"Probably quicker this way. Did you get the note back to Lecter all right?"

"Yeah," Crawford said. "I just got back. We poured water on the hall floor. Faked a broken pipe with electrical short. We had

Simmons—he's the Assistant S.A.C. Baltimore now—we had him mopping when Lecter was brought back to his cell. Simmons thinks he bought it."

"I kept wondering on the plane if Lecter wrote it himself."

"That bothered me too until I looked at it. Bite-mark in the paper matches the ones on the women. Also it's ball-point, which Lecter doesn't have. The person who wrote it had read the *Tattler* and Lecter hasn't had a *Tattler*. Rankin and Willingham tossed the cell. Beautiful job, but they didn't find diddly. They took Polaroids first to get everything back just right. Then the cleaning man went in and did what he always does."

"So what do you think?"

"As far as physical evidence towards an I.D., the note is pretty much dreck," Crawford said. "Some way we've got to make the contact work for us, but damn if I know how yet. We'll get the rest of the lab results in a few minutes."

"You've got the mail and phone covered at the hospital?"

"Standing trace-and-tape order for any time Lecter's on the phone. He made a call Saturday afternoon. He told Chilton he was calling his lawyer. It's a damn W.A.T.S. line and I can't be sure."

"What did his lawyer say?"

"Nothing. We got a leased line to the hospital switchboard for Lecter's convenience in the future, so that won't get by us again. We'll fiddle his mail both ways starting next delivery. No problem with warrants, thank God."

Crawford bellied up to a door and stuck the tag on his waistcoat into the lock slot. "My new office. Come on in. Decorator had some paint left over from a battleship he was doing. Here's the note. The print is exactly to size."

Graham read it twice. Seeing the spidery lines spell his name started a high tone ringing in his head.

"The library confirms the *Tattler* is the only paper that carried a story about Lecter and you," Crawford said, fixing himself an Alka-Seltzer. "Want one of these? Good for you. It was published Monday night a week ago. It was on the stands Tuesday nationwide—some areas not till Wednesday—Alaska and Maine and places. The Tooth Fairy got one—couldn't have done it before Tuesday. He reads it, writes to Lecter. Rankin and Willingham are still sifting the hospital trash for the envelope. Whew, bad job. They don't separate the paper from the diapers at Chesapeake.

"All right, Lecter gets the note from the Tooth Fairy no sooner than Wednesday. He tears out the part about how to reply and scratches over and pokes out one earlier reference—I don't know why he didn't tear that out too."

"It was in the middle of a paragraph full of compliments," Graham said. "He couldn't stand to ruin them. That's why he didn't throw the whole thing away." He rubbed his temples with his knuckles.

"Bowman thinks Lecter will use the *Tattler* to answer the Tooth Fairy. He says that's probably the set-up. You think he'd answer this thing?"

"Sure. He's a great correspondent. Pen-pals all over."

"If they're using the *Tattler*, Lecter would barely have time to get his answer in the issue they'll print tonight, even if he sent it special delivery to the paper the same day he got the Tooth Fairy's note. Chester from the Chicago office is down at the *Tattler* checking the ads. The printers are putting the paper together right now."

"Please God don't stir the *Tattler* up," Graham said.

"The shop foreman thinks Chester's a realtor trying to get a jump on the ads. He's selling him the proof sheets under the table, one by one as they come off. We're getting everything, all the classifieds, just to blow some smoke. All right, say we find out how Lecter was to answer and we can duplicate the method. Then we can fake a message to the Tooth Fairy—but what do we say? How do we use it?"

"The obvious thing is to try to get him to come to a mail drop,"

Graham said. "Bait him with something he'd like to see. 'Important evidence' that Lecter knows about from talking to me. Some mistake he made that we're waiting for him to repeat."

"He'd be an idiot to go for it."

"I know. Want to hear what the best bait would be?"

"I'm not sure I do."

"Lecter would be the best bait," Graham said.

"Set up how?"

"It would be hell to do. I know that. We'd take Lecter into federal custody – Chilton would never sit still for this at Chesapeake—and we stash him in maximum security at a V.A. psychiatric hospital. We fake an escape."

"Oh, Jesus."

"We send the Tooth Fairy a message in next week's *Tattler*, after the big 'escape'. It would be Lecter asking him for a rendezvous."

"Why in God's name would anybody want to meet Lecter? I mean even the Tooth Fairy?"

"To kill him, Jack." Graham got up. There was no window to look out of as he talked. He stood in front of the "Ten Most Wanted", Crawford's only wall decoration. "See, the Tooth Fairy could absorb him that way, engulf him, become more than he is."

"You sound pretty sure."

"I'm not sure. Who's sure? What he said in the note was 'I have some things I'd love to show you. Someday, perhaps, if circumstances permit.' Maybe it was a serious invitation. I don't think he was just being polite."

"Wonder what he's got to show? The victims were intact. Nothing missing but a little skin and hair, and that was probably—how did Bloom put it?"

"Ingested," Graham said. "God knows what he's got. Tremont, remember Tremont's costumes in Spokane? While he was strapped to a stretcher he was pointing with his chin, still trying to show them to the Spokane P.D. I'm not sure Lecter would draw the Tooth Fairy, Jack. I say it's the best shot."

"We'd have a goddam *stampede* if people thought Lecter was out. Papers all over us screaming. Best shot, maybe, but we'll save it for last."

"He probably wouldn't come near a mail drop, but he might be curious enough to *look* at a mail drop to see if Lecter had sold him. If he could do it from a distance. We could pick a drop that could be watched from only a few places a long way off and stake out the observation points." It sounded weak to Graham even as he said it.

"Secret Service has a set-up they've never used. They'd let us have it. But if we don't put an ad in today, we'll have to wait until Monday before the next issue comes out. Presses roll at five our time. That gives Chicago another hour and fifteen minutes to come up with Lecter's ad, if there *is* one."

"What about Lecter's ad *order*, the letter he'd have sent the *Tattler* ordering the ad, could we get that quicker?"

"Chicago put out some general feelers to the shop foreman," Crawford said. "The mail stays in the classified advertising manager's office. They sell the names and return addresses to mailing lists— outfits that sell products for lonely people, love charms, rooster pills, squack dealers, 'meet beautiful Asian girls', personality courses, that sort of stuff.

"We might appeal to the ad manager's citizenship and all and get a look, request him to be quiet, but I don't want to chance it and risk the *Tattler* slobbering all over us. It would take a warrant to go in there and Bogart the mail. I'm thinking about it."

"If Chicago turns up nothing we could put an ad in anyway. If we're wrong about the *Tattler* we wouldn't lose anything," Graham said.

"And if we're right that the *Tattler* is the medium and we make up a reply based on what we have in this note and screw it up—if it doesn't look right to him—we're down the tubes. I didn't ask you about Birmingham. Anything?"

"Birmingham's shut down and over with. The Jacobi house has been painted and redecorated and it's on the market. Their stuff is in storage waiting for probate. I went through the crates. The people I talked to didn't know the Jacobis very well. The one thing they always mentioned was how affectionate the Jacobis were to each other. Always patting. Nothing left of them now but five pallet-loads of stuff in a warehouse. I wish I had—"

"Quit wishing, you're on it now."

"What about the mark on the tree?"

"'You hit it on the head'? Means nothing to me," Crawford said. "The Red Dragon neither. Beverly knows Mah-Jongg. She's sharp and she can't see it. We know from his hair he's not Chinese."

"He cut the limb with a bolt-cutter. I don't see—"

Crawford's telephone rang. He spoke into it briefly.

"Lab's ready on the note, Will. Let's go up to Zeller's office. It's bigger and not so grey."

Lloyd Bowman, dry as a document in spite of the heat, caught up with them in the corridor. He was flapping damp photographs in each hand and held a sheaf of Datafax sheets under his arm. "Jack, I have to be in court at four-fifteen," he said as he flapped ahead. "It's that paperhanger Nilton Eskew and his sweetheart, Nan. She could draw a Treasury note freehand. They've been driving me crazy for two years making their own traveller's cheques on a colour Xerox. Won't leave home without them. Will I make it in time or should I tell the prosecutor?"

"You'll make it," Crawford said. "Here we are."

Beverly Katz smiled at Graham from the couch in Zeller's office, making up for the scowl of Price beside her.

Scientific Analysis Section Chief Brian Zeller was young for his job, but already his hair was thinning and he wore bifocals. On the shelf behind Zeller's desk Graham saw H. J. Wall's forensic science text, Tedeschi's great *Forensic Medicine* in three volumes and an antique edition of Hopkins's *The Wreck of the Deutschland.*

"Will, we met once at G.W.U., I think," he said. "Do you know everybody? Fine."

Crawford leaned against the corner of Zeller's desk, his arms folded. "Anybody got a block-buster? Okay, does anything you found indicate the note did *not* come from the Tooth Fairy?"

"No," Bowman said. "I talked to Chicago a few minutes ago to give them some numerals I picked up from an impression on the back of the note. Six six six. I'll show you when we get to it. Chicago has over 200 personal adds so far." He handed Graham a sheaf of Datafax copies. "I've read them and they're all the usual stuff—marriage offers, appeals to runaways. I'm not sure how we'd recognize the ad if it's here."

Crawford shook his head. "I don't know either. Let's break down the physical. Now Jimmy Price did everything we could do and there was no print. What about you, Bev?"

"I got one whisker. Scale-count and core-size match sample from Hannibal Lecter. So does colour. The colour's markedly different from samples taken in Birmingham and Atlanta. Three blue grains and some dark flecks went to Brian's end." She raised her eyebrows at Brian Zeller.

"The grains were commercial granulated cleanser with chlorine," he said. "It must have come off the cleaning man's hands. There were several very minute particles of dried blood. It's definitely blood, but there's not enough to type."

"The tears at the end of the pieces wandered off the perforations," Beverly Katz continued. "If we find the roll in somebody's possession and he hasn't torn it again, we can get a definite match. I recommend issuing an advisory now, so the arresting officers will be sure to search for the roll."

Crawford nodded. "Bowman?"

"Sharon from my office went after the paper and got samples to match. It's toilet tissue for marine heads and motor homes. The texture matches brand-name Wedeker manufactured in Minneapolis. It has nationwide distribution."

Bowman set up his photographs on an easel near the windows. His voice was surprisingly deep for his slight stature and his bow-tie moved slightly when he talked. "On the handwriting itself, this is a right-handed person using his left hand and printing in a deliberate block pattern. You can see the unsteadiness in the strokes and varying letter sizes.

"The proportions make me think our man has a touch of uncorrected astigmatism.

"The inks on both pieces of the note look like the same standard ball-point Royal Blue in natural light, but a slight difference appears under coloured filters. He used two pens, changing somewhere in the missing section of the note. You can see where the first one began to skip. The first pen is not used frequently—see the blob it starts with? It might have been stored point down and uncapped in a pencil jar or canister, which suggests a desk situation. Also the surface the paper lay on was soft enough to be a blotter. A blotter might retain impressions if you find it. I want to add the blotter to Beverly's advisory."

Bowman flipped to a photograph of the back of the note. The extreme enlargement made the paper look fuzzy. It was grooved with shadowed impressions. "He folded the note to write the bottom part, including what was later torn out. In this enlargement of the back side, oblique light reveals a few impressions. We can make out '666 an'. Maybe that's where he had pen trouble and had to bear down and overwrite. I didn't spot it until I had this high-contrast print. There's no 666 in any ad so far.

"The sentence structure is orderly and there's no rambling. The folds suggest it was delivered in a standard letter-size envelope. These two dark places are printing-ink smudges. The note was probably folded inside some innocuous printed matter in the envelope.

"That's about it," Bowman said. "Unless you have questions, Jack, I'd better go to the courthouse. I'll check in after I testify."

"Sink 'em deep," Crawford said.

Graham studied the *Tattler* personals column. ("Attractive queen-size lady, young 52, seeks Christian Leo non-smoker 40–70. No children please. Artificial limb welcome. No phonies. Send photo first letter.")

Lost in the pain and desperation of the ads, he didn't notice that the others were leaving until Beverly Katz spoke to him.

"I'm sorry, Beverly. What did you say?" He looked up at her bright eyes and kindly, well-worn face.

"I just said I'm glad to see you back, champ. You're looking good."

"Thanks, Beverly."

"Saul's going to cooking school. He's still hit or miss, but when the dust settles come over and let him practice on you."

"I'll do it."

Zeller went away to prowl his laboratory. Only Crawford and Graham were left, looking at the clock.

"Forty minutes to *Tattler* press-time," Crawford said. "I'm going after their mail. What do you say?"

"I think you have to."

Crawford passed the word to Chicago on Zeller's telephone. "Will, we need to be ready with a substitute ad if Chicago bingos."

"I'll work on it."

"I'll set up the drop." Crawford called the Secret Service and talked at some length. Graham was still scribbling when he finished.

"Okay, the mail drop's a beauty," Crawford said at last. "It's an outside message box on a fire extinguisher service outfit in Annapolis. That's Lecter territory. The Tooth Fairy will see that it's something

Lecter could know about. Alphabetical pigeon-holes. The service people drive up to it and get assignments and mail. Our boy can check it out from a park across the street. Secret Service swears it looks good. They set it up to catch a counterfeiter, but it turned out they didn't need it. Here's the address. What about the message?"

"We have to use two messages in the same edition. The first one warns the Tooth Fairy that his enemies are closer than he thinks. It tells him he made a bad mistake in Atlanta and if he repeats the mistake he's doomed. It tells him Lecter has mailed 'secret information' I showed Lecter about what we're doing, how close we are, the leads we have. It directs the Tooth Fairy to a second message that begins with 'your signature'.

"The second message begins 'Avid Fan—' and contains the address of the mail drop. We have to do it that way. Even in roundabout language the warning in the first message is going to excite some casual nuts. If they can't find out the address they can't come to the drop and screw things up."

"Good. Damn good. Want to wait it out in my office?"

"I'd rather be doing something. I need to see Brian Zeller."

"Go ahead, I can get you in a hurry if I have to."

Graham found the Section Chief in Serology.

"Brian, could you show me a couple of things?"

"Sure, what?"

"The samples you used to type the Tooth Fairy."

Zeller looked at Graham through the close-range section of his bifocals. "Was there something in the report you didn't understand?"

"No."

"Was something unclear?"

"No."

"Something *incomplete*?" Zeller mouthed the word as if it had an unpleasant taste.

"Your report was fine, couldn't ask for better. I just want to hold the evidence in my hand."

"*Ah*, certainly. We can do that." Zeller believed that all field men retain the superstitions of the hunt. He was glad to humour Graham. "It's all together down at that end."

Graham followed him between the long counters of apparatus. "You're reading Tedeschi."

"Yes," Zeller said over his shoulder, "we don't do any forensic medicine here, as you know, but Tedeschi has a lot of useful things in there. Graham. Will Graham. You wrote the standard monograph on determining time of death by insect activity, didn't you? Or do I have the right Graham?"

"I did it." A pause. "You're right, Mant and Nuorteva in Tedeschi are better on insects."

Zeller was surprised to hear his thought spoken. "Well, it does have more pictures and tables of invasion waves. No offence."

"Of course not. They're better. I told them so."

Zeller gathered his phials and slides from a cabinet and a refrigerator and set them on the laboratory counter. "If you want to ask me anything, I'll be where you found me. The stage light on this microscope is on the side here."

Graham did not want the microscope. He doubted none of Zeller's findings. He didn't know what he wanted. He raised the phials and slides to the light, and a glassine envelope with two blond hairs found in Birmingham. A second envelope held three hairs found on Mrs. Leeds.

There were spit and hair and semen on the table in front of Graham and empty air where he tried to see an image, a face, something to replace the shapeless dread he carried.

A woman's voice came from a speaker in the ceiling. "Graham, Will Graham, to Special Agent Crawford's office. On Red."

He found Sarah in her headset typing with Crawford looking over her shoulder.

"Chicago's got an ad order with 666 in it," Crawford said out of the side of his mouth. "They're dictating it to Sarah now. They said part of it looks like code."

The lines were climbing out of Sarah's typewriter:

Dear Pilgrim, you honour me . . .

"That's it. That's it," Graham said. "Lecter called him a pilgrim when he was talking to me."

you're very beautiful . . .

"Christ," Crawford said.

I offer 100 prayers for your safety.
Find help in John 6:22, 8:16, 9:1; Luke 1:7, 3:1; Galatians 6:11, 15:2; Acts 3:3; Revelation 18:7; Jonah 6:8 . . .

The typing slowed as Sarah read back each pair of numbers to the agent in Chicago. When she had finished the list of scriptural references covered a quarter of a page. It was signed "Bless you, 666."

"That's it," Sarah said.

Crawford picked up the phone. "Okay, Chester, how did it go down with the ad manager? No, you did right. A complete clam, right. Stand by at that phone, I'll get back to you."

"Code," Graham said.

"Has to be. We've got 22 minutes to get a message in if we can break it. Shop foreman needs ten minutes' notice and $300 to shoehorn one in this edition. Bowman's in his office, he got a recess. If you'll get him cracking I'll talk to cryptography at Langley. Sarah, shoot a telex of the ad to CIA cryptography section. I'll tell 'em it's coming."

Bowman put the message on his desk and aligned it precisely with the corners of his blotter. He polished his rimless spectacles for what seemed to Graham a very long time.

Bowman had a reputation for being quick. Even the explosives section forgave him for not being an ex-Marine and granted him that.

"We have twenty minutes," Graham said.

"I understand. You called Langley?"

"Crawford did."

Bowman read the message many times, looked at it upside down and sideways, ran down the margins with his finger. He took a Bible from his shelves. For five minutes the only sounds were the two men breathing and the crackle of onion-skin pages.

"No," he said. "We won't make it in the time. Better use what's left for whatever else you can do."

Graham showed him an empty hand.

Bowman swivelled round to face Graham and took off his glasses. He had a pink spot on each side of his face. "Do you feel fairly confident the note to Lecter is the only communication he's had from your Tooth Fairy?"

"Right."

"The code is something simple then. They only needed cover against casual readers. Measuring by the perforations in the note to Lecter, only about three inches is missing. That's not much room for instructions. The numbers aren't right for a jailhouse alphabet grid—the tap-code. I'm guessing it's a book-code."

Crawford joined them. "Book-code?"

"Looks like it. The first numeral, that '100 prayers', could be the page number. The paired numbers in the Scriptural references could be line and letter. But what book?"

"Not the Bible?" Crawford said.

"No, not the Bible. I thought it might be at first. Galatians 6:11 threw me off. 'Ye see how large a letter I have written unto you with mine own hand.' That's appropriate, but it's coincidence because next he has Galatians 15:2. Galatians has only six chapters. Same with Jonah 6:8—Jonah has four chapters. He wasn't using a Bible."

"Maybe a book title could be concealed in the clear part of Lecter's message," Crawford said.

Bowman shook his head. "I don't think so."

"Then the Tooth Fairy named the book to use. He specified it in his note to Lecter," Graham said.

"It would appear so," Bowman said. "What about sweating Lecter? In a mental hospital I would think drugs—"

"They tried sodium amytal on him three years ago trying to find out where he buried a Princeton student," Graham said. "He gave them a recipe for dip. Besides, if we sweat him we lose the connection. If the Tooth Fairy picked the book, it's something he knew Lecter would have in his cell."

"I know for sure he didn't order one or borrow one from Chilton," Crawford said.

"What have the papers carried about that, Jack? About Lecter's books?"

"That he has medical books, psychology books, cookbooks."

"Then it could be one of the standards in those areas, something so basic the Tooth Fairy knew Lecter definitely would have it," Bowman said. "We need a list of Lecter's books. Do you have one?"

"No." Graham stared at his shoes. "I could get Chilton—wait. Rankin and Willingham, when they tossed his cell, they took Polaroids so they could get everything back in place."

"Would you ask them to meet me with the pictures of the books?" Bowman said, packing his briefcase.

"Where?"

"The Library of Congress."

Crawford checked the with C.I.A. cryptography section one last time. The computer at Langley was trying consistent and progressive number-letter substitutions and a staggering variety of alphabet grids. No progress. The cryptographer agreed with Bowman that it was probably a book-code.

Crawford looked at his watch. "Will, we're left with three choices and we've got to decide right now. We can pull Lecter's message out of the paper and run nothing. We can substitute our messages in plain language inviting the Tooth Fairy to the mail drop. Or, we can let Lecter's ad run as is."

"Are you sure we can still get Lecter's message out of the *Tattler?*"

"Chester thinks the shop foreman would chisel it for about $500."

"I hate to put in a plain-language message, Jack. Lecter would probably never hear from him again."

"Yeah, but I'm leery of letting Lecter's message run without knowing what it says," Crawford said. "What would Lecter tell him that he doesn't know already? If he found out we have a partial thumb-print and his prints aren't on file anywhere, he could whittle his thumb and pull his teeth and give us a big gummy laugh in court."

"The thumb-print wasn't in the case summary Lecter saw. We better let Lecter's message run. At least it'll encourage the Tooth Fairy to contact him again."

"What if it encourages him to do something besides write?"

"We'll feel sick for a long time," Graham said. "We have to do it."

Fifteen minutes later in Chicago the *Tattler*'s big presses rolled, gathering speed until their thunder raised the dust in the pressroom. The F.B.I. agent waiting in the smell of ink and hot newsprint took one of the first ones.

The cover lines included "HEAD TRANSPLANT!" and "ASTRO-NOMERS GLIMPSE GOD!"

The agent checked to see that Lecter's personal ad was in place and slipped the paper into an express pouch for Washington. He would see that paper again and remember his thumb smudge on the front page, but it would be years later when he took his children through the special exhibits on a tour of F.B.I. headquarters.

IN THE hour before dawn Crawford woke from a deep sleep. He saw the room dark, felt his wife's ample bottom comfortably settled against the small of his back. He did not know why he had awakened until the telephone rang a second time. He found it with no fumbling.

"Jack, this is Lloyd Bowman. I solved the code. You need to know what it says right now."

"Okay, Lloyd." Crawford's feet searched for his slippers.

"It says: *Graham home Marathon, Florida. Save yourself. Kill them all.*"

"Goddammit. Gotta go."

"I know."

Crawford went to his den without stopping for his robe. He called Florida twice, the airport once, then called Graham at his hotel.

"Will, Bowman just broke the code."

"What did it say?"

"I'll tell you in a second. Now listen to me. Everything is okay. I've taken care of it, so stay on the phone when I tell you."

"Tell me now."

"It's your home address. Lecter gave the bastard your home address.

Wait, Will. Sheriff's department has two cars on the way to Sugarloaf right now. Customs launch from Marathon is taking the ocean side. The Tooth Fairy couldn't have done anything in this short time. Hold on. You can move faster with me helping you. Now listen to this.

"The deputies aren't going to scare Molly. The sheriff's cars are just closing the road to the house. Two deputies will move up close enough to watch the house. You can call her when she wakes up. I'll pick you up in half an hour."

"I won't be here."

"The next plane in that direction doesn't go until eight. It'll be quicker to bring them up here. My brother's house on the Chesapeake is available to them. I've got a good plan, Will, wait and hear it. If you don't like it I'll put you on the plane myself."

"I need some things from the armoury."

"We'll get it soon as I pick you up."

Molly and Willy were among the first off the plane at National Airport in Washington. She spotted Graham in the crowd, did not smile, but turned to Willy and said something as they walked swiftly ahead of the stream of tourists returning from Florida.

She looked Graham up and down and came to him with a light kiss. Her brown fingers were cold on his cheek.

Graham felt the boy watching. Willy shook hands from a full arm's length away.

Graham made a joke about the weight of Molly's suitcase as they walked to the car.

"I'll carry it," Willy said.

A brown Chevrolet with Maryland plates moved in behind them as they pulled out of the parking lot.

Graham crossed the bridge at Arlington and pointed out the Lincoln and Jefferson Memorials and the Washington monument before heading east toward the Chesapeake Bay. Ten miles outside Washington the brown Chevrolet pulled up beside them in the inside lane. The driver looked across with his hand to his mouth and a voice from nowhere crackled in the car.

"Fox Edward, you're clean as a whistle. Have a nice trip."

Graham reached under the dash for the concealed microphone. "Roger, Bobby. Much obliged."

The Chevrolet dropped behind them and its turn signal came on.

"Just making sure no press cars or anything were following," Graham said.

"I see," Molly said.

They stopped in the late afternoon and ate crabs at a road-side restaurant. Willy went to look at the lobster tank.

"I hate it, Molly. I'm sorry," Graham said.

"Is he after you now?"

"We've no reason to think so. Lecter just suggested it to him, urged him to do it."

"It's a clammy, sick feeling."

"I know it is. You and Willy are safe at Crawford's brother's house. Nobody in the world knows you're there but me and Crawford."

"I'd just as soon not talk about Crawford."

"It's a nice place, you'll see."

She took a deep breath and when she let it out the anger seemed to go with it, leaving her tired and calm. She gave him a crooked smile. "Hell, I just got mad there for a while. Do we have to put up with any Crawfords?"

"Nope." He moved the cracker basket to take her hand. "How much does Willy know?"

"Plenty. His buddy Tommy's mother had a trash newspaper from the supermarket at their house. Tommy showed it to Willy. It had a lot of stuff about you, apparently pretty distorted. About Hobbs—

the place you were after that, Lecter, everything. It upset him. I asked
him if he wanted to talk about it. He just asked me if I knew it all
along. I said yes, that you and I talked about it once, that you told
me everything before we got married. I asked him if he wanted me
to tell him about it, the way it really was. He said he'd ask you to
your face."

"Damn good. Good for him. What was it, the *Tattler*?"

"I don't know, I think so."

"Thanks a lot, Freddy." A swell of anger at Freddy Lounds lifted him
from his seat. He washed his face with cold water in the rest-room.

Sarah was saying good night to Crawford in the office when the
telephone rang. She put down her purse and umbrella to answer it.

"Special Agent Crawford's office. No, Mr. Graham is not in the
office, but let me see . . . Wait, I'll be glad to . . . Yes, he'll be in
tomorrow afternoon but let me . . ."

The tone of her voice brought Crawford around his desk.

She held the receiver as though it had died in her hand. "He asked
for Will and said he might call back tomorrow afternoon. I tried to
hold him."

"Who?"

"He said 'Just tell Graham it's the Pilgrim.' That's what Dr. Lecter
called—"

"The Tooth Fairy," Crawford said.

Graham went to the grocery store while Molly and Willy unpacked.
He found canary melons at the market and a ripe cranshaw. He parked
across the street from the house and sat for a few minutes still gripping
the wheel. He was ashamed that because of him Molly was rooted out
of the house she loved and put among strangers.

Crawford had done his best. This was no faceless federal safe house with chair arms bleached by palm sweat. It was a pleasant cottage, freshly whitewashed, with Impatiens blooming around the steps. It was the product of careful hands and a sense of order. The rear yard sloped down to the Chesapeake Bay and there was a swimming raft.

Blue-green television light pulsed behind the curtains. Molly and Willy were watching baseball, Graham knew.

Willy's father had been a baseball player and a good one. He and Molly met on the school bus, married in college.

They trooped around the Florida State League while he was in the Cardinals' farm system. They took Willy with them and had a terrific time. Spam and spirit. He got a tryout with the Cardinals and hit safely in his first two games. Then he began to have difficulty swallowing. The surgeon tried to get it all, but it metastasized and ate him up. He died five months later, when Willy was six.

Willy still watched baseball whenever he could. Molly watched baseball when she was upset.

Graham had no key. He knocked.

"I'll get it." Willy's voice.

"Wait." Molly's voice between the curtains. "All right."

Willy opened the door. In his fist, held close to his leg, was a fish billy.

Graham's eyes stung at the sight. The boy must have brought it in his suitcase.

Molly took the bag from him. "Want some coffee? There's gin, but not the kind you like."

When she was in the kitchen, Willy asked Graham to come outside.

From the back porch they could see the riding-lights of boats anchored in the bay.

"Will, is there any stuff I need to know to see about Mom?"

"You're both safe here, Willy. Remember the car that followed us from the airport making sure nobody saw where we went? Nobody can find out where you and your mother are."

"This crazy guy wants to kill you, does he?"

"We don't know that. I just didn't feel easy with him knowing where the house is."

"You gonna kill him?"

Graham closed his eyes for a moment. "No. It's just my job to find him. They'll put him in a mental hospital so they can treat him and keep him from hurting anybody."

"Tommy's mother had this little newspaper, Will. It said you killed a guy in Minnesota and you were in a mental hospital. I never knew that. Is it true?"

"Yes."

"I started to ask Mom, but I figured I'd ask you."

"I appreciate you asking me straight out. It wasn't just a mental hospital; they treat everything." The distinction seemed important. "I was in the psychiatric wing. It bothers you, finding out I was in there. Because I'm married to your mom."

"I told my dad I'd take care of her. I'll do it too."

Graham felt he had to tell Willy enough. He didn't want to tell him too much.

The lights went out in the kitchen. He could see Molly's dim outline inside the screen door and he felt the weight of her judgement. Dealing with Willy he was handling her heart.

Willy clearly did not know what to ask next. Graham did it for him.

"The hospital part was after the business with Hobbs."

"You shot him?"

"Yes."

"How'd it happen?"

"To begin with, Garrett Hobbs was insane. He was attacking college girls and he . . . killed them."

"How?"

"With a knife; anyway, I found a little curly piece of metal in the clothes one of the girls had on. It was the kind of shred a pipe threader makes—remember when we fixed the shower outside?

"I was taking a look at a lot of steam-fitters, plumbers and people. It took a long time. Hobbs had left this resignation letter at a construction job I was checking. I saw it and it was . . . peculiar. He wasn't working anywhere and I had to find him at home.

"I was going up the stairs in Hobbs's apartment house. A uniformed officer was with me. Hobbs must have seen us coming. I was half-way up to his landing when he shoved his wife out the door and she came falling down the stairs dead."

"He had killed her?"

"Yeah. So I asked the officer I was with to call for S.W.A.T., to get some help. But then I could hear kids in there and some screaming. I wanted to wait, but I couldn't."

"You went in the apartment?"

"I did. Hobbs had caught this girl from behind and he had a knife. He was cutting her with it. And I shot him."

"Did the girl die?"

"No."

"She got all right?"

"After a while, yes. She's all right now."

Willy digested this silently. Faint music came from an anchored sailboat.

Graham could leave things out for Willy, but he couldn't help seeing them again himself.

He left out Mrs. Hobbs on the landing clutching at him, stabbed so many times. Seeing she was gone, hearing the screaming from the apartment, prying the slick red fingers off and cracking his shoulder before the door gave in. Hobbs holding his own daughter, busy cutting her neck when he could get to it, her struggling with her chin tucked

down, the .38 knocking chunks out of him and him still cutting and
he wouldn't go down. Hobbs sitting on the floor crying and the girl
rasping. Holding her down and seeing Hobbs had gotten through the
windpipe, but not the arteries. The daughter looked at him with wide
glazed eyes and at her father sitting on the floor crying "See? See?"
until he fell over dead.

That was where Graham lost his faith in .38s.

"Willy, the business with Hobbs, it bothered me a lot. You know,
I kept it on my mind and I saw it over and over. I got so I couldn't
think about much else. I kept thinking there must be some way I could
have handled it better. And then I quit feeling anything. I couldn't eat
and I stopped talking to anybody. I got really depressed. So a doctor
asked me to go into the hospital and I did. After a while I got some
distance on it. The girl that got hurt in Hobbs's apartment came to
see me. She was okay and we talked a lot. Finally I put it aside, and
went back to work."

"Killing somebody, even if you have to do it, it feels that bad?"

"Willy, it's one of the ugliest things in the world."

"Say, I'm going in the kitchen for a minute. You want something,
a Coke?" Willy liked to bring Graham things, but he always made it
a casual adjunct to something he was going to do anyway. No special
trip or anything.

"Sure, a Coke."

"Mom ought to come out and look at the lights."

Late in the night Graham and Molly sat in the back porch swing.
Light rain fell and the boat lights cast grainy halos on the mist. The
breeze off the bay raised goosebumps on their arms.

"This could take a while, couldn't it?" Molly said.

"I hope it won't, but it might."

"Will, Evelyn said she could keep the shop for this week and four days next week. But I've got to go back to Marathon at least for a day or two when my buyers come. I could stay with Evelyn and Sam. I should go to market in Atlanta myself. I need to be ready for September."

"Does Evelyn know where you are?"

"I just told her Washington."

"Good."

"It's hard to have anything, isn't it? Rare to get it, hard to keep it. This is a damn slippery planet."

"Slick as hell."

"We'll be back in Sugarloaf, won't we?"

"Yes we will."

"Don't get in a hurry and hang it out too far. You won't do that?"

"No."

"Are you going back early?"

He had talked to Crawford for half an hour on the phone.

"A little before lunch. If you're going to Marathon at all, there's something we need to tend to in the morning. Willy can fish."

"He had to ask you about the other."

"I know, I don't blame him."

"Damn that reporter, what's his name?"

"Lounds. Freddy Lounds."

"I think maybe you hate him. And I wish I hadn't brought it up. Let's go to bed and I'll rub your back."

Resentment raised a minute blister in Graham. He had justified himself to an eleven-year-old. The kid said it was okay that he had been in the rubber Ramada. Now she was going to rub his back. Let's go to bed—it's okay with Willy.

When you feel strain, keep your mouth shut if you can.

"If you want to think awhile, I'll let you alone," she said.

He didn't want to think. He definitely did not. "You rub my back and I'll rub your front," he said.

"Go to it, Buster."

Winds aloft carried the thin rain out over the bay and by 9 a.m. the ground steamed. The far targets on the sheriff's department range seemed to flinch in the wavy air.

The range-master watched through his binoculars until he was sure the man and woman at the far end of the firing line were observing the safety rules.

The Justice Department credentials the man showed when he asked to use the range said "Investigator". That could be anything. The range-master did not approve of anyone other than a qualified instructor teaching pistol-craft.

Still, he had to admit the fed knew what he was doing.

They were only using a .22 calibre revolver but he was teaching the woman combat shoot from the Weaver stance, left foot slightly forward, a good two-handed grip on the revolver with isometric tension in the arms. She was firing at the silhouette target seven yards in front of her. Again and again she brought the weapon up from the outside pocket of her shoulder bag. It went on until the range-master was bored with it.

A change in the sound brought the range-master's glasses up again. They had the ear-muffs on now and she was working with a short, chunky revolver. The range-master recognized the pop of the light target loads.

He could see the pistol extended in her hands and it interested him. He strolled along the firing line and stood a few yards behind them.

He wanted to examine the pistol, but this was not a good time to interrupt. He got a good look at it as she shucked out the empties and popped in five from a speed-loader.

Odd arm for a fed. It was a Bulldog .44 Special, short and ugly with its startlingly big bore. It had been extensively modified by Mag Na Port. The barrel was vented near the muzzle to help keep the muzzle down on recoil, the hammer was bobbed and it had a good set of fat grips. He suspected it was throated for the speed-loader. One hell of a mean pistol when it was loaded with what the fed had waiting. He wondered how the woman would stand up to it.

The ammunition on the stand beside them was an interesting progression. First there was a box of lightly loaded wadcutters. Then came regular service hardball and last was something the range-master had read much about but had rarely seen. A row of Glaser Safety Slugs. The tips looked like pencil erasers. Behind each tip was a copper jacket containing No. 12 shot suspended in liquid Teflon.

The light projectile was designed to fly at tremendous velocity, smash into the target and release the shot. In meat the results were devastating. The range-master even recalled the figures. Ninety Glasers had been fired at men so far. All ninety were instant one-shot stops. In eighty-nine of the cases immediate death resulted. One man survived, surprising the doctors. The Glasers round had a safety advantage too—no ricochets and it would not go through a wall and kill someone in the next room.

The man was very gentle with her and encouraging, but he seemed sad about something.

The woman had worked up to the full service loads now and the range-master was pleased to see she handled the recoil very well, both eyes open and no flinch. True, it took her maybe four seconds to get the first one off, coming up from the bag, but three were in the X ring. Not bad for a beginner. She had some talent.

He had been back in the tower for some time when he heard the hellish racket of the Glasers going off.

She was pumping all five. It was not standard federal practice.

The range-master wondered what in God's name they saw in the silhouette that it would take five Glasers to kill.

Graham came to the tower to turn in the ear-muffs, leaving his pupil sitting on a bench, head down, her elbows on her knees.

The range-master thought he should be pleased with her and told him so. She had come a long way in one day. Graham thanked him absently. His expression puzzled the range-master. He looked like a man who had witnessed an irrevocable loss.

16

THE CALLER, "Mr. Pilgrim," had said to Sarah that he might call again on the following afternoon. At F.B.I. headquarters certain arrangements were made to receive the call.

Who was Mr. Pilgrim? Not Lecter—Crawford had made sure of that. Was Mr. Pilgrim the Tooth Fairy? Maybe so, Crawford thought.

The desks and telephones from Crawford's office had been moved overnight to a larger room across the hall.

Graham stood in the open doorway of a soundproof booth. Behind him in the booth was Crawford's telephone. Sarah had cleaned it with Windex. With the voiceprint spectrograph, tape recorders and stress evaluator taking up most of her desk and another table beside it, and Beverly Katz sitting in her chair, Sarah needed something to do.

The big clock on the wall showed ten minutes before noon.

Dr. Alan Bloom and Crawford stood with Graham. They had adopted a sidelines stance, hands in their pockets.

A technician seated across from Beverly Katz drummed his fingers on the desk until a frown from Crawford stopped him.

Crawford's desk was cluttered with two new telephones, an open line to the Bell System's electronic switching centre (E.S.S.) and a hot line to the F.B.I. communications room.

"How much time do you need for a trace?" Dr. Bloom asked.

"With the new switching it's a lot quicker than most people think," Crawford said. "Maybe a minute if it comes through all-electronic switching. More if it's from some place where they have to swarm the frame."

Crawford raised his voice to the room. "If he calls at all, it'll be short, so let's play him perfect. Want to go over the drill, Will?"

"Sure. When we get to the point where I talk, I want to ask you a couple of things, Doctor."

Bloom had arrived after the others. He was scheduled to speak to the Behavioural Science section at Quantico later in the day. Bloom could smell cordite on Graham's clothes.

"Okay," Graham said. "The phone rings. The circuit's completed immediately and the trace starts at E.S.S., but the tone generator continues the ringing noise so he doesn't know we've picked up. That gives us about twenty seconds on him." He pointed to the technician. "Tone generator to 'off' at the end of the fourth ring, got it?"

The technician nodded. "End of the fourth ring."

"Now, Beverly picks up the phone. Her voice is different from the one he heard yesterday. No recognition in the voice. Beverly sounds bored. He asks for me. Bev says 'I'll have to page him, may I put you on hold?' Ready with that, Bev?" Graham thought it would be better not to rehearse the lines. They might sound flat by rote.

"All right, the line is open to us, dead to him. I think he'll hold longer than he'll talk."

"Sure you don't want to give him the hold music?" the technician asked.

"Hell no," Crawford said.

"We give him about twenty seconds of hold, then Beverly comes back on and tells him, 'Mr. Graham's coming to the phone, I'll connect you now.' I pick up." Graham turned to Dr. Bloom. "How would you play him, Doctor?"

"He'll expect you to be sceptical about it really being him. I'd give him some polite scepticism. I'd make a strong distinction between the nuisance of fake callers and the significance, the importance, of a call from the real person. The fakes are easy to recognize because they lack the *capacity* to understand what has happened, that sort of thing.

"Make him tell something to prove who he is." Dr. Bloom looked at the floor and kneaded the back of his neck.

"You don't know what he wants. Maybe he wants understanding, maybe he's fixed on you as the adversary and wants to gloat—we'll see. Try to pick up his mood and give him what he's after, a little at a time. I'd be very leery of appealing to him to come to us for help, unless you sense he's asking for that.

"If he's paranoid you'll pick it up fast. In that case I'd play into his suspicion or grievance. Let him air it. If he gets rolling on that, he may forget how long he's talked. That's all I know to tell you." Bloom put his hand on Graham's shoulder and spoke quietly. "Listen, this is not a pep talk or any bullshit; you can take him over the jumps. Never mind advice, do what seems right to you."

Waiting. Half an hour of silence was enough.

"Call or no call, we've got to decide where to go from here," Crawford said. "Want to try the mail drop?"

"I can't see anything better," Graham said.

"That would give us two baits, a stake-out at your house in the Keys and the drop."

The telephone was ringing.

Tone generator on. At E.S.S. the trace began. Four rings. The technician hit the switch and Beverly picked up. Sarah was listening.

"Special Agent Crawford's office."

Sarah shook her head. She knew the caller, one of Crawford's cronies at Alcohol, Tobacco and Firearms. Beverly got him off in a hurry, and stopped the trace. Everyone in the F.B.I. building knew to keep the line clear.

Crawford went over the details of the mail drop again. They were bored and tense at the same time. Lloyd Bowman came around to show them how the number pairs in Lecter's Scriptures fitted page 100 of the softcover *Joy of Cooking*. Sarah passed around coffee in paper cups.

The telephone was ringing.

The tone generator took over and at E.S.S. the trace began. Four rings. The technician hit the switch. Beverly picked up.

"Special Agent Crawford's office."

Sarah was nodding her head. Big nods.

Graham went into his booth and closed the door. He could see Beverly's lips moving. She punched "hold" and watched the second hand on the wall clock.

Graham could see his face in the polished receiver. Two floated faces in the ear-piece and mouth-piece. He could smell cordite from the firing range in his shirt. *Don't hang up. Sweet Jesus, don't hang up.* Forty seconds had elapsed. The telephone moved slightly on his table when it rang. *Let it ring. Once more.* Forty-five seconds. *Now.*

"This is Will Graham, can I help you?"

Low laughter. A muffled voice, "I expect you can."

"Could I ask who's calling, please?"

"Didn't your secretary tell you?"

"No, but she did call me out of a meeting, sir, and—"

"If you tell me you won't talk to Mr. Pilgrim, I'll hang up right now. Yes or no?"

"Mr. Pilgrim, if you have some problem I'm equipped to deal with, I'll be glad to talk with you."

"I think you have the problem, Mr. Graham."

"I'm sorry, I didn't understand you."

The second hand crawled toward one minute.

"You've been a busy boy, haven't you?" the caller said.

"Too busy to stay on the phone unless you state your business."

"My business is in the same place yours is. Atlanta and Birmingham."

"Do you know something about that?"

Soft laughter. "Know something about it? Are you interested in Mr. Pilgrim? Yes or no? I'll hang up if you lie."

Graham could see Crawford through the glass. He had a telephone receiver in each hand.

"Yes. But see, I get a lot of calls and most of them are from people who say they know things." One minute.

Crawford put one receiver down and scrawled on a piece of paper.

"You'd be surprised how many pretenders there are," Graham said. "Talk to them a few minutes and you can tell they don't have the capacity to even understand what's going on. Do you?"

Sarah held a sheet of paper to the glass for Graham to see. It said, "Chicago phone booth. P.D. scrambling."

"I'll tell you what, you tell me one thing you know about Mr. Pilgrim and maybe I'll tell you whether you're right or not," the muffled voice said.

"Let's get straight who we're talking about," Graham said.

"We're talking about Mr. Pilgrim."

"How do I know Mr. Pilgrim has done anything I'm interested in. Has he?"

"Let's say, yes."

"Are you Mr. Pilgrim?"

"I don't think I'll tell you that."

"Are you his friend?"

"Sort of."

"Well, prove it then. Tell me something that shows me how well you know him."

"You first. You show me yours." A nervous giggle. "First time you're wrong, I hang up."

"All right, Mr. Pilgrim is right-handed."

"That's a safe guess. Most people are."

"Mr. Pilgrim is misunderstood."

"No general crap, please."

"Mr. Pilgrim is really strong physically."

"Yes, you could say that."

Graham looked at the clock. A minute and a half. Crawford nodded encouragement.

Don't tell him anything that he could change.

"Mr. Pilgrim is white and about, say, five feet eleven. You haven't told me anything, you know. I'm not so sure you even know him at all."

"Want to stop talking?"

"No, but you said we'd trade. I was just going along with you."

"Do you think Mr. Pilgrim is crazy?"

Bloom was shaking his head.

"I don't think anybody who is as careful as he is could be crazy. I think he's different. I think a lot of people do believe he's crazy, and the reason for that is he hasn't let people understand much about him."

"Describe exactly what you think he did to Mrs. Leeds and maybe I'll tell you if you're right or not."

"I don't want to do that."

"Goodbye."

Graham's heart jumped, but he could still hear breathing on the other end.

"I can't go into that until I know—"

Graham heard the telephone booth door slam open in Chicago and the receiver fall with a clang. Faint voices and bangs as the receiver swung on its cord. Everyone in the office heard it on the speaker-phone.

"Freeze. Don't even twitch. Now lock your fingers behind your head and back out of the booth slowly. Slowly. Hands on the glass and spread 'em."

Sweet relief was flooding Graham.

"I'm not armed, Stan. You'll find my I.D. in my breast pocket. That tickles."

A confused voice loud on the telephone. "Who am I speaking to?"

"Will Graham, F.B.I."

"This is Sgt. Stanley Riddle, Chicago Police Department." Irritated now. "Would you tell me what the hell's going on?"

"You tell me. You have a man in custody?"

"Damn right. Freddy Lounds, the reporter. I've known him for ten years. (Here's your notebook, Freddy.) Are you preferring charges against him?"

Graham's face was pale. Crawford's was red. Dr. Bloom watched the tape reels go around.

"Can you hear me?"

"Yes, I'm preferring charges." Graham's voice was strangled. "Obstruction of justice. Please take him in and hold him for the U.S. Attorney."

Suddenly Lounds was on the telephone. He spoke fast and clearly with the cotton wads out of his cheeks.

"Will, listen—"

"Tell it to the U.S. Attorney. Put Sgt. Riddle on the phone."

"I know something—"

"*Put Riddle on the goddamned telephone.*"

Crawford's voice came on the line. "Let me have it, Will."

Graham slammed his receiver down with a bang that made everyone in range of the speaker-phone flinch. He came out of the booth and left the room without looking at anyone.

"Lounds, you have hubbed Hell, my man," Crawford said.

"You want to catch him or not? I can help you. Let me talk one minute." Lounds hurried into Crawford's silence. "Listen, you just showed how bad you need the *Tattler*. Before I wasn't sure—now I am. That ad's part of the Tooth Fairy case or you wouldn't have gone balls-out to nail this call. Great. The *Tattler*'s here for you. Anything you want."

"How did you find out?"

"The ad manager came to me. Said your Chicago office sent this suit-of-clothes over to check the ads. Your guy took five letters from the incoming ads. Said it was 'pursuant to mail fraud.' Mail fraud nothing. The ad manager Xeroxed the letters and envelopes before he let your guy have them.

"I looked them over. I knew he took five letters to smoke-screen the one he really wanted. Took a day or two to check them all out. The answer was on the envelope. Chesapeake postmark. The postage-meter number was for Chesapeake State Hospital. I was over there, you know, behind your friend with the wild hair up his ass. What else could it be?

"I had to be sure, though. That's why I called, to see if you'd come down on 'Mr. Pilgrim' with both feet, and you did."

"You made a large mistake, Freddy."

"You need the *Tattler* and I can open it up for you. Ads, editorial, monitoring incoming mail, anything. You name it. I can be discreet. I can. Cut me in, Crawford."

"There's nothing to cut you in on."

"Okay, then it won't make any difference if somebody happened to put in six personal ads next issue. All to 'Mr. Pilgrim' and signed the same way."

"I'll get an injunction slapped on you and a sealed indictment for obstruction of justice."

"And it might leak to every paper in the country." Lounds knew he was talking on tape. He didn't care any more. "I swear to God, I'll do it, Crawford. I'll tear up your chance before I lose mine."

"Add interstate transmission of a threatening message to what I just said."

"Let me *help* you, Jack. I can, believe me."

"Run along to the police station, Freddy. Now put the sergeant back on the phone."

Freddy Lounds's Lincoln Versailles smelled of hair tonic and after-shave, socks and cigars, and the police sergeant was glad to get out of it when they reached the station house.

Lounds knew the captain commanding the precinct and many of the patrolmen. The captain gave Lounds coffee and called the U.S. Attorney's office to "try and clear this shit up".

No federal marshal came for Lounds. In half an hour he took a call from Crawford in the precinct commander's office. Then he was free to go. The captain walked him to his car.

Lounds was keyed up and his driving was fast and jerky as he crossed the Loop eastward to his apartment overlooking Lake Michigan. There were several things he wanted out of this story and he knew that he could get them. Money was one, and most of that would come from the paperback. He would have an instant paperback on the stands thirty-six hours after the capture. An exclusive story in the daily press would be a news coup. He would have the satisfaction of seeing the straight press— the *Chicago Tribune*, the *Los Angeles Times*, the sanctified *Washington Post* and the holy *New York Times*—run his copyrighted material under his byline with his picture credits.

And then the correspondents of those august journals, who looked down on him, who would not drink with him, could eat their fucking hearts out.

Lounds was a pariah to them because he had taken a different faith. Had he been incompetent, a fool with no other resource, the veterans of the straight press could have forgiven him for working on the *Tattler*, as one forgives a retarded geek. But Lounds was good. He had the qualities of a good reporter—intelligence, guts and the good eye. He had great energy and patience.

Against him was the fact that he was obnoxious and therefore disliked by news executives, and his inability to keep himself out of his stories.

In Lounds was the lunging need to be noticed that is often miscalled ego. Lounds was lumpy and ugly and small. He had buck teeth and his rat eyes had the sheen of spit on asphalt.

He had worked in straight journalism for ten years when he realized that no one would ever send him to the White House. He saw that his publishers would wear his legs out, use him until it was time for him to become a broken-down old drunk manning a dead-end desk, drifting inevitably toward cirrhosis or a mattress fire.

They wanted the information he could get, but they didn't want Freddy. They paid him top scale, which is not very much money if you have to buy women. They patted his back and told him he had a lot of balls and they refused to put his name on a parking place.

One evening in 1969 while in the office working rewrite, Freddy had an epiphany.

Frank Larkin was seated near him taking dictation on the telephone. Dictation was the glue factory for old reporters on the paper where Freddy worked. Frank Larkin was fifty-five, but he looked seventy. He was oyster-eyed and he went to his locker every half-hour for a drink. Freddy could smell him from where he sat.

Larkin got up and shuffled over to the slot and spoke in a hoarse whisper to the news editor, a woman. Freddy always listened to other people's conversations.

Larkin asked the woman to get him a Kotex from the machine in the ladies room. He had to use them on his bleeding behind.

Freddy stopped typing. He took the story out of his typewriter, replaced the paper and wrote a letter of resignation.

A week later he was working for the *Tattler*.

He started as Cancer Editor at a salary nearly double what he had earned before. Management was impressed with his attitude.

The *Tattler* could afford to pay him well because the paper found cancer very lucrative.

One in five Americans die of it. The relatives of the dying, worn out, prayed out, trying to fight a raging carcinoma with pats and banana pudding and copper-tasting jokes, are desperate for anything hopeful.

Marketing surveys showed that a bold "NEW CURE FOR CANCER" or "CANCER MIRACLE DRUG" cover line boosted supermarket sales of any *Tattler* issue by 22.3 per cent. There was a six percentile drop in those sales when the story ran on Page One beneath the cover line, as the reader had time to scan the empty text while the groceries were being totalled.

Marketing experts discovered it was better to have the big cover line in colour on the front and play the story in the middle pages where it was difficult to hold the paper open and manage a purse and grocery cart at the same time.

The standard story featured an optimistic five paragraphs in ten point type, then a drop to eight point, then to six point before mentioning that the "miracle drug" was unavailable or that animal research was just beginning.

Freddy earned his money turning them out and the stories sold a lot of *Tattlers*.

In addition to increased readership, there were many spin-off sales of miracle medallions and healing cloths. Manufacturers of these paid a premium to get their ads located close to the weekly cancer story.

Many readers wrote to the paper for more information. Some additional revenue was realized by selling their names to a radio "evangelist", a screaming sociopath who wrote to them for money, using envelopes stamped "Someone You Love Will Die Unless . . ."

Freddy Lounds was good for the *Tattler* and the *Tattler* was good to him. Now, after eleven years with the paper, he earned $72,000 a year. He covered pretty much what he pleased and spent the money trying to have a good time. He lived as well as he knew how to live.

The way things were developing, he believed he could raise the ante on his paperback deal and there was movie interest. He had heard that Hollywood was a fine place for obnoxious fellows with money.

Freddy felt good. He shot down the ramp to the underground garage in his building and wheeled into his parking place with a spirited squeal of rubber. There on the wall was his name in letters a foot high, marking his private spot. Mr. Frederick Lounds.

Wendy was here already—her Datsun was parked next to his space. Good. He wished he could take her to Washington with him. That would make those flatfeets' eyes pop. He whistled in the elevator on his way upstairs.

Wendy was packing for him. She had lived out of suitcases and she did a good job.

Neat in her jeans and plaid shirt, her brown hair gathered in a chipmunk tail on her neck, she might have been a farm girl except for her pallor and her shape. Wendy's figure was almost a caricature of puberty.

She looked at Lounds with eyes that had not registered surprise in years. She saw that he was trembling.

"You're working too hard, Roscoe." She liked to call him Roscoe and it pleased him for some reason. "What are you taking, the six o'clock shuttle?" She brought him a drink and moved her sequinned jump suit and wig case off the bed so he could lie down. "I can take you to the airport. I'm not going to the club 'til six."

"Wendy City" was her own topless bar and she didn't have to dance any more. Lounds had co-signed the note.

"You sounded like Morocco Mole when you called me," she said.

"Who?"

"You know, on television Saturday morning, he's real mysterious and he helps Secret Squirrel. We watched it when you had the flu . . . you really pulled one off today, didn't you? You're really pleased with yourself."

"Damn straight. I took a chance today, baby, and it paid off. I've got a chance at something sweet."

"You've got time for a nap before you go. You're running yourself in the ground."

Lounds lit a cigarette. He already had one burning in the ashtray.

"You know what?" she said. "I bet if you drink your drink and get it off, you could go to sleep."

Lounds's face, like a fist pressed against her neck, relaxed at last, became mobile as suddenly as a fist becomes a hand. His trembling stopped. He told her all about it, whispering into the buck jut of her augmented breasts, she tracing eights on the back of his neck with a finger.

"That is some kind of smart, Roscoe," she said. "You go to sleep now. I'll get you up for the plane. It'll be all right, all of it. And then we'll have a high old time."

They whispered about the places they would go. He went to sleep.

CHAPTER

17

DR. ALAN BLOOM and Jack Crawford sat on folding chairs, the only furniture left in Crawford's office.

"The cupboard is bare, Doctor."

Dr. Bloom studied Crawford's simian face and wondered what was coming. Behind Crawford's grousing and his Alka-Seltzers the doctor saw an intelligence as cold as an X-ray table.

"Where did Will go?"

"He'll walk around and cool off," Crawford said. "He hates Lounds."

"Did you think you might lose Will after Lecter published his home address? That he might go back to his family?"

"For a minute, I did. It shook him."

"Understandably," Dr. Bloom said.

"Then I realized—he can't go home and neither can Molly and Willy, never, until the Tooth Fairy is out of the way."

"You've met Molly?"

"Yeah. She's great. I like her. She'd be glad to see me in Hell with my back broken, of course. I'm having to duck her right now."

"She thinks you use Will?"

Crawford looked at Dr. Bloom sharply. "I've got some things I have to talk to him about. We'll need to check with you. When do you have to be at Quantico?"

"Not until Tuesday morning. I put it off." Dr. Bloom was a guest lecturer at the Behavioural Science section of the F.B.I. Academy.

"Graham likes you. He doesn't think you run any mind games on him," Crawford said. Bloom's remark about using Graham stuck in his craw.

"I don't. I wouldn't try," Dr. Bloom said. "I'm as honest with him as I'd be with a patient."

"Exactly."

"No, I want to be his friend and I am. Jack, I owe it to my field of study to observe. Remember, though, when *you* asked me to give you a study on him I refused."

"That was Petersen upstairs, wanted the study."

"You were the one who asked for it. No matter, if I ever did anything on Graham, if there were ever anything that might be of therapeutic benefit to others, I'd abstract it in a form that would be totally unrecognizable. If I ever do anything in a scholarly way, it'll only be published posthumously."

"After you or after Graham?"

Dr. Bloom didn't answer.

"One thing I've noticed—I'm curious about this: you're never alone in a room with Graham, are you? You're smooth about it, but you're never one-on-one with him. Why's that? Do you think he's psychic, is that it?"

"No. He's an *eideteker*—he has a remarkable visual memory—but I don't think he's psychic. He wouldn't let Duke test him—that doesn't mean anything, though. He hates to be prodded and poked. So do I."

"But—"

"Will wants to think of this as purely an intellectual exercise and, in the narrow definition of forensics, that's what it is. He's good at that, but there are other people just as good I imagine."

"Not many," Crawford said.

"What he has in addition is pure empathy and projection," Dr. Bloom said. "He can assume your point of view or mine—and maybe some other points of view that scare and sicken him. It's an uncomfortable gift, Jack. Perception's a tool that's pointed on both ends."

"Why aren't you ever alone with him?"

"Because I have some professional curiosity about him and he'd pick that up in a hurry. He's fast."

"If he caught you peeking, he'd snatch down the shades."

"An unpleasant analogy, but accurate, yes. You've had sufficient revenge now, Jack. We can get to the point. Let's make it short, I don't feel very well."

"A psychosomatic manifestation probably," Crawford said.

"Actually it's my gall bladder—what do you want?"

"I have a medium where I can speak to the Tooth Fairy."

"The *Tattler*," Dr. Bloom said.

"Right. Do you think there's any way to push him in a self-destructive way by what we say to him?"

"Push him toward suicide?"

"Suicide would suit me fine."

"I doubt it. In certain kinds of mental illness that might be possible. Here, I doubt it. If he were self-destructive he wouldn't be so careful. He wouldn't protect himself so well. If he were a classic paranoid schizophrenic you might be able to influence him to blow up and become visible. You might even get him to hurt himself. I wouldn't help you though." Suicide was Bloom's mortal enemy.

"No, I suppose you wouldn't," Crawford said. "Could we enrage him?"

"Why do you want to know? To what purpose?"

"Let me ask you this: could we enrage him and focus his attention?"

"He's already fixed on Graham as his adversary and you know it. Don't fool around. You've decided to stick Graham's neck out, haven't you?"

"I think I have to do it. It's that or he gets his feet sticky on the 25th. Help me."

"I'm not sure you know what you're asking."

"Advice—that's what I'm asking."

"I don't mean from me," Dr. Bloom said. "What you're asking from Graham. I don't want you to misinterpret this, and normally I wouldn't say it, but you ought to know: what do you think one of Will's strongest drives is?"

Crawford shook his head.

"It's fear, Jack. The man deals with a huge amount of fear."

"Because he got hurt?"

"No, not entirely. Fear comes with imagination, it's a penalty, it's the price of imagination."

Crawford stared at his blunt hands folded on his stomach. He reddened. It was embarrassing to talk about it. "Sure. It's what you don't ever mention on the big boys' side of the playground, right? Don't worry about telling me he's afraid. I won't think he's not a 'stand-up guy'. I'm not a total asshole, Doctor."

"I never thought you were, Jack."

"I wouldn't put him out there if I couldn't cover him. Okay, if I couldn't cover him 80 per cent. He's not bad himself. Not the best, but he's quick. Will you help us stir up the Tooth Fairy, Doctor? A lot of people are dead."

"Only if Graham knows the entire risk ahead of time and assumes it voluntarily. I have to hear him say that."

"I'm like you, Doctor. I never bullshit him. No more than we all bullshit each other."

★   ★   ★

Crawford found Graham in the small workroom near Zeller's lab which he had commandeered and filled with photographs and personal papers belonging to the victims.

Crawford waited until Graham put down the Law Enforcement Bulletin he was reading.

"Let me fill you in on what's up for the 25th." He did not have to tell Graham that the 25th would bring the next full moon.

"When he does it again?"

"Yeah, if we have a problem on the 25th."

"Not if. When."

"Both times it's been on Saturday night. Birmingham, June 28th, a full moon falling on a Saturday night. It was July 26th in Atlanta, that's one day short of a full moon, but also Saturday night. This time the full moon falls on Monday, August 25th. He likes the weekend, though, so we're ready from Friday on."

"Ready? We're *ready*?"

"Correct. You know how it is in the textbooks—the ideal way to investigate a homicide?"

"I never saw it done that way," Graham said. "It never works out like that."

"No. Hardly ever. It would be great to be able to do it, though: send one guy in. Just one. Let him go over the place. He's wired and dictating all the time. He gets the place absolutely cherry for as long as he needs. Just him . . . just you."

A long pause.

"What are you telling me?"

"Starting the night of Friday 22nd we have a Grumman Gulfstream standing by at Andrews Air Force Base. I borrowed it from Interior. The basic lab stuff will be on it. We stand by—me, you, Zeller, Jimmy Price, a photographer and two people to do interrogations. Soon as the call comes in, we're on our way. Anywhere in the east or south, we can be there in an hour and fifteen minutes."

"What about the locals? They don't have to co-operate. They won't wait."

"We're blanketing the chiefs of police and sheriffs' departments. Every one of them. We're asking orders to be posted on the dispatchers' consoles and the duty officers' desks."

Graham shook his head. "Balls. They'd never hold off. They couldn't."

"This is what we're asking—it's not so much. We're asking that when a report comes in the first officers at the scene go in and look. Medical personnel go in and make sure nobody's left alive. They come back out. Road-blocks, interrogations go on any way they like, but the *scene*, that's sealed off until we get there. We drive up, you go in. You're wired. You talk it out to us when you feel like it, don't say anything when you don't feel like it. Take as long as you want. Then we'll come in."

"The locals won't wait."

"Of course they won't. They'll send in some guys from homicide. But the request will have *some* effect. It'll cut down on traffic in there and you'll get it fresh."

Fresh. Graham tilted his head back against his chair and stared at the ceiling.

"Of course," Crawford said, "we've still got thirteen days before that weekend."

"Aw, Jack."

"'Jack' what?" Crawford said.

"You kill me, you really do."

"I don't follow you."

"Yes you do. What you've done, you've decided to use me for bait because you don't have anything else. So before you pop the question, you pump me up about how bad next time will be. Not bad psychology. To use on a fucking idiot. What did you think I'd say? You worried I don't have the onions for it since that with Lecter?"

"No."

"I wouldn't blame you for wondering. We both know people it happened to. I don't like walking around in a Kevlar vest with my butt puckered up. But hell, I'm in it now. We can't go home as long as he's loose."

"I never doubted you'd do it."

Graham saw that this was true. "It's something more then, isn't it?"

Crawford said nothing.

"No Molly. *No way.*"

"Jesus, Will, even *I* wouldn't ask you that."

Graham stared at him for a moment. "Oh, for Christ's sake, Jack. You've decided to play ball with Freddy Lounds, haven't you? You and little Freddy have cut a deal."

Crawford frowned at a spot on his tie. He looked up at Graham. "You know yourself it's the best way to bait him. The Tooth Fairy's gonna watch the *Tattler*. What else have we got?"

"It has to be Lounds doing it?"

"He's got the corner on the *Tattler*."

"So I really bad-mouth the Tooth Fairy in the *Tattler* and then we give him a shot. You think it's better than the mail drop? Don't answer that, I know it is. Have you talked to Bloom about it?"

"Just in passing. We'll both get together with him. And Lounds. We'll run the mail drop on him at the same time."

"What about the set-up? I think we'll have to give him a pretty good shot at it. Something open. Some place where he can get close. I don't think he'd snipe. He might fool me, but I can't see him with a rifle."

"We'll have stillwatches on the high places."

They both were thinking the same thing. Kevlar body armour would stop the Tooth Fairy's 9mm and his knife unless Graham got hit in the face. There was no way to protect him against a head shot if a hidden rifleman got the chance to fire.

"You talk to Lounds. I don't have to do that."

"He needs to interview you, Will," Crawford said gently. "He has to take your picture."

Bloom had warned Crawford he'd have trouble on that point.

18

WHEN THE time came, Graham surprised both Crawford and Bloom. He seemed willing to meet Lounds half-way and his expression was affable beneath the cold blue eyes.

Being inside F.B.I. headquarters had a salutary effect on Lounds's manners. He was polite when he remembered to be, and he was quick and quiet with his equipment.

Graham baulked only once: he flatly refused to let Lounds see Mrs. Leeds's diary or any of the families' private correspondence.

When the interview began, he answered Lounds's questions in a civil tone. Both men consulted notes taken in conference with Dr. Bloom. The questions and answers were often rephrased.

Alan Bloom had found it difficult to scheme toward hurt. In the end, he simply laid out his theories about the Tooth Fairy. The others listened like karate students at an anatomy lecture.

Dr. Bloom said the Tooth Fairy's acts and his letter indicated a projective delusional scheme which compensated for intolerable feelings of inadequacy. Smashing the mirrors tied these feelings to his appearance.

The killer's objection to the name "Tooth Fairy" was grounded in the homosexual implications of the word "fairy." Bloom believed he had an unconscious homosexual conflict, a terrible fear of being gay. Dr. Bloom's opinion was reinforced by one curious observation in the Leeds house: fold marks and covered bloodstains indicated the Tooth Fairy put a pair of shorts on Charles Leeds after he was dead. Dr. Bloom believed he did this to emphasize his lack of interest in Leeds.

The psychiatrist talked about the strong bonding of aggression and sexual drives that occurs in sadists at a very early age.

The savage attacks aimed primarily at the women and performed in the presence of their families were clearly strikes at a maternal figure. (Bloom, pacing, talking half to himself, called his subject "the child of a nightmare." Crawford's eyelids drooped at the compassion in his voice.)

In the interview with Lounds, Graham made statements no investigator would make and no straight newspaper would credit.

He speculated that the Tooth Fairy was ugly, impotent with persons of the opposite sex, and he claimed falsely that the killer had sexually molested his male victims. Graham said that the Tooth Fairy was doubtless the laughing-stock of his acquaintances and the product of an incestuous home.

He emphasized that the Tooth Fairy was obviously not as intelligent as Hannibal Lecter. He promised to provide the *Tattler* with more observations and insights about the killer as they occurred to him. Many law enforcement people disagreed with him, he said, but as long as he was heading the investigation the *Tattler* could count on getting the straight stuff from him.

Lounds took a lot of pictures.

The key shot was taken in Graham's "Washington hide-away," an apartment he had "borrowed to use until he squashed the Fairy." It was the only place where he could "find solitude" in the "carnival atmosphere" of the investigation.

The photograph showed Graham in a bath-robe at a desk, studying late into the night. He was poring over a grotesque "artist's conception of the Fairy."

Behind him a slice of the floodlit Capitol dome could be seen through the window. Most importantly, in the lower left corner of the window, blurred but readable, was the sign of a popular motel across the street.

The Tooth Fairy could find the apartment if he wanted to.

At F.B.I. headquarters, Graham was photographed in front of a mass spectrometer. If had nothing to do with the case, but Lounds thought it looked impressive.

Graham even consented to have his picture taken with Lounds interviewing him. They did it in front of the vast gun racks in Firearms and Toolmarks. Lounds held a 9mm automatic of the same type as the Tooth Fairy's weapon. Graham pointed to the home-made silencer, fashioned from a length of television antenna mast.

Dr. Bloom was surprised to see Graham put a comradely hand on Lounds's shoulder just before Crawford clicked the shutter.

The interview and pictures were set to appear in the *Tattler* published the next day, Monday, August 11th. As soon as he had the material, Lounds left for Chicago. He said he wanted to supervise the layout himself. He made arrangements to meet Crawford on Tuesday afternoon five blocks from the trap.

Starting Tuesday, when the *Tattler* became generally available, two traps would be baited for the monster.

Graham would go each evening to his "temporary residence" shown in the *Tattler* picture.

A coded personal notice in the same issue invited the Tooth Fairy to a mail drop in Annapolis watched around the clock. If he were suspicious of the mail drop, he might think the effort to catch him was concentrated there. Then Graham would be a more appealing target, the F.B.I. reasoned.

Florida authorities provided a stillwatch at Sugarloaf Key.

There was an air of dissatisfaction among the hunters—two major stake-outs took manpower that could be used elsewhere, and Graham's presence at the trap each night would limit his movement to the Washington area.

Though Crawford's judgement told him this was the best move, the whole procedure was too passive for his taste. He felt they were playing games with themselves in the dark of the moon with less than two weeks to go before it rose full again.

Sunday and Monday passed in curiously jerky time. The minutes dragged and the hours flew.

Spurgen, chief S.W.A.T. instructor at Quantico, circled the apartment block on Monday afternoon. Graham rode beside him. Crawford was in the back seat.

"The pedestrian traffic falls off around 7.15. Everybody's settled in for dinner," Spurgen said. With his wiry compact body and his baseball cap tipped back on his head, he looked like an infielder. "Give us a toot on the clear band tomorrow night when you cross the B. &. O. railroad tracks. You ought to try to make it about 8.30, 8.40 or so."

He pulled into the apartment parking lot. "This set-up ain't heaven, but it could be worse. You'll park here tomorrow night. We'll arrange the space you use every night after that, but it'll always be on this side. It's 75 yards to the apartment entrance. Let's walk it."

Spurgen, short and bandy-legged, went ahead of Graham and Crawford.

He's looking for places where he could get the bad hop, Graham thought.

"The walk is probably where it'll happen, if it happens," the S.W.A.T. leader said. "See, from here the direct line from your car to the entrance, the natural route, is across the centre of the lot. It's as far as you can get from the line of cars that are here all day. He'll have to come across open asphalt to get close. How well do you hear?"

"Pretty well," Graham said. "Damn well on this parking lot."

Spurgen looked for something in Graham's face, found nothing he could recognize.

He stopped in the middle of the lot. "We're reducing the wattage on these street lights a little to make it tougher on a rifleman."

"Tougher on your people too," Crawford said.

"Two of ours have Startron night scopes," Spurgen said. "I've got some clear spray I'll ask you to use on your suit jackets, Will. By the way, I don't care how hot it is, you will wear body armour each and every time. Correct?"

"Yes."

"What is it?"

"It's Kevlar—what, Jack?—Second Chance?"

"Second Chance," Crawford said.

"It's pretty likely he will come up to you, probably from behind, or he may figure on meeting you and then turning around to shoot when he's passed you," Spurgen said. "Seven times he's gone for the head shot, right? He's seen that work. He'll do it with you too if you give him the time. *Don't give him the time.* After I show you a couple of things in the lobby and the flop, let's go to the range. Can you do that?"

"He can do that," Crawford said.

Spurgen was high priest on the range. He made Graham wear ear-plugs under the ear-muffs and flashed targets at him from every angle. He was relieved to see that Graham didn't carry regulation arms, but he worried about the flash from the ported barrel. They worked for two hours. The man insisted on checking the cylinder crane and cylinder latch screws on Graham's .44 when he had finished firing.

Graham showered and changed clothes to get the smell of gunsmoke off him before he drove to the bay for his last free night with Molly and Willy.

He took his wife and stepson to the grocery store after dinner and made a considerable to-do over selecting melons. He made sure they bought plenty of groceries—the old *Tattler* was still on the racks beside the checkout stands and he hoped Molly would not see the new issue coming in the morning. He didn't want to tell her what was happening.

When she asked him what he wanted for dinner in the coming week, he had to say he'd be away, that he was going back to Birmingham. It was the first real lie he had ever told her and telling it made him feel as greasy as old currency.

He watched her in the aisles: Molly, his pretty baseball wife, with her ceaseless vigilance for lumps, her insistence on quarterly medical check-ups for him and Willy, her controlled fear of the dark; her hard-bought knowledge that time is luck. She knew the value of their days. She could hold a moment by its stem. She had taught him to relish.

Pachelbel's Canon filled the sun-drowned room where they learned each other and there was the exhilaration too big to hold and even then the fear flickered across him like an osprey's shadow: this is too good to live for long.

Molly switched her bag often from shoulder to shoulder in the grocery aisles as though the gun in it weighed much more than its 19 ounces.

Graham would have been offended had he heard the ugly thing he mumbled to the melons: "I have to put that bastard in a rubber sack, that's all. I have to do that."

Variously weighted with lies, guns and groceries, the three of them were a small and solemn troop.

Molly smelled a rat. She and Graham did not speak after the lights were out. Molly dreamed of heavy crazy footsteps coming in a house of changing rooms.

19

THERE IS a news-stand in Lambert St. Louis International Airport which carries many of the major daily newspapers from all over the United States. The New York, Washington, Chicago and Los Angeles papers come in by air-freight and you can buy them on the same day they are published.

Like many news-stands, this one is owned by a chain and, along with the standard magazines and papers, the operator is required to take a certain amount of trash.

When the *Chicago Tribune* was delivered to the stand at 10 p.m. on Monday night, a bundle of *Tattler*s thumped to the floor beside it. The bundle was still warm in the centre.

The news-stand operator squatted in front of his shelves arranging the *Tribune*s. He had enough else to do. The day guys never did their share of straightening.

A pair of black zippered boots came into the corner of his vision. A browser. No, the boots were pointed at him. Somebody wanted some damn thing. The newsie wanted to finishing arranging his *Tribune*s but the insistent attention made the back of his head prickle.

His trade was transient. He didn't have to be nice.

"What is it?" he said to the knees.

"A *Tattler*."

"You'll have to wait until I bust the bundle."

The boots did not go away. They were too close.

"I said you'll have to wait until I bust the bundle. Understand? See I'm working here?"

A hand and a flash of bright steel and the twine on the bundle beside him parted with a pop. A Susan B. Anthony dollar rang on the floor in front of him. A clean copy of the *Tattler*, jerked from the centre of the bundle, spilled the top ones to the floor.

The news-stand operator got to his feet. His cheeks were flushed. The man was leaving with the paper under his arm.

"Hey. Hey you."

The man turned to face him. "Me?"

"Yeah, you. I told you—"

"You told me what?" He was coming back. He stood too close. "You told me what?"

Usually a rude merchant can fluster his customers. There was something awful in this one's calm.

The newsie looked at the floor. "You got a quarter coming back."

Dolarhyde turned his back and walked out. The news-stand operator's cheeks burned for half an hour. *Yeah, that guy was in here last week too. He comes in here again, I'll tell him where to fuckin' get off. I got somethin' under the counter for wiseasses.*

Dolarhyde did not look at the *Tattler* in the airport. Last Thursday's message from Lecter had left him with mixed feelings. Dr. Lecter had been right, of course, in saying that he was beautiful and it was thrilling to read. He *was* beautiful. He felt some contempt for the doctor's fear of the policeman. Lecter did not understand much better than the public.

Still, he was on fire to know if Lecter had sent him another message. He would wait until he got home to look. Dolarhyde was proud of his self-control.

He mused about the news-stand operator as he drove.

There was a time when he would have apologized for disturbing the man and never come back to the news-stand. For years he had taken shit unlimited from people. Not any more. The man could have insulted Francis Dolarhyde: he could not face the Dragon. It was all part of Becoming.

At midnight, the light above his desk still burned. The message from the *Tattler* was decoded and wadded on the floor. Pieces of the *Tattler* were scattered where Dolarhyde had clipped it for his journal. The great journal stood open beneath the painting of the Dragon, glue still drying where the new clippings were fastened. Beneath them, freshly attached, was a small plastic bag, empty as yet.

The legend beside the bag said: *With These He Offended Me.*

But Dolarhyde had left his desk.

He was sitting on the basement stairs in the cool must of earth and mildew. The beam from his electric lantern moved over draped furniture, the dusty backs of the great mirrors that once hung in the house and now leaned against the walls, the trunk containing his case of dynamite.

The beam stopped on a tall draped shape, one of several in the far corner of the cellar. Cobwebs touched his face as he went to it. Dust made him sneeze when he pulled off the cloth cover.

He blinked back the tears and shined his light on the old oak wheelchair he had uncovered. It was high-backed, heavy and strong, one of three in the basement. The county had provided them to Grandmother in the 1940s when she ran her nursing home here.

The wheels creaked as he rolled the chair across the floor. Despite its weight, he carried it easily up the stairs. In the kitchen he oiled the wheels. The small front wheels still squeaked, but the back ones had good bearings and spun freely at a flip of his finger.

The searing anger in him was eased by the wheels' soothing hum. As he spun them, Dolarhyde hummed too.

W HEN F REDDY Lounds left the *Tattler* office at noon on Tuesday he was tired and high. He had put together the *Tattler* story on the plane to Chicago and laid it out in the composing room in thirty minutes flat.

The rest of the time he had worked steadily on his paperback, brushing off all callers. He was a good organizer and now he had 50,000 words of solid background.

When the Tooth Fairy was caught, he'd do a whammo lead and an account of the capture. The background material would fit in neatly. He had arranged to have three of the *Tattler*'s reporters ready to go on short notice. Within hours of the capture they could be digging for details wherever the Tooth Fairy lived.

His agent talked very big numbers. Discussing the project with the agent ahead of time was, strictly speaking, a violation of his agreement with Crawford. All contracts and memos would be post-dated after the capture to cover that up.

Crawford held a big stick—he had Lounds's threat on tape. Interstate transmission of a threatening message was an indictable offence outside any protection Lounds enjoyed under the First Amendment. Lounds also knew that Crawford, with one phone call, could give him a permanent problem with the Internal Revenue Service.

There were polyps of honesty in Lounds; he had few illusions about the nature of his work. But he had developed a near-religious fervour about this project.

He was possessed with a vision of a better life on the other side of the money. Buried under all the dirt he had ever done, his old hopes still faced east. Now they stirred and strained to rise.

Satisfied that his cameras and recording equipment were ready, he drove home to sleep for three hours before the flight to Washington where he would meet Crawford near the trap.

A damned nuisance in the underground garage. The black van, parked in the space next to his, was over the line. It crowded into the space clearly marked Mr. Frederick Lounds.

Lounds opened his door hard, banging the side of the van and leaving a dent and a mark. That would teach the inconsiderate bastard.

Lounds was locking his car when the van door opened behind him. He was turning, had half-turned when the flat sap thocked over his car. He got his hands up, but his knees were going and there was tremendous pressure around his neck and the air was shut off. When his heaving chest could fill again it sucked chloroform.

Dolarhyde parked the van behind his house, climbed out and stretched. He had fought a crosswind all the way from Chicago and his arms were tired. He studied the night sky. The Perseid meteor shower was due soon and he must not miss it.

Revelation: And his tail drew the third part of the stars of heaven, and did cast them down to the earth . . .

His doing in another time. He must see it and remember.

Dolarhyde unlocked the back door and made his routine search of the house. When he came outside again he wore a stocking mask.

He opened the van and attached a ramp. Then he rolled out Freddy Lounds. Lounds wore nothing but his shorts and a gag and blindfold. Though he was only semi-conscious, he did not slump. He sat up very straight, his head against the high back of the old oak wheelchair. From the back of his head to the soles of his feet he was bonded to the chair with epoxy glue.

Dolarhyde rolled him into the house and parked him in a corner of the parlour with his back to the room as though he had misbehaved.

"Are you too cool? Would you like a blanket?"

Dolarhyde peeled off the sanitary napkins covering Lounds's eyes and mouth. Lounds didn't answer. The odour of chloroform hung on him.

"I'll get you a blanket." Dolarhyde took an afghan from the sofa and tucked it around Lounds up to the chin, then pressed an ammonia bottle under his nose.

Lounds's eyes opened wide on a blurred joining of walls. He coughed and started talking.

"Accident? Am I hurt bad?"

The voice behind him: "No, Mr. Lounds. You'll be just fine."

"My back hurts. My skin. Did I get burned? I hope to God I'm not burned."

"Burned? Burned? No. You just rest there. I'll be with you in a little while."

"Let me lie down. Listen, I want you to call my office. My God, I'm in a Striker frame. My back's broken—tell me the truth!"

Footsteps going away.

"What am I doing here?" The question shrill at the end.

The answer came from far behind him. "Atoning, Mr. Lounds."

Lounds heard footsteps mounting stairs. He heard a shower running. His head was clearer now. He remembered leaving the office and driving, but he couldn't remember after that. The side of his head throbbed and the smell of chloroform made him gag. Held rigidly erect, he was afraid he would vomit and drown. He opened his mouth wide and breathed deep. He could hear his heart.

Lounds hoped he was asleep. He tried to raise his arm from the armrest, increasing the pull deliberately until the pain in his palm and arm was enough to wake him from any dream. He was not asleep. His mind gathered speed.

By straining he could turn his eyes enough to see his arm for seconds at a time. He saw how he was fastened. This was no device to protect broken backs. This was no hospital. Someone had him.

Lounds thought he heard footsteps on the floor above, but they might have been his heartbeats.

He tried to think. Strained to think. *Keep cool and think,* he whispered. Cool and think.

The stairs creaked as Dolarhyde came down.

Lounds felt the weight of him in every step. A presence behind him now.

Lounds spoke several words before he could adjust the volume of his voice.

"I haven't seen your face. I couldn't identify you. I don't know what you look like. The *Tattler,* I work for the *National Tattler,* would pay a reward—a big reward for me. Half a million, a million maybe. A million dollars."

Silence behind him. Then a squeak of couch springs. He was sitting down, then.

"What do you think, Mr. Lounds?"

Put the pain and fear away and think. Now. For all time. To have some time. To have years. He hasn't decided to kill me. He hasn't let me see his face.

"What do you think, Mr. Lounds?"

"I don't know what's happened to me."

"Do you know Who I Am, Mr. Lounds?"

"No. I don't want to know, believe me."

"According to you, I'm a vicious, perverted sexual failure. An animal, you said. Probably turned loose from an asylum by a do-good judge." Ordinarily, Dolarhyde would have avoided the sibilant "s" in "sexual". In the presence of this audience, very far from laughter, he was freed. "You know now, don't you?"

Don't lie. Think fast. "Yes."

"Why do you write lies, Mr. Lounds? Why do you say I'm crazy? Answer now."

"When a person . . . when a person does things that most people can't understand, they call him . . ."

"Crazy."

"They called, like—the Wright Brothers. All through history—"

"History. Do you understand what I'm doing, Mr. Lounds?"

Understand. There it was. A chance. Swing hard. "No, but I think I've got an opportunity to understand and then *all my readers could understand too.*"

"Do you feel privileged?"

"It's a privilege. But I have to tell you, man to man, that I'm scared. It's hard to concentrate when you're scared. If you have a great idea you wouldn't have to scare me for me to really be impressed."

"Man to man. Man to man. You use that expression to imply frankness, Mr. Lounds, I appreciate that. But you see, I am not a man. I began as one but, by the Grace of God and my own Will, I have become Other and More than a man. You say you're frightened. Do you believe that God is in attendance here, Mr. Lounds?"

"I don't know."

"Are you praying to Him now?"

"Sometimes I pray. I have to tell you, I just pray mostly when I'm scared."

"And does God help you?"

"I don't know. I don't think about it after. I ought to."

"You ought to. Um hmmmm. There are so many things you ought

to understand. In a little while I'll help you understand. Will you excuse me now?"

"Certainly."

Footsteps out of the room. The slide and rattle of a kitchen drawer. Lounds had covered many murders committed in kitchens where things are handy. Police reporting can change forever your view of kitchens. Water running now.

Lounds thought it must be night. Crawford and Graham were expecting him. Certainly he had been missed by now. A great, hollow sadness pulsed briefly with his fear.

Breathing behind him, a flash of white caught by his rolling eyes. A hand, powerful and pale. It held a cup of tea with honey. Lounds sipped it through a straw.

"I'd do a big true story," he said between sips. "Anything you want to say. Describe you any way you want, or no description, no description."

"Shhhh." A single finger tapped the top of his head. The lights brightened. The chair began to turn.

"No. I don't want to see you."

"Oh, but you must, Mr. Lounds. You're a reporter. You're here to report. When I turn you around, open your eyes and look at me. If you won't open them yourself, I'll staple your eyelids to your forehead."

A wet mouth noise, a snapping click and the chair spun. Lounds faced the room, his eyes tight shut. A finger tapped insistently on his chest. A touch on his eyelids. He looked.

To Lounds, seated, he seemed very tall standing in his kimono. A stocking mask was rolled up to his nose. He turned his back to Lounds and dropped the robe. The great back muscles flexed above the brilliant tattoo of the tail that ran down his lower back and wrapped around the leg.

The Dragon turned his head slowly, looked over his shoulder at Lounds and smiled, all jags and stains.

"Oh my dear God Jesus," Lounds said.

Lounds is now in the centre of the room where he can see the screen. Dolarhyde, behind him, has put on his robe and put in the teeth that allow him to speak.

"Do you want to know What I Am?"

Lounds tried to nod, jerked his scalp. "More than anything. I was afraid to ask."

"Look."

The first slide was Blake's painting, the great Man-Dragon, wings flared and tail lashing, poised above the Woman Clothed with the Sun.

"Do you see now?"

"I see."

Rapidly, Dolarhyde ran through his other slides.

Click. Mrs. Jacobi alive. "Do you see?"

"Yes."

Click. Mrs. Leeds alive. "Do you see?"

"Yes."

Click. Dolarhyde, the Dragon rampant, muscles flexed and tail tattoo above the Jacobis' bed. "Do you see?"

"Yes."

Click. Mrs. Jacobi waiting. "Do you see?"

"Yes."

Click. Mrs. Jacobi after. "Do you see?"

"Yes."

Click. The Dragon rampant. "Do you see?"

"Yes."

Click. Mrs. Leeds waiting, her husband slack beside her. "Do you see?"

"Yes."

Click. Mrs. Leeds after, harlequined with blood. "Do you see?"

"Yes."

Click. Freddy Lounds, a copy of a *Tattler* photograph. "Do you see?"

"Oh God."

"Do you see?"

"Oh my God." The words drawn out, as a child speaks crying.

"Do you see?"

"Please no."

"No what?"

"Not me."

"No what? You're a man, Mr. Lounds. Are you a man?"

"Yes."

"Do you imply that I'm some kind of queer?"

"God no."

"Are you a queer, Mr. Lounds?"

"No."

"Are you going to write more lies about me, Mr. Lounds?"

"Oh no, no."

"Why did you write lies, Mr. Lounds?"

"The police told me. It was what they said."

"You quote Will Graham."

"Graham told me the lies. Graham."

"Will you tell the truth now? About Me. My Work. My Becoming. My *Art*, Mr. Lounds. Is this Art?"

"Art."

The fear in Lounds's face freed Dolarhyde to speak and he could fly on sibilants and fricatives, plosives were his great webbed wings.

"You said that I, who see more than you, am insane. I, who pushed the world so much further than you, am insane. I have dared more than you, I have pressed my unique seal so much deeper in the earth where it will last longer than your dust. Your life to mine is a slug track on stone. A thin silver mucus track in and out of the letters on my monument." The words Dolarhyde had written in his journal swarmed in him now.

"I am the Dragon and you call me *insane*? My movements are followed and recorded as avidly as those of a mighty guest star. Do you know about the guest star in 1054? Of course not. Your readers follow you like a child follows a slug track with his finger and in the same tired loops of reason. Back to your shallow skull and potato face as a slug follows his own slime back home.

"Before Me you are a slug in the sun. You are privy to a great Becoming and you recognize nothing. You are an ant in the afterbirth.

"It is in your nature to do one thing correctly: before Me you rightly tremble. Fear is not what you owe Me, Lounds, you and the other pismires. *You owe Me awe.*"

Dolarhyde stood with his head down, his thumb and forefinger against the bridge of his nose. Then he left the room.

He didn't take off the mask, Lounds thought. *He didn't take off the mask. If he comes back with it off, I'm dead. God, I'm wet all over.* He rolled his eyes toward the doorway and waited through the sounds from the back of the house.

When Dolarhyde returned, he still wore the mask. He carried a lunch-box and two thermoses. "For your trip back home." He held up a thermos. "Ice, we'll need that. Before we go, we'll tape a little while."

He clipped a microphone to the afghan near Lounds's face. "Repeat after me."

They taped for half an hour. Finally, "That's all, Mr. Lounds. You did very well."

"You'll let me go now?"

"I will. There's one way though that I can help you better understand and remember." Dolarhyde turned away.

"I want to understand. I want you to know I appreciate you turning me loose. I'm really going to be fair from now on, you know that."

Dolarhyde could not answer. He had changed his teeth.

The tape recorder was running again.

He smiled at Lounds, a brown stained smile. He placed his hand on Lounds's heart and, leaning to him intimately as though to kiss him, he bit Lounds's lips off and spat them on the floor.

DAWN IN Chicago, heavy air and the grey sky low.

A security guard came out of the lobby of the *Tattler* building and stood at the kerb smoking a cigarette and rubbing the small of his back. He was alone in the street and in the quiet he could hear the clack of the traffic-light changing at the top of the hill, a long block away.

Half a block north of the light, out of the guard's sight, Francis Dolarhyde squatted beside Lounds in the back of the van. He arranged the blanket in a deep cowl that hid Lounds's head.

Lounds was in great pain. He appeared stuporous but his mind was racing. There were things he must remember. The blindfold was tented across his nose and he could see Dolarhyde's fingers checking the crusted gag.

Dolarhyde put on the white jacket of a medical orderly, laid a thermos in Lounds's lap and rolled him out of the van. When he locked the wheels of the chair and turned to put the ramp back in the van, Lounds could see the end of the van's bumper beneath his blindfold.

Turning now, seeing the bumper guard, yes! the licence plate. Only a flash, but Lounds burned it into his mind.

Rolling now. Sidewalk seams. Around a corner and down a kerb. Paper crackled under the wheels.

Dolarhyde stopped the wheelchair in a bit of littered shelter between a garbage dumpster and a parked truck. He pulled at the blindfold. Lounds closed his eyes. An ammonia bottle under his nose.

The soft voice close beside him.

"Can you hear me? You're almost there." The blindfold off now. "Blink if you can hear me."

Dolarhyde opened his eye with a thumb and forefinger. Lounds was looking at Dolarhyde's face.

"I told you one fib." Dolarhyde tapped the thermos. "I don't *really* have your lips on ice." He whipped off the blanket and opened the thermos.

Lounds strained hard when he smelled the gasoline, separating the skin from under his forearms and making the stout chair groan. The gas was cold all over him, fumes filling his throat and they were rolling toward the centre of the street.

"Do you like being Graham's pet, Freeeeedeeeee?"

Lit with a whump and shoved, sent rolling down on the *Tattler*, eeek, eeek, eeekeeekeeek the wheels.

The guard looked up as a scream blew the burning gag away. He saw the fireball coming, bouncing on the potholes, trailing smoke and sparks and the flames blown back like wings, disjointed reflections leaping along the shop windows.

It veered, struck a parked car and overturned in front of the building, one wheel spinning and flames through the spokes, blazing arms rising in the fighting posture of the burned.

The guard ran back into the lobby. He wondered if it would blow up, if he should get away from the windows. He pulled the fire alarm. What else? He grabbed the fire extinguisher off the wall and looked outside. It hadn't blown up yet.

The guard approached cautiously through the greasy smoke spreading low over the pavement and, at last, sprayed foam on Freddy Lounds.

22

THE SCHEDULE called for Graham to leave the staked-out apartment in Washington at 6.45 a.m., well ahead of the morning rush.

Crawford called while he was shaving.

"Good morning."

"Not so good," Crawford said. "The Tooth Fairy got Lounds in Chicago."

"Oh hell no."

"He's not dead yet and he's asking for you. He can't wait long."

"I'll go."

"Meet me at the airport. United 245. It leaves in forty minutes. You can be back for the stake-out, if it's still on."

Special Agent Chester from the Chicago F.B.I. office met them at O'Hare in a downpour. Chicago is a city used to sirens. The traffic parted reluctantly in front of them as Chester howled down the expressway, his red light flashing pink on the driving rain.

He raised his voice above the siren. "Chicago P.D. says he was jumped in his garage. My stuff is second-hand. We're not popular around here today."

"How much is out?" Crawford asked.

"The whole thing, trap, all of it."

"Did Lounds get a look at him?"

"I haven't heard a description. Chicago P.D. put out an all-points bulletin for a licence number about 6.20."

"Did you get hold of Dr. Bloom for me?"

"I got his wife, Jack. Dr. Bloom had his gall bladder taken out this morning."

"Glorious," Crawford said.

Chester pulled under the dripping hospital portico. He turned in his seat. "Jack, Will, before you go up—I hear this fruit really trashed Lounds. You ought to be ready for that."

Graham nodded. All the way to Chicago he had tried to choke his hope that Lounds would die before he had to see him.

The corridor of Paege Burn Center was a tube of spotless tile. A tall doctor with a curiously old-young face beckoned Graham and Crawford away from the knot of people at Lounds's door.

"Mr. Lounds's burns are fatal," the doctor said. "I *can* help him with the pain and I intend to do it. He breathed flames and his throat and lungs are damaged. He may not regain consciousness. In his condition, that would be a blessing.

"In the event that he does regain consciousness, the city police have asked me to take the airway out of his throat so that he might possibly answer questions. I've agreed to try that—briefly.

"At the moment his nerve endings are anaesthetized by fire. A lot of pain is coming, if he lives that long. I made this clear to the police and I want to make it clear to you: I'll interrupt any attempted questioning to sedate him if he wants me to. Do you understand me?"

"Yes," Crawford said.

With a nod to the patrolman in front of the door, the doctor clasped his hands behind his white lab coat and moved away like a wading egret.

Crawford glanced at Graham. "You okay?"

"I'm okay. *I* had the S.W.A.T. team."

Lounds's head was elevated in the bed. His hair and ears were gone and compresses over his sightless eyes replaced the burned-off lids. His gums were puffed with blisters.

The nurse beside him moved an I.V. stand so Graham could come close. Lounds smelled like a stable fire.

"Freddy, it's Will Graham."

Lounds arched his neck against the pillow.

"The movement's just reflex, he's not conscious," the nurse said.

The plastic airway holding open his scorched and swollen throat hissed in time with the respirator.

A pale detective sergeant sat in the corner with a tape recorder and a clipboard on his lap. Graham didn't notice him until he spoke.

"Lounds said your name in the emergency room before they put the airway in."

"You were there?"

"Later I was there. But I've got what he said on tape. He gave the firemen a licence number when they first got to him. He passed out, and he was out in the ambulance, but he came around for a minute in the emergency room when they gave him a shot in the chest. Some *Tattler* people had followed the ambulance—they were there. I have a copy of their tape."

"Let me hear it."

The detective fiddled with his tape recorder. "I think you want to use the ear-phone," he said, his face carefully blank. He punched the button.

Graham heard voices, the rattle of casters, "put him in three," the bump of a litter on a swinging door, a retching cough and a voice croaking, speaking without lips.

"*Tooth Hairy.*"

"Freddy, did you see him? What did he look like, Freddy?"

"*Wendy? Hlease Wendy. Graham set ne uh. The cunt knew it. Graham set ne uh. Cunt tut his hand on ne in the ticture like a hucking tet. Wendy?*"

A noise like a drain sucking. A doctor's voice, "That's it. Let me get there. Get out of the way. *Now.*"

That was all.

Graham stood over Lounds while Crawford listened to the tape.

"We're running down the licence number," the detective said. "Could you understand what he was saying?"

"Who's Wendy?" Crawford asked.

"That hooker in the hall. The blonde with the chest. She's been trying to see him. She doesn't know anything."

"Why don't you let her in?" Graham said from the bedside. His back was to them.

"No visitors."

"The man's dying."

"Think I don't know it? I've been here since a quarter to fucking six o'clock – excuse me, nurse."

"Take a few minutes," Crawford said. "Get some coffee, put some water on your face. He can't say anything. If he does I'll be here with the recorder."

"Okay, I could use it."

When the detective was gone, Graham left Crawford at the bedside and approached the woman in the hall.

"Wendy?"

"Yeah."

"If you're sure you want to go in there, I'll take you."

"I want to. Maybe I ought to go comb my hair."

"It doesn't matter," Graham said.

When the policeman returned, he didn't try to put her out.

Wendy of Wendy City held Lounds's blackened claw and looked straight at him. He stirred once, a little before noon.

"It's gonna be fine, Roscoe," she said. "We'll have us some high old times."

Lounds stirred again and died.

23

CAPTAIN OSBORNE of Chicago Homicide had the grey pointed face of a stone fox. Copies of the *Tattler* were all over the police station. One was on his desk.

He didn't ask Crawford and Graham to sit down.

"You had nothing at all working with Lounds in the city of Chicago?"

"No, he was coming to Washington," Crawford said. "He had a plane reservation. I'm sure you checked it."

"Yeah, I got it. He left his office about 1.30 yesterday. Got jumped in the garage of his building, must have been about ten to two."

"Anything in the garage?"

"His keys got kicked under his car. There's no garage attendant—they had a radio-operated door but it came down on a couple of cars and they took it out. Nobody saw it happen. That's getting to be the refrain today. We're working on his car."

"Can we help you there?"

"You can have the results when I get 'em. You haven't said much, Graham. You had plenty to say in the paper."

"I haven't heard much either, listening to you."

"You pissed off, Captain?" Crawford said.

"Me? Why should I be? We run down a phone trace for you and collar a fucking news-reporter. Then you've got no charges against him. You *have* got some deal with him, gets him cooked in front of this scandal sheet. Now the other papers adopt him like he was their own.

"Now we've got our own Tooth Fairy murder right here in Chicago. That's great. 'Tooth Fairy in Chicago,' boy. Before midnight we'll have six accidental domestic shootings, guy trying to sneak in his own house drunk, wife hears him, bang. The Tooth Fairy may like Chicago, decide to stick around, have some fun."

"We can do like this," Crawford said. "Butt heads, get the Police Commissioner and the U.S. Attorney stirred up, get all the assholes stirred up, yours and mine. Or we can settle down and try to catch the bastard. This was my operation and it went to shit, I know that. You ever have that happen right here in Chicago? I don't want to fight you, Captain. We want to catch him and go home. What do you want?"

Osborne moved a couple of items on his desk, a penholder, a picture of a fox-faced child in band uniform. He leaned back in his chair, pursed his lips and blew out some air.

"Right now I want some coffee. You guys want some?"

"I'd like some," Crawford said.

"So would I," Graham said.

Osborne passed around the styrofoam cups. He pointed to some chairs.

"The Tooth Fairy had to have a van or a panel truck to move Lounds around in that wheelchair," Graham said.

Osborne nodded. "The licence plate Lounds saw was stolen off a T.V. repair truck in Oak Park. He took a commercial plate, so he was getting it for a truck or a van. He *replaced* the plate on the T.V. truck with another stolen plate so it wouldn't be noticed so fast. Very sly, this boy. One thing we do know—he got the plate off the T.V. truck sometime after 8.30 yesterday morning. The T.V. repair guy bought gas first thing yesterday and he used a credit card. The attendant copied the correct licence number on the slip, so the plate was stolen after that."

"Nobody saw any kind of truck or van?" Crawford said.

"Nothing. The guard at the *Tattler* saw zip. He could referee wrestling he sees so little. The fire department responded first to the *Tattler*. They were just looking for fire. We're canvassing the overnight workers in the *Tattler* neighbourhood and the neighbourhoods where the T.V. guy worked Tuesday morning. We hope somebody saw him cop the plate."

"I'd like to see the chair again," Graham said.

"It's in our lab. I'll call them for you." Osborne paused. "Lounds was a ballsy little guy, you have to give him that. Remembering the licence number and spitting it out, the shape he was in. You listened to what Lounds said at the hospital?"

Graham nodded.

"I don't mean to rub this in, but I want to know if we hear it the same way. What does it sound like to you?"

"'Tooth Fairy. Graham set me up. The cunt knew it. Graham set me up. Cunt put his hand on me in the picture like a fucking pet'."

A monotone recital: Osborne could not tell how Graham felt about it. He asked another question.

"He was talking about the picture of you and him in the *Tattler*?"

"Had to be."

"Where would he get that idea?"

"Lounds and I had a few run-ins."

"But you looked friendly towards Lounds in the picture. The Tooth Fairy kills the pet first, is that it?"

"That's it." The stone fox was pretty fast, Graham thought.

"Too bad you didn't stake him out."

Graham said nothing.

"Lounds was supposed to be with us by the time the Tooth Fairy saw the *Tattler*," Crawford said.

"Does what he said mean anything else to you, anything we can use?"

Graham came back from somewhere and had to repeat Osborne's question in his mind before he answered. "We know from what Lounds said that the Tooth Fairy saw the *Tattler* before he hit Lounds, right?"

"Right."

"If you start with the idea that the *Tattler* set him off, does it strike you that he set this up in a hell of a hurry? The thing came off the press Monday night, he's in Chicago stealing licence plates sometime Tuesday, probably Tuesday morning, and he's on top of Lounds Tuesday afternoon. What does that say to you?"

"That he saw it early and he didn't have far to come," Crawford said. "Either he saw it here in Chicago or he saw it some place else Monday night. Bear in mind, he'd be watching for it to get the personal column."

"Either he was already here, or he came from driving distance," Graham said. "He was on top of Lounds too fast with a big old wheelchair you couldn't carry on a plane—it doesn't even fold. And he didn't fly here, steal a van, steal plates for it, and go around looking for an antique wheelchair to use. He had to have an old wheelchair— a new one wouldn't work for what he did." Graham was up, fiddling with the cord on the venetian blinds, staring at the brick wall across the airshaft. "He already had the wheelchair or he saw it all the time."

Osborne started to ask a question, but Crawford's expression cautioned him to wait.

Graham was tying knots in the blind cord. His hands were not steady.

"He saw it all the time," Crawford prompted.

"Um humm," Graham said. "You can see how . . . the idea starts with the wheelchair. From the sight and thought of the wheelchair. That's where the idea would come from when he's thinking what he'll do to those fuckers. Freddy rolling down the street on fire, it must have been quite a sight."

"Do you think he watched it?"

"Maybe. He certainly saw it before he did it, when he was making up his mind what he'd do."

Osborne watched Crawford. Crawford was solid. Osborne knew Crawford was solid and Crawford was going along with this.

"If he had the chair, or he saw it all the time—we can check around the nursing homes, the V.A.," Osborne said.

"It was perfect to hold Freddy still," Graham said.

"For a long time. He was gone fifteen hours and twenty-five minutes, more or less," Osborne said.

"If he had just wanted to snuff Freddy, he could have done that in the garage," Graham said. "He could have burned him in his car. He wanted to talk to Freddy, or hurt him for a while."

"Either he did it in the back of the van or he took him some-where," Crawford said. "That length of time, I'd say he took him somewhere."

"It had to be somewhere safe. If he bundled him up good, he wouldn't attract much notice around a nursing home, going in and out," Osborne said.

"He'd have the racket though," Crawford said. "A certain amount of cleaning up to do. Assume he had the chair, and he had access to the van, and he had a safe place to take him to work on him. Does that sound like . . . home?"

Osborne's telephone rang. He growled into it.

"What? No, I don't want to talk to the *Tattler* . . . Well it better not be bullshit. Put her on . . . Captain Osborne, yes . . . what time? Who answered the phone initially—at the switchboard? Take her off the switchboard, please. Tell me again what he said . . . I'll have an officer there in five minutes."

Osborne looked at his telephone thoughtfully after he hung up.

"Lounds's secretary got a call about five minutes ago," he said. "She swears it was Lounds's voice. He said something, something she didn't get, 'strength of the Great Red Dragon'. That's what she thought he said."

24

Dr. Frederick Chilton stood in the corridor outside Hannibal Lecter's cell. With Chilton were three large orderlies. One carried a strait jacket and leg restraints and another held a can of Mace. The third loaded a tranquilizer dart into his air rifle.

Lecter was reading an actuarial chart at his table and taking notes. He had heard the footsteps coming. He heard the rifle breech close behind him, but he continued to read and gave no sign that he knew Chilton was there.

Chilton had sent him the newspapers at noon and let him wait until night to find out his punishment for helping the Dragon.

"Dr. Lecter," Chilton said.

Lecter turned around. "Good evening, Dr. Chilton." He didn't acknowledge the presence of the guards. He looked only at Chilton.

"I've come for your books. *All* your books."

"I see. May I ask how long you intend to keep them?"

"That depends on your attitude."

"Is this *your* decision?"

"I decide the punitive measures here."

"Of course you do. It's not the sort of thing Will Graham would request."

"Back up to the net and slip these on, Dr. Lecter. I won't ask you twice."

"Certainly, Dr. Chilton. I hope that's a 39—the 37's are snug around the chest."

Dr. Lecter put on the restraints as though they were dinner clothes. An orderly reached through the barrier and fastened them from the back.

"Help him to his cot," Chilton said.

While the orderlies stripped the bookshelves, Chilton polished his glasses and stirred Lecter's personal papers with a pen.

Lecter watched from the shadowed corner of his cell. There was a curious grace about him, even in restraints.

"Beneath the yellow folder," Lecter said quietly, "you'll find a rejection slip the *Archives* sent you. It was brought to me by mistake with some of my *Archives* mail and I'm afraid I opened it without looking at the envelope. Sorry."

Chilton reddened. He spoke to an orderly. "I think you'd better take the seat off Dr. Lecter's toilet."

Chilton looked at the actuarial table. Lecter had written his age at the top: forty-one. "And what do you have here?" Chilton asked.

"Time," Dr. Lecter said.

Section Chief Brian Zeller took the courier's case and the wheelchair wheels into Instrumental Analysis, walking at a rate that made his gabardine pants whistle.

The staff, held over from the day shift, knew that whistling sound very well; Zeller in a hurry.

There had been enough delays. The weary courier, his flight from Chicago delayed by weather and then diverted to Philadelphia, had rented a car and driven down to the F.B.I. laboratory in Washington.

The Chicago police laboratory is efficient, but there are things it is not equipped to do. Zeller prepared to do them now.

At the mass spectrometer he dropped off the paint flecks from Lounds's car door.

Beverly Katz in Hair and Fibre got the wheels to share with others in the section.

Zeller's last stop was the small hot room where Liza Lake bent over her gas chromatograph. She was testing ashes from a Florida arson case, watching the stylus trace its spiky line on the moving graph.

"Ace lighter fluid," she said. "That's what he lit it with." She had looked at so many samples that she could distinguish brands without searching through the manual.

Zeller took his eyes off Liza Lake and rebuked himself severely for feeling pleasure in the office. He cleared his throat and held up the two shiny paint cans.

"Chicago?" she said.

Zeller nodded.

She checked the condition of the cans and the seal of the lids. One can contained ashes from the wheelchair; the other charred material from Lounds.

"How long has it been in the cans?"

"Six hours anyway," Zeller said.

"I'll headspace it."

She pierced the lid with a heavy-duty syringe, extracted air that had been confined with the ashes and injected the air directly into the gas chromatograph. She made minute adjustments. As the sample moved along the machine's 500-foot column, the stylus juggled on the wide graph paper.

"Unleaded . . ." she said. "It's gasohol, unleaded gasohol. Don't see much of that." She flipped quickly through a loose-leaf file of sample graphs. "I can't give you a brand yet. Let me do it with pentane and I'll get back to you."

"Good," Zeller said. Pentane would dissolve the fluids in the ashes, then fractionate early in the chromatograph, leaving the fluids for fine analysis.

By 1 a.m. Zeller had all he could get.

Liza Lake succeeded in naming the gasohol: Freddy Lounds was burned with a "Servico Supreme" blend.

Patient brushing in the grooves of the wheelchair treads yielded two kinds of carpet fibre—wool and synthetic. Mould in dirt from the treads indicated the chair had been stored in a cool, dark place.

The other results were less satisfactory. The paint flecks were not original factory paint. Blasted in the mass spectrometer and compared with the national automotive paint file, the paint proved to be high-quality Duco enamel manufactured in a lot of 186,000 gallons during the first quarter of 1978 for sale to several auto-paint shop chains.

Zeller had hoped to pinpoint the make of vehicle and the approximate time of manufacture.

He telexed the results to Chicago.

The Chicago Police Department wanted its wheels back. The wheels made an awkward package for the courier. Zeller put written lab reports in his pouch along with mail and a package that had come for Graham.

"Federal Express I'm not," the courier said when he was sure Zeller wouldn't hear him.

The Justice Department maintains several small apartments near Seventh District court in Chicago for use of jurists and favoured expert witnesses when court is in session. Graham stayed in one of these with Crawford across the hall.

He came in at 9 p.m., tired and wet. He had not eaten since

breakfast on the plane from Washington and the thought of food repelled him.

Rainy Wednesday was over at last. It was as bad a day as he could remember.

With Lounds dead, it seemed likely that he was next and all day Chester had watched his back; while he was in Lounds's garage, while he stood in the rain on the scorched pavement where Lounds was burned. With strobe lights flashing in his face, he told the press he was "grieved at the loss of his friend Frederick Lounds."

He was going to the funeral, too. So were a number of federal agents and police, in the hope that the killer would come to see Graham grieve.

Actually he felt nothing he could name, just cold nausea and an occasional wave of sickly exhilaration that he had not burned to death instead of Lounds.

It seemed to Graham that he had learned nothing in forty years; he had just gotten tired.

He made a big martini and drank it while he undressed. He had another after his shower while he watched the news.

("An F.B.I. trap to catch the Tooth Fairy backfires and a veteran reporter is dead. We'll be back with details on *Eyewitness News* after this.")

They were referring to the killer as "the Dragon" before the newscast was over. The *Tattler* had spilled it all to the networks. Graham wasn't surprised. Thursday's edition should sell well.

He made a third martini and called Molly.

She had seen the television news at six and eleven o'clock and she had seen a *Tattler*. She knew that Graham had been the bait in a trap.

"You should have told me, Will."

"Maybe. I don't think so."

"Will he try to kill you now?"

"Sooner or later. It would be hard for him now since I'm moving around. I'm covered all the time, Molly, and he knows it. I'll be okay."

"You sound a little slurry, have you been to see your friend in the fridge?"

"I've had a couple."

"How do you feel?"

"Fairly rotten."

"The news said the F.B.I. didn't have any protection for the reporter."

"He was supposed to be with Crawford by the time the Tooth Fairy got the paper."

"The news is calling him the Dragon now."

"That's what he calls himself."

"Will, there's something—I want to take Willy and leave here."

"And go where?"

"His grandparents. They haven't seen him in a while, they'd like to see him."

"Oh, um hmm."

Willy's father's parents had a ranch on the Oregon coast.

"It's creepy here. I know it's supposed to be safe—but we're not sleeping a whole lot. Maybe the shooting lessons spooked me, I don't know."

"I'm sorry, Molly. I wish I could tell you how sorry."

"I'll miss you. We both will."

So she had made up her mind.

"When are you going?"

"In the morning."

"What about the shop?"

"Evelyn wants to take it. I'll underwrite the fall stuff with the wholesalers, just for the interest, and she can keep what she makes."

"The dogs?"

"I asked her to call the county, Will. I'm sorry, but maybe somebody will take some of them."

"Molly, I—"

"If staying here I could keep something bad from happening to you, I'd stay. But you can't save anybody, Will, I'm not helping you here. With us up there, you can just think about taking care of yourself. I'm not carrying this damned pistol the rest of my life, Will."

"Maybe you can get down to Oakland and watch the A's." Didn't mean to say that. Oh boy, this silence is getting pretty long.

"Well, look, I'll call you," she said, "or, I guess you'll have to call me up there."

Graham felt something tearing. He felt short of breath.

"Let me get the office to make the arrangements. Have you made a reservation yet?"

"I didn't use my name. I thought maybe the newspapers—"

"Good. Good. Let me get somebody to see you off. You wouldn't have to board through the gate and you'd get out of Washington absolutely clean. Can I do that? Let me do that. What time does the plane go?"

"9.40. American 118."

"Okay, 8.30 behind the Smithsonian. There's a Park-Rite. Leave the car there. Somebody'll meet you. He'll listen to his watch, put it to his ear when he gets out of his car, okay?"

"That's fine."

"Say, do you change at O'Hare? I could come out—"

"No. Change in Minneapolis."

"Oh, Molly. Maybe I could come up there and get you when it's over?"

"That would be very nice."

Very nice.

"Do you have enough money?"

"The bank's wiring me some."

"What?"

"To Barclay's at the airport. Don't worry."

"I'll miss you."

"Me too, but that'll be the same as now. Same distance by phone. Willy says hi."

"Hi to Willy."

"Be careful, darling."

She had never called him darling before. He didn't care for it. He didn't care for new names; darling, Red Dragon.

The night duty officer in Washington was glad to make the arrangements for Molly.

Graham pressed his face to the cool window and watched sheets of rain whip over the muffled traffic below him, the street leaping from grey to sudden colour in the lightning flashes. His face left a print of forehead, nose, lips and chin on the glass.

Molly was gone.

The day was over and there was only the night to face, and the lipless voice accusing him.

Lounds's woman held what was left of his hand until it was over.

"Hello, this is Valerie Leeds. I'm sorry I can't come to the phone right now . . ."

"I'm sorry too," Graham said.

Graham filled his glass again and sat at the table by the window, staring at the empty chair across from him. He stared until the space in the opposite chair assumed a man-shape filled with dark and swarming motes, a presence like a shadow on suspended dust. He tried to make the image coalesce, to see a face. It would not move, had no countenance but, faceless, faced him with palpable attention.

"I know it's tough," Graham said. He was intensely drunk. "You've got to try to stop, just hold off until we find you. If you've got to do something, fuck, come after me. I don't give a shit. It'll be better after that. They've got some things now to help you make it stop. To help you stop *wanting to* so bad. Help me. Help me a little. Molly's gone, old Freddy's dead. It's you and me now, sport." He leaned across the table, his hand extended to touch, and the presence was gone.

Graham put his head down on the table, his cheek on his arm. He could see the print of his forehead, nose, mouth and chin on the window as the lightning flashed behind it; a face with drops crawling through it down the glass. Eyeless. A face full of rain.

Graham had tried hard to understand the Dragon.

At times, in the breathing silence of the victims' houses, the very spaces the Dragon had moved through tried to speak.

Sometimes Graham felt close to him. A feeling he remembered from other investigations had settled over him in recent days: the taunting sense that he and the Dragon were doing the same things at various times of the day, that there were parallels in the quotidian details of their lives. Somewhere the Dragon was eating, or showering, or sleeping at the same time he did.

Graham tried hard to know him. He tried to see him past the blinding glint of slides and phials, beneath the lines of police reports, tried to see his face through the louvers of print. He tried as hard as he knew how.

But to begin to understand the Dragon, to hear the cold drips in his darkness, to watch the world through his red haze, Graham would have had to see things he could never see, and he would have had to fly through time . . .

CHAPTER

25

Springfield, Mo., June 14th, 1938

MARIAN DOLARHYDE Trevane, tired and in pain, got out of a taxi at City Hospital. Hot wind whipped grit against her ankles as she climbed the steps. The suitcase she lugged was better than her loose wash dress and so was the mesh evening bag she pressed to her swollen belly. She had two quarters and a dime in her bag. She had Francis Dolarhyde in her belly.

She told the admitting officer her name was Betty Johnson, a lie. She said her husband was a musician, but she did not know his whereabouts, which was true.

They put her in the charity section of the maternity ward. She did not look at the patients on either side of her. She looked across the aisle at the soles of feet.

In four hours she was taken to the delivery room where Francis Dolarhyde was born. The obstetrician remarked that he looked "more like a leaf-nosed bat than a baby", another truth. He was born with bilateral fissures in his upper lip and in his hard and soft palates. The centre section of his mouth was unanchored and protruded. His nose was flat.

The hospital supervisors decided not to show him to his mother immediately. They waited to see if the infant could survive without oxygen. They put him in a bed at the rear of the infant ward and faced him away from the viewing window. He could breath, but he could not feed. With his palate cleft, he could not suck.

His crying on the first day was not as continuous as that of a heroin-addicted baby, but it was as piercing.

By the afternoon of the second day a thin keening was all he could produce.

When the shifts changed at 3 p.m., a wide shadow fell across his bed. Prince Easter Mize, 260 pounds, cleaning woman and aide in the maternity ward, stood looking at him, her arms folded on top of her bosom. In twenty-six years in the nursery she had seen about 39,000 infants. This one would live if he ate.

Prince Easter had received no instructions from the Lord about letting this infant die. She doubted that the hospital had received any either. She took from her pocket a rubber stopper pierced with a curved glass drinking straw. She pushed the stopper into a bottle of milk. She could hold the baby and support his head in one great hand. She held him to her breast until she knew he felt her heart beat. Then she flipped him over and popped the tube down his throat. He took about two ounces and went to sleep.

"Um hum," she said. She put him down and went about her assigned duties with the diaper pails.

On the fourth day the nurses moved Marian Dolarhyde Trevane to a private room. Hollyhocks left over from a previous occupant were in an enamel pitcher on the wash-stand. They had held up pretty well.

Marian was a handsome girl and the puffiness was leaving her face. She looked at the doctor when he started talking to her, his hand on her shoulder. She could smell strong soap on his hand and she thought about the crinkles at the corners of his eyes until she realized what he was saying. Then she closed her eyes and did not open them while they brought the baby in.

Finally she looked. They shut the door when she screamed. Then they gave her a shot.

On the fifth day she left the hospital alone. She didn't know where to go. She could never go home again, her mother had made that clear.

Marian Dolarhyde Trevane counted the steps between the light poles. Each time she passed three poles, she sat on the suitcase to rest. At least she had the suitcase. In every town there was a pawn shop near the bus station. She had learned that travelling with her husband.

Springfield in 1938 was not a centre for plastic surgery. In Springfield, you wore your face as it was.

A surgeon at City Hospital did the best he could for Francis Dolarhyde, first retracting the front section of his mouth with an elastic band, then closing the clefts in his lip by a rectangular flap technique that is now outmoded. The cosmetic results were not good.

The surgeon had troubled to read up on the problem and decided, correctly, that repair of the infant's hard palate should wait until he was five. To operate sooner would distort the growth of his·face.

A local dentist volunteered to make an obturator which plugged the baby's palate and permitted him to feed without flooding his nose.

The infant went to the Springfield Foundling Home for a year and a half and then to Morgan Lee Memorial Orphanage.

Rev. S. B. "Buddy" Lomax was head of the orphanage. Brother Buddy called the other boys and girls together and told them that Francis was a harelip but they must be careful never to call him a harelip.

Brother Buddy suggested they pray for him.

Francis Dolarhyde's mother learned to take care of herself in the years following his birth.

Marian Dolarhyde first found a job typing in the office of a ward boss in the St. Louis Democratic machine. With his help she had her marriage to the absent Mr. Trevane annulled.

There was no mention of a child in the annulment proceedings.

She had nothing to do with her mother. ("I didn't raise you to slut for that Irish trash," were Mrs. Dolarhyde's parting words to Marian when she left home with Trevane.)

Marian's ex-husband called her once at the office. Sober and pious, he told her he had been saved and wanted to know if he, Marian, and the child he "never had the joy of knowing" might make a new life together. He sounded broke.

Marian told him the child was born dead and she hung up.

He showed up drunk at her boarding-house with his suitcase.

When she told him to go away, he observed that it was her fault the marriage had failed and the child was stillborn. He expressed doubt that the child was his.

In a rage Marian Dolarhyde told Michael Trevane exactly what he had fathered and told him he was welcome to it. She reminded him that there were two cleft palates in the Trevane family.

She put him in the street and told him never to call her again. He didn't. But years later, drunk and brooding over Marian's rich new husband and her fine life, he did call Marian's mother.

He told Mrs. Dolarhyde about the deformed child and said her snag teeth proved the hereditary fault lay with the Dolarhydes.

A week later a Kansas City streetcar cut Michael Trevane in two.

When Trevane told Mrs. Dolarhyde that Marian had a hidden son, she sat up most of the night. Tall and lean in her rocker, Grandmother

Dolarhyde stared into the fire. Toward dawn she began a slow and purposeful rocking.

Somewhere upstairs in the big house, a cracked voice called out of sleep. The floor above Grandmother Dolarhyde creaked as someone shuffled toward the bathroom.

A heavy thump on the ceiling—someone falling—and the cracked voice called in pain.

Grandmother Dolarhyde never took her eyes off the fire. She rocked faster and, in time, the calling stopped.

Near the end of his fifth year, Francis Dolarhyde had his first and only visitor at the orphanage.

He was sitting in the thick reek of the cafeteria when an older boy came for him and took him to Brother Buddy's office.

The lady waiting with Brother Buddy was tall and middle-aged, dredged in powder, her hair in a tight bun. Her face was stark white. There were touches of yellow in the grey hair and in the eyes and teeth.

What struck Francis, what he would always remember: she smiled with pleasure when she saw his face. That had never happened before. No one would ever do it again.

"This is your grandmother," Brother Buddy said.

"Hello," she said.

Brother Buddy wiped his own mouth with a long hand. "Say 'hello'. Go ahead."

Francis had learned to say some things by occluding his nostrils with his upper lip, but he did not have much occasion for hello. "Lhho," was the best he could do.

Grandmother seemed even more pleased with him. "Can you say 'grandmother'?"

"Try to say 'grandmother'," Brother Buddy said.

The plosive G defeated him. Francis strangled easily on tears.

A red wasp buzzed and tapped against the ceiling.

"Never mind," his grandmother said. "I'll just bet you can say your name. I just know a big boy like you can say his name. Say it for me."

The child's face brightened. The big boys had helped him with this. He wanted to please. He collected himself.

"Cunt Face," he said.

Three days later Grandmother Dolarhyde called for Francis at the orphanage and took him home with her. She began at once to help him with his speech. They concentrated on a single word. It was "mother."

Within two years of the annulment, Marian Dolarhyde met and married Howard Vogt, a successful lawyer with solid connections to the St. Louis machine and what was left of the old Pendergast machine in Kansas City.

Vogt was a widower with three young children, an affable ambitious man fifteen years older than Marian Dolarhyde. He hated nothing in the world except the *St. Louis Post-Dispatch*, which had singed his feathers in the voter registration scandal of 1936 and blasted the attempt in 1940 by the St. Louis machine to steal the governorship.

By 1943 Vogt's star was rising again. He was a brewery candidate for the state legislature and was mentioned as a possible delegate to the upcoming state constitutional convention.

Marian was a useful and attractive hostess and Vogt bought her a handsome, half-timbered house on Olive Street that was perfect for entertaining.

Francis Dolarhyde had lived with his grandmother for a week when she took him there.

Grandmother had never seen her daughter's house. The maid who answered the door did not know her.

"I'm Mrs. Dolarhyde," she said, barging past the servant. Her slip was showing three inches in the back. She led Francis into a big living-room with a pleasant fire.

"Who is it, Viola?" A woman's voice from upstairs.

Grandmother cupped Francis's face in her hand. He could smell the cold leather glove. An urgent whisper. "Go see Mother, Francis. Go see Mother. Run!"

He shrank from her, twisting on the tines of her eyes.

"Go see Mother. Run!" She gripped his shoulders and marched him towards the stairs. He trotted up to the landing and looked back down at her. She motioned upward with her chin.

Up to the strange hallway toward the open bedroom door.

Mother was seated at her dressing-table checking her make-up in a mirror framed with lights. She was getting ready for a political rally and too much rouge wouldn't do.

Her back was to the door.

"Muhner," Francis piped, as he had been taught. He tried hard to get it right. "Muhner."

She saw him in the mirror then. "If you're looking for Ned, he isn't home from . . ."

"Muhner." He came into the heartless light.

Marian heard her mother's voice downstairs demanding tea. Her eyes widened and she sat very still. She did not turn around. She turned out the make-up lights and vanished from the mirror. In the darkened room she gave a single low keening that ended in a sob. It might have been for herself, or it might have been for him.

★   ★   ★

Grandmother took Francis to all the political rallies after that and explained who he was and where he came from. She had him say hello to everyone. They did not work on "hello" at home.

Mr. Vogt lost the election by 1,800 votes.

26

AT GRANDMOTHER'S house, Francis Dolarhyde's new world was a forest of blue-veined legs.

Grandmother Dolarhyde had been running her nursing home for three years when he came to live with her. Money had been a problem since her husband's death in 1936; she had been brought up a lady and she had no marketable skills.

What she had was a big house and her late husband's debts. Taking in boarders was out. The place was too isolated to be a successful boarding-house. She was threatened with eviction.

The announcement in the newspaper of Marian's marriage to the affluent Mr. Howard Vogt had seemed a godsend to Grandmother. She wrote to Marian repeatedly for help, but received no answer. Every time she telephoned, a servant told her Mrs. Vogt was out.

Finally, bitterly, Grandmother Dolarhyde made an arrangement with the county and began to take in elderly indigent persons. For each one she received a sum from the county and erratic payments from such relatives as the county could locate. It was hard until she began to get some private patients from middle-class families.

No help from Marian all this time—and Marian could have helped.

Now Francis Dolarhyde played on the floor in the forest of legs. He played cars with Grandmother's Mah-Jongg pieces, pushing them among feet twisted like gnarled roots. Mrs. Dolarhyde could keep clean wash dresses on her residents, but she despaired at trying to make them keep on their shoes.

The old people sat all day in the living-room listening to the radio. Mrs. Dolarhyde had put in a small aquarium for them to watch as well, and a private contributor had helped her cover her parquet floors with linoleum against the inevitable incontinence.

They sat in a row on the couches and in wheelchairs listening to the radio, their faded eyes fixed on the fish or on nothing or something they saw long ago.

Francis would always remember the shuffle of feet on linoleum in the hot and buzzing day, and the smell of stewed tomatoes and cabbage from the kitchen, the smell of the old people like meat wrappers dried in the sun, and always the radio.

Rinso white, Rinso bright

Happy little washday song.

Francis spent as much time as he could in the kitchen because his friend was there. The cook, Queen Mother Bailey, had grown up in the service of the late Mr. Dolarhyde's family. She sometimes brought Francis a plum in her apron pocket and she called him "Little Possum, always dreamin'." The kitchen was warm and safe. But Queen Mother Bailey went home at night . . .

December, 1943: Francis Dolarhyde, five years old, lay in bed in his upstairs room in Grandmother's house. The room was pitch dark with its blackout curtains against the Japanese. He could not say Japanese. He needed to pee. He was afraid to get up in the dark.

He called to his grandmother in bed downstairs.

"Aayma. Aayma." He sounded like an infant goat. He called until he was tired. "Mleedse Aayma."

It got away from him then, hot on his legs and under his seat and then cold, his nightdress sticking to him. He didn't know what to do. He took a deep breath and rolled over to face the door. Nothing happened to him. He put his foot on the floor. He stood up in the dark, nightdress plastered to his legs, face burning. He ran for the door. The doorknob caught him over the eye and he sat down in wetness, jumped up and ran down the stairs, fingers squealing on the bannister. To his grandmother's room. Crawling across her in the dark and under the covers, warm against her now.

Grandmother stirred, tensed, her back hardened against his cheek, voice hissing, "I've never sheen—" a clatter on the bedside table as she found her teeth, clacket as she put them in. "I've never seen a child as disgusting and dirty as you. Get *out*, get out of this bed."

She turned on the bedside lamp. He stood on the carpet shivering. She wiped her thumb across his eyebrow. Her thumb came away bloody.

"Did you break something?"

He shook his head so fast droplets of blood fell on Grandmother's nightgown.

"Upstairs. Go on."

The dark came down over him as he climbed the stairs. He couldn't turn on the lights because Grandmother had cut the cords off short so only she could reach them. He did not want to get back in the wet bed. He stood in the dark holding on to the footboard for a long time. He thought she wasn't coming. The blackest corners in the room knew she wasn't coming.

She came, snatching the short cord on the ceiling light, her arms full of sheets. She did not speak to him as she changed the bed.

She gripped his upper arm and pulled him down the hall to the bathroom. The light was over the mirror and she had to stand on tiptoe to reach it. She gave him a washcloth, wet and cold.

"Take off your nightshirt and wipe yourself off."

Smell of adhesive tape and the bright sewing scissors clicking. She snipped out a butterfly of tape, stood him on the toilet lid and closed the cut over his eye.

"Now," she said. She held the sewing scissors under his round belly and he felt cold down there.

"Look," she said. She grabbed the back of his head and bent him over to see his little penis lying across the bottom blade of the open scissors. She closed the scissors until they began to pinch him.

"Do you want me to cut it off?"

He tried to look up at her, but she gripped his head. He sobbed and spit fell on his stomach.

"*Do* you?"

"No, Aayma. No, Aayma."

"I pledge you my word, if you ever make your bed dirty again I'll cut it off. Do you understand?"

"Yehn, Aayma."

"You can find the toilet in the dark and you can sit on it like a good boy. You don't have to stand up. Now go back to bed."

At 2 a.m. the wind rose, gusting warm out of the southeast, clacking together the branches of the dead apple trees, rustling the leaves of the live ones. The wind drove warm rain against the side of the house where Francis Dolarhyde, forty-two years old, lay sleeping.

He lay on his side sucking his thumb, his hair damp and flat on his forehead and his neck.

Now he awakes. He listens to his breathing in the dark and the tiny clicks of his blinking eyes. His fingers smell faintly of gasoline. His bladder is full.

He feels on the bedside table for the glass containing his teeth.

Dolarhyde always puts in his teeth before he rises. Now he walks to the bathroom. He does not turn on the light. He finds the toilet in the dark and sits down on it like a good boy.

THE CHANGE in Grandmother first became apparent in the winter of 1947 when Francis was nine.

She stopped taking meals in her room with Francis. They moved to the common table in the dining-room where she presided over meals with the elderly residents.

Grandmother had been trained as a girl to be a charming hostess and now she unpacked and polished her silver bell and put it beside her plate.

Keeping a luncheon table going, pacing the service, managing conversation, batting easy conversation lobs to the strong points of the shy ones, turning the best facets of the bright ones in the light of the other guests' attention is a considerable skill and one now sadly in decline.

Grandmother had been good at it in her time. Her efforts at this table did brighten meals initially for the two or three among the residents who were capable of linear conversation.

Francis sat in the host's chair at the other end of the avenue of nodding heads as Grandmother drew out the recollections of those who could remember. She expressed keen interest in Mrs. Floder's

honeymoon trip to Kansas City, went through the yellow fever with
Mr. Eaton a number of times, and listened brightly to the random,
unintelligible sounds of the others.

"Isn't that interesting, Francis?" she said, and rang the bell for
the next course. The food was a variety of vegetable and meat
mushes, but she divided it into courses, greatly inconveniencing the
kitchen help.

Mishaps at the table were never mentioned. A ring of the bell and
a gesture in mid-sentence took care of those who had spilled or gone
to sleep or forgotten why they were at the table. Grandmother always
kept as large a staff as she could pay.

As Grandmother's general health declined she lost weight and was
able to wear dresses that had long been packed away. Some of them
were elegant. In the cast of her features and her hairstyle, she bore a
marked resemblance to George Washington on the dollar bill.

Her manners had slipped somewhat by spring. She ruled the table
and permitted no interruptions as she told of her girlhood in St.
Charles, even revealing personal matters to inspire and edify Francis
and the others.

It was true that Grandmother had enjoyed a season as a belle in
1907 and was invited to some of the better balls across the river in
St. Louis.

There was an "object lesson" in this for everyone, she said. She
looked pointedly at Francis, who crossed his legs beneath the table.

"I came up at a time when little could be done medically to
overcome the little accidents of nature," she said. "I had lovely
skin and hair and I took full advantage of them. I overcame my
teeth with force of personality and bright spirits—so successfully in
fact that they became my 'beauty spot'. I think you might even call
them my 'charming trademark'. I wouldn't have traded them for the
world."

She distrusted doctors, she explained at length, but when it became clear that gum problems would cost her her teeth, she sought out one of the most renowned dentists in the Midwest, Dr. Felix Bertl, a Swiss. Dr. Bertl's "Swiss teeth" were very popular with a certain class of people, Grandmother said, and he had a remarkable practice.

Opera singers fearing that new shapes in their mouths would affect their tone, actors, and others in public life came from as far away as San Francisco to be fitted.

Dr. Bertl could reproduce a patient's natural teeth exactly and had experimented with various compounds and their effect on resonance.

When Dr. Bertl had completed her dentures, her teeth appeared just as they had before. She overcame them with personality and lost none of her unique charm, she said with a spiky smile.

If there was an object lesson here, Francis did not appreciate it until later; there would be no surgery for him until he could pay for it himself.

Francis could make it through dinner because there was something he looked forward to afterward.

Queen Mother Bailey's husband came for her each evening in the mule-drawn waggon he used to haul firewood. If Grandmother was occupied upstairs, Francis could ride with them down the lane to the main road.

He waited all day for the evening rise: sitting on the waggon seat beside Queen Mother, her tall flat husband silent and almost invisible in the dark, the iron tyres of the waggon loud in the gravel behind the jingle of the bits. Two mules, brown and sometimes muddy, their cropped manes standing up like brushes, swishing their tails across their rumps. The smell of sweat and boiled cotton cloth, snuff and warm harness. There was the smell of woodsmoke when Mr. Bailey had been clearing new ground and sometimes, when he took his shotgun to the new ground, a couple of rabbits or squirrels lay in the waggon box, stretched long as though they were running.

They did not talk on the ride down the lane; Mr. Bailey spoke only to the mules. The waggon motion bumped the boy pleasantly against the Baileys. Dropped off at the end of the lane, he gave his nightly promise to walk straight back to the house and watched the lantern on the waggon move away. He could hear them talking down the road. Sometimes Queen Mother made her husband laugh and she laughed with him. Standing in the dark it was pleasant to hear them and know they were not laughing at him.

Later he would change his mind about that . . .

Francis Dolarhyde's occasional playmate was the daughter of a share-cropper who lived three fields away. Grandmother let her come to play because it amused her now and then to dress the child in the clothing Marian had worn when she was small.

She was a red-haired listless child and she was too tired to play much of the time.

One hot June afternoon, bored with fishing for doodlebugs in the chicken yard with straws, she asked to see Francis's private parts.

In a corner between the chicken-house and a low hedge that shielded them from the lower windows of the house, he showed her. She reciprocated by showing him her own, standing with her pilled cotton underwear around her ankles.

As he squatted on his heels to see, a headless chicken flapped around the corner, travelling on its back, flapping up the dust. The hobbled girl hopped backward as it spattered blood on her feet and legs.

Francis jumped to his feet, his trousers still down, as Queen Mother Bailey came around the corner after the chicken and saw them.

"Look here, boy," she said calmly, "you want to see what's what, well now you see, so go on and find yourselves something else to do. Occupy yourself with children's doings and keep your clothes on. You and that child help me catch that rooster."

The children's embarrassment quickly passed as the rooster eluded them. But Grandmother was watching from the upstairs window . . .

Grandmother watched Queen Mother come back inside. The children went into the chicken-house. Grandmother waited five minutes, then came up on them silently. She flung open the door and found them gathering feathers for head-dresses.

She sent the girl home and led Francis into the house.

She told him he was going back to Brother Buddy's orphanage after she had punished him. "Go upstairs. Go to your room and take your trousers off and wait for me while I get my scissors."

He waited for hours in his room, lying on the bed with his trousers off, clutching the bedspread and waiting for the scissors. He waited through the sounds of supper downstairs and he heard the creak and clop of the firewood waggon and the snort of the mules as Queen Mother's husband came for her.

Sometime toward morning he slept and woke in starts to wait.

Grandmother never came. Perhaps she had forgotten.

He waited through the routine of the days that followed, remembering many times a day in a rush of freezing dread. He would never cease from waiting.

He avoided Queen Mother Bailey, would not speak to her and wouldn't tell her why: he mistakenly believed that she had told Grandmother what she saw in the chicken-yard. Now he was convinced that the laughter he heard while he watched the waggon lantern diminish down the road was about him. Clearly he could trust no one.

It was hard to lie still and go to sleep when it was there to think about. It was hard to lie still on such a bright night.

Francis knew that Grandmother was right. He had hurt her so. He had shamed her. Everyone must know what he had done—even as far away as St. Charles. He was not angry at Grandmother. He was not angry at Grandmother. He knew that he Loved her very much. He wanted to do right.

He imagined that burglars were breaking in and he protected Grandmother and she took back what she said. "You're not a Child of the Devil after all, Francis. You are my good boy."

He thought about a burglar breaking in. Coming in the house determined to show Grandmother his private parts.

How would Francis protect her? He was too small to fight a big burglar.

He thought about it. There was Queen Mother's hatchet in the pantry. She wiped it with newspaper after she killed a chicken. He should see about the hatchet. It was his responsibility. He would fight his fear of the dark. If he really Loved Grandmother, he should be the thing to be afraid of in the dark. The thing for the *burglar* to be afraid of.

He crept downstairs and found the hatchet hanging on its nail. It had a strange smell, like the smell at the sink when they were drawing a chicken. It was sharp and its weight was reassuring in his hand.

He carried the hatchet to Grandmother's room to be sure there were no burglars.

Grandmother was asleep. It was very dark but he knew exactly where she was. If there was a burglar he would hear him breathing just as he could hear Grandmother breathing. He would know where his neck was just as surely as he knew where Grandmother's neck was. It was just below the breathing.

If there was a burglar, he would come up on him quietly like this. He would raise the hatchet over his head with both hands like this.

Francis stepped on Grandmother's slipper beside the bed. The hatchet swayed in the dizzy dark and pinged against the metal shade of her reading-lamp.

Grandmother rolled over and made a wet noise with her mouth.

Francis stood still. His arms trembled from the effort of holding up the hatchet. Grandmother began to snore.

The Love Francis felt almost burst him. He crept out of the room. He was frantic to be ready to protect her. He must do something. He did not fear the dark house now, but it was choking him.

He went out the back door and stood in the brilliant night, face upturned, gasping as though he could breathe the light. A tiny disc of moon, distorted on the whites of his rolled-back eyes, rounded as the eyes rolled down and was centred at last in his pupils.

The Love swelled in him unbearably tight and he could not gasp it out. He walked toward the chicken-house, hurrying now, the ground cold under his feet, the hatchet bumping cold against his leg, running now before he burst . . .

Francis, scrubbing himself at the chicken-yard pump, had never felt such sweet and easy peace. He felt his way cautiously into it and found that the peace was endless and all around him.

What Grandmother had kindly not cut off was still there like a prize when he washed the blood off his belly and legs. His mind was clear and calm.

He should do something about the nightshirt. Better hide it under the sacks in the smokehouse.

Discovery of the dead chicken puzzled Grandmother. She said it didn't look like a fox job.

A month later Queen Mother found another one when she went to gather eggs. This time the head had been wrung off.

Grandmother said at the dinner table that she was convinced it was done for spite by some "sorry help I ran off". She said she had called the sheriff about it.

Francis sat silent at his place, opening and closing his hand on the memory of an eye blinking against his palm. Sometimes in bed he held himself to be sure he hadn't been cut. Sometimes when he held himself he thought he felt a blink.

Grandmother was changing rapidly. She was increasingly contentious and could not keep household help. Though she was short of housekeepers, it was the kitchen where she took personal charge, directing Queen Mother Bailey to the detriment of the food. Queen Mother, who had worked for the Dolarhydes all her life, was the only constant on the staff.

Red-faced in the kitchen heat, Grandmother moved restlessly from one task to the next, often leaving dishes half-made, never to be served. She made casseroles of leftovers while vegetables wilted in the pantry.

At the same time, she became fanatical about waste. She reduced soap and bleach in the wash until the sheets were dingy grey.

In the month of November she hired five different black women to help in the house. They would not stay.

Grandmother was furious the evening the last one left. She went through the house yelling. She came into the kitchen and saw that Queen Mother Bailey had left a teaspoonful of flour on the board after rolling out some dough.

In the steam and heat of the kitchen a half-hour before dinner she walked up to Queen Mother and slapped her face.

Queen Mother dropped her ladle, shocked. Tears sprang in her eyes. Grandmother drew back her hand again. A big pink palm pushed her away.

"Don't you *ever* do that. You're not yourself, Mrs. Dolarhyde, but don't *ever* do that."

Screaming insults, Grandmother with her bare hand shoved over a kettle of soup to slop and hiss down through the stove. She went to her room and slammed the door. Francis heard her cursing in her room and objects thrown against the walls. She didn't come out again all evening.

Queen Mother cleaned up the soup and fed the old people. She got her few things together in a basket and put on her old sweater and stocking cap. She looked for Francis but couldn't find him.

She was in the waggon when she saw the boy sitting in the corner of the porch. He watched her climb down heavily and come back to him.

"Possum, I'm going now. I won't be back here. Sironia at the feed store, she'll call your mama for me. You need me before your mama get here, you come to my house."

He twisted away from the touch on his cheek.

Mr. Bailey clucked to the mules. Francis watched the waggon lantern move away. He had watched it before, with a sad and empty feeling since he understood that Queen Mother betrayed him. Now he didn't care. He was glad. A feeble kerosene waggon light fading down the road. It was nothing to the moon.

He wondered how it feels to kill a mule.

Marian Dolarhyde Vogt did not come when Queen Mother Bailey called her.

She came two weeks later after a call from the sheriff in St. Charles. She arrived in mid-afternoon, driving herself in a pre-war Packard. She wore gloves and a hat.

A deputy sheriff met her at the end of the lane and stooped to the car window.

"Mrs. Vogt, your mother called our office around noon saying something about the help stealing. When I come out here, you'll excuse me but she was talking out of her head and it looked like things wasn't tended to. Sheriff thought he ought to get ahold of y'all first, if you understand me. Mr. Vogt being before the public and all."

Marian understood him. Mr. Vogt was Commissioner of Public Works in St. Louis now and was not in the party's best graces.

"To my knowledge nobody else has saw the place," the deputy said.

Marian found her mother asleep. Two of the old people were still sitting at the table waiting for lunch. One woman was out in the backyard in her slip.

Marian telephoned her husband. "How often do they inspect these places . . . they must not have seen anything . . . I don't *know* if any relatives have complained, I don't think these people have any relatives . . . No. You stay away, I need some Negroes. Get me some Negroes . . . and Dr. Waters. I'll take care of it."

The doctor with an orderly in white arrived in forty-five minutes, followed by a panel truck bringing Marian's maid and five other domestics.

Marian, the doctor and the orderly were in Grandmother's room when Francis came home from school. Francis could hear his grandmother cursing. When they rolled her out in one of the nursing home wheelchairs she was glassy-eyed and a piece of cotton was taped to her arm. Her face looked sunken and strange without her teeth. Marian's arm was bandaged too; she had been bitten.

Grandmother rode away in the doctor's car, sitting in the back seat with the orderly. Francis watched her go. He started to wave, but let his hand fall back to his side.

Marian's cleaning crew scrubbed and aired the house, did a tremendous wash and bathed the old people. Marian worked alongside them and supervised a sketchy meal.

She spoke to Francis only to ask where things were.

Then she sent the crew away and called the county authorities. Mrs. Dolarhyde had suffered a stroke, she explained.

It was dark when the welfare workers came for the patients in a school bus. Francis thought they would take him too. He was not discussed.

Only Marian and Francis remained in the house. She sat at the dining-room table with her head in her hands. He went outside and climbed a crabapple tree.

Finally Marian called him. She had packed a small suitcase with his clothes.

"You'll have to come with me," she said, walking to the car. "Get in. Don't put your feet on the seat."

They drove away in the Packard and left the empty wheelchair standing in the yard.

There was no scandal. The county authorities said it was sure a shame about Mrs. Dolarhyde, she sure kept things nice. The Vogts remained untarnished.

Grandmother was confined to a private nerve sanatorium. It would be fourteen years before Francis went home to her again.

"Francis, here are your stepsisters and stepbrother," his mother said. They were in the Vogts' library.

Ned Vogt was twelve, Victoria thirteen and Margaret, nine. Ned and Victoria looked at each other. Margaret looked at the floor.

Francis was given a room at the top of the servants' stairs. Since the disastrous election of 1944 the Vogts no longer employed an upstairs maid.

He was enrolled in Potter Gerard Elementary School, within walking distance of the house and far from the Episcopal private school the other children attended.

The Vogt children ignored him as much as possible during the first few days, but at the end of the first week Ned and Victoria came up the servants' stairs to call.

Francis heard them whispering for minutes before the knob turned on his door. When they found it bolted they didn't knock. Ned said, "Open this door."

Francis opened it. They did not speak to him again while they looked through his clothes in the wardrobe. Ned Vogt opened the drawer in the small dressing-table and picked up the things he found with two fingers: birthday handkerchiefs with FD embroidered on them, a capo for a guitar, a bright beetle in a pill bottle, a copy of *Baseball Joe in the World Series* which had once been wet and a get-well card signed "Your classmate, Sarah Hughes."

"What's this?" Ned asked.

"A capo."

"What's it for?"

"A guitar."

"Do you have a guitar?"

"No."

"What do you have it for?" Victoria asked.

"My father used it."

"I can't understand you. What did you say? Make him say it again, Ned."

"He said it belonged to his father." Ned blew his nose on one of the handkerchiefs and dropped it back in the drawer.

"They came for the ponies today," Victoria said. She sat on the narrow bed. Ned joined her, his back against the wall, his feet on the quilt.

"No more ponies," Ned said. "No more lake house for the summer. Do you know why? Speak up, you little bastard."

"Father is sick a lot and doesn't make as much money," Victoria said. "Some days he doesn't go to the office at all."

"Know why he's sick, you little bastard?" Ned asked. "Talk where I can understand you."

"Grandmother said he's a drunk. Understand that all right?"

"He's sick because of your ugly face," Ned said.

"That's why people didn't vote for him too," Victoria said.

"Get out," Francis said. When he turned to open the door, Ned kicked him in the back. Francis tried to reach his kidney with both hands, which saved his fingers as Ned kicked him in the stomach.

"Oh, Ned," Victoria said. "Oh, Ned."

Ned grabbed Francis by the ears and held him close to the mirror over the dressing-table.

"That's why he's sick!" Ned slammed his face into the mirror. "That's why he's sick!" Slam. "That's why he's sick!" Slam. The mirror was smeared with blood and mucus. Ned let him go and he sat on the floor. Victoria looked at him, her eyes wide, holding her lower lip between her teeth. They left him there. His face was wet with blood and spit. His eyes watered from the pain, but he did not cry.

CHAPTER

28

RAIN IN Chicago drums through the night on the canopy over the open grave of Freddy Lounds.

Thunder jars Will Graham's pounding head as he weaves from the table to a bed where dreams coil beneath the pillow.

The old house above St. Charles, shouldering the wind, repeats its long sigh over the hiss of rain against the windows and the bump of thunder.

The stairs are creaking in the dark. Mr. Dolarhyde is coming down them, his kimono whispering over the treads, his eyes wide with recent sleep.

His hair is wet and neatly combed. He has brushed his nails. He moves smoothly and slowly, carrying his concentration like a brimming cup.

Film beside his projector. Two subjects. Other reels are piled in the wastebasket for burning. Two left, chosen from the dozens of home movies he has copied at the plant and brought home to audition.

Comfortable in his reclining chair with a tray of cheese and fruit beside him, Dolarhyde settles in to watch.

The first film is a picnic from the Fourth of July weekend. A handsome family; three children, the father bull necked, dipping into the pickle jar with his thick fingers. And the mother.

The best view of her is in the softball game with the neighbour's children. Only about fifteen seconds of her; she takes a lead off second base, faces the pitcher and the plate, feet apart ready to dash either way, her breasts swaying beneath her pullover as she leans forward from the waist. An annoying interruption as a child swings a bat. The woman again, walking back to tag up. She puts one foot on the boat cushion they use for a base and stands hipshot, the thigh muscle tightening in her locked leg.

Over and over Dolarhyde watches the frames of the woman. Foot on the base, pelvis tilts, thigh muscle tightens under the cut-off jeans.

He freezes the last frame. The woman and her children. They are dirty and tired. They hug and a dog wags among their legs.

A terrific crash of thunder clinks the cut crystal in Grandmother's tall case. Dolarhyde reaches for a pear.

The second film is in several segments. The title, *The New House*, is spelled out in pennies on a shirt cardboard above a broken piggy bank. It opens with Father pulling up the "For Sale" sign in the yard. He holds it up and faces the camera with an embarrassed grin. His pockets are turned out.

An unsteady long shot of Mother and three children on the front steps. It is a handsome house. A cut to the swimming-pool. A child, sleek-headed and small, pads around to the diving-board leaving wet footprints on the tile. Heads bob in the water. A small dog paddles toward a daughter, his ears back, chin high, and the whites of his eyes showing.

Mother in the water holds to the ladder and looks up at the camera. Her curly black hair has a gloss of pelt, her bosom swelling shining wet above her suit, her legs wavy below the surface, scissoring.

Night. A badly exposed shot across the pool to the lighted house, the lights reflected in the water.

Indoors and family fun. Boxes everywhere and packing materials. An old trunk, not yet stored in the attic.

A small daughter is trying on Grandmother's clothes. She has on a big garden hat. Father is on the sofa. He looks a little drunk. Now Father must have the camera. It is not quite level. Mother is at the mirror in the hat.

The children jostle around her, the boys laughing and plucking at the old finery. The girl watches her mother coolly, appraising herself in time to come.

A close-up. Mother turns and strikes a pose for the camera with an arch smile, her hand at the back of her neck. She is quite lovely. There is a cameo at her throat.

Dolarhyde freezes the frame. He backs up the film. Again and again she turns from the mirror and smiles.

Absently, Dolarhyde picks up the film of the softball game and drops it into the wastebasket.

He takes the reel from the projector and looks at the Gateway label on the box: *Bob Sherman, Star Route 7, Box 603, Tulsa, Okla.*

An easy drive too.

Dolarhyde holds the film in his palm and covers it with his other hand as though it were a small living thing that might struggle to escape. It seems to jump against his palm like a cricket.

He remembers the jerkiness, the haste at the Leeds house when the lights came on. He had to deal with Mr. Leeds before turning on his movie lights.

This time he wants a smoother progression. It would be wonderful to crawl in between the sleepers with the camera going and snuggle up a little while. Then he could strike in the dark and sit up between them happily getting wet.

He can do that with infra-red film, and he knows where to get some.

The projector is still on. Dolarhyde sits holding the film between his hands while on the bright blank screen other images move for him to the long sigh of the wind.

There is no sense of vengeance in him, only Love and thoughts of the Glory to come; hearts becoming faint and fast, like footsteps fleeing into silence.

Him rampant. Him rampant, filled with Love, the Shermans opening to him.

The past does not occur to him at all; only the Glory to come. He does not think of his mother's house. In fact, his conscious memories of that time are remarkably few and indistinct.

Sometime in his twenties Dolarhyde's memories of his mother's house sank out of sight, leaving a slick on the surface of his mind. He knew that he had lived there only a month. He did not recall that he was sent away at the age of nine for hanging Victoria's cat.

One of the few images he retained was the house itself, lighted, viewed from the street in winter twilight as he passed it going from Potter Gerard Elementary School to the house where he was boarded a mile away.

He could remember the smell of the Vogt library, like a piano just opened, when his mother received him there to give him holiday things. He did not remember the faces at the upstairs windows as he walked away, down the frozen sidewalk, the practical gifts burning hateful under his arm; hurrying home to a place inside his head that was quite different from St. Louis.

At the age of eleven his fantasy life was active and intense and when the pressure of his Love grew too great, he relieved it. He preyed on pets, carefully, with a cool eye to consequence. They were so tame that it was easy. The authorities never linked him with the sad little bloodstains soaked into the dirt floors of garages.

At forty-two he did not remember that. Nor did he ever think about the people in his mother's house; his mother, stepsisters or stepbrother.

Sometimes he saw them in his sleep, in the brilliant fragments of a fever dream; altered and tall, faces and bodies in bright parrot colours, they poised over him in a mantis stance.

When he chose to reflect, which was seldom, he had many satisfactory memories. They were of his military service.

Caught at seventeen entering the window of a woman's house for a purpose never established, he was given the choice of enlisting in the Army or facing criminal charges. He took the Army.

After basic training he was sent to specialist school in dark-room operation and shipped to San Antonio where he worked on medical corps training-films at Brooke Army Hospital.

Surgeons at Brooke took an interest in him and decided to improve his face.

They performed a Z-plasty on his nose, using ear cartilage to lengthen the columella, and repaired his lip with an interesting Abbé flap procedure that drew an audience of doctors to the operating theatre.

The surgeons were proud of the result. Dolarhyde declined the mirror and looked out the window.

Records at the film library show Dolarhyde checked out many films, mainly on trauma, and kept them overnight.

He re-enlisted in 1958 and in his second hitch he found Hong Kong. Stationed at Seoul, Korea, developing film from the tiny spotter planes the Army floated over the 38th Parallel in the late 1950s, he was able to go to Hong Kong twice on leave. Hong Kong and Kowloon could satisfy any appetite in 1959.

Grandmother was released from the sanatorium in 1961 in a vague Thorazine peace. Dolarhyde asked for and received a hardship discharge two months before his scheduled separation date and went home to take care of her.

It was a curiously peaceful time for him as well. With his new job at Gateway, Dolarhyde could hire a woman to stay with Grandmother in the daytime. At night they sat in the parlour together, not speaking. The tick of the old clock and its chimes were all that broke the silence.

He saw his mother once, at Grandmother's funeral in 1970. He looked through her, past her, with his yellow eyes so startlingly like her own. She might have been a stranger.

His appearance surprised his mother. He was deep chested and sleek, with her fine colouring and a neat moustache which she suspected was hair transplanted from his head.

She called him once in the next week and heard the receiver slowly replaced.

For nine years after Grandmother's death Dolarhyde was untroubled and he troubled no one. His forehead was as smooth as a seed. He knew that he was waiting. For what, he didn't know.

One small event, which occurs to everyone, told the seed in his skull it was Time: standing by a north window, examining some film, he noticed ageing in his hands. It was as though his hands, holding the film, had suddenly appeared before him and he saw in that good north light that the skin had slackened over the bones and tendons and his hands were creased in diamonds as small as lizard scales.

As he turned them in the light, an intense odour of cabbage and stewed tomatoes washed over him. He shivered though the room was warm. That evening he worked out harder than usual.

A full-length mirror was mounted on the wall of Dolarhyde's attic gym beside his barbells and weight bench. It was the only mirror hanging in his house and he could admire his body in it comfortably because he always worked out in a mask.

He examined himself carefully while his muscles were pumped

up. At forty, he could have competed successfully in regional body-building competition. He was not satisfied.

Within the week he came upon the Blake painting. It seized him instantly.

He saw it in a large, full-colour photograph in *Time Magazine* illustrating a report on the Blake retrospective at the Tate Gallery in London. The Brooklyn Museum had sent *The Great Red Dragon and the Woman Clothed with the Sun* to London for the show.

Time's critic said "Few demonic images in Western art radiate such a nightmarish charge of sexual energy . . ." Dolarhyde didn't have to read the text to find that out.

He carried the picture with him for days, photographed and enlarged it in the dark-room at night. He was agitated much of the time. He posted the painting beside his mirror in the weight room and stared at it while he pumped. He could sleep only when he had worked out to exhaustion and watched his medical films to aid him in sexual relief.

He had known since the age of nine that essentially he was alone and that he would always be alone, a conclusion more common to the forties.

Now, in his forties, he was seized by a fantasy life with the brilliance and freshness and immediacy of childhood. It took him a step beyond Alone.

At a time when other men first see and fear their isolation, Dolarhyde's became understandable to him: he was alone because he was Unique. With the fervour of conversion he saw that if he worked at it, if he followed the true urges he had kept down for so long—cultivated them as the inspirations they truly were—he could Become.

The Dragon's face is not visible in the painting, but increasingly Dolarhyde came to know how it looked.

Watching his medical films in the parlour, pumped up from lifting, he stretched his jaw wide to hold in Grandmother's teeth. They did not fit his distorted gums and his jaw cramped quickly.

He worked on his jaw in private moments, biting on a hard rubber block until the muscles stood out in his cheeks like walnuts.

In the fall of 1979, Francis Dolarhyde withdrew part of his considerable savings and took a three-month leave of absence from Gateway. He went to Hong Kong and he took with him his grandmother's teeth.

When he returned, red-haired Eileen and his other fellow workers agreed that the vacation had done him good. He was calm. They hardly noticed that he never used the employees' locker-room or shower any more—he had never done that often anyway.

His grandmother's teeth were back in the glass beside her bed. His own new ones were locked in his desk upstairs.

If Eileen could have seen him before his mirror, teeth in place, new tattoo in the harsh gym light, she would have screamed. Once.

There was time now, he did not have to hurry now. He had forever. It was five months before he selected the Jacobis.

The Jacobis were the first to help him, the first to lift him into the Glory of his Becoming. The Jacobis were better than anything, better than anything he ever knew.

Until the Leeds.

And now, as he grew in strength and Glory, there were the Shermans to come and the new intimacy of infra-red. Most promising.

CHAPTER

29

FRANCIS DOLARHYDE had to leave his own territory at Gateway Film Processing to get what he needed.

Dolarhyde was production chief of Gateway's largest division—home movie processing—but there were four other divisions.

The recessions of the 1970s cut deeply into home movie-making and there was increasing competition from home video recorders. Gateway had to diversify.

The company added departments which transferred film to videotape, printed aerial survey maps and offered custom services to small-format commercial film-makers.

In 1979 a plum fell to Gateway. The company contracted jointly with the Department of Defence and the Department of Energy to develop and test new emulsions for infra-red photography.

The Department of Energy wanted sensitive infra-red film for its heat conservation studies. Defence wanted it for night reconnaissance.

Gateway bought a small company next door, Baeder Chemicals, in late 1979 and set up the project there.

Dolarhyde walked across to Baeder in his lunch-hour under a

scrubbed blue sky, carefully avoiding the reflecting puddles on the asphalt. Lounds's death had put him in an excellent humour.

Everyone at Baeder seemed to be out for lunch.

He found the door he wanted at the end of a labyrinth of halls. The sign beside the door said "Infra-red Sensitive Materials in Use. NO Safelights, NO Smoking, NO hot beverages." The red light was on above the sign.

Dolarhyde pushed a button and, in a moment, the light turned green. He entered the light trap and rapped on the inner door.

"Come." A woman's voice.

Cool, absolute darkness. The gurgle of water, the familiar smell of D-76 developer and a trace of perfume.

"I'm Francis Dolarhyde. I came about the dryer."

"Oh, good. Excuse me, my mouth's full. I was just finishing lunch."

He heard papers wadded and dropped in a wastebasket.

"Actually, Ferguson wanted the dryer," said the voice in the dark. "He's on vacation, but I know where it goes. You have one over at Gateway?"

"I have two. One is larger. He didn't say how much room he has." Dolarhyde had seen a memo about the dryer problem weeks ago.

"I'll show you if you don't mind a short wait."

"All right."

"Put your back to the door—" Her voice took on a touch of the lecturer's practiced tone—"come forward three steps, until you feel the tile under your feet, and there'll be a stool just to your left."

He found it. He was closer to her now. He could hear the rustle of her lab apron.

"Thanks for coming down," she said. Her voice was clear with a faint ring of iron in it. "You're head of processing over in the big building, right?"

"Um humm."

"The same 'Mr. D.' who sends the rockets when the requisitions are filed wrong?"

"The very one."

"I'm Reba McClane. Hope there's nothing wrong over here."

"Not my project any more. I just planned the dark-room construction when we bought this place. I haven't been over here in six months." A long speech for him, easier in the dark.

"Just a minute more and we'll get you some light. Do you need a tape measure?"

"I have one."

Dolarhyde found it rather pleasant, talking to the woman in the dark. He heard the rattle of a purse being rummaged, the click of a compact.

He was sorry when the timer rang.

"There we go. I'll put this stuff in the Black Hole," she said.

He felt a breath of cold air, heard a cabinet close on rubber seals and the hiss of a vacuum lock. A puff of air and fragrance touched him as she passed.

Dolarhyde pressed his knuckle under his nose, put on his thoughtful expression and waited for the light.

The lights came on. She stood by the door smiling in his approximate direction. Her eyes made small random movements behind the closed lids.

He saw her white cane propped in the corner. He took his hand away from his face and smiled.

"Do you think I could have a plum?" he said. There were several on the counter where she had been sitting.

"Sure, they're really good."

Reba McClane was about thirty with a handsome prairie face shaped by good bones and resolution. She had a small star-shaped scar on the bridge of her nose. Her hair was a mixture of wheat and red-gold, cut in a page-boy that looked slightly out of date and her hands were pleasantly freckled by the sun. Against the tile and stainless steel of the darkroom she was as bright as Fall.

He was free to look at her. His gaze could move over her as freely as the air. She had no way to parry eyes.

Dolarhyde often felt warm spots, stinging spots on his skin when he talked to a woman. They moved over him to wherever he thought the woman was looking. Even when a woman looked away from him, he suspected that she saw his reflection. He was always aware of reflective surfaces, knew the angles of reflection as a pool shark knows the banks.

His skin was cool now. Hers was freckled, pearly on her throat and the insides of her wrists.

"I'll show you the room where he wants to put it," she said. "We can get the measuring done."

They measured.

"Now I want to ask you a favour," Dolarhyde said.

"Okay."

"I need some infra-red movie film. Hot film, sensitive up around 1,000 nanometers."

"You'll have to keep it in the freezer and put it back in the cold after you shoot."

"I know."

"Could you give me an idea of the conditions, maybe I—"

"Shooting at maybe eight feet, with a pair of Wratten filters over the lights." It sounded too much like a surveillance rig. "At the zoo," he said. "In the 'World of Darkness'. They want to photograph the nocturnal animals."

"They must really be spooky if you can't use commercial infra-red."

"Ummm hmmmm."

"I'm sure we can fix you up. One thing, though. You know a lot of our stuff is under the D.D. contract. Anything that goes out of here, you have to sign for."

"Right."

"When do you need it?"

"About the 20th. No later."

"I don't have to tell you—the more sensitive it is, the meaner it is to handle. You get into coolers, dry ice, all that. They're screening some samples about four o'clock if you want to look. You can pick the tamest emulsion that'll do what you want."

"I'll come."

Reba McClane counted her plums after Dolarhyde left. He had taken one.

Strange man, Mr. Dolarhyde. There had been no awkward pause of sympathy and concern in his voice when she turned on the lights. Maybe he already knew she was blind. Better yet, maybe he didn't give a damn.

That would be refreshing.

30

In Chicago, Freddy Lounds's funeral was underway. The *National Tattler* paid for the elaborate service, rushing the arrangements so that it could be held on Thursday, the day after his death. Then the pictures would be available for the *Tattler* edition published Thursday night.

The funeral was long in the chapel and it was long at the graveside.

A radio evangelist went on and on in fulsome eulogy. Graham rode the greasy swells of his hangover and tried to study the crowd.

The hired choir at the graveside gave full measure for the money while the *Tattler* photographers' motor-driven cameras whizzed. Two T.V. crews were present with fixed cameras and creepy-peepys. Police photographers with press credentials photographed the crowd.

Graham recognized several plainclothes officers from Chicago Homicide. Theirs were the only faces that meant anything to him.

And there was Wendy of Wendy City, Lounds's girlfriend. She was seated beneath the canopy, nearest the coffin. Graham hardly recognized her. Her blonde wig was drawn back in a bun and she wore a black tailored suit.

During the last hymn she rose, went forward unsteadily, knelt and lay her head on the casket, her arms outstretched in the pall of chrysanthemums as the strobe lights flashed.

The crowd made little noise moving over the spongy grass to the cemetery gates.

Graham walked beside Wendy. A crowd of the uninvited stared at them through the bars of the high iron fence.

"Are you all right?" Graham asked.

They stopped among the tombstones. Her eyes were dry, her gaze level.

"Better than you," she said. "Got drunk, didn't you?"

"Yep. Is somebody keeping an eye on you?"

"The precinct sent some people over. They've got plainclothes in the club. Lot of business now. More weirdos than usual."

"I'm sorry you had this. You did—I thought you were fine at the hospital. I admired that."

She nodded. "Freddy was a sport. He shouldn't have to go out that hard. Thanks for getting me in the room." She looked into the distance, blinking, thinking, eye shadow like stone dust on her lids. She faced Graham. "Look, the *Tattler*'s giving me some money. You figured that, right? For an interview and the dive at the graveside. I don't think Freddy would mind."

"He'd have been mad if you passed it up."

"That's what I thought. They're jerks but they pay. What it is, they tried to get me to say that I think you deliberately turned this freak on to Freddy, chumming with him in that picture. I didn't say it. If they print that I did say it, well that's bullshit."

Graham said nothing as she scanned his face.

"You didn't like him, maybe—it doesn't matter. But if you thought this could happen you wouldn't have missed the shot at the Fairy, right?"

"Yeah, Wendy, I'd have staked him out."

"Do you have anything at all? I hear noise from these people and that's about it."

"We don't have much. A few things from the lab we're following up. It was a clean job and he's lucky."

"Are you?"

"What?"

"Lucky?"

"Off and on."

"Freddy was never lucky. He told me he'd clean up on this. Big deals everywhere."

"He probably would have too."

"Well look, Graham, if you ever, you know, feel like a drink, I've got one."

"Thanks."

"But stay sober on the streets."

"Oh yes."

Two policemen cleared a path for Wendy through the crowd of curiosity-seekers outside the gate. One of the gawkers wore a printed tee-shirt reading "The Tooth Fairy is a One-Night Stand." He whistled at Wendy. The woman beside him slapped his face.

A big policeman squeezed into the 280ZX beside Wendy and she pulled into the traffic. A second policeman followed in an unmarked car.

Chicago smelled like a spent skyrocket in the hot afternoon.

Graham was lonely and he knew why; funerals often make us want sex—it's one in the eye for death.

The wind rattled the dry stalks of a funeral arrangement near his feet. For a hard second he remembered palm fronds rustling in the sea wind. He wanted very much to go home, knowing he would not, could not until the Dragon was dead.

31

THE PROJECTION room at Baeder Chemicals was small—five rows of folding chairs with an aisle in the middle.

Dolarhyde arrived late. He stood at the back with his arms folded while they screened grey cards, coloured cards and cubes variously lighted, filmed on a variety of infra-red emulsions.

His presence disturbed Dandridge, the young man in charge. Dolarhyde carried an air of authority at work. He was the recognized dark-room expert from the parent company next door and he was known to be a perfectionist.

Dandridge had not consulted him in months, a petty rivalry that had gone on since Gateway bought Baeder Chemicals.

"Reba, give us the development dope on sample . . . eight," Dandridge said.

Reba McClane sat at the end of a row, a clipboard in her lap. Speaking in a clear voice, her fingers moving over the clipboard in the semi-darkness, she outlined the mechanics of the development—chemicals, temperature and time, and storage procedures before and after filming.

Infra-red sensitive film must be handled in total darkness. She had done all the dark-room work, keeping the many samples straight by touch code and keeping a running record in the dark. It was easy to see her value to Baeder.

The screening ran through quitting time.

Reba McClane kept her seat as the others were filing out. Dolarhyde approached her carefully. He spoke to her at a distance while there were others in the room. He didn't want her to feel watched.

"I thought you hadn't made it," she said.

"I had a machine down. It made me late."

The lights were on. Her clean scalp glistened in the parting of her hair as he stood over her.

"Did you get to see the 1000C sample?"

"I did."

"They said it looked all right. It's a lot easier to handle than the 1200 series. Think it'll do?"

"It will."

She had her purse with her and a light raincoat. He stood back when she came into the aisle behind her searching cane. She didn't seem to expect help. He didn't offer any.

Dandridge stuck his head back into the room.

"Reba, dear, Marcia had to fly. Can you manage?"

Spots of colour appeared in her cheeks. "I can manage very well, thank you, Danny."

"I'd drop you, love, but I'm late already. Say, Mr. Dolarhyde, if it wouldn't be too much trouble could you—"

"Danny—I have a ride home." She held in her anger. The nuances of expression were denied her, so she kept her face relaxed. She couldn't control her colour, though.

Watching with his cold yellow eyes, Dolarhyde understood her anger perfectly; he knew that Dandridge's limp sympathy felt like spit on her cheek.

"I'll take you," he said, rather late.

"No, but thank you." She had thought he might offer and had intended to accept. She wouldn't have anybody forced into it. Damn Dandridge, damn his fumbling, she'd ride the damned bus, dammit. She had the fare and she knew the way and she could go anywhere she fucking pleased.

She stayed in the women's room long enough for the others to leave the building. The janitor let her out.

She followed the edge of a dividing strip across the parking lot toward the bus stop, her raincoat over her shoulders, tapping the edge with her cane and feeling for the slight resistance of the puddles when the cane swished through them.

Dolarhyde watched her from his van. His feelings made him uneasy; they were dangerous in daylight.

For a moment under the lowering sun, windshields, puddles, high steel wires splintered the sunlight into the glint of scissors.

Her white cane comforted him. It swept the light of scissors, swept scissors away, and the memory of her harmlessness eased him. He was starting the engine.

Reba McClane heard the van behind her. It was beside her now.

"Thank you for inviting me."

She nodded, smiled, tapped along.

"Ride with me."

"Thanks, but I take the bus all the time."

"Dandridge is a fool. Ride with me . . ."—*what would someone say?*—
". . . for my pleasure."

She stopped. She heard him get out of the van.

People usually grasped her upper arm, not knowing what else to do. Blind people do not like to have their balance disturbed by a firm hold on their triceps. It is as unpleasant for them as standing on wiggly scales to weigh. Like anyone else, they don't like to be propelled.

He didn't touch her. In a moment she said, "It's better if *I* take *your* arm."

She had wide experience of forearms, but his surprised her fingers. It was as hard as an oak bannister.

She could not know the amount of nerve he summoned to let her touch him.

The van felt big and high. Surrounded by resonances and echoes unlike those of a car, she held to the edges of the bucket seat until Dolarhyde fastened her safety belt. The diagonal shoulder belt pressed one of her breasts. She moved the belt until it lay between them.

They said little during the drive. Waiting at the red lights, he could look at her.

She lived in the left side of a duplex on a quiet street near Washington University.

"Come in and I'll give you a drink."

In his life, Dolarhyde had been in less than a dozen private homes. In the past ten years he had been in four; his own, Eileen's briefly, the Leeds's and the Jacobis'. Other people's houses were exotic to him.

She felt the van rock as he got out. Her door opened. It was a long step down from the van. She bumped into him lightly. It was like bumping into a tree. He was much heavier, more solid than she would have judged from his voice and his footfalls. Solid and light on his feet. She had known a Bronco linebacker once in Denver who came out to film a United Way appeal with some blind kids . . .

Once inside her front door, Reba McClane stood her cane in the corner and was suddenly free. She moved effortlessly, turning on music, hanging up her coat.

Dolarhyde had to reassure himself that she was blind. Being in a home excited him.

"How about a gin and tonic?"

"Tonic will be fine."

"Would you rather have juice?"

"Tonic."

"You're not a drinker, are you?"

"No."

"Come on in the kitchen." She opened the refrigerator. "How about . . ."—she made a quick inventory with her hands—"a piece of pie, then? Karo pecan, it's dynamite."

"Fine."

She took a whole pie from the icebox and put it on the counter.

Hands pointing straight down, she spread her fingers along the edge of the pie tin until its circumference told her that her middle fingers were at nine and three o'clock. Then she touched her thumb-tips together and brought them down to the surface of the pie to locate its exact centre. She marked the centre with a toothpick.

Dolarhyde tried to make conversation to keep her from feeling his stare. "How long have you been at Baeder?" No "s"s in that one.

"Three months. Didn't you know?"

"They tell me the minimum."

She grinned. "You probably stepped on some toes when you laid out the dark-rooms. Listen, the techs love you for it. The plumbing works and there are plenty of outlets. Two-twenty wherever you need it."

She put the middle finger of her left hand on the toothpick, her thumb on the edge of the tin and cut him a slice of pie, guiding the knife with her left index finger.

He watched her handle the bright knife. Strange to look at the front of a woman as much as he liked. How often in company can one look where one wants to look?

She made herself a stiff gin and tonic and they went into the living-room. She passed her hand over a floor lamp, felt no heat, switched it on.

Dolarhyde ate his pie in three bites and sat stiffly on the couch, his sleek hair shining under the lamp, his powerful hands on his knees.

She put her head back in her chair and propped her feet on an ottoman.

"When will they film at the zoo?"

"Maybe next week." He was glad he had called the zoo and offered the infra-red film: Dandridge might check.

"It's a great zoo. I went there with my sister and my niece when they came to help me move in. They have the contact area, you know. I hugged this llama. It felt nice but talk about *aroma*, boy . . . I thought I was being followed by a llama until I changed my shirt."

This was Having a Conversation. He had to say something or leave. "How did you come to Baeder?"

"They advertised at the Reiker Institute in Denver where I was working. I was checking the bulletin board one day and just happened to come across this job. Actually, what happened, Baeder had to shape up their employment practices to keep this Defence contract. They managed to pack seven women, three blacks, three chicanos, an oriental, a paraplegic and me into a total of eight hirings. Each of us counts in two categories, you see."

"You worked out well for Baeder."

"The others did too. Baeder's not giving anything away."

"Before that?" He was sweating a little. Conversation was hard. Looking was good though. She had good legs. She had nicked an ankle shaving. Along his arms a sense of the weight of her legs, limp.

"I trained newly-blind people at the Reiker Institute in Denver for ten years after I finished school. This is my first job on the outside."

"Outside of what?"

"Out in the big world. It was really insular at Reiker. I mean, we were training people to live in the sighted world and we didn't live in it ourselves. We talked to each other too much. I thought I'd get out and knock around a little. Actually, I had intended to go into speech therapy, for speech and hearing impaired children. I expect I'll go back to that one of these days." She drained her glass. "Say, I've got some Mrs. Paul's crab ball miniatures in here. They're pretty good. I shouldn't have served dessert first. Want some?"

"Um hmmmm."

"Do you cook?"

"Um hmmm."

A tiny crease appeared in her forehead. She went into the kitchen. "How about coffee?" she called.

"Uh uh."

She made small talk about grocery prices and got no reply. She came back into the living-room and sat on the ottoman, her elbows on her knees.

"Let's talk about something for a minute and get it out of the way, okay?"

Silence.

"You haven't said anything lately. In fact, you haven't said anything since I mentioned speech therapy." Her voice was kind, but firm. It carried no taint of sympathy. "I understand you fine because you speak very well and because I listen. People don't pay attention. They ask me *what? what?* all the time. If you don't want to talk, okay. But I hope you will talk. Because you can, and I'm interested in what you have to say."

"Ummm. That's good," Dolarhyde said softly. Clearly this little speech was very important to her. Was she inviting him into the two-category club with her and the Chinese paraplegic? He wondered what his second category was.

Her next statement was incredible to him.

"May I touch your face? I want to know if you're smiling or frowning." Wryly, now. "I want to know whether to just shut up or not."

She raised her hand and waited.

How well would she get around with her fingers bitten off, Dolarhyde mused. Even in street teeth he could do it as easily as biting off breadsticks. If he braced his heels on the floor, his weight back on the couch, and locked both hands on her wrist she could never pull away from him in time. Crunch, crunch, crunch, crunch, maybe leave the thumb. For measuring pies.

He took her wrist between his thumb and forefinger and turned her shapely, hard-used hand in the light. There were many small scars on it and several new nicks and abrasions. A smooth scar on the back might have been a burn.

Too close to home. Too early in his Becoming. She wouldn't be there to look at any more.

To ask this incredible thing, she could know nothing personal about him. She had not gossiped.

"Take my word that I'm smiling," he said. Okay on the "s". It was true that he had a sort of smile which exposed his handsome public teeth.

He held her wrist above her lap and released it. Her hand settled to her thigh and half-closed, fingers trailing on the cloth like an averted glance.

"I think the coffee's ready," she said.

"I'm going." Had to go. Home for relief.

She nodded. "If I offended you, I didn't mean to."

"No."

She stayed on the ottoman, listened to be sure the lock clicked as he left.

Reba McClane made herself another gin and tonic. She put on some Segovia records and curled up on the couch. Dolarhyde left a warm dent in the cushion. Traces of him remained in the air—shoe polish, a new leather belt, good shaving lotion.

What an intensely private man. She had heard only a few references to him at the office—Dandridge saying "that son of a bitch Dolarhyde" to one of his toadies.

Privacy was important to Reba. As a child, learning to cope after she lost her sight, she had had no privacy at all.

Now, in public, she could never be sure that she was not watched. So Francis Dolarhyde's sense of privacy appealed to her. She felt not one ion of sympathy from him, and that was good.

So was this gin.

Suddenly the Segovia sounded busy. She put on her whale songs.

Three tough months in a new town. The winter to face, finding kerbs in the snow. Reba McClane, leggy and brave, damned self-pity. She would not have it. She was aware of a deep vein of cripple's anger in her and, while she could not get rid of it, she made it work for her, fueling her drive for independence, strengthening her determination to wring all she could from every day.

In her way, she was a hard one. Faith in any sort of natural justice was nothing but a night light, she knew that. Whatever she did, she would end the same way everyone else does: flat on her back with a tube in her nose, wondering, "Is this all?"

She knew that she would never have the light, but there were things she *could* have. There were things to enjoy. She had gotten pleasure from helping her students, and the pleasure was oddly intensified by the knowledge that she would be neither rewarded nor punished for helping them.

In making friends she was ever wary of people who foster dependence and feed on it. She had been involved with a few—the blind attract them and they are the enemy.

Involved. Reba knew that she was physically attractive to men—God knows enough of them copped a feel with their knuckles when they grabbed her upper arm.

She liked sex very much, but years ago she had learned something basic about men; most of them are terrified of entailing a burden. Their fear was augmented in her case.

She did not like for a man to creep in and out of her bed as though he were stealing chickens.

Ralph Mandy was coming to take her to dinner. He had a particularly cowardly mew about being so scarred by life that he was incapable of love. Careful Ralph told her that too often and it scalded her. Ralph was amusing, but she didn't want to own him.

She didn't want to see Ralph. She didn't feel like making conversation and hearing the hitches in conversations around them as people watched her eat.

It would be so nice to be wanted by someone with the courage to get his hat or stay as he damn pleased, and who gave her credit for the same. Someone who didn't worry about her.

Francis Dolarhyde—shy, with a linebacker's body and no bullshit.

She had never seen or touched a cleft lip and had no visual associations with the sound. She wondered if Dolarhyde thought she understood him easily because "blind people hear so much better than we do." That was a common myth. Maybe she should have explained to him that it was not true, that blind people simply pay more attention to what they hear.

There were so many misconceptions about the blind. She wondered if Dolarhyde shared the popular belief that the blind are "purer in spirit" than most people, that they are somehow sanctified by their affliction. She smiled to herself. That one wasn't true either.

CHAPTER

32

THE CHICAGO police worked under the media blitz, a nightly news "countdown" to the next full moon. Eleven days were left.

Chicago families were frightened.

At the same time, attendance rose at horror movies that should have died at the drive-ins in a week. Fascination and horror. The entrepreneur who hit the punk rock market with "Tooth Fairy" tee-shirts came out with an alternate line that said "The Red Dragon is a One-Night Stand." Sales were divided about equally between the two.

Jack Crawford himself had to appear at a news conference with police officials after the funeral. He had received orders from Above to make the federal presence more visible; he did not make it more audible, as he said nothing.

When heavily manned investigations have little to feed on, they tend to turn upon themselves, covering the same ground over and over, beating it flat. They take on the circular shape of a hurricane or a zero.

Everywhere Graham went he found detectives, cameras, a rush of uniformed men and the incessant crackle of radios. He needed to be still.

Crawford, ruffled from his news conference, found Graham at nightfall in the quiet of an unused jury room on the floor above the U.S. Prosecutor's office.

Good lights hung low over the green felt jury table where Graham spread out his papers and photographs. He had taken off his coat and tie and he was slumped in a chair staring at two photographs. The Leeds's framed picture stood before him and beside it, on a clipboard propped against a carafe, was a picture of the Jacobis.

Graham's pictures reminded Crawford of a bullfighter's folding shrine, ready to be set up in any hotel room. There was no photograph of Lounds. He suspected that Graham had not been thinking about the Lounds case at all. He didn't need trouble with Graham.

"Looks like a pool room in here," Crawford said.

"Did you knock 'em dead?" Graham was pale but sober. He had a quart of orange juice in his fist.

"Jesus." Crawford collapsed in a chair. "You try to think out there, it's like trying to take a piss on the train."

"Any news?"

"The commissioner was popping sweat over a question and scratched his balls on television, that's the only notable thing I saw. Watch at six and eleven if you don't believe it."

"Want some juice?"

"I'd just as soon swallow barbed wire."

"Good. More for me." Graham's face was drawn. His eyes were too bright. "How about the gas?"

"God bless Liza Lake. There're forty-one Servco Supreme franchise stations in greater Chicago. Captain Osborne's boys swarmed those, checking sales in containers to people driving vans and trucks. Nothing yet, but they haven't seen all shifts. Servco has 186 other stations— they're scattered over eight states. We've asked for help from the local jurisdictions. It'll take a while. If God loves me he used a credit card. There's a chance."

"Not if he can suck a siphon hose, there isn't."

"I asked the commissioner not to say anything about the Tooth Fairy maybe living in this area. These people are spooked enough. If he told them that, this place would sound like Korea tonight when the drunks come home."

"You still think he's close?"

"Don't you? It figures, Will." Crawford picked up the Lounds autopsy report and peered at it through his half-glasses.

"The bruise on his head was older than the mouth injuries. Five to eight hours older, they're not sure. Now the mouth injuries were hours old when they got Lounds to the hospital. They were burned over too, but inside his mouth they could tell. He retained some chloroform in this—hell, some place in his wheeze. You think he was unconscious when the Tooth Fairy bit him?"

"No. He'd want him awake."

"That's what I figure. All right, he takes him out with a lick on the head – that's in the garage. He has to keep him quiet with chloroform until he gets him some place where the noise won't matter. Brings him back and gets here hours after the bite."

"He could have done it all in the back of the van, parked way out somewhere," Graham said.

Crawford massaged the sides of his nose with his fingers, giving his voice a megaphone effect. "You're forgetting about the wheels on the chair. Bev got two kinds of carpet fuzz, wool and synthetic. Synthetic's from a van, maybe, but when have you ever seen a wool rug in a van? How many wool rugs have you seen in some place you can rent? Damn few. Wool rug is a house, Will. And the dirt and mould was from a dark place where the chair was stored, a dirt-floored cellar."

"Maybe."

"Now look at this." Crawford pulled a Rand McNally Road Atlas out of his briefcase. He had drawn a circle on the "United States mileage and driving time" map. "Freddy was gone a little over fifteen hours and his injuries were spaced over that time. I'm going to make a couple of assumptions, I don't like to do that but here goes—what are you laughing at?"

"I just remembered when you ran those field exercises at Quantico—when that trainee told you he *assumed* something."

"I don't remember that. Here's—"

"You made him write 'ASSUME' on the blackboard. You took the chalk and started underlining and yelling in his face. 'When you ASSUME you make an *ASS* out of *U* and *ME* both,' that's what you told him, as I recall."

"He needed a boot in the ass to shape up, now look at this. Figure he had Chicago traffic on Tuesday afternoon, going out of town with Lounds. Allow a couple of hours to fool with Lounds at the location where he took him, and then the time driving back. He couldn't have gone much further than six hours' driving time out of Chicago. Okay, this circle around Chicago is six hours' driving time. See, it's wavy because some roads are faster than others."

"Maybe he just stayed here."

"Sure, but this is the farthest away he *could* be."

"So you've narrowed it down to Chicago, or inside a circle covering Milwaukee, Madison, Dubuque, Peoria, St. Louis, Indianapolis, Cincinnati, Toledo and Detroit, to name a few."

"Better than that. We know he got a *Tattler* very fast. Monday night probably."

"He could have done that in Chicago."

"I know it, but once you get out of town the *Tattlers* aren't available on Monday night in a lot of locations. Here's a list from the *Tattler* circulation department—places *Tattlers* are air-freighted or trucked inside the circle on Monday night. See, that leaves Milwaukee, St. Louis, Cincinnati, Indianapolis and Detroit. They go to the airports and maybe ninety news-stands that stay open all night, not counting the ones in Chicago. I'm using the field offices to check them. Some newsie might remember an odd customer on Monday night."

"Maybe. That's a good move, Jack."

Clearly Graham's mind was elsewhere.

If Graham were a regular agent, Crawford would have threatened him with a lifetime appointment to the Aleutians. Instead he said, "My brother called this afternoon. Molly left his house, he said."

"Yeah."

"Some place safe, I guess?"

Graham was confident that Crawford knew exactly where she went.

"Willy's grandparents."

"Well, they'll be glad to see the kid." Crawford waited.

No comment from Graham.

"Everything's okay, I hope."

"I'm working, Jack. Don't worry about it. No, look, it's just that she got jumpy over there."

Graham pulled a flat package tied with string from beneath a stack of funeral pictures and began to pick at the knot.

"What's that?"

"It's from Byron Metcalf, the Jacobis' lawyer. Brian Zeller sent it on. It's okay."

"Wait a minute, let me see." Crawford turned the package in his hairy fingers until he found the stamp and signature of S. F. "Semper Fidelis" Aynesworth, head of the F.B.I.'s explosives section, certifying that the package had been fluoroscoped.

"Always check. Always check."

"I always check, Jack."

"Did Chester bring you this?"

"Yes."

"Did he show you the stamp before he handed it to you?"

"He checked it and showed me."

Graham cut the string. "It's copies of all the probate business in the Jacobi estate. I asked Metcalf to send it to me—we can compare with the Leeds stuff when it comes in."

"We have a lawyer doing that."

"*I* need it. I don't know the Jacobis, Jack. They were new in town. I got to Birmingham a month late and their stuff was scattered to shit and gone. I've got a feel for the Leeds. I don't for the Jacobis. I need to know them. I want to talk to people they knew in Detroit and I want a couple of days more in Birmingham."

"I need you here."

"Listen, Lounds was a straight snuff. We made him mad at Lounds. The only connection to Lounds is one *we* made. There's a little hard evidence with Lounds and the police are handling it. Lounds was just an annoyance to him, but the Leeds and the Jacobis are *what he needs*. We've got to have the connection between them. If we ever get him that's how we'll do it."

"So you have the Jacobi papers to use here," Crawford said. "What are you looking for? What kind of thing?"

"Any damn thing, Jack. Right now, a medical deduction." Graham pulled the I.R.S. Estate Tax form from the package. "Lounds was in a wheelchair. Medical. Valerie Leeds had surgery about six weeks before she died—remember in her diary? A small cyst in her breast. Medical again. I was wondering if Mrs. Jacobi had surgery too."

"I don't remember anything about surgery in the autopsy report."

"No, but it might have been something that didn't show. Her medical history was split between Detroit and Birmingham. Something might have gotten lost there. If she had anything done, there'll be a deduction claimed and maybe an insurance claim."

"Some itinerant orderly, you're thinking? Worked both places—Detroit or Birmingham and Atlanta."

"If you spend time in a mental hospital you pick up the drill. You could pass as an orderly, get a job doing it when you got out," Graham said.

"Want some dinner?"

"I'll wait till later. I get dumb after I eat."

Leaving, Crawford looked back at Graham from the gloom of the doorway. He didn't care for what he saw. The hanging lights deepened the hollows in Graham's face as he studied with the victims staring at him from the photographs. The room smelled of desperation.

Would it be better for the case to put Graham back on the street? Crawford couldn't afford to let him burn himself out in here for nothing. But for something?

Crawford's excellent administrative instincts were not tempered by mercy. They told him to leave Graham alone.

33

By 10 P.M. Dolarhyde had worked out to near-exhaustion with the weights, had watched his films and tried to satisfy himself. Still he was restless.

Excitement bumped his chest like a cold medallion when he thought of Reba McClane. He should not think of Reba McClane.

Stretched out in his recliner, his torso pumped up and reddened by the workout, he watched the television news to see how the police were coming along with Freddy Lounds.

There was Will Graham standing near the casket with the choir howling away. Graham was slender. It would be easy to break his back. Better than killing him. Break his back and twist it just to be sure. They could roll him to the next investigation.

There was no hurry. Let Graham dread it.

Dolarhyde felt a quiet sense of power all the time now.

The Chicago Police Department made some noise at a news conference. Behind the racket about how hard they were working the essence was: no progress on Freddy. Jack Crawford was in the group behind the microphones. Dolarhyde recognized him from a *Tattler* picture.

A spokesman from the *Tattler*, flanked by two bodyguards, said, "This savage and senseless act will only make the *Tattler*'s voice ring louder."

Dolarhyde snorted. Maybe so. It had certainly shut Freddy up.

The news-readers were calling him "the Dragon" now. His acts were "what the police *had* termed the 'Tooth Fairy murders'."

Definite progress.

Nothing but local news left. Some prognathous lout was reporting from the zoo. Clearly they'd send him anywhere to keep him out of the office.

Dolarhyde had reached for his remote control when he saw on the screen someone he had talked with only hours ago on the telephone: Zoo Director Dr. Frank Warfield, who had been so pleased to have the film Dolarhyde offered.

Dr. Warfield and a dentist were working on a tiger with a broken tooth. Dolarhyde wanted to see the tiger but the reporter was in the way. Finally the newsman moved.

Rocked back in his recliner, looking along his own powerful torso at the screen, Dolarhyde saw the great tiger stretched unconscious on a heavy work-table.

Today they were preparing the tooth. In a few days they would cap it, the oaf reported.

Dolarhyde watched them calmly working between the jaws of the tiger's terrible striped face.

"May I touch your face?" said Miss Reba McClane.

He wanted to tell Reba McClane something. He wished she had one inkling of what she had almost done. He wished she had one flash of his glory. But she could not have that and live. She must live: he had been seen with her and she was too close to home.

He had tried to share with Lecter and Lecter had betrayed him.

Still, he would like to share. He would like to share with her a little, in a way she could survive.

34

"I KNOW IT'S political, *you* know it's political, but it's pretty much what you're doing anyway," Crawford told Graham. They were walking down the State Street Mall toward the federal office building in the late afternoon. "Do what you're doing, just write out the parallels and I'll do the rest."

The Chicago Police Department had asked the F.B.I.'s Behavioural Science Section for a detailed victim profile. Police officials said they would use it in planning disposition of extra patrols during the period of the full moon.

"Covering their ass is what they're doing," Crawford said, waving his bag of Tater Tots. "The victims have been affluent people, they need to stack the patrols in affluent neighbourhoods. They know there'll be a squawk about that—the ward bosses have been fighting over the extra manpower ever since Freddy lit off. If they patrol the upper-middle class neighbourhoods and he hits the South Side, God help the city fathers. But if it happens, they can point at the damned feds. I can hear it now—'They told us to do it that way. That's what *they* said do'."

"I don't think he's any more likely to hit Chicago than anywhere else," Graham said. "There's no reason to think so. It's a jerkoff. Why can't Bloom do the profile? He's a consultant to Behavioural Science."

"They don't want it from Bloom, they want it from us. It wouldn't do them any good to blame Bloom. Besides, he's still in the hospital. I'm instructed to do this. Somebody on the Hill has been on the phone with Justice. Above says do it. Will you just do it?"

"I'll do it. It's what I'm doing anyway."

"That's what I know," Crawford said. "Just keep doing it."

"I'd rather go back to Birmingham."

"No," Crawford said. "Stay with me on this."

The last of Friday burned down the west.

Ten days to go.

35

"READY TO tell me what kind of an 'outing' this is?" Reba McClane asked Dolarhyde on Saturday morning when they had ridden in silence for ten minutes. She hoped it was a picnic.

The van stopped. She heard Dolarhyde roll down his window.

"Dolarhyde," he said. "Dr. Warfield left my name."

"Yes, sir. Would you put this under your wiper when you leave the vehicle?"

They moved forward slowly. Reba felt a gentle curve in the road. Strange and heavy odours on the wind. An elephant trumpeted.

"The zoo," she said. "Terrific." She would have preferred a picnic. What the hell, this was okay. "Who's Dr. Warfield?"

"The zoo director."

"Is he a friend of yours?"

"No. We did the zoo a favour with the film. They're paying back."

"How?"

"You get to touch the tiger."

"Don't surprise me too much!"

"Did you ever look at a tiger?"

She was glad he could ask the question. "No. I remember a puma when I was little. That's all they had at the zoo in Red Deer. I think we better talk about this."

"They're working on the tiger's tooth. They have to put him to . . . sleep. If you want to, you can touch him."

"Will there be a crowd, people watching?"

"No. No audience. Warfield, me, a couple of people. T.V.'s coming in after we leave. Want to do it?" An odd urgency in the question.

"Hell fuzzy yes, I do! Thank you . . . that's a fine surprise."

The van stopped.

"Uh, how do I know he's sound asleep?"

"Tickle him. If he laughs, run for it."

The floor of the treatment room felt like linoleum under Reba's shoes. The room was cool with large echoes. Radiant heat was coming from the far side.

A rhythmic shuffling of burdened feet and Dolarhyde guided her to one side until she felt the forked pressure of a corner.

It was in here now, she could smell it.

A voice. "Up now. Easy. Down. Can we leave the sling under him, Dr. Warfield?"

"Yeah, wrap that cushion in one of the green towels and put it under his head. I'll send John for you when we've finished."

Footsteps leaving.

She waited for Dolarhyde to tell her something. He didn't.

"It's in here," she said.

"Ten men carried it in on a sling. It's big. Ten feet. Dr. Warfield's listening to its heart. Now he's looking under one eyelid. Here he comes."

A body damped the noise in front of her.

"Dr. Warfield, Reba McClane," Dolarhyde said.

She held out her hand. A large, soft hand took it.

"Thanks for letting me come," she said. "It's a treat."

"Glad you *could* come. Enlivens my day. We appreciate the film, by the way."

Dr. Warfield's voice was middle-aged, deep, cultured, black. Virginia, she guessed.

"We're waiting to be sure his respiration and heartbeat are strong and steady before Dr. Hassler starts. Hassler's over there adjusting his head-mirror. Just between us, he only wears it to hold down his toupee. Come meet him. Mr. Dolarhyde?"

"You go ahead."

She put out her hand to Dolarhyde. The pat was slow in coming, light when it came. His palm left sweat on her knuckles.

Dr. Warfield placed her hand on his arm and they walked forward slowly.

"He's sound asleep. Do you have a general impression—I'll describe as much as you like." He stopped, uncertain how to put it.

"I remember pictures in books when I was a child, and I saw a puma once in a zoo near home."

"This tiger is like a super puma," he said. "Deeper chest, more massive head and a heavier frame and musculature. He's a four-year-old male Bengal. He's about ten feet long, from his nose to the tip of his tail and he weighs eight hundred and fifteen pounds. He's lying on his right side under bright lights."

"I can feel the lights."

"He's striking, orange and black stripes, the orange is so bright it seems almost to bleed into the air around him." Suddenly Dr. Warfield feared that it was cruel to talk of colours. A glance at her face reassured him.

"He's six feet away, can you smell him?"

"Yes."

"Mr. Dolarhyde may have told you, some dimwit poked at him through the barrier with one of our gardener's spades. He snapped off the long fang on the upper side on the blade. Okay, Dr. Hassler?"

"He's fine. We'll give it another minute or two."

Warfield introduced the dentist to Reba.

"My dear, you're the first *pleasant* surprise I've ever had from Frank Warfield," Hassler said. "You might like to examine this. It's a gold tooth, fang actually." He put it in her hand. "Heavy, isn't it? I cleaned up the broken tooth and took an impression several days ago and today I'll cap it with this one. I could have done it in white of course, but I thought this would be more fun. Dr. Warfield will tell you I never pass up an opportunity to show off. He's too inconsiderate to let me put an advertisement on the cage."

She felt the taper, curve and point with her sensitive battered fingers. "What a nice piece of work!" She heard deep, slow breathing nearby.

"It'll give the kids a start when he yawns," Hassler said. "And I don't think it'll tempt any thieves. Now for the fun. You're not apprehensive, are you? Your muscular gentleman over there is watching us like a ferret. He's not making you do this?"

"No! No, I want to."

"We're facing his back," Dr. Warfield said. "He's just sleeping away about two and a half feet from you, waist-high on a work-table. Tell you what: I'll put your left hand—you're right-handed, aren't you?— I'll put you left hand on the edge of the table and you can explore with your right. Take your time. I'll be right here beside you."

"So will I," Dr. Hassler said. They were enjoying this. Under the hot lights her hair smelled like fresh sawdust in the sun.

Reba could feel the heat on the top of her head. It made her scalp tingle. She could smell her warm hair, Warfield's soap, alcohol and disinfectant and the cat. She felt a touch of faintness, quickly over.

She gripped the edge of the table and reached out tentatively until her fingers touched the tips of fur, warm from the lights, a cooler layer and then a deep steady warmth from below. She flattened her hand on the thick coat and moved it gently, feeling the fur slide across her palm, with and against the lay, felt the hide slide over the wide ribs as they rose and fell.

She gripped the pelt and fur sprang between her fingers. In the very presence of the tiger her face grew pink and she lapsed into blindisms, inappropriate facial movements she had schooled herself against.

Warfield and Hassler saw her forget herself and were glad. They saw her through a wavy window, a pane of new sensation she pressed her face against.

As he watched from the shadows, the great muscles in Dolarhyde's back quivered. A drop of sweat bounded down his ribs.

"The other side's all business," Dr. Warfield said close to her ear.

He led her around the table, her hand trailing down the tail.

A sudden constriction in Dolarhyde's chest as her fingers trailed over the furry testicles. She cupped them and moved on.

Warfield lifted a great paw and put it in her hand. She felt the roughness of the pads and smelled faintly the cage floor. He pressed a toe to make the claw slide out.

The heavy, supple muscles of the shoulders filled her hands.

She felt the tiger's ears, the width of its head and, carefully, the veterinarian guiding her, touched the roughness of its tongue. Hot breath stirred the hair on her forearms.

Last, Dr. Warfield put the stethoscope in her ears. Her hands on the rhythmic chest, her face upturned, she was filled with the tiger heart's bright thunder.

Reba McClane was quiet, flushed, elated as they drove away. She turned to Dolarhyde once and said, slowly, "Thank you . . . very much. If you don't mind, I would dearly love a martini."

"Wait here a minute," Dolarhyde said as he parked in his yard.

She was glad they hadn't gone back to her apartment. It was stale and safe. "Don't tidy up. Take me in and tell me it's neat."

"Wait here."

He carried in the sack from the liquor store and made a fast inspection tour. He stopped in the kitchen and stood for a moment with his hands over his face. He wasn't sure what he was doing. He felt danger, but not from the woman. He couldn't look up the stairs. He had to do something and he didn't know how. He should take her back home.

Before his Becoming he would not have dared any of this.

Now he realized he could do anything. Anything. Anything.

He came outside, into the sunset, into the long blue shadow of the van. Reba McClane held on to his shoulders until her foot touched the ground.

She felt the loom of the house. She sensed its height in the echo of the van door closing.

"Four steps on the grass. Then there's a ramp," he said.

She took his arm. A tremor through him. Clean perspiration in cotton.

"You *do* have a ramp. What for?"

"Old people were here."

"Not now, though."

"No."

"It feels cool and tall," she said in the parlour. Museum air. And was that incense? A clock ticked far away. "It's a big house, isn't it? How many rooms?"

"Fourteen."

"It's old. The things in here are old." She brushed against a fringed lampshade and touched it with her fingers.

Shy Mr. Dolarhyde. She was perfectly aware that it had excited him to see her with the tiger; he had shuddered like a horse when she took his arm leaving the treatment room.

An elegant gesture, his arranging that. Maybe eloquent as well, she wasn't sure.

"Martini?"

"Let me go with you and do it," she said, taking off her shoes.

She flicked vermouth from her finger into the glass. Two and a half ounces of gin on top and two olives. She picked up points of reference quickly in the house—the ticking clock, the hum of a window air-conditioner. There was a warm place on the floor near the kitchen door where the sunlight had fallen through the afternoon.

He took her to his big chair. He sat on the couch.

There was a charge in the air. Like fluorescence in the sea, it limned movement; she found a place for her drink on the stand beside her, he put on music.

To Dolarhyde the room seemed changed. She was the first voluntary company he ever had in the house and now the room was divided into her part and his.

There was music, Debussy, as the light failed.

He asked her about Denver and she told him a little, absently, as though she thought of something else. He described the house and the big hedged yard. There wasn't much need to talk.

In the silence while he changed records, she said, "That wonderful tiger, this house, you're full of surprises, D. I don't think anybody knows you at all."

"Did you ask them?"

"Who?"

"Anybody."

"No."

"Then how do you know that nobody knows me?" His concentration on the tongue-twister kept the tone of the question neutral.

"Oh, some of the women from Gateway saw us getting into your van the other day. Boy, were they curious. All of a sudden I have company at the Coke machine."

"What do they want to know?"

"They just wanted some juicy gossip. When they found out there isn't any, they went away. They were just fishing."

"And what did they say?"

She had meant to make the women's avid curiosity into humour directed at herself. It was not working out that way.

"They wonder about everything," she said. "They find you very mysterious and interesting. Come on, it's a compliment."

"Did they tell you how I look?"

The question was spoken lightly, very well done, but Reba knew that nobody is ever kidding. She met it head on.

"I didn't ask them. But, yes, they told me how they think you look. Want to hear it? Verbatim? Don't ask if you don't." She was sure he would ask.

No reply.

Suddenly Reba felt that she was alone in the room, that the place where he had stood was emptier than empty, a black hole swallowing everything and emanating nothing. She knew he could not have left without her hearing him.

"I think I'll tell you," she said. "You have a kind of hard clean neatness that they like. They said you have a remarkable body." Clearly she couldn't leave it at that. "They say you're very sensitive about your face and that you shouldn't be. Okay, here's the dippy one with the Dentine, is it Eileen?"

"Eileen."

Ah, a return signal. She felt like a radio astronomer.

Reba was an excellent mimic. She could have reproduced Eileen's speech with startling fidelity, but she was too wise to mimic anyone's speech for Dolarhyde. She quoted Eileen as though she read from a transcript.

"'He's not a bad-looking guy. Honest to God I've gone out with lots of guys didn't look that good. I went out with a hockey player one time—played for the Blues?—had a little dip in his lip where his gum shrank back from his bridge? They all have that, hockey players. It's kind of, you know, *macho*, I think. Mr. D.'s got the nicest skin and what I wouldn't give for his hair.' Satisfied? Oh, and she asked me if you're as strong as you look."

"And?"

"I said I didn't know." She drained her glass and got up. Where the hell are you anyway, D.?" She knew when he moved between her and a stereo speaker. "Aha. Here you are. Do you want to know what I think about it?"

She found his mouth with her fingers and kissed it, lightly pressing his lips against his clenched teeth. She registered instantly that it was shyness and not distaste that held him rigid.

He was astonished.

"Now, would you show me where the bathroom is?"

She took his arm and went with him down the hall.

"I can find my own way back."

In the bathroom she patted her hair and ran her fingers along the top of the basin, hunting toothpaste or mouthwash. She tried to find the door of the medicine cabinet and found there was no door, only hinges and exposed shelves. She touched the objects on them carefully, leery of a razor, until she found a bottle. She took off the cap, smelled to verify mouthwash, and swished some around.

When she returned to the parlour, she heard a familiar sound—the whirr of a projector rewinding.

"I have to do a little homework," Dolarhyde said, handing her a fresh martini.

"Sure," she said. She didn't know how to take it. "If I'm keeping you from working, I'll go. Will a cab come up here?"

"No. I want you to be here. I do. It's just some film I need to check. It won't take long."

He started to take her to the big chair. She knew where the couch was. She went to it instead.

"Does it have a sound track?"

"No."

"May I keep the music?"

"Um hmmmm."

She felt his attention. He wanted her to stay, he was just frightened. He shouldn't be. All right. She sat down.

The martini was wonderfully cold and crisp.

He sat on the other end of the couch, his weight clinking the ice in her glass. The projector was still rewinding.

"I think I'll stretch out for a few minutes if you don't mind," she said. "No, don't move, I have plenty of room. Wake me if I drop off, okay?"

She lay on the couch, holding the glass on her stomach, the tips of her hair just touching his hand beside his thigh.

He flicked the remote switch and the film began.

Dolarhyde had wanted to watch his Leeds film or his Jacobi film with this woman in the room. He wanted to look back and forth from the screen to Reba. He knew she would never survive that. The women saw her getting into his van. Don't even think about that. The women saw her getting into his van.

He would watch his film of the Shermans, the people he would visit next. He would see the promise of relief to come, and do it in Reba's presence, looking at her all he liked.

On the screen, *The New House* spelled in pennies on a shirt cardboard. A long shot of Mrs. Sherman and the children. Fun in the pool. Mrs. Sherman holds to the ladder and looks up at the camera, bosom swelling shining wet above her suit, pale legs scissoring.

Dolarhyde was proud of his self-control. He would think of this film, not the other ones. But in his mind he began to speak to Mrs. Sherman as he had spoken to Valerie Leeds in Atlanta.

You see me now, yes

That's how you feel to see me, yes

Fun with old clothes. Mrs. Sherman has the wide hat on. She is before the mirror. She turns with an arch smile and strikes a pose for the camera, her hand at the back of her neck. There is a cameo at her throat.

Reba McClane stirs on the couch. She sets her glass on the floor. Dolarhyde feels a weight and warmth. She has rested her head on his thigh. The nape of her neck is pale and the movie light plays on it.

He sits very still, moves only his thumb to stop the film, back it up. On the screen, Mrs. Sherman poses before the mirror in that hat. She turns to the camera and smiles.

You see me now, yes
That's how you feel to see me, yes
Do you feel me now? yes

Dolarhyde is trembling. His trousers are mashing him so hard. He feels heat. He feels warm breath through the cloth. Reba has made a discovery.

Convulsively his thumb works the switch.

You see me now, yes
That's how you feel to see me, yes
Do you feel me now? yes

Reba has unzipped his trousers.

A stab of fear in him; he has never been erect before in the presence of a living woman. He is the Dragon, he doesn't have to be afraid.

Busy fingers spring him free.

OH.

Do you feel me now? yes
Do you feel this yes
You do I know it yes
Your heart is loud yes

He must keep his hands off Reba's neck. Keep them off. The women saw them in the van. His hand is squeezing the arm of the couch. His fingers pop through the upholstery.

Your heart is loud yes
and fluttering now
It's fluttering now
It's trying to get out yes
And now it's quick and light and quicker and light and . . .
Gone.
Oh, Gone.

Reba rests her head on his thigh and turns her gleaming cheek to him. She runs her hand inside his shirt and rests it warm on his chest.

"I hope I didn't shock you," she said.

It was the sound of her living voice that shocked him and he felt to see if her heart was going and it was. She held his hand there gently.

"My goodness, you're not through yet, are you?"

A living woman. How bizarre. Filled with power, the Dragon's or his own, he lifted her from the couch easily. She weighed nothing, so much easier to carry because she wasn't limp. Not upstairs. Not upstairs. Hurrying now. Somewhere. Quick. Grandmother's bed, the satin comforter sliding under them.

"Oh, wait, I'll get them off. Oh now it's torn. I don't care. Come on. My God, man. That's so sweeet. Don't please hold me down, let me come up to you and take it."

With Reba, his only living woman, held with her in this one bubbleskin of time, he felt for the first time that it was all right: it was his life he was releasing, himself past all mortality that he was sending into her starry darkness, away from this pain planet, ringing harmonic distances away to peace and the promise of rest.

Beside her in the dark, he put his hand on her and pressed her together gently to seal the way back. As she slept Dolarhyde, damned murderer of eleven, listened time and again to her heart.

Images. Baroque pearls flying through the friendly dark. A Very pistol he had fired at the moon. A great firework he saw in Hong Kong called "The Dragon Sows His Pearls."

The Dragon.

He felt stunned, cloven. And all the long night beside her he listened, fearful, for himself coming down the stairs in the kimono.

She stirred once in the night, searching sleepily until she found the bedside glass. Grandmother's teeth rattled in it.

Dolarhyde brought her water. She held him in the dark. When she slept again, he took her hand off his great tattoo and put it on his face.

He slept hard at dawn.

Reba McClane woke at nine and heard his steady breathing. She stretched lazily in the big bed. He didn't stir. She reviewed the layout of the house, the order of rugs and floor, the direction of the ticking clock. When she had it straight, she rose quietly and found the bathroom.

After her long shower, he was still asleep. Her torn underclothes were on the floor. She found them with her feet and stuffed them in her purse. She pulled her cotton dress on over her head, picked up her cane and walked outside.

He had told her the yard was large and level, bounded by hedges grown wild, but she was cautious at first.

The morning breeze was cool, the sun warm. She stood in the yard and let the wind toss the seed heads of the elderberry through her hands. The wind found the creases of her body, fresh from the shower. She raised both arms to it and the wind blew cool beneath her breasts and arms and between her legs. Bees went by. She was not afraid of them and they left her alone.

Dolarhyde woke, puzzled for an instant because he was not in his room upstairs. His yellow eyes grew wide as he remembered. An owlish turn of his head to the other pillow. Empty.

Was she wandering around the house? What might she find? Or had something happened in the night? Something to clean up. He would be suspected. He might have to run.

He looked in the bathroom, in the kitchen. Down in the basement where his other wheelchair stood. The upper floor. He didn't want to go upstairs. He had to look. His tattoo flexed as he climbed the stairs. The Dragon glowed at him from the picture in his bedroom. He could not stay in the room with the Dragon.

From an upstairs window he spotted her in the yard.

"*FRANCIS.*" He knew the voice came from his room. He knew it was the voice of the Dragon. This new twoness with the Dragon disorientated him. He first felt it when he put his hand on Reba's heart.

The Dragon had never spoken *to* him before. It was frightening.

"*FRANCIS, COME HERE.*"

He tried to shut out the voice calling him, calling him as he hurried down the stairs.

What could she have found? Grandmother's teeth had rattled in the glass, but he put them away when he brought her water. She couldn't see anything.

Freddy's tape. It was in a cassette recorder in the parlour. He checked it. The cassette was rewound to the beginning. He couldn't remember if he had rewound it after he played it on the telephone to the *Tattler.*

She must not come back in the house. He didn't know what might happen in the house. She might get a surprise. The Dragon might come down. He knew how easily she would tear.

The women saw her getting in his van. Warfield would remember them together. Hurriedly he dressed.

Reba McClane felt the cool bar of a tree trunk's shadow, and then the sun again as she wandered across the yard. She could always tell where she was by the heat of the sun and the hum of the window air-conditioner. Navigation, her life's discipline, was easy here. She turned around and around, trailing her hands on the shrubs and overgrown flowers.

A cloud blocked the sun and she stopped, not knowing in which direction she faced. She listened for the air-conditioner. It was off. She felt a moment of uneasiness, then clapped her hands and heard the reassuring echo from the house. Reba slipped up her watch crystal and felt the time. She'd have to wake D. soon. She needed to go home.

The screen door slammed.

"Good morning," she said.

His keys tinkled as he came across the grass.

He approached her cautiously, as though the wind of his coming might blow her down, and saw that she was not afraid of him.

She didn't seem embarrassed or ashamed of what they had done in the night. She didn't seem angry. She didn't run from him or threaten him. He wondered if it was because she had not seen his private parts.

Reba put her arms around him and laid her head on his hard chest. His heart was going fast.

He managed to say "Good morning."

"I've had a really terrific time, D."

Really? What would someone say back? "Good. Me too." *That seemed all right. Get her away from here.*

"But I need to go home now," she was saying. "My sister's coming to pick me up for lunch. You could come too if you like."

"I have to go to the plant," he said, modifying the lie he had ready.

"I'll get my purse."

Oh no. "I'll get it."

Almost blind to his own true feelings, no more able to express them than a scar can blush, Dolarhyde did not know what had happened to him with Reba McClane, or why. He was confused, spiked with new fright at being Two.

She threatened him, she did not threaten him.

There was the matter of her startling live movements of acceptance in Grandmother's bed.

Often Dolarhyde did not find out what he felt until he acted. He didn't know how he felt toward Reba McClane.

An ugly incident as he drove her home enlightened him a little.

Just past the Lindbergh Boulevard exit off Interstate 70, Dolarhyde pulled into a Servco Supreme station to fill his van.

The attendant was a heavyset, sullen man with muscatel on his breath. He made a face when Dolarhyde asked him to check the oil.

The van was a quart low. The attendant jammed the oil spout into the can and stuck the spout into the engine.

Dolarhyde climbed out to pay.

The attendant seemed enthusiastic about wiping the windshield; the passenger side of the windshield. He wiped and wiped.

Reba McClane sat in the high bucket seat, her legs crossed, her skirt riding up over her knee. Her white cane lay between the seats.

The attendant started over on the windshield. He was looking up her dress.

Dolarhyde glanced up from his wallet and caught him. He reached in through the window of the van and turned the wipers on high speed, batting the attendant's fingers.

"Hey, watch that." The attendant got busy removing the oil can from the engine compartment. He knew he was caught and he wore a sly grin until Dolarhyde came around the van to him.

"You son of a bitch." Fast over the "s".

"What the hell's the matter with you?" The attendant was about Dolarhyde's weight and height, but he had nowhere near the muscle. He was young to have dentures and he didn't take care of them.

Their greenness disgusted Dolarhyde. "What happened to your teeth?" he asked softly.

"What's it to you?"

"Did you pull them for your boyfriend, you rotten prick?" Dolarhyde stood too close.

"Get the hell away from me."

Quietly. "Pig. Idiot. Trash. Fool."

With a one-hand shove Dolarhyde sent him flying back to slam against the van. The oil can and spout clattered on the asphalt.

Dolarhyde picked it up.

"Don't run. I can catch you." He pulled the spout from the can and looked at its sharp end.

The attendant was pale. There was something in Dolarhyde's face that he had never seen before, anywhere.

For a red instant Dolarhyde saw the spout jammed in the man's chest, draining his heart. He saw Reba's face through the windshield. She was shaking her head, saying something. She was trying to find the handle to roll her window down.

"Ever had anything broken, ass eyes?"

The attendant shook his head fast. "I didn't mean no offence, now. Honest to God."

Dolarhyde held the curved metal spout in front of the man's face. He held it in both hands and his chest muscles bunched as he bent it double. He pulled out the man's waistband and dropped the spout down the front of his pants.

"Keep your pig eyes to yourself." He stuffed money for the gas in the man's shirt pocket. "You can run now," he said. "But I could catch you any time."

36

THE TAPE came on Saturday in a small package addressed to Will Graham c/o F.B.I. Headquarters, Washington. It had been mailed in Chicago on the day Lounds was killed.

The laboratory and Latent Prints found nothing useful on the cassette case or the wrapper.

A copy of the tape went to Chicago in the afternoon pouch. Special Agent Chester brought it to Graham in the jury room at mid-afternoon. A memo from Lloyd Bowman was attached.

Voiceprints verify this is Lounds. Obviously he was repeating dictation [Bowman wrote]. *It's a new tape, manufactured in the last three months and never used before. Behavioural Science is picking at the content. Dr. Bloom should hear that when he's well enough—you decide about that.*

Clearly the killer's trying to rattle you.

He'll do that once too often, I think.

A dry vote of confidence, much appreciated.

Graham knew he had to listen to the tape. He waited until Chester left.

He didn't want to be closed up in the jury room with it. The empty courtroom was better—some sun came in the tall windows.

The cleaning women had been in and dust still hung in the sunlight.

The tape recorder was small and grey. Graham put it on a counsel table and pushed the button.

A technician's monotone: "Case number 426238, item 814, tagged and logged, a tape cassette. This is a re-recording."

A shift in the quality of sound.

Graham held on to the railing of the jury box with both hands.

Freddy Lounds sounded tired and frightened.

"I have had a great privilege. I have seen . . . I have seen with wonder . . . wonder and awe . . . awe . . . the strength of the Great Red Dragon."

The original recording had been interrupted frequently as it was made. The machine caught the clack of the stop key each time. Graham saw the finger on the key. Dragon finger.

"I lied about Him. All I wrote was lies from Will Graham. He made me write them. I have . . . I have blasphemed against the Dragon. Even so . . . the Dragon is merciful. Now I want to serve Him. He . . . has helped me understand . . . His Splendour and I will praise Him. Newspapers, when you print this always capitalize the H in 'Him'.

"He knows you made me lie, Will Graham. Because I was forced to lie, He will be more . . . more merciful to me than to you, Will Graham.

"Reach behind you, Will Graham . . . and feel for the small . . . knobs on the top of your pelvis. Feel your spine between them . . . that is the precise spot . . . where the Dragon will snap your spine."

Graham kept his hands on the railing. Damn if I'll feel. Did the Dragon now know the nomenclature of the iliac spine, or did he choose not to use it?

"There's much . . . for you to dread. From . . . from my own lips you'll learn a little more to dread."

A pause before the awful screaming. Worse, the blubbering lipless cry, "You Goddanned astard you romised."

Graham put his head between his knees until the bright spots stopped dancing in front of his eyes. He opened his mouth and breathed deep.

An hour passed before he could listen to it again.

He took the recorder into the jury room and tried to listen there. Too close. He left the tape recorder turning and went back into the courtroom. He could hear through the open door.

"I have had a great privilege . . ."

Someone was at the courtroom door. Graham recognized the young clerk from the Chicago F.B.I. office and motioned him to come in.

"A letter came for you," the clerk said. "Mr. Chester sent me with it. He told me to be sure and say the postal inspector fluoroscoped it."

The clerk pulled the letter out of his breast pocket. Heavy mauve stationery. Graham hoped it was from Molly.

"It's stamped, see?"

"Thank you."

"Also it's payday." The clerk handed him his cheque.

On the tape, Freddy screamed.

The young man flinched.

"Sorry," Graham said.

"I don't see how you stand it," the young man said.

"Go home," Graham said.

He sat in the jury box to read his letter. He wanted some relief. The letter was from Dr. Hannibal Lecter.

Dear Will.

A brief note of congratulations for the job you did on Mr. Lounds. I admired it enormously. What a cunning boy you are!

Mr. Lounds often offended me with his ignorant drivel, but he did enlighten me on one thing—your confinement in the mental hospital. My inept attorney should have brought that out in court, but never mind.

You know, Will, you worry too much. You'd be so much more comfortable if you relaxed with yourself.

We don't invent our natures, Will; they're issued to us along with our lungs and pancreas and everything else. Why fight it?

I want to help you, Will, and I'd like to start by asking you this: when you were so depressed after you shot Mr. Garrett Jacob Hobbs to death, it wasn't the *act* that got you down, was it? Really, didn't you feel so bad *because killing him felt so good?*

Think about it, but don't worry about it. Why shouldn't it feel good? It must feel good to God—He does it all the time, and are we not made in His image?

You may have noticed in the paper yesterday, God dropped a church roof on thirty-four of His worshippers in Texas Wednesday night—just as they were grovelling through a hymn. Don't you think that felt good? *Thirty-four.* He'd let you have Hobbs.

He got 160 Filipinos in one plane crash last week—He'll let you have measly Hobbs. He won't begrudge you one measly murder. Two now. That's all right.

Watch the papers. God always stays ahead.

Best,

Hannibal Lecter, M.D.

Graham knew that Lecter was dead wrong about Hobbs, but for a half-second he wondered if Lecter might be a little bit right in the case of Freddy Lounds. The enemy inside Graham agreed with any accusations.

He had put his hand on Freddy's shoulder in the *Tattler* photographs to establish that he really had told Freddy those insulting things about the Dragon. Or had he wanted to put Freddy at risk, just a little? He wondered.

The certain knowledge that he would not knowingly miss a chance at the Dragon reprieved him.

"I'm just about worn out with you crazy sons of bitches," Graham said aloud.

He wanted a break. He called Molly but no one answered the telephone at Willy's grandparents' house. "Probably out in their damned motor-home," he mumbled.

He went out for coffee, partly to assure himself that he was not hiding in the jury room.

In the window of a jewellery store he saw a delicate antique gold bracelet. It cost him most of his pay cheque. He had it wrapped and stamped for mailing. Only when he was sure he was alone at the mail drop did he address it to Molly in Oregon. Graham did not realize, as Molly did, that he gave presents when he was angry.

He didn't want to go back to his jury room and work, but he had to. The thought of Valerie Leeds spurred him.

I'm sorry I can't come to the phone right now, Valerie Leeds had said.

He wished that he had known her. He wished—useless, childish thought.

Graham was tired, selfish, resentful, fatigued to a child-minded state in which his standards of measurement were the first ones he learned; where the direction "north" was Highway 61 and "six feet" was forever the length of his father.

He made himself settle down to the minutely detailed victim profile he was putting together from a fan of reports and his own observations.

Affluence. That was one parallel. Both families were affluent. Odd that Valerie Leeds saved money on pantyhose.

Graham wondered if she had been a poor child. He thought so; her own children were a little too well turned out.

Graham had been a poor child, following his father from the

boat-yards in Biloxi and Greenville to the lake boats on Erie. Always the new boy at school, always the stranger. He had a half-buried grudge against the rich.

Valerie Leeds might have been a poor child. He was tempted to watch his film of her again. He could do it in the courtroom. No. The Leeds were not his immediate problem. He knew the Leeds. He did not know the Jacobis.

His lack of intimate knowledge about the Jacobis plagued him. The house fire in Detroit had taken everything—family albums, probably diaries too.

Graham tried to know them through the objects they had wanted, bought and used. That was all he had.

The Jacobi probate file was three inches thick and a lot of it was lists of possessions—since the move to Birmingham. *Look at all this shit.* It was all insured, listed with serial numbers as the insurance companies required. Trust a man who has been burned out to buy plenty of insurance for next time.

The attorney, Byron Metcalf, had sent him carbons instead of Xeroxes of the insurance declarations. The carbons were fuzzy and hard to read.

Jacobi had a ski-boat, Leeds had a ski-boat. Jacobi had a three-wheeler, Leeds had a trail-bike. Graham licked his thumb and turned the page.

The fourth item on the second page was a Chinon Pacific movie projector.

Graham stopped. How had he missed it? He had looked through every crate on every pallet in the Birmingham warehouse, alert for anything that would give him an intimate view of the Jacobis.

Where was the projector? He could cross-check this insurance declaration against the inventory Byron Metcalf had prepared as executor when he stored the Jacobis' things. The items had been checked off by the warehouse supervisor who signed the storage contract.

It took fifteen minutes to go down the list of stored items. No projector, no camera, no film.

Graham leaned back in his chair and stared at the Jacobis smiling from the picture propped before him.

What the hell did you do with it?

Was it stolen?

Did the killer steal it?

If the killer stole it, did he fence it?

Dear God, give me a traceable fence.

Graham wasn't tired any more. He wanted to know if anything else was missing. He looked for an hour, comparing the warehouse storage inventory with the insurance declarations. Everything was accounted for except the small precious items. They should all be on Byron Metcalf's own lock box list of things he had put in the bank vault in Birmingham.

All of them were on the list. Except two.

"Crystal oddment box, 4″ × 3″, sterling silver lid" appeared on the insurance declaration, but was not in the lock box. "Sterling picture-frame, 9″ × 11″, worked with vines and flowers" wasn't in the vault either.

Stolen? Mislaid? They were small items, easily concealed. Usually fenced silver is melted down immediately. It would be hard to trace. But movie equipment had serial numbers inside and out. It could be traced.

Was the killer the thief?

As he stared at his stained photograph of the Jacobis, Graham felt the sweet jolt of a new connection. But when he saw the answer whole it was seedy and disappointing and small.

There was a telephone in the jury room. Graham called Birmingham Homicide. He got the three-to-eleven watch commander.

"In the Jacobi case I noticed you kept an in-and-out log at the house after it was sealed off, right?"

"Let me get somebody to look," the watch commander said.

Graham knew they kept one. It was good procedure to record every person entering or leaving a murder scene, and Graham had been pleased to see that Birmingham did it. He waited five minutes before a clerk picked up the telephone.

"Okay, in-and-out, what do you want to know?"

"Is Niles Jacobi, son of the deceased—is he on it?"

"Umm hmmm, yep. July 2nd, 7 p.m. He had permission to get personal items."

"Did he have a suitcase, does it say?"

"Nope. Sorry."

Byron Metcalf's voice was husky and his breathing heavy when he answered the telephone. Graham wondered what he was doing.

"Hope I didn't disturb you."

"What can I do for you, Will?"

"I need a little help with Niles Jacobi."

"What's he done now?"

"I think he lifted a few things out of the Jacobi house after they were killed."

"Ummm."

"There's a sterling picture-frame missing from your lock box inventory. When I was in Birmingham I picked up a loose photograph of the family in Niles's dormitory room. It used to be in a frame—I can see the impression that mat left on it."

"The little bastard. I gave permission for him to get his clothes and some books he needed," Metcalf said.

"Niles has expensive friendships. This is mainly what I'm after though—a movie projector and a movie camera are missing too. I want to know if he got them. Probably he did, but if he *didn't*, maybe the killer got them. In that case we need to get the serial numbers out to the hock shops. We need to put 'em on the national hot sheet. The frame's probably melted down by now."

"He'll think 'frame' when I get through with him."

"One thing—if Niles took the projector he might have kept the film. He couldn't get anything for it. I want the film. I need to see it. If you come at him from the front, he'll deny everything and flush the film if he has any."

"Okay," Metcalf said. "His car title reverted to the estate. I'm executor so I can search it without a warrant. My friend the judge won't mind papering his room for me. I'll call you."

Graham went back to his work.

Affluence. Put affluence in the profile the police could use.

Graham wondered if Mrs. Leeds and Mrs. Jacobi ever did their marketing in tennis clothes. That was a fashionable thing to do in some areas. It was a dumb thing to do in some areas because it was doubly provocative—arousing class resentment and lust at the same time.

Graham imagined them pushing grocery carts, short pleated skirts brushing the brown thighs, the little balls on their sweat socks winking—passing the husky man with the barracuda eyes who was buying cold lunch meat to gnaw in his car.

How many families were there with three children and a pet, and only common locks between them and the Dragon as they slept?

When Graham pictured possible victims, he saw clever, successful people in graceful houses.

But the next person to confront the Dragon did not have children or a pet, and there was no grace in his house. The next person to confront the Dragon was Francis Dolarhyde.

37

THE THUMP of weights on the attic floor carried through the old house.

Dolarhyde was lifting, straining, pumping more weight than he had ever lifted. His costume was different; sweatpants covered his tattoo. The sweatshirt hung over *The Great Red Dragon and the Woman Clothed with the Sun*. The kimono hung on the wall like the shed skin of a tree snake. It covered the mirror.

Dolarhyde wore no mask.

Up. Two hundred and eighty pounds from the floor to his chest in one heave. Now over his head.

"WHOM ARE YOU THINKING ABOUT?"

Startled by the voice, he nearly dropped the weight, swayed beneath it. Down. The plates thudded and clanked on the floor.

He turned, his great arms hanging, and stared in the direction of the voice.

"WHOM ARE YOU THINKING ABOUT?"

It seemed to come from behind the sweatshirt, but its rasp and volume hurt his throat.

"WHOM ARE YOU THINKING ABOUT?"

He knew who spoke and he was frightened. From the beginning, he and the Dragon had been one. He was Becoming and the Dragon was his higher self. Their bodies, voices, wills were one.

Not now. Not since Reba. Don't think Reba.

"*WHO IS ACCEPTABLE?*" the Dragon asked.

"Mrs. . . . erhman—Sherman." It was hard for Dolarhyde to say.

"*SPEAK UP. I CAN'T UNDERSTAND YOU. WHOM ARE YOU THINKING ABOUT?*"

Dolarhyde, his face set, turned to the barbell. Up. Over his head. Much harder this time.

"Mrs. . . . erhman wet in the water."

"*YOU THINK ABOUT YOUR LITTLE BUDDY, DON'T YOU? YOU WANT HER TO BE YOUR LITTLE BUDDY, DON'T YOU?*"

The weight came down with a thud.

"I 'ont have a lil . . . huddy." With the fear his speech was failing. He had to occlude his nostrils with his upper lip.

"*A STUPID LIE.*" The Dragon's voice was strong and clear. He said the "s" without effort. "*YOU FORGET THE BECOMING. PREPARE FOR THE SHERMANS. LIFT THE WEIGHT.*"

Dolarhyde seized the barbell and strained. His mind strained with his body. Desperately he tried to think of the Shermans. He forced himself to think of the weight of Mrs. Sherman in his arms. Mrs. Sherman was next. It was Mrs. Sherman. He was fighting Mr. Sherman in the dark. Holding him down until loss of blood made Sherman's heart quiver like a bird. It was the only heart he heard. He didn't hear Reba's heart. He didn't.

Fear leeched his strength. He got the weight up to his thighs, could not make the turn up to his chest. He thought of the Shermans ranged around him, eyes wide, as he took the Dragon's due. It was no good. It was hollow, empty. The weight thudded down.

"NOT ACCEPTABLE."

"Mrs. . . ."

"YOU CAN'T EVEN SAY MRS. SHERMAN. YOU NEVER INTEND TO TAKE THE SHERMANS. YOU WANT REBA McCLANE. YOU WANT HER TO BE YOUR LITTLE BUDDY, DON'T YOU? YOU WANT TO BE 'FRIENDS'."

"No."

"LIE!"

"Nyus mhor a niddow wyow."

"JUST FOR A LITTLE WHILE? YOU SNIVELLING HARELIP, WHO WOULD BE FRIENDS WITH YOU? COME HERE. I'LL SHOW YOU WHAT YOU ARE."

Dolarhyde did not move.

"I'VE NEVER SEEN A CHILD AS DISGUSTING AND DIRTY AS YOU. COME HERE."

He went.

"TAKE DOWN THE SWEATSHIRT."

He took it down.

"LOOK AT ME."

The Dragon glowed from the wall.

"TAKE DOWN THE KIMONO. LOOK IN THE MIRROR."

He looked. He could not help himself or turn his face from the scalding light. He saw himself drool.

"LOOK AT YOURSELF. I'M GOING TO GIVE YOU A SUR-PRISE FOR YOUR LITTLE BUDDY. TAKE OFF THAT RAG."

Dolarhyde's hands fought each other at the waistband of the sweatpants. The sweatpants tore. He stripped them away from him with his right hand, held the rags to him with his left.

His right hand snatched the rags away from his trembling, failing left. He threw them into the corner and fell back on the mat, curling himself like a lobster split live. He hugged himself and groaned, breathing hard, his tattoo brilliant in the harsh gym lights.

*"I'VE NEVER SEEN A CHILD AS DISGUSTING AND DIRTY
AS YOU. GO GET THEM."*

"Aaaymah."

"GET THEM."

He padded from the room and returned with the Dragon's teeth.

*"PUT THEM IN YOUR PALMS. LOCK YOUR FINGERS AND
SQUEEZE MY TEETH TOGETHER."*

Dolarhyde's pectoral muscles bunched.

*"YOU KNOW HOW THEY CAN SNAP. NOW HOLD THEM
UNDER YOUR BELLY. HOLD YOURSELF BETWEEN THE
TEETH."*

"No."

"DO IT . . . NOW LOOK."

The teeth were beginning to hurt him. Spit and tears fell on
his chest.

"Mleadse."

*"YOU ARE OFFAL LEFT BEHIND IN THE BECOMING.
YOU ARE OFFAL AND I WILL NAME YOU. YOU ARE CUNT
FACE. SAY IT."*

"I am cunt face." He occluded his nostrils with his lip to say
the words.

"SOON I WILL BE CLEANSED OF YOU," the Dragon said
effortlessly. *"WILL THAT BE GOOD?"*

"Good."

"WHO WILL BE NEXT WHEN IT IS TIME?"

"Mrs. . . . erhman—"

Sharp pain shot through Dolarhyde, pain and terrible fear.

"I'LL TEAR IT OFF."

"Reba. Reba. I'll give you Reba." Already his speech was improving.

*"YOU'LL GIVE ME NOTHING. SHE IS MINE. THEY ARE
ALL MINE. REBA McCLANE AND THEN THE SHERMANS."*

"Reba and then the Shermans, the law will know."

"*I HAVE PROVIDED FOR THAT DAY. DO YOU DOUBT IT?*"

"No."

"*WHO ARE YOU?*"

"Cunt face."

"*YOU MAY PUT AWAY MY TEETH. YOU PITIFUL WEAK HARELIP, YOU'D KEEP YOUR LITTLE BUDDY FROM ME, WOULD YOU? I'LL TEAR HER APART AND RUB THE PIECES IN YOUR UGLY FACE. I'LL HANG YOU WITH HER LARGE INTESTINE IF YOU OPPOSE ME. YOU KNOW I CAN. PUT 300 POUNDS ON THE BAR.*"

Dolarhyde added the plates to the bar. He had never lifted as much as 280 until today.

"*LIFT IT.*"

If he were not as strong as the Dragon, Reba would die. He knew it. He strained until the room turned red before his bulging eyes.

"I can't."

"*NO YOU CAN'T. BUT I CAN.*"

Dolarhyde gripped the bar. It bowed as the weight rose to his shoulders. UP. Above his head easily. "*GOODBYE, CUNT FACE,*" he said, proud Dragon, quivering in the light.

38

FRANCIS DOLARHYDE never got to work on Monday morning.

He started from his house exactly on time, as he always did. His appearance was impeccable, his driving precise. He put on his dark glasses when he made the turn at the Missouri River bridge and drove into the morning sun.

His styrofoam cooler squeaked as it jiggled against the passenger seat. He leaned across and set it on the floor, remembering that he must pick up the dry ice and get the film from . . .

Crossing the Missouri channel now, moving water under him. He looked at the whitecaps on the sliding river and suddenly felt that he was sliding and the river was still. A strange, disjointed, collapsing feeling flooded him. He let up on the accelerator.

The van slowed in the outside lane and stopped. Traffic behind him was stacking up, honking. He didn't hear it.

He sat, sliding slowly northward over the still river, facing the morning sun. Tears leaked from beneath his sunglasses and fell hot on his forearms.

Someone was pecking on the window. A driver, face early-morning pale and puffed with sleep, had gotten out of a car behind him. The driver was yelling something through the window.

Dolarhyde looked at the man. Flashing blue lights were coming from the other side of the bridge. He knew he should drive. He asked his body to step on the gas and it did. The man beside the van skipped backward to save his feet.

Dolarhyde pulled into the parking lot of a big motel near the U.S. 270 interchange. A school bus was parked in the lot, the bell of a tuba leaning against its back window.

Dolarhyde wondered if he was supposed to get on the bus with the old people.

No, that wasn't it. He looked around for his mother's Packard.

"*Get in. Don't put your feet on the seat,*" his mother said.

That wasn't it either.

He was in a motel parking lot on the west side of St. Louis and he wanted to be able to Choose and he couldn't.

In six days, if he could wait that long, he would kill Reba McClane. He made a sudden high sound through his nose.

Maybe the Dragon would be willing to take the Shermans first and wait another moon.

No. He wouldn't.

Reba McClane didn't know about the Dragon. She thought she was with Francis Dolarhyde. She wanted to put her body on Francis Dolarhyde. She welcomed Francis Dolarhyde in Grandmother's bed.

"*I've had a really terrific time, D,*" Reba McClane said in the yard.

Maybe she liked Francis Dolarhyde. That was a perverted, despicable thing for a woman to do. He understood that he should despise her for it, but Oh God it was good.

Reba McClane was guilty of liking Francis Dolarhyde. Demonstrably guilty.

If it weren't for the power of his Becoming, if it weren't for the Dragon, he could never have taken her into his house. He would not have been capable of sex. Or would he?

"*Oh my God, man, that's so sweeet.*"

That's what she said. She said "man".

The breakfast crowd was coming out of the motel, passing his van. Their idle glances walked on him with many tiny feet.

He needed to think. He couldn't go home. He checked into the motel, called his office and reported himself sick. The room he got was bland and quiet. The only decorations were bad steamboat prints. Nothing glowed from the walls.

Dolarhyde lay down in his clothes. The ceiling had sparkling flecks in the spackle. Every few minutes he had to get up and urinate. He shivered, then he sweated. An hour passed.

He did not want to give Reba McClane to the Dragon. He thought about what the Dragon would do to him if he didn't serve her up.

Intense fear comes in waves; the body can't stand it for long at a time. In the heavy calm between the waves, Dolarhyde could think.

How could he keep from giving her to the Dragon? One way kept nudging him. He got up.

The light switch clacked loud in the tiled bathroom. Dolarhyde looked at the shower curtain-rod, a solid piece of one-inch pipe bolted to the bathroom walls. He took down the shower curtain and hung it over the mirror.

Grasping the pipe he chinned himself with one arm, his toes dragging up the side of the bathtub. It was stout enough. His belt was stout enough too. He could make himself do it. He wasn't afraid of *that*.

He tied the end of his belt around the pipe in a bowline knot. The buckle end formed a noose. The thick belt didn't swing, it hung down in a stiff noose.

He sat on the toilet lid and looked at it. He wouldn't get any drop, but he could stand it. He could keep his hands off the noose until he was too weak to raise his arms.

But how could he be sure his death would affect the Dragon, now that he and the Dragon were Two? Maybe it wouldn't. How could he be sure the Dragon then would leave her alone?

It might be days before they found his body. She would wonder where he was. In that time would she go to his house and feel around for him? Go upstairs and feel around for him and get a surprise?

The Great Red Dragon would take an hour spitting her down the stairs.

Should he call her and warn her? What could she do against Him, even warned? Nothing. She could hope to die quickly, hope that in His rage He would quickly bite deep enough.

Upstairs in Dolarhyde's house, the Dragon waited in pictures he had framed with his own hands. The Dragon waited in art books and magazines beyond number, reborn every time a photographer . . . did what?

Dolarhyde could hear in his mind the Dragon's powerful voice cursing Reba. He would curse her first, before he bit. He would curse Dolarhyde too—tell her he was nothing.

"Don't do that. Don't . . . do that," Dolarhyde said to the echoing tile. He listened to his voice, the voice of Francis Dolarhyde, the voice that Reba McClane understood easily, his own voice. He had been ashamed of it all his life, had said bitter and vicious things to others with it.

But he had never heard the voice of Francis Dolarhyde curse him. "Don't do that."

The voice he heard now had never, ever cursed him. It had repeated the Dragon's abuse. The memory shamed him.

He was probably not much of a man, he thought. It occurred to him that he had never really found out about that and now he was curious.

He had one rag of pride that Reba McClane had given him. It told him dying in a bathroom was a sorry end.

What else? What other way was there?

There was a way and when it came to him it was blasphemy, he knew. But it was a way.

He paced the motel room, paced between the beds, and from the door to the windows. As he walked he practiced speaking. The words came out all right if he breathed deep between the sentences and didn't hurry.

He could talk very well between the rushes of fear. Now he had a bad one, he had one that made him retch. A calm was coming after. He waited for it and when it came he hurried to the telephone and placed a call to Brooklyn.

A junior high school band was getting on the bus in the motel parking lot. The children saw Dolarhyde coming. He had to go through them to get to his van.

A fat, round-faced boy with his Sam Browne belt all crooked put on a scowl, puffed up his chest and flexed his biceps after Dolarhyde passed. Two girls giggled. The tuba blatted out the bus window as Dolarhyde went by and he never heard the laughter behind him.

In twenty minutes he stopped the van in the lane three hundred yards from Grandmother's house.

He mopped his face, inhaled deeply three or four times. He gripped his house key in his left hand, the steering wheel with his right.

A high keening sounded through his nose. And again louder. Louder, louder again. Go.

Gravel showered behind the van as it shot forward, the house bouncing bigger in the windshield. The van slid sideways into the yard and Dolarhyde was out of it, running.

Inside, not looking left or right, pounding down the basement stairs, fumbling at the padlocked trunk in the basement, looking at his keys.

The trunk keys were upstairs. He didn't give himself time to think.

A high humming through his nose as loud as he could to numb thought, drown out voices as he climbed the stairs at a run.

At the bureau now, fumbling in the drawer for the keys, not looking at the picture of the Dragon at the foot of the bed. "*WHAT ARE YOU DOING?*"

Where were the keys, where were they keys?

"*WHAT ARE YOU DOING? STOP. I'VE NEVER SEEN A CHILD AS DISGUSTING AND DIRTY AS YOU. STOP.*"

His searching hands slowed.

"*LOOK . . . LOOK AT ME.*"

He gripped the edge of the bureau—tried not to turn to the wall. He cut his eyes painfully away as his head turned in spite of him.

"*WHAT ARE YOU DOING?*"

"Nothing."

The telephone was ringing, telephone ringing, telephone ringing. He picked it up, his back to the picture.

"Hey, D., how are you feeling?" Reba McClane's voice.

He cleared his throat. "Okay"—hardly a whisper.

"I tried to call you down here. Your office said you were sick— you sound terrible."

"Talk to me."

"Of course I'll talk to you. What do you think I called you for? What's wrong?"

"Flu," he said.

"Are you going to the doctor? . . . Hello? I said are you going to the doctor?"

"Talk loud." He scrabbled in the drawer, tried the drawer next to it.

"Have we got a bad connection? D., you shouldn't be there sick by yourself."

"*TELL HER TO COME OVER TONIGHT AND TAKE CARE OF YOU.*"

Dolarhyde almost got his hand over the mouth-piece in time.

"My God, what was that? Is somebody with you?"

"The radio, I grabbed the wrong knob."

"Hey, D., do you want me to send somebody? You don't sound so hot. I'll come myself. I'll get Marcia to bring me lunch."

"No." The keys were under a belt coiled in the drawer. He had them now. He backed into the hall, carrying the telephone. "I'm okay. I'll see you soon." The "s's nearly foundered him. He ran down the stairs. The phone cord jerked out of the wall and the telephone tumbled down the stairs behind him.

A scream of savage rage. "*COME HERE, CUNT FACE.*"

Down to the basement. In the trunk beside his case of dynamite was a small valise packed with cash, credit cards and driver's licences in various names, his pistol, knife and blackjack.

He grabbed the valise and ran up to the ground floor, quickly passed the stairs, ready to fight if the Dragon came down them. Into the van and driving hard, fishtailing in the gravel lane.

He slowed on the highway and pulled over to the shoulder to heave yellow bile. Some of the fear went away. Proceeding at legal speed, using his flashers well ahead of turns, carefully he drove to the airport.

39

DOLARHYDE PAID his taxi fare in front of an apartment house on Eastern Parkway two blocks from the Brooklyn Museum. He walked the rest of the way. Joggers passed him, heading for Prospect Park.

Standing on the traffic island near the I.R.T. subway station, he got a good view of the Greek Revival building. He had never seen the Brooklyn Museum before, though he had read its guidebook— he had ordered the book when he first saw "Brooklyn Museum" in the tiny letters beneath photographs of *The Great Red Dragon and the Woman Clothed with the Sun.*

The names of the great thinkers from Confucius to Demosthenes were carved in stone above the entrance. It was an imposing building with botanical gardens beside it, a fitting house for the Dragon.

The subway rumbled beneath the street, tingling the soles of his feet. Stale air puffed from the gratings and mixed with the smell of the dye in his moustache.

Only an hour left before closing-time. He crossed the street and went inside. The checkroom attendant took his valise.

"Will the checkroom be open tomorrow?" he asked.

"The museum's closed tomorrow." The attendant was a wizened

woman in a blue smock. She turned away from him.

"The people who come in tomorrow, do they use the check-room?"

"No. The museum's closed, the checkroom's closed."

Good. "Thank you."

"Don't mention it."

Dolarhyde cruised among the great glass cases in the Oceanic Hall and the Hall of the Americas on the ground floor—Andes pottery, primitive edged weapons, artifacts and powerful masks from the Indians of the Northwest coast.

Now there were only forty minutes left before the museum closed. There was no more time to learn the ground floor. He knew where the exits and the public elevators were.

He rode up to the fifth floor. He could feel that he was closer to the Dragon now, but it was all right—he wouldn't turn a corner and run into him.

The Dragon was not on public display; the painting had been locked away in the dark since its return from the Tate Gallery in London.

Dolarhyde had learned on the telephone that *The Great Red Dragon and the Woman Clothed with the Sun* was rarely displayed. It was almost two hundred years old and a watercolour—light would fade it.

Dolarhyde stopped in front of Albert Bierstadt's *A Storm in the Rocky Mountains—Mt. Rosalie 1866*. From there he could see the locked doors of the Painting Study and Storage Department. That's where the Dragon was. Not a copy, not a photograph: the Dragon. This is where he would come tomorrow when he had his appointment.

He walked around the perimeter of the fifth floor, past the corridor of portraits, seeing nothing of the paintings. The exits were what interested him. He found the fire exits and the main stairs, and marked the location of the public elevators.

The guards were polite middle-aged men in thick-soled shoes, years of standing in the set of their legs. None was armed, Dolarhyde noted; one of the guards in the lobby was armed. Maybe he was a moonlighting cop.

The announcement of closing-time came over the public address system.

Dolarhyde stood on the pavement under the allegorical figure of Brooklyn and watched the crowd come out into the pleasant summer evening.

Joggers ran in place, waiting while the stream of people crossed the sidewalk toward the subway.

Dolarhyde spent a few minutes in the botanical gardens. Then he flagged a taxi and gave the driver the address of a store he had found in the Yellow Pages.

40

AT 9 P.M. Monday Graham set his briefcase on the floor outside the Chicago apartment he was using and rooted in his pocket for the keys.

He had spent a long day in Detroit interviewing staff and checking employment records at the hospital where Mrs. Jacobi did volunteer work before the family moved to Birmingham. He was looking for a drifter, someone who might have worked in both Detroit and Atlanta or Birmingham and Atlanta; someone with access to a van and a wheelchair who saw Mrs. Jacobi and Mrs. Leeds before he broke into their houses.

Crawford thought the trip was a waste of time, but humoured him. Crawford had been right. Damn Crawford. He was right too much.

·Graham could hear the telephone ringing in the apartment. The keys caught in the lining of his pocket. When he jerked them out, a long thread came with them. Change spilled down the inside of his trouser leg and scattered on the floor.

"Son of a bitch."

He made it halfway across the room before the phone stopped ringing. Maybe that was Molly trying to reach him.

He called her in Oregon.

Willy's grandfather answered the telephone with his mouth full. It was supper time in Oregon.

"Just ask Molly to call me when she's finished," Graham told him.

He was in the shower with shampoo in his eyes when the telephone rang again. He sluiced his head and went dripping to grab the receiver. "Hello, Hotlips."

"You silver-tongued devil, this is Byron Metcalf in Birmingham."

"Sorry."

"I've got good news and bad. You were right about Niles Jacobi. He took the stuff out of the house. He'd gotten rid of it, but I squeezed him with some hash that was in his room and he owned up. That's the bad news—I know you hoped the Tooth Fairy stole it and fenced it.

"The good news is there's some film. I don't have it yet. Niles says there are two reels stuffed under the seat of his car. You still want it, right?"

"Sure, sure I do."

"Well, his intimate friend Randy's using the car and we haven't caught up with him yet, but it won't be long. Want me to put the film on the first plane to Chicago and call you when it's coming?"

"Please do. That's good, Byron, thanks."

"Nothing to it."

Molly called just as Graham was drifting off to sleep. After they assured each other that they were all right, there didn't seem to be much to say.

Willy was having a real good time, Molly said. She let Willy say good night.

Willy had plenty more to say than just good night—he told Will the exciting news: Grandpa bought him a pony.

Molly hadn't mentioned it.

THE BROOKLYN Museum is closed to the general public on Tuesdays, but art classes and refreshers are admitted.

The museum is an excellent facility for serious scholarship. The staff members are knowledgeable and accommodating; they often allow researchers to come by appointment on Tuesdays to see items not on public display.

Francis Dolarhyde came out of the I.R.T. subway station shortly after 2 p.m. on Tuesday carrying his scholarly materials. He had a notebook, a Tate Gallery catalogue and a biography of William Blake under his arm.

He had a flat 9mm pistol, a leather sap and his razor-edged filleting knife under his shirt. An elastic bandage held the weapons against his flat belly. His sport coat would button over them. A cloth soaked in chloroform and sealed in a plastic bag was in his coat pocket.

In his hand he carried a new guitar case.

Three pay telephones stand near the subway exit in the centre of Eastern Parkway. One of the telephones has been ripped out. One of the others works.

Dolarhyde fed it quarters until Reba said "Hello."

He could hear dark-room noises over her voice.

"Hello, Reba," he said.

"Hey, D. How're you feeling?"

Traffic passing on both sides made it hard for him to hear. "Okay."

"Sounds like you're at a pay phone. I thought you were home sick."

"I want to talk to you later."

"Okay. Call me late, all right?"

"I need to . . . see you."

"I want you to see me, but I can't tonight. I have to work. Will you call me?"

"Yeah. If nothing . . ."

"Excuse me?"

"I'll call."

"I do want you to come soon, D."

"Yeah. Goodbye . . . Reba."

All right. Fear trickled from his breastbone to his belly. He squeezed it and crossed the street.

Entrance to the Brooklyn Museum on Tuesdays is through a single door on the extreme right. Dolarhyde went in behind four art students. The students piled their knapsacks and satchels against the wall and got out their passes. The guard behind the desk checked them.

He came to Dolarhyde.

"Do you have an appointment?"

Dolarhyde nodded. "Painting Study, Miss Harper."

"Sign the register, please." The guard offered a pen.

Dolarhyde had his own pen ready. He signed "Paul Crane."

The guard dialed an upstairs extension. Dolarhyde turned his back to the desk and studied Robert Blum's *Vintage Festival* over the entrance while the guard confirmed his appointment. From the corner of his eye he could see one more security officer in the lobby. Yes, that was the one with the gun.

"Back of the lobby by the shop there's a bench next to the main elevators," the desk officer said. "Wait there. Miss Harper's coming down for you." He handed Dolarhyde a pink on white plastic badge.

"Okay if I leave my guitar here?"

"I'll keep an eye on it."

The museum was different with the lights turned down. There was twilight among the great glass cases.

Dolarhyde waited on the bench for three minutes before Miss Harper got off the public elevator.

"Mr. Crane? I'm Paula Harper."

She was younger than she had sounded on the telephone when he called from St. Louis; a sensible-looking woman, severely pretty. She wore her blouse and skirt like a uniform.

"You called about the Blake watercolour," she said. "Let's go upstairs and I'll show it to you. We'll take the staff elevator—this way."

She led him past the dark museum shop and through a small room lined with primitive weapons. He looked around fast to keep his bearings. In the corner of the Americas section was a corridor which led to the small elevator.

Miss Harper pushed the button. She hugged her elbows and waited. The clear blue eyes fell on the pass, pink on white, clipped to Dolarhyde's lapel.

"That's a sixth-floor pass he gave you," she said. "It doesn't matter—there aren't any guards on five today. What kind of research are you doing?"

Dolarhyde had made it on smiles and nods until now. "A paper on Butts," he said.

"On William Butts?"

He nodded.

"I've never read much on him. You only see him in footnotes as a patron of Blake's. Is he interesting?"

322   THOMAS HARRIS

"I'm just beginning. I'll have to go to England."

"I think the National Gallery has two watercolours he did for Butts. Have you seen them yet?"

"Not yet."

"Better write ahead of time."

He nodded. The elevator came.

Fifth floor. He was tingling a little, but he had blood in his arms and legs. Soon it would be just yes or no. If it went wrong he wouldn't let them take him.

She led him down the corridor of American portraits. This wasn't the way he came before. He could tell where he was. It was all right.

But something waited in the corridor for him and when he saw it he stopped dead still.

Paula Harper realized he wasn't following and turned around.

He was rigid before a niche in the wall of portraits.

She came back to him and saw what he was staring at.

"That's a Gilbert Stuart portrait of George Washington," she said.

No it wasn't.

"You see a similar one on the dollar bill. They call it a Lansdowne portrait because Stuart did one for the Marquis of Lansdowne to thank him for his support in the American Revolution—are you all right, Mr. Crane?"

Dolarhyde was pale. This was worse than all the dollar bills he had ever seen. Washington with his hooded eyes and bad false teeth stared out of the frame. My God he looked like Grandmother. Dolarhyde felt like a child with a rubber knife.

"Mr. Crane, are you okay?"

Answer or blow it all. Get past this *My God, man, that's so sweeet.* YOU'RE THE DIRTIEST—no.

Say something.

"I'm taking cobalt," he said.

"Would you like to sit down for a few minutes?" There *was* a faint medicinal smell about him.

"No. Go ahead. I'm coming."

And you are not going to cut me, Grandmother. God damn you, I'd kill you if you weren't already dead. Already dead. Already dead. Grandmother was already dead! Dead now, dead for always. My God, man, that's so sweeet.

The other wasn't dead though and Dolarhyde knew it.

He followed Miss Harper through thickets of fear.

They went through double doors into the Painting Study and Storage Department. Dolarhyde looked around quickly. It was a long, peaceful room, well-lighted and filled with carousel racks of draped paintings. A row of small office cubicles were partitioned off along the wall. The door to the cubicle on the far end was ajar and he heard typing.

He saw no one but Paula Harper.

She took him to a counter-height work-table and brought him a stool.

"Wait here. I'll bring the painting to you."

She disappeared behind the racks.

Dolarhyde undid a button at his belly.

Miss Harper was coming. She carried a flat black case no bigger than a briefcase. It was in there. How did she have the strength to carry the picture? He had never thought of it as flat. He had seen the dimensions in the catalogues—17⅛" × 13½"—but he had paid no attention to them. He expected it to be immense. But it was small. It was small and it was *here* in a quiet room. He had never realized how much strength the Dragon drew from the old house in the orchard.

Miss Harper was saying something "—have to keep it in this solander box because light will fade it. That's why it's not on display very often."

She put the case on the table and unclasped it. A noise at the double doors. "Excuse me, I have to get the door for Julio." She refastened the case and carried it with her to the glass doors. A man with a wheeled dolly waited outside. She held the doors open while he rolled it in.

"Over here okay?"

"Yes, thank you, Julio."

The man went out.

Here came Miss Harper with the solander box.

"I'm sorry, Mr. Crane. Julio's dusting today and getting the tarnish off some frames." She opened the case and took out a white cardboard folder. "You understand that you aren't allowed to touch it. I'll display it for you—that's the rule. Okay?"

Dolarhyde nodded. He couldn't speak.

She opened the folder and removed the covering plastic sheet and mat.

There it was. *The Great Red Dragon and the Woman Clothed with the Sun*—the Man-Dragon rampant over the prostrate pleading woman caught in a coil of his tail.

It was small all right, but it was powerful. Stunning. The best reproductions didn't do justice to the details and the colours.

Dolarhyde saw it clear, saw it all in an instant—Blake's handwriting on the borders, two brown spots at the right edge of the paper. It seized him hard. It was too much . . . the colours were so much stronger.

Look at the woman wrapped in the Dragon's tail. Look.

He saw that her hair was the exact colour of Reba McClane's. He saw that he was twenty feet from the door. He held in voices.

I hope I didn't shock you, said Reba McClane.

"It appears that he used chalk as well as watercolour," Paula Harper was saying. She stood at an angle so that she could see what he was doing. Her eyes never left the painting.

Dolarhyde put his hand inside his shirt.

Somewhere a telephone was ringing. The typing stopped. A woman stuck her head out of the far cubicle.

"Paula, telephone for you. It's your mother."

Miss Harper did not turn her head. Her eyes never left Dolarhyde or the painting. "Would you take a message?" she said. "Tell her I'll call back."

The woman disappeared into the office. In a moment the typing started again.

Dolarhyde couldn't hold it any more. Play for it all, right now.

But the Dragon moved first. "*I'VE NEVER SEEN*—"

"What?" Miss Harper's eyes were wide.

"—a rat that big!" Dolarhyde said, pointing. "Climbing that frame!"

Miss Harper was turning. "Where?"

The blackjack slid out of his shirt. With his wrist more than his arm, he tapped the back of her skull. She sagged as Dolarhyde grabbed a handful of her blouse and clapped the chloroform rag over her face. She made a high sound once, not overloud, and went limp.

He eased her to the floor between the table and the racks of paintings, pulled the folder with the watercolour to the floor and squatted over her. Rustling, wadding, hoarse breathing and a telephone ringing.

The woman came out of the far office.

"Paula?" She looked around the room. "It's your mother," she called. "She needs to talk to you *now*."

She walked behind the table. "I'll take care of the visitor if you—" She saw them then. Paula Harper on the floor, her hair across her face, and squatting over her, his pistol in his hand, Dolarhyde stuffing the last bite of the watercolour in his mouth. Rising, chewing, running. Toward her.

She ran for her office, slammed the flimsy door, grabbed at the phone and knocked it to the floor, scrambled for it on her hands and knees and tried to dial on the busy line as her door caved in. The lighted dial burst in bright colours at the impact behind her ear. The receiver fell quaking to the floor.

Dolarhyde in the staff elevator watched the indicator lights blink down, his gun held flat across his stomach, covered by his books.

First floor.

Out into the deserted galleries. He walked fast, his running shoes whispering on the terrazzo. A wrong turn and he was passing the whale masks, the great mask of Sisuit, losing seconds, running now into the presence of the Haida high totems and lost. He ran to the totems, looked left, saw the primitive edged weapons and knew where he was.

He peered around the corner at the lobby.

The desk officer stood at the bulletin board, thirty feet from the reception desk.

The armed guard was closer to the door. His holster creaked as he bent to rub a spot on the toe of his shoe.

If they fight drop him first. Dolarhyde put the gun under his belt and buttoned his coat over it. He walked across the lobby, unclipping his pass.

The desk officer turned when he heard the footsteps.

"Thank you," Dolarhyde said. He held up his pass by the edges, then dropped it on the desk.

The guard nodded. "Would you put it through the slot there, please?"

The reception desk telephone rang.

The pass was hard to pick up off the glass top.

The telephone rang again. Hurry.

Dolarhyde got hold of the pass, dropped it through the slot. He picked up his guitar case from the pile of knapsacks.

The guard was coming to the telephone.

Out the door now, walking fast for the botanical gardens, he was ready to turn and fire if he heard pursuit.

Inside the gardens and to the left, Dolarhyde ducked into a space between a small shed and a hedge. He opened the guitar case and dumped out a tennis racket, a tennis ball, a towel, a folded grocery sack and a big bunch of leafy celery.

Buttons flew as he tore off his coat and shirt in one move and stepped out of his trousers. Underneath he wore a Brooklyn College tee-shirt and warm-up pants. He stuffed his books and clothing into the grocery bag, then the weapons. The celery stuck out the top. He wiped the handle and clasps of the case and shoved it under the hedge.

Cutting across the gardens now toward Prospect Park, the towel around his neck, he came out on to Empire Boulevard. Joggers were ahead of him. As he followed the joggers into the park, the first police cruisers screamed past. None of the joggers paid any attention to them. Neither did Dolarhyde.

He alternated jogging and walking, carrying his grocery bag and racket and bouncing his tennis ball, a man cooling off from a hard workout who had stopped by the store on the way home.

He made himself slow down; he shouldn't run on a full stomach. He could choose his pace now.

He could choose anything.

CRAWFORD SAT in the back row of the jury box eating Redskin peanuts while Graham closed the courtroom blinds.

"You'll have the profile for me later this afternoon, I take it," Crawford said. "You told me Tuesday; this is Tuesday."

"I'll finish it. I want to watch this first."

Graham opened the express envelope from Byron Metcalf and dumped out the contents—two dusty rolls of home movie film, each in a plastic sandwich bag.

"Is Metcalf pressing charges against Niles Jacobi?"

"Not for theft—he'll probably inherit anyway—he and Jacobi's brother," Graham said. "On the hash, I don't know. Birmingham D.A.'s inclined to break his chops."

"Good," Crawford said.

The movie screen swung down from the courtroom ceiling to face the jury box, an arrangement which made it easy to show jurors filmed evidence.

Graham threaded the projector.

"On checking the news-stands where the Tooth Fairy could have gotten the *Tattler* so fast—I've had reports back from Cincinnati,

Detroit, and a bunch from Chicago," Crawford said. "Various weirdos to run down."

Graham started the film. It was a fishing movie.

The Jacobi children hunkered on the bank of a pond with cane poles and bobbers.

Graham tried not to think of them in their small boxes in the ground. He tried to think of them just fishing.

The girl's cork bobbed and disappeared. She had a bite.

Crawford crackled his peanut sack. "Indianapolis is dragging ass on questioning newsies and checking the Servco Supreme stations," he said.

"Do you want to watch this, or what?" Graham said.

Crawford was silent until the end of the two-minute film. "Terrific, she caught a perch," he said. "Now the profile—"

"Jack, you were in Birmingham right after it happened. I didn't get there for a month. You saw the house while it was still their house—I didn't. It was stripped and remodelled when I got there. Now for Christ's sake let me look at these people and then I'll finish the profile."

He started the second film.

A birthday party appeared on the screen in the courtroom. The Jacobis were seated around a dining-table. They were singing.

Graham lip-read "Haaappy Birth-day to you."

Eleven-year-old Donald Jacobi faced the camera. He was seated at the end of the table with the cake in front of him. The candles reflected in his glasses.

Around the corner of the table, his brother and sister were side by side watching him as he blew out the candles.

Graham shifted in his seat.

Mrs. Jacobi leaned over, her dark hair swinging, to catch the cat and dump it off the table.

Now Mrs. Jacobi brought a large envelope to her son. A long

ribbon trailed from it. Donald Jacobi opened the envelope and took out a big birthday card. He looked up at the camera and turned the card around. It said "Happy Birthday—follow the ribbon."

Bouncing progress as the camera followed the progression to the kitchen. A door there, fastened with a hook. Down the basement stairs, Donald first, then the others, following the ribbon down the steps. The end of the ribbon was tied around the handlebars of a ten-speed bicycle.

Graham wondered why they hadn't given him the bike outdoors.

A jumpy cut to the next scene and his question was answered. Outdoors now and clearly it had been raining hard. Water stood in the yard. The house looked different. Realtor Geehan had changed the colour when he did it over after the murders. The outside basement door opened and Mr. Jacobi emerged carrying the bicycle. This was the first view of him in the movie. A breeze lifted the hair combed across his bald spot. He set the bicycle ceremoniously on the ground.

The film ended with Donald's cautious first ride.

"Sad damn thing," Crawford said, "but we already knew that."

Graham started the birthday film over.

Crawford shook his head and began to read something from his briefcase with the aid of a penlight.

On the screen Mr. Jacobi brought the bicycle out of the basement. The basement door swung closed behind him. A padlock hung from it.

Graham froze the frame.

"There. That's what he wanted the bolt-cutter for, Jack—to cut that padlock and go in through the basement. Why didn't he go in that way?"

Crawford clicked off his penlight and looked over his glasses at the screen. "What's that?"

"I know he had a bolt-cutter—he used it to trim that branch out of his way when he was watching from the woods. Why didn't he use it to go in through the basement door?"

"He couldn't." With a small crocodile smile, Crawford waited. He loved to catch people in assumptions.

"Did he try? Did he mark it up? I never even saw that door—Geehan had put in a steel one with deadbolts by the time I got there."

Crawford opened his jaws. "You ASSUME Geehan put it in. Geehan didn't put it in. The steel door was there when they were killed. Jacobi must have put it in—he was a Detroit guy, he'd favour deadbolts."

"*When* did Jacobi put it in?"

"I don't know. Obviously after the kid's birthday—when was that? It'll be in the autopsy if you've got it here."

"His birthday was April 14th, a Monday," Graham said, staring at the screen, his chin in his hand. "I want to know when Jacobi changed the door."

Crawford's scalp wrinkled. It smoothed out again as he saw the point. "You think the Tooth Fairy cased the Jacobi house while the old door with the padlock was still there," he said.

"He brought a bolt-cutter, didn't he? How do you break in some place with a bolt-cutter?" Graham said. "You cut padlocks, bars or chain. Jacobi didn't have any bars or chained gates, did he?"

"No."

"Then he went there expecting a padlock. A bolt-cutter's fairly heavy and it's long. He was moving in daylight and from where he parked he had to hike a long way to the Jacobi house. For all he knew, he might be coming back in one hell of a hurry if something went wrong. He wouldn't have carried a bolt-cutter unless he knew he'd need it. He was expecting a padlock."

"You figure he cased the place *before* Jacobi changed the door. Then he shows up to kill them, waits in the woods—"

"You can't see this side of the house from the woods."

Crawford nodded. "He waits in the woods. They go to bed and he moves in with his bolt-cutter and finds the new door with the deadbolts."

"Say he finds the new door. He had it all worked out and now this," Graham said, throwing up his hands. "He's really pissed off, frustrated, he's hot to get in there. So he does a fast, loud pry job on the patio door. It was messy the way he went in—he woke Jacobi up and had to blow him away on the stairs. That's not like the Dragon. He's not messy that way. He's careful and he leaves nothing behind. He did a neat job at the Leeds's going in."

"Okay, all right," Crawford said. "If we find out when Jacobi changed his door, maybe we'll establish the interval between when he cased it and when he killed them. The *minimum* time that elapsed, anyway. That seems like a useful thing to know. Maybe it'll match some interval the Birmingham Convention and Visitors' Bureau could show us. We can check car rentals again. This time we'll do vans too. I'll have a word with the Birmingham field office."

Crawford's word must have been emphatic: in forty minutes flat a Birmingham F.B.I. agent, with realtor Geehan in tow, was shouting to a carpenter working in the rafters of a new house. The carpenter's information was relayed in a radio patch to Chicago.

"Last week in April," Crawford said, putting down the telephone. "That's when they put in the new door. My God, that's two months before the Jacobis were hit. Why would he case it two months in advance?"

"I don't know, but I promise you he saw Mrs. Jacobi or saw the whole family before he checked out their house. Unless he followed them down there from Detroit, he spotted Mrs. Jacobi sometime between April 10th when they moved to Birmingham and the end of April when the door was changed. Some time in that period he was in Birmingham. The Bureau's going on with it down there?"

"Cops too," Crawford said. "Tell me this: how did he know there was an inside door from the basement into the house? You couldn't count on that—not in the south."

"He saw the inside of the house, no question."

"Has your buddy Metcalf got the Jacobi bank statements?"

"I'm sure he does."

"Let's see what service calls they paid for between April 10th and the end of the month. I know the service calls have been checked for a couple of weeks back from the killings, but maybe we aren't looking back far enough. Same for the Leeds."

"We always figured he looked around inside the *Leeds's* house," Graham said. "From the alley he couldn't have seen the glass in the kitchen door. That's a latticed porch back there. But he was ready with his glass-cutter. And they didn't have any service calls for three months before they were killed."

"If he's casing this far ahead, maybe we didn't check back far enough. We will now. At the Leeds's though—when he was in the alley reading meters behind the Leeds house two days before he killed them—maybe he saw them going in the house. He could have looked in there while the porch door was open."

"No, the doors don't line up—remember? Look here."

Graham threaded the projector with the Leeds's home movie.

The Leeds's grey Scottie perked up his ears and ran to the kitchen door. Valerie Leeds and the children came in carrying groceries. Through the kitchen door nothing but lattice was visible.

"All right, you want to get Byron Metcalf busy on the bank statement for April? Any kind of service call or purchase that a door-to-door salesman might handle. No—I'll do that while you wind up the profile. Have you got Metcalf's number?"

Seeing the Leeds preoccupied Graham. Absently, he told Crawford three numbers for Byron Metcalf.

He ran the films again while Crawford used the phone in the jury room.

The Leeds film first.

There was the Leeds's dog. It wore no collar and the neighbourhood was full of dogs, but the Dragon knew which dog was theirs.

Here was Valerie Leeds. The sight of her tugged at Graham. There was the door behind her, vulnerable with its big glass pane. Her children played on the courtroom screen.

Graham had never felt as close to the Jacobis as he did to the Leeds. Their movie disturbed him now. It bothered him that he had thought of the Jacobis as chalk marks on a bloody floor.

There were the Jacobi children, ranged around the corner of the table, the birthday candles flickering on their faces.

For a flash Graham saw the blob of candle wax on the Jacobis' bedside table, the bloodstains around the corner of the bedroom at the Leeds's. Something . . .

Crawford was coming back. "Metcalf said to ask you—"

"*Don't talk to me!*"

Crawford wasn't offended. He waited stock-still and his little eyes grew narrow and bright.

The film ran on, its light and shadows playing over Graham's face.

There was the Jacobis' cat. The Dragon knew it was the Jacobis' cat.

There was the inside basement door.

There was the outside basement door with its padlock. The Dragon had brought a bolt-cutter.

The film ended. Finally it came off the reel and the end flapped around and around.

Everything the Dragon needed to know was on the two films.

They hadn't been shown in public, there wasn't any film club, film festi . . .

Graham looked at the familiar green box the Leeds movie came in. Their name and address were on it. And Gateway Film Laboratory, St. Louis, Mo., 63102.

His mind retrieved "St. Louis" just as it would retrieve any telephone number he had ever seen. What about St. Louis? It was one of the places where the *Tattler* was available on Monday night, the same day it was printed—the day before Lounds was abducted.

"Oh me," Graham said. "Oh Jesus."

He clamped his hands on the sides of his head to keep the thought from getting away.

"Do you still have Metcalf on the phone?"

Crawford handed him the receiver.

"Byron, it's Graham. Listen, did those reels of Jacobi film you sent—were they in any containers—sure, sure, I know you would have sent 'em along. I need help bad on something. Do you have the Jacobi bank statements there? Okay, I want to know where they got movie film developed. Probably a store sent it off for them. If there're any cheques to pharmacies or camera stores, we can find out where they did business. It's urgent, Byron. I'll tell you about it first chance. Birmingham F.B.I. will start checking the stores now. If you find something, shoot it straight to them, then to us. Will you do that? Great. *No,* I will *not* introduce you to Hotlips."

Birmingham F.B.I. agents checked four camera stores before they found the one where the Jacobis traded. The manager said all customers' film was sent to one place for processing.

Crawford had watched the films twelve times before Birmingham called back. He took the message.

Curiously formal, he held out his hand to Graham. "It's Gateway," he said.

43

CRAWFORD WAS stirring an Alka-Seltzer in a plastic glass when the stewardess's voice came over the 727's public-address system.

"Passenger Crawford, please?"

When he waved from his aisle seat, she came aft to him. "Mr. Crawford, would you go up to the cockpit please?"

Crawford was gone for four minutes. He slid back into the seat beside Graham.

"Tooth Fairy was in New York today."

Graham winced and his teeth clicked together.

"No. He just tapped a couple of women on the head at the Brooklyn Museum and, listen to this, he *ate* a painting."

"Ate it?"

"Ate it. The Art Squad in New York snapped to it when they found out what he ate. They got two partial prints off the plastic pass he used and they flashed them down to Price a little while ago. When Price put 'em together on the screen he rang the cherries. No I.D., but it's the same thumb that was on the Leeds's kid's eye."

"New York," Graham said.

"Means nothing, he was in New York today. He could still work at Gateway. If he does, he was off the job today. Makes it easier."

"What did he eat?"

"It was a thing called *The Great Red Dragon and the Woman Clothed with the Sun*. William Blake drew it, they said."

"What about the women?"

"He's got a sweet touch with the sap. Younger one's just at the hospital for observation. The older one had to have four stitches. Mild concussion."

"Could they give a description?"

"The younger one did. Quiet, husky, dark moustache and hair— a wig, I think. The guard at the door said the same thing. The older woman—he could've been in a rabbit suit for all she saw."

"But he didn't kill anybody."

"Odd," Crawford said. "He'd have been better off to wax 'em both—he could have been sure of his lead time leaving and saved himself a description or two. Behavioural Science called Bloom in the hospital about it. You know what he said? Bloom said maybe he's trying to stop."

44

DOLARHYDE HEARD the flaps moan down. The lights of St. Louis wheeled slowly beneath the black wing. Under his feet the landing gear rumbled into a rush of air and locked down with a thud.

He rolled his head on his shoulders to ease the stiffness in his powerful neck.

Coming home.

He had taken a great risk and the prize he brought back was the power to choose. He could choose to have Reba McClane alive. He could have her to talk to, and he could have her startling and harmless mobility in his bed.

He did not have to dread his house. He had the Dragon in his belly now. He could go into his house, walk up to a copy Dragon on the wall and wad him up if he wanted to.

He did not have to worry about feeling Love for Reba. If he felt Love for her, he could toss the Shermans to the Dragon and ease it that way, go back to Reba calm and easy, and treat her well.

From the terminal Dolarhyde telephoned her apartment. Not home yet. He tried Baeder Chemicals. The night-line was busy. He thought of Reba walking toward the bus stop after work, tapping alone with the cane, her raincoat over her shoulders.

He drove to the film laboratory through the light evening traffic in less than fifteen minutes.

She wasn't at the bus stop. He parked on the street behind Baeder Chemicals, near the entrance closest to the dark-rooms. He'd tell her he was here, wait until she had finished working and drive her home. He was proud of his new power to choose. He wanted to use it.

There were things he could catch up on in his office while he waited.

Only a few lights were on in Baeder Chemicals.

Reba's dark-room was locked. The light above the door was neither red nor green. He pressed the buzzer. No response.

Maybe she had left a message in his office.

He heard footsteps in the corridor.

The Baeder supervisor, Dandridge, passed the dark-room area and never looked up. He was walking fast and carrying a thick bundle of buff personnel files under his arm.

A small crease appeared in Dolarhyde's forehead.

Dandridge was half-way across the parking lot, heading for the Gateway building, when Dolarhyde came out of Baeder behind him.

Two delivery vans and half a dozen cars were on the lot. That Buick belonged to Fisk, Gateway's personnel director. What were they doing?

There was no night shift at Gateway. Much of the building was dark. Dolarhyde could see by the red exit signs in the corridor as he went toward his office. The lights were on behind the frosted glass door of the personnel department. Dolarhyde heard voices in there, Dandridge's for one, and Fisk's.

A woman's footsteps coming. Fisk's secretary turned the corner into the corridor ahead of Dolarhyde. She had a scarf tied over her curlers and she carried ledgers from Accounting. She was in a hurry.

The ledgers were heavy, a big armload. She pecked on Fisk's office door with her toe.

Will Graham opened it for her.

Dolarhyde froze in the dark hall. His gun was in his van.

The office door closed again.

Dolarhyde moved fast, his running shoes quiet on the smooth floor. He put his face close to the glass of the exit door and scanned the parking lot. Movement now under the floodlights. A man moving. He was beside one of the delivery vans and he had a flashlight. Flicking something. He was dusting the outside mirror for fingerprints.

Behind Dolarhyde, somewhere in the corridors, a man was walking. Get away from the door. He ducked around the corner and down the stairs to the basement and the furnace room on the opposite side of the building.

By standing on a workbench he could reach the high windows that opened at ground level behind the shrubbery. He rolled over the sill and came up on his hands and knees in the bushes ready to run or fight.

Nothing moved on this side of the building. He stood up, put a hand in his pocket and strolled across the street. Running when the sidewalk was dark, walking as cars went by, he made a long loop around Gateway and Baeder Chemicals.

His van stood at the kerb behind Baeder. There was no place to hide close to it. All right. He sprinted across the street and leaped in, clawing at his valise.

Full clip in the automatic. He jacked a round into the chamber and laid the pistol on the console, covering it with a tee-shirt.

Slowly he drove away—don't catch the red light—slowly around the corner and into the scattered traffic.

He had to think now and it was hard to think.

It had to be the films. Graham knew about the films somehow. Graham knew *where*. He didn't know *who*. If he knew who he wouldn't need personnel records. Why accounting records too? Absences, that's why. Match absences against the dates when the Dragon struck. No, those were Saturdays, except for Lounds. Absences on the days before those Saturdays, he'd look for those. Fool him there—no workmen's compensation slips were kept for management.

Dolarhyde drove slowly up Lindbergh Boulevard, gesturing with his free hand as he ticked off the points.

They were looking for fingerprints. He'd given them no chance for fingerprints – except maybe on the plastic pass at Brooklyn Museum. He'd picked it up in a hurry, mostly by the edges.

They must have a print. Why fingerprint if they didn't have something to match it to?

They were checking that van for prints. No time to see if they were checking cars too.

Van. Carrying the wheelchair with Lounds in it—that tipped them. Or maybe somebody in Chicago saw the van. There were a lot of vans at Gateway, private vans, delivery vans.

No, Graham just knew he had a van. Graham knew because he knew. Graham knew. Graham knew. The son of a bitch was a monster.

They'd fingerprint everyone at Gateway and Baeder too. If they didn't spot him tonight, they'd do it tomorrow. He had to run forever with his *face* on every bulletin board in every post office and police station. It was all coming to pieces. He was puny and small before them.

"Reba," he said aloud. Reba couldn't save him now. They were closing in on him and he was nothing but a puny harelip—

"ARE YOU SORRY NOW THAT YOU BETRAYED ME?"

The Dragon's voice rumbled from deep within him, deep as the shredded painting in his bowels.

"I didn't—I just wanted to choose. You called me—"

"GIVE ME WHAT I WANT AND I'LL SAVE YOU."

"No. I'll run."

"*GIVE ME WHAT I WANT AND YOU'LL HEAR GRAHAM'S SPINE SNAP.*"

"No."

"*I ADMIRE WHAT YOU DID TODAY. WE'RE CLOSE NOW. WE CAN BE ONE AGAIN. DO YOU FEEL ME INSIDE YOU? YOU DO, DON'T YOU?*"

"Yes."

"*AND YOU KNOW I CAN SAVE YOU. YOU KNOW THEY'LL SEND YOU TO A PLACE WORSE THAN BROTHER BUDDY'S. GIVE ME WHAT I WANT AND YOU'LL BE FREE.*"

"No."

"*THEY'LL KILL YOU. YOU'LL JERK ON THE GROUND.*"

"No."

"*WHEN YOU'RE GONE SHE'LL FUCK OTHER PEOPLE, SHE'LL—*"

"No! Shut up."

"*SHE'LL FUCK OTHER PEOPLE, PRETTY PEOPLE, SHE'LL PUT THEIR—*"

"Stop it. Shut up."

"*SLOW DOWN AND I WON'T SAY IT.*"

Dolarhyde's foot lifted on the accelerator.

"*THAT'S GOOD. GIVE ME WHAT I WANT AND IT CAN'T HAPPEN. GIVE IT TO ME AND THEN I'LL ALWAYS LET YOU CHOOSE, YOU CAN ALWAYS CHOOSE, AND YOU'LL SPEAK WELL, I WANT YOU TO SPEAK WELL, SLOW DOWN, THAT'S RIGHT, SEE THE SERVICE STATION? PULL OVER THERE AND LET ME TALK TO YOU . . .*"

45

GRAHAM CAME out of the office suite and rested his eyes for a moment in the dim hallway. He was restive, uneasy. This was taking too long.

Crawford was sifting the 380 Gateway and Baeder employees as fast and well as it could be done—the man was a marvel at this kind of job—but time was passing and secrecy could only be maintained so long.

Crawford had kept the working group at Gateway to a minimum. ("We want to find him, not spook him," Crawford had told them. "If we spot him tonight, we can take him outside the plant, maybe at his house or on the lot.")

The St. Louis Police Department was co-operating. Lt. Fogel of St. Louis Homicide and one sergeant came quietly in an unmarked car, bringing a Datafax.

Wired to a Gateway telephone, in minutes the Datafax was transmitting the employment roll simultaneously to the F.B.I. Identification Section in Washington and the Missouri Department of Motor Vehicles.

In Washington, the names would be checked against both the civil and criminal fingerprint records. Names of Baeder employees with security clearances were flagged for faster handling.

The Department of Motor Vehicles would check for ownership of vans.

Only four employees were brought in—the personnel manager, Fisk; Fisk's secretary; Dandridge from Baeder Chemicals; and Gateway's chief accountant.

No telephones were used to summon the employees to this late-night meeting at the plant. Agents called at their houses and stated their business privately. ("Look 'em over before you tell 'em why you want 'em," Crawford said. "And don't let them use the telephone after. This kind of news travels fast.")

They had hoped for a quick identification from the teeth. None of the four employees recognized them.

Graham looked down the long corridors lit with red exit signs. Damn it felt right.

What else could they do tonight?

Crawford had requested that the woman from Brooklyn Museum—Miss Harper—be flown out as soon as she could travel. Probably that would be in the morning. The St. Louis Police Department had a good surveillance van. She could sit in it and watch the employees go in.

If they didn't hit it tonight, all traces of the operation would be removed from Gateway before work started in the morning. Graham didn't kid himself—they'd be lucky to have a whole day to work before the word got out at Gateway. The Dragon would be watching for anything suspicious. He would fly.

46

A LATE SUPPER with Ralph Mandy had seemed all right. Reba McClane knew she had to tell him some time and she didn't believe in leaving things hanging.

Actually, she thought Mandy knew what was coming when she insisted on going Dutch.

She told him in the car as he took her home; that it was no big deal, she'd had a lot of fun with him and wanted to be his friend, but she was involved with somebody now.

Maybe he was hurt a little, but she knew he was relieved a little too. He was pretty good about it, she thought.

At her door he didn't ask to come in. He did ask to kiss her goodbye and she responded gladly. He opened her door and gave her the keys. He waited until she was inside and had closed the door and locked it.

When he turned around Dolarhyde shot him in the throat and twice in the chest. Three putts from the silenced pistol. A scooter is louder.

Dolarhyde lifted Mandy's body easily, laid him between the shrubs and the house and left him there.

Seeing Reba kiss Mandy had stabbed Dolarhyde deep. Then the pain left him for good.

He still looked and sounded like Francis Dolarhyde—the Dragon was a very good actor; he played Dolarhyde well.

Reba was washing her face when she heard the doorbell. It rang four times before she got there. She touched the chain, but didn't take it off.

"Who is it?"

"Francis Dolarhyde."

She eased the door open, still on the chain. "Tell me again."

"Dolarhyde. It's me."

She knew it was. She took off the chain.

Reba did not like surprises. "I thought you said you'd call me, D."

"I would have. But this is an emergency, really," he said, clapping the chloroformed cloth over her face as he stepped inside.

The street was empty. Most of the houses were dark. He carried her to the van. Ralph Mandy's feet stuck out of the shrubbery into the yard. Dolarhyde didn't bother with him any more.

She woke on the ride. She was on her side, her cheek in the dusty carpet of the van, transmission whine loud in her ear.

She tried to bring her hands to her face. The movement mashed her bosom. Her forearms were stuck together.

She felt them with her face. They were bound together from her elbows to her wrists with what felt like soft strips of cloth. Her legs were tied the same way from knees to ankles. Something was across her mouth.

What . . . what . . . D. was at the door and then . . . she remembered twisting her face away and the terrible strength of him. Oh Lord . . . what was it . . . D. was at the door and then she was choking something cold and she tried to twist her face away but there was a terrible grip on her head.

She was in D.'s van now. She recognized the resonances. The van was going. Fear ballooned in her. Her instinct said be quiet, but the fumes were in her throat, chloroform and gasoline. She retched against the gag.

D.'s voice. "It won't be long now."

She felt a turn and they were on gravel now, rocks pinging under the fenders and floorboard.

He's crazy. All right. That's it: crazy.

Crazy is a fearsome word.

What was it? Ralph Mandy. He must have seen them at her house. It set him off.

Christ Jesus, get it all ready. A man had tried to slap her once at Reiker Institute. She was quiet and he couldn't find her—he couldn't see either. This one could fucking well see. Get it all ready. Get ready to talk. God he could kill me with this gag in my mouth. God he could be killing me and not understand what I was saying.

Be ready. Have it all ready and don't say "huh?" Tell him he can back out, no damage. I won't tell. Be passive as long as you can. If you can't be passive, wait until you can find his eyes.

The van stopped. The van rocked as he got out. Side door sliding open. Grass and hot tyres on the air. Crickets. He came in the van.

In spite of herself she squealed into the gag and twisted her face away from him when he touched her.

Soft pats on the shoulder didn't help stop her writhing. A stinging slap across the face did.

She tried to talk into the gag. She was lifted, carried. His footsteps hollow on the ramp. She was sure where she was now. His house. Where in his house? Clock ticking to the right. Rug then floor. The bedroom where they did it. She was sinking in his arms, felt the bed under her.

She tried to talk into the gag. He was leaving. Noise outside. Van door slammed. Here he comes. Setting something on the floor— metal cans.

She smelled gasoline.

"Reba." D.'s voice all right, but so calm. So terribly calm and strange. "Reba, I don't know what to . . . say to you. You felt so good, and you don't know what I did for you. And I was wrong, Reba. You made me weak and then you hurt me."

She tried to talk into the gag.

"If I untie you and let you sit up, will you be good? Don't try to run. I can catch you. Will you be good?"

She twisted her head toward the voice to nod.

A touch of cold steel against her skin, whisper of a knife through cloth and her arms were free. Now her legs. Her cheeks were wet where the gag came off.

Carefully and slowly she sat up in the bed. *Take your best shot.*

"D.," she said, "I didn't know you cared this much about me. I'm glad you feel that way way but, see, you scared me with this."

No answer. She knew he was there.

"D., was it old dumb Ralph Mandy that made you mad? Did you see him at my house? That's it, isn't it? I was telling him I don't want to see him any more. Because I want to see you. I'm never going to see Ralph again."

"Ralph died," Dolarhyde said. "I don't think he liked it very much."

Fantasy. He's making it up Jesus do I hope. "I've never hurt you, D. I never wanted to. Let's just be friends and fuck and have a good time and forget all this."

"Shut up," he said calmly. "I'll tell you something. The most important thing you'll ever hear. Sermon-on-the-Mount important. Ten-Commandments important. Got it?"

"Yes, D. I—"

"Shut up. Reba, some remarkable events have happened in Birmingham and Atlanta. Do you know what I'm talking about?"

She shook her head.

"It's been on the news a lot. Two groups of people were changed. Leeds. And Jacobi. The police think they were murdered. Do you know now?"

She started to shake her head. Then she did know and slowly she nodded.

"Do you know what they call the Being that visited those people? You can say."

"The Tooth—"

A hand gripped her face, shutting off the sound.

"Think carefully and answer correctly."

"It's Dragon something. Dragon—Red Dragon."

He was close to her. She could feel his breath on her face.

"*I AM THE DRAGON.*"

Leaping back, driven back by the volume and terrible timbre of the voice, she slammed against the headboard.

"The Dragon wants you, Reba. He always has. I didn't want to give you to Him. I did a thing for you today so He couldn't have you. And I was wrong."

This was D., she could talk to D. "Please. Please don't let him have me. You won't, please don't, you wouldn't—I'm for *you*. Keep me with you. You like me, I know you do."

"I haven't made up my mind yet. Maybe I can't help giving you to him. I don't know. I'm going to see if you do as I tell you. Will you? Can I depend on you?"

"I'll try. I will try. Don't scare me too much or I can't."

"Get up, Reba. Stand by the bed. Do you know where you are in the room?"

She nodded.

"You know where you are in the house, don't you? You wandered around in the house while I was asleep, didn't you?"

"Asleep?"

"Don't be stupid. When we spent the night here. You went through the house, didn't you? Did you find something odd? Did you take it and show it to somebody? Did you do that, Reba?"

"I just went outside. You were asleep and I went outside. I promise."

"Then you know where the front door is, don't you?"

She nodded.

"Reba, feel on my chest. Bring your hands up slowly."

Try for his eyes?

His thumb and fingers touched lightly on each side of her windpipe. "Don't do what you're thinking, or I'll squeeze. Just feel on my chest. Just at my throat. Feel the key on the chain? Take it off over my head. Careful . . . that's right. Now I'm going to see if I can trust you. Go close the front door and lock it and bring me back the key. Go ahead. I'll wait right here. Don't try to run. I can catch you."

She held the key in her hand, the chain tapping against her thigh. It was harder navigating in her shoes, but she kept them on. The ticking clock helped.

Rug, then floor, rug again. Loom of the sofa. Go to the right.

What's my best shot? Which? Fool along with him or go for it? Did the others fool along with him? She felt dizzy from deep breathing. Don't be dizzy. Don't be dead.

It depends on whether the door is open. Find out where he is.

"Am I going right?" She knew she was.

"It's about five more steps." The voice was from the bedroom all right.

She felt air on her face. The door was half-open. She kept her body between the door and the voice behind her. She slipped the key in the keyhole below the knob. On the outside.

Now. Through the door fast making herself pull it to and turn the key. Down the ramp, no cane, trying to remember where the van was, running. Running. Into what—a bush—screaming now. Screaming, "Help me. Help me. Help me, help me." On gravel running. A truck horn far away. Highway that way, a fast walk and trot and run, fast as she could, veering when she felt grass instead of gravel, zigging down the lane.

Behind her footsteps coming fast and hard, running in the gravel. She stooped and picked up a handful of rocks, waited until he was close and flung them, heard them thump on him.

A shove on the shoulder spun her, a big arm under her chin, around her neck squeezing, blood roared in her ears. She kicked backward, hit a shin as it became increasingly quiet.

C H A P T E R

47

IN TWO hours, the list of white male employees twenty to fifty years old who owned vans was completed. There were twenty-six names on it.

Missouri D.M.V. provided hair colour from driver's licence information, but it was not used as an exclusionary factor; the Dragon might wear a wig.

Fisk's secretary, Miss Trillman, made copies of the list and passed them round.

Lt. Fogel was going down the list of names when his beeper went off.

Fogel spoke to his headquarters briefly on the telephone, then put his hand over the receiver. "Mr. Crawford—Jack, one Ralph Mandy, white male, 38, was found shot to death a few minutes ago in University City—that's in the middle of town, close to Washington University—he was in the front yard of a house occupied by a woman named Reba McClane. The neighbours said she works for Baeder. Her door's unlocked, she's not home."

"Dandridge!" Crawford called. "Reba McClane, what about her?"

"She works in the dark-room. She's blind. She's from some place in Colorado—"

"You know a Ralph Mandy?"

"Mandy?" Dandridge said. "Randy Mandy."

"*Ralph* Mandy, he work here?"

A check of the roll showed he didn't.

"Coincidence maybe," Fogel said.

"Maybe," Crawford said.

"I hope nothing's happened to Reba," Miss Trillman said.

"You know her?" Graham asked.

"I've talked with her several times."

"What about Mandy?"

"I don't know him. The only man I've seen her with, I saw her getting into Mr. Dolarhyde's van."

"Mr. Dolarhyde's van, Miss Trillman? What colour is Mr. Dolarhyde's van?"

"Let's see. Dark brown, or maybe black."

"Where does Mr. Dolarhyde work?" Crawford asked.

"He's production supervisor," Fisk said.

"Where's his office?"

"Right down the hall."

Crawford turned to speak to Graham, but he was already moving.

Mr. Dolarhyde's office was locked. A pass-key from maintenance worked.

Graham reached in and flipped on the light. He stood still in the doorway while his eyes went over the room. It was extremely neat. No personal items were anywhere in sight. The bookshelf held only technical manuals.

The desk-lamp was on the left side of the chair, so he was right-handed. Need a left thumbprint fast off a right-handed man.

"Let's toss it for a clipboard," he said to Crawford, behind him in the hall. "He'll use his left thumb on the clip."

They had started on the drawers when the desk appointment

calendar caught Graham's eye. He flipped back through the scribbled pages to Saturday 28th, the date of the Jacobi killings.

The calendar was unmarked on the Thursday and Friday before that weekend.

He flipped forward to the last week in July. The Thursday and Friday were blank. There was a note on Wednesday. It said "Am 552 3.45–6.15."

Graham copied the entry. "I want to find out where this flight goes."

"Let me do it, you go ahead here," Crawford said. He went to a telephone across the hall.

Graham was looking at a tube of denture adhesive in the bottom desk drawer when Crawford called from the door.

"It goes to Atlanta, Will. Let's take him."

48

WATER, COLD on Reba's face, running in her hair. Dizzy. Something hard under her, sloping. She turned her head. Wood under her. A cold wet towel wiped her face.

"Are you all right, Reba?" Dolarhyde's calm voice.

She shied from the sound. "Uhhhh."

"Breathe deeply."

A minute passed.

"Do you think you can stand up? Try to stand up."

She could stand with his arm around her. Her stomach heaved. He waited until the spasm passed.

"Up the ramp. Do you remember where you are?"

She nodded.

"Take the key out of the door, Reba. Come inside. Now lock it and put the key around my neck. Hang it around my neck. Good. Let's just be sure it's locked."

She heard the knob rattle.

"That's good. Now go in the bedroom, you know the way."

She stumbled and went down on her knees, her head bowed. He lifted her by the arms and supported her into the bedroom.

"Sit in this chair."

She sat.

"*GIVE HER TO ME NOW.*"

She struggled to rise, big hands on her shoulders held her down.

"Sit still or I can't keep Him off you," Dolarhyde said.

Her mind was coming back. It didn't want to.

"Please try," she said.

"Reba, it's all over for me."

He was up, doing something. The odour of gasoline was very strong.

"Put out your hand. Feel this. Don't grab it, feel it."

She felt something like steel nostrils, slick inside. The muzzle of a gun.

"That's a shotgun, Reba. A 12-gauge magnum. Do you know what it will do?"

She nodded.

"Take your hand down." The cold muzzle rested in the hollow of her throat.

"Reba, I wish I could have trusted you. I wanted to trust you."

He sounded like he was crying.

"You felt so good."

He *was* crying.

"So did you, D. I love it. Please don't hurt me now."

"It's all over for me. I can't leave you to Him. You know what He'll do?"

Bawling now.

"Do you know what He'll do? He'll bite you to death. Better you go with me."

She heard a match struck, smelled sulphur, heard a whoosh. Heat in the room. Smoke. Fire. The thing she feared most in the world. Fire. Anything was better than that. She hoped the first shot killed her. She tensed her legs to run.

Blubbering.

"Oh, Reba, I can't stand to watch you burn."

The muzzle left her throat.

Both barrels of the shotgun went off at once as she came to her feet.

Ears numbed, she thought she was shot, thought she was dead, felt the heavy thump on the floor more than she heard it.

Smoke now and the crackle of flames. Fire. Fire brought her to herself. She felt heat on her arms and face. Out. She stepped on legs, stumbled choking into the foot of the bed.

Stoop low, they said, under the smoke. Don't run, you'll bump into things and die.

She was locked in. Locked in. Walking, stooping low, fingers trailing on the floor, she found legs—other end—she found hair, a hairy flap, put her hand in something soft below the hair. Only pulp, sharp bone splinters and a loose eye in it.

Key around his neck, hurry. Both hands on the chain, legs under her, snatch. The chain broke and she fell backward, scrambling up again. Turned around. Confused. Trying to feel, trying to listen with her numbed ears over the crackle of the flames. Side of the bed, which side? She stumbled on the body, tried to listen.

BONG BONG, the clock striking, BONG BONG, into the living-room, BONG BONG, take a right.

Throat seared with smoke. BONG BONG. Door here. Under the knob. Don't drop it. Click the lock. Snatch it open. Air. Down the ramp. Air. Collapsed in the grass. Up again on hands and knees, crawling.

She came up on her knees to clap, picked up the house echo and crawled away from it, breathing deep until she could stand, walk, run until she hit something, run again.

49

LOCATING FRANCIS Dolarhyde's house was not so easy. The address listed at Gateway was a post-office box in St. Charles.

Even the St. Charles Sheriff's Department had to check a service map at the power company office to be sure.

The sheriff's department welcomed St. Louis S.W.A.T. to the other side of the river and the caravan moved quietly up State Highway 94. A deputy beside Graham in the lead car showed the way. Crawford leaned between them from the back seat and sucked at something in his teeth. They met light traffic at the north end of St. Charles, a pick-up full of children, a Greyhound bus, a tow-truck.

They saw the glow as they cleared the northern city limits.

"That's *it!*" the deputy said. "That's where it is!"

Graham put his foot down. The glow brightened and swelled as they roared up the highway.

Crawford snapped his fingers for the microphone.

"All units, that's his house burning. Watch it now. He may be coming out. Sheriff, let us have a road-block here, if you will."

A thick column of sparks and smoke leaned southeast over the fields, hanging over them now.

"Here," the deputy said, "turn in on this gravel."

They saw the woman then, silhouetted black against the fire, saw her as she heard them and raised her arms to them.

And then the great fire blasted upward, outward, burning beams and window frames describing slow high arcs into the night sky, the blazing van rocked over on its side, orange tracery of the burning trees suddenly blown out and dark. The ground shuddered as the explosion whump rocked the police cars.

The woman was face down in the road. Crawford and Graham and the deputies out, running to her as fire rained in the road, some running past her with their weapons drawn.

Crawford took Reba from a deputy batting sparks from her hair.

He held her arms, face close to hers, red in the firelight.

"Francis Dolarhyde," he said. He shook her gently. "Francis Dolarhyde, where is he?"

"He's in there," she said, raising her stained hand toward the heat, letting it fall. "He's dead in there."

"You *know* that?" Crawford peered into her sightless eyes.

"I was with him."

"Tell me, please."

"He shot himself in the face. I put my hand in it. He set fire to the house. He shot himself. I put my hand in it. He was on the floor. I put my hand in it. Can I sit down?"

"Yes," Crawford said. He got into the back of the police car with her. He put his arms around her and let her cry into his jowl.

Graham stood in the road and watched the flames until his face was red and sore.

The winds aloft whipped smoke across the moon.

50

THE WIND in the morning was warm and wet. It blew wisps of cloud over the blackened chimneys where Dolarhyde's house had stood. Thin smoke blew flat across the fields.

A few raindrops struck coals and exploded in tiny puffs of steam and ashes.

A fire truck stood by, its light revolving.

S. F. Aynesworth, F.B.I. Section Chief, Explosives, stood with Graham upwind of the ruins pouring coffee from a thermos.

Aynesworth winced as the local fire marshal reached into the ashes with a rake.

"Thank God it's still too hot for him in there," he said out of the side of his mouth. He had been carefully cordial to the local authorities. To Graham, he spoke his mind. "I got to wade it, hell. This place'll look like a fucking turkey farm soon as all the special duties and constables finish their pancakes and take a crap. They'll be right on down to help."

Until Aynesworth's beloved bomb van arrived from Washington, he had to make do with what he could bring on the plane. He pulled a faded Marine Corps duffel bag out of the trunk of a patrol car and unpacked his Nomex underwear and asbestos boots and coveralls.

"What did it look like when it went up, Will?"

"A flash of intense light that died down. Then it looked darker at the base. A lot of stuff was going up, window frames, flat pieces of the roof, and chunks flying sideways, tumbling in the fields. There was a shock wave, and the wind after. It blew out and sucked back in again. It looked like it almost blew the fire out."

"The fire was going good when it blew?"

"Yeah, it was through the roof and out the windows upstairs and down. The trees were burning."

Aynesworth recruited two local firemen to stand by with a hose and a third dressed in asbestos stood by with a winch line in case something fell on him.

He cleared the basement steps, now open to the sky, and went down into the tangle of black timbers. He could only stay a few minutes at a time. He made eight trips.

All he got for his effort was one flat piece of torn metal, but it seemed to make him happy.

Red-faced and wet with sweat, he stripped off his asbestos clothing and sat on the running-board of the fire truck with a fireman's raincoat over his shoulders.

He laid the flat piece of metal on the ground and blew away a film of ash.

"Dynamite," he told Graham. "Look here, see the fern pattern in the metal? This stuff's the right gauge for a trunk or a foot locker. That's probably it. Dynamite in a foot locker. It didn't go off in the basement though. Looks like the ground floor to me. See where the tree's cut there, where that marble table-top hit it? Blown out sideways. The dynamite was in something that kept the fire off of it for a while."

"How about remains?"

"There may not be a lot, but there's always something. We've got a lot of sifting to do. We'll find him. I'll give him to you in a small sack."

A sedative had finally put Reba McClane to sleep at DePaul Hospital shortly after dawn. She wanted the policewoman to sit close beside her bed. Several times through the morning she woke and reached out for the officer's hand.

When she asked for breakfast, Graham brought it in.

Which way to go? Sometimes it was easier for them if you were impersonal. With Reba McClane, he didn't think so.

He told her who he was.

"Do you know him?" she asked the policewoman.

Graham passed the officer his credentials. She didn't need them.

"I know he's a federal officer, Miss McClane."

She told him everything, finally. All about her time with Francis Dolarhyde. Her throat was sore and she stopped frequently to suck cracked ice.

He asked her the unpleasant questions and she took him through it, once waving him out the door while the policewoman held the basin to catch her breakfast.

She was pale and her face was scrubbed and shiny when he came back into the room.

He asked the last of it and closed his notebook.

"I won't put you through this again," he said, "but I'd like to come back by. Just to say hi and see how you're doing."

"How could you help it?—a charmer like me."

For the first time he saw tears and realized where it ate her.

"Would you excuse us for a minute, officer?" Graham said. He took Reba's hand.

"Look here. There was plenty wrong with Dolarhyde, but there's nothing wrong with you. You said he was kind and thoughtful to you. I believe it. That's what you brought out in him. At the end, he couldn't kill you and he couldn't watch you die. People who study this kind of thing say he was trying to stop. Why? Because you helped him. That probably saved some lives. You didn't draw a freak. You drew a man with a freak on his back. Nothing wrong with you, kid. If you let yourself believe there is, you're a sap. I'm coming back to see you in a day or so. I have to look at cops all the time and I need relief—try to do something about your hair there."

She shook her head and waved him toward the door. Maybe she grinned a little, he couldn't be sure.

Graham called Molly from the St. Louis F.B.I. office. Willy's grandfather answered the telephone.

"It's Will Graham, Mama," he said. "Hello, Mr. Graham."

Willy's grandparents always called him "Mr. Graham."

"Mama said he killed himself. She was looking at Donahue and they broke in with it. Damn lucky thing. Saved you fellows a lot of trouble catching him. Saves us taxpayers footing any more bills for this thing too. Was he really white?"

"Yes, sir. Blond. Looked Scandinavian."

Willy's grandparents were Scandinavian.

"May I speak to Molly please?"

"Are you going back down to Florida now?"

"Soon. Is Molly there?"

"Mama, he wants to speak to Molly. She's in the bathroom, Mr. Graham. My grandboy's eating breakfast again. Been out riding in that good air. You ought to see that little booger eat. I bet he's gained ten pounds. Here she is."

"Hello."

"Hi, hotshot."

"Good news, huh?"

"Looks like it."

"I was out in the garden. Mamamma came out and told me when she saw it on T.V. When did you find out?"

"Late last night."

"Why didn't you call me?"

"Mamamma was probably asleep."

"No, she was watching Johnny Carson. I can't tell you, Will. I'm so glad you didn't have to catch him."

"I'll be here a little longer."

"Four or five days?"

"I'm not sure. Maybe not that long. I want to see you, kid."

"I want to see you too, when you get through with everything you need to do."

"Today's Wednesday. By Friday I ought to—"

"Will, Mamamma has all Willy's uncles and aunts coming down from Seattle next week and—"

"Fuck Mamamma. What is this 'Mamamma' anyway?"

"When Willy was real little, he couldn't say—"

"Come home with me."

"Will, *I've* waited for *you*. They never get to see Willy and a few more days—"

"Come yourself. Leave Willy there and your ex-mother-in-law can stick him on a plane next week. Tell you what—let's stop in New Orleans. There's a place called—"

"I don't think so. I've been working—just part-time—at this western store in town and I have to give them a little notice."

"What's wrong, Molly?"

"Nothing. Nothing's wrong . . . I got so sad, Will. You know I came up here after Willy's father died." She always said "Willy's father" as though it were an office. She never used his name. "And we were all together—I got myself together, I got calm. I've gotten myself together now, too, and I—"

"Small difference: I'm not dead."

"Don't be that way."

"What way? Don't be what way?"

"You're mad."

Graham closed his eyes for a moment.

"Hello."

"I'm not mad, Molly. You do what you want to. I'll call you when things wind up here."

"You could come up here."

"I don't think so."

"Why not? There's plenty of room. Mamamma would—"

"Molly, they don't like me and you know why. Every time they look at me I remind them."

"That's not fair and it's not true either."

Graham was very tired.

"Okay. They're full of shit and they make me sick—try that one."

"Don't say that."

"They want the boy. Maybe they like you all right, probably they do if they ever think about it. But they want the boy and they'll take you. They don't want me and I couldn't care less. *I* want *you.* In Florida. Willy too, when he gets tired of his pony."

"You'll feel better when you get some sleep."

"I doubt it. Look, I'll call you when I know something here."

"Sure." She hung up.

"*Ape* shit," Graham said. "*Ape* shit."

Crawford stuck his head in the door. "Did I hear you say 'ape shit'?"

"You did."

"Well, cheer up. Aynesworth called in from the site. He has something for you. He said we ought to come on out, he's got some static from the locals."

51

AYNESWORTH WAS pouring ashes carefully into new paint cans when Graham and Crawford got to the black ruin where Dolarhyde's house had stood.

He was covered with soot and a large blister puffed under his ear. Special Agent Janowitz from Explosives Section was working down in the cellar.

A tall sack of a man fidgeted beside a dusty Oldsmobile in the drive. He intercepted Crawford and Graham as they crossed the yard.

"Are you Crawford?"

"That's right."

"I'm Robert L. Dulaney. I'm the coroner and this is my jurisdiction." He showed them his card. It said "Vote for Robert L. Dulaney."

Crawford waited.

"Your man there has some evidence that should have been turned over to me. He's kept me waiting for nearly an hour."

"Sorry for the inconvenience, Mr. Dulaney. He was following my instructions. Why don't you have a seat in your car and I'll clear this up."

Dulaney started after them.

Crawford turned around. "You'll excuse us, Mr. Dulaney. Have a seat in your car."

Section Chief Aynesworth was grinning, his teeth white in his sooty face. He had been sieving ashes all morning.

"As Section Chief, it gives me great pleasure—"

"To pull your prong, we all know that," Janowitz said, climbing from the black tangle of the cellar.

"Silence in the ranks, Indian Janowitz. Fetch the items of interest." He tossed Janowitz a set of car keys.

From the trunk of an F.B.I. sedan, Janowitz brought a long cardboard box. A shotgun, the stock burned off and barrels twisted by the heat, was wired to the bottom of the box. A smaller box contained a blacked automatic pistol.

"The pistol came out better," Aynesworth said. "Ballistics may be able to make a match with it. Come on, Janowitz, get to it."

Aynesworth took three plastic freezer bags from him.

"Front and centre, Graham." For a moment the humour left Aynesworth's face. This was a hunter's ritual, like smearing Graham's forehead with blood.

"That was a real sly show, podna." Aynesworth put the bags in Graham's hands.

One bag contained five inches of a charred human femur and the ball of a hip. Another contained a wristwatch. The third held the teeth.

The plate was black and broken and only half was there, but that half contained the unmistakable pegged lateral incisor.

Graham supposed he should say something. "Thanks. Thanks a lot."

His head swam briefly and he relaxed all over.

". . . museum piece," Aynesworth was saying. "We have to turn it over to the turkey, don't we, Jack?"

"Yeah. But there're some pros in the St. Louis coroner's office. They'll come over and make good impressions. We'll have those."

Crawford and the others huddled with the coroner beside his car.

Graham was alone with the house. He listened to the wind in the chimneys. He hoped Bloom would come here when he was well. Probably he would.

Graham wanted to know about Dolarhyde. He wanted to know what happened here, what bred the Dragon. But he had had enough for now.

A mocking-bird lit on the top of a chimney and whistled.

Graham whistled back.

He was going home.

GRAHAM SMILED when he felt the jet's big push rocket him up and away from St. Louis, turning across the sun's path south and east at last toward home.

Molly and Willy would be there.

"Let's don't jack around about who's sorry for what. I'll pick you up in Marathon, kiddo," she said on the phone.

In time he hoped he would remember the few good moments— the satisfaction of seeing people at work who were deeply committed to their skills. He supposed you could find that anywhere if you knew enough about what you were watching.

It would have been presumptuous to thank Lloyd Bowman and Beverly Katz, so he just told them on the telephone that he was glad to have worked with them again.

One thing bothered him a little: the way he felt when Crawford turned from the telephone in Chicago and said "It's Gateway."

Possibly that was the most intense and savage joy that had ever burst in him. It was unsettling to know that the happiest moment of his life had come then, in that stuffy jury room in the city of Chicago. *When even before he knew, he knew.*

He didn't tell Lloyd Bowman how it felt; he didn't have to.

"You know, when his theorem rang the cherries, Pythagoras gave one hundred oxen to the Muse," Bowman said.

"Nothing sweeter, is there? Don't answer—it lasts better if you don't spend it talking."

Graham grew more impatient the closer he got to home and to Molly. In Miami he had to go out on the apron to board "Aunt Lula", the old DC-3 that flew to Marathon.

He liked DC-3s. He liked everything today.

Aunt Lula was built when Graham was five years old and her wings were always dirty with a film of oil that blew back from the engine. He had great confidence in her. He ran to her as though she had landed in a jungle clearing to rescue him.

Islamorada's lights were coming on as the island passed under the wing. Graham could still see whitecaps on the Atlantic side. In minutes they were descending to Marathon.

It was like the first time he came to Marathon. He had come aboard Aunt Lula that time too, and often afterward he went to the airfield at dusk to watch her coming in, slow and steady, flaps down, fire flickering out her exhausts and all the passengers safe behind their lighted windows.

The take-offs were good to watch as well, but when the old aeroplane made her great arc to the north it left him sad and empty and the air acrid with goodbyes. He learned to watch only the landings and hellos.

That was before Molly.

With a final grunt, the aeroplane swung on to the apron. Graham saw Molly and Willy standing behind the fence, under the floodlights.

Willy was solidly planted in front of her. He'd stay there until Graham joined them. Only then would he wander along, examining whatever interested him. Graham liked him for that.

Molly was the same height as Graham, five feet ten inches. A level

kiss in public carries a pleasant jolt, possibly because level kisses are
usually exchanged in bed.

Willy offered to carry his suitcase. Graham gave him the suitbag
instead.

Riding home to Sugarloaf Key, Molly driving, Graham remembered
the things picked out by the headlights, imagining the rest.

When he opened the car door in the yard, he could hear the sea.

Willy went into the house, holding the suitbag on top of his head,
the bottom flapping against the back of his legs.

Graham stood in the yard absently brushing mosquitoes away from
his face.

Molly put her hand on his cheek. "What you ought to do is come
on in the house before you get eaten up."

He nodded. His eyes were wet.

She waited a moment longer, tucked her head and peered up at
him, wiggling her eyebrows. "Tanqueray martinis, steaks, hugging
and stuff. Right this way . . . and the light bill and the water bill and
lengthy conversations with my child," she added out of the side of
her mouth.

GRAHAM AND Molly wanted very much for it to be the same again between them, to go on as they had before.

When they saw that it was not the same, the unspoken knowledge lived with them like unwanted company in the house. The mutual assurances they tried to exchange in the dark and in the day passed through some refraction that made them miss the mark.

Molly had never looked better to him. From a painful distance, he admired her unconscious grace.

She tried to be good to him, but she had been to Oregon and she had raised the dead.

Willy felt it and he was cool to Graham, maddeningly polite.

A letter came from Crawford. Molly brought it in the mail and did not mention it.

It contained a picture of the Sherman family, printed from movie film. Not everything had burned, Crawford's note explained. A search of the fields around the house had turned this picture up, along with a few other things the explosion had blown far from the fire.

"These people were probably on his itinerary," Crawford wrote. "Safe now. Thought you'd like to know."

Graham showed it to Molly.

"See? That's why," he said. "That's why it was worth it."

"I know," she said. "I understand that, really I do."

The bluefish were running under the moon. Molly packed suppers and they fished and they built fires and none of it was any good.

Grandpa and Mamamma sent Willy a picture of his pony and he tacked it to the wall of his room.

The fifth day home was the last day before Graham and Molly would go back to work in Marathon. They fished in the surf, walking a quarter-mile around the curving beach to a place where they had luck before.

Graham had decided to talk to both of them together.

The expedition did not begin well. Willy pointedly put aside the rod Graham had rigged for him and brought the new surf-casting rod his grandfather sent home with him.

They fished for three hours in silence. Graham opened his mouth to speak several times, but it didn't seem right.

He was tired of being disliked.

Graham caught four snappers, using sand fleas for bait. Willy caught nothing. He was casting a big Rapala with three treble hooks which his grandfather had given him. He was fishing too fast, casting again and again, retrieving too fast, until he was red-faced and his tee-shirt stuck to him.

Graham waded into the water, scooped sand in the backwash of a wave and came up with two sand fleas, their legs waving from their shells.

"How about one of these, partner?" He held out a sand flea to Willy.

"I'll use the Rapala. It was my father's, did you know that?"

"No," Graham said. He glanced at Molly.

She hugged her knees and looked far off at a frigate bird sailing high.

She got up and brushed off the sand. "I'll go fix some sandwiches," she said.

When Molly had gone, Graham was tempted to talk to the boy by himself. No. Willy would feel whatever his mother felt. He'd wait and get them both together when she came back. He'd do it this time.

She wasn't gone long and she came back without the sandwiches, walking swiftly on the packed sand above the surf.

"Jack Crawford's on the phone. I told him you'd call him back, but he said it's urgent," she said, examining a fingernail. "Better hurry."

Graham blushed. He stuck the butt of his rod in the sand and trotted toward the dunes. It was quicker than going around the beach if you carried nothing to catch in the brush.

He heard a low whirring sound carried on the wind and, wary of a rattler, he scanned the ground as he went into the scrub cedar.

He saw boots beneath the brush, the glint of a lens and a flash of khaki rising.

He looked into the yellow eyes of Francis Dolarhyde and fear raised the hammers of his heart.

Snick of a pistol action working, an automatic coming up and Graham kicked at it, struck it as the muzzle bloomed pale yellow in the sun, and the pistol flew into the brush. Graham on his back, something burning in the left side of his chest, slid headfirst down the dune on to the beach.

Dolarhyde leaped high to land on Graham's stomach with both feet and he had the knife out now and never looked up at the thin screaming from the water's edge. He pinned Graham with his knees, raised the knife high and grunted as he brought it down. The blade missed Graham's eye and crunched deep into his cheek.

Dolarhyde rocked forward and put his weight on the handle of the knife to shove it through Graham's head.

The rod whistled as Molly swung it hard at Dolarhyde's face. The big Rapala's hooks sank solidly in his cheek and the reel screamed, paying out line as she drew back to strike again.

He growled, grabbed at his face as she hit him, and the treble hooks jammed into his hand as well. One hand free, one hand hooked to his face, he tugged the knife out and started after her.

Graham rolled over, got to his knees, then his feet, eyes wild and choking blood he ran, ran from Dolarhyde, ran until he collapsed.

Molly ran for the dunes, Willy ahead of her. Dolarhyde was coming, dragging the rod. It caught on a bush and pulled him howling to a stop before he thought to cut the line.

"Run, baby, run, baby, run, baby! Don't look back," she gasped. Her legs were long and she shoved the boy ahead of her, the crashing ever closer in the brush behind them.

They had one hundred yards on him when they left the dunes, seventy yards when they reached the house. Scrambling up the stairs. Clawing in Will's closet.

To Willy, "Stay here."

Down again to meet him. Down to the kitchen, not ready, fumbling with the speedloader.

She forgot the stance and she forgot the front sight but she got a good two-handed grip on the pistol and as the door exploded inward she blew a rat hole through his thigh—"Muhner!"—and she shot him in the face as he slid down the door facing and she shot him in the face as he sat on the floor and she ran to him and shot him twice in the face as he sprawled against the wall, scalp down to his chin and his hair on fire.

Willy tore up a sheet and went to look for Will. His legs were shaking and he fell several times crossing the yard.

The sheriff's deputies and ambulances came before Molly ever thought to call them. She was taking a shower when they came in the house behind their pistols. She was scrubbing hard at the flecks of blood and bone on her face and hair and she couldn't answer when a deputy tried to talk to her through the shower curtain.

One of the deputies finally picked up the dangling telephone receiver and talked to Crawford in Washington, who had heard the shots and summoned them.

"I don't know, they're bringing him in now," the deputy said. He looked out the window as the litter passed. "It don't look good to me," he said.

54

ON THE wall at the foot of the bed there was a clock with numbers large enough to read through the drugs and the pain.

When Will Graham could open his right eye, he saw the clock and knew where he was—an intensive care unit. He knew to watch the clock. Its movement assured him that this was passing, would pass.

That's what it was there for.

It said four o'clock. He had no idea which four o'clock and he didn't care, as long as the hands were moving. He drifted away.

The clock said eight when he opened his eye again.

Someone was to the side of him. Cautiously he turned his eye. It was Molly, looking out the window. She was thin. He tried to speak, but a great ache filled the left side of his head when he moved his jaw. His head and his chest did not throb together. It was more of a syncopation. He made a noise as she left the room.

The window was light when they pulled and tugged at him and did things that made the cords in his neck stand out.

Yellow light when he saw Crawford's face over him.

Graham managed to wink. When Crawford grinned, Graham could see a piece of spinach between his teeth.

Odd. Crawford eschewed most vegetables.

Graham made writing motions on the sheet beneath his hand.

Crawford slid his notebook under Graham's hand and put a pen between his fingers.

"Willy OK?" he wrote.

"Yeah, he's fine," Crawford said. "Molly too. She's been in here while you were asleep. Dolarhyde's dead, Will. I promise you, he's dead. I took the prints myself and had Price match them. There's no question. He's dead."

Graham drew a question mark on the pad.

"We'll get into it. I'll be here, I can tell you the whole thing when you feel good. They only give me five minutes."

"Now," Graham wrote.

"Has the doctor talked to you? No? About you first—you'll be okay. Your eye's just swelled shut from the deep stab wound in the face. They've got it fixed, but it'll take time. They took out your spleen. But who needs a spleen? Price left his in Burma in '41."

A nurse pecked on the glass.

"I've got to go. They don't respect credentials, nothing, around here. They just throw you out when the time's up. See you later."

Molly was in the I.C.U. waiting-room. A lot of tired people were.

Crawford went to her. "Molly—"

"Hello, Jack," she said. "*You're* looking really well. Want to give him a face transplant."

"Don't, Molly."

"Did you look at him?"

"Yes."

"I didn't think I could look at him, but I did."

"They'll fix him up. The doctor told me. They can do it. You want somebody to stay with you, Molly? I brought Phyllis down, she—"

"No. Don't do anything else for me."

She turned away, fumbling for a tissue. He saw the letter when she opened her purse: expensive mauve stationery that he had seen before.

Crawford hated this. He had to do it.

"Molly."

"What is it?"

"Will got a letter?"

"Yes."

"Did the nurse give it to you?"

"*Yes* she gave it to me. They're holding some flowers from all his *friends* in Washington too."

"May I see the letter?"

"I'll give it to him when he feels like it."

"Please let me see it."

"Why?"

"Because he doesn't need to hear from—that particular person."

Something was wrong with the expression on his face and she looked down at the letter and dropped it, purse and all. A lipstick rolled across the floor.

Stooping to pick up Molly's things, Crawford heard her heels tap fast as she left him, abandoning her purse.

He gave the purse to the charge nurse.

Crawford knew it would be nearly impossible for Lecter to get what he'd need, but with Lecter he took no chances.

He had an intern fluoroscope the letter in the X-ray department.

Crawford split the envelope on all sides with a penknife and examined its inside surface and the note for any stain or dust—they would have lye for scrubbing at Chesapeake Hospital and there was a pharmacy.

Satisfied at last, he read it:

Dear Will,

Here we are, you and I, languishing in our hospitals. You have your pain and I am without my books—the learned Dr. Chilton has seen to that.

We live in a primitive time—don't we, Will?—neither savage nor wise. Half measures are the curse of it. Any rational society would either kill me or give me my books.

I wish you a speedy convalescence and hope you won't be very ugly.

I think of you often.

Hannibal Lecter.

The intern looked at his watch. "Do you need me any more?"

"No," Crawford said. "Where's the incinerator?"

When Crawford returned in four hours for the next visiting period, Molly wasn't in the waiting-room and she wasn't in the Intensive Care Unit.

Graham was awake. He drew a question mark on the pad at once. "D dead how?" he wrote under it.

Crawford told him. Graham lay still for a full minute. Then he wrote "Lammed how?"

"Okay," Crawford said. "St. Louis. Dolarhyde must have been looking for Reba McClane. He came in the lab while we were there and spotted us. His prints were on an open furnace room window—it wasn't reported until yesterday."

Graham tapped the pad. "Body?"

"We think it was a guy named Arnold Lang—he's missing. His car was found in Memphis. It had been wiped down. They'll run me out in a minute, let me give it to you in order.

"Dolarhyde knew we were there. He gave us the slip at the plant and drove to a Servco Supreme station at Lindbergh and U.S. 270. Arnold Lang worked there.

"Reba McClane said Dolarhyde had a tiff with a service station attendant on Saturday before last. We think it was Lang.

"He snuffed Lang and took his body to the house. Then he went by Reba McClane's. She was in a clinch with Ralph Mandy at the door. He shot Mandy and dragged him into the hedge."

The nurse came in.

"For God's sake, it's police business," Crawford said. He talked fast as she pulled him by the coat sleeve to the door. "He chloroformed Reba McClane and took her to the house. The body was there," Crawford said from the hall.

Graham had to wait four hours to find out the rest.

"He gave her this and that, you know, will I kill you or not," Crawford said as he came in the door.

"You know the routine about the key hanging around his neck— that was to make sure she felt the body. So she could tell *us* she certainly did feel a body. All right, it's this way and that way, 'I can't stand to see you burn,' he says and blows Lang's head off with a 12-gauge.

"Lang was perfect. He didn't have any teeth anyway. Maybe Dolarhyde knew the maxillary arch survives fires a lot of times— who knows what he knew? Anyway, Lang didn't have any maxillary arch after Dolarhyde got through with him. He shot the head off Lang's body and he must have tipped the chair or something for the thud of the body falling. He'd hung the key around Lang's neck.

"Now Reba's scrambling around looking for the key. Dolarhyde's in the corner watching. Her ears are ringing from the shotgun. She won't hear his little noises.

"He's started a fire, but he hasn't put the gas to it yet. He's got gas in the room. She got out of the house okay. If she had panicked too much, run into a wall or something, or frozen, I guess he'd have sapped her and dragged her outside. She wouldn't have known how she got out. But she had to get out for it to work. Oh hell, here comes that nurse."

Graham wrote fast. "How vehicle?"

"You have to admire this," Crawford said. "He knew he'd have to leave his van at the house. He couldn't drive two vehicles out there and he needed a getaway piece.

"This is what he did: he made *Lang* hook up the service station tow-truck to his van. He snuffed Lang, locked the station and towed his van out to his house. Then he left the tow-truck on a dirt road back in the fields behind the house, got back in his van and went after Reba. When she got out of the house all right, he dragged out his dynamite, put the gasoline around the fire and lammed out the back. He drove the tow-truck *back* to the service station, left it and got Lang's car. No loose ends.

"It drove me crazy until we figured it out. I know it's right because he left a couple of prints on the towbar.

"We probably met him in the road when we were going up there to the house – yes, ma'am. I'm coming. Yes, Ma'am."

Graham wanted to ask a question but it was too late.

Molly took the next five-minute visit.

Graham wrote "I love you" on Crawford's pad.

She nodded and held his hand.

A minute later he wrote again.

"Willy okay?"

She nodded.

"Here?"

She looked up at him too quickly from the pad. She made a kiss with her mouth and pointed to the approaching nurse.

He tugged her thumb.

"*Where?*" he insisted, underlining twice.

"Oregon," she said.

Crawford came a final time.

Graham was ready with his note. It said "Teeth?"

"His grandmother's," Crawford said. "The ones we found in the house were his grandmother's. St. Louis P.D. located one Ned Vogt—

Dolarhyde's mother was Vogt's stepmother. Vogt saw Mrs. Dolarhyde when he was a kid and he never forgot the teeth.

"That's what I was calling you about when you ran into Dolarhyde. The Smithsonian had just called me. They finally had gotten the teeth from the Missouri authorities, just to examine for their own satisfaction. They noticed the upper part was made of vulcanite instead of acrylic like they use now. Nobody's made vulcanite plates in thirty-five years.

"Dolarhyde had a new acrylic pair just like them made to fit him. The new ones were on his body. Smithsonian looked at some features on them—the fluting, they said, and rugae. Chinese manufacture. The old ones were Swiss.

"He had a key on him too, for a locker in Miami. Big book in there. Kind of a diary—hell of a thing. I'll have it when you want to see it.

"Look, sport, I have to go back to Washington. I'll get back down here the week-end, if I can. You gonna be okay?"

Graham drew a question mark, then scratched it out and wrote "Sure".

The nurse came after Crawford left. She shot some Demerol into his intravenous line and the clock grew fuzzy. He couldn't keep up with the second hand.

He wondered if Demerol would work on your feelings. He could hold Molly a while with his face. Until they finished fixing it anyway. That would be a cheap shot. Hold her for what? He was drifting off and he hoped he wouldn't dream.

He did drift between memory and dream, but it wasn't so bad. He didn't dream of Molly leaving, or of Dolarhyde. It was a long memory-dream of Shiloh, interrupted by lights shined in his face and the gasp and hiss of the blood pressure cuff . . .

It was spring, soon after he shot Garrett Jacob Hobbs, when Graham visited Shiloh.

On a soft April day he walked across the asphalt road to Bloody Pond. The new grass, still light green, grew down the slope to the water. The clear water had risen into the grass and the grass was visible in the water, growing down, down as though it covered the bottom of the pond.

Graham knew what had happened there in April, 1862.

He sat down in the grass, felt the damp ground through his trousers.

A tourist's automobile went by and after it had passed, Graham saw movement behind it in the road. The car had broken a chicken snake's back. It slid in endless figure eights across itself in the centre of the asphalt road, sometimes showing its black back, sometimes its pale belly.

Shiloh's awesome presence hooded him with cold, though he was sweating in the mild spring sun.

Graham got up off the grass, his trousers damp behind. He was light-headed.

The snake looped on itself. He stood over it, picked it by the end of its smooth dry tail, and with a long fluid motion cracked it like a whip.

Its brains zinged into the pond. A bream rose to them.

He had thought Shiloh haunted, its beauty sinister like flags.

Now, drifting between memory and narcotic sleep, he saw that Shiloh was not sinister; it was indifferent. Beautiful Shiloh could witness anything. Its unforgivable beauty simply underscored the indifference of nature, the Green Machine. The loveliness of Shiloh mocked our plight.

He roused and watched the mindless clock, but he couldn't stop thinking.

In the Green Machine there is no mercy; *we* make mercy, manufacture it in the parts that have overgrown our basic reptile brain.

There is no murder. We make murder, and it matters only to us.

Graham knew too well that he contained all the elements to make murder; perhaps mercy too.

He understood murder uncomfortably well though.

He wondered if, in the great body of humankind, in the minds of men set on civilization, the vicious urges we control in ourselves and the dark instinctive knowledge of those urges function like the crippled virus the body arms against.

He wondered if old, awful urges are the virus that makes vaccine.

Yes, he had been wrong about Shiloh. Shiloh isn't haunted—men are haunted.

Shiloh doesn't care.

And I gave my heart to know wisdom, and to know madness and folly: I perceived that this also is vexation of spirit.

Ecclesiastes 1:17

The Silence of the Lambs

To the memory of my father

If after the manner of men I have fought with beasts at Ephesus, what advantageth it me, if the dead rise not?

– 1 Corinthians

Need I look upon a death's head in a ring, that have one in my face?

– John Donne, "Devotions"

CHAPTER

1

BEHAVIORAL SCIENCE, the F.B.I. section that deals with serial murder, is on the bottom floor of the Academy building at Quantico, half-buried in the earth. Clarice Starling reached it flushed after a fast walk from Hogan's Alley on the firing range. She had grass in her hair and grass stains on her F.B.I. Academy windbreaker from diving to the ground under fire in an arrest problem on the range.

No one was in the outer office, so she fluffed briefly by her reflection in the glass doors. She knew she could look all right without primping. Her hands smelled of gunsmoke, but there was no time to wash—Section Chief Crawford's summons had said *now.*

She found Jack Crawford alone in the cluttered suite of offices. He was standing at someone else's desk talking on the telephone and she had a chance to look him over for the first time in a year. What she saw disturbed her.

Normally, Crawford looked like a fit, middle-aged engineer who might have paid his way through college playing baseball—a crafty catcher, tough when he blocked the plate. Now he was thin, his shirt collar was too big, and he had dark puffs under his reddened eyes. Everyone who could read the papers knew Behavioral Science

Section was catching hell. Starling hoped Crawford wasn't on the juice. That seemed most unlikely here.

Crawford ended his telephone conversation with a sharp "No." He took her file from under his arm and opened it.

"Starling, Clarice M., good morning," he said.

"Hello." Her smile was only polite.

"Nothing's wrong. I hope the call didn't spook you."

"No." *Not totally true*, Starling thought.

"Your instructors tell me you're doing well, top quarter of the class."

"I hope so, they haven't posted anything."

"I ask them from time to time."

That surprised Starling; she had written Crawford off as a two-faced recruiting sergeant son of a bitch.

She had met Special Agent Crawford when he was a guest lecturer at the University of Virginia. The quality of his criminology seminars was a factor in her coming to the Bureau. She wrote him a note when she qualified for the Academy, but he never replied, and for the three months she had been a trainee at Quantico, he had ignored her.

Starling came from people who do not ask for favors or press for friendship, but she was puzzled and regretful at Crawford's behavior. Now, in his presence, she liked him again, she was sorry to note.

Clearly something was wrong with him. There was a peculiar cleverness in Crawford, aside from his intelligence, and Starling had first noticed it in his color sense and the textures of his clothing, even within the F.B.I.-clone standards of agent dress. Now he was neat but drab, as though he were molting.

"A job came up and I thought about you," he said. "It's not really a job, it's more of an interesting errand. Push Berry's stuff off that chair and sit down. You put down here that you want to come directly to Behavioral Science when you get through with the Academy."

"I do."

"You have a lot of forensics, but no law-enforcement background. We look for six years, minimum."

"My father was a marshal, I know the life."

Crawford smiled a little. "What you *do* have is a double major in psychology and criminology, and how many summers working in a mental health center—two?"

"Two."

"Your counselor's license, is it current?"

"It's good for two more years. I got it before you had the seminar at U.V.A.—before I decided to do this."

"You got stuck in the hiring freeze."

Starling nodded. "I was lucky though—I found out in time to qualify as a Forensic Fellow. Then I could work in the lab until the Academy had an opening."

"You wrote to me about coming here, didn't you, and I don't think I answered—I know I didn't. I should have."

"You've had plenty else to do."

"Do you know about VI-CAP?"

"I know it's the Violent Criminal Apprehension Program. The *Law Enforcement Bulletin* says you're working on a database, but you aren't operational yet."

Crawford nodded. "We've developed a questionnaire. It applies to all the known serial murderers in modern times." He handed her a thick sheaf of papers in a flimsy binding. "There's a section for investigators, and one for surviving victims, if any. The blue is for the killer to answer if he will, and the pink is a series of questions an examiner asks the killer, getting his reactions as well as his answers. It's a lot of paperwork."

Paperwork. Clarice Starling's self-interest snuffled ahead like a keen beagle. She smelled a job offer coming—probably the drudgery of feeding raw data into a new computer system. It was tempting to get into Behavioral Science in any capacity she could, but she knew what happens to a woman if she's ever pegged as a secretary—it sticks until the end of time. A choice was coming, and she wanted to choose well.

Crawford was waiting for something—he must have asked her a question. Starling had to scramble to recall it:

"What tests have you given? Minnesota Multiphasic, ever? Rorschach?"

"Yes, MMPI, never Rorschach," she said. "I've done Thematic Apperception and I've given children Bender-Gestalt."

"Do you spook easily, Starling?"

"Not yet."

"See, we've tried to interview and examine all the thirty-two known serial murderers we have in custody, to build up a database for psychological profiling in unsolved cases. Most of them went along with it—I think they're driven to show off, a lot of them. Twenty-seven were willing to cooperate. Four on death row with appeals pending clammed up, understandably. But the one we want the most, we haven't been able to get. I want you to go after him tomorrow in the asylum."

Clarice Starling felt a glad knocking in her chest and some apprehension too.

"Who's the subject?"

"The psychiatrist—Dr. Hannibal Lecter," Crawford said.

A brief silence follows the name, always, in any civilized gathering.

Starling looked at Crawford steadily, but she was too still. "Hannibal the Cannibal," she said.

"Yes."

"Yes, well—okay, right. I'm glad of the chance, but you have to know I'm wondering—why me?"

"Mainly because you're available," Crawford said. "I don't expect him to cooperate. He's already refused, but it was through an intermediary—the director of the hospital. I have to be able to say our qualified examiner went to him and asked him personally. There are reasons that don't concern you. I don't have anybody left in this section to do it."

"You're jammed—Buffalo Bill—and the things in Nevada," Starling said.

"You got it. It's the old story—not enough warm bodies."

"You said tomorrow—you're in a hurry. Any bearing on a current case?"

"No. I wish there were."

"If he balks on me, do you still want a psychological evaluation?"

"No. I'm waist-deep in inaccessible-patient evaluations of Dr. Lecter and they're all different."

Crawford shook two vitamin C tablets into his palm, and mixed an Alka-Seltzer at the water cooler to wash them down. "It's ridiculous, you know; Lecter's a psychiatrist and he writes for the psychiatric journals himself—extraordinary stuff—but it's never about his own little anomalies. He pretended to go along with the hospital director, Chilton, once in some tests—sitting around with a blood-pressure cuff on his penis, looking at wreck pictures—then Lecter published first what he'd learned about Chilton and made a fool out of him. He responds to serious correspondence from psychiatric students in fields unrelated to his case, and that's all he does. If he won't talk to you, I just want straight reporting. How does he look, how does his cell look, what's he doing. Local color, so to speak. Watch out for the press going in and coming out. Not the real press, the supermarket press. They love Lecter even better than Prince Andrew."

"Didn't a sleazo magazine offer him fifty thousand dollars for some recipes? I seem to remember that," Starling said.

Crawford nodded. "I'm pretty sure the *National Tattler* has bought somebody inside the hospital and they may know you're coming after I make the appointment."

Crawford leaned forward until he faced her at a distance of two feet. She watched his half-glasses blur the bags under his eyes. He had gargled recently with Listerine.

"Now. I want your full attention, Starling. Are you listening to me?"

"Yes, sir."

"Be very careful with Hannibal Lecter. Dr. Chilton, the head of the mental hospital, will go over the physical procedure you use to deal with him. Don't deviate from it. *Do not deviate from it one iota for any reason.* If Lecter talks to you at all, he'll just be trying to find out about you. It's the kind of curiosity that makes a snake look in a bird's nest. We both know you have to back-and-forth a little in interviews, but you tell him no specifics about yourself. You don't want any of your personal facts in his head. You know what he did to Will Graham."

"I read about it when it happened."

"He gutted Will with a linoleum knife when Will caught up with him. It's a wonder Will didn't die. Remember the Red Dragon? Lecter turned Francis Dolarhyde onto Will and his family. Will's face looks like damn Picasso drew him, thanks to Lecter. He tore a nurse up in the asylum. Do your job, just don't ever forget what he is."

"And what's that? Do you know?"

"I know he's a monster. Beyond that, nobody can say for sure. Maybe you'll find out; I didn't pick you out of a hat, Starling. You asked me a couple of interesting questions when I was at U.V.A. The Director will see your own report over your signature—if it's clear and tight and organized. I decide that. And I *will* have it by 0900 Sunday. Okay, Starling, carry on in the prescribed manner."

Crawford smiled at her, but his eyes were dead.

DR. FREDERICK CHILTON, fifty-eight, administrator of the Baltimore State Hospital for the Criminally Insane, has a long, wide desk upon which there are no hard or sharp objects. Some of the staff call it "the moat." Other staff members don't know what the word *moat* means. Dr. Chilton remained seated behind his desk when Clarice Starling came into his office.

"We've had a lot of detectives here, but I can't remember one so attractive," Chilton said without getting up.

Starling knew without thinking about it that the shine on his extended hand was lanolin from patting his hair. She let go before he did.

"It is *Miss* Sterling, isn't it?"

"It's *Star*ling, Doctor, with an *a*. Thank you for your time."

"So the F.B.I. is going to the girls like everything else, ha, ha." He added the tobacco smile he uses to separate his sentences.

"The Bureau's improving, Dr. Chilton. It certainly is."

"Will you be in Baltimore for several days? You know, you can have just as good a time here as you can in Washington or New York, if you know the town."

She looked away to spare herself his smile and knew at once that he had registered her distaste. "I'm sure it's a great town, but my instructions are to see Dr. Lecter and report back this afternoon."

"Is there someplace I could call you in Washington for a follow-up, later on?"

"Of course. It's kind of you to think of it. Special Agent Jack Crawford's in charge of this project, and you can always reach me through him."

"I see," Chilton said. His cheeks, mottled with pink, clashed with the improbable red-brown of his coif. "Give me your identification, please." He let her remain standing through his leisurely examination of her I.D. card. Then he handed it back and rose. "This won't take much time. Come along."

"I understood you'd brief me, Dr. Chilton," Starling said.

"I can do that while we walk." He came around his desk, looking at his watch. "I have a lunch in half an hour."

Dammit, she should have read him better, quicker. He might not be a total jerk. He might know something useful. It wouldn't have hurt her to simper once, even if she wasn't good at it.

"Dr. Chilton, I have an appointment with you now. It was set at your convenience, when you could give me some time. Things could come up during the interview—I may need to go over some of his responses with you."

"I really, really doubt it. Oh, I need to make a telephone call before we go. I'll catch up with you in the outer office."

"I'd like to leave my coat and umbrella here."

"Out there," Chilton said. "Give them to Alan in the outer office. He'll put them away."

Alan wore the pajama-like garment issued to the inmates. He was wiping out ashtrays with the tail of his shirt.

He rolled his tongue around in his cheek as he took Starling's coat.

"Thank you," she said.

"You're more than welcome. How often do you shit?" Alan asked.

"What did you say?"

"Does it come out lo-o-o-o-nnng?"

"I'll hang these somewhere myself."

"You don't have anything in the way—you can bend over and watch it come out and see if it changes color when the air hits it, do you do that? Does it look like you have a big brown tail?" He wouldn't let go of the coat.

"Dr. Chilton wants you in his office, right now," Starling said.

"No I don't," Dr. Chilton said. "Put the coat in the closet, Alan, and don't get it out while we're gone. *Do it.* I had a full-time office girl, but the cutbacks robbed me of her. Now the girl who let you in types three hours a day, and then I have Alan. Where are all the office girls, Miss Starling?" His spectacles flashed at her. "Are you armed?"

"No, I'm not armed."

"May I see your purse and briefcase?"

"You saw my credentials."

"And they say you're a student. Let me see your things, please."

Clarice Starling flinched as the first of the heavy steel gates clashed shut behind her and the bolt shot home. Chilton walked slightly ahead, down the green institutional corridor in an atmosphere of Lysol and distant slammings. Starling was angry at herself for letting Chilton put his hand in her purse and briefcase, and she stepped hard on the anger so that she could concentrate. It was all right. She felt her control solid beneath her, like a good gravel bottom in a fast current.

"Lecter's a considerable nuisance," Chilton said over his shoulder. "It takes an orderly at least ten minutes a day to remove the staples from the publications he receives. We tried to eliminate or reduce his subscriptions, but he wrote a brief and the court overruled us. The volume of his personal mail used to be enormous. Thankfully, it's dwindled since he's been overhadowed by other creatures in the news. For a while it seemed that every little student doing a master's thesis in psychology wanted something from Lecter in it. The medical journals still publish him, but it's just for the freak value of his byline."

"He did a good piece on surgical addiction in the *Journal of Clinical Psychiatry*, I thought," Starling said.

"You did, did you? *We* tried to study Lecter. We thought, 'Here's an opportunity to make a landmark study'—it's so rare to get one alive."

"One what?"

"A pure sociopath, that's obviously what he is. But he's impenetrable, much too sophisticated for the standard tests. And, my, does he hate us. He thinks I'm his nemesis. Crawford's very clever—isn't he?—using you on Lecter."

"How do you mean, Dr. Chilton?"

"A young woman to 'turn him on,' I believe you call it. I don't believe Lecter's seen a woman in several years—he may have gotten a glimpse of one of the cleaning people. We generally keep women out of there. They're trouble in detention."

Well fuck off, Chilton. "I graduated from the University of Virginia with honors, Doctor. It's not a charm school."

"Then you should be able to remember the rules: Do not reach through the bars, do not touch the bars. You pass him nothing but soft paper. No pens, no pencils. He has his own felt-tipped pens some of the time. The paper you pass him must be free of staples, paper clips, or pins. Items come back out through the sliding food carrier. No exceptions. Do not accept anything he attempts to hold out to you through the barrier. Do you understand me?"

"I understand."

They had passed through two more gates and left the natural light behind. Now they were beyond the wards where inmates can mix together, down in the region where there can be no windows and no mixing. The hallway lights are covered with heavy grids, like the lights in the engine rooms of ships. Dr. Chilton paused beneath one. When their footfalls stopped, Starling could hear somewhere beyond the wall the ragged end of a voice ruined by shouting.

"Lecter is never outside his cell without wearing full restraints and a mouthpiece," Chilton said. "I'm going to show you why. He was a model of cooperation for the first year after he was committed. Security around him was slightly relaxed—this was under the previous administration, you understand. On the afternoon of July 8, 1976, he complained of chest pain and he was taken to the dispensary. His restraints were removed to make it easier to give him an electrocardiogram. When the nurse bent over him, he did this to her." Chilton handed Clarice Starling a dog-eared photograph. "The doctors managed to save one of her eyes. Lecter was hooked up to the monitors the entire time. He broke her jaw to get at her tongue. His pulse never got over eighty-five, even when he swallowed it."

Starling didn't know which was worse, the photograph or Chilton's attention as he gleaned her face with fast grabby eyes. She thought of a thirsty chicken pecking tears off her face.

"I keep him in here," Chilton said, and pushed a button beside heavy double doors of security glass. A big orderly let them into the block beyond.

Starling made a tough decision and stopped just inside the doors. "Dr. Chilton, we really need these test results. If Dr. Lecter feels you're his enemy—if he's fixed on you, just as you've said—we might have more luck if I approached him by myself. What do you think?"

Chilton's cheek twitched. "That's perfectly fine with me. You might have suggested that in my office. I could have sent an orderly with you and saved the time."

"I could have suggested it there if you'd briefed me there."

"I don't expect I'll see you again, Miss *Star*ling—Barney, when she's finished with Lecter, ring for someone to bring her out."

Chilton left without looking at her again.

Now there was only the big impassive orderly and the soundless clock behind him and his wire mesh cabinet with the Mace and restraints, mouthpiece and tranquilizer gun. A wall rack held a long pipe device with a U on the end for pinioning the violent to the wall.

The orderly was looking at her. "Dr. Chilton told you, don't touch the bars?" His voice was both high and hoarse. She was reminded of Aldo Ray.

"Yes, he told me."

"Okay. It's past the others, the last cell on the right. Stay toward the middle of the corridor as you go down, and don't mind anything. You can take him his mail, get off on the right foot." The orderly seemed privately amused. "You just put it in the tray and let it roll through. If the tray's inside, you can pull it back with the cord, or he can send it back. He can't reach you where the tray stops outside." The orderly gave her two magazines, their loose pages spilling out, three newspapers and several opened letters.

The corridor was about thirty yards long, with cells on both sides. Some were padded cells with an observation window, long and narrow like an archery slit, in the center of the door. Others were standard prison cells, with a wall of bars opening on the corridor. Clarice Starling was aware of figures in the cells, but she tried not to look at them. She was more than halfway down when a voice hissed, "I can smell your cunt." She gave no sign that she had heard it, and went on.

The lights were on in the last cell. She moved toward the left side of the corridor to see into it as she approached, knowing her heels announced her.

3

DR. LECTER'S cell is well beyond the others, facing only a closet across the corridor, and it is unique in other ways. The front is a wall of bars, but within the bars, at a distance greater than the human reach, is a second barrier, a stout nylon net stretched from floor to ceiling and wall to wall. Behind the net, Starling could see a table bolted to the floor and piled high with softcover books and papers, and a straight chair, also fastened down.

Dr. Hannibal Lecter himself reclined on his bunk, perusing the Italian edition of *Vogue*. He held the loose pages in his right hand and put them beside him one by one with his left. Dr. Lecter has six fingers on his left hand.

Clarice Starling stopped a little distance from the bars, about the length of a small foyer.

"Dr. Lecter." Her voice sounded all right to her.

He looked up from his reading.

For a steep second she thought his gaze hummed, but it was only her blood she heard.

"My name is Clarice Starling. May I talk with you?" Courtesy was implicit in her distance and her tone.

Dr. Lecter considered, his finger pressed against his pursed lips. Then he rose in his own time and came forward smoothly in his cage, stopping short of the nylon web without looking at it, as though he chose the distance.

She could see that he was small, sleek; in his hands and arms she saw wiry strength like her own.

"Good morning," he said, as though he had answered the door. His cultured voice has a slight metallic rasp beneath it, possibly from disuse.

Dr. Lecter's eyes are maroon and they reflect the light in pinpoints of red. Sometimes the points of light seem to fly like sparks to his center. His eyes held Starling whole.

She came a measured distance closer to the bars. The hair on her forearms rose and pressed against her sleeves.

"Doctor, we have a hard problem in psychological profiling. I want to ask you for your help."

"'We' being Behavioral Science at Quantico. You're one of Jack Crawford's, I expect."

"I am, yes."

"May I see your credentials?"

She hadn't expected this. "I showed them at the . . . office."

"You mean you showed them to Frederick Chilton, Ph.D.?"

"Yes."

"Did you see *his* credentials?"

"No."

"The academic ones don't make extensive reading, I can tell you. Did you meet Alan? Isn't he charming? Which of them had you rather talk with?"

"On the whole, I'd say Alan."

"You could be a reporter Chilton let in for money. I think I'm entitled to see your credentials."

"All right." She held up her laminated I.D. card.

"I can't read it at this distance, send it through, please."

"I can't."

"Because it's hard."

"Yes."

"Ask Barney."

The orderly came and considered. "Dr. Lecter, I'll let this come through. But if you don't return it when I ask you to—if we have to bother everybody and secure you to get it—then I'll be upset. If you upset me, you'll have to stay bundled up until I feel better toward you. Meals through the tube, dignity pants changed twice a day—the works. And I'll hold your mail for a week. Got it?"

"Certainly, Barney."

The card rolled through on the tray and Dr. Lecter held it to the light.

"A trainee? It says 'trainee.' Jack Crawford sent a *trainee* to interview me?" He tapped the card against his small white teeth and breathed in its smell.

"Dr. Lecter," Barney said.

"Of course." He put the card back in the tray carrier and Barney pulled it to the outside.

"I'm still in training at the Academy, yes," Starling said, "but we're not discussing the F.B.I.—we're talking about psychology. Can you decide for yourself if I'm qualified in what we talk about?"

"Ummmm," Dr. Lecter said. "Actually . . . that's rather slippery of you. Barney, do you think Officer Starling might have a chair?"

"Dr. Chilton didn't tell me anything about a chair."

"What do your manners tell you, Barney?"

"Would you like a chair?" Barney asked her. "We could have had one, but he never—well, usually nobody needs to stay that long."

"Yes, thank you," Starling said.

Barney brought a folding chair from the locked closet across the hall, set it up, and left them.

"Now," Lecter said, sitting sideways at his table to face her, "what did Miggs say to you?"

"Who?"

"Multiple Miggs, in the cell down there. He hissed at you. What did he say?"

"He said, 'I can smell your cunt.'"

"I see. I myself cannot. You use Evyan skin cream, and sometimes you wear L'Air du Temps, but not today. Today you are determinedly unperfumed. How do you feel about what Miggs said?"

"He's hostile for reasons I couldn't know. It's too bad. He's hostile to people, people are hostile to him. It's a loop."

"Are you hostile to him?"

"I'm sorry he's disturbed. Beyond that, he's noise. How did you know about the perfume?"

"A puff from your bag when you got out your card. Your bag is lovely."

"Thank you."

"You brought your best bag, didn't you?"

"Yes." It was true. She had saved for the classic casual handbag, and it was the best item she owned.

"It's much better than your shoes."

"Maybe they'll catch up."

"I have no doubt of it."

"Did you do the drawings on your walls, Doctor?"

"Do you think I called in a decorator?"

"The one over the sink is a European city?"

"It's Florence. That's the Palazzo Vecchio and the Duomo, seen from the Belvedere."

"Did you do it from memory, all the detail?"

"Memory, Officer Starling, is what I have instead of a view."

"The other one is a crucifixion? The middle cross is empty."

"It's Golgotha after the Deposition. Crayon and Magic Marker on butcher paper. It's what the thief who had been promised Paradise really got, when they took the paschal lamb away."

"And what was that?"

"His legs broken of course, just like his companion who mocked Christ. Are you entirely innocent of the Gospel of St John? Look at Duccio, then—he paints accurate crucifixions. How is Will Graham? How does he look?"

"I don't know Will Graham."

"You know who he is. Jack Crawford's protégé. The one before you. How does his face look?"

"I've never seen him."

"This is called 'cutting up a few old touches,' Officer Starling, you don't mind, do you?"

Beats of silence and she plunged.

"Better than that, we could touch up a few old cuts here. I brought—"

"No. No, that's stupid and wrong. Never use wit in a segue. Listen, understanding a witticism and replying to it makes your subject perform a fast, detached scan that is inimical to mood. It is on the plank of mood that we proceed. You were doing fine, you'd been courteous and receptive to courtesy, you'd established trust by telling the embarrassing truth about Miggs, and then you come in with a ham-handed segue into your questionnaire. It won't do."

"Dr. Lecter, you're an experienced clinical psychiatrist. Do you think I'm dumb enough to try to run some kind of mood scam on you? Give me some credit. I'm asking you to respond to the questionnaire, and you will or you won't. Would it hurt to look at the thing?"

"Officer Starling, have you read any of the papers coming out of Behavioral Science recently?"

"Yes."

"So have I. The F.B.I. stupidly refused to send me the *Law Enforcement Bulletin*, but I get it from secondhand dealers and I have the *News* from

John Jay, and the psychiatric journals. They're dividing the people who practice serial murder into two groups—organized and disorganized. What do you think of that?"

"It's . . . fundamental, they evidently—"

"*Simplistic* is the word you want. In fact, most psychology is puerile, Officer Starling, and that practiced in Behavioral Science is on a level with phrenology. Psychology doesn't get very good material to start with. Go to any college psychology department and look at the students and faculty: ham-radio enthusiasts and other personality-deficient buffs. Hardly the best brains on the campus. *Organized* and *disorganized*—a real bottom-feeder thought of that."

"How would you change the classification?"

"I wouldn't."

"Speaking of publications, I read your pieces on surgical addiction and left-side, right-side facial displays."

"Yes, they were first-rate," Dr. Lecter said.

"I thought so, and so did Jack Crawford. He pointed them out to me. That's one reason he's anxious for you—"

"Crawford the Stoic is anxious? He must be busy if he's recruiting help from the student body."

"He is, and he wants—"

"Busy with Buffalo Bill."

"I expect so."

"No. Not 'I expect so.' Officer Starling, you know perfectly well it's Buffalo Bill. I thought Jack Crawford might have sent you to ask me about that."

"No."

"Then you're not working around to it."

"No, I came because we need your—"

"What do you know about Buffalo Bill?"

"Nobody knows much."

"Has everything been in the papers?"

"I think so. Dr. Lecter, I haven't seen any confidential material on that case, my job is—"

"How many women has Buffalo Bill used?"

"The police have found five."

"All flayed?"

"Partially, yes."

"The papers have never explained his name. Do you know why he's called Buffalo Bill?"

"Yes."

"Tell me."

"I'll tell you if you'll look at this questionnaire."

"I'll look, that's all. Now, why?"

"It started as a bad joke in Kansas City homicide."

"Yes . . ."

"They call him Buffalo Bill because he skins his humps."

Starling discovered that she had traded feeling frightened for feeling cheap. Of the two, she preferred feeling frightened.

"Send through the questionnaire."

Starling rolled the blue section through on the tray. She sat still while Lecter flipped through it.

He dropped it back in the carrier. "Oh, Officer Starling, do you think you can dissect me with this blunt little tool?"

"No. I think you can provide some insight and advance this study."

"And what possible reason could I have to do that?"

"Curiosity."

"About what?"

"About why you're here. About what happened to you."

"Nothing happened to me, Officer Starling. I happened. You can't reduce me to a set of influences. You've given up good and evil for behaviorism, Officer Starling. You've got everybody in moral dignity pants—nothing is ever anybody's fault. Look at me, Officer Starling. Can you stand to say I'm evil? Am I evil, Officer Starling?"

"I think you've been destructive. For me it's the same thing."

"Evil's just destructive? Then *storms* are evil, if it's that simple. And we have *fire*, and then there's *hail*. Underwriters lump it all under 'Acts of God.'"

"Deliberate—"

"I collect church collapses, recreationally. Did you see the recent one in Sicily? Marvelous! The façade fell on sixty-five grandmothers at a special Mass. Was that evil? If so, who did it? If He's up there, He just loves it, Officer Starling. Typhoid and swans—it all comes from the same place."

"I can't explain you, Doctor, but I know who can."

He stopped her with his upraised hand. The hand was shapely, she noted, and the middle finger perfectly replicated. It is the rarest form of polydactyly.

When he spoke again, his tone was soft and pleasant. "You'd like to quantify me, Officer Starling. You're so ambitious, aren't you? Do you know what you look like to me, with your good bag and your cheap shoes? You look like a rube. You're a well-scrubbed, hustling rube with a little taste. Your eyes are like cheap birthstones—all surface shine when you stalk some little answer. And you're bright behind them, aren't you? Desperate not to be like your mother. Good nutrition has given you some length of bone, but you're not more than one generation out of the mines, *Officer* Starling. Is it the West Virginia Starlings or the Okie Starlings, Officer? It was a toss-up between college and the opportunities in the Women's Army Corps, wasn't it? Let me tell you something specific about yourself, Student Starling. Back in your room, you have a string of gold add-a-beads and you feel an ugly little thump when you look at how tacky they are now, isn't that so? All those tedious thank-yous, permitting all that sincere fumbling, getting all sticky once for every bead. Tedious. Tedious. Bo-o-o-o-r-i-ing. Being smart spoils a lot of things, doesn't it? And taste isn't kind. When you think about this conversation, you'll remember the dumb animal hurt in his face when you got rid of him.

"If the add-a-beads got tacky, what else will as you go along? You wonder, don't you, at night?" Dr. Lecter asked in the kindest of tones.

Starling raised her head to face him. "You see a lot, Dr. Lecter. I won't deny anything you've said. But here's the question you're answering for me right now, whether you mean to or not: Are you strong enough to point that high-powered perception at yourself? It's hard to face. I've found that out in the last few minutes. How about it? Look at yourself and write down the truth. What more fit or complex subject could you find? Or maybe you're afraid of yourself."

"You're tough, aren't you, Officer Starling?"

"Reasonably so, yes."

"And you'd hate to think you were common. Wouldn't that sting? My! Well you're far from common, Officer Starling. All you have is fear of it. What are your add-a-beads, seven millimeter?"

"Seven."

"Let me make a suggestion. Get some loose, drilled tiger's eyes and string them alternately with the gold beads. You might want to do two-and-three or one-and-two, however looks best to you. The tiger's eyes will pick up the color of your own eyes and the highlights in your hair. Has anyone ever sent you a Valentine?"

"Yep."

"We're already into Lent. Valentine's Day is only a week away, hummmm, are you expecting some?"

"You never know."

"No, you never do . . . I've been thinking about Valentine's Day. It reminds me of something funny. Now that I think of it, I could make you very happy on Valentine's Day, *Clarice* Starling."

"How, Doctor Lecter?"

"By sending you a wonderful Valentine. I'll have to think about it. Now, please excuse me. Good-bye, Officer Starling."

"And the study?"

"A census taker tried to quantify me once. I ate his liver with some fava beans and a big Amarone. Go back to school, little Starling."

Hannibal Lecter, polite to the last, did not give her his back. He stepped backward from the barrier before he turned to his cot again, and lying on it, became as remote from her as a stone crusader lying on a tomb.

Starling felt suddenly empty, as though she had given blood. She took longer than necessary to put the papers back in her briefcase because she didn't immediately trust her legs. Starling was soaked with the failure she detested. She folded her chair and leaned it against the utility-closet door. She would have to pass Miggs again. Barney in the distance appeared to be reading. She could call him to come for her. Damn Miggs. It was no worse than passing construction crews or delivery louts every day in the city. She started back down the corridor.

Close beside her, Miggs's voice hissed, "I bit my wrist so I can diiiieeeeeeeee—see how it bleeds?"

She should have called Barney but, startled, she looked into the cell, saw Miggs flick his fingers and felt the warm spatter on her cheek and shoulder before she could turn away.

She got away from him, registered that it was semen, not blood, and Lecter was calling to her, she could hear him. Dr. Lecter's voice behind her, the cutting rasp in it more pronounced.

"Officer Starling."

He was up and calling after her as she walked. She rummaged in her purse for tissues.

Behind her, "Officer Starling."

She was on the cold rails of her control now, making steady progress toward the gate.

"Officer Starling." A new note in Lecter's voice.

She stopped. *What in God's name do I want this bad?* Miggs hissed something she didn't listen to.

She stood again in front of Lecter's cell and saw the rare spectacle of the doctor agitated. She knew that he could smell it on her. He could smell everything.

"I would not have had that happen to you. Discourtesy is unspeakably ugly to me."

It was as though committing murders had purged him of lesser rudeness. Or perhaps, Starling thought, it excited him to see her marked in this particular way. She couldn't tell. The sparks in his eyes flew into his darkness like fireflies down a cave.

Whatever it is, use it, Jesus! She held up her briefcase. "Please do this for me."

Maybe she was too late; he was calm again.

"No. But I'll make you happy that you came. I'll give you something else. I'll give you what you love the most, Clarice Starling."

"What's that, Dr. Lecter?"

"Advancement, of course. It works out perfectly—I'm so glad. Valentine's Day made me think of it." The smile over his small white teeth could have come for any reason. He spoke so softly she could barely hear. "Look in Raspail's car for your Valentines. Did you hear me? Look in *Raspail's car* for your Valentines. You'd better go now; I don't think Miggs could manage again so soon, even if he *is* crazy, do you?"

4

CLARICE STARLING was excited, depleted, running on her will. Some of the things Lecter had said about her were true, and some only clanged on the truth. For a few seconds she had felt an alien consciousness loose in her head, slapping things off the shelves like a bear in a camper.

She hated what he'd said about her mother and she had to get rid of the anger. This was business.

She sat in her old Pinto across the street from the hospital and breathed deeply. When the windows fogged she had a little privacy from the sidewalk.

Raspail. She remembered the name. He was a patient of Lecter's and one of his victims. She'd had only one evening with the Lecter background material. The file was vast and Raspail one of many victims. She needed to read the details.

Starling wanted to run with it, but she knew that the urgency was of her own manufacture. The Raspail case was closed years ago. No one was in danger. She had time. Better to be well informed and well advised before she went further.

Crawford might take it away from her and give it to someone else. She'd have to take that chance.

She tried to call him from a phone booth, but found he was budget-begging for the Justice Department before the House Subcommittee on Appropriations.

She could have gotten details of the case from the Baltimore Police Department's homicide division, but murder is not a federal crime and she knew they'd snatch it away from her immediately, no question.

She drove back to Quantico, back to Behavioral Science with its homey brown-checked curtains and its gray files full of hell. She sat there into the evening, after the last secretary had left, cranking through the Lecter microfilm. The contrary old viewer glowed like a jack-o'-lantern in the darkened room, the words and the negatives of pictures swarming across her intent face.

Raspail, Benjamin René, WM, 46, was first flutist for the Baltimore Philharmonic Orchestra. He was a patient in Dr. Hannibal Lecter's psychiatric practice.

On March 22, 1975, he failed to appear for a performance in Baltimore. On March 25 his body was discovered seated in a pew in a small rural church near Falls Church, Virginia, dressed only in a white tie and a tailcoat. Autopsy revealed that Raspail's heart was pierced and that he was short of his thymus and pancreas.

Clarice Starling, who from early life had known much more than she wished to know about meat processing, recognized the missing organs as the sweetbreads.

Baltimore Homicide believed that these items appeared on the menu of a dinner Lecter gave for the president and the conductor of the Baltimore Philharmonic on the evening following Raspail's disappearance.

Dr. Hannibal Lecter professed to know nothing about these matters. The president and the conductor of the Philharmonic testified that they could not recall the fare at Dr. Lecter's dinner, though Lecter was known for the excellence of his table and had contributed numerous articles to gourmet magazines.

The president of the Philharmonic subsequently was treated for anorexia and problems related to alcohol dependency at a holistic nerve sanitarium in Basel.

Raspail was Lecter's ninth known victim, according to the Baltimore police.

Raspail died intestate, and the lawsuits among his relatives over the estate were followed by the newspapers for a number of months before public interest flagged.

Raspail's relatives had also joined with the families of other victims in Lecter's practice in a successful lawsuit to have the errant psychiatrist's case files and tapes destroyed. There was no telling what embarrassing secrets he might blab, their reasoning went, and the files were documentation.

The court had appointed Raspail's lawyer, Everett Yow, to be executor of his estate.

Starling would have to apply to the lawyer to get at the car. The lawyer might be protective of Raspail's memory and, with enough advance notice, might destroy evidence to cover for his late client.

Starling preferred to pounce, and she needed advice and authorization. She was alone in Behavioral Science and had the run of the place. She found Crawford's home number in the Rolodex.

She never heard the telephone ringing, but suddenly his voice was there, very quiet and even.

"Jack Crawford."

"This is Clarice Starling. I hope you weren't eating dinner . . ." She had to continue into silence. ". . . Lecter told me something about the Raspail case today, I'm in the office following it up. He tells me there's something in Raspail's car. I'd have to get at it through his lawyer, and since tomorrow's Saturday—no school—I wanted to ask you if—"

"Starling, do you have any recollection of what I told you to do with the Lecter information?" Crawford's voice was so terribly quiet.

"Give you a report by 0900 Sunday."

"Do that, Starling. Do just exactly that."

"Yes, sir."

The dial tone stung in her ear. The sting spread over her face and made her eyes burn.

"Well God fucking shit," she said. "You old creep. Creepo son of a bitch. Let Miggs squirt *you* and see how you like it."

Starling, scrubbed shiny and wearing the F.B.I. Academy nightgown, was working on the second draft of her report when her dormitory roommate, Ardelia Mapp, came in from the library. Mapp's broad, brown, eminently sane countenance was one of the more welcome sights of her day.

Ardelia Mapp saw the fatigue in her face.

"What did you do today, girl?" Mapp always asked questions as if the answers could make no possible difference.

"Wheedled a crazy man with come all over me."

"I wish *I* had time for a social life—I don't know how you manage it, and school too."

Starling found that she was laughing. Ardelia Mapp laughed with her, as much as the small joke was worth. Starling did not stop, and she heard herself from far away, laughing and laughing. Through Starling's tears, Mapp looked strangely old and her smile had sadness in it.

5

JACK CRAWFORD, fifty-three, reads in a wing chair by a low lamp in the bedroom of his home. He faces two double beds, both raised on blocks to hospital height. One is his own; in the other lies his wife, Bella. Crawford can hear her breathing through her mouth. It has been two days since she last could stir or speak to him.

She misses a breath. Crawford looks up from his book, over his half-glasses. He puts the book down. Bella breathes again, a flutter and then a full breath. He rises to put his hand on her, to take her blood pressure and her pulse. Over the months he has become expert with the blood-pressure cuff.

Because he will not leave her at night, he has installed a bed for himself beside her. Because he reaches out to her in the dark, his bed is high, like hers.

Except for the height of the beds and the minimal plumbing necessary for Bella's comfort, Crawford has managed to keep this from looking like a sickroom. There are flowers, but not too many. No pills are in sight—Crawford emptied a linen closet in the hall and filled it with her medicines and apparatus before he brought her home from the hospital. (It was the second time he had carried her across the threshold of that house, and the thought nearly unmanned him.)

A warm front has come up from the south. The windows are open and the Virginia air is soft and fresh. Small frogs peep to one another in the dark.

The room is spotless, but the carpet has begun to nap—Crawford will not run the noisy vacuum cleaner in the room and uses a manual carpet sweeper that is not as good. He pads to the closet and turns on the light. Two clipboards hang on the inside of the door. On one he notes Bella's pulse and blood pressure. His figures and those of the day nurse alternate in a column that stretches over many yellow pages, many days and nights. On the other clipboard, the day-shift nurse has signed off Bella's medication.

Crawford is capable of giving any medication she may need in the night. Following a nurse's directions, he practiced injections on a lemon and then on his thighs before he brought her home.

Crawford stands over her for perhaps three minutes, looking down into her face. A lovely scarf of silk moiré covers her hair like a turban. She insisted on it, for as long as she could insist. Now he insists on it. He moistens her lips with glycerine and removes a speck from the corner of her eye with his broad thumb. She does not stir. It is not yet time to turn her.

At the mirror, Crawford assures himself that he is not sick, that he doesn't have to go into the ground with her, that he himself is well. He catches himself doing this and it shames him.

Back at his chair he cannot remember what he was reading. He feels the books beside him to find the one that is warm.

6

ON MONDAY morning, Clarice Starling found this message from Crawford in her mailbox:

CS:

Proceed on the Raspail car. On your own time. My office will provide you a credit-card number for long-distance calls. Ck with me before you contact estate or go anywhere. Report Wednesday 1600 hours.

The Director got your Lecter report over your signature. You did well.

JC
SAIC/Section 8

Starling felt pretty good. She knew Crawford was just giving her an exhausted mouse to bat around for practice. But he wanted to teach her. He wanted her to do well. For Starling, that beat courtesy every time.

Raspail had been dead for eight years. What evidence could have lasted in a car that long?

She knew from family experience that, because automobiles depreciate so rapidly, an appellate court will let survivors sell a car before probate, the money going into escrow. It seemed unlikely that even an estate as tangled and disputed as Raspail's would hold a car this long.

There was also the problem of time. Counting her lunch break, Starling had an hour and fifteen minutes a day free to use the telephone during business hours. She'd have to report to Crawford on Wednesday afternoon. So she had a total of three hours and forty-five minutes to trace the car, spread over three days, if she used her study periods and made up the study at night.

She had good notes from her Investigative Procedures classes, and she'd have a chance to ask general questions of her instructors.

During her Monday lunch, personnel at the Baltimore County Courthouse put Starling on hold and forgot her three times. During her study period she reached a friendly clerk at the courthouse, who pulled the probate records on the Raspail estate.

The clerk confirmed that permission had been granted for sale of an auto and gave Starling the make and serial number of the car, and the name of a subsequent owner off the title transfer.

On Tuesday, she wasted half her lunch hour trying to chase down that name. It cost her the rest of her lunch period to find out that the Maryland Department of Motor Vehicles is not equipped to trace a vehicle by serial number, only by registration number or current tag number.

On Tuesday afternoon, a downpour drove the trainees in from the firing range. In a conference room steamy with damp clothing and sweat, John Brigham, the ex-Marine firearms instructor, chose to test Starling's hand strength in front of the class by seeing how many times she could pull the trigger on a Model 19 Smith & Wesson in sixty seconds.

She managed seventy-four with her left hand, puffed a strand of hair out of her eyes, and started over with her right while another student counted. She was in the Weaver stance, well braced, the front sight in sharp focus, the rear sight and her makeshift target properly blurred. Midway through her minute, she let her mind wander to get it off the pain. The target on the wall came into focus. It was a certificate of appreciation from the Interstate Commerce enforcement division made out to her instructor, John Brigham.

She questioned Brigham out of the side of her mouth while the other student counted the clicks of the revolver.

"How do you trace the current registration . . ."

". . . *sixtyfivesixtysixsixtysevensixtyeightsixty* . . ."

". . . of a car when you've only got the serial number . . ."

". . . *seventyeightseventynineeightyeightyone* . . ."

". . . and the make? You don't have a current tag number."

". . . *eightynineninety. Time.*"

"All right, you people," the instructor said, "I want you to take note of that. Hand strength's a major factor in steady combat shooting. Some of you gentlemen are worried I'll call on you next. Your worries would be justified—Starling is well above average with both hands. That's because she works at it. She works at it with the little squeezy things you all have access to. Most of you are not used to squeezing anything harder than your"—ever vigilant against his native Marine terminology, he groped for a polite simile—"zits," he said at last. "Get serious, Starling, you're not good enough either. I want to see that left hand over ninety before you graduate. Pair up and time each other—chop-chop.

"Not you, Starling, come here. What else have you got on the car?"

"Just the serial number and make, that's it. One prior owner five years ago."

"All right, listen. Where most people f—fall into error is trying to leapfrog through the registrations from one owner to the next. You get fouled up between states. I mean, cops even do that sometimes. And registrations and tag numbers are all the computer's got. We're all accustomed to using tag numbers or registration numbers, not vehicle serial numbers."

The clicking of the blue-handled practice revolvers was loud all over the room and he had to rumble in her ear.

"There's one way it's easy. R. L. Polk and Company, that publishes city directories—they also put out a list of current car registrations by make and consecutive serial number. It's the only place. Car dealers steer their advertising with them. How'd you know to ask me?"

"You were ICC enforcement, I figured you'd traced a lot of vehicles. Thanks."

"Pay me back—get that left hand up where it ought to be and let's shame some of these lilyfingers."

Back in her phone booth during study period, her hands trembled so that her notes were barely legible. Raspail's car was a Ford. There was a Ford dealer near the University of Virginia who for years had patiently done what he could with her Pinto. Now, just as patiently, the dealer poked through his Polk listings for her. He came back to the telephone with the name and address of the person who had last registered Benjamin Raspail's car.

Clarice is on a roll, Clarice has got control. Quit being silly and call the man up at his home in, lemme see, Number Nine Ditch, Arkansas. Jack Crawford will never let me go down there, but at least I can confirm who's got the ride.

No answer, and again no answer. The ring sounded funny and far away, a double rump-rump like a party line. She tried at night and got no answer.

At Wednesday lunch period, a man answered Starling's call:

"WPOQ Plays the Oldies."

"Hello, I'm calling to—"

"I wouldn't care for any aluminum siding and I don't want to live in no trailer court in Florida, what else you got?"

Starling heard a lot of the Arkansas hills in the man's voice. She could speak that with anybody when she wanted to, and her time was short.

"Yessir, if you could help me out I'd be much obliged. I'm trying to get ahold of Mr. Lomax Bardwell? This is Clarice Starling?"

"It's Starling somebody," the man yelled to the rest of his household. "What do you want with Bardwell?"

"This is the Mid-South regional office of the Ford recall division? He's entitled to some warranty work on his L.T.D. free of charge?"

"I'm Bardwell. I thought you was trying to sell me something on that cheap long distance. It's way too late for any adjustment, I need the whole thing. Me and the wife was in Little Rock, pulling out of the Southland Mall there?"

"Yessir."

"Durn rod come out through the oil pan. Oil all over everywhere and that Orkin truck that's got the big bug on top of it? He hit that oil and got sideways."

"Lord have mercy."

"Knocked the Fotomat booth slap off the blocks and the glass fell out. Fotomat fella come wandering out addled. Had to keep him out of the road."

"Well I'll be. What happened to it then?"

"What happened to what?"

"The car."

"I told Buddy Sipper at the wrecking yard he could have it for fifty if he'd come get it. I expect he's parted it out."

"Could you tell me what his telephone number is, Mr. Bardwell?"

"What do you want with Sipper? If anybody gets something out of it, it ought to be me."

"I understand that, sir. I just do what they tell me till five o'clock, and they said find the car. Have you got that number, please?"

"I can't find my phone book. It's been gone a good while now. You know how it is with these grandbabies. Central ought to give it to you, it's Sipper Salvage."

"Much oblige, Mr. Bardwell."

The salvage yard confirmed that the automobile had been stripped and pressed into a cube to be recycled. The foreman read Starling the vehicle serial number from his records.

Shit House Mouse, thought Starling, not entirely out of the accent. Dead end. Some Valentine.

Starling rested her head against the cold coin box in the telephone booth. Ardelia Mapp, her books on her hip, pecked on the door of the booth and handed in an Orange Crush.

"Much oblige, Ardelia. I got to make one more call. If I can get done with that in time, I'll catch up with you in the cafeteria, okay?"

"I was *so* in hopes you'd overcome that ghastly dialect," Mapp said. "Books are available to help. *I* never use the colorful patois of my housing project anymore. You come talking that mushmouth, people say you eat up with the dumb-ass, girl." Mapp closed the phone-booth door.

Starling felt she had to try for more information from Lecter. If she already had the appointment, maybe Crawford would let her return to the asylum. She dialed Dr. Chilton's number, but she never got past his secretary.

"Dr. Chilton is with the coroner and the assistant district attorney," the woman said. "He's already spoken to your supervisor and he has nothing to say to you. Good-bye."

"YOUR FRIEND Miggs is dead," Crawford said. "Did you tell me everything, Starling?" Crawford's tired face was as sensitive to signals as the dished ruff of an owl, and as free of mercy.

"How?" She felt numb and she had to handle it.

"Swallowed his tongue sometime before daylight. Lecter suggested it to him, Chilton thinks. The overnight orderly heard Lecter talking softly to Miggs. Lecter knew a lot about Miggs. He talked to him for a little while, but the overnight couldn't hear what Lecter said. Miggs was crying for a while, and then he stopped. Did you tell me everything, Starling?"

"Yes, sir. Between the report and my memo, there's everything, almost verbatim."

"Chilton called up to complain about you . . ." Crawford waited, and seemed pleased when she wouldn't ask. "I told him I found your behavior satisfactory. Chilton's trying to forestall a civil rights investigation."

"Will there be one?"

"Sure, if Miggs's family want it. Civil Rights Division will do probably eight thousand this year. They'll be glad to add Miggs to the list." Crawford studied her. "You okay?"

"I don't know how to feel about it."

"You don't have to feel any particular way about it. Lecter did it to amuse himself. He knows they can't really touch him for it, so why not? Chilton takes his books and his toilet seat for a while is all, and he doesn't get any Jell-O." Crawford laced his fingers over his stomach and compared his thumbs. "Lecter asked you about me, didn't he?"

"He asked if you were busy. I said yes."

"That's all? You didn't leave out anything personal because I wouldn't want to see it?"

"No. He said you were a Stoic, but I put that in."

"Yes, you did. Nothing else?"

"No, I didn't leave anything out. You don't think I traded some kind of gossip, and that's why he talked to me?"

"No."

"I don't know anything personal about you, and if I did I wouldn't discuss it. If you've got a problem believing that, let's get it straight now."

"I'm satisfied. Next item."

"You thought *something*, or—"

"Proceed to the next item, Starling."

"Lecter's hint about Raspail's car is a dead end. It was mashed into a cube four months ago in Number Nine Ditch, Arkansas, and sold for recycling. Maybe if I go back in and talk to him, he'll tell me more."

"You've exhausted the lead?"

"Yes."

"Why do you think the car Raspail drove was his only car?"

"It was the only one registered, he was single, I assumed—"

"Aha, hold it." Crawford's forefinger pointed to some principle invisible in the air between them. "You assumed. You *assumed*, Starling. Look here." Crawford wrote *assume* on a legal pad. Several of Starling's instructors had picked this up from Crawford and used it, but Starling didn't reveal that she'd seen it before.

Crawford began to underline. "If you *assume* when I send you on a job, Starling, you can make an *ass* out of *u* and *me* both." He leaned back, pleased. "Raspail collected cars, did you know that?"

"No, does the estate still have them?"

"I don't know. Do you think you could manage to find out?"

"Yes, I can."

"Where would you start?"

"His executor."

"A lawyer in Baltimore, a Chinese, I seem to remember," Crawford said.

"Everett Yow," Starling said. "He's in the Baltimore phone book."

"Have you given any thought to the question of a warrant to search Raspail's car?"

Sometimes Crawford's tone reminded Starling of the know-it-all caterpillar in Lewis Carroll.

Starling didn't dare give it back, much. "Since Raspail is deceased and not suspected of anything, if we have permission of his executor to search the car, then it is a valid search, and the fruit admissible evidence in other matters at law," she recited.

"Precisely," Crawford said. "Tell you what: I'll advise the Baltimore field office you'll be up there. Saturday, Starling, on your own time. Go feel the fruit, if there is any."

Crawford made a small, successful effort not to look after her as she left. From his wastebasket he lifted in the fork of his fingers a wad of heavy mauve notepaper. He spread it on his desk. It was about his wife and it said, in an engaging hand:

O wrangling schools, that search what fire
   Shall burn this world, had none the wit
Unto this knowledge to aspire
   That this her fever might be it?

I'm so sorry about Bella, Jack.

Hannibal Lecter

8

EVERETT YOW drove a black Buick with a De Paul University sticker on the back window. His weight gave the Buick a slight list to the left as Clarice Starling followed him out of Baltimore in the rain. It was almost dark; Starling's day as an investigator was nearly gone and she didn't have another day to replace it. She dealt with her impatience, tapping the wheel in time with the wipers as the traffic crawled down Route 301.

Yow was intelligent, fat, and had a breathing problem. Starling guessed his age at sixty. So far he was accommodating. The lost day was not his fault; returning in the late afternoon from a week-long business trip to Chicago, the Baltimore lawyer had come directly from the airport to his office to meet Starling.

Raspail's classic Packard had been stored since long before his death, Yow explained. It was unlicensed and never driven. Yow had seen it once, covered and in storage, to confirm its existence for the estate inventory he made shortly after his client's murder. If Investigator Starling would agree to "frankly disclose at once" anything she found that might be damaging to his late client's interests, he would show her the automobile, he said. A warrant and the attendant stir would not be necessary.

Starling was enjoying the use for one day of an F.B.I. motor pool
Plymouth with a cellular telephone, and she had a new I.D. card
provided by Crawford. It simply said FEDERAL INVESTIGATOR—and
expired in a week, she noticed.

Their destination was Split City Mini-Storage, about four miles
past the city limits. Creeping along with the traffic, Starling used her
telephone to find out what she could about the storage facility. By the
time she spotted the high orange sign, SPLIT CITY MINI-STORAGE—
YOU KEEP THE KEY, she had learned a few facts.

Split City had an Interstate Commerce Commission freight-forwarder's
license, in the name of Bernard Gary. A federal grand jury had barely
missed Gary for interstate transportation of stolen goods three years
ago, and his license was up for review.

Yow turned in beneath the sign and showed his keys to a spotty
young man in uniform at the gate. The gatekeeper logged their license
numbers, opened up and beckoned impatiently, as though he had more
important things to do.

Split City is a bleak place the wind blows through. Like the Sunday
divorce flight from La Guardia to Juárez, it is a service industry to the
mindless Brownian movement in our population; most of its business
is storing the sundered chattels of divorce. Its units are stacked with
living-room suites, breakfast ensembles, spotted mattresses, toys, and
the photographs of things that didn't work out. It is widely believed
among Baltimore County sheriff's officers that Split City also hides
good and valuable consideration from the bankruptcy courts.

It resembles a military installation: thirty acres of long buildings
divided by fire walls into units the size of a generous single garage,
each with its roll-up overhead door. The rates are reasonable and some
of the property has been there for years. Security is good. The place is
surrounded by a double row of high hurricane fence, and dogs patrol
between the fences twenty-four hours a day.

Six inches of sodden leaves, mixed with paper cups and small trash, had banked against the bottom of the door of Raspail's storage unit, number 31. A hefty padlock secured each side of the door. The left-side hasp also had a seal on it. Everett Yow bent stiffly over the seal. Starling held the umbrella and a flashlight in the early dark.

"It doesn't appear to have been opened since I was here five years ago," he said. "You see the impression of my notary seal here in the plastic. I had no idea at the time that the relatives would be so contentious and would drag out the probate for so many years."

Yow held the flashlight and umbrella while Starling took a picture of the lock and seal.

"Mr. Raspail had an office-studio in the city, which I closed down to save the estate from paying rent," he said. "I had the furnishings brought here and stored them with Raspail's car and other things that were already here. We brought an upright piano, books and music, a bed, I think."

Yow tried a key. "The locks may be frozen. At least this one's very stiff." It was hard for him to bend over and breathe at the same time. When he tried to squat, his knees creaked.

Starling was glad to see that the padlocks were big chrome American Standards. They looked formidable, but she knew she could pop the brass cylinders out easily with a sheet-metal screw and a claw hammer— her father had showed her how burglars do it when she was a child. The problem would be finding the hammer and screw; she did not even have the benefit of the resident junk in her Pinto.

She poked through her purse and found the de-icer spray she used on her Pinto's door locks.

"Want to rest a second in your car, Mr. Yow? Why don't you warm up for a few minutes and I'll give this a try. Take the umbrella, it's only a drizzle now."

Starling moved the F.B.I. Plymouth up close to the door to use its headlights. She pulled the dipstick out of the car and dripped oil into the keyholes of the padlocks, then sprayed in de-icer to thin the oil.

Mr. Yow smiled and nodded from his car. Starling was glad Yow was an intelligent man; she could perform her task without alienating him.

It was dark now. She felt exposed in the glare of the Plymouth's headlights and the fan belt squealed in her ear as the car idled. She'd locked the car while it was running. Mr. Yow appeared to be harmless, but she saw no reason to take a chance on being mashed against the door.

The padlock jumped like a frog in her hand and lay there open, heavy and greasy. The other lock, having soaked, was easier.

The door would not come up. Starling lifted on the handle until bright spots danced before her eyes. Yow came to help, but between the small, inadequate door handle and his hernia, they exerted little additional force.

"We might return next week, with my son, or with some workmen," Mr. Yow suggested. "I would like very much to go home soon."

Starling was not at all sure she'd ever get back to this place; it would be less trouble to Crawford if he just picked up the telephone and had the Baltimore field office handle it. "Mr. Yow, I'll hurry. Do you have a bumper jack in this car?"

With the jack under the handle of the door, Starling used her weight on top of the lug wrench that served as a jack handle. The door squealed horribly and went up a half-inch. It appeared to be bending upward in the center. The door went up another inch and another until she could slide the spare tire under it, to hold it up while she moved Mr Yow's jack and her own to the sides of the door, placing them under the bottom edge, close to the tracks the door ran in.

Alternating at the jacks on each side, she inched the door up a foot and a half, where it jammed solidly and her full weight on the jack handles would not raise it.

Mr. Yow came to peer under the door with her. He could only bend over for a few seconds at a time.

"It smells like mice in there," he said. "I was assured they used rodent poison here. I believe it is specified in the contract. Rodents are almost unknown, they said. But I hear them, do you?"

"I hear them," Starling said. With her flashlight, she could pick out cardboard boxes and one big tire with a wide whitewall beneath the edge of a cloth cover. The tire was flat.

She backed the Plymouth up until part of the headlight pattern shone under the door, and she took out one of the rubber floor mats.

"You're going in there, Officer Starling?"

"I have to take a look, Mr. Yow."

He took out his handkerchief. "May I suggest you tie your cuffs snugly around your ankles? To prevent mouse intrusion."

"Thank you, sir, that's a very good idea. Mr. Yow, if the door should come down, ha ha, or something else should occur, would you be kind enough to call this number? It's our Baltimore field office. They know I'm here with you right now, and they'll be alarmed if they don't hear from me in a little while, do you follow me?"

"Yes, of course. Absolutely, I do." He gave her the key to the Packard.

Starling put the rubber mat on the wet ground in front of the door and lay down on it, her hand cupping a pack of plastic evidence bags over the lens of her camera and her cuffs tied snugly with Yow's handkerchief and her own. A mist of rain fell in her face, and the smell of mold and mice was strong in her nose. What occurred to Starling was, absurdly, Latin.

Written on the blackboard by her forensics instructor on her first day in training, it was the motto of the Roman physician: *Primum non nocere*. First do no harm.

He didn't say that in a garage full of fucking mice.

And suddenly her father's voice, speaking to her with his hand on her brother's shoulder, "If you can't play without squawling, Clarice, go on to the house."

Starling fastened the collar button of her blouse, scrunched her shoulders up around her neck and slid under the door.

She was beneath the rear of the Packard. It was parked close to the left side of the storage room, almost touching the wall. Cardboard boxes were stacked high on the right side of the room, filling the space beside the car. Starling wriggled along on her back until her head was out in the narrow gap left between the car and the boxes. She shined her flashlight up the cliff face of boxes. Many spiders had spanned the narow space with their webs. Orb weavers, mostly, the webs dotted with small shriveled carcasses tightly bound.

Well, a brown recluse spider is the only kind to worry about, and it wouldn't build out in the open, Starling said to herself. *The rest don't raise much of a welt.*

There would be space to stand beside the rear fender. She wriggled around until she was out from under the car, her face close beside the wide whitewall tire. It was hatched with dry rot. She could read the words GOODYEAR DOUBLE EAGLE on it. Careful of her head, she got to her feet in the narrow space, hand before her face to break the webs. Was this how it felt to wear a veil?

Mr. Yow's voice from outside. "Okay, Miss Starling?"

"Okay," she said. There were small scurryings at the sound of her voice, and something inside a piano climbed over a few high notes. The car lights from outside lit her legs up to the calf.

"So you found the piano, Officer Starling," Mr. Yow called.

"That wasn't me."

"Oh."

The car was big, tall and long. A 1938 Packard limousine, according to Yow's inventory. It was covered with a rug, the plush side down. She played her flashlight over it.

"Did you cover the car with this rug, Mr. Yow?"

"I found it that way and I never uncovered it," Yow called under the door. "I can't deal with a dusty rug. That's the way Raspail had it. I just made sure the car was there. My movers put the piano against the wall and covered it and stacked more boxes beside the car and left. I was paying them by the hour. The boxes are sheet music and books, mostly."

The rug was thick and heavy and as she tugged at it, dust swarmed in the beam of her flashlight. She sneezed twice. Standing on tiptoe, she could fold the rug over to the midline of the tall old car. The curtains were drawn in the back windows. The door handle was covered with dust. She had to lean forward over cartons to reach it. Touching only the end of the handle, she tried to turn it downward. Locked. There was no keyhole in the rear door. She'd have to move a lot of boxes to get to the front door, and there was damn little place to put them. She could see a small gap between the curtain and the post of the rear window.

Starling leaned over boxes to put her eye close to the glass and shined her light through the crack. She could only see her reflection until she cupped her hand on top of the light. A splinter of the beam, diffused by the dusty glass, moved across the seat. An album lay open on the seat. The colors were poor in the bad light, but she could see Valentines pasted on the pages. Lacy old Valentines, fluffy on the page.

"Thanks a lot, Dr. Lecter." When she spoke, her breath stirred the fuzz of dust on the windowsill and fogged the glass. She didn't want to wipe it, so she had to wait for it to clear. The light moved on, over a lap rug crumpled on the floor of the car and onto the dusty wink of a pair of men's patent leather evening shoes. Above the shoes, black socks and above the socks were tuxedo trousers with legs in them.

Nobodysbeeninthatdoorinfiveyears—easy, easy, hold it, baby.

"Oh, Mr. Yow. Say, Mr. Yow?"

"Yes, Officer Starling?"

"Mr. Yow, looks like somebody's sitting in this car."

"Oh my. Maybe you better come out, Miss Starling."

"Not quite yet, Mr. Yow. Just wait there, if you will, please."

Now is when it's important to think. Now is more important than all the crap you tell your pillow for the rest of your life. Suck it up and do this right. I don't want to destroy evidence. I do want some help. But most of all I don't want to cry wolf. If I scramble the Baltimore office and the cops out here for nothing, I've had it. I see what looks like some legs. Mr. Yow would not have brought me here if he'd known there was a cool one in the car. She managed to smile at herself. "Cool one" was bravado. *Nobody's been here since Yow's last visit. All right, that means the boxes were put here after whatever's in the car. And that means I can move the boxes without losing anything important.*

"All right, Mr. Yow."

"Yes. Do we have to call the police, or are you sufficient, Officer Starling?"

"I've got to find that out. Just wait right there, please."

The box problem was as maddening as Rubik's Cube. She tried to work with the flashlight under her arm, dropped it twice, and finally put it on top of the car. She had to put boxes behind her, and some of the shorter book cartons would slide under the car. Some kind of bite or splinter made the ball of her thumb itch.

Now she could see through the dusty glass of the front passenger's side window into the chauffeur's compartment. A spider had spun between the big steering wheel and the gearshift. The partition between the front and back compartments was closed.

She wished she had thought to oil the Packard key before she came under the door, but when she stuck it in the lock, it worked.

There was hardly room to open the door more than a third of the way in the narrow passage. It swung against the boxes with a thump that sent the mice scratching and brought additional notes from the piano. A stale smell of decay and chemicals came out of the car. It jogged her memory in a place she couldn't name.

She leaned inside, opened the partition behind the chauffeur's seat, and shined her flashlight into the rear compartment of the car. A formal shirt with studs was the bright thing the light found first, quickly up the shirtfront to the face, no face to see, and down again, over glittering shirt studs and satin lapels to a lap with zipper open, and up again to the neat bow tie and the collar, where the white stub neck of a mannequin protruded. But above the neck, something else that reflected little light. Cloth, a black hood, where the head should be, big, as though it covered a parrot's cage. Velvet, Starling thought. It sat on a plywood shelf extending over the neck of the mannequin from the parcel shelf behind.

She took several pictures from the front seat, focusing with the flashlight and closing her eyes against the flash of the strobe. Then she straightened up outside the car. Standing in the dark, wet, with cobwebs on her, she considered what to do.

What she was *not* going to do was summon the special agent in charge of the Baltimore field office to look at a mannequin with its fly open and a book of Valentines.

Once she decided to get in the backseat and take the hood off the thing, she didn't want to think about it very long. She reached through the chauffeur's partition, unlocked the rear door, and rearranged some boxes to get it open. It all seemed to take a long time. The smell from the rear compartment was much stronger when she opened the door. She reached in and, carefully lifting the Valentine album by the corners, moved it onto an evidence bag on top of the car. She spread another evidence bag on the seat.

The car springs groaned as she got inside and the figure shifted a little when she sat down beside it. The right hand in its white glove slid off the thigh and lay on the seat. She touched the glove with her finger. The hand inside was hard. Gingerly she pushed the glove down from the wrist. The wrist was some white synthetic material. There was a lump in the trousers that for a silly instant reminded her of certain events in high school.

Small scrambling noises came from under the seat.

Gentle as a caress, her hand touching the hood. The cloth moved easily over something hard and slick beneath. When she felt the round knob on the top, she knew. She knew that it was a big laboratory specimen jar and she knew what would be in it. With dread, but little doubt, she pulled off the cover.

The head inside the jar had been severed neatly close beneath the jaw. It faced her, the eyes long burned milky by the alcohol that preserved it. The mouth was open and the tongue protruded slightly, very gray. Over the years, the alcohol had evaporated to the point that the head rested on the bottom of the jar, its crown protruding through the surface of the fluid in a cap of decay. Turned at an owlish angle to the body beneath, it gaped stupidly at Starling. Even in the play of light over the features, it remained dumb and dead.

Starling, in this moment, examined herself. She was pleased. She was exhilarated. She wondered for a second if those were worthy feelings. Now, at this moment, sitting in this old car with a head and some mice, she could think clearly, and she was proud of that.

"Well, Toto," she said, "we're not in Kansas anymore." She'd always wanted to say that under stress, but doing it left her feeling phony, and she was glad nobody had heard. Work to do.

She sat back gingerly and looked around.

This was somebody's environment, chosen and created, a thousand light-years across the mind from the traffic crawling down Route 301.

Dried blossoms drooped from the cut-crystal bud vases on the pillars. The limousine's table was folded down and covered with a linen cloth. On it, a decanter gleamed through dust. A spider had built between the decanter and the short candlestick beside it.

She tried to picture Lecter, or someone, sitting here with her present companion and having a drink and trying to show him the Valentines. And what else? Working carefully, disturbing the figure as little as possible, she frisked it for identification. There was none. In a jacket pocket she found the bands of material left over from adjusting the length of the trousers—the dinner clothes were probably new when they were put on the figure.

Starling poked the lump in the trousers. Too hard, even for high school, she reflected. She spread the fly with her fingers and shined her light inside, on a dildo of polished, inlaid wood. Good-sized one too. She wondered if she was depraved.

Carefully she turned the jar and examined the sides and back of the head for wounds. There were none visible. The name of a laboratory supply company was cast in the glass.

Considering the face again, she believed she learned something that would last her. Looking with purpose at this face, with its tongue changing color where it touched the glass, was not as bad as Miggs swallowing his tongue in her dreams. She felt she could look at anything, if she had something positive to do about it. Starling was young.

In the ten seconds after her WPIK-T.V. mobile news unit slid to a stop, Jonetta Johnson put in her earrings, powdered her beautiful brown face, and cased the situation. She and her news crew, monitoring the Baltimore County police radio, had arrived at Split City ahead of the patrol cars.

All the news crew saw in their headlights was Clarice Starling, standing in front of the garage door with her flashlight and her little laminated I.D. card, her hair plastered down by the drizzle.

Jonetta Johnson could spot a rookie every time. She climbed out with the camera crew behind her and approached Starling. The bright lights came on.

Mr. Yow sank so far down in his Buick that only his hat was visible above the windowsill.

"Jonetta Johnson, WPIK news, did you report a homicide?"

Starling did not look like very much law and she knew it. "I'm a federal officer, this is a crime scene. I have to secure it until the Baltimore authorities—"

The assistant cameraman had grabbed the bottom of the garage door and was trying to lift it.

"Hold it," Starling said. "I'm talking to *you*, sir. Hold it. Back off, please. I'm not kidding with you. Help me out here." She wished hard for a badge, a uniform, anything.

"Okay, Harry," the newswoman said. "Ah, officer, we want to cooperate in every way. Frankly, this crew costs money and I just want to know whether to even keep them here until the other authorities arrive. Will you tell me if there's a body in there? Camera's off, just between us. Tell me and we'll wait. We'll be good, I promise. How about it?"

"I'd wait if I were you," Starling said.

"Thanks, you won't be sorry," Jonetta Johnson said. "Look, I've got some information on Split City Mini-Storage that you could probably use. Would you shine your light on the clipboard? Let's see if I can find it here."

"WEYE mobile unit just turned in at the gate, Joney," the man Harry said.

"Let's see if I can find it here, Officer, here it is. There was a scandal about two years ago when they tried to prove this place was trucking and storing—was it fireworks?" Jonetta Johnson glanced over Starling's shoulder once too often.

Starling turned to see the cameraman on his back, his head and shoulders in the garage, the assistant squatting beside him, ready to pass the minicam under the door.

"Hey!" Starling said. She dropped to her knees on the wet ground beside him and tugged at his shirt. "You can't go in there. Hey! I told you not to do that."

And all the time the men were talking to her, constantly, gently.

"We won't touch anything. We're pros, you don't have to worry. The cops will let us in anyway. It's all right, honey."

Their cozening backseat manner put her over.

She ran to a bumper jack at the end of the door and pumped the handle. The door came down two inches, with a grinding screech. She pumped it again. Now the door was touching the man's chest. When he didn't come out, she pulled the handle out of the socket and carried it back to the prone cameraman. There were other bright television lights now, and in the glare of them she banged the door above him hard with the jack handle, showering dust and rust down on him.

"Give me your attention," she said. "You don't listen, do you? Come out of there. Now. You're one second from arrest for obstruction of justice."

"Take it easy," the assistant said. He put his hand on her. She turned on him. There were shouted questions from behind the glare and she heard sirens.

"Hands off and back off, buster." She stood on the cameraman's ankle and faced the assistant, the jack handle hanging by her side. She did not raise the jack handle. It was just as well. She looked bad enough on television as it was.

THE ODORS of the violent ward seemed more intense in the semi-darkness. A T.V. set playing without sound in the corridor threw Starling's shadow on the bars of Dr. Lecter's cage.

She could not see into the dark behind the bars, but she didn't ask the orderly to turn up the lights from his station. The whole ward would light at once and she knew the Baltimore County police had had the lights full on for hours while they shouted questions at Lecter. He had refused to speak, but responded by folding for them an origami chicken that pecked when the tail was manipulated up and down. The senior officer, furious, had crushed the chicken in the lobby ashtray as he gestured for Starling to go in.

"Dr. Lecter?" She heard her own breathing, and breathing down the hall, but from Miggs's empty cell, no breathing. Miggs's cell was vastly empty. She felt its silence like a draft.

Starling knew Lecter was watching her from the darkness. Two minutes passed. Her legs and back ached from her struggle with the garage door, and her clothes were damp. She sat on her coat on the floor, well back from the bars, her feet tucked under her, and lifted her wet, bedraggled hair over her collar to get it off her neck.

Behind her on the T.V. screen, an evangelist waved his arms.

"Dr. Lecter, we both know what this is. They think you'll talk to me."

Silence. Down the hall, someone whistled "Over the Sea to Skye."

After five minutes, she said, "It was strange going in there. Sometime I'd like to talk to you about it."

Starling jumped when the food carrier rolled out of Lecter's cell. There was a clean, folded towel in the tray. She hadn't heard him move.

She looked at it and, with a sense of falling, took it and toweled her hair. "Thanks," she said.

"Why don't you ask me about Buffalo Bill?" His voice was close, at her level. He must be sitting on the floor too.

"Do you know something about him?"

"I might if I saw the case."

"I don't have the case," Starling said.

"You won't have this one, either, when they're through using you."

"I know."

"You could get the files on Buffalo Bill. The reports and the pictures. I'd like to see it."

I'll bet you would. "Dr. Lecter, you started this. Now please tell me about the person in the Packard."

"You found an entire person? Odd. I only saw a head. Where do you suppose the rest came from?"

"All right. Whose *head* was it?"

"What can you tell?"

"They've only done the preliminary stuff. White male, about twenty-seven, both American and European dentistry. Who was he?"

"Raspail's lover. Raspail, of the gluey flute."

"What were the circumstances—how did he die?"

"Circumlocution, Officer Starling?"

"No, I'll ask it later."

"Let me save you some time. I didn't do it; Raspail did. Raspail liked sailors. This was a Scandinavian one named Klaus something. Raspail never told me the last name."

Dr. Lecter's voice moved lower. Maybe he was lying on the floor, Starling thought.

"Klaus was off a Swedish boat in San Diego. Raspail was out there teaching for a summer at the conservatory. He went berserk over the young man. The Swede saw a good thing and jumped his boat. They bought some kind of awful camper and sylphed through the woods naked. Raspail said the young man was unfaithful and he strangled him."

"Raspail told you this?"

"Oh yes, under the confidential seal of therapy sessions. I think it was a lie. Raspail always embellished the facts. He wanted to seem dangerous and romantic. The Swede probably died in some banal erotic asphyxia transaction. Raspail was too flabby and weak to have strangled him. Notice how closely Klaus was trimmed under the jaw? Probably to remove a high ligature mark from hanging."

"I see."

"Raspail's dream of happiness was ruined. He put Klaus's head in a bowling bag and came back East."

"What did he do with the rest?"

"Buried it in the hills."

"He showed you the head in the car?"

"Oh yes, in the course of therapy he came to feel he could tell me anything. He went out to sit with Klaus quite often and showed him the Valentines."

"And then Raspail himself . . . died. Why?"

"Frankly, I got sick and tired of his whining. Best thing for him, really. Therapy wasn't going anywhere. I expect most psychiatrists have a patient or two they'd like to refer to me. I've never discussed this before, and now I'm getting bored with it."

"And your dinner for the orchestra officials."

"Haven't you ever had people coming over and no time to shop? You have to make do with what's in the fridge, *Clarice*. May I call you Clarice?"

"Yes. I think I'll just call you—"

"Dr. Lecter—that seems most appropriate to your age and station," he said.

"Yes."

"How did you feel when you went into the garage?"

"Apprehensive."

"Why?"

"Mice and insects."

"Do you have something you use when you want to get up your nerve?" Dr. Lecter asked.

"Nothing I know of that works, except wanting what I'm after."

"Do memories or tableaux occur to you then, whether you try for them or not?"

"Maybe. I haven't thought about it."

"Things from your early life."

"I'll have to watch and see."

"How did you feel when you heard about my late neighbor, Miggs? You haven't asked me about it."

"I was getting to it."

"Weren't you *glad* when you heard?"

"No."

"Were you *sad*?"

"No. Did you talk him into it?"

Dr. Lecter laughed quietly. "Are you asking me, Officer Starling, if

I *suborned* Mr. Miggs's felony suicide? Don't be silly. It has a certain pleasant symmetry, though, his swallowing that offensive tongue, don't you agree?"

"No."

"Officer Starling, that was a lie. The first one you've told me. A *triste* occasion, Truman would say."

"President Truman?"

"Never mind. Why do you think I helped you?"

"I don't know."

"Jack Crawford likes you, doesn't he?"

"I don't know."

"That's probably untrue. Would you like for him to like you? Tell me, do you feel an urge to please him and does it worry you? Are you *wary* of your urge to please him?"

"Everyone wants to be liked, Dr. Lecter."

"Not everyone. Do you think Jack Crawford wants you sexually? I'm sure he's very frustrated now. Do you think he visualizes . . . scenarios, transactions . . . fucking with you?"

"That's not a matter of curiosity to me, Dr. Lecter, and it's the sort of thing Miggs would ask."

"Not anymore."

"Did you suggest to him that he swallow his tongue?"

"Your interrogative case often has that proper subjunctive in it. With your accent, it stinks of the lamp. Crawford clearly likes you and believes you competent. Surely the odd confluence of events hasn't escaped you, Clarice—you've had Crawford's help and you've had mine. You say you don't know why Crawford helps you—do you know why I did?"

"No, tell me."

"Do you think it's because I like to look at you and think about eating you up—about how you would taste?"

"Is that it?"

"No. I want something Crawford can give me and I want to trade him for it. But he won't come to see me. He won't ask for my help with Buffalo Bill, even though he knows it means more young women will die."

"I can't believe that, Dr. Lecter."

"I only want something very simple, and he could get it." Lecter turned up the rheostat slowly in his cell. His books and drawings were gone. His toilet seat was gone. Chilton had stripped the cell to punish him for Miggs.

"I've been in this room eight years, Clarice. I know that they will never, ever let me out while I'm alive. What I want is a view. I want a window where I can see a tree, or even water."

"Has your attorney petitioned—"

"Chilton put that television in the hall, set to a religious channel. As soon as you leave the orderly will turn the sound back up, and my attorney can't stop it, the way the court is inclined toward me now. I want to be in a federal institution and I want my books back and a view. I'll give good value for it. Crawford could do that. Ask him."

"I can tell him what you've said."

"He'll ignore it. And Buffalo Bill will go on and on. Wait until he scalps one and see how you like it. Ummmm . . . I'll tell you one thing about Buffalo Bill without ever seeing the case, and years from now when they catch him, if they ever do, you'll see that I was right and I could have helped. I could have saved lives. Clarice?"

"Yes?"

"Buffalo Bill has a two-story house," Dr. Lecter said, and turned out his light.

He would not speak again.

10

CLARICE STARLING leaned against a dice table in the F.B.I.'s casino and tried to pay attention to a lecture on money-laundering in gambling. It had been thirty-six hours since the Baltimore County police took her deposition (via a chain-smoking two-finger typist: "See if you can get that window open if the smoke bothers you.") and dismissed her from its jurisdiction with a reminder that murder is not a federal crime.

The network news on Sunday night showed Starling's scrap with the television cameramen and she felt sure she was deep in the glue. Through it all, no word from Crawford or from the Baltimore field office. It was as though she had dropped her report down a hole.

The casino where she now stood was small—it had operated in a moving trailer truck until the F.B.I. seized it and installed it in the school as a teaching aid. The narrow room was crowded with police from many jurisdictions; Starling had declined with thanks the chairs of two Texas Rangers and a Scotland Yard detective.

The rest of her class were down the hall in the Academy building, searching for hairs in the genuine motel carpet of the "Sex-Crime Bedroom" and dusting the "Anytown Bank" for fingerprints. Starling had spent so many hours on searches and fingerprints as a Forensic

Fellow that she was sent instead to this lecture, part of a series for visiting lawmen.

She wondered if there was another reason she had been separated from the class: maybe they isolate you before you get the ax.

Starling rested her elbows on the pass line of the dice table and tried to concentrate on money-laundering in gambling. What she thought about instead was how much the F.B.I. hates to see its agents on television, outside of official news conferences.

Dr. Hannibal Lecter was catnip to the media, and the Baltimore police had happily supplied Starling's name to reporters. Over and over she saw herself on the Sunday-night network news. There was "Starling of the F.B.I." in Baltimore, banging the jack handle against the garage door as the cameraman tried to slither under it. And here was "Federal Agent Starling" turning on the assistant with the jack handle in her hand.

On the rival network, station WPIK, lacking film of its own, had announced a personal-injury lawsuit against "Starling of the F.B.I." and the Bureau itself because the cameraman got dirt and rust particles in his eyes when Starling banged the door.

Jonetta Johnson of WPIK was on coast-to-coast with the revelation that Starling had found the remains in the garage through an "eerie bonding with a man authorities have branded . . . a *monster!*" Clearly, WPIK had a source at the hospital.

BRIDE OF FRANKENSTEIN!! screamed the *National Tattler* from its supermarket racks.

There was no public comment from the F.B.I., but there was plenty inside the Bureau, Starling was sure.

At breakfast, one of her classmates, a young man who wore a lot of Canoe after-shave, had referred to Starling as "Melvin Pelvis," a stupid play on the name of Melvin Purvis, Hoover's number one G-man in the thirties. What Ardelia Mapp said to the young man made his face turn white, and he left his breakfast uneaten on the table.

Now Starling found herself in a curious state in which she could not be surprised. For a day and a night she'd felt suspended in a diver's ringing silence. She intended to defend herself, if she got the chance.

The lecturer spun the roulette wheel as he talked, but he never let the ball drop. Looking at him, Starling was convinced that he had never let the ball drop in his life. He was saying something now: "Clarice Starling." Why was he saying "Clarice Starling"? *That's me.*

"Yes," she said.

The lecturer pointed with his chin at the door behind her. Here it came. Her fate shied under her as she turned to see. But it was Brigham, the gunnery instructor, leaning into the room to point to her across the crowd. When she saw him, he beckoned.

For a second she thought they were throwing her out, but that wouldn't be Brigham's job.

"Saddle up, Starling. Where's your field gear?" he said in the hall.

"My room—C Wing."

She had to walk fast then to keep up with him.

He was carrying the big fingerprint kit from the property room— the good one, not the play-school kit—and a small canvas bag.

"You go with Jack Crawford today. Take stuff for overnight. You may be back, but take it."

"Where?"

"Some duck hunters in West Virginia found a body in the Elk River around daylight. In a Buffalo Bill-type situation. Deputies are bringing it out. It's real boonies, and Jack's not inclined to wait on those guys for details." Brigham stopped at the door to C Wing. "He needs somebody to help him that can print a floater, among other things. You were a grunt in the lab—you can do that, right?"

"Yeee, let me check the stuff."

Brigham held the fingerprint kit open while Starling lifted out the trays. The fine hypodermics and the vials were there, but the camera wasn't.

"I need the one-to-one Polaroid, the CU-5, Mr. Brigham, and film packs and batteries for it."

"From property? You got it."

He handed her the small canvas bag, and when she felt its weight, she realized why it was Brigham who had come for her.

"You don't have a duty piece yet, right?"

"No."

"You gotta have full kit. This is the rig you've been wearing on the range. The gun is my own. It's the same K-frame Smith you're trained with, but the action's cleaned up. Dry-fire it in your room tonight when you get the chance. I'll be in a car behind C Wing in ten minutes flat with the camera. Listen, there's no head in the Blue Canoe. Go to the bathroom while you've got the chance is my advice. Chop-chop, Starling."

She tried to ask him a question, but he was leaving her.

Has to be Buffalo Bill, if Crawford's going himself. What the hell is the Blue Canoe? But you have to think about packing when you pack. Starling packed fast and well.

"Is it—"

"That's okay," Brigham interrupted as she got in the car. "The butt prints against your jacket a little if somebody's looking for it, but it's okay for now." She was wearing the snub-nosed revolver under her blazer in a pancake holster snug against her ribs, with a speedloader straddling her belt on the other side.

Brigham drove at precisely the base speed limit toward the Quantico airstrip.

He cleared his throat. "One good thing about the range, Starling, is there's no politics out there."

"No?"

"You were right to secure that garage up at Baltimore there. You worried about the T.V.?"

"Should I be?"

"We're talking just us, right?"

"Right."

Brigham returned the greeting of a Marine directing traffic.

"Taking you along today, Jack's showing confidence in you where nobody can miss it," he said. "In case, say, somebody in the Office of Professional Responsibility has your jacket in front of him and his bowels in an uproar, understand what I'm telling you?"

"Ummm."

"Crawford's a stand-up guy. He made it clear where it matters that you had to secure the scene. He let you go in there bare—that is, bare of all your visible symbols of authority, and he said that too. And the response time of the Baltimore cops was pretty slow. Also, Crawford needs the help today, and he'd have to wait an hour for Jimmy Price to get somebody here from the lab. So you got it cut out for you, Starling. A floater's no day at the beach, either. It's not punishment for you, but if somebody outside needed to see it that way, they could. See, Crawford is a very subtle guy, but he's not inclined to explain things, that's why I'm telling you . . . If you're working with Crawford, you should know what the deal is with him—do you know?"

"I really don't."

"He's got a lot on his mind besides Buffalo Bill. His wife Bella's real sick. She's . . . in a terminal situation. He's keeping her at home. If it wasn't for Buffalo Bill, he'd have taken compassionate leave."

"I didn't know that."

"It's not discussed. Don't tell him you're sorry or anything, it doesn't help him . . . they had a good time."

"I'm glad you told me."

Brigham brightened as they reached the airstrip. "I've got a couple of important speeches I give at the end of the firearms course,

Starling, try not to miss them." He took a shortcut between some hangars.

"I will."

"Listen, what I teach is something you probably won't ever have to do. I hope you won't. But you've got some aptitude, Starling. If you have to shoot, you can shoot. Do your exercises."

"Right."

"Don't ever put it in your purse."

"Right."

"Pull it a few times in your room at night. Stay so you can find it."

"I will."

A venerable twin-engined Beechcraft stood on the taxiway at the Quantico airstrip with its beacons turning and the door open. One propeller was spinning, riffling the grass beside the tarmac.

"That wouldn't be the Blue Canoe," Starling said.

"Yep."

"It's little and it's old."

"It *is* old," Brigham said cheerfully. "Drug Enforcement seized it in Florida a long time ago, when it flopped in the 'Glades. Mechanically sound now, though. I hope Gramm and Rudman don't find out we're using it—we're supposed to ride the bus." He pulled up beside the airplane and got Starling's baggage out of the backseat. In some confusion of hands he managed to give her the stuff and shake her hand.

And then, without meaning to, Brigham said, "Bless you, Starling." The words felt odd in his Marine mouth. He didn't know where they came from and his face felt hot.

"Thanks . . . thank you, Mr. Brigham."

Crawford was in the copilot's seat, in shirtsleeves and sunglasses. He turned to Starling when he heard the pilot slam the door.

She couldn't see his eyes behind the dark glasses, and she felt she didn't know him. Crawford looked pale and tough, like a root a bulldozer pushes up.

"Take a pew and read," is all he said.

A thick case file lay on the seat behind him. The cover said BUFFALO BILL. Starling hugged it tight as the Blue Canoe blatted and shuddered and began to roll.

THE EDGES of the runway blurred and fell away. To the east, a flash of morning sun off the Chesapeake Bay as the small plane turned out of traffic.

Clarice Starling could see the school down there, and the surrounding Marine base at Quantico. On the assault course, tiny figures of Marines scrambled and ran.

This was how it looked from above.

Once, after a night-firing exercise, walking in the dark along the deserted Hogan's Alley, walking to think, she had heard airplanes roar over and then, in the new silence, voices calling in the black sky above her—airborne troops in a night jump calling to each other as they came down through the darkness. And she wondered how it felt to wait for the jump light at the aircraft door, how it felt to plunge into the bellowing dark.

Maybe it felt like this.

She opened the file.

He had done it five times that they knew of, had Bill. At least five times, and probably more, over the past ten months he had abducted a woman, killed her and skinned her. (Starling's eye raced down the autopsy protocols to the free-histamine tests to confirm that he killed them before he did the rest.)

He dumped each body in running water when he was through with it. Each was found in a different river, downstream from an interstate highway crossing, each in a different state. Everyone knew Buffalo Bill was a traveling man. That was all the law knew about him, absolutely all, except that he had at least one gun. It had six lands and grooves, left-hand twist—possibly a Colt revolver or a Colt clone. Skidmarks on recovered bullets indicated he preferred to fire .38 Specials in the longer chambers of a .357.

The rivers left no fingerprints, no trace evidence of hair or fiber.

He was almost certain to be a white male: white because serial murderers usually kill within their own ethnic group and all the victims were white; male because female serial murderers are almost unknown in our time.

Two big-city columnists had found a headline in e.e. cummings' deadly little poem, "Buffalo Bill": . . . *how do you like your blueeyed boy Mister Death*.

Someone, maybe Crawford, had pasted the quotation inside the cover of the file.

There was no clear correlation between where Bill abducted the young women and where he dumped them.

In the cases where the bodies were found soon enough for an accurate determination of time of death, police learned another thing the killer did: Bill kept them for a while, alive. These victims did not die until a week to ten days after they were abducted. That meant he had to have a place to keep them and a place to work in privacy. It meant he wasn't a drifter. He was more of a trapdoor spider. With his own digs. Somewhere.

That horrified the public more than anything—his holding them for a week or more, knowing he would kill them.

Two were hanged, three shot. There was no evidence of rape or physical abuse prior to death, and the autopsy protocols recorded no evidence of "specifically genital" disfigurement, though pathologists noted it would be almost impossible to determine these things in the more deteriorated bodies.

All were found naked. In two cases, articles of the victims' outer clothing were found beside the road near their homes, slit up the back like funeral suits.

Starling got through the photographs all right. Floaters are the worst kind of dead to deal with, physically. There is an absolute pathos about them too, as there often is about homicide victims out of doors. The indignities the victim suffers, the exposure to the elements and to casual eyes, anger you if your job permits you anger.

Often, at indoor homicides, evidences of a victim's unpleasant personal practices, and the victim's own victims—beaten spouses, abused children—crowd around to whisper that the dead one had it coming, and many times he did.

But nobody had this coming. Here they had not even their skins as they lay on littered riverbanks amid the outboard-oil bottles and sand- wich bags that are our common squalor. The cold-weather ones largely retained their faces. Starling reminded herself that their teeth were not bared in pain, that turtles and fish in the course of feeding had created that expression. Bill peeled the torsos and mostly left the limbs alone.

They wouldn't have been so hard to look at, Starling thought, if this airplane cabin wasn't so warm and if the damned plane didn't have this crawly yaw as one prop caught the air better than the other, and if the God damned sun didn't splinter so on the scratched windows and jab like a headache.

It's possible to catch him. Starling squeezed on that thought to help herself sit in this ever-smaller airplane cabin with her lap full of awful information. She could help stop him cold. Then they could put this slightly sticky, smooth-covered file back in the drawer and turn the key on it.

She stared at the back of Crawford's head. If she wanted to stop Buffalo Bill she was in the right crowd. Crawford had organized successful hunts for three serial murderers. But not without casualties. Will Graham, the keenest hound ever to run in Crawford's pack, was a legend at the Academy; he was also a drunk in Florida now with a face that was hard to look at, they said.

Maybe Crawford felt her staring at the back of his head. He climbed out of the copilot's seat. The pilot touched the trim wheel as Crawford came back to her and buckled in beside her. When he folded his sunglasses and put on his bifocals, she felt she knew him again.

When he looked from her face to the report and back again, something passed behind his face and was quickly gone. A more animated mug than Crawford's would have shown regret.

"I'm hot, are you hot?" he said. "Bobby, it's too damned hot in here," he called to the pilot. Bobby adjusted something and cold air came in. A few snowflakes formed in the moist cabin air and settled in Starling's hair.

Then it was Jack Crawford hunting, his eyes like a bright winter day.

He opened the file to a map of the Central and Eastern United States. Locations where bodies had been found were marked on the map—a scattering of dots as mute and crooked as Orion.

Crawford took a pen from his pocket and marked the newest location, their objective.

"Elk River, about six miles below U.S. 79," he said. "We're lucky on this one. The body was snagged on a trotline—a fishing line set out in the river. They don't think she's been in the water all that long. They're bringing her to Potter, the county seat. I want to know who she is in a hurry so we can sweep for witnesses to the abduction. We'll send the prints back on a land line as soon as we get 'em." Crawford tilted his head to look at Starling through the bottoms of his glasses. "Jimmy Price says you can do a floater."

"Actually, I never had an entire floater," Starling said. "I finger-printed the hands Mr. Price got in his mail every day. A good many of them were from floaters, though."

Those who have never been under Jimmy Price's supervision believe him to be a lovable curmudgeon. Like most curmudgeons, he is really a mean old man. Jimmy Price is a supervisor in Latent Prints at the Washington lab. Starling did time with him as a Forensic Fellow.

"That Jimmy," Crawford said fondly. "What is it they call that job . . ."

"The position is called 'lab wretch,' or some people prefer 'Igor'—that's what's printed on the rubber apron they give you."

"That's it."

"They tell you to pretend you're dissecting a frog."

"I see—"

"Then they bring you a package from UPS. They're all watching—some of them hurry back from coffee, hoping you'll barf. I can print a floater very well. In fact—"

"Good, now look at this. His first victim that we know of was found in the Blackwater River in Missouri, outside of Lone Jack, last June. The Bimmel girl, she'd been reported missing in Belvedere, Ohio, on April 15, two months before. We couldn't tell a lot about it—it took another three months just to get her identified. The next one he grabbed in Chicago the third week in April. She was found in the Wabash in downtown Lafayette, Indiana, just ten days after she was taken, so we could tell what had happened to her. Next we've got a white female, early twenties, dumped in the Rolling Fork near I-65, about thirty-eight miles south of Louisville, Kentucky. She's never been identified. And the Varner woman, grabbed in Evansville, Indiana, and dropped in the Embarras just below Interstate 70 in eastern Illinois.

"Then he moved south and dumped one in the Conasauga below Damascus, Georgia, down from Interstate 75, that was this Kittridge girl from Pittsburgh—here's her graduation picture. His luck's ungodly—nobody's ever seen him make a snatch. Except for the dumps being near an Interstate, we haven't seen any pattern."

"If you trace heaviest-traffic routes backward from the dump sites, do they converge at all?"

"No."

"What if you . . . *postulate* . . . that he's making a dropoff and a new abduction on the same trip?" Starling asked, carefully avoiding the forbidden word *assume*. "He'd drop off the body first, wouldn't he, in case he got in trouble grabbing the next one? Then, if he was caught grabbing somebody, he might get off for assault, plead it down to zip if he didn't have a body in his car. So how about drawing vectors backward from each abduction site through the previous dump site? You've tried it."

"That's a good idea, but he had it too. If he *is* doing both things in one trip, he's zigging around. We've run computer simulations, first with him westbound on the Interstates, then eastbound, then various combinations with the best dates we can put on the dumps and abductions. You put it in the computer and smoke comes out. He lives in the East, it tells us. He's not in a moon cycle, it tells us. No convention dates in the cities correlate. Nothing but feathers. No, he's seen us coming, Starling."

"You think he's too careful to be a suicide."

Crawford nodded. "Definitely too careful. He's found out how to have a meaningful relationship now, and he wants to do it a lot. I'm not getting my hopes up for a suicide."

Crawford passed the pilot a cup of water from a thermos. He gave one to Starling and mixed himself an Alka-Seltzer.

Her stomach lifted as the airplane started down.

"Couple of things, Starling. I look for first-rate forensics from you, but I need more than that. You don't say much, and that's okay, neither do I. But don't ever feel you've got to have a new fact to tell me before you can bring something up. There aren't any silly questions. You'll see things that I won't, and I want to know what they are. Maybe you've got a knack for this. All of a sudden we've got this chance to see if you do."

Listening to him, her stomach lifting and her expression properly rapt, Starling wondered how long Crawford had known he'd use her on this case, how hungry for a chance he had wanted her to be. He was a leader, with a leader's frank-and-open bullshit, all right.

"You think about him enough, you see where he's been, you get a feel for him," Crawford went on. "You don't even dislike him all the time, hard as that is to believe. Then, if you're lucky, out of the stuff you know, part of it plucks at you, tries to get your attention. Always tell me when something plucks, Starling.

"Listen to me, a crime is confusing enough without the investigation mixing it up. Don't let a herd of policemen confuse you. Live right behind your eyes. Listen to yourself. Keep the crime separate from what's going on around you now. Don't try to impose any pattern or symmetry on this guy. Stay open and let him show you.

"One other thing: an investigation like this is a zoo. It's spread out over a lot of jurisdictions, and a few are run by losers. We have to get along with them so they won't hold out on us. We're going to Potter, West Virginia. I don't know about these people we're going to. They may be fine or they may think we're the revenuers."

The pilot lifted an earphone away from his head and spoke over his shoulder. "Final approach, Jack. You staying back there?"

"Yeah," Crawford said. "School's out, Starling."

CHAPTER

12

NOW HERE is the Potter Funeral Home, the largest white frame house on Potter Street in Potter, West Virginia, serving as the morgue for Rankin County. The coroner is a family physician named Dr. Akin. If he rules that a death is questionable, the body is sent on to Claxton Regional Medical Center in the neighboring county, where they have a trained pathologist.

Clarice Starling, riding into Potter from the airstrip in the back of a sheriff's department cruiser, had to lean up close to the prisoner screen to hear the deputy at the wheel as he explained these things to Jack Crawford.

A service was about to get under way at the mortuary. The mourners in their country Sunday best filed up the sidewalk between leggy boxwoods and bunched on the steps, waiting to get in. The freshly painted house and the steps had, each in its own direction, settled slightly out of plumb.

In the private parking lot behind the house, where the hearses waited, two young deputies and one old one stood with two state troopers under a bare elm. It was not cold enough for their breath to steam.

Starling looked at these men as the cruiser pulled into the lot, and at once she knew about them. She knew they came from houses that had chifforobes instead of closets and she knew pretty much what was in the chifforobes. She knew that these men had relatives who hung their clothes in suitbags on the walls of their trailers. She knew that the older deputy had grown up with a pump on the porch and had waded to the road in the muddy spring to catch the school bus with his shoes hanging around his neck by the laces, as her father had done. She knew they had carried their lunches to school in paper sacks with grease spots on them from being used over and over and that after lunch they folded the sacks and slipped them in the back pockets of their jeans.

She wondered how much Crawford knew about them.

There were no handles on the inside of the rear doors in the cruiser, as Starling discovered when the driver and Crawford got out and started toward the back of the funeral home. She had to bat on the glass until one of the deputies beneath the tree saw her, and the driver came back red-faced to let her out.

The deputies watched her sidelong as she passed. One said "ma'am." She gave them a nod and a smile of the correct dim wattage as she went to join Crawford on the back porch.

When she was far enough away, one of the younger deputies, a newlywed, scratched beneath his jaw and said, "She don't look half as good as she thinks she does."

"Well, if she just thinks she looks *pretty God damned good*, I'd have to agree with her, myself," the other young deputy said. "I'd put her on like a Mark Five gas mask."

"I'd just as soon have a big watermelon, if it was cold," the older deputy said, half to himself.

Crawford was already talking to the chief deputy, a small, taut man in steel-rimmed glasses and the kind of elastic-sided boots the catalogs call "Romeos."

They had moved into the funeral home's dim back corridor, where a Coke machine hummed and random odd objects stood against the wall—a treadle sewing machine, a tricycle, and a roll of artificial grass, a striped canvas awning wrapped around its poles. On the wall was a sepia print of Saint Cecilia at the keyboard. Her hair was braided around her head, and roses tumbled onto the keys out of thin air.

"I appreciate your letting us know so fast, Sheriff," Crawford said.

The chief deputy wasn't having any. "It was somebody from the district attorney's office called you," he said. "I know the sheriff didn't call you—Sheriff Perkins is on a guided tour of Hawaii at the present time with Mrs. Perkins. I spoke to him on long distance this morning at eight o'clock, that's three A.M., Hawaii time. He'll get back to me later in the day, but he told me Job One is to find out if this is one of our local girls. It could be something that outside elements has just dumped on us. We'll tend to that before we do anything else. We've had 'em haul bodies here all the way from Phenix City, Alabama."

"That's where we can help you, Sheriff. If—"

"I've been on the phone with the field services commander of the state troopers in Charleston. He's sending some officers from the Criminal Investigation Section—what's known as the CIS. They'll give us all the backup we need." The corridor was filling with deputy sheriffs and troopers; the chief deputy had too much of an audience. "We'll get around to you just as soon as we can, and extend you ever courtesy, work with you ever *way* we can, but right now—"

"Sheriff, this kind of a sex crime has some aspects that I'd rather say to you just between us men, you understand what I mean?" Crawford said, indicating Starling's presence with a small movement of his head. He hustled the smaller man into a cluttered office off the hall and closed the door. Starling was left to mask her umbrage before the gaggle of deputies. Her teeth hard together, she gazed on Saint Cecilia and returned the saint's ethereal smile while eavesdropping through the door. She could hear raised voices, then scraps of a telephone conversation. They were back out in the hall in less than four minutes.

The chief deputy's mouth was tight. "Oscar, go out front and get Dr. Akin. He's kind of obliged to attend those rites, but I don't think they've got started out there yet. Tell him we've got Claxton on the phone."

The coroner, Dr. Akin, came to the little office and stood with his foot on a chair, tapping his front teeth with a Good Shepherd fan while he had a brief telephone conference with the pathologist in Claxton. Then he agreed to everything.

So, in an embalming room with cabbage roses in the wallpaper and a picture molding beneath its high ceiling, in a white frame house of a type she understood, Clarice Starling met with her first direct evidence of Buffalo Bill.

The bright green body bag, tightly zipped, was the only modern object in the room. It lay on an old-fashioned porcelain embalming table, reflected many times in the glass panes of cabinets holding trocars and packages of Rock-Hard Cavity Fluid.

Crawford went to the car for the fingerprint transmitter while Starling unpacked her equipment on the drainboard of a large double sink against the wall.

Too many people were in the room. Several deputies, the chief deputy, all had wandered in with them and showed no inclination to leave. It wasn't right. *Why didn't Crawford come on and get rid of them?*

The wallpaper billowed in a draft, billowed inward as the doctor turned on the big, dusty vent fan.

Clarice Starling, standing at the sink, needed now a prototype of courage more apt and powerful than any Marine parachute jump. The image came to her, and helped her, but it pierced her too:

Her mother, standing at the sink, washing blood out of her father's hat, running cold water over the hat, saying, "We'll be all right, Clarice. Tell your

brothers and sister to wash up and come to the table. We need to talk and then
we'll fix our supper."

Starling took off her scarf and tied it over her hair like a mountain midwife. She took a pair of surgical gloves out of her kit. When she opened her mouth for the first time in Potter, her voice had more than its normal twang and the force of it brought Crawford to the door to listen. "Gentlemen. Gentlemen! You officers and gentlemen! Listen here a minute. Please. Now let me take care of her." She held her hands before their faces as she pulled on the gloves. "There's things we need to do for her. You brought her this far, and I know her folks would thank you if they could. Now please go on out and let me take care of her."

Crawford saw them suddenly go quiet and respectful and urge each other out in whispers: "Come on, Jess. Let's go out in the yard." And Crawford saw that the atmosphere had changed here in the presence of the dead: that wherever this victim came from, whoever she was, the river had carried her into the country, and while she lay helpless in this room in the country, Clarice Starling had a special relationship to her. Crawford saw that in this place Starling was heir to the granny women, to the wise women, the herb healers, the stalwart country women who have always done the needful, who keep the watch and when the watch is over, wash and dress the country dead.

Then there were only Crawford and Starling and the doctor in the room with the victim, Dr. Akin and Starling looking at each other with a kind of recognition. Both of them were oddly pleased, oddly abashed.

Crawford took a jar of Vicks VapoRub out of his pocket and offered it around. Starling watched to see what to do, and when Crawford and the doctor rubbed it around the rims of their nostrils, she did too.

She dug her cameras out of the equipment bag on the drainboard, her back to the room. Behind her she heard the zipper of the body bag go down.

Starling blinked at the cabbage roses on the wall, took a breath and let it out. She turned round and looked at the body on the table.

"They should have put paper bags on her hands," she said. "I'll bag them when we're through." Carefully, overriding the automatic camera to bracket her exposures, Starling photographed the body.

The victim was a heavy-hipped young woman sixty-seven inches long by Starling's tape. The water had leached her gray where the skin was gone, but it had been cold water and she clearly hadn't been in it more than a few days. The body was flayed neatly from a clean line just below the breasts to the knees, about the area that would be covered by a bullfighter's pants and sash.

Her breasts were small and between them, over the sternum, was the apparent cause of death, a ragged, star-shaped wound a hand's breadth across.

Her round head was peeled to the skull from just above the eyebrows and ears to the nape.

"Dr. Lecter said he'd start scalping," Starling said.

Crawford stood with his arms folded while she took the pictures. "Get her ears with the Polaroid," was all he said.

He went so far as to purse his lips as he walked around the body. Starling peeled off her glove to trail her finger up the calf of the leg. A section of the trotline and treble fishhooks that had entangled and held the body in the moving river was still wrapped around the lower leg.

"What do you see, Starling?"

"Well, she's not a local—her ears are pierced three times each, and she wore glitter polish. Looks like town to me. She's got maybe two weeks' or so hair growth on her legs. And see how soft it's grown in? I think she got her legs waxed. Armpits too. Look how she bleached the fuzz on her upper lip. She was pretty careful about herself, but she hasn't been able to take care of it for a while."

"What about the wound?"

"I don't know," Starling said. "I would have said an exit gunshot wound, except that looks like part of an abrasion collar and a muzzle stamp at the top there."

"Good, Starling. It's a contact entrance wound over the sternum. The explosion gases expand between the bone and the skin and blow out the star around the hole."

On the other side of the wall a pipe organ wheezed as the service got under way in the front of the funeral home.

"Wrongful death," Dr. Akins contributed, nodding his head. "I've got to get in there for at least part of this service. The family always expects me to go the last mile. Lamar will be in here to help you as soon as he finishes playing the musical offering. I take you at your word on preserving evidence for the pathologist at Claxton, Mr. Crawford."

"She's got two nails broken off here on the left hand," Starling said when the doctor was gone. "They're broken back up in the quick and it looks like dirt or some hard particles driven up under some of the others. Can we take evidence?"

"Take samples of grit, take a couple of flakes of polish," Crawford said. "We'll tell 'em after we get the results."

Lamar, a lean funeral home assistant with a whiskey bloom in the middle of his face, came in while she was doing it. "You must of been a manicurist one time," he said.

They were glad to see the young woman had no fingernail marks in her palms—an indication that, like the others, she had died before anything else was done to her.

"You want to print her facedown, Starling?" Crawford said.

"Be easier."

"Let's do teeth first, and then Lamar can help us turn her over."

"Just pictures, or a chart?" Starling attached the dental kit to the front of the fingerprint camera, privately relieved that all the parts were in the bag.

"Just pictures," Crawford said. "A chart can throw you off without

X rays. We can eliminate a couple of missing women with the pictures."

Lamar was very gentle with his organist's hands, opening the young woman's mouth at Starling's direction and retracting her lips while Starling placed the one-to-one Polaroid against the face to get details of the front teeth. That part was easy, but she had to shoot the molars with a palatal reflector, watching from the side for the glow through the cheek to be sure the strobe around the lens was lighting the inside of the mouth. She had only seen it done in a forensics class.

Starling watched the first Polaroid print of the molars develop, adjusted the lightness control and tried again. This print was better. This one was very good.

"She's got something in her throat," Starling said.

Crawford looked at the picture. It showed a dark cylindrical object just behind the soft palate. "Give me the flashlight."

"When a body comes out of the water, a lot of times there's, like, leaves and things in the mouth," Lamar said, helping Crawford to look.

Starling took some forceps out of her bag. She looked at Crawford across the body. He nodded. It only took her a second to get it.

"What is it, some kind of seed pod?" Crawford said.

"Nawsir, that's a bug cocoon," Lamar said. He was right.

Starling put it in a jar.

"You might want the county agent to look at that," Lamar said.

Facedown, the body was easy to fingerprint. Starling had been prepared for the worst—but none of the tedious and delicate injection methods or finger stalls were necessary. She took the prints on thin card stock held in a device shaped like a shoehorn. She did a set of plantar prints as well, in case they had only baby footprints from a hospital for reference.

Two triangular pieces of skin were missing from high on the shoulders. Starling took pictures.

"Measure too," Crawford said. "He cut the girl from Akron when he slit her clothes off, not much more than a scratch, but it matched the cut up the back of her blouse when they found it beside the road. This is something new, though. I haven't seen this."

"Looks like a burn across the back of her calf," Starling said.

"Old people gets those a lot," Lamar said.

"What?" Crawford said.

"I SAID OLD PEOPLE GETS THOSE A LOT."

"I heard you fine, I want you to explain it. What about old people?"

"Old people pass away with a heating pad on them, and when they're dead it burns them, even when it's not all that hot. You burn under a heating pad when you're dead. No circulation under it."

"We'll ask the pathologist at Claxton to test it, and see if it's postmortem," Crawford said to Starling.

"Car muffler, most likely," Lamar said.

"What?"

"CAR MUFFL—car muffler. One time Billy Petrie got shot to death and they dumped him in the trunk of his car? His wife drove the car around two or three days looking for him. When they brought him in here, the muffler had got hot under the car trunk and burned him just like that, only across his hip," Lamar said. "I can't put groceries in the trunk of my car for it melting the ice cream."

"That's a good thought, Lamar, I wish you worked for me," Crawford said. "Do you know the fellows that found her in the river?"

"Jabbo Franklin and his brother, Bubba."

"What do they do?"

"Fight at the Moose, make fun of people that's not bothering them—someone just comes in the Moose after a simple drink, worn out from looking at the bereaved all day, and it's 'Set down there, Lamar, and play "Filipino Baby."' Make a person play 'Filipino Baby' over and over on that sticky old bar piano. That's what Jabbo likes. 'Well, make up some damn words if you don't know it,' he says, 'and make the damn thing rhyme this time.' He gets a check from the Veterans and goes to dry out at the VA around Christmas. I been looking for him on this table for fifteen years."

"We'll need serotonin tests on the fishhook punctures," Crawford said. "I'm sending the pathologist a note."

"Them hooks are too close together," Lamar said.

"What did you say?"

"The Franklins was running a trotline with the hooks too close together. It's a violation. That's prob'ly why they didn't call it in until this morning."

"The sheriff said they were duck hunters."

"I expect they did tell him that," Lamar said. "They'll tell you they wrestled Duke Keomuka in Honolulu one time too, tag team with Satellite Monroe. You can believe that too, if you feel like it. Grab a croaker sack and they'll take you on a snipe hunt too, if you favor snipe. Give you a glass of billiards with it."

"What do you think happened, Lamar?"

"The Franklins was running this trotline, it's their trotline with these unlawful hooks, and they was pulling it up to see if they had any fish."

"Why do you think so?"

"This lady's not near ready to float."

"No."

"Then if they hadna been pulling up on the trotline they never would have found her. They prob'ly went off scared and finally called in. I expect you'll want the game warden in on this."

"I expect so," Crawford said.

"Lots of times they've got a crank telephone behind the seat in their Ramcharger, that's a big fine right there, if you don't have to go to the pen."

Crawford raised his eyebrows.

"To telephone fish with," Starling said. "Stun the fish with electric current when you hang the wires in the water and turn the crank. They come to the top and you just dip 'em out."

"Right," Lamar said, "are you from around here?"

"They do it lots of places," Starling said.

Starling felt the urge to say something before they zipped up the bag, to make a gesture or express some kind of commitment. In the end, she just shook her head and got busy packing the samples into her case.

It was different with the body and problem out of sight. In this slack moment, what she'd been doing came in on her. Starling stripped off her gloves and turned the water on in the sink. With her back to the room, she ran water over her wrists. The water in the pipes wasn't all that cool. Lamar, watching, disappeared into the hall. He came back from the Coke machine with an ice-cold can of soda, unopened, and offered it to her.

"No, thanks," Starling said. "I don't believe I'll have one."

"No, hold it under your neck there," Lamar said, "and on that little bump at the back of your head. Cold'll make you feel better. It does me."

By the time Starling had finished taping the memo to the pathologist across the zipper of the body bag, Crawford's fingerprint transmitter was clicking on the office desk.

Finding this victim so soon after the crime was a lucky break. Crawford was determined to identify her quickly and start a sweep around her home for witnesses to the abduction. His method was a lot of trouble to everyone, but it was fast.

Crawford carried a Litton Policefax fingerprint transmitter. Unlike federal-issue facsimile machines, the Policefax is compatible with most big-city police department systems. The fingerprint card Starling had assembled was barely dry.

"Load it, Starling, you've got the nimble fingers."

Don't smear it was what he meant, and Starling didn't. It was hard, wrapping the glued-together composite card around the little drum while six wire rooms waited around the country.

Crawford was on the telephone to the F.B.I. switchboard and wire room in Washington. "Dorothy, is everybody on? Okay, gentlemen, we'll turn it down to one-twenty to keep it nice and sharp—check one-twenty, everybody? Atlanta, how about it? Okay, give me the picture wire . . . now."

Then it was spinning at slow speed for clarity, sending the dead woman's prints simultaneously to the F.B.I. wire room and major police department wire rooms in the East. If Chicago, Detroit, Atlanta, or any of the others got a hit on the fingerprints, a sweep would begin in minutes.

Next Crawford sent pictures of the victim's teeth and photos of her face, the head draped by Starling with a towel in the event the supermarket press got hold of the photographs.

Three officers of the West Virginia State Police Criminal Investigation Section arrived from Charleston as they were leaving. Crawford did a lot of handshaking, passing out cards with the National Crime Information Center hotline number. Starling was interested to see how fast he got them into a male-bonding mode. They sure would call up with anything they got, they sure would. You betcha and much oblige. Maybe it wasn't male bonding, she decided; it worked on her too.

Lamar waved with his fingers from the porch as Crawford and Starling rode away with the deputy toward the Elk River. The Coke was still pretty cold. Lamar took it into the storeroom and fixed a refreshing beverage for himself.

13

"DROP ME at the lab, Jeff," Crawford told the driver. "Then I want you to wait for Officer Starling at the Smithsonian. She'll go on from there to Quantico."

"Yes, sir."

They were crossing the Potomac River against the after-dinner traffic, coming into downtown Washington from National Airport.

The young man at the wheel seemed in awe of Crawford and drove with excessive caution, Starling thought. She didn't blame him; it was an article of faith at the Academy that the last agent who'd committed a Full Fuck-Up in Crawford's command now investigated pilfering at DEW-line installations along the Arctic Circle.

Crawford was not in a good humor. Nine hours had passed since he transmitted the fingerprints and pictures of the victim, and she remained unidentified. Along with the West Virginia troopers, he and Starling had worked the bridge and the river bank until dark without result.

Starling had heard him on the phone from the airplane, arranging for an evening nurse at home.

The F.B.I. plain-jane sedan seemed wonderfully quiet after the Blue Canoe, and talking was easier.

"I'll post the hotline and the Latent Descriptor Index when I take your prints up to I.D.," Crawford said. "You draft me an insert for the file. An insert, not a 302—do you know how to do it?"

"I know how."

"Say I'm the Index, tell me what's new."

It took her a second to get it together—she was glad Crawford seemed interested in the scaffolding on the Jefferson Memorial as they passed by.

The Latent Descriptor Index in the Identification Section's computer compares the characteristics of a crime under investigation to the known proclivities of criminals on file. When it finds pronounced similarities, it suggests suspects and produces their fingerprints. Then a human operator compares the file fingerprints with latent prints found at the scene. There were no prints yet on Buffalo Bill, but Crawford wanted to be ready.

The system requires brief, concise statements. Starling tried to come up with some.

"White female, late teens or early twenties, shot to death, lower torso and thighs flayed—"

"Starling, the Index already knows he kills young white women and skins their torsos—use 'skinned,' by the way, 'flayed' is an uncommon term another officer might not use, and you can't be sure the damned thing will read a synonym. It already knows he dumps them in rivers. It doesn't know what's *new* here. What's new here, Starling?"

"This is the sixth victim, the first one scalped, the first one with triangular patches taken from the back of the shoulders, the first one shot in the chest, the first one with a cocoon in her throat."

"You forgot broken fingernails."

"No, sir, she's the second one with broken fingernails."

"You're right. Listen, in your insert for the file, note that the cocoon is confidential. We'll use it to eliminate false confessions."

"I'm wondering if he's done that before—placed a cocoon or an insect," Starling said. "It would be easy to miss in an autopsy, especially with a floater. You know, the medical examiner sees an obvious cause of death, it's hot in there, and they want to get through . . . can we check back on that?"

"If we have to. You can count on the pathologists to say they didn't miss anything, naturally. The Cincinnati Jane Doe's still in the freezer out there. I'll ask them to look at her, but the other four are in the ground. Exhumation orders stir people up. We had to do it with four patients who passed away under Dr. Lecter's care, just to make sure what killed them. Let me tell you, it's a lot of trouble and it upsets the relatives. I'll do it if I have to, but we'll see what you find out at the Smithsonian before I decide."

"Scalping . . . that's rare, isn't it?"

"Uncommon, yes," Crawford said.

"But Dr. Lecter said Buffalo Bill would do it. How did he know that?"

"He didn't know it."

"He said it, though."

"It's not a big surprise, Starling. I wasn't surprised to see that. I should have said that it was rare until the Mengel case, remember that? Scalped the woman? There were two or three copycats after that. The papers, when they were playing around with the Buffalo Bill tag, they emphasized more than once that this killer doesn't take scalps. It's no surprise after that—he probably follows his press. Lecter was guessing. He didn't say *when* it would happen, so he could never be wrong. If we caught Bill and there was no scalping, Lecter could say we got him just *before* he did it."

"Dr. Lecter also said Buffalo Bill lives in a two-story house. We never got into that. Why do you suppose he said it?"

"That's not a guess. He's very likely right, and he could have told you why, but he wanted to tease you with it. It's the only weakness

I ever saw in him—he has to look smart, smarter than anybody. He's been doing it for years."

"You said ask if I don't know—well, I have to ask you to explain that."

"Okay, two of the victims were hanged, right? High ligature marks, cervical displacement, definite hanging. As Dr. Lecter knows from personal experience, Starling, it's very hard for one person to hang another against his will. People hang *themselves* from doorknobs all the time. They hang themselves sitting down, it's easy. But it's hard to hang somebody else—even when they're bound up, they manage to get their feet under them, if there's any support to find with their feet. A ladder's threatening. Victims won't climb it blindfolded and they sure won't climb it if they can see the noose. The way it's done is in a stairwell. Stairs are familiar. Tell them you're taking them up to use the bathroom, whatever, walk them up with a hood on, slip the noose on, and boot them off the top step with the rope fastened to the landing railing. It's the only good way in a house. Fellow in California popularized it. If Bill didn't have a stairwell, he'd kill them another way. Now give me those names, the senior deputy from Potter and the state police guy, the ranking officer."

Starling found them in her notepad, reading by a penlight held in her teeth.

"Good," Crawford said. "When you're posting a hotline, Starling, always credit the cops by name. They hear their own names, they get more friendly to the hotline. Fame helps them remember to call us if they get something. What does the burn on her leg say to you?"

"Depends if it's postmortem."

"If it is?"

"Then he's got a closed truck or a van or a station wagon, something long."

"Why?"

"Because the burn's across the back of her calf."

They were at Tenth and Pennsylvania, in front of the new F.B.I. headquarters that nobody ever refers to as the J. Edgar Hoover Building.

"Jeff, you can let me out here," Crawford said. "Right here, don't go underneath. Stay in the car, Jeff, just pop the trunk. Come show me, Starling."

She got out with Crawford while he retrieved his datafax and briefcase from the luggage compartment.

"He hauled the body in something big enough for the body to be stretched out on its back," Starling said. "That's the only way the back of her calf would rest on the floor over the exhaust pipe. In a car trunk like this, she'd be curled up on her side and—"

"Yeah, that's how I see it," Crawford said.

She realized then that he'd gotten her out of the car so he could speak with her privately.

"When I told that deputy he and I shouldn't talk in front of a woman, that burned you, didn't it?"

"Sure."

"It was just smoke. I wanted to get him by himself."

"I know that."

"Okay." Crawford slammed the trunk and turned away.

Starling couldn't let it go.

"It matters, Mr. Crawford."

He was turning back to her, laden with his fax machine and briefcase, and she had his full attention.

"Those cops know who you are," she said. "They look at you to see how to act." She stood steady, shrugged her shoulders, opened her palms. There it was, it was true.

Crawford performed a measurement on his cold scales.

"Duly noted, Starling. Now get on with the bug."

"Yes, sir."

She watched him walk away, a middle-aged man laden with cases and rumpled from flying, his cuffs muddy from the riverbank, going home to what he did at home.

She would have killed for him then. That was one of Crawford's great talents.

THE SMITHSONIAN'S National Museum of Natural History had been closed for hours, but Crawford had called ahead and a guard waited to let Clarice Starling in the Constitution Avenue entrance.

The lights were dimmed in the closed museum and the air was still. Only the colossal figure of a South Seas chieftain facing the entrance stood tall enough for the weak ceiling light to shine on his face.

Starling's guide was a big black man in the neat turnout of the Smithsonian guards. She thought he resembled the chieftain as he raised his face to the elevator lights. There was a moment's relief in her idle fancy, like rubbing a cramp.

The second level above the great stuffed elephant, a vast floor closed to the public, is shared by the departments of Anthropology and Entomology. The anthropologists call it the fourth floor. The entomologists contend it is the third. A few scientists from Agriculture say they have proof that it is the sixth. Each faction has a case in the old building with its additions and subdivisions.

Starling followed the guard into a dim maze of corridors walled high with wooden cases of anthropological specimens. Only the small labels revealed their contents.

"Thousands of people in these boxes," the guard said. "Forty thousand specimens."

He found office numbers with his flashlight and trailed the light over the labels as they went along.

Dyak baby carriers and ceremonial skulls gave way to Aphids, and they left Man for the older and more orderly world of Insects. Now the corridor was walled with big metal boxes painted pale green.

"Thirty million insects—and the spiders on top of that. Don't lump the spiders in with the insects," the guard advised. "Spider people jump all over you about that. There, the office that's lit. Don't try to come out by yourself. If they don't say they'll bring you down, call me at this extension, it's the guard office. I'll come get you." He gave her a card and left her.

She was in the heart of Entomology, on a rotunda gallery high above the great stuffed elephant. There was the office with the lights on and the door open.

"Time, Pilch!" A man's voice, shrill with excitement. "Let's go here. Time!"

Starling stopped in the doorway. Two men sat at a laboratory table playing chess. Both were about thirty, one black-haired and lean, the other pudgy with wiry red hair. They appeared to be engrossed in the chessboard. If they noticed Starling, they gave no sign. If they noticed the enormous rhinoceros beetle slowly making its way across the board, weaving among the chessmen, they gave no sign of that either.

Then the beetle crossed the edge of the board.

"Time, Roden," the lean one said instantly.

The pudgy one moved his bishop and immediately turned the beetle around and started it trudging back the other way.

"If the beetle just cuts across the corner, is time up then?" Starling asked.

"Of course time's up then," the pudgy one said loudly, without looking up. "Of *course* it's up then. How do *you* play? Do you make him cross the whole board? Who do you play against, a sloth?"

"I have the specimen Special Agent Crawford called about."

"I can't imagine why we didn't hear your siren," the pudgy one said. "We're waiting all night here to identify a *bug* for the F.B.I. Bugs're all we do. Nobody said anything about Special Agent Crawford's *specimen*. He should show his *specimen* privately to his family doctor. Time, Pilch!"

"I'd love to catch your whole routine another time," Starling said, "but this is urgent, so let's do it now. Time, Pilch."

The black-haired one looked around at her, saw her leaning against the doorframe with her briefcase. He put the beetle on some rotten wood in a box and covered it with a lettuce leaf.

When he got up, he was tall.

"I'm Noble Pilcher," he said. "That's Albert Roden. You need an insect identified? We're happy to help you." Pilcher had a long friendly face, but his black eyes were a little witchy and too close together, and one of them had a slight cast that made it catch the light independently. He did not offer to shake hands. "You are . . . ?"

"Clarice Starling."

"Let's see what you've got."

Pilcher held the small jar to the light.

Roden came to look. "Where did you find it? Did you kill it with your *gun*? Did you see its *mommy*?"

It occurred to Starling how much Roden would benefit from an elbow smash in the hinge of his jaw.

"Shhh," Pilcher said. "Tell us where you found it. Was it attached to anything—a twig or a leaf—or was it in the soil?"

"I see," Starling said. "Nobody's talked to you."

"The Chairman asked us to stay late and identify a bug for the F.B.I.," Pilcher said.

"*Told* us," Roden said. "*Told* us to stay late."

"We do it all the time for Customs and the Department of Agriculture," Pilcher said.

"But not in the middle of the night," Roden said.

"I need to tell you a couple of things involving a criminal case," Starling said. "I'm allowed to do that if you'll keep it in confidence until the case is resolved. It's important. It means some lives, and I'm not just saying that. Dr. Roden, can you tell me seriously that you'll respect a confidence?"

"I'm not a doctor. Do I have to sign anything?"

"Not if your word's any good. You'll have to sign for the specimen if you need to keep it, that's all."

"Of course I'll help you. I'm not *uncaring*."

"Dr. Pilcher?"

"That's true," Pilcher said. "He's not uncaring."

"Confidence?"

"I won't tell."

"Pilch isn't a doctor yet either," Roden said. "We're on an equal educational footing. But notice how he *allowed* you to call him that." Roden placed the tip of his forefinger against his chin, as though pointing to his judicious expression. "Give us all the details. What might seem irrelevant to *you* could be vital information to an expert."

"This insect was found lodged behind the soft palate of a murder victim. I don't know how it got there. Her body was in the Elk River in West Virginia, and she hadn't been dead more than a few days."

"It's Buffalo Bill, I heard it on the radio," Roden said.

"You didn't hear about the insect on the radio, did you?" Starling said.

"No, but they said Elk River—are you coming in from that today, is that why you're so late?"

"Yes," Starling said.

"You must be tired, do you want some coffee?" Roden said.

"No, thank you."

"Water?"

"No."

"A Coke?"

"I don't believe so. We want to know where this woman was held captive and where she was killed. We're hoping this bug has some specialized habitat, or it's limited in range, you know, or it only sleeps on some kind of tree—we want to know where this insect is from. I'm asking for your confidence because—if the perpetrator put the insect there deliberately—then only he would know that fact and we could use it to eliminate false confessions and save time. He's killed six at least. Time's eating us up."

"Do you think he's holding another woman right this minute, while we're looking at his bug?" Roden asked in her face. His eyes were wide and his mouth open. She could see into his mouth, and she flashed for a second on something else.

"*I don't know.*" A little shrill, that. "I don't know," she said again, to take the edge off it. "He'll do it again as soon as he can."

"So we'll do this as soon as we can," Pilcher said. "Don't worry, we're good at this. You couldn't be in better hands." He removed the brown object from the jar with a slender forceps and placed it on a sheet of white paper beneath the light. He swung a magnifying glass on a flexible arm over it.

The insect was long and it looked like a mummy. It was sheathed in a semitransparent cover that followed its general outlines like a sarcophagus. The appendages were bound so tightly against the body, they might have been carved in low relief. The little face looked wise.

"In the first place, it's not anything that would normally infest a body outdoors, and it wouldn't be in the water except by accident," Pilcher said. "I don't know how familiar you are with insects or how much you want to hear."

"Let's say I don't know diddly. I want you to tell me the whole thing."

"Okay, this is a pupa, an immature insect, in a chrysalis—that's the cocoon that holds it while it transforms itself from a larva into an adult," Pilcher said.

"Obtect pupa, Pilch?" Roden wrinkled his nose to hold his glasses up.

"Yeah, I think so. You want to pull down Chu on the immature insects? Okay, this is the pupal stage of a large insect. Most of the more advanced insects have a pupal stage. A lot of them spend the winter this way."

"Book or look, Pilch?" Roden said.

"I'll look." Pilcher moved the specimen to the stage of a microscope and hunched over it with a dental probe in his hand. "Here we go: No distinct respiratory organs on the dorsocephalic region, spiracles on the mesothorax and some abdominals, let's start with that."

"Ummhumm," Roden said, turning pages in a small manual. "Functional mandibles?"

"Nope."

"Paired galeae of maxillae on the ventro meson?"

"Yep, yep."

"Where are the antennae?"

"Adjacent to the mesal margin of the wings. Two pairs of wings, the inside pair are completely covered up. Only the bottom three abdominal segments are free. Little pointy cremaster—I'd say Lepidoptera."

"That's what it says here," Roden said.

"It's the family that includes the butterflies and moths. Covers a lot of territory," Pilcher said.

"It's gonna be tough if the wings are soaked. I'll pull the references," Roden said. "I guess there's no way I can keep you from talking about me while I'm gone."

"I guess not," Pilcher said. "Roden's all right," he told Starling as soon as Roden left the room.

"I'm sure he is."

"Are you now?" Pilcher seemed amused. "We were undergraduates together, working and glomming any kind of fellowship we could. He got one where he had to sit down in a coal mine waiting for proton decay. He just stayed in the dark too long. He's all right. Just don't mention proton decay."

"I'll try to talk around it."

Pilcher turned away from the bright light. "It's a big family, Lepidoptera. Maybe thirty thousand butterflies and a hundred thirty thousand moths. I'd like to take it out of the chrysalis—I'll have to if we're going to narrow it down."

"Okay. Can you do it in one piece?"

"I think so. See, this one had started out on its own power before it died. It had started an irregular fracture in the chrysalis right here. This may take a little while."

Pilcher spread the natural split in the case and eased the insect out. The bunched wings were soaked. Spreading them was like working with a wet, wadded facial tissue. No pattern was visible.

Roden was back with the books.

"Ready?" Pilcher said. "Okay, the prothoracic femur is concealed."

"What about pilifers?"

"No pilifers," Pilcher said. "Would you turn out the light, Officer Starling?"

She waited by the wall switch until Pilcher's penlight came on. He stood back from the table and shined it on the specimen. The insect's eyes glowed in the dark, reflecting the narrow beam.

"Owlet," Roden said.

"Probably, but which one?" Pilcher said. "Give us the lights, please. It's a Noctuid, Officer Starling—a night moth. How many Noctuids are there, Roden?"

"Twenty-six hundred and . . . about twenty-six hundred have been described."

"Not many this big, though. Okay, let's see you shine, my man."

Roden's wiry red head covered the microscope.

"We have to go to chaetaxy now—studying the skin of the insect to narrow it down to one species," Pilcher said. "Roden's the best at it."

Starling had the sense that a kindness had passed in the room.

Roden responded by starting a fierce argument with Pilcher over whether the specimen's larval warts were arranged in circles or not. It raged on through the arrangement of the hairs on the abdomen.

"*Erebus odora*," Roden said at last.

"Let's go look," Pilcher said.

They took the specimen with them, down in the elevator to the level just above the great stuffed elephant and back into an enormous quad filled with pale green boxes. What was formerly a great hall had been split into two levels with decks to provide more storage for the Smithsonian's insects. They were in Neo-tropical now, moving into Noctuids. Pilcher consulted his notepad and stopped at a box chest-high in the great wall stack.

"You have to be careful with these things," he said, sliding the heavy metal door off the box and setting it on the floor. "You drop one on your foot and you hop for weeks."

He ran his finger down the stacked drawers, selected one, and pulled it out.

In the tray Starling saw the tiny preserved eggs, the caterpillar in a tube of alcohol, a cocoon peeled away from a specimen very similar to hers, and the adult—a big brown-black moth with a wingspan of nearly six inches, a furry body, and slender antennae.

"*Erebus odora*," Pilcher said. "The Black Witch Moth."

Roden was already turning pages. "'A tropical species sometimes straying up to Canada in the fall,'" he read.

"'The larvae eat acacia, catclaw, and similar plants. Indigenous West Indies, Southern U.S., considered a pest in Hawaii.'"

Fuckola, Starling thought. "Nuts," she said aloud. "They're all over."

"But they're not all over all the time." Pilcher's head was down. He pulled at his chin. "Do they double-brood, Roden?"

"Wait a second . . . yeah, in extreme south Florida and south Texas."

"When?"

"May and August."

"I was just thinking," Pilcher said. "Your specimen's a little better developed than the one we have, and it's fresh. It had started fracturing its cocoon to come out. In the West Indies or Hawaii, maybe, I could understand it, but it's winter here. In this country it would wait three months to come out. Unless it happened accidentally in a greenhouse, or somebody raised it."

"Raised it how?"

"In a cage, in a warm place, with some acacia leaves for the larvae to eat until they're ready to button up in their cocoons. It's not hard to do."

"Is it a popular hobby? Outside professional study, do a lot of people do it?"

"No, primarily it's entomologists trying to get a perfect specimen, maybe a few collectors. There's the silk industry too, they raise moths, but not this kind."

"Entomologists must have periodicals, professional journals, people that sell equipment," Starling said.

"Sure, and most of the publications come here."

"Let me make you a bundle," Roden said. "A couple of people here subscribe privately to the smaller newsletters—keep 'em locked up and make you give them a quarter just to look at the stupid things. I'll have to get those in the morning."

"I'll see they're picked up, thank you, Mr. Roden."

Pilcher photocopied the references on *Erebus odora* and gave them to her, along with the insect. "I'll take you down," he said.

They waited for the elevator. "Most people love butterflies and hate moths," he said. "But moths are more—interesting, engaging."

"They're destructive."

"Some are, a lot are, but they live in all kinds of ways. Just like we do." Silence for one floor. "There's a moth, more than one in fact, that lives only on tears," he offered. "That's all they eat or drink."

"What kind of tears? Whose tears?"

"The tears of large land mammals, about our size. The old definition of moth was 'anything that gradually, silently eats, consumes, or wastes any other thing.' It was a verb for destruction too . . . Is this what you do all the time—hunt Buffalo Bill?"

"I do it all I can."

Pilcher polished his teeth, his tongue moving behind his lips like a cat beneath the covers. "Do you ever go out for cheeseburgers and beer or the amusing house wine?"

"Not lately."

"Will you go for some with me now? It's not far."

"No, but I'll treat when this is over—and Mr. Roden can go too, naturally."

"There's nothing natural about that," Pilcher said. And at the door, "I hope you're through with this soon, Officer Starling."

She hurried to the waiting car.

Ardelia Mapp had left Starling's mail and half a Mounds candy bar on her bed. Mapp was asleep.

Starling carried her portable typewriter down to the laundry room, put it on the clothes-folding shelf and cranked in a carbon set. She had organized her notes on *Erebus odora* in her head on the ride back to Quantico, and she covered that quickly.

Then she ate the Mounds and wrote a memo to Crawford suggesting they cross-check the entomology publications' computerized mailing lists against the F.B.I.'s known offender files and the files in the cities closest to the abductions, plus felon and sex-offender files of Metro Dade, San Antonio, and Houston, the areas where the moths were most plentiful.

There was another thing, too, that she had to bring up for a second time: *Let's ask Dr. Lecter why he thought the perpetrator would start taking scalps.*

She delivered the paper to the night duty officer and fell into her grateful bed, the voices of the day still whispering, softer than Mapp's breathing across the room. On the swarming dark she saw the moth's wise little face. Those glowing eyes had looked at Buffalo Bill.

Out of the cosmic hangover the Smithsonian leaves came her last thought and a coda for her day: *Over this odd world, this half of the world that's dark now, I have to hunt a thing that lives on tears.*

15

In East Memphis, Tennessee, Catherine Baker Martin and her best boyfriend were watching a late movie on television in his apartment and having a few hits off a bong pipe loaded with hashish. The commercial breaks grew longer and more frequent.

"I've got the munchies, want some popcorn?" she said.

"I'll go get it, give me your keys."

"Sit still. I need to see if Mom called, anyway."

She got up from the couch, a tall young woman, big-boned and well fleshed, nearly heavy, with a handsome face and a lot of clean hair. She found her shoes under the coffee table and went outside.

The February evening was more raw than cold. A light fog off the Mississippi River hung breast-high over the big parking area. Directly overhead she could see the dying moon, pale and thin as a bone fishhook. Looking up made her a little dizzy. She started across the parking field, navigating steadily toward her own front door a hundred yards away.

The brown panel truck was parked near her apartment, among some motor homes and boats on trailers. She noticed it because it resembled the parcel delivery trucks which often brought presents from her mother.

As she passed near the truck, a lamp came on in the fog. It was a floor lamp with a shade, standing on the asphalt behind the truck. Beneath the lamp was an overstuffed armchair in red-flowered chintz, the big red flowers blooming in the fog. The two items were like a furniture grouping in a showroom.

Catherine Baker Martin blinked several times and kept going. She thought the word *surreal* and blamed the bong. She was all right. Somebody was moving in or moving out. In. Out. Somebody was always moving at the Stonehinge Villas. The curtain stirred in her apartment and she saw her cat on the sill, arching and pressing his side against the glass.

She had her key ready, and before she used it she looked back. A man climbed out of the back of the truck. She could see by the lamplight that he had a cast on his hand and his arm was in a sling. She went inside and locked the door behind her.

Catherine Baker Martin peeped around the curtain and saw the man trying to put the chair into the back of the truck. He gripped it with his good hand and tried to boost it with his knee. The chair fell over. He righted it, licked his finger and rubbed at a spot of parking-lot grime on the chintz.

She went outside.

"Help you with that." She got the tone just right—helpful and that's all.

"Would you? Thanks." An odd, strained voice. Not a local accent.

The floor lamp lit his face from below, distorting his features, but she could see his body plainly. He had on pressed khaki trousers and some kind of chamois shirt, unbuttoned over a freckled chest. His chin and cheeks were hairless, as smooth as a woman's, and his eyes only pinpoint gleams above his cheekbones in the shadows of the lamp.

He looked at her too, and she was sensitive to that. Men were often surprised at her size when she got close to them and some concealed it better than others.

"Good," he said.

There was an unpleasant odor about the man, and she noticed with distaste that his chamois shirt still had hairs on it, curly ones across the shoulders and beneath the arms.

It was easy lifting the chair onto the low floor of the truck.

"Let's slide it to the front, do you mind?" He climbed inside and moved some clutter, the big flat pans you can slide under a vehicle to drain the oil, and a small hand winch called a coffin hoist.

They pushed the chair forward until it was just behind the seats.

"Are you about a fourteen?" he said.

"What?"

"Would you hand me that rope? It's just at your feet."

When she bent to look, he brought the plaster cast down on the back of her head. She thought she'd bumped her head and she raised her hand to it as the cast came down again, smashing her fingers against her skull, and down again, this time behind her ear, a succession of blows, none of them too hard, as she slumped over the chair. She slid to the floor of the truck and lay on her side.

The man watched her for a second, then pulled off his cast and the arm sling. Quickly he brought the lamp into the truck and closed the rear doors.

He pulled her collar back and, with a flashlight, read the size tag on her blouse.

"Good," he said.

He slit the blouse up the back with a pair of bandage scissors, pulled the blouse off, and handcuffed her hands behind her. Spreading a mover's pad on the floor of the truck, he rolled her onto her back.

She was not wearing a brassiere. He prodded her big breasts with his fingers and felt their weight and resilience.

"Good," he said.

There was a pink suck mark on her left breast. He licked his finger to rub it as he had done the chintz and nodded when the lividity went away with light pressure. He rolled her onto her face and checked her scalp, parting her thick hair with his fingers. The padded cast hadn't cut her.

He checked her pulse with two fingers on the side of her neck and found it strong.

"Gooood," he said. He had a long way to drive to his two-story house and he'd rather not field-dress her here.

Catherine Baker Martin's cat watched out the window as the truck pulled away, the taillights getting closer and closer together.

Behind the cat the telephone was ringing. The machine in the bedroom answered, its red light blinking in the dark.

The caller was Catherine's mother, the junior U.S. Senator from Tennessee.

16

IN THE 1980s, the Golden Age of Terrorism, procedures were in place to deal with a kidnapping affecting a member of Congress:

At 2:45 A.M. the special agent in charge of the Memphis F.B.I. office reported to headquarters in Washington that Senator Ruth Martin's only daughter had disappeared.

At 3:00 A.M. two unmarked vans pulled out of the damp basement garage at the Washington field office, Buzzard's Point. One van went to the Senate Office Building, where technicians placed monitoring and recording equipment on the telephones in Senator Martin's office and put a Title 3 wiretap on the pay phones closest to the Senator's office. The Justice Department woke the most junior member of the Senate Select Intelligence Committee to provide the obligatory notice of the tap.

The other vehicle, an "eyeball van" with one-way glass and surveillance equipment, was parked on Virginia Avenue to cover the front of the Watergate West, Senator Martin's Washington residence. Two of the van's occupants went inside to install monitoring equipment on the Senator's home telephones.

Bell Atlantic estimated the mean trace time at seventy seconds on any ransom call placed from a domestic digital switching system.

The Reactive Squad at Buzzard's Point went to double shifts in the event of a ransom drop in the Washington area. Their radio procedure changed to mandatory encryption to protect any possible ransom drop from intrusion by news helicoptors—that kind of irresponsibility on the part of the news business was rare, but it had happened.

The Hostage Rescue Team went to an alert status one level short of airborne.

Everyone hoped Catherine Baker Martin's disappearance was a professional kidnapping for ransom; that possibility offered the best chance for her survival.

Nobody mentioned the worst possibility of all.

Then, shortly before dawn in Memphis, a city patrolman investigating a prowler complaint on Winchester Avenue stopped an elderly man collecting aluminum cans and junk along the shoulder of the road. In his cart the patrolman found a woman's blouse, still buttoned in front. The blouse was slit up the back like a funeral suit. The laundry mark was Catherine Baker Martin's.

Jack Crawford was driving south from his home in Arlington at 6:30 A.M. when the telephone in his car beeped for the second time in two minutes.

"Nine twenty-two forty."

"Forty stand by for Alpha 4."

Crawford spotted a rest area, pulled in, and stopped to give his full attention to the telephone. Alpha 4 is the Director of the F.B.I.

"Jack—you up on Catherine Martin?"

"The night duty officer called me just now."

"Then you know about the blouse. Talk to me."

"Buzzard's Point went to kidnap alert," Crawford said. "I'd prefer they didn't stand down yet. When they do stand down I'd like to keep the phone surveillance. Slit blouse or not, we don't know for sure it's Bill. If it's a copycat he might call for ransom. Who's doing taps and traces in Tennessee, us or them?"

"Them. The state police. They're pretty good. Phil Adler called from the White House to tell me about the President's 'intense interest.' We could use a win here, Jack."

"That had occurred to me. Where's the Senator?"

"En route to Memphis. She got me at home a minute ago. You can imagine."

"Yes." Crawford knew Senator Martin from budget hearings.

"She's coming down with all the weight she's got."

"I don't blame her."

"Neither do I," the Director said. "I've told her we're going flat-out, just as we've done all along. She is . . . she's aware of your personal situation and she's offered you a company Lear. Use it—come home at night if you can."

"Good. The Senator's tough, Tommy. If she tries to run it we'll butt heads."

"I know. Do a set-pick off me if you have to. What have we got at the best—six or seven days, Jack?"

"I don't know. If he panics when he finds out who she is—he might just do her and dump her."

"Where are you?"

"Two miles from Quantico."

"Will the strip at Quantico take a Lear?"

"Yes."

"Twenty minutes."

"Yes, sir."

Crawford punched numbers into his phone and pulled back into the traffic.

SORE FROM a troubled sleep, Clarice Starling stood in her bathrobe and bunny slippers, towel over her shoulder, waiting to get in the bathroom she and Mapp shared with the students next door. The news from Memphis on the radio froze her for half a breath.

"Oh God," she said. "Oh boy. ALL RIGHT IN THERE! THIS BATHROOM IS SEIZED. COME OUT WITH YOUR PANTS UP. THIS IS NOT A DRILL!" She climbed into the shower with a startled nextdoor neighbor. "Ooch over, Gracie, and would you pass me that soap."

Ear cocked to the telephone, she packed for overnight and set her forensic kit by the door. She made sure the switchboard knew she was in her room and gave up breakfast to stick by the phone. At ten minutes to class time, with no word, she hurried down to Behavioral Science with her equipment.

"Mr. Crawford left for Memphis forty-five minutes ago," the secretary told her sweetly. "Burroughs went, and Stafford from the lab left from National."

"I put a report here for him last night. Did he leave any message for me? I'm Clarice Starling."

"Yes, I know who you are. I have three copies of your telephone number right here, and there are several more on his desk, I believe. No, he didn't leave a thing for you, Clarice." The woman looked at Starling's luggage. "Would you like me to tell him something when he calls in?"

"Did he leave a Memphis phone number on his three-card?"

"No, he'll call with it. Don't you have classes today, Clarice? You're still in school, aren't you?"

"Yes. Yes, I am."

Starling's entry, late, into the classroom was not eased by Gracie Pitman, the young woman she had displaced in the shower. Gracie Pitman sat directly behind Starling. It seemed a long way to her seat. Gracie Pitman's tongue had time to make two full revolutions in her downy cheek before Starling could submerge into the class.

With no breakfast she sat through two hours of "The Good-Faith Warrant Exception to the Exclusionary Rule in Search and Seizure," before she could get to the vending machine and chug a Coke.

She checked her box for a message at noon and there was nothing. It occurred to her then, as it had on a few other occasions in her life, that intense frustration tastes very much like the patent medicine called Fleet's that she'd had to take as a child.

Some days you wake up changed. This was one for Starling, she could tell. What she had seen yesterday at the Potter Funeral Home had caused in her a small tectonic shift.

Starling had studied psychology and criminology in a good school. In her life she had seen some of the hideously offhand ways in which the world breaks things. But she hadn't really *known* and now she knew: sometimes the family of man produces, behind a human face, a mind whose pleasure is what lay on the porcelain table at Potter, West Virginia, in the room with the cabbage roses. Starling's first apprehension of that mind was worse than anything she could see on the autopsy scales. The knowledge would lie against her skin forever, and she knew she had to form a callus or it would wear her through.

The school routine didn't help her. All day she had the feeling that things were going on just over the horizon. She seemed to hear a vast murmur of events, like the sound from a distant stadium. Suggestions of movement unsettled her, groups passing in the hallway, cloud shadows moving over, the sound of an airplane.

After class Starling ran too many laps and then she swam. She swam until she thought about the floaters and then she didn't want the water on her anymore.

She watched the seven o'clock news with Mapp and a dozen other students in the recreation room. The abduction of Senator Martin's daughter was not the lead item, but it was first after the Geneva arms talks.

There was film from Memphis, starting with the sign of the Stonehinge Villas, shot across the revolving light of a patrol car. The media was blitzing the story and, with little new to report, reporters interviewed each other in the parking lot at Stonehinge. Memphis and Shelby County authorities ducked their heads to unaccustomed banks of microphones. In a jostling, squealing hell of lens flare and audio feedback, they listed the things they didn't know. Still-photographers stooped and darted, back-pedaling into the T.V. minicams whenever investigators entered or left Catherine Baker Martin's apartment.

A brief, ironic cheer went up in the Academy recreation room when Crawford's face appeared briefly in the apartment window. Starling smiled on one side of her mouth.

She wondered if Buffalo Bill was watching. She wondered what he thought of Crawford's face or if he even knew who Crawford was.

Others seemed to think Bill might be watching too.

There was Senator Martin, on television live with Peter Jennings. She stood alone in her child's bedroom, a Southwestern University pennant and posters favoring Wile E. Coyote and the Equal Rights Amendment on the wall behind her.

She was a tall woman with a strong, plain face.

"I'm speaking now to the person who is holding my daughter," she said. She walked closer to the camera, causing an unscheduled refocus, and spoke as she never would have spoken to a terrorist.

"You have the power to let my daughter go unharmed. Her name is Catherine. She's very gentle and understanding. Please let my daughter go, please release her unharmed. You have control of this situation. You have the power. You are in charge. I know you can feel love and compassion. You can protect her against anything that might want to harm her. You now have a wonderful chance to show the whole world that you are capable of great kindness, that you are big enough to treat others better than the world has treated you. Her name is Catherine."

Senator Martin's eyes cut away from the camera as the picture switched to a home movie of a toddler helping herself walk by hanging on to the mane of a large collie.

The Senator's voice went on: "The film you're seeing now is Catherine as a little child. Release Catherine. Release her unharmed anywhere in this country and you'll have my help and my friend-ship."

Now a series of still photographs—Catherine Martin at eight, holding the tiller of a sailboat. The boat was up on blocks and her father was painting the hull. Two recent photographs of the young woman, a full shot and a close-up of her face.

Now back to the Senator in close-up: "I promise you in front of this entire country, you'll have my unstinting aid whenever you need it. I'm well equipped to help you. I am a United States Senator. I serve on the Armed Services Committee. I am deeply involved in the Strategic Defense Initiative, the space weapons systems which everyone calls 'Star Wars.' If you have enemies, I will fight them.

If anyone interferes with you, I can stop them. You can call me at any time, day or night. Catherine is my daughter's name. Please, show us your strength," Senator Martin said in closing, "release Catherine unharmed."

"Boy, is that smart," Starling said. She was trembling like a terrier. "Jesus, that's smart."

"What, the Star Wars?" Mapp said. "If the aliens are trying to control Buffalo Bill's thoughts from another planet, Senator Martin can protect him—is that the pitch?"

Starling nodded. "A lot of paranoid schizophrenics have that specific hallucination—alien control. If that's the way Bill's wired, maybe this approach could bring him out. It's a damn good shot, though, and she stood up there and fired it, didn't she? At the least it might buy Catherine a few more days. They may have time to work on Bill a little. Or they may not; Crawford thinks his period may be getting shorter. They can *try* this, they can try other things."

"Nothing I *wouldn't* try if he had one of mine. Why did she keep saying 'Catherine,' why the name all the time?"

"She's trying to make Buffalo Bill see Catherine as a person. They're thinking he'll have to depersonalize her, he'll have to see her as an object before he can tear her up. Serial murderers talk about that in prison interviews, some of them. They say it's like working on a doll."

"Do you see Crawford behind Senator Martin's statement?"

"Maybe, or maybe Dr. Bloom—there he is," Starling said. On the screen was an interview taped several weeks earlier with Dr. Alan Bloom of the University of Chicago on the subject of serial murder.

Dr. Bloom refused to compare Buffalo Bill with Francis Dolarhyde or Garrett Hobbs, or any of the others in his experience. He refused to use the term "Buffalo Bill." In fact he didn't say much at all, but he was known to be an expert, probably *the* expert on the subject, and the network wanted to show his face.

They used his final statement for the snapper at the end of the report: "There's nothing we can threaten him with that's more terrible than what he faces every day. What we *can* do is ask him to come to us. We can promise him kind treatment and relief, and we can mean it absolutely and sincerely."

"Couldn't we all use some relief," Mapp said. "Damn if I couldn't use some relief myself. Slick obfuscation and facile bullshit, I love it. He didn't tell them anything, but then he probably didn't stir Bill up much either."

"I can stop thinking about that kid in West Virginia for a while," Starling said, "it goes away for, say, a half an hour at a time, and then it pokes me in the throat. Glitter polish on her nails—let me not get into it."

Mapp, rummaging among her many enthusiasms, lightened Starling's gloom at dinner and fascinated eavesdroppers by comparing slant-rhymes in the works of Stevie Wonder and Emily Dickinson.

On the way back to the room, Starling snatched a message out of her box and read this: *Please call Albert Roden*, and a telephone number.

"That just proves my theory," she told Mapp as they flopped on their beds with their books.

"What's that?"

"You meet two guys, right? The wrong one'll call you every God damned time."

"I *been* knowing that."

The telephone rang.

Mapp touched the end of her nose with her pencil. "If that's Hot Bobby Lowrance, would you tell him I'm in the library?" Mapp said. "I'll call him tomorrow, tell him."

It was Crawford calling from an airplane, his voice scratchy on the phone. "Starling, pack for two nights and meet me in an hour."

She thought he was gone, there was only a hollow humming on

the telephone, then the voice came back abruptly "—won't need the kit, just clothes."

"Meet you where?"

"The Smithsonian." He started talking to someone else before he punched off.

"Jack Crawford," Starling said, flipping her bag on the bed.

Mapp appeared over the top of her *Federal Code of Criminal Procedure*. She watched Starling pack, an eyelid dropping over one of her great dark eyes.

"I don't want to put anything on your mind," she said.

"Yes you do," Starling said. She knew what was coming.

Mapp had made the Law Review at the University of Maryland while working at night. Her academic standing at the Academy was number two in the class, her attitude toward the books was pure banzai.

"You're supposed to take the Criminal Code exam tomorrow and the P.E. test in two days. You make sure Supremo Crawford knows you could get recycled if he's not careful. Soon as he says, 'Good work, Trainee Starling,' don't you say, 'The pleasure was mine.' You get right in his old Easter Island face and say, 'I'm counting on you to see to it *yourself* that I'm not recycled for missing school.' Understand what I'm saying?"

"I can get a makeup on the Code," Starling said, opening a barrette with her teeth.

"Right, and you fail it with no time to study, you think they won't recycle you? Are you kidding me? Girl, they'll sail you off the back steps like a dead Easter chick. Gratitude's got a short half-life, Clarice. Make him say *no recycle*. You've got good grades—make him say it. I never would find another roommate that can iron as fast as you can at one minute to class."

Starling had her old Pinto moving up the four-lane at a steady lope, one mile an hour below the speed where the shimmy sets in. The smells of hot oil and mildew, the rattles underneath, the transmission's whine resonated faintly with memories of her father's pickup truck, her memories of riding beside him with her squirming brothers and sister.

She was doing the driving now, driving at night, the white dashes passing under blip blip blip. She had time to think. Her fears breathed on her from close behind her neck; other, recent memories squirmed beside her.

Starling was very much afraid Catherine Baker Martin's body had been found. When Buffalo Bill found out who she was, he might have panicked. He might have killed her and dumped her body with a bug in the throat.

Maybe Crawford was bringing the bug to be identified. Why else would he want her at the Smithsonian? But any agent could carry a bug into the Smithsonian, an F.B.I. messenger could do it for that matter. And he told her to pack for two days.

She could understand Crawford not explaining it to her over an unsecured radio link, but it was maddening to wonder.

She found an all-news station on the radio and waited through the weather report. When the news came, it was no help. The story from Memphis was a rehash of the seven o'clock news. Senator Martin's daughter was missing. Her blouse had been found slit up the back in the style of Buffalo Bill. No witnesses. The victim found in West Virginia remained unidentified.

West Virginia. Among Clarice Starling's memories of the Potter Funeral Home was something hard and valuable. Something durable, shining apart from the dark revelations. Something to keep. She deliberately recalled it now and found that she could squeeze it like a talisman. In the Potter Funeral Home, standing at the sink, she had found strength from a source that surprised and pleased her—the memory of her mother. Starling was a seasoned survivor on hand-me-down grace from her late father through her brothers; she was surprised and moved by this bounty she had found.

She parked the Pinto beneath F.B.I. headquarters at Tenth and Pennsylvania. Two television crews were set up on the sidewalk, reporters looking over-groomed in the lights. They were intoning standup reports with the J. Edgar Hoover Building in the background. Starling skirted the lights and walked the two blocks to the Smithsonian's National Museum of Natural History.

She could see a few lighted windows high in the old building. A Baltimore County Police van was parked in the semicircular drive. Crawford's driver, Jeff, waited at the wheel of a new surveillance van behind it. When he saw Starling coming, he spoke into a hand-held radio.

18

THE GUARD took Clarice Starling to the second level above the Smithsonian's great stuffed elephant. The elevator door opened onto that vast dim floor and Crawford was waiting there alone, his hands in the pockets of his raincoat.

"Evening, Starling."

"Hello," she said.

Crawford spoke over her shoulder to the guard. "We can make it from here by ourselves, Officer, thank you."

Crawford and Starling walked side by side along a corridor in the stacked trays and cases of anthropological specimens. A few ceiling lights were on, not many. As she fell with him into the hunched, reflective attitude of a campus stroll, Starling became aware that Crawford wanted to put his hand on her shoulder, that he would have done it if it were possible for him to touch her.

She waited for him to say something. Finally she stopped, put her hands in her pockets too, and they faced each other across the passage in the silence of the bones.

Crawford leaned his head back against the cases and took a deep breath through his nose. "Catherine Martin's probably still alive," he said.

Starling nodded, kept her head down after the last nod. Maybe he would find it easier to talk if she didn't look at him. He was steady, but something had hold of him. Starling wondered for a second if his wife had died. Or maybe spending all day with Catherine's grieving mother had done it.

"Memphis was pretty much of a wipe," he said. "He got her on the parking lot, I think. Nobody saw it. She went in her apartment and then she came back out for some reason. She didn't mean to stay out long—she left the door ajar and flipped the deadbolt so it wouldn't lock behind her. Her keys were on top of the T.V. Nothing disturbed inside. I don't think she was in the apartment long. She never got as far as her answering machine in the bedroom. The message light was still blinking when her yo-yo boyfriend finally called the police." Crawford idly let his hand fall into a tray of bones, and quickly took it out again.

"So now he's got her, Starling. The networks agreed not to do a countdown on the evening news—Dr. Bloom thinks it eggs him on. A couple of the tabloids'll do it anyway."

In one previous abduction, clothing slit up the back had been found soon enough to identify a Buffalo Bill victim while she was still being held alive. Starling remembered the black-bordered countdown on the front pages of the trash papers. It reached eighteen days before the body floated.

"So Catherine Baker Martin's waiting in Bill's green room, Starling, and we have maybe a week. That's at the outside—Bloom thinks his period's getting shorter."

This seemed like a lot of talk for Crawford. The theatrical "green room" reference smacked of bullshit. Starling waited for him to get to the point, and then he did.

"But this time, Starling, *this* time we may have a little break."

She looked up at him beneath her brows, hopeful and watchful too.

"We've got another insect. Your fellows, Pilcher and that . . . other one."

"Roden."

"They're working on it."

"Where was it—Cincinnati?—the girl in the freezer?"

"No. Come on and I'll show you. Let's see what you think about it."

"Entomology's the other way, Mr. Crawford."

"I know," he said.

They rounded the corner to the door of Anthropology. Light and voices came through the frosted glass. She went in.

Three men in laboratory coats worked at a table in the center of the room beneath a brilliant light. Starling couldn't see what they were doing. Jerry Burroughs from Behavioral Science was looking over their shoulders taking notes on a clipboard. There was a familiar odor in the room.

Then one of the men in white moved to put something in the sink and she could see all right.

In a stainless-steel tray on the workbench was "Klaus," the head she had found in the Split City Mini-Storage.

"Klaus had the bug in his throat," Crawford said. "Hold on a minute, Starling. Jerry, are you talking to the wire room?"

Burroughs was reading from his clipboard into the telephone. He put his hand over the mouthpiece. "Yeah, Jack, they're drying the art on Klaus."

Crawford took the receiver from him. "Bobby, don't wait for the Interpol split. Get a picture wire and transmit the photographs now, along with the medical. Scandinavian countries, West Germany, the Netherlands. Be sure to say Klaus could be a merchant sailor that jumped ship. Mention that their National Health may have a claim for the cheekbone fracture. Call it the what, the zygomatic arch. Make sure you move both dental charts, the universal and the Fédération

Dentaire. They're coming with an age, but emphasize that it's a rough estimate—you can't depend on skull sutures for that." He gave the phone back to Burroughs. "Where's your gear, Starling?"

"The guard office downstairs."

"Johns Hopkins found the insect," Crawford said as they waited for the elevator. "They were doing the head for the Baltimore County police. It was in the throat, just like the girl in West Virginia."

"Just like West Virginia."

"You clucked. Johns Hopkins found it about seven tonight. The Baltimore district attorney called me on the plane. They sent the whole thing over, Klaus and all, so we could see it *in situ*. They also wanted an opinion from Dr. Angel on Klaus's age and how old he was when he fractured his cheekbone. They consult the Smithsonian just like we do."

"I have to deal with this a second. You're saying maybe Buffalo Bill killed *Klaus*? Years ago?"

"Does it seem farfetched, too much of a coincidence?"

"Right this second it does."

"Let it cook a minute."

"Dr. Lecter told me where to find Klaus," Starling said.

"Yes, he did."

"Dr. Lecter told me his patient, Benjamin Raspail, claimed to have killed Klaus. But Lecter said he believed it was probably accidental erotic asphyxia."

"That's what he said."

"You think maybe Dr. Lecter knows exactly how Klaus died, and it wasn't Raspail, and it wasn't erotic asphyxia?"

"Klaus had a bug in his throat, the girl in West Virginia had a bug in her throat. I never saw that anywhere else. Never read about it, never heard of it. What do you think?"

"I think you told me to pack for two days. You want me to ask Dr. Lecter, don't you?"

"You're the one he talks to, Starling." Crawford looked so sad when he said, "I figure you're game."

She nodded.

"We'll talk on the way to the asylum," he said.

"DR. LECTER had a big psychiatric practice for years before we caught him for the murders," Crawford said. "He did a slew of psychiatric evaluations for the Maryland and Virginia courts and some others up and down the East Coast. He's seen a lot of the criminally insane. Who knows what he turned loose, just for fun? That's one way he could know. Also, he knew Raspail socially and Raspail told him things in therapy. Maybe Raspail told him who killed Klaus."

Crawford and Starling faced each other in swivel chairs in the back of the surveillance van, whizzing north on U.S. 95 toward Baltimore, thirty-seven miles away. Jeff, in the driver's compartment, clearly had orders to step on it.

"Lecter offered to help, and I had no part of him. I've had his help before. He gave us nothing useful and he helped Will Graham get a knife jammed through his face last time. For fun.

"But a bug in Klaus's throat, a bug in the girl's throat in West Virginia, I can't ignore that. Alan Bloom's never heard of that specific act before, and neither have I. Have you ever run across it before, Starling? You've read the literature since I have."

"Never. Inserting other objects, yes, but never an insect."

"Two things to begin with. First, we go on the premise that Dr. Lecter really knows something concrete. Second, we remember that Lecter looks only for the fun. Never forget fun. He has to want Buffalo Bill caught while Catherine Martin's still alive. All the fun and benefits have to lie in that direction. We've got nothing to threaten him with—he's lost his commode seat and his books already. That cleans him out."

"What would happen if we just told him the situation and offered him something—a cell with a view. That's what he asked for when he offered to help."

"He offered to *help*, Starling. He didn't offer to snitch. Snitching wouldn't give him enough of a chance to show off. You're doubtful. You favor the truth. Listen, Lecter's in no hurry. He's followed this like it was baseball. We ask him to snitch, he'll wait. He won't do it right away."

"Even for a reward? Something he won't get if Catherine Martin dies?"

"Say we tell him we *know* he's got information and we want him to snitch. He'd have the most fun by waiting and acting like he's trying to remember week after week, getting Senator Martin's hopes up and letting Catherine die, and then tormenting the next mother and the next, getting their hopes up, always just about to remember—that would be better than having a view. It's the kind of thing he lives on. It's his nourishment.

"I'm not sure you get wiser as you get older, Starling, but you do learn to dodge a certain amount of hell. We can dodge some right there."

"So Dr. Lecter has to think we're coming to him strictly for theory and insight," Starling said.

"Correct."

"Why did you tell me? Why didn't you just send me in to ask him that way?"

"I level with you. You'll do the same when you have a command. Nothing else works for long."

"So there's no mention of the insect in Klaus's throat, no connection between Klaus and Buffalo Bill."

"No. You came back to him because you were so impressed that he could predict Buffalo Bill would start scalping. I'm on the record dismissing him and so is Alan Bloom. But I'm letting you fool with it. You have an offer for some privileges—stuff that only somebody as powerful as Senator Martin could get for him. He has to believe he should hurry because the offer ends if Catherine dies. The Senator totally loses interest in him if that happens. And if he fails, it's because he's not smart and knowledgeable enough to do what he said he could do—it's not because he's holding out to spite us."

"*Will* the Senator lose interest?"

"Better you should be able to say under oath that you never knew the answer to that question."

"I see." So Senator Martin hadn't been told. That took some nerve. Clearly, Crawford was afraid of interference, afraid the Senator might make the mistake of appealing to Dr. Lecter.

"*Do* you see?"

"Yes. How can he be specific enough to steer us to Buffalo Bill without showing he's got special knowledge? How can he do that with just theory and insight?"

"I don't know, Starling. He's had a long time to think about it. He's waited through six victims."

The scrambler phone in the van buzzed and blinked with the first of a series of calls Crawford had placed with the F.B.I. switchboard.

Over the next twenty minutes he talked to officers he knew in the Dutch State Police and Royal Marechausee, an *Overstelojtnant* in the Swedish Technical Police who had studied at Quantico, a personal acquaintance who was assistant to the *Rigspolitichef* of the Danish governmental police, and he surprised Starling by breaking into French with the night command desk of the Belgian Police Criminelle. Always he stressed the need for speed in identifying Klaus and his associates. Each jurisdiction would already have the request on its Interpol telex but, with the old-boy network buzzing, the request wouldn't hang from the machine for hours.

Starling could see that Crawford had chosen the van for its com- munications—it had the new Voice Privacy system—but the job would have been easier from his office. Here he had to juggle his notebooks on the tiny desk in marginal light, and they bounced each time the tires hit a tar strip. Starling's field experience was small, but she knew how unusual it was for a section chief to be booming along in a van on an errand like this. He could have briefed her over the radio telephone. She was glad he had not.

Starling had the feeling that the quiet and calm in this van, the time allowed for this mission to proceed in an orderly way, had been purchased at a high price. Listening to Crawford on the phone confirmed it.

He was speaking with the Director at home now. "No, sir. Did they roll over for it? . . . How long? No, sir. No. No wire. Tommy, that's my recommendation, I stand on it. I *do not* want her to wear a wire. Dr. Bloom says the same thing. He's fogged in at O'Hare. He'll come as soon as it clears. Right."

Then Crawford had a cryptic telephone conversation with the night nurse at his house. When he had finished, he looked out the one-way window of the van for perhaps a minute, his glasses held on his knee in the crook of his finger, his face looking naked as the oncoming lights crawled across it. Then he put the glasses on and turned back to Starling.

"We have Lecter for three days. If we don't get any results, Baltimore sweats him until the court pulls them off."

"Sweating him didn't work last time. Dr. Lecter doesn't sweat much."

"What did he give them after all that, a paper chicken?"

"A chicken, yes." The crumpled origami chicken was still in Starling's purse. She smoothed it out on the little desk and made it peck.

"I don't blame the Baltimore cops. He's their prisoner. If Catherine floats, they have to be able to tell Senator Martin they tried it all."

"How is Senator Martin?"

"Game but hurting. She's a smart, tough woman with a lot of sense, Starling. You'd probably like her."

"Will Johns Hopkins and Baltimore County homicide keep quiet about the bug in Klaus's throat? Can we keep it out of the papers?"

"For three days at least."

"That took some doing."

"We can't trust Frederick Chilton, or anybody else at the hospital," Crawford said. "If Chilton knows, the world knows. Chilton has to know you're there, but it's simply a favor you're doing Baltimore Homicide, trying to close the Klaus case—it has nothing to do with Buffalo Bill."

"And I'm doing this late at night?"

"That's the only time I'd give you. I should tell you, the business about the bug in West Virginia will be in the morning papers. The Cincinnati coroner's office spilled it, so that's no secret anymore. It's an inside detail that Lecter can get from you, and it doesn't matter, really, as long as he doesn't know we found one in Klaus too."

"What have we got to trade him?"

"I'm working on it," Crawford said, and turned back to his telephones.

CHAPTER

20

A BIG BATHROOM, all white tile and skylights and sleek Italian fixtures standing against exposed old brick. An elaborate vanity flanked by tall plants and loaded with cosmetics, the mirror beaded by the steam the shower made. From the shower came humming in a key too high for the unearthly voice. The song was Fats Waller's "Cash for Your Trash," from the musical *Ain't Misbehavin'*. Sometimes the voice broke into the words:

"Save up all your old newsPA-PERS.
Save and pile 'em like a high skySCRAPER
DAH DAHDAHDAH DAH DAH DAHDAH DAH DAH . . ."

Whenever there were words, a small dog scratched at the bathroom door.

In the shower was Jame Gumb, white male, thirty-four, six feet one inch, 205 pounds, brown and blue, no distinguishing marks. He pronounces his first name like *James* without the *s*, Jame. He insists on it.

After his first rinse, Gumb applied Friction des Bains, rubbing it over his chest and buttocks with his hands and using a dishmop on the parts he did not like to touch. His legs and feet were a little stubbly, but he decided they would do.

Gumb toweled himself pink and applied a good skin emollient. His full-length mirror had a shower curtain on a bar in front of it.

Gumb used the dishmop to tuck his penis and testicles back between his legs. He whipped the shower curtain aside and stood before the mirror, hitting a hipshot pose despite the grinding it caused in his private parts.

"Do something *for* me, honey. Do something for me SOON." He used the upper range of his naturally deep voice, and he believed he was getting better at it. The hormones he'd taken—Premarin for a while and then diethylstilbestrol, orally—couldn't do anything for his voice, but they had thinned the hair a little across his slightly budding breasts. A lot of electrolysis had removed Gumb's beard and shaped his hairline into a widow's peak, but he did not look like a woman. He looked like a man inclined to fight with his nails as well as his fists and feet.

Whether his behavior was an earnest, inept attempt to swish or a hateful mocking would be hard to say on short acquaintance, and short acquaintances were the only kind he had.

"Whatcha gonna do for meeee?"

The dog scratched on the door at the sound of his voice. Gumb put on his robe and let the dog in. He picked up the little champagne-colored poodle and kissed her plump back.

"Ye-e-e-e-s. Are you *famished*, Precious? I am too."

He switched the little dog from one arm to the other to open the bedroom door. She squirmed to get down.

"Just a mo', sweetheart." With his free hand he picked up a Mini-14 carbine from the floor beside the bed and laid it across the pillows. "*Now*. Now, then. We'll have our supper in a minute." He put the little dog on the floor while he found his nightclothes. She trailed him eagerly downstairs to the kitchen.

Jame Gumb took three T.V. dinners from his microwave oven. There were two Hungry Man dinners for himself and one Lean Cuisine for the poodle.

The poodle greedily ate her entrée and the dessert, leaving the vegetable. Jame Gumb left only the bones on his two trays.

He let the little dog out the back door and, clutching his robe closed against the chill, he watched her squat in the narrow strip of light from the doorway.

"You haven't done Number Two-ooo. All right, I won't watch." But he took a sly peek between his fingers. "Oh, *super*, you little baggage, aren't you a perfect lady? Come on, let's go to bed."

Mr. Gumb liked to go to bed. He did it several times a night. He liked to get up too, and sit in one or another of his many rooms without turning on the light, or work for a little while in the night, when he was hot with something creative.

He started to turn out the kitchen light, but paused, his lips in a judicious pout as he considered the litter of supper. He gathered up the three T.V. trays and wiped off the table.

A switch at the head of the stairs turned on the lights in the basement. Jame Gumb started down, carrying the trays. The little dog cried in the kitchen and nosed open the door behind him.

"All right, Silly Billy." He scooped up the poodle and carried her down. She wriggled and nosed at the trays in his other hand. "No you don't, you've had enough." He put her down and she followed close beside him through the rambling, multilevel basement.

In a basement room directly beneath the kitchen was a well, long dry. Its stone rim, reinforced with modern well rings and cement, rose two feet above the sandy floor. The original wooden safety cover, too heavy for a child to lift, was still in place. There was a trap in the lid big enough to lower a bucket through. The trap was open and Jame Gumb scraped his trays and the dog's tray into it.

The bones and bits of vegetable winked out of sight into the absolute blackness of the well. The little dog sat up and begged.

"No, no, all gone," Gumb said. "You're too fat as it is."

He climbed the basement stairs, whispering "Fatty Bread, Fatty Bread" to his little dog. He gave no sign if he heard the cry, still fairly strong and sane, that echoed up from the black hole:

"PLEEASE."

CLARICE STARLING entered the Baltimore State Hospital for the Criminally Insane at a little after 10:00 P.M. She was alone. Starling had hoped Dr. Frederick Chilton wouldn't be there, but he was waiting for her in his office.

Chilton wore an English-cut sportscoat in windowpane check. The double vent and skirts gave it a peplum effect, Starling thought. She hoped to God he hadn't dressed for her.

The room was bare in front of his desk, except for a straight chair screwed to the floor. Starling stood beside it while her greeting hung in the air. She could smell the cold, rank pipes in the rack beside Chilton's humidor.

Dr. Chilton finished examining his collection of Franklin Mint locomotives and turned to her.

"Would you like a cup of decaf?"

"No, thanks. I'm sorry to interrupt your evening."

"You're still trying to find out something about that head business," Dr. Chilton said.

"Yes. The Baltimore district attorney's office told me they'd made the arrangements with you, Doctor."

"Oh yes. I work *very* closely with the authorities here, Miss Starling. Are you doing an article or a thesis, by the way?"

"No."

"Have you ever been published in any of the professional journals?"

"No, I never have. This is just an errand the U.S. Attorney's office asked me to do for Baltimore County Homicide. We left them with an open case and we're just helping them tidy up the loose ends." Starling found her distaste for Chilton made the lying easier.

"Are you wired, Miss Starling?"

"Am I—"

"Are you wearing a microphone device to record what Dr. Lecter says? The police term is 'wired,' I'm sure you've heard it."

"No."

Dr. Chilton took a small Pearlcorder from his desk and popped a cassette into it. "Then put this in your purse. I'll have it transcribed and forward you a copy. You can use it to augment your notes."

"No, I can't do that, Dr. Chilton."

"Why on earth not? The Baltimore authorities have asked me all along for my analysis of anything Lecter says about this Klaus business."

Get around Chilton if you can, Crawford told her. *We can step on him in a minute with a court order, but Lecter will smell it. He can see through Chilton like a CAT scan.*

"The U.S. Attorney thought we'd try an informal approach first. If I recorded Dr. Lecter without his knowledge, and he found out, it would really, it would be the end of any kind of working atmosphere we had. I'm sure you'd agree with that."

"How would he find out?"

He'd read it in the newspaper with everything else you know, you fucking jerk. She didn't answer. "If this should go anywhere and he has to depose, you'd be the first one to see the material and I'm sure you'd be invited to serve as expert witness. We're just trying to get a lead out of him now."

"Do you know why he talks to you, Miss Starling?"

"No, Dr. Chilton."

He looked at each item in the claque of certificates and diplomas on the walls behind his desk as though he were conducting a poll. Now a slow turn to Starling. "Do you *really* feel you know what you're doing?"

"Sure I do." *Lot of "do's" there.* Starling's legs were shaky from too much exercise. She didn't want to fight with Chilton. She had to have something left when she got to Lecter.

"What you're doing is coming into my hospital to conduct an interview and refusing to share information with me."

"I'm acting on my instructions, Dr. Chilton. I have the U.S. Attorney's night number here. Now please, either discuss it with him or let me do my job."

"I'm not a turnkey here, Miss Starling. I don't come running down here at night just to let people in and out. I had a ticket to *Holiday on Ice*."

He realized he'd said *a* ticket. In that instant Starling saw his life, and he knew it.

She saw his bleak refrigerator, the crumbs on the T.V. tray where he ate alone, the still piles his things stayed in for months until he moved them—she felt the ache of his whole yellow-smiling Sen-Sen lonesome life—and switchblade-quick she knew not to spare him, not to talk on or look away. She stared into his face, and with the smallest tilt of her head, she gave him her good looks and bored her knowledge in, speared him with it, knowing he couldn't stand for the conversation to go on.

He sent her with an orderly named Alonzo.

DESCENDING THROUGH the asylum with Alonzo toward the final keep, Starling managed to shut out much of the slammings and the screaming, though she felt them shiver the air against her skin. Pressure built on her as though she sank through water, down and down.

The proximity of madmen—the thought of Catherine Martin bound and alone, with one of them snuffling her, patting his pockets for his tools—braced Starling for her job. But she needed more than resolution. She needed to be calm, to be still, to be the keenest instrument. She had to use patience in the face of the awful need to hurry. If Dr. Lecter knew the answer, she'd have to find it down among the tendrils of his thought.

Starling found she thought of Catherine Baker Martin as the child she'd seen in the film on the news, the little girl in the sailboat.

Alonzo pushed the buzzer at the last heavy door.

"Teach us to care and not to care, teach us to be still."

"Pardon me?" Alonzo said, and Starling realized she had spoken aloud.

He left her with the big orderly who opened the door. As Alonzo turned away, she saw him cross himself.

"Welcome back," the orderly said, and shot the bolts home behind her.

"Hello, Barney."

A paperback book was wrapped around Barney's massive index finger as he held his place. It was Jane Austen's *Sense and Sensibility*; Starling was set to notice everything.

"How do you want the lights?" he said.

The corridor between the cells was dim. Near the far end she could see bright light from the last cell shining on the corridor floor.

"Dr. Lecter's awake."

"At night, always—even when his lights are off."

"Let's leave them like they are."

"Stay in the middle going down, don't touch the bars, right?"

"I want to shut that T.V. off." The television had been moved. It was at the far end, facing up the center of the corridor. Some inmates could see it by leaning their heads against the bars.

"Sure, turn the sound off, but leave the picture if you don't mind. Some of 'em like to look at it. The chair's right there if you want it."

Starling went down the dim corridor alone. She did not look into the cells on either side. Her footfalls seemed loud to her. The only other sounds were wet snoring from one cell, maybe two, and a low chuckle from another.

The late Miggs's cell had a new occupant. She could see long legs outstretched on the floor, the top of a head resting against the bars. She looked as she passed. A man sat on the cell floor in a litter of shredded construction paper. His face was vacant. The television was reflected in his eyes and a shiny thread of spit connected the corner of his mouth and his shoulder.

She didn't want to look into Dr. Lecter's cell until she was sure he had seen her. She passed it, feeling itchy between the shoulders, went to the television and turned off the sound.

Dr. Lecter wore the white asylum pajamas in his white cell. The only colors in the cell were his hair and eyes and his red mouth, in a face so long out of the sun it leached into the surrounding whiteness; his features seemed suspended above the collar of his shirt. He sat at his table behind the nylon net that kept him back from the bars. He was sketching on butcher paper, using his hand for a model. As she watched, he turned his hand over and, flexing his fingers to great tension, drew the inside of the forearm. He used his little finger as a shading stump to modify a charcoal line.

She came a little closer to the bars, and he looked up. For Starling every shadow in the cell flew into his eyes and widow's peak.

"Good evening, Dr. Lecter."

The tip of his tongue appeared, with his lips equally red. It touched his upper lip in the exact center and went back in again.

"Clarice."

She heard the slight metallic rasp beneath his voice and wondered how long it had been since last he spoke. Beats of silence . . .

"You're up late for a school night," he said.

"This is night school," she said, wishing her voice were stronger. "Yesterday I was in West Virginia—"

"Did you hurt yourself?"

"No, I—"

"You have on a fresh Band-Aid, Clarice."

Then she remembered. "I got a scrape on the side of the pool, swimming today." The Band-Aid was out of sight, on her calf beneath her trousers. He must smell it. "I was in West Virginia yesterday. They found a body over there, Buffalo Bill's latest."

"Not quite his *latest*, Clarice."

"His next-to-latest."

"Yes."

"She was scalped. Just as you said she would be."

"Do you mind if I go on sketching while we talk?"

"No, please."

"You viewed the remains?"

"Yes."

"Had you seen his earlier efforts?"

"No. Only pictures."

"How did you feel?"

"Apprehensive. Then I was busy."

"And after?"

"Shaken."

"Could you function all right?" Dr. Lecter rubbed his charcoal on the edge of his butcher paper to refine the point.

"Very well. I functioned very well."

"For Jack Crawford? Or does he still make house calls?"

"He was there."

"Indulge me a moment, Clarice. Would you let your head hang forward, just let it hang forward as though you were asleep. A second more. Thank you, I've got it now. Have a seat, if you like. You had told Jack Crawford what I said before they found her?"

"Yes. He pretty much pooh-poohed it."

"And after he saw the body in West Virginia?"

"He talked to his main authority, from the University of—"

"Alan Bloom."

"That's right. Dr. Bloom said Buffalo Bill was fulfilling a persona the newspapers created, the Buffalo Bill scalp-taking business the tabloids were playing with. Dr. Bloom said anybody could see that was coming."

"Dr. Bloom saw that coming?"

"He said he did."

"He saw it coming, but he kept it to himself. I see. What do you think, Clarice?"

"I'm not sure."

"You have some psychology, some forensics. Where the two flow together you fish, don't you? Catching anything, Clarice?"

"It's pretty slow so far."

"What do your two disciplines tell you about Buffalo Bill?"

"By the book, he's a sadist."

"Life's too slippery for books, Clarice; anger appears as lust, lupus presents as hives." Dr. Lecter finished sketching his left hand with his right, switched the charcoal and began to sketch his right with his left, and just as well. "Do you mean Dr. Bloom's book?"

"Yes."

"You looked me up in it, didn't you?"

"Yes."

"How did he describe me?"

"A pure sociopath."

"Would you say Dr. Bloom is always right?"

"I'm still waiting for the shallowness of affect."

Dr. Lecter's smile revealed his small white teeth. "We have experts at every hand, Clarice. Dr. Chilton says Sammie, behind you there, is a hebephrenic schizoid and irretrievably lost. He put Sammie in Miggs' old cell, because he thinks Sammie's said bye-bye. Do you know how hebephrenics usually go? Don't worry, he won't hear you."

"They're the hardest to treat," she said. "Usually they go into terminal withdrawal and personality disintegration."

Dr. Lecter took something from between his sheets of butcher paper and put it in the sliding food carrier. Starling pulled it through.

"Only yesterday Sammie sent that across with my supper," he said.

It was a scrap of construction paper with writing in crayon.

Starling read:

I WAN TOO GO TO JESA
I WAN TOO GO WIV CRIEZ
I CAN GO WIV JESA
EF I AC RELL NIZE

SAMMIE

Starling looked back over her right shoulder. Sammie sat vacant-faced against the wall of his cell, his head leaning against the bars.

"Would you read it aloud? He won't hear you."

Starling began. "'I want to go to Jesus, I want to go with Christ, I can go with Jesus if I act real nice.'"

"No, no. Get a more assertive 'Pease porridge hot' quality into it. The meter varies but the intensity is the same." Lecter clapped time softly, "Pease porridge *in* the pot *nine days old.* Intensely, you see. Fervently. 'I *wan* to go to Jesa, I *wan* to go wiv Criez.'"

"I see," Starling said, putting the paper back in the carrier.

"No, you don't see anything at all." Dr. Lecter bounded to his feet, his lithe body suddenly grotesque, bent in a gnomish squat, and he was bouncing, clapping time, his voice ringing like sonar, "I *wan* to go to Jesa—"

Sammie's voice boomed behind her sudden as a leopard's cough, louder than a howler monkey, Sammie up and mashing his face into the bars, livid and straining, the cords standing out in his neck:

"I *WAN* TOO GO TO JESA
I *WAN* TOO GO WIV *CRIEZ*

I CAN *GO* WIV JESA *EF I AC RELL NIIIZE.*"

Silence. Starling found that she was standing and her folding chair was over backwards. Her papers had spilled from her lap.

"Please," Dr. Lecter said, erect and graceful as a dancer once again, inviting her to sit. He dropped easily into his seat and rested his chin on his hand. "You don't see at all," he said again. "Sammie is intensely religious. He's simply disappointed because Jesus is so late. May I tell Clarice why you're here, Sammie?"

Sammie grabbed the lower part of his face and halted its movement.

"Please?" Dr. Lecter said.

"Eaaah," Sammie said between his fingers.

"Sammie put his mother's head in the collection plate at the Highway Baptist Church in Trune. They were singing 'Give of Your Best to the Master' and it was the nicest thing he had." Lecter spoke over her shoulder. "Thank you, Sammie. It's perfectly all right. Watch television."

The tall man subsided to the floor with his head against the bars, just as before, the images from the television worming on his pupils, three streaks of silver on his face now, spit and tears.

"Now. See if you can apply yourself to his problem and perhaps I'll apply myself to yours. Quid pro quo. He's not listening."

Starling had to bear down hard. "The verse changes from 'go to Jesus' to 'go with Christ,'" she said. "That's a reasoned sequence: going to, arriving at, going with."

"Yes. It's a linear progression. I'm particularly pleased that he knows 'Jesa' and 'Criez' are the same. That's progress. The idea of a single Godhead also being a Trinity is hard to reconcile, particularly for Sammie, who's not positive how many people he is himself. Eldridge Cleaver gives us the parable of the 3-in-One Oil, and we find that useful."

"He sees a causal relationship between his behavior and his aims, that's structured thinking," Starling said. "So is the management of a rhyme. He's not blunted—he's crying. You believe he's a catatonic schizoid?"

"Yes. Can you smell his sweat? That peculiar goatish odor is trans-3-methyl-2 hexenoic acid. Remember it, it's the smell of schizo-phrenia."

"And you believe he's treatable?"

"Particularly now, when he's coming out of a stuporous phase. How his cheeks shine!"

"Dr. Lecter, why do you say Buffalo Bill's not a sadist?"

"Because the newspapers have reported the bodies had ligature marks on the wrists, but not the ankles. Did you see any on the person's ankles in West Virginia?"

"No."

"Clarice, recreational flayings are always conducted with the victim inverted, so that blood pressure is maintained longer in the head and chest and the subject remains conscious. Didn't you know that?"

"No."

"When you're back in Washington, go to the National Gallery and look at Titian's *Flaying of Marsyas* before they send it back to Czechoslovakia. Wonderful for details, Titian—look at helpful Pan, bringing the bucket of water."

"Dr. Lecter, we have some extraordinary circumstances here and some unusual opportunities."

"For whom?"

"For you, if we save this one. Did you see Senator Martin on television?"

"Yes, I saw the news."

"What did you think of the statement?"

"Misguided but harmless. She's badly advised."

"She's very powerful, Senator Martin. And determined."

"Let's have it."

"I think you have extraordinary insight. Senator Martin has indicated that if you help us get Catherine Baker Martin back alive and unharmed, she'll help you get transferred to a federal institution, and if there's a view available, you'll get it. You may also be asked to review written psychiatric evaluations of incoming patients—a job, in other words. No relaxing of security restrictions."

"I don't believe that, Clarice."

"You should."

"Oh, I believe *you*. But there are more things you don't know about human behavior than how a proper flaying is conducted.

Would you say that for a United States Senator, you're an odd choice of messenger?"

"I was *your* choice, Dr. Lecter. You chose to speak to me. Would you prefer someone else now? Or maybe you don't think you could help."

"That is both impudent and untrue, Clarice. I don't believe Jack Crawford would allow any compensation ever to reach me . . . Possibly I'll tell you one thing you can tell the Senator, but I operate strictly COD. Maybe I'll trade for a piece of information about you. Yes or no?"

"Let's hear the question."

"Yes or no? Catherine's waiting, isn't she? Listening to the whetstone? What do you think she'd ask you to do?"

"Let's hear the question."

"What's your worst memory of childhood?"

Starling took a deep breath.

"Quicker than that," Dr. Lecter said. "I'm not interested in your worst *invention*."

"The death of my father," Starling said.

"Tell me."

"He was a town marshal. One night he surprised two burglars, addicts, coming out of the back of the drugstore. As he was getting out of his pickup he short-shucked a pump shotgun and they shot him."

"Short-shucked?"

"He didn't work the slide fully. It was an old pump gun, a Remington 870, and the shell hung up in the shell carrier. When it happens the gun won't shoot and you have to take it down to clear it. I think he must have hit the slide on the door getting out."

"Was he killed outright?"

"No. He was strong. He lasted a month."

"Did you see him in the hospital?"

"Dr. Lecter—yes."

"Tell me a detail you remember from the hospital."

Starling closed her eyes. "A neighbor came, an older woman, a single lady, and she recited the end of 'Thanatopsis' to him. I guess that was all she knew to say. That's it. We've traded."

"Yes we have. You've been very frank, Clarice. I always know. I think it would be quite something to know you in private life."

"Quid pro quo."

"In life, was the girl in West Virginia very attractive physically, do you think?"

"She was well-groomed."

"Don't waste my time with loyalty."

"She was heavy."

"Large?"

"Yes."

"Shot in the chest."

"Yes."

"Flat-chested, I expect."

"For her size, yes."

"But big through the hips. Roomy."

"She was, yes."

"What else?"

"She had an insect deliberately inserted in her throat—that hasn't been made public."

"Was it a butterfly?"

Her breath stopped for a moment. She hoped he didn't hear it. "It was a moth," she said. "Please tell me how you anticipated that."

"Clarice, I'm going to tell you what Buffalo Bill wants Catherine Baker Martin for, and then good night. This is my last word under the current terms. You can tell the Senator what he wants with Catherine and she can come up with a more interesting offer for me . . . or she can wait until Catherine bobs to the surface and see that I was right."

"What does he want her for, Dr. Lecter?"

"He wants a vest with tits on it," Dr. Lecter said.

23

CATHERINE BAKER MARTIN lay seventeen feet below the cellar floor. The darkness was loud with her breathing, loud with her heart. Sometimes the fear stood on her chest the way a trapper kills a fox. Sometimes she could think: she knew she was kidnapped, but she didn't know by whom. She knew she wasn't dreaming; in the absolute dark she could hear the tiny clicks her eyes made when she blinked.

She was better now than when she first regained consciousness. Much of the awful vertigo was gone, and she knew there was enough air. She could tell *down* from *up* and she had some sense of her body's position.

Her shoulder, hip, and knee hurt from being pressed against the cement floor where she lay. That side was *down*. *Up* was the rough futon she had crawled beneath during the last interval of blazing, blinding light. The throbbing in her head had subsided now and her only real pain was in the fingers of her left hand. The ring finger was broken, she knew.

She wore a quilted jumpsuit that was strange to her. It was clean and smelled of fabric softener. The floor was clean too, except for the chicken bones and bits of vegetable her captor had raked into the hole. The only other objects with her were the futon and a plastic sanitation bucket with a thin string tied to the handle. It felt like cotton kitchen string and it led up into the darkness as far as she could reach.

Catherine Martin was free to move around, but there was no place to go. The floor she lay on was oval, about eight by ten feet, with a small drain in the center. It was the bottom of a deep covered pit. The smooth cement walls sloped gently inward as they rose.

Sounds from above now or was it her heart? Sounds from above. Sounds came clearly to her from overhead. The oubliette that held her was in the part of the basement directly beneath the kitchen. Footsteps now across the kitchen floor, and running water. The scratching of dog claws on linoleum. Nothing then until a weak disc of yellow light through the open trap above as the basement lights came on. Then blazing light in the pit, and this time she sat up into the light, the futon across her legs, determined to look around, trying to peer through her fingers as her eyes adjusted, her shadow swaying around her as a flood-lamp lowered into the pit swung on its cord high above.

She flinched as her toilet bucket moved, lifted, swayed upward on its flimsy string, twisting slowly as it rose toward the light. She tried to swallow down her fear, got too much air with it, but managed to speak.

"My family will pay," she said. "Cash. My mother will pay it now, no questions asked. This is her private—*oh!*" a flapping shadow down on her, only a towel. "This is her private number. It's 202—"

"Wash yourself."

It was the same unearthly voice she'd heard talking to the dog.

Another bucket coming down on a thin cord. She smelled hot, soapy water.

"Take it off and wash yourself all over, or you'll get the hose." And an aside to the dog as the voice faded, "Yes it will get the hose, won't it, Darlingheart, yes it *will!*"

Catherine Martin heard the footsteps and the claws on the floor above the basement. The double vision she'd had the first time the lights went on was gone now. She could see. How high was the top, was the floodlight on a strong cord? Could she snag it with the jumpsuit, catch something with the towel? Do *something*, hell. The walls were so smooth, a smooth tube upward.

A crack in the cement a foot above her reach, the only blemish she could see. She rolled the futon as tightly as she could and tied the roll with the towel. Standing on it, wobbly, reaching for the crack, she got her fingernails in it for balance and peered up into the light. Squinting into the glare. It's a floodlight with a shade, hanging just a foot down into the pit, almost ten feet above her upstretched hand, it might as well be the moon, and he was coming, the futon was wobbling, she scrabbling at the crack in the wall for balance, hopping down, something, a flake falling past her face.

Something coming down past the light, a hose. A single spatter of icy water, a threat.

"Wash yourself. All over."

There was a washcloth in the bucket and floating in the water was a plastic bottle of an expensive foreign skin emollient.

She did it, goosebumps on her arms and thighs, nipples sore and shriveled in the cool air, she squatted beside the bucket of warm water as close to the wall as she could get and washed.

"Now dry off and rub the cream all over. Rub it all over."

The cream was warm from the bath water. Its moisture made the jumpsuit stick to her skin.

"Now pick up your litter and wash the floor."

She did that too, gathering the chicken bones and picking up the English peas. She put them in the bucket, and dabbed the little spots of grease on the cement. Something else here, near the wall. The flake that had fluttered down from the crack above. It was a human fingernail, covered with glitter polish and torn off far back in the quick.

The bucket was pulled aloft.

"My mother will pay," Catherine Martin said. "No questions asked. She'll pay enough for you all to be rich. If it's a cause, Iran or Palestine, or Black Liberation, she'll give the money for that. All you have to do—"

The lights went out. Sudden and total darkness.

She flinched and went "Uhhhhhh!" when her sanitation bucket settled beside her on its string. She sat on the futon, her mind racing. She believed now that her captor was alone, that he was a white American. She'd tried to give the impression she had no idea what he was, what color or how many, that her memory of the parking lot was wiped out by the blows on her head. She hoped that he believed he could safely let her go. Her mind was working, working, and at last it worked too well:

The fingernail, someone else was here. A woman, a girl was here. Where was she now? What did he do to her?

Except for shock and disorientation, it would not have been so long in coming to her. As it was, the skin emollient did it. Skin. She knew who had her then. The knowledge fell on her like every scalding awful thing on earth and she was screaming, screaming, under the futon, up and climbing, clawing at the wall, screaming until she was coughing something warm and salty in her mouth, hands to her face, drying sticky on the backs of her hands and she lay rigid on the futon, arching off the floor from head to heels, her hands clenched in her hair.

CLARICE STARLING'S quarter bonged down through the telephone in the shabby orderlies' lounge. She dialed the van.

"Crawford."

"I'm at a pay phone outside the maximum-security ward," Starling said. "Dr. Lecter asked me if the insect in West Virginia was a butterfly. He wouldn't elaborate. He said Buffalo Bill needs Catherine Martin because, I'm quoting, 'He wants a vest with tits on it.' Dr. Lecter wants to trade. He wants a 'more interesting' offer from the Senator."

"Did he break it off?"

"Yes."

"How soon do you think he'll talk again?"

"I think he'd like to do this over the next few days, but I'd rather hit him again now, if I can have some kind of urgent offer from the Senator."

"Urgent is right. We got an I.D. on the girl in West Virginia, Starling. A missing-person fingerprint card from Detroit rang the cherries in I.D. section about a half hour ago. Kimberly Jane Emberg, twenty-two, missing from Detroit since February seventh. We're canvassing her neighborhood for witnesses. The Charlottesville medical examiner says she died not later than February eleventh, and possibly the day before, the tenth."

"He only kept her alive three days," Starling said.

"His period's getting shorter. I don't think anybody's surprised." Crawford's voice was even. "He's had Catherine Martin about twenty-six hours. I think if Lecter can deliver, he'd better do it in your next conversation. I'm set up in the Baltimore field office, the van patched you through. I have a room for you in the HoJo two blocks from the hospital if you need a catnap later on."

"He's leery, Mr. Crawford, he's not sure you'd let him have anything good. What he said about Buffalo Bill, he traded for personal information about me. I don't think there's any textual correlation between his questions and the case . . . Do you want to know the questions?"

"No."

"That's why you didn't make me wear a wire, isn't it? You thought it'd be easier for me, I'd be more likely to tell him stuff and please him if nobody else could hear."

"Here's another possibility for you: What if I trusted your judgment, Starling? What if I thought you were my best shot, and I wanted to keep a lot of second-guessers off your back? Would I have you wear a wire then?"

"No, sir." *You're famous for handling agents, aren't you, Mr. Crawfish?* "What can we offer Dr. Lecter?"

"A couple of things I'm sending over. It'll be there in five minutes, unless you want to rest a little first."

"I'd rather do it now," Starling said. "Tell them to ask for Alonzo. Tell Alonzo I'll meet him in the corridor outside Section 8."

"Five minutes," Crawford said.

Starling walked up and down the linoleum of the shabby lounge far underground. She was the only brightness in the room.

We rarely get to prepare ourselves in meadows or on graveled walks;

we do it on short notice in places without windows, hospital corridors, rooms like this lounge with its cracked plastic sofa and Cinzano ashtrays, where the café curtains cover blank concrete. In rooms like this, with so little time, we prepare our gestures, get them by heart so we can do them when we're frightened in the face of Doom. Starling was old enough to know that; she didn't let the room affect her.

Starling walked up and down. She gestured to the air. "Hold on, girl," she said aloud. She said it to Catherine Martin and she said it to herself. "We're better than this room. We're better than this fucking place," she said aloud. "We're better than wherever he's got you. Help me. Help me. Help me." She thought for an instant of her late parents. She wondered if they would be ashamed of her now—just that question, not its pertinence, no qualifications—the way we always ask it. The answer was no, they would not be ashamed of her.

She washed her face and went out into the hall.

The orderly Alonzo was in the corridor with a sealed package from Crawford. It contained a map and instructions. She read them quickly by the corridor light and pushed the button for Barney to let her in.

25

DR. LECTER was at his table, examining his correspondence. Starling
found it easier to approach the cage when he wasn't looking at her.

"Doctor."

He held up a finger for silence. When he had finished reading his
letter, he sat musing, the thumb of his six-fingered hand beneath his
chin, his index finger beside his nose. "What do you make of this?"
he said, putting the document into the food carrier.

It was a letter from the U.S. Patent Office.

"This is about my crucifixion watch," Dr. Lecter said. "They won't
give me a patent, but they advise me to copyright the face. Look here."
He put a drawing the size of a dinner napkin in the carrier and Starling
pulled it through. "You may have noticed that in most crucifixions the
hands point to, say, a quarter to three, or ten till two at the earliest,
while the feet are at six. On this watch face, Jesus is on the cross, as
you see there, and the arms revolve to indicate the time, just like the
arms on the popular Disney watches. The feet remain at six and at the
top a small second hand revolves in the halo. What do you think?"

The quality of the anatomical sketching was very good. The head
was hers.

"You'll lose a lot of detail when it's reduced to watch size," Starling said.

"True, unfortunately, but think of the clocks. Do you think this is safe without a patent?"

"You'd be buying quartz watch movements—wouldn't you?—and they're already under patent. I'm not sure, but I think patents only apply to unique mechanical devices and copyright applies to design."

"But you're not a lawyer, are you? They don't require that in the F.B.I. anymore."

"I have a proposal for you," Starling said, opening her briefcase.

Barney was coming. She closed the briefcase again. She envied Barney's enormous calm. His eyes read negative for dope and there was considerable intelligence behind them.

"Excuse me," Barney said. "If you've got a lot of papers to wrestle, there's a one-armed desk, a school desk, in the closet here that the shrinks use. Want it?"

School image. Yes or no?

"May we talk now, Dr. Lecter?"

The doctor held up an open palm.

"Yes, Barney. Thank you."

Seated now and Barney safely away.

"Dr. Lecter, the Senator has a remarkable offer."

"I'll decide that. You spoke to her so soon?"

"Yes. She's not holding anything back. This is all she's got, so it's not a matter for bargaining. This is it, everything, one offer." She glanced up from her briefcase.

Dr. Lecter, murderer of nine, had his fingers steepled beneath his nose and he was watching her. Behind his eyes was endless night.

"If you help us find Buffalo Bill in time to save Catherine Martin unharmed, you get the following: transfer to the Veterans' Administration hospital at Oneida Park, New York, to a cell with a view of the woods around the hospital. Maximum security measures still apply. You'll be asked to help evaluate written psychological tests on some federal inmates, though not necessarily those sharing your own institution. You'll do the evaluations blind. No identities. You'll have reasonable access to books." She glanced up.

Silence can mock.

"The best thing, the remarkable thing: one week a year, you will leave the hospital and go here." She put a map in the food carrier. Dr. Lecter did not pull it through.

"Plum Island," she continued. "Every afternoon of that week you can walk on the beach or swim in the ocean with no surveillance closer than seventy-five yards, but it'll be S.W.A.T. surveillance. That's it."

"If I decline?"

"Maybe you could hang some café curtains in there. It might help. We don't have anything to threaten you with, Dr. Lecter. What I've got is a way for you to see the daylight."

She didn't look at him. She didn't want to match stares now. This was not a confrontation.

"Will Catherine Martin come and talk to me—only about her captor—if I decide to publish? Talk *exclusively* to me?"

"Yes. You can take that as a given."

"How do you know? *Given* by whom?"

"I'll bring her myself."

"If she'll come."

"We'll have to ask her first, won't we?"

He pulled the carrier through. "Plum Island."

"Look off the tip of Long Island, the north finger there."

"Plum Island. 'The Plum Island Animal Disease Center. (Federal, hoof and mouth disease research),' it says. Sounds charming."

"That's just part of the island. It has a nice beach and good quarters. The terns nest there in the spring."

"Terns." Dr. Lecter sighed. He cocked his head slightly and touched the center of his red lip with his red tongue. "If we talk about this,

Clarice, I have to have something on account. Quid pro quo. I tell you things, and you tell me."

"Go," Starling said.

She had to wait a full minute before he said, "A caterpillar becomes a pupa in a chrysalis. Then it emerges, comes out of its secret changing room as the beautiful imago. Do you know what an imago is, Clarice?"

"An adult winged insect."

"But what else?"

She shook her head.

"It's a term from the dead religion of psychoanalysis. An imago is an image of the parent buried in the unconscious from infancy and bound with infantile affect. The word comes from the wax portrait busts of their ancestors the ancient Romans carried in funeral processions . . . Even the phlegmatic Crawford must see some significance in the insect chrysalis."

"Nothing to jump on except checking the entomology journals' subscription lists against known sex offenders in the descriptor index."

"First, let's drop Buffalo Bill. It's a misleading term and has nothing to do with the person you want. For convenience we'll call him Billy. I'll give you a precis of what I think. Ready?"

"Ready."

"The significance of the chrysalis is change. Worm into butterfly, or moth. Billy thinks he wants to change. He's making himself a girl suit out of real girls. Hence the large victims—he has to have things that fit. The number of victims suggests he may see it as a series of molts. He's doing this in a two-story house, did you find out why two stories?"

"For a while he was hanging them on the stairs."

"Correct."

"Dr. Lecter, there's no correlation that I ever saw between trans-sexualism and violence—transsexuals are passive types, usually."

"That's true, Clarice. Sometimes you see a tendency to surgical addiction—cosmetically, transsexuals are hard to satisfy—but that's about all. Billy's not a real transsexual. You're very close, Clarice, to the way you're going to catch him, do you realize that?"

"No, Dr. Lecter."

"Good. Then you won't mind telling me what happened to you after your father's death."

Starling looked at the scarred top of the school desk.

"I don't imagine the answer's in your papers, Clarice."

"My mother kept us together for more than two years."

"Doing what?"

"Working as a motel maid in the daytime, cooking at a café at night."

"And then?"

"I went to my mother's cousin and her husband in Montana."

"Just you?"

"I was the oldest."

"The town did nothing for your family?"

"A check for five hundred dollars."

"Curious there was no insurance. Clarice, you said your father hit the shotgun slide on the door of his pickup."

"Yes."

"He didn't have a patrol car?"

"No."

"It happened at night."

"Yes."

"Didn't he have a pistol?"

"No."

"Clarice, he was working at night, in a pickup truck, armed only with a shotgun . . . Tell me, did he wear a time clock on his belt, by any chance? One of those things where they have keys screwed to posts all over town and you have to drive to them and stick them in your clock? So the town fathers know you weren't asleep. Tell me if he wore one, Clarice."

"Yes."

"He was a night watchman, wasn't he, Clarice, he wasn't a marshal at all. I'll know if you lie."

"The job description said night marshal."

"What happened to it?"

"What happened to what?"

"The time clock. What happened to it after your father was shot?"

"I don't remember."

"If you do remember, will you tell me?"

"Yes. Wait—the mayor came to the hospital and asked my mother for the clock and the badge." She hadn't known she knew that. The mayor in his leisure suit and Navy-surplus shoes. The cocksucker. "Quid pro quo, Dr. Lecter."

"Did you think for a second you'd made that up? No, if you'd made it up, it wouldn't sting. We were talking about transsexuals. You said violence and destructive aberrant behavior are not statistical correlatives of transsexualism. True. Do you remember what we said about anger expressed as lust, and lupus presenting as hives? Billy's not a transsexual, Clarice, but he thinks he is, he tries to be. He's tried to be a lot of things, I expect."

"You said that was close to the way we'd catch him."

"There are three major centers for transsexual surgery: Johns Hopkins, the University of Minnesota, and Columbus Medical Center. I wouldn't be surprised if he's applied for sex reassignment at one or all of them and been denied."

"On what basis would they reject him, what would show up?"

"You're very quick, Clarice. The first reason would be criminal record. That disqualifies an applicant, unless the crime is relatively harmless and related to the gender-identity problem. Cross-dressing in public, something like that. If he lied successfully about a serious criminal record, then the personality inventories would get him."

"How?"

"You have to know how in order to sieve them, don't you?"

"Yes."

"Why don't you ask Dr. Bloom?"

"I'd rather ask you."

"What will you get out of this, Clarice, a promotion and a raise? What are you, a G-9? What do little G-9s get nowadays?"

"A key to the front door, for one thing. How would he show up on the diagnostics?"

"How did you like Montana, Clarice?"

"Montana's fine."

"How did you like your mother's cousin's husband?"

"We were different."

"How were they?"

"Worn out from work."

"Were there other children?"

"No."

"Where did you live?"

"On a ranch."

"A sheep ranch?"

"Sheep and horses."

"How long were you there?"

"Seven months."

"How old were you?"

"Ten."

"Where did you go from there?"

"The Lutheran Home in Bozeman."

"Tell me the truth."

"I am telling you the truth."

"You're hopping around the truth. If you're tired, we could talk toward the end of the week. I'm rather bored myself. Or had you rather talk now?"

"Now, Dr. Lecter."

"All right. A child is sent away from her mother to a ranch in Montana. A sheep and horse ranch. Missing the mother, excited by the animals . . ." Dr. Lecter invited Starling with his open hands.

"It was great. I had my own room with an Indian rug on the floor. They let me ride a horse—they led me around on this horse— she couldn't see very well. There was something wrong with all the horses. Lame or sick. Some of them had been raised with children and they would, you know, nicker at me in the mornings when I went out to the school bus."

"But then?"

"I found something strange in the barn. They had a little tack room out there. I thought this thing was some kind of old helmet. When I got it down, it was stamped 'W. W. Greener's Humane Horse Killer.' It was sort of a bell-shaped metal cap and it had a place in the top to chamber a cartridge. Looked like about a .32."

"Did they feed out slaughter horses on this ranch, Clarice?"

"Yes, they did."

"Did they kill them at the ranch?"

"The glue and fertilizer ones they did. You can stack six in a truck if they're dead. The ones for dog food they hauled away alive."

"The one you rode around the yard?"

"We ran away together."

"How far did you get?"

"I got about as far as I'm going until you break down the diagnostics for me."

"Do you know the procedure for testing male applicants for trans-sexual surgery?"

"No."

"It may help if you bring me a copy of the regimen from any of the centers, but to begin: the battery of tests usually includes Wechsler Adult Intelligence Scale, House-Tree-Person, Rorschach, Drawing of Self-Concept, Thematic Apperception, MMPI, of course, and a couple of others—the Jenkins, I think, that NYU developed. You need something you can see quickly, don't you? Don't you, Clarice?"

"That would be the best, something quick."

"Let's see . . . our hypothesis is we're looking for a male who will test differently from the way a true transsexual would test. All right— on House-Tree-Person, look for someone who didn't draw the female figure first. Male transsexuals almost always draw the female first and, typically, they pay a lot of attention to adornments on the females they draw. Their male figures are simple stereotypes—there are some notable exceptions where they draw Mr. America—but not much in between.

"Look for a house drawing without the rosy-future embellish- ments—no baby carriage outside, no curtains, no flowers in the yard.

"You get two kinds of trees with real transsexuals—flowing, copious willows and castration themes. The trees that are cut off by the edge of the drawing or the edge of the paper, the castration images, are full of life in the drawings of true transsexuals. Flowering and fruitful stumps. That's an important distinction. They're very unlike the frightened, dead, mutilated trees you see in drawings by people with mental disturbances. That's a good one—Billy's tree will be frightful. Am I going too fast?"

"No, Dr. Lecter."

"On his drawing of himself, a transsexual will almost never draw himself naked. Don't be misled by a certain amount of paranoid ideation in the TAT cards—that's fairly common among transsexual subjects who cross-dress a lot; oftentimes they've had bad experiences with the authorities. Shall I summarize?"

"Yes, I'd like a summary."

"You should try to obtain a list of people rejected from all three gender-reassignment centers. Check first the ones rejected for criminal record—and among those look hard at the burglars. Among those who tried to conceal criminal records, look for severe childhood disturbances associated with violence. Possibly internment in childhood. Then go to the tests. You're looking for a white male, probably under thirty-five and sizable. He's not a transsexual, Clarice. He just thinks he is, and he's puzzled and angry because they won't help him. That's all I want to say, I think, until I've read the case. You *will* leave it with me."

"Yes."

"And the pictures."

"They're included."

"Then you'd better run with what you have, Clarice, and we'll see how you do."

"I need to know how you—"

"No. Don't be grabby or we'll discuss it next week. Come back when you've made some progress. Or not. And Clarice?"

"Yes."

"Next time you'll tell me two things. What happened with the horse is one. The other thing I wonder is . . . how do you manage your rage?"

Alonzo came for her. She held her notes against her chest, walking head bent, trying to hold it all in her mind. Eager for the outside air, she didn't even glance toward Chilton's office as she hurried out of the hospital.

Dr. Chilton's light was on. You could see it under the door.

FAR BENEATH the rusty Baltimore dawn, stirrings in the maximum-security ward. Down where it is never dark the tormented sense beginning day as oysters in a barrel open to their lost tide. God's creatures who cried themselves to sleep stirred to cry again and the ravers cleared their throats.

Dr. Hannibal Lecter stood stiffly upright at the end of the corridor, his face a foot from the wall. Heavy canvas webbing bound him tightly to a mover's tall hand truck as though he were a grandfather clock. Beneath the webbing he wore a straitjacket and leg restraints. A hockey mask over his face precluded biting; it was as effective as a mouthpiece, and not so wet for the orderlies to handle.

Behind Dr. Lecter, a small, round-shouldered orderly mopped Lecter's cage. Barney supervised the thrice-weekly cleaning and searched for contraband at the same time. Moppers tended to hurry, finding it spooky in Dr. Lecter's quarters. Barney checked behind them. He checked everything and he neglected nothing.

Only Barney supervised the handling of Dr. Lecter, because Barney never forgot what he was dealing with. His two assistants watched taped hockey highlights on television.

Dr. Lecter amused himself—he has extensive internal resources and can entertain himself for years at a time. His thoughts were no more bound by fear or kindness than Milton's were by physics. He was free in his head.

His inner world has intense colors and smells, and not much sound. In fact, he had to strain a bit to hear the voice of the late Benjamin Raspail. Dr. Lecter was musing on how he would give Jame Gumb to Clarice Starling, and it was useful to remember Raspail. Here was the fat flutist on the last day of his life, lying on Lecter's therapy couch, telling him about Jame Gumb:

"Jame had the most atrocious room imaginable in this San Francisco flophouse, sort of aubergine walls with smears of psychedelic Day-Glo here and there from the hippie years, terribly battered everything.

"Jame—you know, it's actually spelled that way on his birth certificate, that's where he got it and you have to pronounce it 'Jame,' like 'name,' or he gets livid, even though it was a mistake at the hospital—they were hiring cheap help even then that couldn't even get a name right. It's even worse today, it's worth your life to go in a hospital. Anyway, here was Jame sitting on his bed with his head in his hands in that awful room, and he'd been fired from the curio store and he'd done the bad thing again.

"I'd told him I simply couldn't put up with his behavior, and Klaus had just come into my life, of course. Jame is not really gay, you know, it's just something he picked up in jail. He's not anything, really, just a sort of total lack that he wants to fill, and so angry. You always felt the room was a little emptier when he came in. I mean, he killed his grandparents when he was twelve, you'd think a person that volatile would have some presence, wouldn't you?

"And here he was, no job, he'd done the bad thing again to some luckless bag person. I was gone. He'd gone by the post office and picked up his former employer's mail, hoping there was something he could sell. And there was a package from Malaysia, or somewhere over there. He

eagerly opened it up and it was a suitcase full of dead butterflies, just in there loose.

"His boss sent money to postmasters on all those islands and they sent him boxes and boxes of dead butterflies. He set them in Lucite and made the tackiest ornaments imaginable—and he had the gall to call them objets. *The butterflies were useless to Jame and he dug his hands in them, thinking there might be jewellery underneath—sometimes they got bracelets from Bali—and he got butterfly powder on his fingers. Nothing. He sat on the bed with his head in his hands, butterfly colors on his hands and face and he was at the bottom, just as we've all been, and he was crying. He heard a little noise and it was a butterfly in the open suitcase. It was struggling out of a cocoon that had been thrown in with the butterflies and it climbed out. There was dust in the air from the butterflies and dust in the sun from the window—you know how terribly* vivid *it all is when somebody's describing it to you stoned. He watched it pump up its wings. It was a big one, he said. Green. And he opened the window and it flew away and he felt so light, he said, and he knew what to do.*

"Jame found the little beach house Klaus and I were using, and when I came home from rehearsal, there he was. But I didn't see Klaus. Klaus wasn't there. I said where's Klaus and he said swimming. I knew that was a lie, Klaus never swam, the Pacific's much too crashy-bangy. And when I opened the refrigerator, well, you know what I found. Klaus's head looking out from behind the orange juice. Jame had made himself an apron too, you know, from Klaus, and he put it on and asked me how I liked him now. I know you must be appalled that I'd ever have anything else to do with Jame—he was even more unstable when you met him, I think he was just astounded that you weren't afraid of him."

And then, the last words Raspail ever said: "I wonder why my parents didn't kill me before I was old enough to fool them."

The slender handle of the stiletto wiggled as Raspail's spiked heart tried to keep beating, and Dr. Lecter said, "Looks like a straw down a doodlebug hole, doesn't it?" but it was too late for Raspail to answer.

Dr. Lecter could remember every word, and much more too. Pleasant thoughts to pass the time while they cleaned his cell.

Clarice Starling was astute, the doctor mused. She might get Jame Gumb with what he had told her, but it was a long shot. To get him in time, she would need more specifics. Dr. Lecter felt sure that when he read the details of the crimes, hints would suggest themselves—possibly having to do with Gumb's job training in the juvenile correction facility after he killed his grandparents. He'd give her Jame Gumb tomorrow, and make it clear enough so that even Jack Crawford couldn't miss it. Tomorrow should see it done.

Behind him, Dr. Lecter heard footsteps and the television was turned off. He felt the hand truck tilt back. Now would begin the long, tedious process of freeing him within the cell. It was always done the same way. First Barney and his helpers laid him gently on his cot, face down. Then Barney tied his ankles to the bar at the foot of the cot with towels, removed the leg restraints, and, covered by his two helpers armed with Mace and riot batons, undid the buckles on the back of the straitjacket and backed out of the cell, locking the net and the barred door in place, and leaving Dr. Lecter to work his way out of his bonds. Then the doctor traded the equipment for his breakfast. The procedure had been in effect ever since Dr. Lecter savaged the nurse, and it worked out nicely for everyone.

Today the process was interrupted.

A SLIGHT BUMP as the hand truck carrying Dr. Lecter rolled over the threshold of the cage. And here was Dr. Chilton, sitting on the cot, looking through Dr. Lecter's private correspondence. Chilton had his tie and coat off. Dr. Lecter could see some kind of medal hanging from his neck.

"Stand him up beside the toilet, Barney," Dr. Chilton said without looking up. "You and the others wait at your station."

Dr. Chilton finished reading Dr. Lecter's most recent exchange with the General Archives of Psychiatry. He tossed the letters on the cot and went outside the cell. A glint from behind the hockey mask as Dr. Lecter's eyes tracked him, but Lecter's head didn't move.

Chilton went to the school desk in the hall and, bending stiffly, removed a small listening device from beneath the seat.

He waggled it in front of the eye holes in Dr. Lecter's mask and resumed his seat on the cot.

"I thought she might be looking for a civil rights violation in Miggs' death, so I listened," Chilton said. "I hadn't heard your voice in years— I suppose the last time was when you gave me all the misleading answers in my interviews and then ridiculed me in your *Journal* articles. It's hard to believe an inmate's opinions could count for anything in the professional community, isn't it? But I'm still here. And so are you."

Dr. Lecter said nothing.

"Years of silence, and then Jack Crawford sends down his girl and you just went to jelly, didn't you? What was it that got you, Hannibal? Was it those good, hard ankles? The way her hair shines? She's glorious, isn't she? Remote and glorious. A winter sunset of a girl, that's the way I think of her. I know it's been some time since you've seen a winter sunset, but take my word for it.

"You only get one more day with her. Then Baltimore Homicide takes over the interrogation. They're screwing a chair to the floor for you in the electroshock therapy room. The chair has a commode seat for your convenience, and for their convenience when they attach the wires. I won't know a thing.

"Do you get it yet? They *know*, Hannibal. They know that you know exactly who Buffalo Bill is. They think you probably treated him. When I heard Miss Starling ask about Buffalo Bill, I was puzzled. I called a friend at Baltimore Homicide. They found an insect in Klaus's throat, Hannibal. They know Buffalo Bill killed him. Crawford's letting you think you're smart. I don't think you know how much Crawford hates you for cutting up his protégé. He's got you now. Do you feel *smart* now?"

Dr. Lecter watched Chilton's eyes moving over the straps that held on the mask. Clearly Chilton wanted to remove it so he could watch Lecter's face. Lecter wondered if Chilton would do it the safe way, from behind. If he did it from the front, he'd have to reach around Dr. Lecter's head, with the blue-veined insides of his forearms close to Lecter's face. Come, Doctor. Come close. No, he's decided against it.

"Do you still think you're going someplace with a window? Do you think you'll walk on the beach and see the birds? I don't think so. I called Senator Ruth Martin and she never heard of any deal with you. I had to remind her who you were. She never heard of Clarice

Starling, either. It's a scam. We have to expect *small* dishonesties in a woman, but that's a shocker, wouldn't you say?

"When they get through milking you, Hannibal, Crawford's charging you with misprision of a felony. You'll duck it on *M'Naghten,* of course, but the judge won't like it. You sat through six deaths. The judge won't take such interest in your welfare anymore.

"No window, Hannibal. You'll spend the rest of your life sitting on the floor in a state institution watching the diaper cart go by. Your teeth will go and your strength and nobody will be afraid of you anymore and you'll be out in the ward at someplace like Flendauer. The young ones will just push you around and use you for sex when they feel like it. All you'll get to read is what you write on the wall. You think the court will care? You've seen the old ones. They cry when they don't like the stewed apricots.

"Jack Crawford and his fluff. They'll get together openly after his wife dies. He'll dress younger and take up some sport they can enjoy together. They've been intimate ever since Bella Crawford got sick, they're certainly not fooling anybody about that. They'll get their promotions and they won't think about you once a year. Crawford probably wants to come personally at the end to tell you what *you're* getting. Up the booty. I'm sure he has a speech all prepared.

"Hannibal, he doesn't know you as well as I do. He thought if he asked you for the information, you'd just torment the mother with it."

Quite right, too, Dr. Lecter reflected. *How wise of Jack—that obtuse Scotch-Irish mien is misleading. His face is all scars if you know how to look. Well, possibly there's room for a few more.*

"I know what you're afraid of. It's not pain, or solitude. It's *indignity* you can't stand, Hannibal, you're like a cat that way. I'm on my honor to look after you, Hannibal, and I do it. No personal considerations have ever entered into our relationship, from my end. And I'm looking after you now.

"There never was a deal for you with Senator Martin, but there is now. Or there could be. I've been on the phone for hours on your behalf and for the sake of that girl. I'm going to tell you the first condition: you speak only through me. I alone publish a professional account of this, my successful interview with you. You publish nothing. I have exclusive access to any material from Catherine Martin, if she should be saved.

"That condition is non-negotiable. You'll answer me now. Do you accept that condition?"

Dr. Lecter smiled to himself.

"You'd better answer me now or you can answer Baltimore Homicide. This is what you get: If you identify Buffalo Bill and the girl is found in time, Senator Martin—and she'll confirm this by telephone—Senator Martin will have you installed in Brushy Mountain State Prison in Tennessee, out of the reach of the Maryland authorities. You'll be in her bailiwick, away from Jack Crawford. You'll be in a maximum-security cell with a view of the woods. You get books. Any outdoor exercise, the details will have to be worked out, but she's amenable. Name him and you can go at once. The Tennessee State Police will take custody of you at the airport, the governor has agreed."

At last Dr. Chilton has said something interesting, and he doesn't even know what it is. Dr. Lecter pursed his red lips behind the mask. *The custody of police. Police are not as wise as Barney. Police are accustomed to handling criminals. They're inclined to use leg irons and handcuffs. Handcuffs and leg irons open with a handcuff key. Like mine.*

"His first name is Billy," Dr. Lecter said. "I'll tell the rest to the Senator. In Tennessee."

28

JACK CRAWFORD declined Dr. Danielson's coffee, but took the cup to mix himself an Alka-Seltzer at the stainless-steel sink behind the nursing station. Everything was stainless steel, the cup dispenser, the counter, the waste bin, the rims of Dr. Danielson's spectacles. The bright metal suggested the wink of instruments and gave Crawford a distinct twinge in the area of his inguinal ring.

He and the doctor were alone in the little gallery.

"Not without a court order, you don't," Dr. Danielson said again. He was brusque this time, to counter the hospitality he'd shown with the coffee.

Danielson was head of the Gender Identity Clinic at Johns Hopkins and he had agreed to meet Crawford at first light, long before morning rounds. "You'll have to show me a separate court order for each specific case and we'll fight every one. What did Columbus and Minnesota tell you—same thing, am I right?"

"The Justice Department's asking them right now. We have to do this fast, Doctor. If the girl's not dead already, he'll kill her soon—tonight or tomorrow. Then he'll pick the next one," Crawford said.

"To even mention Buffalo Bill in the same breath with the problems we treat here is ignorant and unfair and dangerous, Mr. Crawford. It makes my hair stand on end. It's taken years—we're not through yet—showing the public that transsexuals aren't crazy, they aren't perverts, they aren't *queers*, whatever that is—"

"I agree with you—"

"Hold on. The incidence of violence among transsexuals is a lot lower than in the general population. These are decent people with a real problem—a famously intransigent problem. They deserve help and we can give it. I'm not having a witch hunt here. We've never violated a patient's confidence, and we never will. Better start from there, Mr. Crawford."

For months now in his private life, Crawford had been cultivating his wife's doctors and nurses, trying to weasel every minute advantage for her. He was pretty sick of doctors. But this was not his private life. This was Baltimore and it was business. Be nice now.

"Then I haven't made myself clear, Doctor. My fault—it's early, I'm not a morning person. The whole idea is, the man we want is *not your patient*. It would be someone you *refused* because you recognized that he was *not a transsexual*. We're not flying blind here—I'll show you some specific ways he'd deviate from typical transsexual patterns in your personality inventories. Here's a short list of things your staff could look for among your rejects."

Dr. Danielson rubbed the side of his nose with his finger as he read. He handed the paper back. "That's original, Mr. Crawford. In fact it's extremely bizarre, and that's a word I don't use very often. May I ask who provided you with that piece of . . . conjecture?"

I don't think you'd like to know that, Dr. Danielson. "The Behavioral Science staff," Crawford said, "in consultation with Dr. Alan Bloom at the University of Chicago."

"*Alan Bloom* endorsed that?"

"And we don't just depend on the tests. There's another way Buffalo Bill's likely to stand out in your records—he probably tried to conceal a record of criminal violence, or falsified other background material. Show me the ones you turned away, Doctor."

Danielson was shaking his head the whole time. "Examination and interview materials are confidential."

"Dr. Danielson, how can fraud and misrepresentation be confidential? How does a criminal's real name and real background fall under the doctor-patient relationship when he never told it to you, you had to find it out for yourself? I know how thorough Johns Hopkins is. You've got cases like that, I'm sure of it. Surgical addicts apply every place surgery's performed. It's no reflection on the institution or the legitimate patients. You think nuts don't apply to the F.B.I.? We get 'em all the time. A man in a Moe hairpiece applied in St Louis last week. He had a bazooka, two rockets, and a bearskin shako in his golf bag."

"Did you hire him?"

"Help me, Dr. Danielson. Time's eating us up. While we're standing here, Buffalo Bill may be turning Catherine Martin into one of these." Crawford put a photograph on the gleaming counter.

"Don't even do that," Dr. Danielson said. "That's a childish, bullying thing to do. I was a battle surgeon, Mr. Crawford. Put your picture back in your pocket."

"Sure, a surgeon can stand to look at a mutilated body," Crawford said, crumpling his cup and stepping on the pedal of the covered wastebasket. "But I don't think a doctor can stand to see a life wasted." He dropped in his cup and the lid of the wastebasket came down with a satisfactory clang. "Here's my best offer: I won't ask you for patient information, only application information selected by you, with reference to these guidelines. You and your psychiatric review board can handle your rejected applications a lot faster than I can. If we find Buffalo Bill through your information, I'll suppress that fact. I'll find another way we could have done it and we'll walk through it that way, for the record."

"Could Johns Hopkins be a protected witness, Mr. Crawford? Could we have a new identity? Move us to Bob Jones College, say? I doubt very much that the F.B.I. or any other government agency can keep a secret very long."

"You'd be surprised."

"I doubt it. Trying to crawl out from under an inept bureaucratic lie would be more damaging than just telling the truth. Please don't ever protect us that way, thank you very much."

"Thank *you*, Dr. Danielson, for your humorous remarks. They're very helpful to me—I'll show you how in a minute. You like the truth—try this. He kidnaps young women and rips their skins off. He puts on these skins and capers around in them. We don't want him to do that anymore. If you don't help me as fast as you can, this is what I'll do to you: this morning the Justice Department will ask publicly for a court order, saying you've refused to help. We'll ask twice a day, in plenty of time for the A.M. and P.M. news cycles. Every news release from Justice about this case will say how we're coming along with Dr. Danielson at Johns Hopkins, trying to get him to pitch in. Every time there's news in the Buffalo Bill case—when Catherine Martin floats, when the next one floats, and the next one floats—we'll issue a news release right away about how we're doing with Dr. Danielson at Johns Hopkins, complete with your humorous comments about Bob Jones College. One more thing, Doctor. You know, Health and Human Services is right here in Baltimore. My thoughts are running to the Office of Eligibility Policy, and I expect *your* thoughts got there first, didn't they? What if Senator Martin, sometime after her daughter's funeral, asked the fellows over at Eligibility this question: Should the sex-change operations you perform here be considered cosmetic surgery? Maybe they'll scratch their heads and decide, 'Why, you know, Senator Martin's *right*. Yes. We think it's cosmetic surgery,' then this program won't qualify for federal assistance any more than a nose-job clinic."

"That's insulting."

"No, it's just the truth."

"You don't frighten me, you don't intimidate me—"

"Good. I don't want to do either one, Doctor. I just want you to know I'm serious. Help me, Doctor. Please."

"You said you're working with Alan Bloom."

"Yes. The University of Chicago—"

"I know Alan Bloom, and I'd rather discuss this on a professional level. Tell him I'll be in touch with him this morning. I'll tell you what I've decided before noon. I do care about the young woman, Mr. Crawford. And the others. But there's a lot at stake here, and I don't think it's as important to you as it ought to be . . . Mr. Crawford, have you had your blood pressure checked recently?"

"I do it myself."

"And do you prescribe for yourself?"

"That's against the law, Dr. Danielson."

"But you have a doctor."

"Yes."

"Share your findings with him, Mr. Crawford. What a loss to us all if you dropped dead. You'll hear from me later in the morning."

"How much later, Doctor? How about an hour?"

"An hour."

Crawford's beeper sounded as he got off the elevator at the ground floor. His driver, Jeff, was beckoning as Crawford trotted to the van. *She's dead and they found her*, Crawford thought as he grabbed the phone. It was the Director calling. The news wasn't as bad as it could get, but it was bad enough: Chilton had butted into the case and now Senator Martin was stepping in. The attorney general of the state of Maryland, on instructions from the governor, had authorized the extradition to Tennessee of Dr. Hannibal Lecter. It would take all the muscle of the Federal Court, District of Maryland, to prevent or delay the move. The Director wanted a judgment call from Crawford and he wanted it now.

"Hold on," Crawford said. He held the receiver on his thigh and looked out the van window. There wasn't much color in February for the first light to find. All gray. So bleak.

Jeff started to say something and Crawford hushed him with a motion of his hand.

Lecter's monster ego. Chilton's ambition. Senator Martin's terror for her child. Catherine Martin's life. Call it.

"Let them go," he said into the phone.

29

DR. CHILTON and three well-pressed Tennessee state troopers stood close together on the windy tarmac at sunrise, raising their voices over a wash of radio traffic from the open door of the Grumman Gulfstream and from the ambulance idling beside the airplane.

The trooper captain in charge handed Dr. Chilton a pen. The papers blew over the end of the clipboard and the policeman had to smooth them down.

"Can't we do this in the air?" Chilton asked.

"Sir, we have to do the documentation at the moment of physical transfer. That's my instructions."

The copilot finished clamping the ramp over the airplane steps. "Okay," he called.

The troopers gathered with Dr. Chilton at the back of the ambulance. When he opened the back doors, they tensed as though they expected something to jump out.

Dr. Hannibal Lecter stood upright on his hand truck, wrapped in canvas webbing and wearing his hockey mask. He was relieving his bladder while Barney held the urinal.

One of the troopers snorted. The other two looked away.

"Sorry," Barney said to Dr. Lecter, and closed the doors again.

"That's all right, Barney," Dr. Lecter said. "I'm quite finished, thank you."

Barney rearranged Lecter's clothing and rolled him to the back of the ambulance.

"Barney?"

"Yes, Dr. Lecter?"

"You've been decent to me for a long time. Thank you."

"You're welcome."

"Next time Sammie's at himself, would you say goodbye for me?"

"Sure."

"Good-bye, Barney."

The big orderly pushed open the doors and called to the troopers. "You want to catch the bottom there, fellows? Take it on both sides. We'll set him on the ground. Easy."

Barney rolled Dr. Lecter up the ramp and into the airplane. Three seats had been removed on the craft's right side. The copilot lashed the hand truck to the seat brackets in the floor.

"He's gonna fly laying down?" one trooper asked. "Has he got rubber britches on?"

"You'll just have to hold your water to Memphis, buddy ruff," the other trooper said.

"Dr. Chilton, could I speak to you?" Barney said.

They stood outside the airplane while the wind made little twisters of dust and trash around them.

"These fellows don't know anything," Barney said.

"I'll have some help on the other end—experienced psychiatric orderlies. He's their responsibility now."

"You think they'll treat him all right? You know how he is—you have to threaten him with boredom. That's all he's afraid of. Slapping him around's no good."

"I'd never allow that, Barney."

"You'll be there when they question him?"

"Yes." *And you won't,* Chilton added privately.

"I could get him settled on the other end and be back here just a couple of hours behind my shift," Barney said.

"He's not your job anymore, Barney. I'll be there. I'll show them how to manage him, every step."

"They better pay attention," Barney said. "*He* will."

30

CLARICE STARLING sat on the side of her motel bed and stared at the black telephone for almost a minute after Crawford hung up. Her hair was tousled and she had twisted her F.B.I. Academy nightgown about her, tossing in her short sleep. She felt like she had been kicked in the stomach.

It had only been three hours since she left Dr. Lecter, and two hours since she and Crawford finished working out the sheet of characteristics to check against applications at the medical centers. In that short time, while she slept, Dr. Frederick Chilton had managed to screw it up.

Crawford was coming for her. She needed to get ready, had to think about getting ready.

God dammit. God DAMMIT. GOD DAMMIT. You've killed her, Dr. Chilton. You've killed her, Dr. Fuck Face. Lecter knew some more and I could have gotten it. All gone, all gone, now. All for nothing. When Catherine Martin floats, I'll see that you have to look at her, I swear I will. You took it away from me. I really have to have something useful to do. Right now. What can I do right now, what can I do this minute? Get clean.

In the bathroom, a little basket of paper-wrapped soaps, tubes of shampoo and lotion, a little sewing kit, the favors you get at a good motel.

Stepping into the shower, Starling saw in a flash herself at eight, bringing in the towels and the shampoo and paper-wrapped soap to her mother when her mother cleaned motel rooms. When she was eight, there was a crow, one of a flock on the gritty wind of that sour town, and this crow liked to steal from the motel cleaning carts. It took anything bright. The crow would wait for its chance, and then rummage among the many housekeeping items on the cart. Sometimes, in an emergency takeoff, it crapped on the clean linens. One of the other cleaning women threw bleach at it, to no effect except to mottle its feathers with snow-white patches. The black-and-white crow was always watching for Clarice to leave the cart, to take things to her mother, who was scrubbing bathrooms. Her mother was standing in the door of a motel bathroom when she told Starling she would have to go away, to live in Montana. Her mother put down the towels she was holding and sat down on the side of the motel bed and held her. Starling still dreamed about the crow, saw it now with no time to think why. Her hand came up in a shooing motion and then, as though it needed to excuse the gesture, her hand continued to her forehead to slick back the wet hair.

She dressed quickly. Slacks, blouse, and a light sweater vest, the snub-nosed revolver tucked tight against her ribs in the pancake holster, the speedloader straddling her belt on the other side. Her blazer needed a little work. A seam in the lining was fraying over the speedloader. She was determined to be busy, be busy, until she cooled off. She got the motel's little paper sewing kit and tacked the lining down. Some agents sewed washers into the tail of the jacket so it would swing away cleanly, she'd have to do that . . .

Crawford was knocking on the door.

31

IN CRAWFORD'S experience, anger made women look tacky. Rage made their hair stick out behind and played hell with their color and they forgot to zip. Any unattractive feature was magnified. Starling looked herself when she opened the door of her motel room, but she was mad all right.

Crawford knew he might learn a large new truth about her now.

Fragrance of soap and steamy air puffed at him as she stood in the doorway. The covers on the bed behind her had been pulled up over the pillow.

"What do you *say*, Starling?"

"I say God dammit, Mr. Crawford, what do *you* say?"

He beckoned with his head. "Drugstore's open on the corner already. We'll get some coffee."

It was a mild morning for February. The sun, still low in the east, shone red on the front of the asylum as they walked past. Jeff trailed them slowly in the van, the radios crackling. Once he handed a phone out the window to Crawford for a brief conversation.

"Can I file obstruction of justice on Chilton?"

Starling was walking slightly ahead. Crawford could see her jaw muscles bunch after she asked.

"No, it wouldn't stick."

"What if he's wasted her, what if Catherine dies because of him? I really want to get in his face . . . Let me stay with this, Mr. Crawford. Don't send me back to school."

"Two things. If I keep you, it won't be to get in Chilton's face, that comes later. Second, if I keep you much longer, you'll be recycled. Cost you some months. The Academy cuts nobody any slack. I can guarantee you get back in, but that's all—there'll be a place for you, I can tell you that."

She leaned her head far back, then put it down again, walking. "Maybe this isn't a polite question to ask the boss, but are you in the glue? Can Senator Martin do anything to you?"

"Starling, I have to retire in two years. If I find Jimmy Hoffa and the Tylenol killer I still have to hang it up. It's not a consideration."

Crawford, ever wary of desire, knew how badly he wanted to be wise. He knew that a middle-aged man can be so desperate for wisdom he may try to make some up, and how deadly that can be to a youngster who believes him. So he spoke carefully, and only of things he knew.

What Crawford told her on that mean street in Baltimore he had learned in a succession of freezing dawns in Korea, in a war before she was born. He left the Korea part out, since he didn't need it for authority.

"This is the hardest time, Starling. Use this time and it'll temper you. Now's the hardest test—not letting rage and frustration keep you from thinking. It's the core of whether you can command or not. Waste and stupidity get you the worst. Chilton's a God damned fool and he may have cost Catherine Martin her life. But maybe not. We're her chance. Starling, how cold is liquid nitrogen in the lab?"

"What? Ah, liquid nitrogen . . . minus two hundred degrees Centigrade, about. It boils at a little more than that."

"Did you ever freeze stuff with it?"

"Sure."

"I want you to freeze something now. Freeze the business with Chilton. Keep the information you got from Lecter and freeze the feelings. I want you to keep your eyes on the prize, Starling. That's all that matters. You worked for some information, paid for it, got it, now we'll use it. It's just as good—or as worthless—as it was before Chilton messed in this. We just won't get any more from Lecter, probably. Take the knowledge of Buffalo Bill you got from Lecter and keep fit. Freeze the rest. The waste, the loss, your anger, Chilton. Freeze it. When we have time, we'll kick Chilton's butt up between his shoulder blades. Freeze it now and slide it aside. So you can see past it to the prize, Starling. Catherine Martin's life. And Buffalo Bill's hide on the barn door. Keep your eyes on the prize. If you can do that, I need you."

"To work with the medical records?"

They were in front of the drugstore now.

"Not unless the clinics stonewall us and we have to take the records. I want you in Memphis. We have to hope Lecter tells Senator Martin something useful. But I want you to be close by, just in case—if he gets tired of toying with her, maybe he'll talk to you. In the meantime, I want you to try to get a feel for Catherine, how Bill might have spotted her. You're not a lot older than Catherine, and her friends might tell you things they wouldn't tell somebody that looks more like a cop.

"We've still got the other things going. Interpol's working on identifying Klaus. With an I.D. on Klaus we can take a look at his associates in Europe and in California where he had his romance with Benjamin Raspail. I'm going to the University of Minnesota—we got off on the wrong foot up there—and I'll be in Washington tonight. I'll get the coffee now. Whistle up Jeff and the van. You're on a plane in forty minutes."

THE SILENCE OF THE LAMBS 575

The red sun had reached three-quarters of the way down the telephone poles. The sidewalks were still violet. Starling could reach up into the light as she waved for Jeff.

She felt lighter, better. Crawford really was very good. She knew that his little nitrogen question was a nod to her forensic background, meant to please her and to trigger ingrained habits of disciplined thinking. She wondered if men actually regard that kind of manipulation as subtle. Curious how things can work on you even when you recognize them. Curious how the gift of leadership is often a coarse gift.

Across the street, a figure coming down the steps of the Baltimore State Hospital for the Criminally Insane. It was Barney, looking even larger in his lumber jacket. He was carrying his lunchpail.

Starling mouthed "Five minutes" to Jeff waiting in the van. She caught Barney as he was unlocking his old Studebaker.

"Barney."

He turned to face her, expressionless. His eyes may have been a bit wider than usual. He had his weight on both feet.

"Did Dr. Chilton tell you you'd be all right from this?"

"What else would he tell me?"

"You believe it?"

The corner of his mouth turned down. He didn't say yes or no.

"I want you to do something for me. I want you to do it now, with no questions. I'll ask you nicely—we'll start with that. What's left in Lecter's cell?"

"A couple of books—*Joy of Cooking*, medical journals. They took his court papers."

"The stuff on the walls, the drawings?"

"It's still there."

"I want it all and I'm in a hell of a hurry."

He considered her for a second. "Hold on," he said and trotted back up the steps, lightly for such a big man.

Crawford was waiting for her in the van when Barney came

back out with rolled drawings and the papers and books in a shopping bag.

"You sure I knew the bug was in that desk I brought you?" Barney said as he handed her the stuff.

"I have to give that some thought. Here's a pen, write your phone numbers on the bag. Barney, you think they can *handle* Dr. Lecter?"

"I got my doubts and I said so to Dr. Chilton. Remember I told you that, in case it slips his mind. You're all right, Officer Starling. Listen, when you get Buffalo Bill?"

"Yeah?"

"Don't bring him to me just because I got a vacancy, all right?" He smiled. Barney had little baby teeth.

Starling grinned at him in spite of herself. She flapped a wave back over her shoulder as she ran to the van.

Crawford was pleased.

32

THE GRUMMAN GULFSTREAM carrying Dr. Hannibal Lecter touched down in Memphis with two puffs of blue tire smoke. Following directions from the tower, it taxied fast toward the Air National Guard hangars, away from the passenger terminal. An Emergency Service ambulance and a limousine waited inside the first hangar.

Senator Ruth Martin watched through the smoked glass of the limousine as the state troopers rolled Dr. Lecter out of the airplane. She wanted to run up to the bound and masked figure and tear the information out of him, but she was smarter than that.

Senator Martin's telephone beeped. Her assistant, Brian Gossage, reached it from the jump seat.

"It's the F.B.I.—Jack Crawford," Gossage said.

Senator Martin held out her hand for the phone without taking her eyes off Dr. Lecter.

"Why didn't you tell me about Dr. Lecter, Mr. Crawford?"

"I was afraid you'd do just what you're doing, Senator."

"I'm not fighting you, Mr. Crawford. If you fight me, you'll be sorry."

"Where's Lecter now?"

"I'm looking at him."

"Can he hear you?"

"No."

"Senator Martin, listen to me. You want to make personal guarantees to Lecter—all right, fine. But do this for me. Let Dr. Alan Bloom brief you before you go up against Lecter. Bloom can help you, believe me."

"I've got professional advice."

"Better than Chilton, I hope."

Dr. Chilton was pecking on the window of the limousine. Senator Martin sent Brian Gossage out to take care of him.

"Infighting wastes time, Mr. Crawford. You sent a green recruit to Lecter with a phony offer. I can do better than that. Dr. Chilton says Lecter's capable of responding to a straight offer and I'm giving him one—no red tape, no personalities, no questions of credit. If we get Catherine back safe, everybody smells like a rose, you included. If she . . . dies, I don't give a God damn about excuses."

"*Use* us, then, Senator Martin."

She heard no anger in his voice, only a professional, cut-your-losses cool that she recognized. She responded to it. "Go on."

"If you get something, let us act on it. Make sure we have everything. Make sure the local police share. Don't let them think they'll please you by cutting us out."

"Paul Krendler from Justice is coming. He'll see to it."

"Who's your ranking officer there now?"

"Major Bachman from the Tennessee Bureau of Investigation."

"Good. If it's not too late, try for a media blackout. You better threaten Chilton about that—he likes attention. We don't want Buffalo Bill to know anything. When we find him, we want to use the Hostage Rescue Team. We want to hit him fast and avoid a standoff. You mean to question Lecter yourself?"

"Yes."

"Will you talk to Clarice Starling first? She's on the way."

"To what purpose? Dr. Chilton's summarized that material for me. We've fooled around enough."

Chilton was pecking on the window again, mouthing words through the glass. Brian Gossage put a hand on his wrist and shook his head.

"I want access to Lecter after you've talked to him," Crawford said.

"Mr. Crawford, he's promised he'll name Buffalo Bill in exchange for privileges—amenities, really. If he doesn't do that, you can have him forever."

"Senator Martin, I know this is sensitive, but I have to say it to you: whatever you do, don't beg him."

"Right, Mr. Crawford. I really can't talk right now." She hung up the phone. "If I'm wrong, she won't be any deader than the last six you handled," she said under her breath, and waved Gossage and Chilton into the car.

Dr. Chilton had requested an office setting in Memphis for Senator Martin's interview with Hannibal Lecter. To save time, an Air National Guard briefing room in the hangar had been rearranged hastily for the meeting.

Senator Martin had to wait out in the hangar while Dr. Chilton got Lecter settled in the office. She couldn't stand to stay in the car. She paced in a small circle beneath the great roof of the hangar, looking up at the high, latticed rafters and down again at the painted stripes on the floor. Once she stopped beside an old Phantom F-4 and rested her head against its cold side where the stencil said NO STEP. *This airplane must be older than Catherine. Sweet Jesus, come on.*

"Senator Martin." Major Bachman was calling her. Chilton beckoned from the door.

There was a desk for Chilton in the room, and chairs for Senator Martin and her assistant and for Major Bachman. A video cameraman was ready to record the meeting. Chilton claimed it was one of Lecter's requirements.

Senator Martin went in looking good. Her navy suit breathed power. She had put some starch in Gossage too.

Dr. Hannibal Lecter sat alone in the middle of the room in a stout oak armchair bolted to the floor. A blanket covered his straitjacket and leg restraints and concealed the fact that he was chained to the chair. But he still wore the hockey mask that kept him from biting.

Why? the Senator wondered—the idea had been to permit Dr. Lecter some dignity in an office setting. Senator Martin gave Chilton a look and turned to Gossage for papers.

Chilton went behind Dr. Lecter and, with a glance at the camera, undid the straps and removed the mask with a flourish.

"Senator Martin, meet Dr. Hannibal Lecter."

Seeing what Dr. Chilton had done for showmanship frightened Senator Martin as much as anything that had happened since her daughter disappeared. Any confidence she might have had in Chilton's judgment was replaced with the cold fear that he was a fool.

She'd have to wing it.

A lock of Dr. Lecter's hair fell between his maroon eyes. He was as pale as the mask. Senator Martin and Hannibal Lecter considered each other, one extremely bright and the other not measurable by any means known to man.

Dr. Chilton returned to his desk, looked around at everyone, and began:

"Dr. Lecter has indicated to me, Senator, that he wants to contribute to the investigation some special knowledge, in return for considerations regarding the conditions of his confinement."

Senator Martin held up a document. "Dr. Lecter, this is an affidavit which I'll now sign. It says I'll help you. Want to read it?"

She thought he wasn't going to reply and turned to the desk to sign, when he said:

"I won't waste your time and Catherine's time bargaining for petty privileges. Career climbers have wasted enough already. Let me help you now, and I'll trust you to help me when it's over."

"You can count on it. Brian?"

Gossage raised his pad.

"Buffalo Bill's name is William Rubin. He goes by Billy Rubin. He was referred to me in April or May 1975, by my patient Benjamin Raspail. He said he lived in Philadelphia, I can't remember an address, but he was staying with Raspail in Baltimore."

"Where are your records?" Major Bachman broke in.

"My records were destroyed by court order shortly after—"

"What did he look like?" Major Bachman said.

"Do you *mind*, Major? Senator Martin, the only—"

"Give me an age and a physical description, anything else you can remember," Major Bachman said.

Dr. Lecter simply went away. He thought about something else— Géricault's anatomical studies for *The Raft of the Medusa*—and if he heard the questions that followed, he didn't show it.

When Senator Martin regained his attention, they were alone in the room. She had Gossage's pad.

Dr. Lecter's eyes focused on her. "That flag smells like cigars," he said. "Did you nurse Catherine?"

"Pardon me? Did I . . ."

"Did you breast-feed her?"

"Yes."

"Thirsty work, isn't it . . . ?"

When her pupils darkened, Dr. Lecter took a single sip of her pain and found it exquisite. That was enough for today. He went on: "William Rubin is about six feet one, and would be thirty-five years old now. He's strongly built—about one hundred ninety pounds when I knew him and he's gained since then, I expect. He has brown hair and pale blue eyes. Give them that much, and then we'll go on."

"Yes, I'll do that," Senator Martin said. She passed her notes out the door.

"I only saw him once. He made another appointment, but he never came again."

"Why do you think he's Buffalo Bill?"

"He was murdering people then, and doing some similar things with them, anatomically. He said he wanted some help to stop, but actually he just wanted to schmooze about it. To *rap*."

"And you didn't—he was sure you wouldn't turn him in?"

"He didn't think I would, and he likes to takes chances. I had honored the confidences of his friend Raspail."

"*Raspail* knew he was doing this?"

"Raspail's appetites ran to the louche—he was covered with scars."

"Billy Rubin told me he had a criminal record, but no details. I took a brief medical history. It was unexceptional, except for one thing: Rubin told me he once suffered from elephant ivory anthrax. That's all I remember, Senator Martin, and I expect you're anxious to go. If anything else occurs to me, I'll send you word."

"Did Billy Rubin kill the person whose head was in the car?"

"I believe so."

"Do you know who that is?"

"No. Raspail called him Klaus."

"Were the other things you told the F.B.I. true?"

"At least as true as what the F.B.I. told *me*, Senator Martin."

"I've made some temporary arrangements for you here in Memphis. We'll talk about your situation and you'll go on to Brushy Mountain when this is . . . when we've got it settled."

"Thank you. I'd like a telephone, if I think of something . . ."

"You'll have it."

"And music. Glenn Gould, the *Goldberg Variations*? Would that be too much?"

"Fine."

"Senator Martin, don't entrust any lead solely to the F.B.I. Jack Crawford never plays fair with the other agencies. It's such a game with those people. He's determined to have the arrest himself. A 'collar,' they call it."

"Thank you, Dr. Lecter."

"Love your suit," he said as she went out the door.

ROOM INTO room, Jame Gumb's basement rambles like the maze that thwarts us in dreams. When he was still shy, lives and lives ago, Mr. Gumb took his pleasure in the rooms most hidden, far from the stairs. There are rooms in the farthest corners, rooms from other lives, that Gumb hasn't opened in years. Some of them are still occupied, so to speak, though the sounds from behind the doors peaked and trailed off to silence long ago.

The levels of the floors vary from room to room by as much as a foot. There are thresholds to step over, lintels to duck. Loads are impossible to roll and difficult to drag. To march something ahead of you—it stumbling and crying, begging, banging its dazed head— is difficult, dangerous even.

As he grew in wisdom and in confidence, Mr. Gumb no longer felt he had to meet his needs in the hidden parts of the basement. He now uses a suite of basement rooms around the stairs, large rooms with running water and electricity.

The basement is in total darkness now.

Beneath the sand-floored room, in the oubliette, Catherine Martin is quiet.

Mr. Gumb is here in the basement, but he is not in this chamber.

The room beyond the stairs is black to human vision, but it is full of small sounds. Water trickles here and small pumps hum. In little echoes the room sounds large. The air is moist and cool. Smell the greenery. A flutter of wings against the cheek, a few clicks across the air. A low nasal sound of pleasure, a human sound.

The room has none of the wavelengths of light the human eye can use, but Mr. Gumb is here and he can see very well, though he sees everything in shades and intensities of green. He's wearing an excellent pair of infrared goggles (Israeli military surplus, less than four hundred dollars) and he directs the beam of an infrared flashlight on the wire cage in front of him. He is sitting on the edge of a straight chair, rapt, watching an insect climb a plant in the screen cage. The young imago has just emerged from a split chrysalis in the moist earth of the cage floor. She climbs carefully on a stalk of night-shade, seeking space to unfurl the damp new wings still wadded on her back. She selects a horizontal twig.

Mr. Gumb must tilt his head to see. Little by little the wings are pumped full of blood and air. They are still stuck together over the insect's back.

Two hours pass. Mr. Gumb has hardly moved. He turns the infrared flashlight on and off to surprise himself with the progress the insect has made. To pass the time he plays the light over the rest of the room— over his big aquariums full of vegetable tanning solution. On forms and stretchers in the tanks, his recent acquisitions stand like broken classic statuary green beneath the sea. His light moves over the big galvanized worktable with its metal pillow block and backsplash and drains, touches the hoist above it. Against the wall, his long industrial sinks. All in the green images of filtered infrared. Flutters, streaks of phosphorescence cross his vision, little comet trails of moths free in the room.

He switches back to the cage just in time. The big insect's wings are held above her back, hiding and distorting her markings. Now she brings down her wings to cloak her body and the famous design is clear. A human skull, wonderfully executed in the furlike scales, stares from the back of the moth. Under the shaded dome of the skull are the black eye holes and prominent cheekbones. Beneath them darkness lies like a gag across the face above the jaw. The skull rests on a marking flared like the top of a pelvis.

A skull stacked upon a pelvis, all drawn on the back of a moth by an accident of nature.

Mr. Gumb feels so good and light inside. He leans forward, puffs soft air across the moth. She raises her sharp proboscis and squeaks angrily.

He walks quietly with his light into the oubliette room. He opens his mouth to quiet his breathing. He doesn't want to spoil his mood with a lot of noise from the pit. The lenses of his goggles on their small protruding barrels look like crab eyes on stalks. Mr. Gumb knows the goggles aren't the least bit attractive, but he has had some great times with them in the black basement, playing basement games.

He leans over and shines his invisible light down the shaft.

The material is lying on her side, curled like a shrimp. She seems to be asleep. Her waste bucket stands beside her. She has not foolishly broken the string again, trying to pull herself up the sheer walls. In her sleep, she clutches the corner of the futon against her face and sucks her thumb.

Watching Catherine, playing the infrared flashlight up and down her, Mr. Gumb prepares himself for the very real problems ahead.

The human skin is fiendishly difficult to deal with if your standards are as high as Mr. Gumb's. There are fundamental structural decisions to make, and the first one is where to put the zipper.

He moves the beam down Catherine's back. Normally he would put the closure in the back, but then how could he do it alone? It won't be the sort of thing he can ask someone to help him with, exciting as that prospect might be. He knows of places, circles, where his efforts would be much admired—there are certain yachts where he could preen—but that will have to wait. He must have things he can use alone. To split the center front would be sacrilege—he puts that right out of his mind.

Mr. Gumb can tell nothing of Catherine's color by infrared, but she looks thinner. He believes she may have been dieting when he took her.

Experience has taught him to wait from four days to a week before harvesting the hide. Sudden weight loss makes the hide looser and easier to remove. In addition, starvation takes much of his subjects' strength and makes them more manageable. More docile. A stuporous resignation comes over some of them. At the same time, it's necessary to provide a few rations to prevent despair and destructive tantrums that might damage the skin.

It definitely has lost weight. This one is so special, so central to what he is doing, he can't stand to wait long, and he doesn't have to. Tomorrow afternoon, he can do it, or tomorrow night. The next day at the latest. Soon.

34

CLARICE STARLING recognized the Stonehinge Villas sign from television news. The East Memphis housing complex, a mix of flats and town houses, formed a large U around a parking field.

Starling parked her rented Chevrolet Celebrity in the middle of the big lot. Well-paid blue-collar workers and bottom-echelon executives lived here—the Trans-Ams and IROC-Z Camaros told her that. Motor homes for the weekends and ski boats bright with glitter paint were parked in their own section of the lot.

Stonehinge Villas—the spelling grated on Starling every time she looked at it. Probably the apartments were full of white wicker and peach shag. Snapshots under the glass of the coffee table. The *Dinner for Two Cookbook* and *Fondue on the Menu*. Starling, whose only residence was a dormitory room at the F.B.I. Academy, was a severe critic of these things.

She needed to know Catherine Baker Martin, and this seemed an odd place for a senator's daughter to live. Starling had read the brief biographical material the F.B.I. had gathered, and it showed Catherine Martin to be a bright underachiever. She'd failed at Farmington and had two unhappy years at Middlebury. Now she was a student at Southwestern and a practice teacher.

Starling could easily have pictured her as a self-absorbed, blunted, boarding-school kid, one of those people who never listen. Starling knew she had to be careful here because she had her own prejudices and resentments. Starling had done her time in boarding schools, living on scholarships, her grades much better than her clothes. She had seen a lot of kids from rich, troubled families, with too much boarding-school time. She didn't give a damn about some of them, but she had grown to learn that inattention can be a stratagem to avoid pain, and that it is often misread as shallowness and indifference.

Better to think of Catherine as a child sailing with her father, as she was in the film they showed with Senator Martin's plea on television. She wondered if Catherine tried to please her father when she was little. She wondered what Catherine was doing when they came and told her that her father was dead, of a heart attack at forty-two. Starling was positive Catherine missed him. Missing your father, the common wound, made Starling feel close to this young woman.

Starling found it essential to like Catherine Martin because it helped her to bear down.

Starling could see where Catherine's apartment was located—two Tennessee Highway Patrol cruisers were parked in front of it. There were spots of white powder on the parking lot in the area closest to the apartment. The Tennessee Bureau of Investigation must have been lifting oil stains with pumice or some other inert powder. Crawford said the T.B.I. was pretty good.

Starling walked over to the recreational vehicles and boats parked in the special section of the lot in front of the apartment. This is where Buffalo Bill got her. Close enough to her door so that she left it unlocked when she came out. Something tempted her out. It must have been a harmless-looking setup.

Starling knew the Memphis police had done exhaustive door-to-door interviews and nobody had seen anything, so maybe it happened among the tall motor homes. He must have watched from here. Sitting in some kind of vehicle, had to be. But Buffalo Bill *knew* Catherine was here. He must have spotted her somewhere and stalked her, waiting for his chance. Girls the size of Catherine aren't common. He didn't just sit around at random locations until a woman of the right size came by. He could sit for days and not see one.

All the victims were big. All of them were big. Some were fat, but all were big. "So he can get something that will fit." Remembering Dr. Lecter's words, Starling shuddered. Dr. Lecter, the new Memphian.

Starling took a deep breath, puffed up her cheeks and let the air out slowly. *Let's see what we can tell about Catherine.*

A Tennessee state trooper wearing his Smokey the Bear hat answered the door of Catherine Martin's apartment. When Starling showed him her credentials, he motioned her inside.

"Officer, I need to look over the premises here." *Premises* seemed a good word to use to a man who had his hat on in the house.

He nodded. "If the phone rings, leave it alone. I'll answer it."

On the counter in the open kitchen Starling could see a tape recorder attached to the telephone. Beside it were two new telephones. One had no dial—a direct line to Southern Bell security, the mid–South tracing facility.

"Can I help you any way?" the young officer asked.

"Are the police through in here?"

"The apartment's been released to the family. I'm just here for the telephone. You can touch stuff, if that's what you want to know."

"Good, I'll look around, then."

"Okay." The young policeman retrieved the newspaper he had stuffed beneath the couch and resumed his seat.

Starling wanted to concentrate. She wished she were alone in the apartment, but she knew she was lucky the place wasn't full of cops.

She started in the kitchen. It was not equipped by a serious cook. Catherine had come for popcorn, the boyfriend had told police.

Starling opened the freezer. There were two boxes of microwave popcorn. You couldn't see the parking lot from the kitchen.

"Where you from?"

Starling didn't register the question the first time.

"Where you from?"

The trooper on the couch was watching her over his newspaper.

"Washington," she said.

Under the sink—yep, scratches on the pipe joint, they'd taken the trap out and examined it. Good for the T.B.I. The knives were not sharp. The dishwasher had been run, but not emptied. The refrigerator was devoted to cottage cheese and deli fruit salad. Catherine Martin shopped for fast-food groceries, probably had a regular place, a drive-in she used close by. Maybe somebody cruised the store. That's worth checking.

"You with the Attorney General?"

"No, the F.B.I."

"The Attorney General's coming. That's what I heard at turnout. How long you been in the F.B.I.?"

Starling looked at the young policeman.

"Officer, tell you what. I'll probably need to ask you a couple of things after I've finished looking around here. Maybe you could help me out then."

"Sure. If I can—"

"Good, okay. Let's wait and talk then. I have to think about this right now."

"No problem, there."

The bedroom was bright, with a sunny, drowsy quality Starling liked. It was done with better fabrics and better furnishings than most young women could afford. There were a Coromandel screen, two pieces of cloisonné on the shelves, and a good secretary in burled walnut. Twin beds. Starling lifted the edge of the coverlets. Rollers were locked on the left bed, but not on the right-hand one. *Catherine must push them together when it suits her. May have a lover the boyfriend doesn't know about. Or maybe they stay over here sometimes. There's no remote beeper on her answering machine. She may need to be here when her mom calls.*

The answering machine was like her own, the basic Phone-Mate. She opened the top panel. Both incoming and outgoing tapes were gone. In their place was a note, TAPES TBI PROPERTY #6.

The room was reasonably neat but it had the ruffled appearance left by searchers with big hands, men who try to put things back exactly, but miss just a little bit. Starling would have known the place had been searched even without the traces of fingerprint powder on all the smooth surfaces.

Starling didn't believe that any part of the crime had happened in the bedroom. Crawford probably was right, Catherine had been grabbed in the parking lot. But Starling wanted to know her, and this is where she lived. *Lives,* Starling corrected herself. She *lives* here.

In the cabinet of the nightstand were a telephone book, Kleenex, a box of grooming items and, behind the box, a Polaroid SX-70 camera with a cable release and a short tripod folded beside it. Ummmm. Intent as a lizard, Starling looked at the camera. She blinked as a lizard blinks and didn't touch it.

The closet interested Starling most. Catherine Baker Martin, laundry mark C-B-M, had a lot of clothes and some of them were very good. Starling recognized many of the labels, including Garfinkel's and Britches in Washington. *Presents from Mommy,* Starling said to herself. Catherine had fine, classic clothes in two sizes, made to fit her at about 145 and 165 pounds, Starling guessed, and there were a few pairs of crisis fat pants and pullovers from the Statuesque Shop. In a hanging rack were twenty-three pairs of shoes. Seven pairs were Ferragamos in 10C, and there were some Reeboks and run-over loafers. A light backpack and a tennis racket were on the top shelf.

The belongings of a privileged kid, a student and practice teacher who lived better than most.

Lots of letters in the secretary. Loopy backhand notes from former classmates in the East. Stamps, mailing labels. Gift wrapping paper in the bottom drawer, a sheaf in various colors and patterns. Starling's fingers walked through it. She was thinking about questioning the clerks at the local drive-in market when her fingers found a sheet in the stack of gift wrap that was too thick and stiff. Her fingers went past it, walked back to it. She was trained to register anomalies and she had it half pulled out when she looked at it. The sheet was blue, of a material similar to a lightweight blotter, and the pattern printed on it was a crude imitation of the cartoon dog Pluto. The little rows of dogs all looked like Pluto, they were the proper yellow, but they weren't exactly right in their proportions.

"Catherine, Catherine," Starling said. She took some tweezers from her bag and used them to slide the sheet of colored paper into a plastic envelope. She placed it on the bed for the time being.

The jewelry box on the dresser was a stamped-leather affair, the kind you see in every girl's dormitory room. The two drawers in front and the tiered lid contained costume jewelry, no valuable pieces. Starling wondered if the best things had been in the rubber cabbage in the refrigerator, and if so, who took them.

She hooked her finger under the side of the lid and released the secret drawer in the back of the jewelry box. The secret drawer was empty. She wondered whom these drawers were a secret from—certainly not burglars. She was reaching behind the jewelry box, pushing the drawer back in, when her fingers touched the envelope taped to the underside of the secret drawer.

Starling pulled on a pair of cotton gloves and turned the jewelry box around. She took out the empty drawer and inverted it. A brown envelope was taped to the bottom of the drawer with masking tape. The flap was just tucked in, not sealed. She held the paper close to her nose. The envelope had not been fumed for fingerprints. Starling used the tweezers to open it and extract the contents. There were five

Polaroid pictures in the envelope and she took them out one by one. The pictures were of a man and a woman coupling. No heads or faces appeared. Two of the pictures were taken by the woman, two by the man, and one appeared to have been shot from the tripod set up on the nightstand.

It was hard to judge scale in a photograph, but with that spectacular 145 pounds on a long frame, the woman had to be Catherine Martin. The man wore what appeared to be a carved ivory ring on his penis. The resolution of the photograph was not sharp enough to reveal the details of it. The man had had his appendix out. Starling bagged the photographs, each in a sandwich bag, and put them in her own brown envelope. She returned the drawer to the jewelry box.

"I have the good stuff in my pocketbook," said a voice behind her. "I don't think anything was taken."

Starling looked in the mirror. Senator Ruth Martin stood in the bedroom door. She looked drained.

Starling turned around. "Hello, Senator Martin. Would you like to lie down? I'm almost finished."

Even exhausted, Senator Martin had a lot of presence. Under her careful finish, Starling saw a scrapper.

"Who are you, please? I thought the police were through in here."

"I'm Clarice Starling, F.B.I. Did you talk to Dr. Lecter, Senator?"

"He gave me a name." Senator Martin lit a cigarette and looked Starling up and down. "We'll see what it's worth. And what did you find in the jewelry box, Officer Starling? What's *it* worth?"

"Some documentation we can check out in just a few minutes," was the best Starling could do.

"In my daughter's jewelry box? Let's see it."

Starling heard voices in the next room and hoped for an interruption. "Is Mr. Copley with you, the Memphis special agent in—"

"No, he's not, and that's not an answer. No offense, Officer, but

I'll see what you got out of my daughter's jewelry box." She turned her head and called over her shoulder. "Paul. Paul, would you come in here? Officer Starling, you may know Mr. Krendler from the Department of Justice. Paul, this is the girl Jack Crawford sent in to Lecter."

Krendler's bald spot was tanned and he looked fit at forty.

"Mr. Krendler, I know who you are. Hello," Starling said. *DeeJay Criminal Division congressional liaison, troubleshooter, at least an Assistant Deputy Attorney General, Jesus God, save my bod.*

"Officer Starling found something in my daughter's jewelry box and she put it in her brown envelope. I think we'd better see what it is, don't you?"

"Officer," Krendler said.

"May I speak to you, Mr. Krendler?"

"Of course you can. Later." He held out his hand.

Starling's face was hot. She knew Senator Martin was not herself, but she would never forgive Krendler for the doubt in his face. Never.

"You got it," Starling said. She handed him the envelope.

Krendler looked in at the first picture and had closed the flap again when Senator Martin took the envelope out of his hands.

It was painful to watch her examine the pictures. When she finished, she went to the window and stood with her face turned up to the overcast sky, her eyes closed. She looked old in the daylight and her hand trembled when she tried to smoke.

"Senator, I—" Krendler began.

"The police searched this room," Senator Martin said. "I'm sure they found those pictures and had sense enough to put them back and keep their mouths shut."

"No they did *not*," Starling said. The woman was wounded but, hell. "Mrs. Martin, we need to know who this man is, you can see that. If it's the boyfriend, fine. I can find that out in five minutes. Nobody else needs to see the pictures and Catherine never needs to know."

"I'll tend to it." Senator Martin put the envelope in her purse, and Krendler let her do it.

"Senator, did you take the jewelry out of the rubber cabbage in the kitchen?" Starling asked.

Senator Martin's aide, Brian Gossage, stuck his head in the door. "Excuse me, Senator, they've got the terminal set up. We can watch them search the William Rubin name at the F.B.I."

"Go ahead, Senator Martin," Krendler said. "I'll be out in a second."

Ruth Martin left the room without answering Starling's question.

Starling had a chance to look Krendler over as he was closing the bedroom door. His suit was a triumph of single-needle tailoring and he was not armed. The shine was buffed off the bottom half-inch of his heels from walking on much deep carpet, and the edges of the heels were sharp.

He stood for a moment with his hand on the doorknob, his head down.

"That was a good search," he said when he turned around.

Starling couldn't be had that cheap. She looked back at him.

"They turn out good rummagers at Quantico," Krendler said.

"They don't turn out thieves."

"I know that," he said.

"Hard to tell."

"Drop it."

"We'll follow up on the pictures and the rubber cabbage, right?" she said.

"Yes."

"What's the 'William Rubin' name, Mr. Krendler?"

"Lecter says that's Buffalo Bill's name. Here's our transmission to I.D. Section and NCIC. Look at this." He gave her a transcript of the Lecter interview with Senator Martin, blurry copy from a dot-matrix printer.

"Any thoughts?" he said when she finished reading.

"There's nothing here he'll ever have to eat," Starling said. "He says it's a white male named Billy Rubin who had elephant ivory anthrax. You couldn't catch him in a lie here, no matter what happens. At the worst he'd just be mistaken. I hope this is true. But he could be having fun with her. Mr. Krendler, he's perfectly capable of that. Have you ever . . . met him?"

Krendler shook his head and snorted air from his nose.

"Dr. Lecter killed nine people we know of. He's not walking, no matter—he could raise the dead and they wouldn't let him out. So all that's left for him is *fun*. That's why we were playing him—"

"I know how you were playing him. I heard Chilton's tape. I'm not saying it was wrong—I'm saying it's over. Behavioral Science can follow up what you got—the transsexual angle—for what it's worth. And you'll be back in school at Quantico tomorrow."

Oh boy. "I found something else."

The sheet of colored paper had lain on the bed unnoticed. She gave it to him.

"What is it?"

"Looks like a sheet of Plutos." She made him ask the rest.

He beckoned for the information with his hand.

"I'm pretty sure it's blotter acid. LSD. From maybe the middle seventies or before. It's a curiosity now. It's worth finding out where she got it. We should test it to be sure."

"You can take it back to Washington and give it to the lab. You'll be going in a few minutes."

"If you don't want to wait, we can do it now with a field kit. If the police've got a standard Narcotics Identification Kit, it's test J, take two seconds, we can—"

"Back to Washington, back to school," he said, opening the door.

"Mr. Crawford instructed me—"

"Your *instructions* are what I'm telling you. You're not under Jack

Crawford's direction now. You're back under the same supervision as any other trainee forthwith, and your business is at Quantico, do you understand me? There's a plane at two-ten. Be on it."

"Mr. Krendler, Dr. Lecter talked to me after he refused to talk to the Baltimore police. He might do that again. Mr. Crawford thought—"

Krendler closed the door again, harder than he had to. "Officer Starling, I don't have to explain myself to you, but listen to me. Behavioral Science's brief is advisory, always has been. It's going back to that. Jack Crawford should be on compassionate leave anyway. I'm surprised he's been able to perform as well as he has. He took a foolish chance with this, keeping it from Senator Martin, and he got his butt sawed off. With his record, this close to retirement, even *she* can't hurt him that much. So I wouldn't worry about his pension, if I were you."

Starling lost it a little. "You've got somebody else who's caught three serial murderers? You know anybody else who's caught one? You shouldn't let her run this, Mr. Krendler."

"You must be a bright kid, or Crawford wouldn't bother with you, so I'll tell you one time: do something about that mouth or it'll put you in the typing pool. Don't you understand—the only reason you were ever sent to Lecter in the first place was to get some news for your Director to use on Capitol Hill. Harmless stuff on major crimes, the 'inside scoop' on Dr. Lecter, he hands that stuff out like pocket candy while he's trying to get the budget through. Congressmen eat it up, they dine out on it. You're out of line, Officer Starling, and you're out of this case. I know you got supplementary I.D. Let's have it."

"I need the I.D. to fly with the gun. The gun belongs at Quantico."

"Gun. *Jesus.* Turn in the I.D. as soon as you get back."

Senator Martin, Gossage, a technician, and several policemen were gathered around a video display terminal with a modem connected to the telephone. The National Crime Information Center's hotline kept a running account of progress as Dr. Lecter's information was processed in Washington. Here was news from the National Center for Disease Control in Atlanta: Elephant ivory anthrax is contracted by breathing dust from grinding African ivory, usually for decorative handles. In the United States it is a disease of knifemakers.

At the word "knifemakers," Senator Martin closed her eyes. They were hot and dry. She squeezed the Kleenex in her hand.

The young trooper who had let Starling into the apartment was bringing the Senator a cup of coffee. He still had on his hat.

Starling was damned if she'd slink out. She stopped before the woman and said, "Good luck, Senator. I hope Catherine's all right."

Senator Martin nodded without looking at her. Krendler urged Starling out.

"I didn't know she wasn't s'posed to be in here," the young trooper said as she left the room.

Krendler stepped outside with her. "I have nothing but respect for Jack Crawford," he said. "Please tell him how sorry we all are about . . . Bella's problem, all that. Now let's get back to school and get busy, all right?"

"Good-bye, Mr. Krendler."

Then she was alone on the parking lot, with the unsteady feeling that she understood nothing at all in this world.

She watched a pigeon walk around beneath the motor homes and boats. It picked up a peanut hull and put it back down. The damp wind ruffled its feathers.

Starling wished she could talk to Crawford. *Waste and stupidity get you the worst*, that's what he said. *Use this time and it'll temper you. Now's the hardest test—not letting rage and frustration keep you from thinking. It's the core of whether you can command or not.*

She didn't give a damn about commanding. She found she didn't give a damn, or a shit for that matter, about being Special Agent Starling. Not if you play this way.

She thought about the poor, fat, sad, dead girl she saw on the table in the funeral home at Potter, West Virginia. *Painted her nails with glitter just like these God damned redneck ski boats.*

What was her name? Kimberly.

Damn if these assholes are gonna see me cry.

Jesus, everybody was named Kimberly, four in her class. Three guys named Sean. Kimberly with her soap-opera name tried to fix herself, punched all those holes in her ears trying to look pretty, trying to decorate herself. And Buffalo Bill looked at her sad flat tits and stuck the muzzle of a gun between them and blew a starfish on her chest.

Kimberly, her sad, fat sister who waxed her legs. No wonder— judging from her face and her arms and legs, her skin was her best feature. *Kimberly, are you angry somewhere?* No senators looking out for her. No jets to carry crazy men around. *Crazy* was a word she wasn't supposed to use. Lot of stuff she wasn't supposed to do. *Crazy men.*

Starling looked at her watch. She had an hour and a half before the plane, and there was one small thing she could do. She wanted to look in Dr. Lecter's face when he said "Billy Rubin." If she could stand to meet those strange maroon eyes for long enough, if she looked deeply where the dark sucks in the sparks, she might see something useful. She thought she might see glee.

Thank God I've still got the I.D.

She laid twelve feet of rubber pulling out of the parking lot.

35

CLARICE STARLING driving in a hurry through the perilous Memphis traffic, two tears of anger dried stiff on her cheeks. She felt oddly floaty and free now. An unnatural clarity in her vision warned her that she was inclined to fight, so she was careful of herself.

She had passed the old courthouse earlier on her way from the airport, and she found it again without trouble.

The Tennessee authorities were taking no chances with Hannibal Lecter. They were determined to hold him securely without exposing him to the dangers of the city jail.

Their answer was the former courthouse and jail, a massive Gothic-style structure built of granite back when labor was free. It was a city office building now, somewhat over-restored in this prosperous, history-conscious town.

Today it looked like a medieval stronghold surrounded by police.

A mix of law-enforcement cruisers—highway patrol, Shelby County Sheriff's Department, Tennessee Bureau of Investigation, and Department of Corrections—crowded the parking lot. There was a police post to pass before Starling even could get in to park her rented car.

Dr. Lecter presented an additional security problem from outside.

Threatening calls had been coming in ever since the mid-morning newscasts reported his whereabouts; his victims had many friends and relatives who would love to see him dead.

Starling hoped the resident F.B.I. agent, Copley, wasn't here. She didn't want to get him in trouble.

She saw the back of Chilton's head in a knot of reporters on the grass beside the main steps. There were two television minicams in the crowd. Starling wished her head were covered. She turned her face away as she approached the entrance to the tower.

A state trooper stationed in front of the door examined her I.D. card before she could go into the foyer. The foyer of the tower looked like a guardroom now. A city policeman was stationed at the single tower elevator, and another at the stairs. State troopers, the relief for the patrol units stationed around the building, read the *Commercial Appeal* on the couches where the public could not see them.

A sergeant manned the desk opposite the elevator. His name tag said TATE, C.L.

"No press," Sergeant Tate said when he saw Starling.

"No," she said.

"You with the Attorney General's people?" he said when he looked at her card.

"Deputy Assistant Attorney General Krendler," she said. "I just left him."

He nodded. "We've had every kind of cop in West Tennessee in here wanting to look at Dr. Lecter. Don't see something like that very often, thank God. You'll need to talk to Dr. Chilton before you go up."

"I saw him outside," Starling said. "We were working on this in Baltimore earlier today. Is this where I log in, Sergeant Tate?"

The sergeant briefly checked a molar with his tongue. "Right there," he said. "Detention rules, miss. Visitors check weapons, cops or not."

Starling nodded. She dumped the cartridges from her revolver, the sergeant glad to watch her hands move on the gun. She gave it to him butt first, and he locked it in his drawer.

"Vernon, take her up." He dialed three digits and spoke her name into the phone.

The elevator, an addition from the 1920s, creaked up to the top floor. It opened onto a stair landing and a short corridor.

"Right straight across, ma'am," the trooper said.

Painted on the frosted glass of the door was SHELBY COUNTY HISTORICAL SOCIETY.

Almost all the top floor of the tower was one octagonal room painted white, with a floor and moldings of polished oak. It smelled of wax and library paste. With its few furnishings, the room had a spare, Congregational feeling. It looked better now than it ever had as a bailiff's office.

Two men in the uniform of the Tennessee Department of Corrections were on duty. The small one stood up at his desk when Starling came in. The bigger one sat in a folding chair at the far end of the room, facing the door of a cell. He was the suicide watch.

"You're authorized to talk with the prisoner, ma'am?" the officer at the desk said. His nameplate read PEMBRY, T.W. and his desk set included a telephone, two riot batons, and Chemical Mace. A long pinion stood in the corner behind him.

"Yes, I am," Starling said. "I've questioned him before."

"You know the rules? Don't pass the barrier."

"Absolutely."

The only color in the room was the police traffic barrier, a brightly striped sawhorse in orange and yellow mounted with round yellow flashers, now turned off. It stood on the polished floor five feet in front of the cell door. On a coat tree nearby hung the doctor's things— the hockey mask and something Starling had never seen before, a Kansas gallows vest. Made of heavy leather, with double-locking wrist shackles at the waist and buckles in the back, it may be the most infallible restraint garment in the world. The mask and the black vest suspended by its nape from the coat tree made a disturbing composition against the white wall.

Starling could see Dr. Lecter as she approached the cell. He was reading at a small table bolted to the floor. His back was to the door. He had a number of books and the copy of the running file on Buffalo Bill she had given him in Baltimore. A small cassette player was chained to the table leg. How strange to see him outside the asylum.

Starling had seen cells like this before, as a child. They were prefabricated by a St Louis company around the turn of the century, and no one has ever built them better—a tempered steel modular cage that turns any room into a cell. The floor was sheet steel laid over bars, and the walls and ceiling of cold-forged bars completely lined the room. There was no window. The cell was spotlessly white and brightly lit. A flimsy paper screen stood in front of the toilet.

These white bars ribbed the walls. Dr. Lecter had a sleek dark head.

He's a cemetery mink. He lives down in a ribcage in the dry leaves of a heart.

She blinked it away.

"Good morning, Clarice," he said without turning around. He finished his page, marked his place and spun in his chair to face her, his forearms on the chair back, his chin resting on them. "Dumas tells us that the addition of a crow to bouillon in the fall, when the crow has fattened on juniper berries, greatly improves the color and flavor of stock. How do *you* like it in the soup, Clarice?"

"I thought you might want your drawings, the stuff from your cell, just until you get your view."

"How thoughtful. Dr. Chilton's euphoric about you and Jack Crawford being put off the case. Or did they send you in for one last wheedle?"

The officer on suicide watch had strolled back to talk to Officer Pembry at the desk. Starling hoped they couldn't hear.

"They didn't send me. I just came."

"People will say we're in love. Don't you want to ask about Billy Rubin, Clarice?"

"Dr. Lecter, without in any way . . . impugning what you've told Senator Martin, would you advise me to go on with your idea about—"

"*Impugning*—I love it. I wouldn't advise you at all. You tried to fool me, Clarice. Do you think I'm playing with these people?"

"I think you were telling me the truth."

"Pity you tried to fool me, isn't it?" Dr. Lecter's face sank behind his arms until only his eyes were visible. "Pity Catherine Martin won't ever see the sun again. The sun's a mattress fire her God died in, Clarice."

"Pity you have to pander now and lick a few tears when you can," Starling said. "It's a pity we didn't get to finish what we were talking about. Your idea of the imago, the structure of it, had a kind of . . . elegance that's hard to get away from. Now it's like a ruin, half an arch standing there."

"Half an arch won't stand. Speaking of arches, will they still let you pound a beat, Clarice? Did they take your badge?"

"No."

"What's that under your jacket, a watchman's clock just like Dad's?"

"No, that's a speedloader."

"So you go around armed?"

"Yes."

"Then you should let your jacket out. Do you sew at all?"

"Yes."

"Did you make that costume?"

"No. Dr. Lecter, you find out everything. You couldn't have talked intimately with this 'Billy Rubin' and come out knowing so little about him."

"You think not?"

"If you met him, you know *everything*. But today you happened to remember just one detail. He'd had elephant ivory anthrax. You should have seen them jump when Atlanta said it's a disease of knifemakers. They ate it up, just like you knew they would. You should have gotten a suite at the Peabody for that. Dr. Lecter, if you met him you know about him. I think maybe you didn't meet him and Raspail told you about him. Secondhand stuff wouldn't sell as well to Senator Martin, would it?"

Starling took a quick look over her shoulder. One of the officers was showing the other something in *Guns & Ammo* magazine. "You had more to tell me in Baltimore, Dr. Lecter. I believe that stuff was valid. Tell me the rest."

"I've read the cases, Clarice, have you? Everything you need to know to find him is right there, if you're paying attention. Even Inspector Emeritus Crawford should have figured it out. Incidentally, did you read Crawford's *stupefying* speech last year to the National Police Academy? Spouting Marcus Aurelius on duty and honor and fortitude—we'll see what kind of a Stoic Crawford is when Bella bites the big one. He copies his philosophy out of *Bartlett's Familiar*, I think. If he understood Marcus Aurelius, he might solve his case."

"Tell me how."

"When you show the odd flash of contextual intelligence, I forget your generation can't read, Clarice. The Emperor counsels simplicity. First principles. Of each particular thing, ask: What is it in itself, in its own constitution? What is its causal nature?"

"That doesn't mean anything to me."

"What does he do, the man you want?"

"He kills—"

"Ah—" he said sharply, averting his face for a moment from her wrongheadedness. "That's incidental. What is the first and principal thing he does, what need does he serve by killing?"

"Anger, social resentment, sexual frus—"

"No."

"What, then?"

"He covets. In fact, he covets being the very thing you are. It's his nature to covet. How do we begin to covet, Clarice? Do we seek out things to covet? Make an effort at an answer."

"No. We just—"

"No. Precisely so. We begin by coveting what we see every day. Don't you feel eyes moving over you every day, Clarice, in chance encounters? I hardly see how you could not. And don't your eyes move over things?"

"All right, then tell me how—"

"It's your turn to tell *me*, Clarice. You don't have any beach vacations at the Hoof and Mouth Disease Station to offer me anymore. It's strictly quid pro quo from here on out. I have to be careful doing business with you. Tell me, Clarice."

"Tell you what?"

"The two things you owe me from before. What happened to you and the horse, and what you do with your anger."

"Dr. Lecter, when there's time I'll—"

"We don't reckon time the same way, Clarice. This is all the time you'll ever have."

"Later, listen, I'll—"

"I'll *listen now*. Two years after your father's death, your mother sent you to live with her cousin and her husband on a ranch in Montana. You were ten years old. You discovered they fed out slaughter horses. You ran away with a horse that couldn't see very well. And?"

"—It was summer and we could sleep out. We got as far as Bozeman by a back road."

"Did the horse have a name?"

"Probably, but they don't—you don't find that out when you're feeding out slaughter horses. I called her Hannah, that seemed like a good name."

"Were you leading her or riding?"

"Some of both. I had to lead her up beside a fence to climb on."

"You rode and walked to Bozeman."

"There was a livery stable, dude ranch, riding academy sort of thing just outside of town. I tried to see about them keeping her. It was twenty dollars a week in the corral. More for a stall. They could tell right off she couldn't see. I said okay, I'll lead her around. Little kids can sit on her and I'll lead her around while their parents are, you know, regular riding. I can stay right here and muck out stalls. One of them, the man, agreed to everything I said while his wife called the sheriff."

"The sheriff was a policeman, like your father."

"That didn't keep me from being scared of him, at first. He had a big red face. The sheriff finally put up twenty dollars for a week's board while he 'straightened things out.' He said there was no use going for the stall in warm weather. The papers picked it up. There was a flap. My mother's cousin agreed to let me go. I wound up going to the Lutheran Home in Bozeman."

"It's an orphanage?"

"Yes."

"And Hannah?"

"She went too. A big Lutheran rancher put up the hay. They already had a barn at the orphanage. We plowed the garden with her. You had to watch where she was going, though. She'd walk through the butterbean trellises and step on any kind of plant that was too short for her to feel it against her legs. And we led her around pulling kids in a cart."

"She died though."

"Well, yes."

"Tell me about that."

"It was last year, they wrote me at school. They think she was about twenty-two. Pulled a cart full of kids the last day she lived, and died in her sleep."

Dr. Lecter seemed disappointed. "How heartwarming," he said. "Did your foster father in Montana fuck you, Clarice?"

"No."

"Did he try?"

"No."

"What made you run away with the horse?"

"They were going to kill her."

"Did you know when?"

"Not exactly. I worried about it all the time. She was getting pretty fat."

"What triggered you then? What set you off on that particular day?"

"I don't know."

"I think you do."

"I had worried about it all the time."

"What set you off, Clarice? You started what time?"

"Early. Still dark."

"Then something woke you. What woke you up? Did you dream? What was it?"

"I woke up and heard the lambs screaming. I woke up in the dark and the lambs were screaming."

"They were slaughtering the spring lambs?"

"Yes."

"What did you do?"

"I couldn't do anything for them. I was just a—"

"What did you do with the *horse*?"

"I got dressed without turning on the light and went outside. She was scared. All the horses in the pen were scared and milling around. I blew in her nose and she knew it was me. Finally she'd put her nose in my hand. The lights were on in the barn and in the shed by the sheep pen. Bare bulbs, big shadows. The refrigerator truck had come and it was idling, roaring. I led her away."

"Did you saddle her?"

"No. I didn't take their saddle. Just a rope hackamore was all."

"As you went off in the dark, could you hear the lambs back where the lights were?"

"Not long. There weren't but twelve."

"You still wake up sometimes, don't you? Wake up in the iron dark with the lambs screaming?"

"Sometimes."

"Do you think if you caught Buffalo Bill yourself and if you made Catherine all right, you could make the lambs stop screaming, do you think they'd be all right too and you wouldn't wake up again in the dark and hear the lambs screaming? Clarice?"

"Yes. I don't know. Maybe."

"Thank you, Clarice." Dr. Lecter seemed oddly at peace.

"Tell me his name, Dr. Lecter," Starling said.

"Dr. Chilton," Lecter said, "I believe you know each other."

For an instant, Starling didn't realize Chilton was behind her. Then he took her elbow.

She took it back. Officer Pembry and his big partner were with Chilton.

"In the elevator," Chilton said. His face was mottled red.

"Did you know Dr. Chilton has no medical degree?" Dr. Lecter said. "Please bear that in mind later on."

"Let's go," Chilton said.

"You're not in charge here, Dr. Chilton," Starling said.

Officer Pembry came around Chilton. "No, ma'am, but I am. He called my boss and your boss both. I'm sorry, but I've got orders to see you out. Come on with me, now."

"Good-bye, Clarice. Will you let me know if ever the lambs stop screaming?"

"Yes."

Pembry was taking her arm. It was go or fight him.

"Yes," she said. "I'll tell you."

"Do you promise?"

"Yes."

"Then why not finish the arch? Take your case file with you, Clarice, I won't need it anymore." He held it at arm's length through the bars, his forefinger along the spine. She reached across the barrier and took it. For an instant the tip of her forefinger touched Dr. Lecter's. The touch crackled in his eyes.

"Thank you, Clarice."

"Thank you, Dr. Lecter."

And that is how he remained in Starling's mind. Caught in the instant when he did not mock. Standing in his white cell, arched like a dancer, his hands clasped in front of him and his head slightly to the side.

She went over a speed bump at the airport fast enough to bang her head on the roof of the car, and had to run for the airplane Krendler had ordered her to catch.

36

Officers Pembry and Boyle were experienced men brought especially from Brushy Mountain State Prison to be Dr. Lecter's warders. They were calm and careful and did not feel they needed their job explained to them by Dr. Chilton.

They had arrived in Memphis ahead of Lecter and examined the cell minutely. When Dr. Lecter was brought to the old court-house, they examined him as well. He was subjected to an internal body search by a male nurse while he was still in restraints. His clothing was searched thoroughly and a metal detector run over the seams.

Boyle and Pembry came to an understanding with him, speaking in low, civil tones close to his ears as he was examined.

"Dr. Lecter, we can get along just fine. We'll treat you just as good as you treat us. Act like a gentleman and you get the Eskimo Pie. But we're not pussyfooting around with you, buddy. Try to bite, and we'll leave you smooth-mouthed. Looks like you got something good going here. You don't want to fuck it up, do you?"

Dr. Lecter crinkled his eyes at them in a friendly fashion. If he had been inclined to reply he would have been prevented by the wooden peg between his molars as the nurse shone a flashlight in his mouth and ran a gloved finger into his cheeks.

The metal detector beeped at his cheeks.

"What's that?" the nurse asked.

"Fillings," Pembry said. "Pull his lip back there. You've put some miles on them back ones, haven't you, Doc?"

"Strikes me he's pretty much of a broke-dick," Boyle confided to Pembry after they had Dr. Lecter secure in his cell. "He won't be no trouble if he don't flip out."

The cell, while secure and strong, lacked a rolling food carrier. At lunchtime, in the unpleasant atmosphere that followed Starling's visit, Dr. Chilton inconvenienced everyone, making Boyle and Pembry go through the long process of securing the compliant Dr. Lecter in the straitjacket and leg restraints as he stood with his back to the bars, Chilton poised with the Mace, before they opened the door to carry in his tray.

Chilton refused to use Boyle's and Pembry's names, though they wore nameplates, and addressed them indiscriminately as "you, there."

For their part, after the warders heard Chilton was not a real M.D., Boyle observed to Pembry that he was just "some kind of a God damned schoolteacher."

Pembry tried once to explain to Chilton that Starling's visit had been approved not by them but by the desk downstairs, and saw that in Chilton's anger it didn't matter.

Dr. Chilton was absent at supper and, with Dr. Lecter's bemused cooperation, Boyle and Pembry used their own method to take in his tray. It worked very well.

"Dr. Lecter, you not gonna be needing your dinner jacket tonight," Pembry said. "I'll ask you to sit on the floor and scoot backwards till you can just stick your hands out through the bars, arms extended backward. There you go. Scoot up a little and straighten 'em out more behind you, elbows straight." Pembry handcuffed Dr. Lecter tightly outside the bars, with a bar between his arms, and a low crossbar above them. "That hurts just a little bit, don't it? I know it does and they won't be on there but a minute, save us both a lot of trouble."

Dr. Lecter could not rise, even to a squat, and with his legs straight in front of him on the floor, he couldn't kick.

Only when Dr. Lecter was pinioned did Pembry return to the desk for the key to the cell door. Pembry slid his riot baton in the ring at his wrist, put a canister of Mace in his pocket, and returned to the cell. He opened the door while Boyle took in the tray. When the door was secured, Pembry took the key back to the desk before he took the cuffs off Dr. Lecter. At no time was he near the bars with the key while the doctor was free in the cell.

"Now that was pretty easy, wasn't it?" Pembry said.

"It was very convenient, thank you, Officer," Dr. Lecter said. "You know, I'm just trying to get by."

"We all are, brother," Pembry said.

Dr. Lecter toyed with his food while he wrote and drew and doodled on his pad with a felt-tipped pen. He flipped over the cassette in the tape player chained to the table leg and punched the play button. Glenn Gould playing Bach's *Goldberg Variations* on the piano. The music, beautiful beyond plight and time, filled the bright cage and the room where the warders sat.

For Dr. Lecter, sitting still at the table, time slowed and spread as it does in action. For him the notes of music moved apart without losing tempo. Even Bach's silver pounces were discrete notes glittering off the steel around him. Dr. Lecter rose, his expression abstracted, and watched his paper napkin slide off his thighs to the floor. The napkin was in the air a long time, brushed the table leg, flared, sideslipped, stalled and turned over before it came to rest on the steel floor. He made no effort to pick it up, but took a stroll across his cell, went behind the paper screen and sat on the lid of his toilet, his only private place. Listening to the music, he leaned sideways on the sink, his chin in his hand, his strange maroon eyes half-closed. The *Goldberg Variations* interested him structurally. Here it came again, the bass progression from the saraband repeated, repeated. He nodded along, his tongue moving over the edges of his teeth. All the way around on top, all the way around on the bottom. It was a long and interesting trip for his tongue, like a good walk in the Alps.

He did his gums now, sliding his tongue high in the crevice between his cheek and gum and moving it slowly around as some men do when ruminating. His gums were cooler than his tongue. It was cool up in the crevice. When his tongue got to the little metal tube, it stopped.

Over the music he heard the elevator clank and whir as it started up. Many notes of music later, the elevator door opened and a voice he did not know said, "I'm s'posed to get the tray."

Dr. Lector heard the smaller one coming, Pembry. He could see through the crack between the panels in his screen. Pembry was at the bars.

"Dr. Lecter. Come sit on the floor with your back to the bars like we did before."

"Officer Pembry, would you mind if I just finish up here? I'm afraid my trip's gotten my digestion a little out of sorts." It took a very long time to say.

"All right." Pembry calling down the room, "We'll call down when we got it."

"Can I look at him?"

"We'll call you."

The elevator again and then only the music.

Dr. Lecter took the tube from his mouth and dried it on a piece of toilet tissue. His hands were steady, his palms perfectly dry.

In his years of detention, with his unending curiosity, Dr. Lecter had learned many of the secret prison crafts. In all the years after he savaged the nurse in the Baltimore asylum, there had been only two lapses in the security around him, both on Barney's days off. Once a psychiatric researcher loaned him a ballpoint pen and then forgot it. Before the man was out of the ward, Dr. Lecter had broken up the plastic barrel of the pen and flushed it down his toilet. The metal ink tube went in the rolled seam edging his mattress.

The only sharp edge in his cell at the asylum was a burr on the head of a bolt holding his cot to the wall. It was enough. In two months of rubbing, Dr. Lecter cut the required two incisions, parallel and a quarter-inch long, running along the tube from its open end. Then he cut the ink tube in two pieces one inch from the open end and flushed the long piece with the point down the toilet. Barney did not spot the calluses on his fingers from the nights of rubbing.

Six months later, an orderly left a heavy-duty paper clip on some documents sent to Dr. Lecter by his attorney. One inch of the steel clip went inside the tube and the rest went down the toilet. The little tube, smooth and short, was easy to conceal in seams of clothing, between the cheek and gum, in the rectum.

Now, behind his paper screen, Dr. Lecter tapped the little metal tube on his thumbnail until the wire inside it slipped out. The wire was a tool and this was the difficult part. Dr. Lecter stuck the wire halfway into the little tube and with infinite care used it as a lever to bend down the strip of metal between the two incisions. Sometimes they break. Carefully, with his powerful hands, he bent the metal and it was coming. Now. The minute strip of metal was at right angles to the tube. Now he had a handcuff key.

Dr. Lecter put his hands behind him and passed the key back and forth between them fifteen times. He put the key back in his mouth while he washed his hands and meticulously dried them. Then, with his tongue, he hid the key between the fingers of his right hand, knowing Pembry would stare at his strange left hand when it was behind his back.

"I'm ready when you are, Officer Pembry," Dr. Lecter said. He sat on the floor of the cell and stretched his arms behind him, his hands and wrists through the bars. "Thank you for waiting." It seemed a long speech, but it was leavened by the music.

He heard Pembry behind him now. Pembry felt his wrist to see if he had soaped it. Pembry felt his other wrist to see if he had soaped it. Pembry put the cuffs on tight. He went back to the desk for the key to the cell. Over the piano, Dr. Lecter heard the clink of the key ring as Pembry took it from the desk drawer. Now he was coming back, walking through the notes, parting the air that swarmed with crystal notes. This time Boyle came back with him. Dr. Lecter could hear the holes they made in the echoes of the music.

Pembry checked the cuffs again. Dr. Lecter could smell Pembry's breath behind him. Now Pembry unlocked the cell and swung the door open. Boyle came in. Dr. Lecter turned his head, the cell moving by his vision at a rate that seemed slow to him, the details wonderfully sharp—Boyle at the table gathering the scattered supper things onto the tray with a clatter of annoyance at the mess. The tape player with its reels turning, the napkin on the floor beside the bolted-down leg of the table. Through the bars, Dr. Lecter saw in the corner of his eye the back of Pembry's knee, the tip of the baton hanging from his belt as he stood outside the cell holding the door.

Dr. Lecter found the keyhole in his left cuff, inserted the key and turned it. He felt the cuff spring loose on his wrist. He passed the key to his left hand, found the keyhole, put in the key and turned it.

Boyle bent for the napkin on the floor. Fast as a snapping turtle the handcuff closed on Boyle's wrist and as he turned his rolling eye to Lecter the other cuff locked around the fixed leg of the table. Dr. Lecter's legs under him now, driving to the door, Pembry trying to come from behind it and Lecter's shoulder drove the iron door into him, Pembry going for the Mace in his belt, his arm mashed to his body by the door. Lecter grabbed the long end of the baton and lifted. With the leverage twisting Pembry's belt tight around him, he hit Pembry in the throat with his elbow and sank his teeth in Pembry's face. Pembry trying to claw at Lecter, his nose and upper lip caught between the tearing teeth. Lecter shook his head like a rat-killing dog and pulled the riot baton from Pembry's belt. In the cell Boyle bellowing now, sitting on the floor, digging desperately in his pocket for his handcuff key, fumbling, dropping it, finding it again. Lecter drove the end of the baton into Pembry's stomach and throat and he went to his knees. Boyle got the key in a lock of the handcuffs, he was bellowing, Lecter coming to him now. Lecter shut Boyle up with a shot of the Mace and as he wheezed, cracked his upstretched arm with two blows of the baton. Boyle tried to get under the table, but blinded by the Mace he crawled the wrong way and it was easy, with five judicious blows, to beat him to death.

Pembry had managed to sit up and he was crying. Dr. Lecter looked down at him with his red smile. "I'm ready if you are, Officer Pembry," he said.

The baton, whistling in a flat arc, caught Pembry *pock* on the back of the head and he shivered out straight like a clubbed fish.

Dr. Lecter's pulse was elevated to more than one hundred by the exercise, but quickly slowed to normal. He turned off the music and listened.

He went to the stairs and listened again. He turned out Pembry's pockets, got the desk key and opened all its drawers. In the bottom drawer were Boyle's and Pembry's duty weapons, a pair of .38 Special revolvers. Even better, in Boyle's pocket he found a pocket knife.

37

THE LOBBY was full of policemen. It was 6:30 P.M. and the police at the outside guard posts had just been relieved at their regular two-hour interval. The men coming into the lobby from the raw evening warmed their hands at several electric heaters. Some of them had money down on the Memphis State basketball game in progress and were anxious to know how it was going.

Sergeant Tate would not allow a radio to be played aloud in the lobby, but one officer had a Walkman plugged in his ear. He reported the score often, but not often enough to suit the bettors.

In all there were fifteen armed policemen in the lobby plus two Corrections officers to relieve Pembry and Boyle at 7:00 P.M. Sergeant Tate himself was looking forward to going off duty with the eleven-to-seven shift.

All posts reported quiet. None of the nut calls threatening Lecter had come to anything.

At 6:45, Tate heard the elevator start up. He saw the bronze arrow above the door begin to crawl around the dial. It stopped at five.

Tate looked around the lobby. "Did Sweeney go up for the tray?"

"Naw, I'm here, Sarge. You mind calling, see if they're through? I need to get going."

Sergeant Tate dialed three digits and listened. "Phone's busy," he said. "Go ahead up and see." He turned back to the log he was completing for the eleven-to-seven shift.

Patrolman Sweeney pushed the elevator button. It didn't come.

"Had to have *lamb chops* tonight, rare," Sweeney said. "What you reckon he'll want for breakfast, some fucking thing from the zoo? And who'll have to catch it for him? Sweeney."

The bronze arrow above the door stayed on five.

Sweeney waited another minute. "What *is* this shit?" he said.

The .38 boomed somewhere above them, the reports echoing down the stone stairs, two fast shots and then a third.

Sergeant Tate, on his feet at the third one, microphone in his hand. "CP, shots fired upstairs at the tower. Outside posts, look sharp. We're going up."

Yelling, milling in the lobby.

Tate saw the bronze arrow of the elevator moving then. It was already down to four. Tate roared over the racket, "Hold it! Guard mount, double up at your outside posts, first squad stays with me. Berry and Howard cover that fucking elevator if it comes—" The needle stopped at three.

"First squad, here we go. Don't pass a door without checking it. Bobby, outside—get a shotgun and the vests and bring 'em up."

Tate's mind was racing on the first flight of stairs. Caution fought with the terrible need to help the officers upstairs. *God, don't let him be out. Nobody wearing vests, shit. Fucking Corrections screws.*

The offices on two, three and four were supposed to be empty and locked. You could get from the tower to the main building on those floors, if you went through the offices. You couldn't on five.

Tate had been to the excellent Tennessee S.W.A.T. school and he knew how to do it. He went first and took the young ones in hand. Fast and careful they took the stairs, covering each other from landing to landing.

"You turn your back on a door before you check it, I'll ream your ass."

The doors off the second-floor landing were dark and locked.

Up to three now, the little corridor dim. One rectangle of light on the floor from the open elevator car. Tate moved down the wall opposite the open elevator, no mirrors in the car to help him. With two pounds' pressure on a nine-pound trigger, he looked inside the car. Empty.

Tate yelled up the stairs, "*Boyle! Pembry!* Shit." He posted a man on three and moved up.

Four was flooded with the music of the piano coming from above. The door into the offices opened at a push. Beyond the offices, the beam of the long flashlight shone on a door open wide into the great dark building beyond.

"*Boyle! Pembry!*" He left two on the landing. "Cover the door. Vests are coming. Don't show your ass in that doorway."

Tate climbed the stone stairs into the music. At the top of the tower now, the fifth-floor landing, light dim in the short corridor. Bright light through the frosted glass that said SHELBY COUNTY HISTORICAL SOCIETY.

Tate moved low beneath the door glass to the side opposite the hinges. He nodded to Jacobs on the other side, turned the knob and shoved hard, the door swinging all the way back hard enough for the glass to shatter, Tate inside fast and out of the doorframe, covering the room over the wide sights of his revolver.

Tate had seen many things. He had seen accidents beyond reckoning, fights, murders. He had seen six dead policemen in his time. But he thought that what lay at his feet was the worst thing he had ever seen happen to an officer. The meat above the uniform collar no longer resembled a face. The front and top of the head were a slick of blood peaked with torn flesh and a single eye was stuck beside the nostrils, the sockets full of blood.

Jacobs passed Tate, slipping on the bloody floor as he went in to the cell. He bent over Boyle, still handcuffed to the table leg. Boyle, partly eviscerated, his face hacked to pieces, seemed to have exploded blood in the cell, the walls and the stripped cot covered with gouts and splashes.

Jacobs put his fingers on the neck. "This one's dead," he called over the music. "Sarge?"

Tate, back at himself, ashamed of a second's lapse, and he was talking into his radio. "Command post, two officers down. Repeat, two officers down. Prisoner is missing. Lecter is missing. Outside posts, watch the windows, subject has stripped the bed, he may be making a rope. Confirm ambulances en route."

"Pembry dead, Sarge?" Jacobs shut the music off.

Tate knelt and as he reached for the neck to feel, the awful thing on the floor groaned and blew a bloody bubble.

"Pembry's alive." Tate didn't want to put his mouth in the bloody mess, knew he would if he had to to help Pembry breathe, knew he wouldn't make one of the patrolmen do it. Better if Pembry died, but he would help him breathe. But there was a heartbeat, he found it, there was breathing. It was ragged and gurgling but it was breathing. The ruin was breathing on its own.

Tate's radio crackled. A patrol lieutenant set up on the lot outside took command and wanted news. Tate had to talk.

"Come here, Murray," Tate called to a young patrolman. "Get down here with Pembry and take ahold of him where he can feel your hands on him. Talk to him."

"What's his name, Sarge?" Murray was green.

"It's Pembry, now talk to him, God dammit." Tate on the radio. "Two officers down, Boyle's dead and Pembry's bad hurt. Lecter's missing and armed—he took their guns. Belts and holsters are on the desk."

The lieutenant's voice was scratchy through the thick walls. "Can you confirm the stairway clear for stretchers?"

"Yes, sir. Call up to four before they pass. I have men on every landing."

"Roger, Sergeant. Post Eight out here thought he saw some movement behind the windows in the main building on four. We've got the exits covered, he's not getting out. Hold your positions on the landings. S.W.A.T.'s rolling. We're gonna let S.W.A.T. flush him out. Confirm."

"I understand. S.W.A.T.'s play."

"What's he got?"

"Two pistols and a knife, Lieutenant—Jacobs, see if there's any ammo in the gunbelts."

"Dump pouches," the patrolman said. "Pembry's still full, Boyle's too. Dumb shit didn't take the extra rounds."

"What are they?"

"Thirty-eight + Ps JHP."

Tate was back on the radio. "Lieutenant, it looks like he's got two six-shot .38s. We heard three rounds fired and the dump pouches on the gunbelts are still full, so he may just have nine left. Advise S.W.A.T. its + Ps jacketed hollowpoints. This guy favors the face."

Plus Ps were hot rounds, but they would not penetrate S.W.A.T.'s body armor. A hit in the face would very likely be fatal, a hit on a limb would maim.

"Stretchers coming up, Tate."

The ambulances were there amazingly fast, but it did not seem fast enough to Tate, listening to the pitiful thing at his feet. Young Murray was trying to hold the groaning, jerking body, trying to talk reassuringly and not look at him, and he was saying, "You're just fine, Pembry, looking good," over and over in the same sick tone.

As soon as he saw the ambulance attendants on the landing, Tate yelled, "Corpsman!" as he had in war.

He got Murray by the shoulder and moved him out of the way. The ambulance attendants worked fast, expertly securing the clenched, blood-slick fists under the belt, getting an airway in and peeling a nonstick surgical bandage to get some pressure on the bloody face and head. One of them popped an intravenous plasma pack, but the other, taking blood pressure and pulse, shook his head and said, "Downstairs."

Orders on the radio now. "Tate, I want you to clear the offices in the tower and seal it off. Secure the doors from the main building. Then cover from the landings. I'm sending up vests and shotguns. We'll get him alive if he wants to come, but we take no special risks to preserve his life. Understand me?"

"I got it, Lieutenant."

"I want S.W.A.T. and nobody but S.W.A.T. in the main building. Let me have that back."

Tate repeated the order.

Tate was a good sergeant and he showed it now as he and Jacobs shrugged into their heavy armored vests and followed the gurney as the orderlies carried it down the stairs to the ambulance. A second crew followed with Boyle. The men on the landings were angry, seeing the gurneys pass, and Tate had a word of wisdom for them: "Don't let your temper get your ass shot off."

As the sirens wailed outside, Tate, backed by the veteran Jacobs, carefully cleared the offices and sealed off the tower.

A cool draft blew down the hall on four. Beyond the door, in the vast dark spaces of the main building, the telephones were ringing. In dark offices all over the building, buttons on telephones were winking like fire-flies, the bells sounding over and over.

The word was out that Dr. Lecter was "barricaded" in the building, and radio and television reporters were calling, dialing fast with their modems, trying to get live interviews with the monster. To avoid this, S.W.A.T. usually has the telephones shut off, except for one that the negotiator uses. This building was too big, the offices too many.

Tate closed and locked the door on the rooms of blinking telephones. His chest and back were wet and itching under the hardshell vest.

He took his radio off his belt. "CP, this is Tate, the tower's clear, over."

"Roger, Tate. Captain wants you at the CP."

"Ten-four. Tower lobby, you there?"

"Here, Sarge."

"It's me on the elevator, I'm bringing it down."

"Gotcha, Sarge."

Jacobs and Tate were in the elevator riding down to the lobby when a drop of blood fell on Tate's shoulder. Another hit his shoe.

He looked at the ceiling of the car, touched Jacobs, motioning for silence.

Blood was dripping from the crack around the service hatch in the top of the car. It seemed a long ride down to the lobby. Tate and Jacobs stepped off backwards, guns pointed at the ceiling of the elevator. Tate reached back in and locked the car.

"Shhhh," Tate said in the lobby. Quietly, "Berry, Howard, he's on the roof of the elevator. Keep it covered."

Tate went outside. The black S.W.A.T. van was on the lot. S.W.A.T. always had a variety of elevator keys.

They were set up in moments, two S.W.A.T. officers in black body armor and headsets climbing the stairs to the third-floor landing. With Tate in the lobby were two more, their assault rifles pointed at the elevator ceiling.

Like the big ants that fight, Tate thought.

The S.W.A.T. commander was talking into his headset. "Okay, Johnny."

On the third floor, high above the elevator, Officer Johnny Peterson turned his key in the lock and the elevator door slid open. The shaft was dark. Lying on his back in the corridor, he took a stun grenade from his tactical vest and put it on the floor beside him. "Okay, I'll take a look now."

He took out his mirror with its long handle and stuck it over the edge while his partner shined a powerful flashlight down the shaft.

"I see him. He's on top of the elevator. I see a weapon beside him. He's not moving."

The question in Peterson's earphone, "Can you see his hands?"

"I see one hand, the other one's under him. He's got the sheets around him."

"Tell him."

"PUT YOUR HANDS ON TOP OF YOUR HEAD AND FREEZE," Peterson yelled down the shaft. "He didn't move, Lieu-tenant . . . Right.

"IF YOU DON'T PUT YOUR HANDS ON TOP OF YOUR HEAD I'LL DROP A STUN GRENADE ON YOU. I'LL GIVE YOU THREE SECONDS," Peterson called. He took from his vest one of the doorstops every S.W.A.T. officer carries. "OKAY, GUYS, WATCH OUT DOWN THERE—HERE COMES THE GRENADE." He dropped the doorstop over the edge, saw it bounce on the figure. "He didn't move, Lieutenant."

"Okay, Johnny, we're gonna push the hatch up with a pole from outside the car. Can you get the drop?"

Peterson rolled over. His 10 mm Colt, cocked and locked, pointed straight down at the figure. "Got the drop," he said.

Looking down the elevator shaft, Peterson could see the crack of light appear below as the officers in the foyer pushed up on the hatch with a S.W.A.T. boathook. The still figure was partly over the hatch and one of the arms moved as the officers pushed from below.

Peterson's thumb pressed a shade harder on the safety of the

Colt. "His arm moved, Lieutenant, but I think it's just the hatch moving it."

"Roger. Heave."

The hatch banged backward and lay against the wall of the elevator shaft. It was hard for Peterson to look down into the light. "He hasn't moved. His hand's *not* on the weapon."

The calm voice in his ear, "Okay, Johnny, hold up. We're coming into the car, so watch with the mirror for movement. Any fire will come from us. Affirm?"

"Got it."

In the lobby, Tate watched them go into the car. A rifleman loaded with armor-piercing aimed his weapon at the ceiling of the elevator. A second officer climbed on a ladder. He was armed with a large automatic pistol with a flashlight clamped beneath it. A mirror and the pistol-light went up through the hatch. Then the officer's head and shoulders. He handed down a .38 revolver. "He's dead," the officer called down.

Tate wondered if the death of Dr. Lecter meant Catherine Martin would die too, all the information lost when the lights went out in that monster mind.

The officers were pulling him down now, the body coming upside down through the elevator hatch, eased down into many arms, an odd deposition in a lighted box. The lobby was filling up, policemen crowding up to see.

A corrections officer pushed forward, looked at the body's outflung tattooed arms.

"That's Pembry," he said.

38

IN THE back of the howling ambulance, the young attendant braced himself against the sway and turned to his radio to report to his emergency room supervisor, talking loud above the siren.

"He's comatose but the vital signs are good. He's got good pressure. One-thirty over ninety. Yeah, ninety. Pulse eighty-five. He's got severe facial cuts with elevated flaps, one eye enucleated. I've got pressure on the face and an airway in place. Possible gunshot in the head, I can't tell."

Behind him on the stretcher, the balled and bloody fists relax inside the waistband. The right hand slides out, finds the buckle on the strap across the chest.

"I'm scared to put much pressure on the head—he showed some convulsive movement before we put him on the gurney. Yeah, got him in the Fowler position."

Behind the young man, the hand gripped the surgical bandage and wiped out the eyes.

The attendant heard the airway hiss close behind him, turned and saw the bloody face in his, did not see the pistol descending and it caught him hard over the ear.

The ambulance slowing to a stop in traffic on the six-lane freeway, drivers behind it confused and honking, hesitant to pull around an emergency vehicle. Two small pops like backfires in the traffic and the ambulance started up again, weaving, straightening out, moving to the right lane.

The airport exit coming up. The ambulance piddled along in the right lane, various emergency lights going on and off on the outside of it, wipers on and off, then the siren wailing down, starting up, wailing down to silence and the flashing lights going off. The ambulance proceeding quietly, taking the exit to Memphis International Airport, the beautiful building floodlit in the winter evening. It took the curving drive as far as the automated gates to the vast underground parking field. A bloody hand came out to take a ticket. And the ambulance disappeared down the tunnel to the parking field beneath the ground.

CHAPTER

39

NORMALLY, CLARICE STARLING would have been curious to see Crawford's house in Arlington, but the bulletin on the car radio about Dr. Lecter's escape knocked all that out of her.

Lips numb and scalp prickling, she drove by rote, saw the neat 1950s ranch house without looking at it, and only wondered dimly if the lit, curtained windows on the left were where Bella was lying. The doorbell seemed too loud.

Crawford opened the door on the second ring. He wore a baggy cardigan and he was talking on a wireless phone. "Copley in Memphis," he said. Motioning for her to follow, he led her through the house, grunting into the telephone as he went.

In the kitchen, a nurse took a tiny bottle from the refrigerator and held it to the light. When Crawford raised his eyebrows to the nurse, she shook her head, she didn't need him.

He took Starling to his study, down three steps into what was clearly a converted double garage. There was good space here, a sofa and chairs, and on the cluttered desk a computer terminal glowed green beside an antique astrolabe. The rug felt as though it was laid on concrete. Crawford waved her to a seat.

He put his hand over the receiver. "Starling, this is baloney, but did you hand Lecter anything at all in Memphis?"

"No."

"No object."

"Nothing."

"You took him the drawings and stuff from his cell."

"I never gave it to him. The stuff's still in my bag. He gave *me* the file. That's all that passed between us."

Crawford tucked the phone under his jowl. "Copley, that's unmitigated bullshit. I want you to step on that bastard and do it now. Straight to the chief, straight to the T.B.I. See the hotline's posted with the rest. Burroughs is on it. Yes." He turned off the phone and stuffed it in his pocket.

"Want some coffee, Starling? Coke?"

"What was that about handing things to Dr. Lecter?"

"Chilton's saying you must have given Lecter something he used to slip the ratchet on the cuffs. You didn't do it on purpose, he says—it was just ignorance." Sometimes Crawford had angry little turtle-eyes. He watched how she took it. "Did Chilton try to snap your garters, Starling? Is that what's the matter with him?"

"Maybe. I'll take black with sugar, please."

While he was in the kitchen, she took deep breaths and looked around the room. If you live in a dormitory or a barracks, it's comforting to be in a home. Even with the ground shaking under Starling, her sense of the Crawfords' lives in this house helped her.

Crawford was coming, careful down the steps in his bifocals, carrying the cups. He was half an inch shorter in his moccasins. When Starling stood to take her coffee, their eyes were almost level. He smelled like soap, and his hair looked fluffy and gray.

"Copley said they haven't found the ambulance yet. Police barracks are turning out all over the South."

She shook her head. "I don't know any details. The radio just had the bulletin—Dr. Lecter killed two policemen and got away."

"Two corrections officers." Crawford punched up the crawling text on his computer screen. "Names were Boyle and Pembry. You deal with them?"

She nodded. "They . . . put me out of the lockup. They were okay about it." *Pembry coming around Chilton, uncomfortable, determined, but country-courteous. Come on with me, now, he said. He had liver spots on his hands and forehead. Dead now, pale beneath his spots.*

Suddenly Starling had to put her coffee down. She filled her lungs deep and looked at the ceiling for a moment. "How'd he do it?"

"He got away in an ambulance, Copley said. We'll go into it. How did you make out with the blotter acid?"

Starling had spent the late afternoon and early evening walking the sheet of Plutos through Scientific Analysis on Krendler's orders. "Nothing. They're trying the DEA files for a batch-match, but the stuff's ten years old. Documents may do better with the printing than DEA can do with the dope."

"But it *was* blotter acid."

"Yes. How'd he do it, Mr. Crawford?"

"Want to know?"

She nodded.

"Then I'll tell you. They loaded Lecter into an ambulance by mistake. They thought he was Pembry, badly injured."

"Did he have on Pembry's uniform? They were about the same size."

"He put on Pembry's uniform and part of Pembry's face. And about a pound off Boyle too. He wrapped Pembry's body in the waterproof mattress cover and the sheets from his cell to keep it from dripping and stuffed it on top of the elevator. He put on the uniform, got himself fixed up, laid on the floor and fired shots into the ceiling to start the stampede. I don't know what he did with the gun, stuffed it down the back of his pants, maybe. The ambulance comes, cops everywhere with their guns out. The ambulance crew came in fast and did what they're trained to do under fire—they stuffed in an airway, slapped a bandage over the worst of it, pressure to stop bleeding, and hauled out of there. They did their job. The ambulance never made it to the hospital. The police are still looking for it. I don't feel good about those medics. Copley said they're playing the dispatcher's tapes. The ambulances were called a couple of times. They think Lecter called the ambulances himself before he fired the shots, so he wouldn't have to lie around too long. *Dr. Lecter likes his fun.*"

Starling had never heard the bitter snarl in Crawford's voice before. Because she associated bitter with weak, it frightened her.

"This escape doesn't mean Dr. Lecter was lying," Starling said. "Sure, he was lying to somebody—us or Senator Martin—but maybe he wasn't lying to both of us. He told Senator Martin it was Billy Rubin and claimed that's all he knew. He told me it was somebody with delusions of being a transsexual. About the last thing he said to me was, 'Why not finish the arch?' He was talking about following the sex-change theory that—"

"I know, I saw your summary. There's nowhere to go with that until we get names from the clinics. Alan Bloom's gone personally to the department heads. They say they're looking. I have to believe it."

"Mr. Crawford, are you in the glue?"

"I'm directed to take compassionate leave," Crawford said. "There's a new task force of F.B.I., D.E.A., and 'additional elements' from the Attorney General's office—meaning Krendler."

"Who's boss?"

"Officially, F.B.I. Assistant Director John Golby. Let's say he and I are in close consultation. John's a good man. What about you, are *you* in the glue?"

"Krendler told me to turn in my I.D. and the roscoe and report back to school."

"That was all he did *before* your visit to Lecter. Starling, he sent a rocket this afternoon to the Office of Professional Responsibility. It was a request 'without prejudice' that the Academy suspend you pending a reevaluation of your fitness for the service. It's a chicken-shit backshot. The Chief Gunny, John Brigham, saw it in the faculty meeting at Quantico a little while ago. He gave 'em an earful and got on the horn to me."

"How bad is that?"

"You're entitled to a hearing. I'll vouch for your fitness and that'll be enough. But if you spend any more time away, you'll definitely be recycled, regardless of any finding at a hearing. Do you know what happens when you're recycled?"

"Sure, you're sent back to the regional office that recruited you. You get to file reports and make coffee until you get another spot in a class."

"I can promise you a place in a later class, but I can't keep them from recycling you if you miss the time."

"So I go back to school and stop working on this, or . . ."

"Yeah."

"What do you want me to do?"

"Your job was Lecter. You did it. I'm not asking you to take a recycle. It could cost you, maybe half a year, maybe more."

"What about Catherine Martin?"

"He's had her almost forty-eight hours—be forty-eight hours at midnight. If we don't catch him he'll probably do her tomorrow or the next day, if it's like last time."

"Lecter's not all we had."

"They got six William Rubins so far, all with priors of one kind or another. None of 'em look like much. No Billy Rubins on the bug journal subscription lists. The Knifemakers Guild knows about five cases of ivory anthrax in the last ten years. We've got a couple of those left to check. What else? Klaus hasn't been identified—yet. Interpol reports a fugitive warrant outstanding in Marseilles for a Norwegian merchant seaman, a 'Klaus Bjetland,' however you say it. Norway's looking for his dental records to send. If we get anything from the clinics, and you've got the time, you can help with it. Starling?"

"Yes, Mr. Crawford?"

"Go back to school."

"If you didn't want me to chase him you shouldn't have taken me in that funeral home, Mr. Crawford."

"No," Crawford said. "I suppose I shouldn't. But then we wouldn't have the insect. You don't turn in your roscoe. Quantico's safe enough, but you'll be armed any time you're off the base at Quantico until Lecter's caught or dead."

"What about you? He hates you. I mean, he's given this some thought."

"Lot of people have, Starling, in a lot of jails. One of these days he might get around to it, but he's way too busy now. It's sweet to be out and he's not ready to waste it that way. And this place is safer than it looks."

The phone in Crawford's pocket buzzed. The one on the desk purred and blinked. He listened for a few moments, said "Okay," and hung up.

"They found the ambulance in the underground garage at the Memphis airport." He shook his head. "No good. Crew was in the back. Dead, both of them." Crawford took off his glasses, rummaged for his handkerchief to polish them.

"Starling, the Smithsonian called Burroughs asking for you. The Pilcher fellow. They're pretty close to finishing up on the bug. I want you to write a 302 on that and sign it for the permanent file. You found the bug and followed up on it and I want the record to say so. You up to it?"

Starling was as tired as she had ever been. "Sure," she said.

"Leave your car at the garage, and Jeff'll drive you back to Quantico when you're through."

On the steps she turned her face toward the lighted, curtained windows where the nurse kept watch, and then looked back at Crawford.

"I'm thinking about you both, Mr. Crawford."

"Thank you, Starling," he said.

"OFFICER STARLING, Dr. Pilcher said he'd meet you in the Insect Zoo. I'll take you over there," the guard said.

To reach the Insect Zoo from the Constitution Avenue side of the museum, you must take the elevator one level above the great stuffed elephant and cross a vast floor devoted to the study of man.

Tiers of skulls were first, rising and spreading, representing the explosion of human population since the time of Christ.

Starling and the guard moved in a dim landscape peopled with figures illustrating human origin and variation. Here were displays of ritual—tattoos, bound feet, tooth modification, Peruvian surgery, mummification.

"Did you ever see Wilhelm von Ellenbogen?" the guard asked, shining his light into a case.

"I don't believe I have," Starling said without slowing her pace.

"You should come sometime when the lights are up and take a look at him. Buried him in Philadelphia in the eighteenth century? Turned right to soap when the ground water hit him."

The Insect Zoo is a large room, dim now and loud with chirps and whirs. Cages and cases of live insects fill it. Children particularly like the zoo and troop through it all day. At night, left to themselves, the insects are busy. A few of the cases were lit with red, and the fire exit signs burned fiercely red in the dim room.

"Dr. Pilcher?" the guard called from the door.

"Here," Pilcher said, holding a penlight up as a beacon.

"Will you bring this lady out?"

"Yes, thank you, Officer."

Starling took her own small flashlight out of her purse and found the switch already on, the batteries dead. The flash of anger she felt reminded her that she was tired and she had to bear down.

"Hello, Officer Starling."

"Dr. Pilcher."

"How about 'Professor Pilcher'?"

"*Are* you a professor?"

"No, but I'm not a doctor either. What I *am* is glad to see you. Want to look at some bugs?"

"Sure. Where's Dr. Roden?"

"He made most of the progress over the last two nights with chaetaxy and finally he had to crash. Did you see the bug before we started on it?"

"No."

"It was just mush, really."

"But you got it, you figured it out."

"Yep. Just now." He stopped at a mesh cage. "First let me show you a moth like the one you brought in Monday. This is not exactly the same as yours, but the same family, an owlet." The beam of his flashlight found the large sheeny blue moth sitting on a small branch, its wings folded. Pilcher blew air at it and instantly the fierce face of an owl appeared as the moth flared the undersides of its wings at them, the eye-spots on the wings glaring like the last sight a rat ever sees. "This one's *Caligo beltrao*—fairly common. But with this Klaus specimen, you're talking some heavy moths. Come on."

At the end of the room was a case set back in a niche with a rail in front of it. The case was beyond the reach of children and it was covered with a cloth. A small humidifier hummed beside it.

"We keep it behind glass to protect people's fingers—it can fight. It likes the damp too, and glass keeps the humidity in." Pilcher lifted the cage carefully by its handles and moved it to the front of the niche. He lifted off the cover and turned on a small light above the cage.

"This is the Death's-head Moth," he said. "That's nightshade she's sitting on—we're hoping she'll lay."

The moth was wonderful and terrible to see, its large brown-black wings tented like a cloak, and on its wide furry back, the signature device that has struck fear in men for as long as men have come upon it suddenly in their happy gardens. The domed skull, a skull that is both skull and face, watching from its dark eyes, the cheekbones, the zygomatic arch traced exquisitely beside the eyes.

"*Acherontia styx*," Pilcher said. "It's named for two rivers in Hell. Your man, he drops the bodies in a river every time—did I read that?"

"Yes," Starling said. "Is it rare?"

"In this part of the world it is. There aren't any at all in nature."

"Where's it from?" Starling leaned her face close to the mesh roof of the case. Her breath stirred the fur on the moth's back. She jerked back when it squeaked and fiercely flapped its wings. She could feel the tiny breeze it made.

"Malaysia. There's a European type too, called *atropos*, but this one and the one in Klaus's mouth are Malaysian."

"So somebody raised it."

Pilcher nodded. "Yes," he said when she didn't look at him. "It had to be shipped from Malaysia as an egg or more likely as a pupa. Nobody's ever been able to get them to lay eggs in captivity. They mate, but no eggs. The hard part is finding the caterpillar in the jungle. After that, they're not hard to raise."

"You said they can fight."

"The proboscis is sharp and stout, and they'll jam it in your finger if you fool with them. It's an unusual weapon and alcohol doesn't affect it in preserved specimens. That helped us narrow the field so we could identify it so fast." Pilcher seemed suddenly embarrassed, as though he had boasted. "They're tough too," he hurried on to say. "They go in beehives and Bogart honey. One time we were collecting in Sabah, Borneo, and they'd come to the light behind the youth hostel. It was weird to hear them, we'd be—"

"Where did this one come from?"

"A swap with the Malaysian government. I don't know what we traded. It was funny, there we were in the dark, waiting with this cyanide bucket, when—"

"What kind of customs declaration came with this one? Do you have records of that? Do they have to be cleared out of Malaysia? Who would have that?"

"You're in a hurry. Look, I've written down all the stuff we have and the places to put ads if you want to do that kind of thing. Come on, I'll take you out."

They crossed the vast floor in silence. In the light of the elevator, Starling could see that Pilcher was as tired as she was.

"You stayed up with this," she said. "That was a good thing to do. I didn't mean to be abrupt before, I just—"

"I hope they get him. I hope you're through with this soon," he said. "I put down a couple of chemicals he might be buying if he's putting up soft specimens . . . Officer Starling, I'd like to get to know you."

"Maybe I should call you when I can."

"You definitely should, absolutely, I'd like that," Pilcher said.

The elevator closed and Pilcher and Starling were gone. The floor devoted to man was still and no human figure moved, not the tattooed, not the mummified, the bound feet didn't stir.

The fire lights glowed red in the Insect Zoo, reflected in ten thousand active eyes of the older phylum. The humidifier hummed and hissed. Beneath the cover, in the black cage, the Death's-head Moth climbed down the nightshade. She moved across the floor, her wings trailing like a cape, and found the bit of honeycomb in her dish. Grasping the honeycomb in her powerful front legs, she uncoiled her sharp proboscis and plunged it through the wax cap of a honey cell. Now she sat sucking quietly while all around her in the dark the chirps and whirs resumed, and with them the tiny tillings and killings.

41

CATHERINE BAKER MARTIN down in the hateful dark. Dark swarmed behind her eyelids and, in jerky seconds of sleep, she dreamed the dark came into her. Dark came insidious, up her nose and into her ears, damp fingers of dark proposed themselves to each of her body openings. She put her hand over her mouth and nose, put her other hand over her vagina, clenched her buttocks, turned one ear to the mattress and sacrificed the other ear to the intrusion of the dark. With the dark came a sound, and she jerked awake. A familiar busy sound, a sewing machine. Variable speed. Slow, now fast.

Up in the basement the lights were on—she could see a feeble disc of yellow high above her where the small hatch in the well lid stood open. The poodle barked a couple of times and the unearthly voice was talking to it, muffled.

Sewing. Sewing was so wrong down here. Sewing belongs to the light. The sunny sewing room of Catherine's childhood flashed so welcome in her mind . . . the housekeeper, dear Bea Love, at the machine . . . her little cat batted at the blowing curtain.

The voice blew it all away, fussing at the poodle.

"Precious, put that *down*. You'll stick yourself with a pin and *then* where will we be? I'm almost done. Yes, Darlingheart. You get a Chew-wy *when we get through-y*, you get a Chew-wy *doody doody doo.*"

Catherine did not know how long she had been captive. She knew that she had washed twice—the last time she had stood up in the light, wanting him to see her body, not sure if he was looking down from behind the blinding light. Catherine Baker Martin naked was a show-stopper, a girl and a half in all directions, and she knew it. She wanted him to see. She wanted out of the pit. Close enough to fuck is close enough to fight—she said it silently to herself over and over as she washed. She was getting very little to eat and she knew she'd better do it while she had her strength. She knew she would fight him. She knew she could fight. Would it be better to fuck him first, fuck him as many times as he could do it and wear him out? She knew if she could ever get her legs around his neck she could send him home to Jesus in about a second and a half. *Can I stand to do that? You're damned right I can. Balls and eyes, balls and eyes, balls and eyes.* But there had been no sound from above as she finished washing and put on the fresh jumpsuit. There was no reply to her offers as the bath bucket swayed up on its flimsy string and was replaced by her toilet bucket.

She waited now, hours later, listening to the sewing machine. She did not call out to him. In time, maybe a thousand breaths, she heard him going up the stairs, talking to the dog, saying something, "—breakfast when I get back." He left the basement light on. Sometimes he did that.

Toenails and footsteps on the kitchen floor above. The dog whining. She believed her captor was leaving. Sometimes he went away for a long time.

Breaths went by. The little dog walked around in the kitchen above, whining, rattling something along the floor, bonging something along the floor, maybe its bowl. Scratching, scratching above. And barking again, short sharp barks, this time not as clear as the sounds had been when the dog was above her in the kitchen. Because the little dog was not in the kitchen. It had nosed the door open and it was down in the basement chasing mice, as it had done before when he was out.

Down in the dark, Catherine Martin felt beneath her mattress. She found the piece of chicken bone and sniffed it. It was hard not to eat the little shreds of meat and gristle on it. She put it in her mouth to get it warm. She stood up now, swaying a little in the dizzy dark. With her in the sheer pit was nothing but her futon, the jumpsuit she was wearing, the plastic toilet bucket and its flimsy cotton string stretching upward toward the pale yellow light.

She had thought about it in every interval when she could think. Catherine stretched as high as she could and grasped the string. Better to jerk or to pull? She had thought about it through thousands of breaths. Better to pull steadily.

The cotton string stretched more than she expected. She got a new grip as high as she could and pulled, swinging her arm from side to side, hoping the string was fraying where it passed over the wooden lip of the opening above her. She frayed until her shoulder ached. She pulled, the string stretching, now not stretching, no more stretch. Please break high. Pop, and it fell, hanks of it across her face.

Squatting on the floor, the string lying on her head and shoulder, not enough light from the hole far above to see the string piled on her. She didn't know how much she had. Must not tangle. Carefully she laid the string out on the floor in bights, measuring them on her forearm. She counted fourteen forearms. The string had broken at the lip of the well.

She tied the chicken bone with its shredded morsels of flesh securely into the line where it attached to the bucket handle.

Now the harder part.

Work carefully. She was in her heavy-weather mindset. It was like taking care of yourself in a small boat in heavy weather.

She tied the broken end of the string to her wrist, tightening the knot with her teeth.

She stood as clear of the string as possible. Holding the bucket by the handle, she swung it in a big circle and threw it straight upward at the faint disc of light above her. The plastic bucket missed the open hatch, hit the underside of the lid and fell back, hitting her in the face and shoulder. The little dog barked louder.

She took the time to lay out the line and threw again, and again. On the third throw, the bucket hit her broken finger when it fell and she had to lean against the in-sloping wall and breathe until the nausea went away. Throw four banged down on her, but five did not. It was out. The bucket was somewhere on the wooden cover of the well beside the open trap. How far from the hole? Get steady. Gently she pulled. She twitched the string to hear the bucket handle rattle against the wood above her.

The little dog barked louder.

She mustn't pull the bucket over the edge of the hole, but she must pull it close. She pulled it close.

The little dog among the mirrors and the mannequins in a nearby basement room. Sniffing at the threads and shreds beneath the sewing machine. Nosing around the great black armoire. Looking toward the end of the basement where the sounds were coming from. Dashing toward the gloomy section to bark and dash back again.

Now a voice, echoing faintly through the basement.

"Preeeee-cious."

The little dog barked and jumped in place. Its fat little body quivered with the barks.

Now a wet kissing sound.

The dog looked up at the kitchen floor above, but that wasn't where the sound came from.

A smack-smack sound like eating. "Come on, Precious. Come on, Sweetheart."

On its tiptoes, ears up, the dog went into the gloom.

Slurp-slurp. "Come on, Sweetums, come on, Precious."

The poodle could smell the chicken bone tied to the bucket handle. It scratched at the side of the well and whined.

Smack-smack-smack.

The small poodle jumped up onto the wooden cover of the well. The smell was over here, between the bucket and the hole. The little dog barked at the bucket, whined in indecision. The chicken bone twitched ever so slightly.

The poodle crouched with its nose between its front paws, behind in the air, wagging furiously. It barked twice and pounced on the chicken bone, gripping it with its teeth. The bucket seemed to be trying to nose the little dog away from the chicken. The poodle growled at the bucket and held on, straddling the handle, teeth firmly clamped on the bone. Suddenly the bucket bumped the poodle over, off its feet, pushed it, it struggled to get up, bumped again, it struggled with the bucket, a back foot and haunch went off in the hole, its claws scrabbled frantically at the wood, the bucket sliding, wedging in the hole with the dog's hindquarters and the little dog pulled free, the bucket slipping over the edge and plunging, the bucket escaping down the hole with the chicken bone. The poodle barked angrily down the hole, barks ringing down in the well. Then it stopped barking and cocked its head at a sound only it could hear. It scrambled off the top of the well and went up the stairs yipping as a door slammed somewhere upstairs.

Catherine Baker Martin's tears spread hot on her cheeks and fell, plucking at the front of her jumpsuit, soaking through, warm on her breasts, and she believed that she would surely die.

42

CRAWFORD STOOD alone in the center of his study with his hands jammed deep in his pockets. He stood there from 12:30 A.M. to 12:33, demanding an idea. Then he telexed the California Department of Motor Vehicles requesting a trace on the motor home Dr. Lecter said Raspail had bought in California, the one Raspail used in his romance with Klaus. Crawford asked the DMV to check for traffic tickets issued to any driver other than Benjamin Raspail.

Then he sat on the sofa with a clipboard and worked out a proactive personal ad to run in the major papers:

> Junoesque creamy passion flower, 21, model, seeks man who appreciates quality AND quantity. Hand and cosmetic model, you've seen me in the magazine ads, now I'd like to see you. Send pix first letter.

Crawford considered for a moment, scratched out "Junoesque," and substituted "full-figured."

His head dipped and he dozed. The green screen of the computer terminal made tiny squares in the lenses of his glasses. Movement on the screen now, the lines crawling upward, moving on Crawford's lenses. In his sleep he shook his head as though the image tickled him.

The message was:

MEMPHIS POX RECOVERED 2 ITEMS IN SEARCH OF LECTER'S CELL.

(1) IMPROVISED HANDCUFF KEY MADE FROM BALLPOINT TUBE. INCISIONS BY ABRASION, BALTIMORE REQUESTED TO CHECK HOS-PITAL CELL FOR TRACES OF MANUFACTURE, AUTH COPLEY, SAC MEMPHIS.

(2) SHEET OF NOTEPAPER LEFT FLOATING IN TOILET BY FUGIT-IVE. ORIGINAL EN ROUTE TO WX DOCUMENT SECTION/LAB. GRAPHIC OF WRITING FOLLOWS. GRAPHIC SPLIT TO LANGLEY, ATTN: BENSON——CRYPTOGRAPHY.

When the graphic appeared, rising like something peeping over the bottom edge of the screen, it was this:

The soft double beep of the computer terminal did not wake Crawford, but three minutes later the telephone did. It was Jerry Burroughs at the National Crime Information Center hotline.

"See your screen, Jack?"

"Just a second," Crawford said. "Yeah, okay."

"The lab's got it already, Jack. The drawing Lecter left in the john. The numbers between the letters in Chilton's name, it's biochem-istry—$C_{33}H_{36}N_4O_6$—it's the formula for a pigment in human bile called bilirubin. Lab advises it's a chief coloring agent in shit."

"Balls."

"You were right about Lecter, Jack. He was just jerking them around. Too bad for Senator Martin. Lab says bilirubin's just about exactly the color of Chilton's hair. Asylum humor, they call it. Did you see Chilton on the six o'clock news?"

"No."

"Marilyn Sutter saw it upstairs. Chilton was blowing off about 'The Search for Billy Rubin.' Then he went to dinner with a television reporter. That's where he was when Lecter took a walk. What a pluperfect asshole."

"Lecter told Starling to 'bear in mind' that Chilton didn't have a medical degree," Crawford said.

"Yeah, I saw it in the summary. I think Chilton tried to fuck Starling's what I think, and she sawed him off at the knees. He may be dumb but he ain't blind. How is the kid?"

"Okay, I think. Worn down."

"Think Lecter was jerking her off too?"

"Maybe. We'll stay with it, though. I don't know what the clinics are doing, I keep thinking I should've gone after the records in court. I hate to have to depend on them. Midmorning, if we haven't heard anything, we'll go the court route."

"Say, Jack . . . you got some people outside that know what Lecter looks like, right?"

"Sure."

"Don't you know he's laughing somewhere."

"Maybe not for long," Crawford said.

DR. HANNIBAL LECTER stood at the registration desk of the elegant Marcus Hotel in St Louis. He wore a brown hat and a raincoat buttoned to the neck. A neat surgical bandage covered his nose and cheeks.

He signed the register "Lloyd Wyman," a signature he had practiced in Wyman's car.

"How will you be paying, Mr. Wyman?" the clerk said.

"American Express." Dr. Lecter handed the man Lloyd Wyman's credit card.

Soft piano music came from the lounge. At the bar Dr. Lecter could see two people with bandages across their noses. A middle-aged couple crossed to the elevators, humming a Cole Porter tune. The woman wore a gauze patch over her eye.

The clerk finished making the credit-card impression. "You do know, Mr. Wyman, you're entitled to use the hospital garage."

"Yes, thank you," Dr. Lecter said. He had already parked Wyman's car in the garage, with Wyman in the trunk.

The bellman who carried Wyman's bags to the small suite got one of Wyman's five-dollar bills in compensation.

Dr. Lecter ordered a drink and a sandwich and relaxed with a long shower.

The suite seemed enormous to Dr. Lecter after his long confinement. He enjoyed going to and fro in his suite and walking up and down in it.

From his windows he could see across the street the Myron and Sadie Fleischer Pavilion of St Louis City Hospital, housing one of the world's foremost centers for craniofacial surgery.

Dr. Lecter's visage was too well known for him to be able to take advantage of the plastic surgeons here, but it was one place in the world where he could walk around with a bandage on his face without exciting interest.

He had stayed here once before, years ago, when he was doing psychiatric research in the superb Robert J. Brockman Memorial Library.

Heady to have a window, several windows. He stood at his windows in the dark, watching the car lights move across the MacArthur Bridge and savoring his drink. He was pleasantly fatigued by the five-hour drive from Memphis.

The only real rush of the evening had been in the underground garage at Memphis International Airport. Cleaning up with cotton pads and alcohol and distilled water in the back of the parked ambulance was not at all convenient. Once he was in the attendant's whites, it was just a matter of catching a single traveler in a deserted aisle of long-term parking in the great garage. The man obligingly leaned into the trunk of his car for his sample case, and never saw Dr. Lecter come up behind him.

Dr. Lecter wondered if the police believed he was fool enough to fly from the airport.

The only problem on the drive to St Louis was finding the lights, the dimmers, and the wipers in the foreign car, as Dr. Lecter was unfamiliar with stalk controls beside the steering wheel.

Tomorrow he would shop for things he needed, hair bleach, barbering supplies, a sunlamp, and there were other, prescription, items that he would obtain to make some immediate changes in his appearance. When it was convenient, he would move on.

There was no reason to hurry.

ARDELIA MAPP was in her usual position, propped up in bed with a book. She was listening to all-news radio. She turned it off when Clarice Starling trudged in. Looking into Starling's drawn face, blessedly she didn't ask anything except, "Want some tea?"

When she was studying, Mapp drank a beverage she brewed of mixed loose leaves her grandmother sent her, which she called "Smart People's Tea."

Of the two brightest people Starling knew, one was also the steadiest person she knew and the other was the most frightening. Starling hoped that gave her some balance in her acquaintance.

"You were lucky to miss today," Mapp said. "That damn Kim Won ran us right into the *ground*. I'm not lying. I believe they must have more gravity in Korea than we do. Then they come over here and get *light*, see, get jobs teaching P.E. because it's not any work for them . . . John Brigham came by."

"When?"

"Tonight, a little while ago. Wanted to know if you were back yet. He had his hair slicked down. Shifted around like a freshman in the lobby. We had a little talk. He said if you're behind and we need to jam instead of shoot during the range period the next couple of days, he'll open up the range this weekend and let us make it up. I said I'd let him know. He's a nice man."

"Yeah, he is."

"Did you know he wants you to shoot against the DEA and Customs in the interservice match?"

"Nope."

"Not the Women's. The Open. Next question: Do you know the Fourth Amendment stuff for Friday?"

"A lot of it I do."

"Okay, what's *Chimel versus California?*"

"Searches in secondary schools."

"What *about* school searches?"

"I don't know."

"It's the 'immediate reach' concept. Who was *Schneckloth?*"

"Hell, I don't know."

"Schneckloth versus Bustamonte."

"Is it the reasonable expectation of privacy?"

"Boo to you. Expectation of privacy is the *Katz* principle. *Sckneckloth* is consent to search. I can see we've got to jam on the books, my girl. I've got the notes."

"Not tonight."

"No. But tomorrow you'll wake up with your mind fertile and ignorant, and then we'll begin to plant the harvest for Friday. Starling, Brigham said—he's not supposed to tell, so I promised—he said you'll beat the hearing. He thinks that signifying son of a bitch Krendler won't remember you two days from now. Your grades are good, we'll knock this stuff out easy." Mapp studied Starling's tired face. "You did the best anybody could for that poor soul, Starling. You stuck your neck out for her and you got your butt kicked for her and you moved things along. You deserve a chance yourself. Why don't you go ahead and crash? I'm fixing to shut this down myself."

"Ardelia. Thanks."

And after the lights were out.

"Starling?"

"Yeah?"

"Who do you think's prettiest, Brigham or Hot Bobby Lowrance?"

"That's a hard one."

"Brigham's got a tattoo on his shoulder, I could see it through his shirt. What does it say?"

"I wouldn't have any idea."

"Will you let me know soon as you find out?"

"Probably not."

"I told you about Hot Bobby's python briefs."

"You just saw 'em through the window when he was lifting weights."

"Did Gracie tell you that? That girl's mouth is gonna—"

Starling was asleep.

45

SHORTLY BEFORE 3:00 A.M., Crawford, dozing beside his wife, came awake. There was a catch in Bella's breathing and she had stirred on her bed. He sat up and took her hand.

"Bella?"

She took a deep breath and let it out. Her eyes were open for the first time in days. Crawford put his face close before hers, but he didn't think she could see him.

"Bella, I love you, kid," he said in case she could hear.

Fear brushed the walls of his chest, circling inside him like a bat in a house. Then he got hold of it.

He wanted to get something for her, anything, but he did not want her to feel him let go of her hand.

He put his ear to her chest. He heard a soft beat, a flutter, and then her heart stopped. There was nothing to hear, there was only a curious cool rushing. He didn't know if the sound was in her chest or only in his ears.

"God bless you and keep you with Him . . . and with your folks," Crawford said, words he wanted to be true.

He gathered her to him on the bed, sitting against the headboard, held her to his chest while her brain died. His chin pushed back the scarf from the remnants of her hair. He did not cry. He had done all that.

Crawford changed her into her favorite, her best bed gown and sat for a while beside the high bed, holding her hand against his cheek. It was a square, clever hand, marked with a lifetime of gardening, marked by IV needles now.

When she came in from the garden, her hands smelled like thyme.

("Think about it like egg white on your fingers," the girls at school had counseled Bella about sex. She and Crawford had joked about it in bed, years ago, years later, last year. Don't think about that, think about the good stuff, the pure stuff. That *was* the pure stuff. She wore a round hat and white gloves and going up in the elevator the first time he whistled a dramatic arrangement of "Begin the Beguine." In the room she teased him that he had the cluttered pockets of a boy.)

Crawford tried going into the next room—he still could turn when he wanted to and see her through the open door, composed in the warm light of the bedside lamp. He was waiting for her body to become a ceremonial object apart from him, separate from the person he had held upon the bed and separate from the life's companion he held now in his mind. So he could call them to come for her.

His empty hands hanging palms forward at his sides, he stood at the window looking to the empty east. He did not look for dawn; east was only the way the window faced.

C H A P T E R

46

"READY, PRECIOUS?"

Jame Gumb was propped against the headboard of his bed and very comfortable, the little dog curled up warm on his tummy.

Mr. Gumb had just washed his hair and he had a towel wrapped around his head. He rummaged in the sheets, found the remote control for his VCR, and pushed the play button.

He had composed his program from two pieces of videotape copied onto one cassette. He watched it every day when he was making vital preparations, and he always watched it just before he harvested a hide.

The first tape was from scratchy film of *Movietone News*, a black-and-white newsreel from 1948. It was the quarter-finals of the Miss Sacramento contest, a preliminary event on the long road to the Miss America pageant in Atlantic City.

This was the swimsuit competition, and all the girls carried flowers as they came in a file to the stairs and mounted to the stage.

Mr. Gumb's poodle had been through this many times and she squinted her eyes when she heard the music, knowing she'd be squeezed.

The beauty contestants looked very World War II. They wore Rose Marie Reid swimsuits, and some of the faces were lovely. Their legs were nicely shaped too, some of them, but they lacked muscle tone and seemed to lap a little at the knee.

Gumb squeezed the poodle.

"Precious, here she comes, hereshecomes hereshecomes!"

And here she came, approaching the stairs in her white swimsuit, with a radiant smile for the young man who assisted at the stairs, then quick on her high heels away, the camera following the backs of her thighs: Mom. There was Mom.

Mr. Gumb didn't have to touch his remote control, he'd done it all when he dubbed this copy. In reverse, here she came backward, backward down the stairs, took back her smile from the young man, backed up the aisle, now forward again, and back and forward, forward and back.

When she smiled at the young man, Gumb smiled too.

There was one more shot of her in a group, but it always blurred in freeze-frame. Better just to run it at speed and get the glimpse. Mom was with the other girls, congratulating the winners.

The next item he'd taped off cable television in a motel in Chicago— he'd had to rush out and buy a VCR and stay an extra night to get it. This was the loop film they run on seedy cable channels late at night as background for the sex ads that crawl up the screen in print. The loops are made of junk film, fairly innocuous naughty movies from the forties and fifties, and there was nudist camp volleyball and the less explicit parts of thirties sex movies where the male actors wore false noses and still had their socks on. The sound was any music at all. Right now it was "The Look of Love," totally out of sync with the sprightly action.

There was nothing Mr. Gumb could do about the ads crawling up the screen. He just had to put up with them.

Here it is, an outdoor pool—in California, judging from the foliage.

Good pool furniture, everything very fifties. Naked swimming, some graceful girls. A few of them might have appeared in a couple of B-pictures. Sprightly and bouncing, they climbed out of the pool and ran, much faster than the music, to the ladder of a water slide, climbed up—down they came, Wheeee! Breasts lifting as they plunged down the slide, laughing, legs out straight, Splash!

Here came Mom. Here she came, climbing out of the pool behind the girl with the curly hair. Her face was partly covered by a crawl ad from Sinderella, a sex boutique, but here you saw her going away, and there she went up the ladder all shiny and wet, wonderfully buxom and supple, with a small Cesarean scar, and down the slide, Wheeee! So beautiful, and even if he couldn't see her face, Mr. Gumb knew in his heart it was Mom, filmed after the last time in his life that he ever got to really see her. Except in his mind, of course.

The scene switched to a filmed ad for a marital aid and abruptly ended.

The poodle squinted her eyes two seconds before Mr. Gumb hugged her tight.

"Oh, Precious. Come here to Mommy. Mommy's gonna be *so* beautiful."

Much to do, much to do, much to do to get ready for tomorrow.

He could never hear it from the kitchen even at the top of its voice, thank goodness, but he could hear it on the stairs as he went down to the basement. He had hoped it would be quiet and asleep. The poodle, riding beneath his arm, growled back at the sounds from the pit.

"*You've* been raised better than that," he said into the fur on the back of her head.

The oubliette room is through a door to the left at the bottom of the stairs. He didn't spare it a glance, nor did he listen to the words from the pit—as far as he was concerned, they bore not the slightest resemblance to English.

Mr. Gumb turned right into the workroom, put the poodle down and turned on the lights. A few moths fluttered and lit harmlessly on the wire mesh covering the ceiling lights.

Mr. Gumb was meticulous in the workroom. He always mixed his fresh solutions in stainless steel, never in aluminum.

He had learned to do everything well ahead of time. As he worked he admonished himself:

You have to be orderly, you have to be precise, you have to be expeditious, because the problems are formidable.

The human skin is heavy—sixteen to eighteen percent of body weight—and slippery. An entire hide is hard to handle and easy to drop when it's still wet. Time is important too; skin begins to shrink immediately after it has been harvested, most notably from young adults, whose skin is tightest to begin with.

Add to that the fact that the skin is not perfectly elastic, even in the young. If you stretch it, it never regains its original proportions. Stitch something perfectly smooth, then pull it too hard over a tailor's ham, and it bulges and puckers. Sitting at the machine and crying your eyes out won't remove one pucker. Then there are the cleavage lines, and you'd better know where they are. Skin doesn't stretch the same amount in all directions before the collagen bundles deform and the fibers tear; pull the wrong way, and you get a stretch mark.

Green material is simply impossible to work with. Much experimentation went into this, along with much heartbreak, before Mr Gumb got it right.

In the end he found the old ways were best. His procedures were these: First he soaked his items in the aquariums, in vegetable extracts developed by the Native Americans—all-natural substances that contain no mineral salts whatsoever. Then he used the method that produced the matchless butter-soft buckskin of the New World— classic brain tanning. The Native Americans believed that each animal has just enough brains to tan its own hide. Mr. Gumb knew that this was not true and long ago had quit trying it, even with the largest-brained primate. He had a freezer full of beef brains now, so he never ran short.

The problems of processing the material he could manage; practice had made him near perfect.

Difficult structural problems remained, but he was especially well qualified to solve them too.

The workroom opened into a basement corridor leading to a disused bath where Mr. Gumb stored his hoisting tackle and his timepiece, and on to the studio and the vast black warren beyond.

He opened his studio door to brilliant light—floodlights and incandescent tubes, color-corrected to daylight, were fastened to ceiling beams. Mannequins posed on a raised floor of pickled oak. All were partly clad, some in leather and some in muslin patterns for leather garments. Eight mannequins were doubled in the two mirrored walls— good plate mirror too, not tiles. A makeup table held cosmetics, several wig forms, and wigs. This was the brightest of studios, all white and blond oak.

The mannequins wore commercial work in progress, dramatic Armani knockoffs mostly, in fine black cabretta leather, all roll-pleats and pointed shoulders and breastplates.

The third wall was taken up by a large worktable, two commercial sewing machines, two dressmaker's forms, and a tailor's form cast from the very torso of Jame Gumb.

Against the fourth wall, dominating this bright room, was a great black armoire in Chinese lacquer that rose almost to the eight-foot ceiling. It was old and the designs on it had faded; a few gold scales remained where a dragon was, his white eye still clear and staring, and here was the red tongue of another dragon whose body had faded away. The lacquer beneath them remained intact, though it was crackled.

The armoire, immense and deep, had nothing to do with commercial work. It contained on forms and hangers the Special Things, and its doors were closed.

The little dog lapped from her water bowl in the corner and lay down between the feet of a mannequin, her eyes on Mr. Gumb.

He had been working on a leather jacket. He needed to finish it—he'd meant to get everything out of the way, but he was in a creative fever now and his own muslin fitting garment didn't satisfy him yet.

Mr. Gumb had progressed in tailoring far beyond what the California Department of Corrections had taught him in his youth, but this was a true challenge. Even working delicate cabretta leather does not prepare you for really fine work.

Here he had two muslin fitting garments, like white waistcoats, one his exact size and one he had made from measurements he took while Catherine Baker Martin was still unconscious. When he put the smaller one on his tailor's form, the problems were apparent. She was a big girl, and wonderfully proportioned, but she wasn't as big as Mr Gumb, and not nearly so broad across the back.

His ideal was a seamless garment. This was not possible. He was determined, though, that the bodice front be absolutely seamless and without blemish. This meant all figure corrections had to be made on the back. Very difficult. He'd already discarded one fitting muslin and started over. With judicious stretching, he could get by with two underarm darts—not French darts, but vertical inset darts, apexes down. Two waist darts also in the back, just inside his kidneys. He was used to working with only a tiny seam allowance.

His considerations went beyond the visual aspects to the tactile; it was not inconceivable that an attractive person might be hugged.

Mr. Gumb sprinkled talc lightly on his hands and embraced the tailor's form of his body in a natural, comfortable hug.

"Give me a kiss," he said playfully to the empty air where the head should be. "Not *you*, silly," he told the little dog, when she raised her ears.

Gumb caressed the back of the form at the natural reach of his arms. Then he walked behind it to consider the powder marks. Nobody wanted to feel a seam. In an embrace, though, the hands lap over the center of the back. Also, he reasoned, we are accustomed to the center line of a spine. It is not as jarring as an asymmetry in our bodies. Shoulder seams were definitely out, then. A center dart at the top was the answer, apex a little above the center of the shoulder blades. He could use the same seam to anchor the stout yoke built into the lining to provide support. Lycra panels beneath plackets on both sides—he must remember to get the Lycra—and a Velcro closure beneath the placket on the right. He thought about those marvelous Charles James gowns where the seams were staggered to lie perfectly flat.

The dart in back would be covered by his hair, or rather the hair he would have soon.

Mr. Gumb slipped the muslin off the dressmaker's form and started to work.

The sewing machine was old and finely made, an ornate foot-treadle machine that had been converted to electricity perhaps forty years ago. On the arm of the machine was painted in gold-leaf scroll "I Never Tire, I Serve." The foot treadle remained operative, and Gumb started the machine with it for each series of stitches. For fine stitching, he preferred to work barefoot, rocking the treadle delicately with his meaty foot, gripping the front edge of it with his painted toes to prevent overruns. For a while there were only the sounds of the machine, and the little dog snoring, and the hiss of the steam pipes in the warm basement.

When he had finished inserting the darts in the muslin pattern garment, he tried it on in front of the mirrors. The little dog watched from the corner, her head cocked.

He needed to ease it a little under the arm holes. There were a few remaining problems with facings and interfacings. Otherwise it was so nice. It was supple, pliant, bouncy. He could see himself just running up the ladder of a water slide as fast as you please.

Mr. Gumb played with the lights and his wigs for some dramatic effects, and he tried a wonderful choker necklace of shells over the collar line. It would be stunning when he wore a décolleté gown or hostess pajamas over his new thorax.

It was so tempting to just go on with it now, to really get busy, but his eyes were tired. He wanted his hands to be absolutely steady too, and he just wasn't up for the noise. Patiently he picked out the stitches and laid out the pieces. A perfect pattern to cut by.

"Tomorrow, Precious," he told the little dog as he set the beef brains out to thaw. "We'll do it first thing tomooooooorooow. Mommy's gonna be so *beautiful!*"

47

STARLING SLEPT hard for five hours and woke in the pit of the night, driven awake by fear of the dream. She bit the corner of the sheet and pressed her palms over her ears, waiting to find out if she was truly awake and away from it. Silence and no lambs screaming. When she knew she was awake her heart slowed, but her feet would not stay still beneath the covers. In a moment her mind would race, she knew it.

It was a relief when a flush of hot anger rather than fear shot through her.

"Nuts," she said, and put a foot out in the air.

In all the long day, when she had been disrupted by Chilton, insulted by Senator Martin, abandoned, and rebuked by Krendler, taunted by Dr. Lecter and sickened by his bloody escape, and put off the job by Jack Crawford, there was one thing that stung the worst: being called a thief.

Senator Martin was a mother under extreme duress, and she was sick of policemen pawing her daughter's things. She hadn't meant it.

Still, the accusation stuck in Starling like a hot needle.

As a small child, Starling had been taught that thieving is the cheapest, most despicable act short of rape and murder for money. Some kinds of manslaughter were preferable to theft.

As a child in institutions where there were few prizes and many hungers, she had learned to hate a thief.

Lying in the dark, she faced another reason Senator Martin's implication bothered her so.

Starling knew what the malicious Dr. Lecter would say, and it was true: she was afraid there was something tacky that Senator Martin saw in her, something cheap, something thieflike that Senator Martin reacted to. That Vanderbilt bitch.

Dr. Lecter would relish pointing out that class resentment, the buried anger that comes with mother's milk, was a factor too. Starling gave away nothing to any Martin in education, intelligence, drive, and certainly physical appearance, but still it was there and she knew it.

Starling was an isolated member of a fierce tribe with no formal genealogy but the honors list and the penal register. Dispossessed in Scotland, starved out of Ireland, a lot of them were inclined to the dangerous trades. Many generic Starlings had been used up this way, had thumped on the bottom of narrow holes or slid off planks with a shot at their feet, or were commended to glory with a cracked "Taps" in the cold when everyone wanted to go home. A few may have been recalled tearily by the officers on regimental mess nights, the way a man in drink remembers a good bird dog. Faded names in a Bible.

None of them had been very smart, as far as Starling could tell, except for a great-aunt who wrote wonderfully in her diary until she got "brain fever."

They didn't steal, though.

School was the thing in America, don't you know, and the Starlings caught on to that. One of Starling's uncles had his junior college degree cut on his tombstone.

Starling had lived by schools, her weapon the competitive exam, for all the years when there was no place else for her to go.

She knew she could pull out of this. She could be what she had always been, ever since she'd learned how it works: she could be near the top of her class, approved, included, chosen, and not sent away.

It was a matter of working hard and being careful. Her grades would be good. The Korean couldn't kill her in P.E. Her name would be engraved on the big plaque in the lobby, the "Possible Board," for extraordinary performance on the range.

In four weeks she would be a special agent of the Federal Bureau of Investigation.

Would she have to watch out for that fucking Krendler for the rest of her life?

In the presence of the Senator, he had wanted to wash his hands of her. Every time Starling thought about it, it stung. He wasn't positive that he would find evidence in the envelope. That was shocking. Picturing Krendler now in her mind, she saw him wearing Navy oxfords on his feet like the mayor, her father's boss, coming to collect the watchman's clock.

Worse, Jack Crawford in her mind seemed diminished. The man was under more strain than anyone should have to bear. He had sent her in to check out Raspail's car with no support or evidence of authority. Okay, she had asked to go under those terms—the trouble was a fluke. But Crawford had to know there'd be trouble when Senator Martin saw her in Memphis; there would have been trouble even if she hadn't found the fuck pictures.

Catherine Baker Martin lay in this same darkness that held her now. Starling had forgotten it for a moment while she thought about her own best interests.

Pictures of the past few days punished Starling for the lapse, flashed on her in sudden color, too much color, shocking color, the color that leaps out of black when lightning strikes at night.

It was Kimberly that haunted her now. Fat dead Kimberly who had her ears pierced trying to look pretty and saved to have her legs waxed.

Kimberly with her hair gone. Kimberly her sister. Starling did not think Catherine Baker Martin would have much time for Kimberly. Now they were sisters under the skin. Kimberly lying in a funeral home full of state trooper buckaroos.

Starling couldn't look at it anymore. She tried to turn her face away as a swimmer turns to breathe.

All of Buffalo Bill's victims were women, his obsession was women, he lived to hunt women. Not one woman was hunting him full time. Not one woman investigator had looked at every one of his crimes.

Starling wondered if Crawford would have the nerve to use her as a technician when he had to go look at Catherine Martin. Bill would "do her tomorrow," Crawford predicted. *Do her. Do her. Do her.*

"*Fuck* this," Starling said aloud and put her feet on the floor.

"You're over there corrupting a moron, aren't you, Starling?" Ardelia Mapp said. "Sneaked him in here while I was asleep and now you're giving him instructions—don't think I don't hear you."

"Sorry, Ardelia, I didn't—"

"You've got to be a lot more specific with 'em than that, Starling. You can't just say what *you* said. Corrupting morons is just like journalism, you've got to tell 'em *What, When, Where,* and *How.* I think *Why* gets self-explanatory as you go along."

"Have you got any laundry?"

"I thought you said did I have any laundry."

"Yep, I think I'll run a load. Whatcha got?"

"Just those sweats on the back of the door."

"Okay. Shut your eyes, I'm gonna turn on the light for just a second."

It was not the Fourth Amendment notes for her upcoming exam that she piled on top of the clothes basket and lugged down the hall to the laundry room.

She took the Buffalo Bill file, a four-inch-thick pile of hell and pain in a buff cover printed with ink the color of blood. With it was a hotline printout of her report on the Death's-head Moth.

She'd have to give the file back tomorrow and, if she wanted this copy to be complete, sooner or later she had to insert her report. In the warm laundry room, in the washing machine's comforting chug, she took off the rubber bands that held the file together. She laid out the papers on the clothes-folding shelf and tried to do the insert without seeing any of the pictures, without thinking of what pictures might be added soon. The map was on top, that was fine. But there was handwriting on the map.

Dr. Lecter's elegant script ran across the Great Lakes, and it said:

Clarice, does this *random* scattering of sites seem overdone to you? Doesn't it seem *desperately* random? Random past all possible convenience? Does it suggest to you the elaborations of a bad liar?

Ta,

Hannibal Lecter

P.S. Don't bother to flip through, there isn't anything else.

It took twenty minutes of page-turning to be sure there wasn't anything else.

Starling called the hotline from the pay phone in the hall and read the message to Burroughs. She wondered when Burroughs slept.

"I have to tell you, Starling, the market in Lecter information is way down," Burroughs said. "Did Jack call you about Billy Rubin?"

"No."

She leaned against the wall with her eyes closed while he described Dr. Lecter's joke.

"I don't know," he said at last. "Jack says they'll go on with the sex-change clinics, but how hard? If you look at the information in the computer, the way the field entries are styled, you can see that all the Lecter information, yours and the stuff from Memphis, has special prefixes. All the Baltimore stuff or all the Memphis stuff or both can be knocked out of consideration with one button. I think Justice wants to push the button on all of it. I got a memo here suggesting the bug in Klaus's throat was, let's see, 'flotsam.'"

"You'll punch this up for Mr. Crawford, though," Starling said.

"Sure, I'll put it on his screen, but we're not calling him right now. You shouldn't either. Bella died a little while ago."

"Oh," Starling said.

"Listen, on the bright side, our guys in Baltimore took a look at Lecter's cell in the asylum. That orderly, Barney, helped out. They got brass grindings off a bolt head in Lecter's cot where he made his handcuff key. Hang in there, kid. You're gonna come out smelling like a rose."

"Thank you, Mr. Burroughs. Good night."

Smelling like a rose. Putting Vicks VapoRub under her nostrils.

Daylight coming on the last day of Catherine Martin's life.

What could Dr. Lecter mean?

There was no knowing what Dr. Lecter knew. When she first gave him the file, she expected him to enjoy the pictures and use the file as a prop while he told her what he already knew about Buffalo Bill.

Maybe he was always lying to her, just as he lied to Senator Martin. Maybe he didn't know or understand anything about Buffalo Bill.

He sees very clearly—he damn sure sees through me. It's hard to accept that someone can understand you without wishing you well. At Starling's age it hadn't happened to her much.

Desperately random, Dr. Lecter said.

Starling and Crawford and everyone else had stared at the map with its dots marking the abductions and body dumps. It had looked to Starling like a black constellation with a date beside each star, and she knew Behavioral Science had once tried imposing zodiac signs on the map without result.

If Dr. Lecter was reading for recreation, why would he fool with the map? She could see him flipping through the report, making fun of the prose style of some of the contributors.

There was no pattern in the abductions and body dumps, no relationships of convenience, no coordination in time with any known business conventions, any spate of burglaries or clothes-line thefts or other fetish-oriented crimes.

Back in the laundry room, with the dryer spinning, Starling walked her fingers over the map. Here an abduction, there the dump. Here the second abduction, there the dump. Here the third and—But are these dates backward or, no, the second body was discovered first.

That fact was recorded, unremarked, in smudged ink beside the location on the map. The body of the second woman abducted was found first, floating in the Wabash River in downtown Lafayette, Indiana, just below Interstate 65.

The first young woman reported missing was taken from Belvedere, Ohio, near Columbus, and found much later in the Blackwater River in Missouri, outside of Lone Jack. The body was weighted. No others were weighted.

The body of the first victim was sunk in water in a remote area. The second was dumped in a river upstream from a city, where quick discovery was certain.

Why?

The one he started with was well hidden, the second one, not.

Why?

What does "desperately random" mean?

The first, first. What did Dr. Lecter say about "first"? What did anything mean that Dr. Lecter said?

Starling looked at the notes she had scribbled on the airplane from Memphis.

Dr. Lecter said there was enough in the file to locate the killer.

"Simplicity," he said. What about "first," where was first? Here—"First principles" were important. "First Principles" sounded like pretentious bullshit when he said it.

What does he do, Clarice? What is the first and principal thing he does, what need does he serve by killing? He covets. How do we begin to covet? We begin by coveting what we see every day.

It was easier to think about Dr. Lecter's statements when she wasn't feeling his eyes on her skin. It was easier here in the safe heart of Quantico.

If we begin to covet by coveting what we see every day, did Buffalo Bill surprise himself when he killed the first one? Did he do someone close around him? Is that why he hid the first body well, and the second one poorly? Did he abduct the second one far from home and dump her where she'd be found quickly because he wanted to establish early the belief that the abduction sites were random?

When Starling thought of the victims, Kimberly Emberg came first to mind because she had seen Kimberly dead and, in a sense, had taken Kimberly's part.

Here was the first one. Fredrica Bimmel, twenty-two, Belvedere, Ohio. There were two photos. In her yearbook picture she looked large and plain, with good thick hair and a good complexion. In the second photo, taken at the Kansas City morgue, she looked like nothing human.

Starling called Burroughs again. He was sounding a little hoarse by now, but he listened.

"So what are you saying, Starling?"

"Maybe he lives in Belvedere, Ohio, where the first victim lived. Maybe he saw her every day, and he killed her sort of spontaneously. Maybe he just meant to . . . give her a 7-Up and talk about the choir. So he did a good job of hiding the body and then he grabbed another one far from home. He didn't hide that one very well, so it would be found first and the attention would be directed away from him. You know how much attention a missing-person report gets, it gets zip until the body's found."

"Starling, the return's better where the trail is fresh, people remember better, witnesses—"

"That's what I'm saying. He *knows* that."

"For instance, you won't be able to sneeze today without spraying a cop in that last one's hometown—Kimberly Emberg from Detroit. Lot of interest in Kimberly Emberg all of a sudden since little Martin disappeared. All of a sudden they're working the hell out of it. You never heard me say that."

"Will you put it up for Mr. Crawford, about the first town?"

"Sure. Hell, I'll put it on the hotline for everybody. I'm not saying it's bad thinking, Starling, but the town was picked over pretty good as soon as the woman—what's her name, Bimmel, is it?—as soon as Bimmel was identified. The Columbus office worked Belvedere, and so did a lot of locals. You've got it all there. You're not gonna raise much interest in Belvedere or any other theory of Dr. Lecter's this morning."

"All he—"

"Starling, we're sending a gift to U.N.I.C.E.F. for Bella. You want in, I'll put your name on the card."

"Sure, thanks, Mr. Burroughs."

Starling got the clothes out of the dryer. The warm laundry felt good and smelled good. She hugged the warm laundry close to her chest.

Her mother with an armload of sheets.

Today is the last day of Catherine's life.

The black-and-white crow stole from the cart. She couldn't be outside to shoo it and in the room too.

Today is the last day of Catherine's life.

Her father used an arm signal instead of the blinkers when he turned his pickup into the driveway. Playing in the yard, she thought *with his big arm he showed the pickup where to turn, grandly directed it to turn.*

When Starling decided what she would do, a few tears came. She put her face in the warm laundry.

48

CRAWFORD CAME out of the funeral home and looked up and down the street for Jeff with the car. Instead he saw Clarice Starling waiting under the awning, dressed in a dark suit, looking real in the light.

"Send me," she said.

Crawford had just picked out his wife's coffin and he carried in a paper sack a pair of her shoes he had mistakenly brought. He collected himself.

"Forgive me," Starling said. "I wouldn't come now if there were any other time. Send me."

Crawford jammed his hands in his pockets, turned his neck in his collar until it popped. His eyes were bright, maybe dangerous. "Send you where?"

"You sent me to get a feel for Catherine Martin—let me go to the others. All we've got left is to find out how he hunts. How he finds them, how he picks them. I'm as good as anybody you've got at the cop stuff, better at some things. The victims are all women and there aren't any women working this. I can walk in a woman's room and know three times as much about her as a man would know, and *you* know that's a fact. Send me."

"You ready to accept a recycle?"

"Yes."

"Six months of your life, probably."

She didn't say anything.

Crawford stubbed at the grass with his toe. He looked up at her, at the prairie distance in her eyes. She had backbone, like Bella. "Who would you start with?"

"The first one, Fredrica Bimmel, Belvedere, Ohio."

"Not Kimberly Emberg, the one you saw?"

"*He* didn't start with her." *Mention Lecter? No. He'd see it on the hotline.*

"Emberg would be the *emotional* choice, wouldn't she, Starling? Travel's by reimbursement. Got any money?" The banks wouldn't open for an hour.

"I've got some left on my Visa."

Crawford dug in his pockets. He gave her three hundred dollars cash and a personal check.

"Go, Starling. Just to the first one. Post the hotline. Call me."

She raised her hand to him. She didn't touch his face or his hand, there didn't seem to be any place to touch, and she turned and ran for the Pinto.

Crawford patted his pockets as she drove away. He had given her the last cent he had with him.

"Baby needs a new pair of shoes," he said. "My baby doesn't need any shoes." He was crying in the middle of the sidewalk, sheets of tears on his face, a Section Chief of the F.B.I., silly now.

Jeff from the car saw his cheeks shine and backed into an alley where Crawford couldn't see him. Jeff got out of the car. He lit a cigarette and smoked furiously. As his gift to Crawford he would dawdle until Crawford was dried off and pissed off and justified in chewing him out.

ON THE morning of the fourth day, Mr. Gumb was ready to harvest the hide.

He came in from shopping with the last things he needed, and it was hard to keep from running down the basement stairs. In the studio he unpacked his shopping bags, new bias seam-binding, panels of stretchy Lycra to go under the plackets, a box of kosher salt. He had forgotten nothing.

In the workroom, he laid out his knives on a clean towel beside the long sinks. The knives were four: a sway-backed skinning-knife, a delicate drop-point caper that perfectly followed the curve of the index finger in close places, a scalpel for the closest work, and a World War I-era bayonet. The rolled edge of the bayonet is the finest tool for fleshing a hide without tearing it.

In addition he had a Strycker autopsy saw, which he hardly ever used and regretted buying.

Now he greased the head of a wig stand, packed coarse salt over the grease and set the stand in a shallow drip pan. Playfully he tweaked the nose on the face of the wig stand and blew it a kiss.

It was hard to behave in a responsible manner—he wanted to fly about the room like Danny Kaye. He laughed and blew a moth away from his face with a gentle puff of air.

Time to start the aquarium pumps in his fresh tanks of solution. Oh, was there a nice chrysalis buried in the humus in the cage? He poked with his finger. Yes, there was.

The pistol, now.

The problem of killing this one had perplexed Mr. Gumb for days. Hanging her was out because he didn't want the pectoral mottling, and besides, he couldn't risk the knot tearing her behind the ear.

Mr. Gumb had learned from each of his previous efforts, sometimes painfully. He was determined to avoid some of the nightmares he'd gone through before. One cardinal principle: no matter how weak from hunger or faint with fright, they always fought you when they saw the apparatus.

He had in the past hunted young women through the blacked-out basement using his infrared goggles and light, and it was wonderful to do, watching them feel their way around, seeing them try to scrunch into corners. He liked to hunt them with the pistol. He liked to use the pistol. Always they became disoriented, lost their balance, ran into things. He could stand in absolute darkness with his goggles on, wait until they took their hands down from their faces, and shoot them right in the head. Or in the legs first, below the knee so they could still crawl.

That was childish and a waste. They were useless afterward and he had quit doing it altogether.

In his current project, he had offered showers upstairs to the first three, before he booted them down the staircase with a noose around their necks—no problem. But the fourth had been a disaster. He'd had to use the pistol in the bathroom and it had taken an hour to clean up. He thought about the girl, wet, goosebumps on her, and how she shivered when he cocked the pistol. He liked to cock it, snick snick, one big bang and no more racket.

He liked his pistol, and well he should, because it was a very handsome piece, a stainless steel Colt Python with a six-inch barrel. All Python actions are tuned at the Colt custom shop, and this one was a pleasure to feel. He cocked it now and squeezed it off, catching the hammer with his thumb. He loaded the Python and put it on the workroom counter.

Mr. Gumb wanted very much to offer this one a shampoo, because he wanted to watch it comb out the hair. He could learn much for his own grooming about how the hair lay on the head. But this one was tall and probably strong. This one was too rare to risk having to waste the whole thing with gunshot wounds.

No, he'd get his hoisting tackle from the bathroom, offer her a bath, and when she had put herself securely in the hoisting sling he'd bring her halfway up the shaft of the oubliette and shoot her several times low in the spine. When she lost consciousness he could do the rest with chloroform.

That's it. He'd go upstairs now and get out of his clothes. He'd wake up Precious and watch his video with her and then go to work, naked in the warm basement, naked as the day he was born.

He felt almost giddy going up the stairs. Quickly out of his clothes and into his robe. He plugged in his videocassette.

"Precious, come on, Precious. Busybusy day. Come on, Sweetheart." He'd have to shut her up here in the upstairs bedroom while he got through with the noisy part in the basement—she hated the noise and got terribly upset. To keep her occupied, he'd gotten her a whole box of Cheweez while he was out shopping.

"Precious." When she didn't come, he called in the hall, "Precious!" and then in the kitchen, and in the basement, "Precious!" When he called at the door of the oubliette room, he got an answer:

"She's down here, you son of a bitch," Catherine Martin said.

Mr. Gumb sickened all over in a plunge of fear for Precious. Then rage tightened him again and, fists against the sides of his head, he pressed his forehead into the doorframe and tried to get hold of himself. One sound between a retch and a groan escaped him and the little dog answered with a yip.

He went to the workroom and got his pistol.

The string to the sanitation bucket was broken. He still wasn't sure how she'd done it. Last time the string was broken, he'd assumed she'd broken it in an absurd attempt to climb. They had tried to climb it before—they had done every fool thing imaginable.

He leaned over the opening, his voice carefully controlled.

"Precious, are you all right? Answer me."

Catherine pinched the dog's plump behind. It yipped and paid her back with a nip on the arm.

"How's that?" Catherine said.

It seemed very unnatural to Mr. Gumb to speak to Catherine in this way, but he overcame his distaste.

"I'll lower a basket. You'll put her in it."

"You'll lower a telephone or I'll have to break her neck. I don't want to hurt you, I don't want to hurt this little dog. Just give me the telephone."

Mr. Gumb brought the pistol up. Catherine saw the muzzle extending past the light. She crouched, holding the dog above her, weaving it between her and the gun. She heard him cock the pistol.

"You shoot, motherfucker, you better kill me quick or I'll break her fucking neck. I swear to God."

She put the dog under her arm, put her hand around its muzzle, raised its head. "Back off, you son of a bitch." The little dog whined. The gun withdrew.

Catherine brushed the hair back from her wet forehead with her free hand. "I didn't mean to insult you," she said. "Just lower me a phone. I want a live phone. You can go away, I don't care about you, I never saw you. I'll take good care of Precious."

"No."

"I'll see she has everything. Think about her welfare, not just yourself. You shoot in here, she'll be deaf whatever happens. All I want's a live telephone. Get a long extension, get five or six and clip them together—they come with the connections on the ends—and lower it down here. I'd air-freight you the dog anywhere. My family has dogs. My mother loves dogs. You can run, I don't care what you do."

"You won't get any more water, you've had your last water."

"She won't get any either, and I won't give her any from my water bottle. I'm sorry to tell you, I think her leg's broken." This was a lie—the little dog, along with the baited bucket, had fallen onto Catherine and it was Catherine who suffered a scratched cheek from the dog's scrabbling claws. She couldn't put it down or he'd see it didn't limp. "She's in pain. Her leg's all crooked and she's trying to lick it. It just makes me sick," Catherine lied. "I've got to get her to a vet."

Mr. Gumb's groan of rage and anguish made the little dog cry. "You think *she's* in pain," Mr. Gumb said. "You don't know what pain is. You hurt her and I'll scald you."

When she heard him pounding up the stairs Catherine Martin sat down, shaken by gross jerks in her arms and legs. She couldn't hold the dog, she couldn't hold her water, she couldn't hold anything.

When the little dog climbed into her lap she hugged it, grateful for the warmth.

FEATHERS RODE on the thick brown water, curled feathers blown from the coops, carried on breaths of air that shivered the skin of the river. The houses on Fell Street, Fredrica Bimmel's street, were termed waterfront on the weathered realtors' signs because their backyards ended at a slough, a backwater of the Licking River in Belvedere, Ohio, a Rust Belt town of 112,000, east of Columbus.

It was a shabby neighborhood of big, old houses. A few of them had been bought cheap by young couples and renovated with Sears Best enamel, making the rest of the houses look worse. The Bimmel house had not been renovated.

Clarice Starling stood for a moment in Fredrica's backyard looking at the feathers on the water, her hands deep in the pockets of her trenchcoat. There was some rotten snow in the reeds, blue beneath the blue sky on this mild winter day.

Behind her Starling could hear Fredrica's father hammering in the city of pigeon coops, the Orvieto of pigeon coops rising from the water's edge and reaching almost to the house. She hadn't seen Mr. Bimmel yet. The neighbors said he was there. Their faces were closed when they said it.

Starling was having some trouble with herself. At that moment in the night when she knew she had to leave the Academy to hunt Buffalo Bill, a lot of extraneous noises had stopped. She felt a pure new silence in the center of her mind, and a calm there. In a different place, down the front of her, she felt in flashes that she was a truant and a fool.

The petty annoyances of the morning hadn't touched her—not the gymnasium stink of the airplane to Columbus, not the confusion and ineptitude at the rental-car counter. She'd snapped at the car clerk to make him move, but she hadn't felt anything.

Starling had paid a high price for this time and she meant to use it as she thought best. Her time could be up at any moment, if Crawford was overruled and they pulled her credentials.

She should hurry, but to think about why, to dwell on Catherine's plight on this final day, would be to waste the day entirely. To think of her in real time, being processed at this moment as Kimberly Emberg and Fredrica Bimmel had been processed, would jam all other thought.

The breeze fell off, the water still as death. Near her feet a curled feather spun on the surface tension. Hang on, Catherine.

Starling caught her lip between her teeth. If he shot her, she hoped he'd do a competent job of it.

Teach us to care and not to care.

Teach us to be still.

She turned to the leaning stack of coops and followed a path of boards laid on the mud between them, toward the sound of hammering. The hundreds of pigeons were of all sizes and colors; there were tall knock-kneed ones and pouters with their chests stuck out. Eyes bright, heads jerking as they paced, the birds spread their wings in the pale sun and made pleasant sounds as she passed.

Fredrica's father, Gustav Bimmel, was a tall man, flat and wide-hipped with red-rimmed eyes of watery blue. A knit cap was pulled down to his eyebrows. He was building another coop on sawhorses in front of his work shed. Starling smelled vodka on his breath as he squinted at her identification.

"I don't know nothing new to tell you," he said. "The policemen come back here night before last. They went back over my statement with me again. Read it back to me. 'Is that right? Is that right?' I told him, I said hell yes, if that wasn't right I wouldn't have told you in the first place."

"I'm trying to get an idea where the—get an idea where the kidnapper might have seen Fredrica, Mr. Bimmel. Where he might have spotted her and decided to take her away."

"She went into Columbus on the bus to see about a job at that store there. The police said she got to the interview all right. She never came home. We don't know where else she went that day. The F.B.I. got her Master Charge slips, but there wasn't nothing for that day. You know all that, don't you?"

"About the credit card, yes, sir, I do. Mr. Bimmel, do you have Fredrica's things, are they here?"

"Her room's in the top of the house."

"May I see?"

It took him a moment to decide where to lay down his hammer. "All right," he said, "come along."

JACK CRAWFORD'S office in the F.B.I.'s Washington headquarters was painted an oppressive gray, but it had big windows.

Crawford stood at these windows with his clipboard held to the light, peering at a list off a Goddamned fuzzy dot-matrix printer that he'd told them to get rid of.

He'd come here from the funeral home and worked all morning, tweaking the Norwegians to hurry with their dental records on the missing seaman named Klaus, jerking San Diego's chain to check Benjamin Raspail's familiars at the Conservatory where he had taught, and stirring up Customs, which was supposed to be checking for import violations involving living insects.

Within five minutes of Crawford's arrival, F.B.I. Assistant Director John Golby, head of the new interservice task force, stuck his head in the office for a moment to say "Jack, we're all thinking about you. Everybody appreciates you coming in. Has the service been set yet?"

"The wake's tomorrow evening. Service is Saturday at eleven o'clock."

Golby nodded. "There's a U.N.I.C.E.F. memorial, Jack, a fund. You want it to read Phyllis or Bella, we'll do it any way you like."

"Bella, John. Let's make it Bella."

"Can I do anything for you, Jack?"

Crawford shook his head. "I'm just working. I'm just gonna work now."

"Right," Golby said. He waited the decent interval. "Frederick Chilton asked for federal protective custody."

"Grand. John, is somebody in Baltimore talking to Everett Yow, Raspail's lawyer? I mentioned him to you. He might know something about Raspail's friends."

"Yeah, they're on it this morning. I just sent Burroughs my memo on it. The Director's putting Lecter on the Most Wanted. Jack, if you need anything . . ." Golby raised his eyebrows and his hand and backed out of sight.

If you need anything.

Crawford turned to the windows. He had a fine view from his office. There was the handsome old Post Office building where he'd done some of his training. To the left was the old F.B.I. headquarters. At graduation, he'd filed through J. Edgar Hoover's office with the others. Hoover stood on a little box and shook their hands in turn. That was the only time Crawford ever met the man. The next day he married Bella.

They had met in Livorno, Italy. He was Army, she NATO staff, and she was Phyllis then. They walked on the quays and a boatman called "Bella" across the glittering water and she was always Bella to him after that. She was only Phyllis when they disagreed.

Bella's dead. That should change the view from these windows. It wasn't right this view stayed the same. Had to fucking *die* on me. Jesus, kid. I knew it was coming but it *smarts*.

What do they say about forced retirement at fifty-five? You fall in love with the Bureau, but it doesn't fall in love with you. He'd seen it.

Thank God, Bella had saved him from that. He hoped she was

somewhere today and that she was comfortable at last. He hoped she could see in his heart.

The phone was buzzing its intraoffice buzz.

"Mr. Crawford, a Dr. Danielson from—"

"Right." Punch. "Jack Crawford, Doctor."

"Is this line secure, Mr. Crawford?"

"Yes. On this end it is."

"You're not taping, are you?"

"No, Dr. Danielson. Tell me what's on your mind."

"I want to make it clear this has nothing to do with anybody who was ever a patient at Johns Hopkins."

"Understood."

"If anything comes of it, I want you to make it clear to the public he's not a transsexual, he had nothing to do with this institution."

"Fine. You got it. Absolutely." *Come on, you stuffy bastard.* Crawford would have said anything.

"He shoved Dr. Purvis down."

"Who, Dr. Danielson?"

"He applied to the program three years ago as John Grant of Harrisburg, Pennsylvania."

"Description?"

"Caucasian male, he was thirty-one. Six feet one, a hundred and ninety pounds. He came to be tested and did very well on the Wechsler intelligence scale—bright normal—but the psychological testing and the interviews were another story. In fact, his House-Tree-Person and his TAT were spot-on with the sheet you gave me. You let me think Alan Bloom authored that little theory, but it was Hannibal Lecter, wasn't it?"

"Go on with Grant, Doctor."

"The board would have turned him down anyway, but by the time we met to discuss it, the question was moot because the background checks got him."

"Got him how?"

"We routinely check with the police in an applicant's hometown. The Harrisburg police were after him for two assaults on homosexual men. The last one nearly died. He'd given us an address that turned out to be a boarding house he stayed in from time to time. The police got his fingerprints there and a credit-card gas receipt with his license number on it. His name wasn't John Grant at all, he'd just told us that. About a week later he waited outside the building here and shoved Dr. Purvis down, just for spite."

"What was his name, Dr. Danielson?"

"I'd better spell it for you, it's J-A-M-E G-U-M-B."

52

FREDRICA BIMMEL'S house was three stories tall and gaunt, covered with asphalt shingles stained rusty where the gutters had spilled over. Volunteer maples growing in the gutters had stood up to the winter pretty well. The windows on the north side were covered with sheet plastic.

In a small parlor, very warm from a space heater, a middle-aged woman sat on a rug, playing with an infant.

"My wife," Bimmel said as they passed through the room. "We just got married Christmas."

"Hello," Starling said. The woman smiled vaguely in her direction.

Cold in the hall again and everywhere boxes stacked waist-high filling the rooms, passageways among them, cardboard cartons filled with lampshades and canning lids, picnic hampers, back numbers of the *Reader's Digest* and *National Geographic*, thick old tennis rackets, bed linens, a case of dartboards, fiber car-seat covers in a fifties plaid with the intense smell of mouse pee.

"We're moving pretty soon," Mr. Bimmel said.

The stuff near the windows was bleached by the sun, the boxes stacked for years and bellied with age, the random rugs worn bare in the paths through the rooms.

Sunlight dappled the bannister as Starling climbed the stairs behind Fredrica's father. His clothes smelled stale in the cold air. She could see sunlight coming through the sagging ceiling at the top of the stairwell. The cartons stacked on the landing were covered with plastic.

Fredrica's room was small, under the eaves on the third floor.

"You want me anymore?"

"Later, I'd like to talk to you, Mr. Bimmel. What about Fredrica's mother?" The file said "deceased," it didn't say when.

"What do you mean, what about her? She died when Fredrica was twelve."

"I see."

"Did you think that was Fredrica's mother downstairs? After I told you we just been married since Christmas? That what you thought, is it? I guess the law's used to handling a different class of people, missy. She never knew Fredrica at all."

"Mr. Bimmel, is the room pretty much like Fredrica left it?"

The anger wandered somewhere else in him.

"Yah," he said softly. "We just left it alone. Nobody much could wear her stuff. Plug in the heater if you want it. Remember and unplug it before you come down."

He didn't want to see the room. He left her on the landing.

Starling stood for a moment with her hand on the cold porcelain knob. She needed to organize a little, before her head was full of Fredrica's things.

Okay, the premise is Buffalo Bill did Fredrica first, weighted her and hid her well, in a river far from home. He hid her better than the others—she was the only one weighted—because he wanted the later ones found first. He wanted the idea of random selection of victims in widely scattered towns well established before Fredrica, of Belvedere, was found. It was important to take attention away from Belvedere. Because he lives here, or maybe in Columbus.

He started with Fredrica because he coveted her hide. We don't begin to covet with imagined things. Coveting is a very literal sin—we begin to covet with tangibles, we begin with what we see every day. He saw Fredrica in the course of his daily life. He saw her in the course of her daily life.

What was the course of Fredrica's daily life? All right . . .

Starling pushed the door open. Here it was, this still room smelling of mildew in the cold. On the wall, last year's calendar was forever turned to April. Fredrica had been dead ten months.

Cat food, hard and black, was in a saucer in the corner.

Starling, veteran yard-sale decorator, stood in the center of the room and turned slowly around. Fredrica had done a pretty good job with what she had. There were curtains of flowered chintz. Judging from the piped edges, she had recycled some slipcovers to make the curtains.

There was a bulletin board with a sash pinned to it. BHS BAND was printed on the sash in glitter. A poster of the performer Madonna was on the wall, and another of Deborah Harry and Blondie. On a shelf above the desk, Starling could see a roll of the bright self-adhesive wallpaper Fredrica had used to cover her walls. It was not a great job of papering, but better than her own first effort, Starling thought.

In an average home, Fredrica's room would have been cheerful. In this bleak house it was shrill; there was an echo of desperation in it.

Fredrica did not display photographs of herself in the room.

Starling found one in the school yearbook on the small bookcase. Glee Club, Home-Ec Club, Sew 'n' Sew, Band, 4-H Club—maybe the pigeons served as her 4-H project.

Fredrica's school annual had some signatures. "To a great pal," and a "great gal" and "my chemistry buddy," and "Remember the bake sale?!!"

Could Fredrica bring her friends up here? Did she have a friend good enough to bring up those stairs beneath the drip? There was an umbrella beside the door.

Look at this picture of Fredrica, here she's in the front row of the band. Fredrica is wide and fat, but her uniform fits better than the others. She's big and she has beautiful skin. Her irregular features combine to make a pleasant face, but she is not attractive looking by conventional standards.

Kimberly Emberg wasn't what you would call fetching either, not to the mindless gape of high school, and neither were a couple of the others.

Catherine Martin, though, would be attractive to anybody, a big, good-looking young woman who would have to fight the fat when she was thirty.

Remember, he doesn't look at women as a man looks at them. Conventionally attractive doesn't count. They just have to be smooth and roomy.

Starling wondered if he thought of women as "skins," the way some cretins call them "cunts."

She became aware of her own hand tracing the line of credits beneath the yearbook picture, became aware of her entire body, the space she filled, her figure and her face, their effect, the power in them, her breasts above the book, her hard belly against it, her legs below it. What of her experience applied?

Starling saw herself in the full-length mirror on the end wall and was glad to be different from Fredrica. But she knew the difference was a matrix in her thinking. What might it keep her from seeing?

How did Fredrica want to appear? What was she hungry for, where did she seek it? What did she try to do about herself?

Here were a couple of diet plans, the Fruit Juice Diet, the Rice Diet, and a crackpot plan where you don't eat and drink at the same sitting.

Organized diet groups—did Buffalo Bill watch them to find big girls? Hard to check. Starling knew from the file that two of the victims had belonged to diet groups and that the membership rosters had been compared. An agent from the Kansas City office, the F.B.I.'s traditional Fat Boys' Bureau, and some overweight police were sent around to work out at Slenderella, and Diet Center, and join Weight Watchers and other diet denominations in the victims' towns. She didn't know if Catherine Martin belonged to a diet group. Money would have been a problem for Fredrica in organized dieting.

Fredrica had several issues of *Big Beautiful Girl*, a magazine for large women. Here she was advised to "come to New York City, where you can meet newcomers from parts of the world where your size is considered a prized asset." Right. Alternatively, "you could travel to Italy or Germany, where you won't be alone after the first day." You bet. Here's what to do if your toes hang out over the ends of your shoes. Jesus! All Fredrica needed was to meet Buffalo Bill, who considered her size a "prized asset."

How did Fredrica manage? She had some makeup, a lot of skin stuff. Good for you, *use* that asset. Starling found herself rooting for Fredrica as though it mattered anymore.

She had some junk jewelry in a White Owl cigar box. Here was a gold-filled circle pin that most likely had belonged to her late mother. She'd tried to cut the fingers off some old gloves of machine lace, to wear them Madonna-style, but they'd raveled on her.

She had some music, a single-shot Decca record player from the fifties with a jackknife attached to the tone arm with rubber bands for weight. Yard-sale records. Love themes by Zamfir, Master of the Pan Flute.

When she pulled the string to light the closet, Starling was surprised at Fredrica's wardrobe. She had nice clothes, not a great many, but plenty for school, enough to get along in a fairly formal office or even a dressy retail job. A quick look inside them, and Starling saw the reason. Fredrica made her own, and made them well, the seams were bound with a serger, the facings carefully fitted. Stacks of patterns were on a shelf at the back of the closet. Most of them were Simplicity, but there were a couple of Vogues that looked hard.

She probably wore her best thing to the job interview. What had she worn? Starling flipped through her file. Here: last seen wearing a green outfit. Come on, Officer, what the hell is a "green outfit"?

Fredrica suffered from the Achilles' heel of the budget wardrobe—she was short on shoes—and at her weight she was hard on the shoes she had. Her loafers were strained into ovals. She wore Odor-Eaters in her sandals. The eyelets were stretched in her running shoes.

Maybe Fredrica exercised a little—she had some outsized warmups. They were made by Juno.

Catherine Martin also had some fat pants made by Juno.

Starling backed out of the closet. She sat on the foot of the bed with her arms folded and stared into the lighted closet.

Juno was a common brand, sold in a lot of places that handle outsizes, but it raised the question of clothing. Every town of any size has at least one store specializing in clothes for fat people.

Did Buffalo Bill watch fat stores, select a customer and follow her?

Did he go into oversize shops in drag and look around? Every oversize shop in a city gets both transvestites and drag queens as customers.

The idea of Buffalo Bill trying to cross over sexually had just been applied to the investigation very recently, since Dr. Lecter gave Starling his theory. What about his clothes?

All of the victims must have shopped in fat stores—Catherine Martin would wear a twelve, but the others couldn't, and Catherine must have shopped in an oversize store to buy the big Juno sweats.

Catherine Martin could wear a twelve. She was the smallest of the victims. Fredrica, the first victim, was largest. How was Buffalo Bill managing to down-size with the choice of Catherine Martin? Catherine was plenty buxom, but she wasn't that big around. Had

T H O M A S   H A R R I S

he lost weight himself? Might he have joined a diet group lately? Kimberly Emberg was sort of in-between, big, but with a good waist indention . . .

Starling had specifically avoided thinking about Kimberly Emberg, but now the memory swamped her for a second. Starling saw Kimberly on the slab in Potter. Buffalo Bill hadn't cared about her waxed legs, her carefully glittered fingernails: he looked at Kimberly's flat bosom and it wasn't good enough and he took his pistol and blew a starfish in her chest.

The door to the room pushed open a few inches. Starling felt the movement in her heart before she knew what it was. A cat came in, a large tortoiseshell cat with one eye gold, the other blue. It hopped up on the bed and rubbed against her. Looking for Fredrica.

Loneliness. Big lonesome girls trying to satisfy somebody.

The police had eliminated lonely-hearts clubs early. Did Buffalo Bill have another way to take advantage of loneliness? Nothing makes us more vulnerable than loneliness except greed.

Loneliness might have permitted Buffalo Bill an opening with Fredrica, but not with Catherine. Catherine wasn't lonesome.

Kimberly was lonesome. *Don't start this.* Kimberly, obedient and limp, past rigor mortis, being rolled over on the mortician's table so Starling could fingerprint her. *Stop it. Can't stop it.* Kimberly lonesome, anxious to please, had Kimberly ever rolled over obediently for someone, just to feel his heart beat against her back? She wondered if Kimberly had felt whiskers grating between her shoulder blades.

Staring into the lighted closet, Starling remembered Kimberly's plump back, the triangular patches of skin missing from her shoulders.

Staring into the lighted closet, Starling saw the triangles on Kimberly's shoulders outlined in the blue dashes of a dressmaking pattern. The idea swam away and circled and came again, came close enough for her to grab it this time and she did with a fierce pulse of joy: THEY'RE DARTS—HE TOOK THOSE TRIANGLES TO MAKE DARTS

SO HE COULD LET OUT HER WAIST. MOTHERFUCKER CAN SEW. BUFFALO BILL'S TRAINED TO SERIOUSLY SEW —HE'S NOT JUST PICKING OUT READY-TO-WEAR.

What did Dr. Lecter say? "He's making himself a girl suit out of real girls." What did he say to me? "Do you sew, Clarice?" Damn straight I do.

Starling put her head back, closed her eyes for one second. Problem-solving is hunting; it is savage pleasure and we are born to it.

She'd seen a telephone in the parlor. She started downstairs to use it, but Mrs. Bimmel's reedy voice was calling up to her already, calling her to the phone.

MRS. BIMMEL gave Starling the telephone and picked up the fretting baby. She didn't leave the parlor.

"Clarice Starling."

"Jerry Burroughs, Starling—"

"Good, Jerry, listen I think Buffalo Bill can sew. He cut the triangles—just a sec—Mrs. Bimmel, could I ask you to take the baby in the kitchen? I need to talk here. Thank you . . . Jerry, he can sew. He took—"

"Starling—"

"He took those triangles off of Kimberly Emberg to make darts, dressmaking darts, do you know what I'm saying? He's skilled, he's not just making caveman stuff. I.D. Section can search Known Offenders for tailors, sailmakers, drapers, upholsterers—run a scan on the Distinguishing Marks field for a tailor's notch in his teeth—"

"Right, right, right, I'm punching up a line now to I.D. Now listen up—I may have to get off the phone here. Jack wanted me to brief you. We got a name and a place that looks not bad. The Hostage Rescue Team's airborne from Andrews. Jack's briefing them on the scrambler."

"Going where?"

"Calumet City, edge of Chicago. Subject's Jame, like 'Name' with a *J*, last name Gumb, a.k.a. John Grant, WM, thirty-four, one-ninety, brown and blue. Jack got a beep from Johns Hopkins. Your thing—your profile on how he'd be different from a transsexual—it rang the cherries at Johns Hopkins. Guy applied for sex reassignment three years ago. Roughed up a doctor after they turned him down. Hopkins had the Grant alias and a flop address in Harrisburg, Pennsylvania. The cops had a gas receipt with his tag number and we went from there. Big jacket in California as a juvenile—he killed his grandparents when he was twelve and did six years in Tulare Psychiatric. The state let him out sixteen years ago when they shut down the asylum. He disappeared a long time. He's a fag-basher. Had a couple of scrapes in Harrisburg and faded out again."

"Chicago, you said. How do you know Chicago?"

"Customs. They had some paper on the John Grant alias. Customs stopped a suitcase at LAX a couple of years ago shipped from Surinam with live 'pupae'—is that how you say it?—insects anyway, moths, in it. The addressee was John Grant, care of a business in Calumet called—get this—called 'Mr. Hide.' Leather goods. Maybe the sewing fits with that; I'm relaying the sewing to Chicago and Calumet. No home address yet on Grant, or Gumb—the business is closed, but we're close."

"Any pictures?"

"Just the juveniles from Sacramento PD so far. They're not much use—he was twelve. Looked like Beaver Cleaver. The wire room's faxing them around anyway."

"Can I go?"

"No. Jack said you'd ask. They've got two female marshals from Chicago and a nurse to take charge of Martin if they get her. You'd never be in time anyway, Starling."

"What if he's barricaded? It could take—"

"There won't be any standoff. They find him, they fall on him— Crawford's authorized an explosive entry. Special problems with this guy, Starling, he's been in a hostage situation before. His juvenile homicides, they got him in a barricade situation in Sacramento with his grandmother as hostage—he'd already killed his grandfather—and it came out gruesome, let me tell you. He walked her out in front of the cops, they had this preacher talking to him. He's a kid, nobody took the shot. He was behind her and he did her kidneys. Medical attention no avail. At twelve, he did this. So this time no negotiations, no warning. Martin's probably dead already, but say we're lucky. Say he had a lot on his mind, one thing and another he didn't get around to it yet. If he sees us coming, he'll do her right in our faces for spite. Costs him nothing, right? So they find him and—Boom!—the door's down."

The room was too damned hot and it smelled of baby ammonia.

Burroughs was still talking. "We're looking for both names on the entomology magazine subscription lists, Knifemakers Guild, Known Offenders, the works—nobody stands down until it's over. You're doing Bimmel's acquaintances, right?"

"Right."

"Justice says it's a tricky case to make if we don't catch him dirty. We need him with Martin or with something identifiable—something with teeth or fingers, frankly. Goes without saying, if he's dumped Martin already, we need witnesses to put him with a victim before the fact. We can use your stuff from Bimmel regardless . . . Starling, I wish to God this had happened yesterday for more reasons than the Martin kid. They throw the switch on you at Quantico?"

"I think so. They put in somebody else that was waiting out a recycle—that's what they tell me."

"If we get him in Chicago, you made a lot of contribution here. They're hardasses at Quantico like they're supposed to be, but they have to see *that*. Wait a minute."

Starling could hear Burroughs barking, away from the phone. Then he was back again.

"Nothing—they can deploy in Calumet City in forty to fifty-five, depends on the winds aloft. Chicago SWAT's deputized in case they find him sooner. Calumet Power and Light's come up with four possible addresses. Starling, watch for anything they can use up there to narrow it down. You see anything about Chicago or Calumet, get to me fast."

"Righto."

"Now listen—this and I gotta go. If it happens, if we get him in Calumet City, you fall in at Quantico 0800 *mañana* with your Mary Janes shined. Jack's going before the board with you. So is the chief gunny, Brigham. It don't hurt to ask."

"Jerry, one other thing: Fredrica Bimmel had some warmups made by Juno, it's a brand of fat clothes. Catherine Martin had some too, for what it's worth. He might watch fat stores to find large victims. We could ask Memphis, Akron, the other places."

"Got it. Keep smiling."

Starling walked out in the junky yard in Belvedere, Ohio, 380 long miles from the action in Chicago. The cold air felt good on her face. She threw a small punch in the air, rooting hard for the Hostage Rescue Team. At the same time, she felt a little trembly in her chin and cheeks. What the hell was this? What the hell would she have done if she'd found anything? She'd have called the cavalry, the Cleveland field office, and Columbus SWAT, the Belvedere PD too.

Saving the young woman, saving the daughter of Senator Fuck-You Martin and the ones that might come after—truly, that was what mattered. If they did it, everybody was right.

If they weren't in time, if they found something awful, please God they got Buffa—got Jame Gumb or Mr. Hide or whatever they wanted to call the damned thing.

Still, to be so close, to get a hand on the rump of it, to have a good idea a day late and wind up far from the arrest, busted out of school, it all smacked of losing. Starling had long suspected, guiltily, that the Starlings' luck had been sour for a couple of hundred years now—that all the Starlings had been wandering around pissed off and confused back through the mists of time. That if you could find the tracks of the first Starling, they would lead in a circle. This was classic loser thinking, and she was damned if she'd entertain it.

If they caught him because of the profile she'd gotten from Dr. Lecter, it had to help her with the Department of Justice. Starling had to think about that a little; her career hopes were twitching like a phantom limb.

Whatever happened, having the flash on the dressmaking pattern had felt nearly as good as anything ever had. There was stuff to keep here. She'd found courage in the memory of her mother as well as her father. She'd earned and kept Crawford's confidence. These were things to keep in her own White Owl cigar box.

Her job, her duty, was to think about Fredrica and how Gumb might have gotten her. A criminal prosecution of Buffalo Bill would require all the facts.

Think about Fredrica, stuck here all her young life. Where would she look for the exit? Did her longings resonate with Buffalo Bill's? Did that draw them together? Awful thought, that he might have understood her out of his own experience, empathized even, and still helped himself to her skin.

Starling stood at the edge of the water.

Almost every place has a moment of the day, an angle and intensity of light, in which it looks its best. When you're stuck someplace, you learn that time and you look forward to it. This, midafternoon, was probably the time for the Licking River behind Fell Street. Was this the Bimmel girl's time to dream? The pale sun raised enough vapor off the water to blur the old refrigerators and ranges dumped in the brush on the far side of the backwater. The northeast wind, opposite the light, pushed the cattails toward the sun.

A piece of white PVC pipe led from Mr. Bimmel's shed toward the river. It gurgled and a brief rush of bloody water came out, staining the old snow. Bimmel came out into the sun. The front of his trousers was flecked with blood and he carried some pink and gray lumps in a plastic food bag.

"Squab," he said, when he saw Starling looking. "Ever eat squab?"

"No," Starling said, turning back to the water, "I've eaten doves."

"Never have to worry about biting on a shot in these."

"Mr. Bimmel, did Fredrica know anybody from Calumet City or the Chicago area?"

He shrugged and shook his head.

"Had she ever been to Chicago, to your knowledge?"

"What do you mean, 'to my knowledge'? You think a girl of mine's going off to Chicago and I don't know it? She didn't go to *Columbus* I didn't know it."

"Did she know any men that sew, tailors or sailmakers?"

"She sewed for everybody. She could sew like her mother. I don't know of any men. She sewed for stores, for ladies, I don't know who."

"Who was her best friend, Mr. Bimmel? Who did she hang out with?" *Didn't mean to say "hang." Good, it didn't stick him—he's just pissed off.*

"She didn't hang out like the good-for-nothings. She always had some work. God didn't make her pretty, he made her busy."

"Who would you say was her best friend?"

"Stacy Hubka, I guess, since they were little. Fredrica's mother used to say Stacy went around with Fredrica just to have somebody to wait on her, I don't know."

"Do you know where I could get in touch with her?"

"Stacy worked at the insurance, I guess she still does. The Franklin Insurance."

Starling walked to her car across the rutted yard, her head down, hands deep in her pockets. Fredrica's cat watched her from the high window.

CHAPTER

54

F.B.I. CREDENTIALS get a snappier response the farther west you go. Starling's I.D., which might have raised one bored eyebrow on a Washington functionary, got the undivided attention of Stacy Hubka's boss at the Franklin Insurance Agency in Belvedere, Ohio. He relieved Stacy Hubka at the counter and the telephones himself, and offered Starling the privacy of his cubicle for the interview.

Stacy Hubka had a round, downy face and stood five-four in heels. She wore her hair in frosted wings and used a Cher Bono move to brush them back from her face. She looked Starling up and down whenever Starling wasn't facing her.

"Stacy—may I call you Stacy?"

"Sure."

"I'd like you to tell me, Stacy, how you think this might have happened to Fredrica Bimmel—where this man might have spotted Fredrica."

"Freaked me *out*. Get your *skin* peeled off, is that a bummer? Did you see her? They said she was just like *rags*, like somebody let the air out of—"

"Stacy, did she ever mention anybody from Chicago or Calumet City?"

Calumet City. The clock above Stacy Hubka's head worried Starling. If the Hostage Rescue Team makes it in forty minutes, they're just ten minutes from touchdown. Did they have a hard address? Tend to your business.

"Chicago?" Stacy said. "No, we marched at Chicago one time in the Thanksgiving parade."

"When?"

"Eighth grade, that would be what?—nine years ago. The band just went there and back on the bus."

"What did you think last spring when she first disappeared?"

"I just didn't know."

"Remember where you were when you first found it out? When you got the news? What did you think then?"

"That first night she was gone, Skip and me went to the show and then we went to Mr. Toad's for a drink and Pam and them, Pam Malavesi, came in and said Fredrica had disappeared, and Skip goes, *Houdini* couldn't make Fredrica disappear. And then he's got to tell everybody who Houdini was, he's always showing off how much he knows, and we just sort of blew it off. I thought she was just mad at her dad. Did you *see* her house? Is *that* the pits? I mean, wherever she is, I know she's embarrassed you saw it. Wouldn't *you* run away?"

"Did you think maybe she'd run away *with* somebody, did anybody pop into your mind—even if it was wrong?"

"Skip said maybe she'd found her a chubby-chaser. But no, she never had anybody like that. She had one boyfriend, but that's, like, ancient history. He was in the band in the tenth grade, I say 'boyfriend' but they just talked and giggled like a couple of girls and did homework. He was a big sissy though, wore one of these little Greek fisherman's caps? Skip thought he was a, you know, a queer. She got kidded about going out with a queer. Him and his sister got killed in a car wreck though, and she never got anybody else."

"What did you think when she didn't come back?"

"Pam thought maybe it was some Moonies got her, I didn't know,

I was scared every time I thought about it. I wouldn't any more go out at night without Skip, I told him, I said uh-uh, buddy, when the sun goes down, *we* go out."

"Did you ever hear her mention anybody named Jame Gumb? Or John Grant?"

"Ummmm . . . no."

"Do you think she could have had a friend you didn't know about? Were there gaps in time, days when you didn't see her?"

"No. She had a guy, I'd of known, believe me. She never had a guy."

"Do you think it might be just possible, let's say, she could have had a friend and didn't say anything about it?"

"Why wouldn't she?"

"Scared she'd get kidded, maybe?"

"Kidded by us? What are you saying, because of the other time? The sissy kid in high school?" Stacy reddened. "No. No way we would hurt her. I just mentioned that together. She didn't . . . everybody was, like, *kind* to her after he died."

"Did you work with Fredrica, Stacy?"

"Me and her and Pam Malavesi and Jaronda Askew all worked down at the Bargain Center summers in high school. Then Pam and me went to Richards' to see could we get on, it's real nice clothes, and they hired me and then Pam, so Pam says to Fredrica come on they need another girl and she came, but Mrs. Burdine—the merchandizing manager?— she goes, 'Well, Fred*ri*ca, we need somebody that, you know, people can relate to, that they come in and say I want to look like *her*, and you can give them advice how they look in this and stuff. And if you get yourself together and lose your weight I want you to come right back here and see me,' she says. 'But right now, if you want to take over some of our alterations I'll try you at that, I'll put in a word with Mrs. Lippman.' Mrs. Burdine talked in this sweety voice but she turned out to be a bitch really, but I didn't know it right at first."

"So Fredrica did alterations for Richards', the store where you worked?"

"It hurt her feelings, but sure. Old Mrs. Lippman did everybody's alterations. She had the business and she had more than she could do, and Fredrica worked for her. She did them for old Mrs. Lippman. Mrs. Lippman sewed for everybody, made dresses. After Mrs. Lippman retired, her kid or whatever didn't want to do it and Fredrica got it all and just kept sewing for everybody. That's all she did. She'd meet me and Pam, we'd go to Pam's house on lunch and watch *The Young and the Restless* and she'd bring something and be working in her lap the whole time."

"Did Fredrica ever work at the store, taking measurements? Did she meet customers or the wholesale people?"

"Sometimes, not much. I didn't work every day."

"Did Mrs. Burdine work every day, would she know?"

"Yeah, I guess."

"Did Fredrica ever mention sewing for a company called Mr. Hide in Chicago or Calumet City, maybe lining leather goods?"

"I don't know, Mrs. Lippman might have."

"Did you ever see the Mr. Hide brand? Did Richards' ever carry it, or one of the boutiques?"

"No."

"Do you know where Mrs. Lippman is? I'd like to talk to her."

"She died. She went to Florida to retire and she died down there, Fredrica said. I never did know her, me and Skip just picked up Fredrica over there sometimes when she had a bunch of clothes. You might talk to her family or something. I'll write it down for you."

This was extremely tedious, when what Starling wanted was news from Calumet City. Forty minutes was up. The Hostage Rescue Team ought to be on the ground. She shifted so she didn't have to look at the clock, and pressed on.

"Stacy, where did Fredrica buy clothes, where did she get those oversize Juno workout clothes, the sweats?"

"She made just about everything. I expect she got the sweats at Richards', you know, when everybody started wearing them real big, so they came down over tights like that? A lot of places carried them then. She got a discount at Richards' because she sewed for them."

"Did she ever shop at an oversize store?"

"We went in every place to look, you know how you do. We'd go in Personality Plus and she'd look for ideas, you know, flattering patterns for big sizes."

"Did anybody ever come up and bug you around an oversize store, or did Fredrica ever feel somebody had his eye on her?"

Stacy looked at the ceiling for a second and shook her head.

"Stacy, did transvestites ever come into Richards', or men buying large dresses, did you ever run into that?"

"No. Me and Skip saw some at a bar in Columbus one time."

"Was Fredrica with you?"

"Not *hardly*. We'd gone, like, for the weekend."

"Would you write down the oversize places you went with Fredrica, do you think you could remember all of them?"

"Just here, or here and Columbus?"

"Here and Columbus. And Richards' too, I want to talk to Mrs Burdine."

"Okay. Is it a pretty good job, being a F.B.I. agent?"

"I think it is."

"You get to travel around and stuff? I mean places better than this."

"Sometimes you do."

"Got to look good every day, right?"

"Well, yeah. You have to try to look businesslike."

"How do you get into that, being a F.B.I. agent?"

"You have to go to college first, Stacy."

"That's tough to pay for."

"Yeah, it is. Sometimes there are grants and fellowships that help out, though. Would you like me to send you some stuff?"

"Yeah. I was just thinking, Fredrica was so *happy* for me when I got this job. She really got her rocks off—she never had a real office job—she thought this was getting somewhere. *This*—cardboard files and Barry Manilow on the speakers all day—she thought it was hot shit. What did she know, big dummy." Tears stood in Stacy Hubka's eyes. She opened them wide and held her head back to keep from having to do her eyes over.

"How about my list now?"

"I better do it at my desk, I got my word processor and I need my phone book and stuff." She went out with her head back, navigating by the ceiling.

It was the telephone that was tantalizing Starling. The moment Stacy Hubka was out of the cubicle, Starling called Washington collect to get the news.

AT THAT moment, over the southern tip of Lake Michigan, a twenty-four-passenger business jet with civilian markings came off maximum cruise and began the long curve down to Calumet City, Illinois.

The twelve men of the Hostage Rescue Team felt the lift in their stomachs. There were a few elaborately casual tension yawns up and down the aisle.

Team commander Joel Randall, at the front of the passenger compartment, took off the headset and glanced over his notes before he got up to talk. He believed he had the best-trained S.W.A.T. team in the world, and he may have been right. Several of them had never been shot at, but as far as simulations and tests could tell, these were the best of the best.

Randall had spent a lot of time in airplane aisles, and kept his balance easily in the bumpy descent.

"Gentlemen, our ground transportation's courtesy of DEA under-cover. They've got a florist's truck and a plumbing van. So, Vernon, Eddie, into your long handles and your civvies. If we go in behind stun grenades, remember you've got no flash protection on your faces."

Vernon muttered to Eddie, "Make sure you cover up your cheeks."

"Did he say don't moon? I thought he said don't flash," Eddie murmured back.

Vernon and Eddie, who would make the initial approach to the door, had to wear thin ballistic armor beneath civilian clothes. The rest could go in hardshell armor, proof against rifle fire.

"Bobby, make sure and put one of your handsets in each van for the driver, so we don't get fucked up talking to those DEA guys," Randall said.

The Drug Enforcement Administration uses UHF radios in raids, while the F.B.I. has VHF. There had been problems in the past.

They were equipped for most eventualities, day or night: for walls they had basic rappelling equipment, to listen they had Wolf's Ears and a VanSleek Farfoon, to see they had night-vision devices. The weapons with night scopes looked like band instruments in their bulging cases.

This was to be a precise surgical operation and the weapons reflected it—there was nothing that fired from an open bolt.

The team shrugged into their web gear as the flaps went down.

Randall got news from Calumet on his headset. He covered the microphone and spoke to the team again. "Guys, they got it down to two addresses. We take the best one and Chicago S.W.A.T.'s on the other."

The field was Lansing Municipal, the closest to Calumet on the southeast side of Chicago. The plane was cleared straight in. The pilot brought it to a stop in a stink of brakes beside two vehicles idling at the end of the field farthest from the terminal.

There were quick greetings beside the florist's truck. The DEA commander handed Randall what looked like a tall flower arrangement. It was a twelve-pound door-buster sledgehammer, the head wrapped in colored foil like a flowerpot, foliage attached to the handle.

"You might want to deliver this," he said. "Welcome to Chicago."

MR. GUMB went ahead with it in the late afternoon.

With dangerous steady tears standing in his eyes, he'd watched his video again and again and again. On the small screen, Mom climbed the waterslide and whee down into the pool, whee down into the pool. Tears blurred Jame Gumb's vision as though he were in the pool himself.

On his middle a hot-water bottle gurgled, as the little dog's stomach had gurgled when she lay on him.

He couldn't stand it any longer—what he had in the basement holding Precious prisoner, threatening her. Precious was in pain, he knew she was. He wasn't sure he could kill it before it fatally injured Precious, but he had to try. Right now.

He took off his clothes and put on the robe—he always finished a harvest naked and bloody as a newborn.

From his vast medicine cabinet he took the salve he had used on Precious when the cat scratched her. He got out some little Band-Aids and Q-tips and the plastic "Elizabethan collar" the vet gave him to keep her from worrying a sore place with her teeth. He had tongue depressors in the basement to use for splints on her little broken leg, and a tube of Sting-Eez to take the hurt away if the stupid thing scratched her thrashing around before it died.

A careful head shot, and he'd just sacrifice the hair. Precious was worth more to him than the hair. The hair was a sacrifice, an offering for her safety.

Quietly down the stairs now, to the kitchen. Out of his slippers and down the dark basement stairs, staying close to the wall to keep the stairs from creaking.

He didn't turn on the light. At the bottom of the stairs, he took a right into the workroom, moving by touch in the familiar dark, feeling the floor change under his feet.

His sleeve brushed the cage and he heard the soft angry chirp of a brood moth. Here was the cabinet. He found his infrared light and slipped the goggles on his head. Now the world glowed green. He stood for a moment in the comforting burble of the tanks, in the warm hiss of the steam pipes. Master of the dark, queen of the dark.

Moths free in the air left green trails of fluorescence across his vision, faint breaths across his face as their downy wings brushed the darkness.

He checked the Python. It was loaded with .38 Special lead wad-cutters. They would slam into the skull and expand for an instant kill. If it was standing when he shot, if he shot down into the top of the head, the bullet was less likely than a Magnum load to exit the lower jaw and tear the bosom.

Quiet, quiet he crept, knees bent, painted toes gripping the old boards. Silent on the sand floor of the oubliette room. Quiet but not too slow. He didn't want his scent to have time to reach the little dog in the bottom of the well.

The top of the oubliette glowed green, the stones and mortar distinct; the grain of the wooden cover sharp in his vision. Hold the light and lean over. There they were. It was on its side like a giant shrimp. Perhaps asleep. Precious was curled up close against its body, surely sleeping, oh please not dead.

The head was exposed. A neck shot was tempting—save the hair. Too risky.

Mr. Gumb leaned over the hole, the stalk-eyes of his goggles peering down. The Python has a good, muzzle-heavy feel, wonderfully pointable it is. Have to hold it in the beam of infrared. He lined up the sights on the side of its head, just where the hair was damp against the temple.

Noise or smell, he never knew—but Precious up and yipping, jumping straight up in the dark, Catherine Baker Martin doubling around the little dog and pulling the futon over them. Just lumps moving under the futon, he couldn't tell what was dog and what was Catherine. Looking down in infrared, his depth perception was impaired. He couldn't tell which lumps were Catherine.

But he had seen Precious jump. He knew her leg was all right, and at once he knew something more: Catherine Baker Martin wouldn't hurt the dog, any more than he would. Oh, sweet relief. Because of their shared feeling, he could shoot her in the God damned legs and when she clutched her legs, blow her fucking head off. No caution necessary.

He turned on the lights, all the damned lights in the basement, and got the floodlight from the storeroom. He had control of himself, he was reasoning well—on his way through the workroom he remembered to run a little water in the sinks so nothing would clot in the traps.

As he hurried past the stairs, ready to go, carrying the floodlight, the doorbell rang.

The doorbell grating, rasping, he had to stop and think about what it was. He hadn't heard it in years, hadn't even known whether it worked. Mounted in the stairway so it could be heard upstairs and down, clanging now, black metal tit covered with dust. As he looked at it, it rang again, kept ringing, dust flying off it. Someone was at the front, pushing the old button marked SUPERINTENDENT.

They would go away.

He rigged the floodlight.

They didn't go away.

Down in the well, it said something he paid no attention to. The bell was clanging, grating, they were just leaning on the button.

Better go upstairs and peek out the front. The long-barreled Python wouldn't go in the pocket of his robe. He put it on the workroom counter.

He was halfway up the stairs when the bell stopped ringing. He waited a few moments halfway up. Silence. He decided to look anyway. As he went through the kitchen a heavy knock on the back door made him jump. In the pantry near the back door was a pump shotgun. He knew it was loaded.

With the door closed to the basement stairs, nobody could hear it yelling down there, even at the top of its voice, he was sure of that.

Banging again. He opened the door a crack on the chain.

"I tried the front but nobody came," Clarice Starling said. "I'm looking for Mrs. Lippman's family, could you help me?"

"They don't live here," Mr. Gumb said, and closed the door. He had started for the stairs again when the banging resumed, louder this time.

He opened the door on the chain.

The young woman held an I.D. close to the crack. It said Federal Bureau of Investigation. "Excuse me, but I need to talk to you. I want to find the family of Mrs. Lippman. I know she lived here. I want you to help me, please."

"Mrs. Lippman's been dead for ages. She didn't have any relatives that I know of."

"What about a lawyer, or an accountant? Somebody who'd have her business records? Did you know Mrs. Lippman?"

"Just briefly. What's the problem?"

"I'm investigating the death of Fredrica Bimmel. Who are you, please?"

"Jack Gordon."

"Did you know Fredrica Bimmel when she worked for Mrs Lippman?"

"No. Was she a great, fat person? I may have seen her, I'm not sure. I didn't mean to be rude—I was sleeping . . . Mrs. Lippman had a lawyer, I may have his card somewhere, I'll see if I can find it. Do you mind stepping in? I'm freezing and my cat will *streak* through here in a second. She'll be outside like a shot before I can catch her."

He went to a rolltop desk in the far corner of the kitchen, raised the top and looked in a couple of pigeonholes. Starling stepped inside the door and took her notebook out of her purse.

"That horrible business," he said, rummaging the desk. "I shiver every time I think about it. Are they close to catching somebody, do you think?"

"Not yet, but we're working. Mr. Gordon, did you take over this place after Mrs. Lippman died?"

"Yes." Gumb bent over the desk, his back to Starling. He opened a drawer and poked around in it.

"Were there any records left here? Business records?"

"No, nothing at all. Does the F.B.I. have any ideas? The police here don't seem to know the first thing. Do they have a description, or fingerprints?"

Out of the folds in the back of Mr. Gumb's robe crawled a Death's-head Moth. It stopped in the center of his back, about where his heart would be, and adjusted its wings.

Starling dropped her notebook into the bag.

Mister Gumb. Thank God my coat's open. Talk out of here, go to a phone. No. He knows I'm F.B.I., I let him out of my sight he'll kill her. Do her kidneys. They find him, they fall on him. His phone. Don't see it. Not in here, ask for his phone. Get the connection, then throw down on him. Make him lie facedown, wait for the cops. That's it, do it. He's turning around.

"Here's the number," he said. He had a business card.

Take it? No.

"Good, thank you. Mr. Gordon, do you have a telephone I could use?"

As he put the card on the table, the moth flew. It came from behind him, past his head and lit between them, on a cabinet above the sink.

He looked at it. When she didn't look at it, when her eyes never left his face, he knew.

Their eyes met and they knew each other.

Mr. Gumb tilted his head a little to the side. He smiled. "I have a cordless phone in the pantry, I'll get it for you."

No! Do it. She went for the gun, one smooth move she'd done four thousand times and it was right where it was supposed to be, good two-hand hold, her world the front sight and the center of his chest. "Freeze."

He pursed his lips.

"Now. Slowly. Put up your hands."

Move him outside, keep the table between us. Walk him to the front. Facedown in the middle of the street and hold up the badge.

"Mr. Gub—Mr. Gumb, you're under arrest. I want you to walk slowly outside for me."

Instead, he walked out of the room. If he had reached for his pocket, reached behind him, if she'd seen a weapon, she could have fired. He just walked out of the room.

She heard him go down the basement stairs fast, she around the table and to the door at the top of the stairwell. He was gone, the stairwell brightly lit and empty. *Trap.* Be a sitting duck on the stairs.

From the basement then a thin paper cut of a scream.

She didn't like the stairs, didn't like the stairs, Clarice Starling in the quick where you give it or you don't.

Catherine Martin screamed again, he's killing her and Starling went down them anyway, one hand on the bannister, gun arm out, the gun just under her line of vision, floor below bounding over the gunsight, gun arm swinging with her head as she tried to cover the two facing doors open at the bottom of the staircase.

Lights blazing in the basement, she couldn't go through one door without turning her back on the other, do it quick then, to the left toward the scream. Into the sand-floored oubliette room, clearing the doorframe fast, eyes wider than they had ever been. Only place to hide was behind the well, she sliding sideways around the wall, both hands on the gun, arms out straight, a little pressure on the trigger, on around the well and nobody behind it.

A small scream rising from the well like thin smoke. Yipping now, a dog. She approached the well, eyes on the door, got to the rim, looked over the edge. Saw the girl, looked up again, down again, said what she was trained to say, calm the hostage:

"F.B.I., you're safe."

"Safe SHIT, he's got a gun. Getmeout. GETMEOUT."

"Catherine, you'll be all right. Shut up. Do you know where he is?"

"GETMEOUT, I DON'T GIVE A SHIT WHERE HE IS, GETMEOUT."

"I'll get you out. Be quiet. Help me. Be quiet so I can hear. Try and shut that dog up."

Braced behind the well, covering the door, her heart pounded and her breath blew dust off the stone. She could not leave Catherine Martin to get help when she didn't know where Gumb was. She moved up to the door and took cover behind the frame. She could see across the foot of the stairs and into part of the workroom beyond.

Either she found Gumb, or she made sure he'd fled, or she took Catherine out with her, those were the only choices.

A quick look over her shoulder, around the oubliette room.

"Catherine. Catherine. Is there is a ladder?"

"I don't know, I woke up down here. He let the bucket down on strings."

Bolted to a wall beam was a small hand winch. There was no line on the drum of the winch.

"Catherine, I have to find something to get you out with. Can you walk?"

"Yes. Don't leave me."

"I have to leave the room for just a minute."

"You fucking bitch, don't you leave me down here, my mother will tear your goddamn shit brains out—"

"Catherine, shut up. I want you to be quiet so I can hear. To *save* yourself be quiet, do you understand?" Then, louder, "The other officers will be here any minute, now shut up. We won't leave you down there."

He had to have a rope. Where was it? Go see.

Starling moved across the stairwell in one rush, to the door of the workroom, door's the worst place, in fast, back and forth along the near wall until she had seen all the room, familiar shapes swimming in the glass tanks, she too alert to be startled. Quickly through the room, past the tanks, the sinks, past the cage, a few big moths flying. She ignored them.

Approaching the corridor beyond, it blazing with light. The refrigerator turned on behind her and she spun in a crouch, hammer lifting off the frame of the Magnum, eased the pressure off. On to the corridor. She wasn't taught to peek. Head and gun at once, but low. The corridor empty. The studio blazing with light at the end of it. Fast along it, gambling past the closed door, on to the studio door. The room all white and blond oak. Hell to clear from the doorway. Make sure every mannequin is a mannequin, every reflection is a mannequin. Only movement in the mirrors *your* movement.

The great armoire stood open and empty. The far door open onto darkness, the basement beyond. No rope, no ladder anywhere. No lights beyond the studio. She closed the door into the dark part of the basement, pushed a chair under the knob, and pushed a sewing machine against it. If she could be positive he wasn't in this part of the basement, she'd risk going upstairs for a moment to find a phone.

Back down the corridor, one door she'd passed. Get on the side opposite the hinges. All the way open in one move. The door slammed back, nobody behind it. An old bathroom. In it, rope, hooks, a sling. Get Catherine or go for the phone? In the bottom of the well Catherine wouldn't get shot by accident. But if Starling got killed, Catherine was dead too. Take Catherine with her to the phone.

Starling didn't want to stay in the bathroom long. He could come to the door and hose her. She looked both ways and ducked inside for the rope. There was a big bathtub in the room. The tub was almost filled with hard red-purple plaster. A hand and wrist stuck up from the plaster, the hand turned dark and shriveled, the fingernails painted pink. On the wrist was a dainty watch. Starling was seeing everything at once, the rope, the tub, the hand, the watch.

The tiny insect-crawl of the second-hand was the last thing she saw before the lights went out.

Her heart knocked hard enough to shake her chest and arms. *Dizzy dark, need to touch something, the edge of the tub. The bathroom. Get out of the bathroom. If he can find the door he can hose this room, nothing to get behind. Oh dear Jesus, go out. Go out down low and out in the hall. Every light out? Every light. He must have done it at the fuse box, pulled the lever, where would it be? Where would the fuse box be? Near the stairs. Lot of times near the stairs. If it is, he'll come from that way. But he's between me and Catherine.*

Catherine Martin was keening again.

Wait here? Wait forever? Maybe he's gone. He can't be sure no backup's coming. Yes he can. But soon I'll be missed. Tonight. The stairs are in the direction of the screams. Solve it now.

She moved, quietly, her shoulder barely brushing the wall, brushing it too lightly for sound, one hand extended ahead, the gun at waist level, close to her in the confined hallway. Out into the workroom now. Feel the space opening up. Open room. In the crouch in the open room, arms out, both hands on the gun. You know exactly where the gun is, it's just below eye level. Stop, listen. Head and body and arms turning together like a turret. Stop, listen.

In absolute black the hiss of steam pipes, trickle of water.

Heavy in her nostrils the smell of the goat.

Catherine keening.

Against the wall stood Mr. Gumb with his goggles on. There was no danger she'd bump into him—there was an equipment table between them. He played his infrared light up and down her. She was too slender to be of great utility to him. He remembered her hair though, from the kitchen, and it was glorious, and that would only take a minute. He could slip it right off. Put it on himself. He could lean over the well wearing it and tell that thing "Surprise!"

It was fun to watch her trying to sneak along. She had her hip against the sinks now, creeping toward the screams with her gun stuck out. It would have been fun to hunt her for a long time—he'd never hunted one armed before. He would have *thoroughly* enjoyed it. No time for that. Pity.

A shot in the face would be fine and easy at eight feet. Now.

He cocked the Python as he brought it up snick snick and the figure blurred, bloomed, bloomed green in his vision and his gun bucked in his hand and the floor hit him hard in the back and his light was on and he saw the ceiling. Starling on the floor, flash-blind, ears ringing, deafened by the blast of the guns. She worked in the dark while neither could hear, dump the empties, tip it, feel to see they're all out, in with the speedloader, feel it, tip it down, twist, drop it, close the cylinder. She'd fired four. Two shots and two shots. He'd fired once. She found the two good cartridges she'd dumped. Put them where? In the speedloader pouch. She lay still. Move before he can hear?

The sound of a revolver being cocked is like no other. She'd fired at the sound, seen nothing past the great muzzle flashes of the guns. She hoped he'd fire now in the wrong direction, give her the muzzle flash to shoot at. Her hearing was coming back, her ears still rang, but she could hear.

What was that sound? Whistling? Like a teakettle, but interrupted. What was it? Like breathing. Is it me? No. Her breath blew warm off the floor, back in her face. Careful, don't get dust, don't sneeze. It's breathing. It's a sucking chest wound. He's hit in the chest. They'd taught her how to seal one, to put something over it, a rain slicker, a plastic bag, something airtight, strap it tight. Reinflate the lung. She'd hit him in the chest, then. What to do? Wait. Let him stiffen up and bleed. Wait.

Starling's cheek stung. She didn't touch it, if it was bleeding she didn't want her hands slick.

The moaning from the well came again, Catherine talking, crying. Starling had to wait. She couldn't answer Catherine. She couldn't say anything or move.

Mr. Gumb's invisible light played on the ceiling. He tried to move it and he couldn't, any more than he could move his head. A great Malaysian Luna Moth passing close beneath the ceiling picked up the infrared and came down, circled, lit on the light. The pulsing shadows of its wings, enormous on the ceiling, were visible only to Mr. Gumb.

Over the sucking in the dark, Starling heard Mr. Gumb's ghastly voice, choking: "How . . . does . . . it feel . . . to be . . . so beautiful?"

And then another sound. A gurgle, a rattle and the whistling stopped.

Starling knew that sound too. She'd heard it once before, at the hospital when her father died.

She felt for the edge of the table and got to her feet. Feeling her way along, going toward the sound of Catherine, she found the stairwell and climbed the stairs in the dark.

It seemed to take a long time. There was a candle in the kitchen drawer. With it she found the fuse box beside the stairs, jumped when the lights came on. To get to the fuse box and shut off the lights, he must have left the basement another way and come down again behind her.

Starling had to be positive he was dead. She waited until her eyes were well adjusted to the light before she went back in the workroom, and then she was careful. She could see his naked feet and legs sticking out from under the worktable. She kept her eyes on the hand beside the gun until she kicked the gun away. His eyes were open. He was dead, shot through the right side of the chest, thick blood under him. He had put on some of his things from the armoire and she couldn't look at him long.

She went to the sink, put the Magnum on the drain-board and ran cold water on her wrists, wiped her face with her wet hand. No blood. Moths batted at the mesh around the lights. She had to step around the body to retrieve the Python.

At the well she said, "Catherine, he's dead. He can't hurt you. I'm going upstairs and call—"

"No! GET ME OUT. GET ME OUT. GET ME OUT."

"Look here. He's dead. This is his gun. Remember it? I'm going to call the police and the fire department. I'm afraid to hoist you out myself, you might fall. Soon as I call them I'll come back down and wait with you. Okay? Okay. Try to shut that dog up. Okay? Okay."

The local television crews arrived just after the fire department and before the Belvedere police. The fire captain, angered at the glare from the lights, drove the television crews back up the stairs and out of the basement while he rigged a pipe frame to hoist out Catherine

Martin, not trusting Mr. Gumb's hook in the ceiling joist. A fireman went down into the well and put her in the rescue chair. Catherine came out holding the dog, kept the dog in the ambulance.

They drew the line on dogs at the hospital and wouldn't let the dog in. A fireman, instructed to drop it off at the animal shelter, took it home with him instead.

57

THERE WERE about fifty people at National Airport in Washington, meeting the red-eye flight from Columbus, Ohio. Most of them were meeting relatives and they looked sleepy and grumpy enough, with their shirttails sticking out below their jackets.

From the crowd, Ardelia Mapp had a chance to look Starling over as she came off the plane. Starling was pasty, dark under the eyes. Some black grains of gunpowder were in her cheek. Starling spotted Mapp and they hugged.

"Hey, Sport," Mapp said. "You check anything?"

Starling shook her head.

"Jeff's outside in the van. Let's go home."

Jack Crawford was outside too, his car parked behind the van in the limousine lane. He'd had Bella's relatives all night.

"I . . ." he started. "You know what you did. You hit a home run, kid." He touched her cheek. "What's this?"

"Burnt gunpowder. The doctor said it'll work out by itself in a couple of days—better than digging for it."

Crawford took her to him and held her very tight for a moment, just a moment, and then put her away from him and kissed her on the forehead. "You know what you did," he said again. "Go home. Go to sleep. Sleep in. I'll talk to you tomorrow."

The new surveillance van was comfortable, designed for long stakeouts. Starling and Mapp rode in the big chairs in the back.

Without Jack Crawford in the van, Jeff drove a little harder. They made good time toward Quantico.

Starling rode with her eyes closed. After a couple of miles, Mapp nudged her knee. Mapp had opened two short-bottle Cokes. She handed Starling a Coke and took a half-pint of Jack Daniel's out of her purse.

They each took a swig out of their Cokes and poured in a shot of sour mash. Then they stuck their thumbs in the necks of the bottles, shook them, and shot the foam in their mouths.

"Ahhh," Starling said.

"Don't spill that in here," Jeff said.

"Don't worry, Jeff," Mapp said. Quietly to Starling, "You should have seen my man Jeff waiting for me outside the liquor store. He looked like he was passing peach seeds." When Mapp saw the whiskey start to work a little, when Starling sank a little deeper in her chair, Mapp said, "How you doing, Starling?"

"Ardelia, I'm damned if I know."

"You don't have to go back, do you?"

"Maybe for one day next week, but I hope not. The U.S. Attorney came over from Columbus to talk to the Belvedere cops. I did depositions out the wazoo."

"Couple of good things," Mapp said. "Senator Martin's been on the phone all evening from Bethesda—you knew they took Catherine to Bethesda? Well, she's okay. He didn't mess her up in any physical way. Emotional damage, they don't know, they have to watch. Don't worry about school. Crawford and Brigham both called. The hearing's canceled. Krendler asked for his memo back. These people have got a heart like a greasy BB, Starling—you get no slack. You don't have to take the Search-and-Seizure exam at 0800 tomorrow, but you take it Monday, and the P.E. test right after. We'll jam over the weekend."

They finished the half-pint just north of Quantico and dumped the evidence in a barrel at a roadside park.

"That Pilcher, Dr. Pilcher at the Smithsonian, called three times. Made me promise to tell you he called."

"He's not a doctor."

"You think you might do something about him?"

"Maybe. I don't know yet."

"He sounds like he's pretty funny. I've about decided funny's the best thing in men, I'm talking about *aside* from money and your basic manageability."

"Yeah, and manners too, you can't leave that out."

"Right. Give me a son of a bitch with some manners every time."

Starling went like a zombie from the shower to the bed.

Mapp kept her reading light on for a while, until Starling's breathing was regular. Starling jerked in her sleep, a muscle in her cheek twitched, and once her eyes opened wide.

Mapp woke sometime before daylight, the room feeling empty. Mapp turned on her light. Starling was not in her bed. Both of their laundry bags were missing, so Mapp knew where to look.

She found Starling in the warm laundry room, dozing against the slow rump-rump of a washing machine in the smell of bleach and soap and fabric softener. Starling had the psychology background—Mapp's was law—yet it was Mapp who knew that the washing machine's rhythm was like a great heartbeat and the rush of its waters was what the unborn hear—our last memory of peace.

JACK CRAWFORD woke early on the sofa in his study and heard the snoring of his in-laws in his house. In the free moments before the weight of the day came on him, he remembered not Bella's death, but the last thing she'd said to him, her eyes clear and calm: "What's going on in the yard?"

He took Bella's grain scoop and, in his bathrobe, went out and fed the birds as he had promised to do. Leaving a note for his sleeping in-laws, he eased out of the house before sunrise. Crawford had always gotten along with Bella's relatives, more or less, and it helped to have the noise in the house, but he was glad to get away to Quantico.

He was going through the overnight telex traffic and watching the early news in his office when Starling pressed her nose to the glass of the door. He dumped some reports out of a chair for her and they watched the news together without saying anything. Here it came.

The outside of Jame Gumb's old building in Belvedere with its empty storefront and soaped windows covered with heavy gates. Starling hardly recognized it.

"Dungeon of Horrors," the news reader called it.

Harsh, jostled pictures of the well and the basement, still cameras held up before the television camera, and angry firemen waving the photographers back. Moths crazed by the television lights, flying into the lights, a moth on the floor on its back, wings beating down to a final tremor.

Catherine Martin refusing a stretcher and walking to the ambulance with a policeman's coat around her, the dog sticking its face out between the lapels.

A side view of Starling walking fast to a car, her head down, hands in the pockets of her coat.

The film was edited to exclude some of the more grisly objects. In the far reaches of the basement, the cameras could show only the low, lime-sprinkled thresholds of the chambers holding Gumb's tableaux. The body count in that part of the basement stood at six so far.

Twice Crawford heard Starling expel air through her nose. The news went to a commercial break.

"Good morning, Starling."

"Hello," she said, as though it were later in the day.

"The U.S. Attorney in Columbus faxed me your depositions overnight. You'll have to sign some copies for him . . . So you went from Fredrica Bimmel's house to Stacy Hubka, and then to the Burdine woman at the store Bimmel sewed for, Richards' Fashions, and Mrs Burdine gave you Mrs. Lippman's old address, the building there."

Starling nodded. "Stacy Hubka had been by the place a couple of times to pick up Fredrica, but Stacy's boyfriend was driving and her directions were vague. Mrs. Burdine had the address."

"Mrs. Burdine never mentioned a man at Mrs. Lippman's?"

"No."

The television news had film from Bethesda Naval Hospital. Senator Ruth Martin's face framed in a limousine window.

"Catherine was rational last night, yes. She's sleeping, she's sedated right now. We're counting our blessings. No, as I said before, she's suffering from shock, but she's rational. Just bruises, and her finger is broken. And she's dehydrated as well. Thank you." She poked her chauffeur in the back. "Thank you. No, she mentioned the dog to me last night, I don't know what we'll do about it, we already *have* two dogs."

The story closed with a nothing quote from a stress specialist who would be talking with Catherine Martin later in the day to assess emotional damage.

Crawford shut it off.

"How're you hittin' 'em, Starling?"

"Kind of numb . . . you too?"

Crawford nodded, quickly moved along. "Senator Martin's been on the phone overnight. She wants to come see you. Catherine does too, as soon as she can travel."

"I'm always home."

"Krendler too, he wants to come down here. He asked for his memo back."

"Come to think of it, I'm not always home."

"Here's some free advice. Use Senator Martin. Let her tell you how grateful she is, let her hand you the markers. Do it soon. Gratitude has a short half-life. You'll need her one of these days, the way you act."

"That's what Ardelia says."

"Your roomie, Mapp? The Superintendent told me Mapp's set to cram you for your makeup exams on Monday. She just pulled a point and a half ahead of her archrival, Stringfellow, he tells me."

"For valedictorian?"

"He's tough, though, Stringfellow—he's saying she can't hold him off."

"He best bring his lunch."

In the clutter on Crawford's desk was the origami chicken Dr. Lecter had folded. Crawford worked the tail up and down. The chicken pecked.

"Lecter's gone platinum—he's at the top of everybody's Most

Wanted list," he said. "Still, he could be out for a while. Off the post, you need some good habits."

She nodded.

"He's busy now," Crawford said, "but when he's not busy, he'll entertain himself. We need to be clear on this: You know he'd do it to you, just like he'd do anybody else."

"I don't think he'd ever bushwhack me—it's rude, and he wouldn't get to ask any questions that way. Sure he'd do it as soon as I bored him."

"Maintain good habits is all I'm saying. When you go off the post, flag your three-card—no phone queries on your whereabouts without positive I.D. I want to put a trace-alert on your telephone, if you don't mind. It'll be private unless you push the button."

"I don't look for him to come after me, Mr. Crawford."

"But you heard what I said."

"I did. I did hear."

"Take these depositions and look 'em over. Add if you want to. We'll witness your signatures here when you're ready. Starling, I'm proud of you. So is Brigham, so is the Director." It sounded stiff, not like he wanted it to sound.

He went to his office door. She was going away from him, down the deserted hall. He managed to hail her from his berg of grief: "Starling, your father sees you."

JAME GUMB was news for weeks after he was lowered into his final hole.

Reporters pieced together his history, beginning with the records of Sacramento County:

His mother had been carrying him a month when she failed to place in the Miss Sacramento Contest in 1948. The "Jame" on his birth certificate apparently was a clerical error that no one bothered to correct.

When her acting career failed to materialize, his mother went into an alcoholic decline; Gumb was two when Los Angeles County placed him in a foster home.

At least two scholarly journals explained that this unhappy childhood was the reason he killed women in his basement for their skins. The words *crazy* and *evil* do not appear in either article.

The film of the beauty contest that Jame Gumb watched as an adult was real footage of his mother, but the woman in the swimming pool film was not his mother, comparative measurements revealed.

Gumb's grandparents retrieved him from an unsatisfactory foster home when he was ten, and he killed them two years later.

Tulare Vocational Rehabilitation taught Gumb to be a tailor during

his years at the psychiatric hospital. He demonstrated definite aptitude
for the work.

Gumb's employment record is broken and incomplete. Reporters
found at least two restaurants where he worked off the books, and he
worked sporadically in the clothing business. It has not been proven
that he killed during this period, but Benjamin Raspail said he did.

He was working at the curio store where the butterfly ornaments
were made when he met Raspail, and he lived off the musician for
some time. It was then that Gumb became obsessed with moths and
butterflies and the changes they go through.

After Raspail left him, Gumb killed Raspail's next lover, Klaus,
beheaded and partially flayed him.

Later he dropped in on Raspail in the East. Raspail, ever thrilled
by bad boys, introduced him to Dr. Lecter.

This was proven in the week after Gumb's death when the F.B.I.
seized from Raspail's next of kin the tapes of Raspail's therapy sessions
with Dr. Lecter.

Years ago, when Dr. Lecter was declared insane, the therapy-session
tapes had been turned over to the families of the victims to be
destroyed. But Raspail's wrangling relatives kept the tapes, hoping
to use them to attack Raspail's will. They had lost interest listening
to the early tapes, which are only Raspail's boring reminiscences of
school life. After the news coverage of Jame Gumb, the Raspail family
listened to the rest. When the relatives called the lawyer Everett Yow
and threatened to use the tapes in a renewed assault on Raspail's will,
Yow called Clarice Starling.

The tapes include the final session, when Lecter killed Raspail.
More important, they reveal how much Raspail told Lecter about
Jame Gumb:

Raspail told Dr. Lecter that Gumb was obsessed with moths, that he
had flayed people in the past, that he had killed Klaus, that he had a
job with the Mr. Hide leather-goods company in Calumet City, but

was taking money from an old lady in Belvedere, Ohio, who had made linings for Mr. Hide, Inc. One day Gumb would take everything the old lady had, Raspail predicted.

"When Lecter read that the first victim was from Belvedere and she was flayed, he knew who was doing it," Crawford told Starling as they listened together to the tape. "He'd have given you Gumb and looked like a genius if Chilton had stayed out of it."

"He hinted to me by writing in the file that the sites were too random," Starling said. "And in Memphis he asked me if I sew. What did he want to happen?"

"He wanted to amuse himself," Crawford said. "He's been amusing himself for a long, long time."

No tape of Jame Gumb was ever found, and his activities in the years after Raspail's death were established piecemeal through business correspondence, gas receipts, interviews with boutique owners.

When Mrs. Lippman died on a trip to Florida with Gumb, he inherited everything—the old building with its living quarters and empty storefront and vast basement, and a comfortable amount of money. He stopped working for Mr. Hide, but maintained an apartment in Calumet City for a while, and used the business address to receive packages in the John Grant name. He kept favored customers, and continued to travel to boutiques around the country, as he had for Mr. Hide, measuring for custom garments he made in Belvedere. He used his trips to scout for victims and to dump them when they were used up—the brown van droning for hours on the Interstate with finished leather garments swaying on racks in the back above the rubberized body bag on the floor.

He had the wonderful freedom of the basement. Room to work and play. At first it was only games—hunting young women through the black warren, creating amusing tableaux in remote rooms and sealing them up, opening the doors again only to throw in a little lime.

Fredrica Bimmel began to help Mrs. Lippman in the last year of the old lady's life. Fredrica was picking up sewing at Mrs. Lippman's when she met Jame Gumb. Fredrica Bimmel was not the first young woman he killed, but she was the first one he killed for her skin.

Fredrica Bimmel's letters to Gumb were found among his things.

Starling could hardly read the letters, because of the hope in them, because of the dreadful need in them, because of the endearments from Gumb that were implied in her responses: "Dearest Secret Friend in my Breast, I love you!—I didn't *ever* think I'd get to say that, and it is best of all to get to say it *back*."

When did he reveal himself? Had she discovered the basement? How did her face look when he changed, how long did he keep her alive?

Worst, Fredrica and Gumb truly were friends to the last; she wrote him a note from the pit.

The tabloids changed Gumb's nickname to Mr. Hide and, sick because they hadn't thought of the name themselves, virtually started over with the story.

Safe in the heart of Quantico, Starling did not have to deal with the press, but the tabloid press dealt with her.

From Dr. Frederick Chilton, the *National Tattler* bought the tapes of Starling's interview with Dr. Hannibal Lecter. The *Tattler* expanded on their conversations for their "Bride of Dracula" series and implied that Starling had made frank sexual revelations to Lecter in exchange for information, spurning an offer to Starling from *Velvet Talks: The Journal of Telephone Sex.*

People magazine did a short, pleasant item on Starling, using yearbook pictures from the University of Virginia and from the Lutheran Home at Bozeman. The best picture was of the horse, Hannah, in her later years, drawing a cart full of children.

Starling cut out the picture of Hannah and put it in her wallet. It was the only thing she saved.

She was healing.

60

ARDELIA MAPP was a great tutor—she could spot a test question in a lecture farther than a leopard can see a limp—but she was not much of a runner. She told Starling it was because she was so weighted with facts.

She had fallen behind Starling on the jogging trail and caught up at the old DC-6 the F.B.I. uses for hijack simulations. It was Sunday morning. They had been on the books for two days, and the pale sun felt good.

"So what did Pilcher say on the phone?" Mapp said, leaning against the landing gear.

"He and his sister have this place on the Chesapeake."

"Yeah, and?"

"His sister's there with her kids and dogs and maybe her husband."

"So?"

"They're in one end of the house—it's a big old dump on the water they inherited from his grandmother."

"Cut to the chase."

"Pilch has the other end of the house. Next weekend, he wants us to go. Lots of rooms, he says. 'As many rooms as anybody might need,' I believe is the way he put it. His sister would call and invite me, he said."

"No kidding. I didn't know people did that anymore."

"He did this nice scenario—no hassles, bundle up and walk on the beach, come in and there's a fire going, dogs jump all over you with their big sandy paws."

"Idyllic, umm-humm, big sandy paws, go on."

"It's kind of much, considering we've never had a date, even. He claims it's best to sleep with two or three big dogs when it gets really cold. He says they've got enough dogs for everybody to have a couple."

"Pilcher's setting you up for the old dog-suit trick, you snapped to that, didn't you?"

"He claims to be a good cook. His sister says he is."

"Oh, she called already."

"Yep."

"How'd she sound?"

"Okay. Sounded like she was in the other end of the house."

"What did you tell her?"

"I said, 'Yes, thank you very much,' is what I said."

"Good," Mapp said. "That's very good. Eat some crabs. Grab Pilcher and smooch him on his face, go wild."

DOWN THE deep carpet in the corridor of the Marcus Hotel, a room-service waiter trundled a cart.

At the door of suite 91, he stopped and rapped softly on the door with his gloved knuckle. He cocked his head and rapped again to be heard above the music from within—Bach, *Two- and Three-Part Inventions*, Glenn Gould at the piano.

"Come."

The gentleman with the bandage across his nose was in a dressing gown, writing at the desk.

"Put it by the windows. May I see the wine?"

The waiter brought it. The gentleman held it under the light of his desk lamp, touched the neck to his cheek.

"Open it, but leave it off the ice," he said, and wrote a generous tip across the bottom of the bill. "I won't taste it now."

He did not want the waiter handing him wine to taste—he found the smell of the man's watchband objectionable.

Dr. Lecter was in an excellent humor. His week had gone well. His appearance was coming right along, and as soon as a few small discolorations cleared, he could take off his bandages and pose for passport photos.

The actual work he was doing himself—minor injections of silicon in his nose. The silicon gel was not a prescription item, but the hypodermics and the Novocaine were. He got around this difficulty by pinching a prescription off the counter of a busy pharmacy near the hospital. He blanked out the chicken scratches of the legitimate physician with typist's correction fluid and photocopied the blank prescription form. The first prescription he wrote was a copy of the one he stole, and he returned it to the pharmacy, so nothing was missing.

The palooka effect in his fine features was not pleasing, and he knew the silicon would move around if he wasn't careful, but the job would do until he got to Rio.

When his hobbies began to absorb him—long before his first arrest—Dr. Lecter had made provisions for a time when he might be a fugitive. In the wall of a vacation cottage on the banks of the Susquehanna River were money and the credentials of another identity, including a passport and the cosmetic aids he'd worn in the passport photos. The passport would have expired by now, but it could be renewed very quickly.

Preferring to be herded through customs with a big tour badge on his chest, he'd already signed up for a ghastly sounding tour called "South American Splendor" that would take him as far as Rio.

He reminded himself to write a check on the late Lloyd Wyman for the hotel bill and get the extra five days' lead while the check plodded through the bank, rather than sending an Amex charge into the computer.

This evening he was catching up on his correspondence, which he would have to send through a remailing service in London.

First, he sent to Barney a generous tip and a thank-you note for his many courtesies at the asylum.

Next, he dropped a note to Dr. Frederick Chilton in federal protective custody, suggesting that he would be paying Dr. Chilton a visit in the near future. After this visit, he wrote, it would make sense for the hospital to tattoo feeding instructions on Chilton's forehead to save paperwork.

Last, he poured himself a glass of the excellent Batard-Montrachet and addressed Clarice Starling:

Well, Clarice, have the lambs stopped screaming?

You owe me a piece of information, you know, and that's what I'd like.

An ad in the national edition of the *Times* and in the *International Herald-Tribune* on the first of any month will be fine. Better put it in the *China Mail* as well.

I won't be surprised if the answer is yes and no. The lambs will stop for now. But, Clarice, you judge yourself with all the mercy of the dungeon scales at Threave; you'll have to earn it again and again, the blessed silence. Because it's the plight that drives you, seeing the plight, and the plight will not end, ever.

I have no plans to call on you, Clarice, the world being more interesting with you in it. Be sure you extend me the same courtesy.

Dr. Lecter touched his pen to his lips. He looked out at the night sky and smiled.

I have windows.

Orion is above the horizon now, and near it Jupiter, brighter than it will ever be again before the year 2000. (I have no intention of telling you the time and how high it is.) But I expect you can see it too. Some of our stars are the same.

Clarice.

Hannibal Lecter

Far to the east, on the Chesapeake shore, Orion stood high in the clear night, above a big old house, and a room where a fire is banked for the night, its light pulsing gently with the wind above the chimneys. On a large bed there are many quilts and on the quilts and under them are several large dogs. Additional mounds beneath the covers may or may not be Noble Pilcher, it is impossible to determine in the ambient light. But the face on the pillow, rosy in the firelight, is certainly that of Clarice Starling, and she sleeps deeply, sweetly, in the silence of the lambs.

Hannibal

I

WASHINGTON, D.C.

You would think that such a day
would tremble to begin . . .

CLARICE STARLING's Mustang boomed up the entrance ramp at the Bureau of Alcohol, Tobacco and Firearms on Massachusetts Avenue, a headquarters rented from the Reverend Sun Myung Moon in the interest of economy.

The strike force waited in three vehicles, a battered undercover van to lead and two black SWAT vans behind it, manned and idling in the cavernous garage.

Starling hoisted the equipment bag out of her car and ran to the lead vehicle, a dirty white panel van with MARCELL'S CRAB HOUSE signs stuck on the sides.

Through the open back doors of the van, four men watched Starling coming. She was slender in her fatigues and moving fast under the weight of her equipment, her hair shining in the ghastly fluorescent lights.

"Women. Always late," a D.C. police officer said.

BATF Special Agent John Brigham was in charge.

"She's not late—I didn't beep her until we got the squeal," Brigham said. "She must have hauled ass from Quantico—Hey, Starling, pass me the bag."

She gave him a fast high five. "Hey, John."

Brigham spoke to the scruffy undercover officer at the wheel and the van was rolling before the back doors closed, out into the pleasant fall afternoon.

Clarice Starling, a veteran of surveillance vans, ducked under the eyepiece of the periscope and took a seat in the back as close as possible to the hundred-fifty-pound block of dry ice that served as air-conditioning when they had to lurk with the engine turned off.

The old van had the monkey-house smell of fear and sweat that never scrubs out. It had borne many labels in its time. The dirty and faded signs on the doors were thirty minutes old. The bullet holes plugged with Bond-O were older.

The back windows were one-way mirror, appropriately tarnished. Starling could watch the big black SWAT vans following. She hoped they wouldn't spend hours buttoned down in the vans.

The male officers looked her over whenever her face was turned to the window.

FBI Special Agent Clarice Starling, thirty-two, always looked her age and she always made that age look good, even in fatigues.

Brigham retrieved his clipboard from the front passenger seat.

"How come you always catch this crap, Starling?" he said, smiling.

"Because you keep asking for me," she said.

"For this I need you. But I see you serving warrants on jump-out squads, for Christ's sake. I don't ask, but somebody at Buzzard's Point hates you, I think. You should come to work with me. These are my guys, Agents Marquez Burke and John Hare, and this is Officer Bolton from the D.C. Police Department."

A composite raid team of the Bureau of Alcohol, Tobacco and Firearms, the Drug Enforcement Administration SWAT teams and the FBI was the force-fit product of budget constraints in a time when even the FBI Academy was closed for lack of funding.

Burke and Hare looked like agents. The D.C. policeman, Bolton, looked like a bailiff. He was about forty-five, overweight and yeasty.

The Mayor of Washington, anxious to appear tough on drugs after his own drug conviction, insisted the D.C. police share credit for every major raid in the city of Washington. Hence, Bolton.

"The Drumgo posse's cooking today," Brigham said.

"Evelda Drumgo, I knew it," Starling said without enthusiasm.

Brigham nodded. "She's opened an ice plant beside the Feliciana Fish Market on the river. Our guy says she's cooking a batch of crystal today. And she's got reservations to Grand Cayman tonight. We can't wait."

Crystal methamphetamine, called "ice" on the street, provides a short powerful high and is murderously addictive.

"The dope's DEA business but we need Evelda on interstate transportation of Class Three weapons. Warrant specifies a couple of Beretta submachine guns and some MAC 10s, and she knows where a bunch more are. I want you to concentrate on Evelda, Starling. You've dealt with her before. These guys will back you up."

"We got the easy job," Officer Bolton said with some satisfaction.

"I think you better tell them about Evelda, Starling," Brigham said.

Starling waited while the van rattled over some railroad tracks. "Evelda will fight you," she said. "She doesn't look like it—she was a model—but she'll fight you. She's Dijon Drumgo's widow. I arrested her twice on RICO warrants, the first time with Dijon.

"This last time she was carrying a nine-millimeter with three magazines and Mace in her purse and she had a balisong knife in her bra. I don't know what she's carrying now.

"The second arrest, I asked her very politely to give it up and she did. Then in D.C. detention, she killed an inmate named Marsha Valentine with a spoon shank. So you don't know . . . her face is hard to read. Grand jury found self-defense.

"She beat the first RICO count and pled the other one down. Some weapons charges were dropped because she had infant children and her husband had just been killed in the Pleasant Avenue drive-by, maybe by the Spliffs.

"I'll ask her to give it up. I hope she will—we'll give her a show. But—listen to me—if we have to subdue Evelda Drumgo, I want some real help. Never mind watching my back, I want some weight on her. Gentlemen, don't think you're going to watch me and Evelda mud-wrestling."

There was a time when Starling would have deferred to these men. Now they didn't like what she was saying, and she had seen too much to care.

"Evelda Drumgo is connected through Dijon to the Trey-Eight Crips," Brigham said. "She's got Crip security, our guy says, and the Crips are distributing on the coast. It's security against the Spliffs, mainly. I don't know what the Crips will do when they see it's us. They don't cross the G if they can help it."

"You should know—Evelda's HIV positive," Starling said. "Dijon gave it to her off a needle. She found out in detention and flipped out. She killed Marsha Valentine that day and she fought the guards in jail. If she's not armed and she fights, you can expect to get hit with whatever fluid she has to throw. She'll spit and bite, she'll wet and defecate on you if you try to pat her down, so gloves and masks are SOP. If you put her in a patrol car, when you put your hand on her head, watch out for a needle in her hair and secure her feet."

Burke's and Hare's faces were growing long. Officer Bolton appeared unhappy. He pointed with his wattled chin at Starling's main sidearm, a well-worn Colt .45 Government Model with a strip of skateboard tape on the grip, riding in a Yaqui slide behind her right hip. "You go around with that thing cocked all the time?" he wanted to know.

"Cocked and locked, every minute of my day," Starling said.

"Dangerous," Bolton said.

"Come out to the range and I'll explain it to you, Officer."

Brigham broke it up. "Bolton, I coached Starling when she was interservice combat pistol champion three years straight. Don't worry about her weapon. Those guys from the Hostage Rescue Team, the Velcro Cowboys, what did they call you after you beat their ass, Starling? Annie Oakley?"

"Poison Oakley," she said, and looked out the window.

Starling felt pierced and lonesome in this goat-smelling surveillance van crowded with men. Chaps, Brut, Old Spice, sweat and leather. She felt some fear, and it tasted like a penny under her tongue. *A mental image: her father, who smelled of tobacco and strong soap, peeling an orange with his pocketknife, the tip of the blade broken off square, sharing the orange with her in the kitchen. The taillights of her father's pickup disappearing as he went off on the night-marshal patrol that killed him. His clothes in the closet. His square-dancing shirt. Some nice stuff in her closet now she never got to wear. Sad party clothes on hangers, like toys in the attic.*

"About another ten minutes," the driver called back.

Brigham looked out the windshield and checked his watch. "Here's the layout," he said. He had a crude diagram drawn hastily with a Magic Marker, and a blurry floor plan faxed to him by the Department of Buildings. "The fish market building is in a line of stores and warehouses along the riverbank. Parcell Street dead-ends into Riverside Avenue in this small square in front of the fish market.

"See, the building with the fish market backs on the water. They've got a dock back there that runs all along the back of the building, right here. Beside the fish market on the ground floor, that's Evelda's lab. Entrance here in front, just beside the fish market awning. Evelda will have the watchers out while she's cooking the dope, at least three blocks around. They've tipped her before in time for her to flush her stuff. So—a regular DEA incursion team in the third van is going in from a fishing boat on the dock side at fifteen hundred hours. We can get closer than anybody in this van, right up to the stret door a couple of minutes before the raid. If Evelda comes out the front, we get her. If she stays in, we hit this streetside door right after they hit the other side. Second van's our backup, seven guys, they come in at fifteen hundred unless we call first."

"We're doing the door how?" Starling said.

Burke spoke up. "If it sounds quiet, the ram. If we hear flash-bangs or gunfire, it's 'Avon calling.'" Burke patted his shotgun.

Starling had seen it done before—"Avon calling" is a three-inch magnum shotgun shell loaded with fine powdered lead to blow the lock out without injuring people inside.

"Evelda's kids? Where are they?" Starling said.

"Our informant saw her drop them off at day care," Brigham said. "Our informant's close to the family situation, like, he's very close, as close as you can get with safe sex."

Brigham's radio chirped in his earphone and he searched the part of the sky he could see out the back window. "Maybe he's just doing traffic," he said into his throat microphone. He called to the driver, "Strike Two saw a news helicopter a minute ago. You seen anything?"

"No."

"He better be doing traffic. Let's saddle up and button up."

One hundred and fifty pounds of dry ice will not keep five humans cool in the back of a metal van on a warm day, especially when they are putting on body armor. When Bolton raised his arms, he demonstrated that a splash of Canoe is not the same as a shower.

Clarice Starling had sewn shoulder pads inside her fatigue shirt to take the weight of the Kevlar vest, hopefully bulletproof. The vest had the additional weight of a ceramic plate in the back as well as the front.

Tragic experience had taught the value of the plate in the back. Conducting a forcible entry raid with a team you do not know, of people with various levels of training, is a dangerous enterprise.

Friendly fire can smash your spine as you go in ahead of a green and frightened column.

Two miles from the river, the third van dropped off to take the DEA incursion team to a rendezvous with their fishing boat, and the backup van dropped a discreet distance behind the white undercover vehicle.

The neighborhood was getting scruffy. A third of the buildings were boarded up, and burned-out cars rested on crates beside the curbs. Young men idled on the corners in front of bars and small markets. Children played around a burning mattress on the sidewalk.

If Evelda's security was out, it was well concealed among the regulars on the sidewalk. Around the liquor stores and in the grocery parking lots, men sat in cars talking.

A low-rider Impala convertible with four young African-American men in it pulled into the light traffic and cruised along behind the van. The low-riders hopped the front end off the pavement for the benefit of the girls they passed and the thump of their stereo buzzed the sheet metal in the van.

Watching through the one-way glass of the back window, Starling could see the young men in the convertible were not a threat—a Crip gunship is almost always a powerful, full-sized sedan or station wagon, old enough to blend into the neighborhood, and the back windows roll all the way down. It carries a crew of three, sometimes four. A basketball team in a Buick can look sinister if you don't keep your mind right.

While they waited at a traffic light, Brigham pulled the cover off the eyepiece of the periscope and tapped Bolton on the knee.

"Look around and see if there are any local celebrities on the sidewalk," Brigham said.

The objective lens of the periscope is concealed in a roof ventilator. It only sees sideways.

Bolton made a full rotation and stopped, rubbing his eyes. "Thing shakes too much with the motor running," he said.

Brigham checked by radio with the boat team. "Four hundred meters downstream and closing," he repeated to his crew in the van.

The van caught a red light a block away on Parcell Street and sat facing the market for what seemed a long time. The driver turned as though checking his right mirror and talked out of the corner of his mouth to Brigham. "Looks like not many people buying fish. Here we go."

The light changed and at 2:57 P.M., exactly three minutes before zero hour, the battered undercover van stopped in front of the Feliciana Fish Market, in a good spot by the curb.

In the back they heard the ratchet as the driver set the hand brake.

Brigham relinquished the periscope to Starling. "Check it out."

Starling swept the periscope across the front of the building. Tables and counters of fish on ice glittered beneath a canvas awning on the pavement. Snappers up from the Carolina banks were arranged artfully in schools on the shaved ice, crabs moved their legs in open crates and lobsters climbed over one another in a tank. The smart fishmonger had moisture pads over the eyes of his bigger fish to keep them bright until the evening wave of cagey Caribbean-born housewives came to sniff and peer.

Sunlight made a rainbow in the spray of water from the fish-cleaning table outside, where a Latin-looking man with big forearms cut up a mako shark with graceful strokes of his curved knife and hosed the big fish down with a powerful handheld spray. The bloody water ran down the gutter and Starling could hear it running under the van.

Starling watched the driver talk to the fishmonger, ask him a question. The fishmonger looked at his watch, shrugged, pointed out a local lunch place. The driver poked around the market for a minute, lit a cigarette and walked off in the direction of the café.

A boom box in the market was playing "La Macarena" loud enough for Starling to hear it clearly in the van; she would never again in her life be able to endure the song.

The door that mattered was on the right, a double metal door in a metal casement with a single concrete step.

Starling was about to give up the periscope when the door opened. A large white man in a luau shirt and sandals came out. He had a satchel across his chest. His other hand was behind the satchel. A wiry black man came out behind him carrying a raincoat.

"Heads up," Starling said.

Behind the two men, with her long Nefertiti neck and handsome face visible over their shoulders, came Evelda Drumgo.

"Evelda's coming out behind two guys, looks like they're both packing," Starling said.

She couldn't give up the periscope fast enough to keep Brigham from bumping her. Starling pulled on her helmet.

Brigham was on the radio. "Strike One to all units. Showdown. Showdown. She's out this side, we're moving.

"Put 'em on the ground as quietly as we can," Brigham said. He racked the slide on his riot gun. "Boat's here in thirty seconds, let's do it."

Starling first out on the ground, Evelda's braids flying out as her head spun toward her. Starling conscious of the men beside her, guns out, barking "Down on the ground, down on the ground!"

Evelda stepping out from between the two men.

Evelda was carrying a baby in a carrier slung around her neck.

"Wait, wait, don't want any trouble," she said to the men beside her. "Wait, wait." She strode forward, posture regal, holding the baby high in front of her at the extent of the sling, blanket hanging down.

Give her a place to go. Starling holstered her weapon by touch, extended her arms, hands open. "Evelda! Give it up. Come to me."

Behind Starling, the roar of a big V8 and squeal of tires. She couldn't turn around. *Be the backup.*

Evelda ignoring her, walking toward Brigham, the baby blanket fluttered as the MAC 10 went off behind it and Brigham went down, his face shield full of blood.

The heavy white man dropped the satchel. Burke saw his machine pistol and fired a puff of harmless lead dust from the Avon round in his shotgun. He racked the slide, but not in time. The big man fired a burst, cutting Burke across the groin beneath his vest, swinging toward Starling as she came up from the leather and shot him twice in the middle of his hula shirt before he could fire.

Gunshots behind Starling. The wiry black man dropped the raincoat off his weapon and ducked back in the building, as a blow like a hard fist in the back drove Starling forward, drove breath out of her. She spun and saw the Crip gunship broadside in the street, a Cadillac sedan, windows open, two shooters sitting Cheyenne-style in the offside windows firing over the top and a third from the backseat. Fire and smoke from three muzzles, bullets slamming the air around her.

Starling dived between two parked cars, saw Burke jerking in the road. Brigham lay still, a puddle spreading out of his helmet. Hare and Bolton fired from between cars someplace across the street and over there auto glass powdered and clanged in the road and a tire exploded as automatic fire from the Cadillac pinned them down. Starling, one foot in the running gutter, popped out to look.

Two shooters sitting up in the windows firing across the car roof, the driver firing a pistol with his free hand. A fourth man in the backseat had the door open, was pulling Evelda in with the baby. She carried the satchel. They were firing at Bolton and Hare across the street, smoke from the Cadillac's back tires and the car began to roll. Starling stood up and swung with it and shot the driver in the side of the head. Fired twice at the shooter sitting up in the front window and he went over backward. She dropped the magazine out of the .45

and slammed another one in before the empty hit the ground without taking her eyes off the car.

The Cadillac sideswiped a line of cars across the street and came to a grinding stop against them.

Starling was walking toward the Cadillac now. A shooter still sat in the back window, his eyes wild and hands pushing against the car roof, his chest compressed between the Cadillac and a parked car. His gun slid off the roof. Empty hands appeared out of the near back window. A man in a blue bandana do-rag got out, hands up, and ran. Starling ignored him.

Gunfire from her right and the runner pitched forward, sliding on his face, and tried to crawl under a car. Helicopter blades blatting above her.

Someone yelling in the fish market, "Stay down. Stay down." People under the counters and water at the abandoned cleaning table showering into the air.

Starling advancing on the Cadillac. Movement in the back of the car. Movement in the Cadillac. The car rocking. The baby screaming in there. Gunfire and the back window shattered and fell in.

Starling held up her arm and yelled without turning around. "HOLD IT. Hold your fire. Watch the door. Behind me. Watch the fish house door."

"Evelda." Movement in the back of the car. The baby screaming in there. "Evelda, put your hands out the window."

Evelda Drumgo was coming out now. The baby was screaming. "La Macarena" pounding on the speakers in the fish market. Evelda was out and walking toward Starling, her fine head down, her arms wrapped around the baby.

Burke twitched on the ground between them. Smaller twitches now that he had about bled out. "La Macarena" jerked along with Burke. Someone, moving low, scuttled to him and, lying beside him, got pressure on the wound.

Starling had her weapon pointed at the ground in front of Evelda. "Evelda, show me your hands, come on, please, show me your hands."

A lump in the blanket. Evelda, with her braids and dark Egyptian eyes, raised her head and looked at Starling.

"Well, it's you, Starling," she said.

"Evelda, don't do this. Think about the baby."

"Let's swap body fluids, bitch."

The blanket fluttered, air slammed. Starling shot Evelda Drumgo through the upper lip and the back of her head blew out.

Starling was somehow sitting down with a terrible stinging in the side of her head and the breath driven out of her. Evelda sat in the road too, collapsed forward over her legs, blood gouting out of her mouth and over the baby, its cries muffled by her body. Starling crawled over to her and plucked at the slick buckles of the baby harness. She pulled the balisong out of Evelda's bra, flicked it open without looking at it and cut the harness off the baby. The baby was slick and red, hard for Starling to hold.

Starling, holding it, raised her eyes in anguish. She could see the water spraying in the air from the fish market and she ran over there carrying the bloody child. She swept away the knives and fish guts and put the child on the cutting board and turned the strong hand-spray on him, this dark child lying on a white cutting board amid the knives and fish guts and the shark's head beside him, being washed of HIV positive blood, Starling's own blood falling on him, washing away with Evelda's blood in a common stream exactly salty as the sea.

Water flying, a mocking rainbow of God's Promise in the spray, sparkling banner over the work of His blind hammer. No holes in this man-child that Starling could see. On the speakers "La Macarena" pounding, a strobe light going off and off and off until Hare dragged the photographer away.

2

A CUL-DE-SAC in a working-class neighborhood in Arlington, Virginia, a little after midnight. It is a warm fall night after a rain. The air moves uneasily ahead of a cold front. In the smell of wet earth and leaves, a cricket is playing a tune. He falls silent as a big vibration reaches him, the muffled boom of a 5.0-liter Mustang with steel tube headers turning into the cul-de-sac, followed by a federal marshal's car. The two cars pull into the driveway of a neat duplex and stop. The Mustang shudders a little at idle. When the engine goes silent, the cricket waits a moment and resumes his tune, his last before the frost, his last ever.

A federal marshal in uniform gets out of the driver's seat of the Mustang. He comes around the car and opens the passenger door for Clarice Starling. She gets out. A white headband holds a bandage over her ear. Red-orange Betadine stains her neck above the green surgical blouse she wears instead of a shirt.

She carries her personal effects in a plastic zip-lock bag—some mints and keys, her identification as a Special Agent of the Federal Bureau of Investigation, a speed-loader containing five rounds of ammunition, a small can of Mace. With the bag she carries a belt and empty holster.

The marshal hands her the car keys.

"Thank you, Bobby."

"You want me and Pharon to come in and sit with you awhile? Would you rather I get Sandra? She waits up for me. I'll bring her over a little while, you need some company . . ."

"No, I'll just go in now. Ardelia will be home after a while. Thank you, Bobby."

The marshal gets in the waiting car with his partner and when he sees Starling safely inside the house, the federal car leaves.

The laundry room in Starling's house is warm and smells of fabric softener. The washing machine and clothes dryer hoses are clamped in place with plastic handcuff strips. Starling puts down her personal effects on top of the washing machine. The car keys make a loud clank on the metal top. She takes a load of wash out of the washing machine and stuffs it into the dryer. She takes off her fatigue pants and throws them in the washer and the surgical greens and her bloodstained bra and turns on the machine. She is wearing socks and underpants and a .38 Special with a shrouded hammer in an ankle holster. There are livid bruises on her back and ribs and an abrasion on her elbow. Her right eye and cheek are puffed.

The washing machine is warming and starting to slosh. Starling wraps herself in a big beach towel and pads into the living room. She comes back with two inches of Jack Daniel's neat in a tumbler. She sits down on the rubber mat before the washing machine and leans back against it in the dark as the warm machine throbs and sloshes. She sits on the floor with her face turned up and sobs a few dry sobs before the tears come. Scalding tears on her cheeks, down her face.

Ardelia Mapp's date brought her home about 12:45 A.M. after a long drive down from Cape May, and she told him good night at the door. Mapp was in her bathroom when she heard the water running, the thud in the pipes as the washing machine advanced its cycle.

She went to the back of the house and turned on the lights in the kitchen she shared with Starling. She could see into the laundry room. She could see Starling sitting on the floor, the bandage around her head.

"*Starling!* Oh, baby." Kneeling beside her quickly. "What is it?"

"I got shot through the ear, Ardelia. They fixed it at Walter Reed. Don't turn the light on, okay?"

"Okay. I'll make you something. I haven't heard—we were playing tapes in the car—tell me."

"John's dead, Ardelia."

"*Not Johnny Brigham!*" Mapp and Starling had both had crushes on Brigham when he was gunnery instructor at the FBI Academy. They had tried to read his tattoo through his shirtsleeve.

Starling nodded and wiped her eyes with the back of her hand like a child. "Evelda Drumgo and some Crips. Evelda shot him. They got Burke too, Marquez Burke from BATF. We all went in together. Evelda was tipped ahead and the TV news got there the same time we did. Evelda was mine. She wouldn't give it up, Ardelia. She wouldn't give it up and she was holding the baby. We shot each other. She's dead."

Mapp had never seen Starling cry before.

"Ardelia, I killed five people today."

Mapp sat on the floor beside Starling and put her arm around her. Together they leaned back against the turning washing machine. "What about Evelda's baby?"

"I got the blood off him, he didn't have any breaks in his skin I could see. The hospital said physically he's all right. They're going to release him to Evelda's mother in a couple of days. You know the last thing Evelda said to me, Ardelia? She said, 'Let's swap body fluids, bitch.'"

"Let me fix you something," Mapp said.

"What?" Starling said.

WITH THE gray dawn came the newspapers and the early network news.

Mapp came over with some muffins when she heard Starling stirring around and they watched together.

CNN and the other networks all bought the copyrighted film from WFUL-TV's helicopter camera. It was extraordinary footage from directly overhead.

Starling watched once. She had to see that Evelda shot first. She looked at Mapp and saw anger in her brown face.

Then Starling ran to throw up.

"That's hard to watch," Starling said when she came back, shaky-legged and pale.

As usual, Mapp got to the point at once. "Your question is, how do I feel about you killing that African-American woman holding that child. This is the answer. She shot you first. I want you to be alive. But Starling, think about who's making this insane policy here. What kind of dumb-ass thinking put you and Evelda Drumgo together in that sorry place so you could solve the drug problem between you with some damn guns? How smart is that? I hope you'll think about whether you want to be their cat's paw anymore." Mapp poured some tea for punctuation. "You want me to stay with you? I'll take a personal day."

"Thanks. You don't need to do that. Call me."

The *National Tattler*, prime beneficiary of the tabloid boom in the nineties, put out an extra that was extraordinary even by its own standards. Someone threw it at the house at midmorning. Starling found it when she went to investigate the thump. She was expecting the worst, and she got it:

"*DEATH ANGEL: CLARICE STARLING, THE FBI'S KILLING MACHINE,*" screamed the *National Tattler's* headline in seventy-two-point Railroad Gothic. The three front-page photos were: Clarice Starling in fatigues firing a .45-caliber pistol in competition, Evelda Drumgo bent over her baby in the road, her head tilted like that of a Cimabue Madonna, with the brains blown out, and Starling again, putting a brown naked baby on a white cutting board amid knives and fish guts and the head of a shark.

The caption beneath the pictures says, "*FBI Special Agent Clarice Starling, slayer of serial killer Jame Gumb, adds at least five notches to her gun. Mother with babe in arms and two police officers among the dead after botched drug raid.*"

The main story covered the drug careers of Evelda and Dijon Drumgo, and the appearance of the Crip gang on the war-torn landscape of Washington, D.C. There was a brief mention of fallen officer John Brigham's military service, and his decorations were cited.

Starling was treated to an entire sidebar, beneath a candid photo of Starling in a restaurant wearing a scoop-necked dress, her face animated.

Clarice Starling, FBI Special Agent, had her fifteen minutes of fame when she shot to death serial murderer Jame Gumb, the "Buffalo Bill" killer, in his basement seven years ago. Now she may face departmental charges and civil liabilities in the death Thursday of a Washington mother accused of manufacturing illegal amphetamines. (See main story Page 1.)

"This may be the end of her career," said one source at the Bureau of Alcohol, Tobacco and Firearms, the FBI's sister agency. "We don't know all the details of how it went down, but John Brigham should be alive today. This is the last thing the FBI needs after Ruby Ridge," said the source, who declined to be identified.

Clarice Starling's colorful career began soon after she arrived at the FBI Academy as a trainee. An honors graduate of the University of Virginia in psychology and criminology, she was assigned to interview the lethal madman Dr. Hannibal Lecter, dubbed by this newspaper "Hannibal the Cannibal," and received information from him that was important in the search for Jame Gumb and the rescue of his hostage, Catherine Martin, daughter of the former U.S. senator from Tennessee.

Agent Starling was the interservice combat pistol champion for three years running before she withdrew from competition. Ironically, Officer Brigham, who died at her side, was firearms instructor at Quantico when Starling trained there and was her coach in competition.

An FBI spokesman said Agent Starling will be relieved of field duties with pay pending the outcome of the FBI's internal investigation. A hearing is expected later this week before the Office of Professional Responsibility, the FBI's own dread inquisition.

Relatives of the late Evelda Drumgo said they will seek civil damages from the U.S. government and from Starling personally in wrongful-death suits.

Drumgo's three-month-old son, seen in his mother's arms in the dramatic pictures of the shoot-out, was not injured.

Attorney Telford Higgins, who has defended the Drumgo family in numerous criminal proceedings, alleged that Special Agent Starling's weapon, a modified Colt .45 semiautomatic pistol, was not approved for use in law enforcement in the city of Washington. "It is a deadly and dangerous instrument not suitable for use in law enforcement," Higgins

*said. "Its very use constitutes reckless endangerment of human life," the
noted defense attorney said.*

The *Tattler* had bought Clarice Starling's very home phone number
from one of her informants and rang it until Starling left it off the
hook, and used her FBI cell phone to talk to the office.

Starling did not have a great deal of pain in her ear and the swollen
side of her face as long as she did not touch the bandage. At least she
didn't throb. Two Tylenol held her. She didn't need the Percocet the
doctor had prescribed. She dozed against the headboard of the bed,
the *Washington Post* sliding off the spread onto the floor, gunpowder
residue in her hands, dried tears stiff on her cheeks.

4

You fall in love with the Bureau, but the Bureau doesn't fall in love with you.

—MAXIM IN FBI SEPARATION COUNSELING

THE FBI gymnasium in the J. Edgar Hoover Building was almost empty at this early hour. Two middle-aged men ran slow laps on the indoor track. The clank of a weight machine in a far corner and the shouts and impacts of a racquetball game echoed in the big room.

The voices of the runners did not carry. Jack Crawford was running with FBI Director Tunberry at the Director's request. They had gone two miles and were beginning to puff.

"Blaylock at ATF has to twist in the wind for Waco. It won't happen right now, but he's done and he knows it," the Director said. "He might as well give the Reverend Moon notice he's vacating the premises." The fact that the Bureau of Alcohol, Tobacco and Firearms rents office space in Washington from the Reverend Sun Myung Moon is a source of amusement to the FBI.

"And Farriday is out for Ruby Ridge," the Director continued.

"I can't see that," Crawford said. He had served in New York with Farriday in the 1970s when the mob was picketing the FBI field office at Third Avenue and 69th Street. "Farriday's a good man. He didn't set the rules of engagement."

"I told him yesterday morning."

"He going quietly?" Crawford asked.

"Let's just say he's keeping his benefits. Dangerous times, Jack."

Both men were running with their heads back. Their pace quickened a little. Out of the corner of his eye, Crawford saw the Director sizing up his condition.

"You're what, Jack, fifty-six?"

"That's right."

"One more year to mandatory retirement. Lot of guys get out at forty-eight, fifty, while they can still get a job. You never wanted that. You wanted to keep busy after Bella died."

When Crawford didn't answer for half a lap, the Director saw he had misspoken.

"I don't mean to be light about it, Jack. Doreen was saying the other day, how much—"

"There's still some stuff to do at Quantico. We want to streamline VICAP on the Web so any cop can use it, you saw it in the budget."

"Did you ever want to be Director, Jack?"

"I never thought it was my kind of job."

"It's not, Jack. You're not a political guy. You could never have been Director. You could never have been an Eisenhower, Jack, or an Omar Bradley." He motioned for Crawford to stop, and they stood wheezing beside the track. "You could have been a Patton, though, Jack. You can lead 'em through hell and make 'em love you. It's a gift that I don't have. I have to drive them." Tunberry took a quick look around him, picked up his towel off a bench and draped it around his shoulders like the vestment of a hanging judge. His eyes were bright.

Some people have to tap their anger to be tough, Crawford reflected as he watched Tunberry's mouth move.

"In the matter of the late Mrs. Drumgo with her MAC 10 and her meth lab, shot to death while holding her baby: Judiciary Oversight wants a meat sacrifice. Fresh, bleating meat. And so do the media. DEA has to throw them some meat. ATF has to throw them some meat. And we have to throw them some. But in our case, they just might be satisfied with poultry. Krendler thinks we can give them Clarice Starling and they'll leave us alone. I agree with him. ATF and DEA take the rap for planning the raid. Starling pulled the trigger."

"On a cop killer who shot her first."

"It's the pictures, Jack. You don't get it, do you? The public didn't see Evelda Drumgo shoot John Brigham. They didn't see Evelda shoot at Starling first. You don't see it if you don't know what you're looking at. Two hundred million people, a tenth of whom vote, saw Evelda Drumgo sitting in the road in a protective posture over her baby, with her brains blown out. Don't say it, Jack—I know you thought for a while Starling would be your protégée. But she's got a smart mouth, Jack, and she got off to the wrong start with certain people—"

"Krendler is a pissant."

"Listen to me and don't say anything until I finish. Starling's career was flat-lining anyway. She'll get an administrative discharge without prejudice, the paperwork won't look any worse than a time-and-attendance rap—she'll be able to get a job. Jack, you've done a great thing in the FBI, the Behavioral Science. A lot of people think if you'd pushed your own interests a little better you'd be a lot more than a section chief, that you deserve a lot more. I'll be the first one to say it. Jack, you're going to retire a deputy Director. You have that from me."

"You mean if I stay out of this?"

"In the normal course of events, Jack. With peace all over the kingdom, that's what will happen. Jack, look at me."

"Yes, Director Tunberry?"

"I'm not asking you, I'm giving you a direct order. Stay out of this.

Don't throw it away, Jack. Sometimes you've just got to turn your face away. I've done it. Listen, I know it's hard, believe me I know how you feel."

"How I feel? I feel like I need a shower," Crawford said.

STARLING WAS an efficient housekeeper, but not a meticulous one. Her side of the duplex was clean and she could find everything, but stuff tended to pile up—clean unsorted laundry, more magazines than places to put them. She was a world-class last-minute ironer and she didn't need to primp, so she got by.

When she wanted order, she went through the shared kitchen to Ardelia Mapp's side of the duplex. If Ardelia was there, she had the benefit of her counsel, which was always useful, though sometimes closer to the bone than she might wish. If Ardelia was not there, it was understood that Starling could sit in the absolute order of Mapp's dwelling to think, as long as she didn't *leave* anything. There she sat today. It is one of those residences that always contains its occupant whether she's there or not.

Starling sat looking at Mapp's grandmother's life insurance policy, hanging on the wall in a handmade frame, just as it had hung in the grandmother's farm tenant house and in the Mapp's project apartment during Ardelia's childhood. Her grandmother had sold garden vegetables and flowers and saved the dimes to pay the premiums, and she had been able to borrow against the paid-up policy to help

Ardelia over the last hump when she was working her way through college. There was a picture, too, of the tiny old woman, making no attempt to smile above her starched white collar, ancient knowlege shining in the black eyes beneath the rim of her straw boater.

Ardelia felt her background, found strength in it every day. Now Starling felt for hers, tried to gather herself. The Lutheran Home at Bozeman had fed and clothed her and given her a decent model of behavior, but for what she needed now, she must consult her blood.

What do you have when you come from a poor-white background? And from a place where Reconstruction didn't end until the 1950s. If you came from people often referred to on campuses as crackers and rednecks or, condescendingly, as blue-collar or poor-white Appalachians. If even the uncertain gentility of the South, who accord physical work no dignity at all, refer to your people as peckerwoods—in what tradition do you find an example? That we whaled the piss out of them that first time at Bull Run? That Great-granddaddy did right at Vicksburg, that a corner of Shiloh is forever Yazoo City?

There is much honor and more sense in having succeeded with what was left, making something with the damned forty acres and a muddy mule, but you have to be able to see that. No one will tell you.

Starling had succeeded in FBI training because she had nothing to fall back on. She survived most of her life in institutions, by respecting them and playing hard and well by the rules. She had always advanced, won the scholarship, made the team. Her failure to advance in the FBI after a brilliant start was a new and awful experience for her. She batted against the glass ceiling like a bee in a bottle.

She had had four days to grieve for John Brigham, shot dead before her eyes. A long time ago John Brigham had asked her something and she said no. And then he asked her if they could be friends, and meant it, and she said yes, and meant it.

She had to come to terms with the fact that she herself had killed five people at the Feliciana Fish Market. She flashed again and again on the Crip with his chest crushed between the cars, clawing at the car top as his gun slid away.

Once, for relief, she went to the hospital to look at Evelda's baby. Evelda's mother was there, holding her grandchild, preparing to take him home. She recognized Starling from the newspapers, handed the baby to the nurse and, before Starling realized what she was about, she slapped Starling's face hard on the bandaged side.

Starling didn't strike back, but pinned the older woman against the maternity ward window in a wristlock until she stopped struggling, her face distorted against the foam and spit-smeared glass. Blood ran down Starling's neck and the pain made her dizzy. She had her ear restitched in the emergency room, and declined to file charges. An emergency room aide tipped the *Tattler* and got three hundred dollars.

She had to go out twice more—to make John Brigham's final arrangements and to attend his funeral at Arlington National Cemetery. Brigham's relatives were few and distant and in his written final requests, he named Starling to take care of him.

The extent of his facial injuries required a closed casket, but she had seen to his appearance as well as she could. She laid him out in his perfect Marine dress blues, with his Silver Star and ribbons for his other decorations.

After the ceremony, Brigham's commanding officer delivered to Starling a box containing John Brigham's personal weapons, his badges, and some items from his ever-cluttered desk, including his silly weather bird that drank from a glass.

In five days Starling faced a hearing that could ruin her. Except for one message from Jack Crawford, her work phone had been silent, and there was no Brigham to talk to anymore.

She called her representative in the FBI Agent's Association. His advice was to not wear dangly earrings or open-toed shoes to the hearing.

Every day television and the newspapers seized the story of Evelda Drumgo's death and shook it like a rat.

Here in the absolute order of Mapp's house, Starling tried to think.

The worm that destroys you is the temptation to agree with your critics, to get their approval.

A noise was intruding.

Starling tried to remember her exact words in the undercover van. Had she said more than was necessary? A noise was intruding.

Brigham told her to brief the others on Evelda. Did she express some hostility, say some slur—

A noise was intruding.

She came to herself and realized she was hearing her doorbell next door. A reporter probably. She was also expecting a civil subpoena. She moved Mapp's front curtain and peeked out to see the mailman returning to his truck. She opened Mapp's front door and caught him, turning her back to the press car across the street with the telephoto lens as she signed for the express mail. The envelope was mauve, with silky threads in the fine linen paper. Distracted as she was, it reminded her of something. Back inside, out of the glare, she looked at the address. A fine copperplate hand.

Above the constant droning note of dread in Starling's mind, a warning went off. She felt the skin on her belly quiver as though she had dripped something cold down her front.

Starling took the envelope by the corners and carried it into the kitchen. From her purse, she took the ever-present white evidence-handling gloves. She pressed the envelope on the hard surface of the kitchen table and felt it carefully all over. Though the paper stock was heavy, she would have detected the lump of a watch battery ready to fire a sheet of C-4. She knew she should take it to a fluoroscope. If she opened it she might get in trouble. Trouble. Right. Balls.

She slit the envelope with a kitchen knife and took out the single, silky sheet of paper. She knew at once, before she glanced at the signature, who had written to her.

Dear Clarice,

I have followed with enthusiasm the course of your disgrace and public shaming. My own never bothered me, except for the inconvenience of being incarcerated, but you may lack perspective.

In our discussions down in the dungeon, it was apparent to me that your father, the dead night watchman, figures large in your value system. I think your success in putting an end to Jame Gumb's career as a couturier pleased you most because you could imagine your father doing it.

Now you are in bad odour with the FBI. Have you always imagined your father ahead of you there, have you imagined him a section chief, or— better even than Jack Crawford—a DEPUTY DIRECTOR, watching your progress with pride? And now do you see him shamed and crushed by your disgrace? Your failure? The sorry, petty end of a promising career? Do you see yourself doing the menial tasks your mother was reduced to, after the addicts busted a cap on your DADDY? Hmmmm? Will your failure reflect on them, will people forever wrongly believe that your parents were trailer camp tornado bait white trash? Tell me truly, Special Agent Starling.

Give it a moment before we proceed.

Now I will show you a quality you have that will help you: You are not blinded by tears, you have the onions to read on.

Here's an exercise you might find useful. I want you physically to do this with me:

Do you have a black iron skillet? You are a southern mountain girl, I can't imagine you would not. Put it on the kitchen table. Turn on the overhead lights.

Mapp had inherited her grandmother's skillet and used it often. It had a glassy black surface that no soap ever touched. Starling put it in front of her on the table.

Look into the skillet, Clarice. Lean over it and look down. If this were your mother's skillet, and it well may be, it would hold among its molecules the vibrations of all the conversations ever held in its presence. All the exchanges, the petty irritations, the deadly revelations, the flat announcements of disaster, the grunts and poetry of love.

Sit down at the table, Clarice. Look into the skillet. If it is well cured, it's a black pool, isn't it? It's like looking down a well. Your detailed reflection is not in the bottom, but you loom there, don't you? The light behind you, there you are in blackface, with a corona like your hair on fire.

We are elaborations of carbon, Clarice. You and the skillet and Daddy dead in the ground, cold as the skillet. It's all still there. Listen. How did they really sound, and live—your struggling parents? The concrete memories, not the imagi that swell your heart.

Why was your father not a deputy sheriff, in tight with the courthouse crowd? Why did your mother clean motels to keep you, even if she failed to keep you all together until you were grown?

What is your most vivid memory of the kitchen? Not the hospital, the kitchen.

My mother washing the blood out of my father's hat.

What is your best memory in the kitchen?

My father peeling oranges with his old pocketknife with the tip broken off, and passing the sections to us.

Your father, Clarice, was a night watchman. Your mother was a chambermaid.

Was a big federal career your hope or theirs? How much would your father bend to get along in a stale bureaucracy? How many buttocks would he kiss? Did you ever in your life see him toady or fawn?

Have your supervisors demonstrated any values, Clarice? How about your parents, did they demonstrate any? If so, are those values the same?

Look into the honest iron and tell me. Have you failed your dead family? Would they want you to suck up? What was their view on fortitude? You can be as strong as you wish to be.

You are a warrior, Clarice. The enemy is dead, the baby safe. You are a warrior.

The most stable elements, Clarice, appear in the middle of the periodic table, roughly between iron and silver.

Between iron and silver. I think that is appropriate for you.

Hannibal Lecter

P.S. You still owe me some information, you know. Tell me if you still wake up hearing the lambs. On any Sunday place an ad in the agony column of the national edition of the Times, *the* International Herald-Tribune, *and the* China Mail. *Address it to A. A. Aaron so it will be first, and sign it Hannah.*

Reading, Starling heard the words in the same voice that had mocked her and pierced her, probed her life and enlightened her in the maximum security ward of the insane asylum, when she had to trade the quick of her life to Hannibal Lecter in exchange for his vital knowledge of Buffalo Bill. The metallic rasp of that seldom-used voice still sounded in her dreams.

There was a new spiderweb in the corner of the kitchen ceiling. Starling stared at it while her thoughts tumbled. Glad and sorry, sorry and glad. Glad of the help, glad she saw a way to heal. Glad and sorry that Dr. Lecter's remailing service in Los Angeles must be hiring cheap help—they had used a postal meter this time. Jack Crawford would be delighted with the letter, and so would the postal authorities and the lab.

THE CHAMBER where Mason spends his life is quiet, but it has its own soft pulse, the hiss and sigh of the respirator that finds him breath. It is dark except for the glow of the big aquarium where an exotic eel turns and turns in an endless figure eight, its cast shadow moving like a ribbon over the room.

Mason's plaited hair lies in a thick coil on the respirator shell covering his chest on the elevated bed. A device of tubes, like panpipes, is suspended before him.

Mason's long tongue slides out from between his teeth. He scrolls his tongue around the end pipe and puffs with the next pulse of the respirator.

Instantly a voice responds from a speaker on the wall. "Yes, sir."

"The *Tattler*." The initial *t*'s are lost, but the voice is deep and resonant, a radio voice.

"Page one has—"

"Don't read to me. Put it up on the elmo." The *d* and *m* and the *p* are lost from Mason's speech.

The large screen of an elevated monitor crackles. Its blue-green glow goes pink as the red masthead of the *Tattler* appears.

*"DEATH ANGEL: CLARICE STARLING, THE FBI'S KILL-
ING MACHINE,"* Mason reads, through three slow breaths of his
respirator. He can zoom on the pictures.

Only one of his arms is out from under the covers of his bed. He has
some movement in the hand. Like a pale spider crab the hand moves,
more by the motion of the fingers than the power of his wasted arm.
Since Mason cannot turn his head much to see, the index and middle
fingers feel ahead like antennae as the thumb, ring and little fingers
scuttle the hand along. It finds the remote, where he can zoom and
turn the pages.

Mason reads slowly. The goggle over his single eye makes a tiny
hiss twice a minute as it sprays moisture on his lidless eyeball, and
often fogs the lens. It takes him twenty minutes to get through the
main article and the sidebar.

"Put up the X ray," he said when he had finished.

It took a moment. The large sheet of X ray film required a light
table to show up well on the monitor. Here was a human hand,
apparently damaged. Here was another exposure, showing the hand
and the entire arm. A pointer pasted on the X ray showed an old
fracture in the humerus about halfway between the elbow and the
shoulder.

Mason looked at it through many breaths. "Put up the letter," he
said at last.

Fine copperplate appeared on the screen, the handwriting absurdly
large in magnification.

Dear Clarice, Mason read, *I have followed with enthusiasm the course
of your disgrace and public shaming. . . .* The very rhythm of the voice
excited in him old thoughts that spun him, spun his bed, spun his
room, tore the scabs off his unspeakable dreams, raced his heart ahead
of his breath. The machine sensed his excitement and filled his lungs
ever faster.

He read it all, at his painful rate, reading over the moving machine, like reading on horseback. Mason could not close his eye, but when he had finished reading, his mind went away from behind his eye for a while to think. The breathing machine slowed down. Then he puffed on his pipe.

"Yes, sir."

"Punch up Congressman Vellmore. Bring me the headphone. Turn off the speakerphone.

"Clarice Starling," he said to himself with the next breath the machine permitted him. The name has no plosive sounds and he managed it very well. None of the sounds was lost. While he waited for the telephone, he dozed a moment, the shadow of the eel crawling over his sheet and his face and his coiled hair.

BUZZARD'S POINT, the FBI's field office for Washington and the District of Columbia, is named for a gathering of vultures at a Civil War hospital on the site.

The gathering today is of middle-management officials of the Drug Enforcement Administration, the Bureau of Alcohol, Tobacco and Firearms and the FBI to discuss Clarice Starling's fate.

Starling stood alone on the thick carpet of her boss's office. She could hear her pulse thump beneath the bandage around her head. Over her pulse she heard the voices of the men, muffled by the frosted-glass door of an adjoining conference room.

The great seal of the FBI with its motto, "Fidelity, Bravery, Integrity," is rendered handsomely in gold leaf on the glass.

The voices behind the seal rose and fell with some passion; Starling could hear her name when no other word was clear.

The office has a fine view across the yacht basin to Fort McNair, where the accused Lincoln assassination conspirators were hanged.

Starling flashed on photos she had seen of Mary Surratt, walking past her own casket and mounting the gallows at Fort McNair, standing hooded on the trap, her skirts tied around her legs to prevent immodesty as she dropped through to the loud crunch and the dark.

Next door, Starling heard the chairs scrape back as the men got to their feet. They were filing into this office now. Some of the faces she recognized. Jesus, there was Noonan, the A/DIC over the whole investigation division.

And there was her nemesis, Paul Krendler from Justice, with his long neck and his round ears set high on his head like the ears of a hyena. Krendler was a climber, the gray eminence at the shoulder of the Inspector General. Since she caught the serial killer Buffalo Bill ahead of him in a celebrated case seven years ago, he had dripped poison into her personnel file at every opportunity, and whispered close to the ears of the Career Board.

None of these men had ever been on the line with her, served a warrant with her, been shot at with her or combed the glass splinters out of their hair with her.

The men did not look at her until they all looked at once, the way a sidling pack turns its attention suddenly on the cripple in the herd.

"Have a chair, Agent Starling." Her boss, Special Agent Clint Pearsall, rubbed his thick wrist as though his watch hurt him.

Without meeting her eyes, he gestured toward an armchair facing the windows. The chair in an interrogation is not the place of honor.

The seven men remained standing, their silhouettes black against the bright windows. Starling could not see their faces now, but below the glare, she could see their legs and feet. Five were wearing the thick-soled tasseled loafers favored by country slicksters who have made it to Washington. A pair of Thom McAn wing tips with Corfam soles and some Florsheim wing tips rounded out the seven. A smell in the air of shoe polish warmed by hot feet.

"In case you don't know everybody, Agent Starling, this is Assistant Director Noonan, I'm sure you know who *he* is; this is John Eldredge from DEA, Bob Sneed, BATF, Benny Holcomb is assistant to the mayor and Larkin Wainwright is an examiner from our Office of

Professional Responsibility," Pearsall said. "Paul Krendler—you know Paul—came over unofficially from the Inspector General's Office at Justice. Paul's here as a favor to us, he's here and he's not here, just to help us head off trouble, if you follow me."

Starling knew what the saying was in the service: a federal examiner is someone who arrives at the battlefield after the battle is over and bayonets the wounded.

The heads of some of the silhouettes bobbed in greeting. The men craned their necks and considered the young woman they were gathered over. For a few beats, nobody spoke.

Bob Sneed broke the silence. Starling remembered him as the BATF spin doctor who tried to deodorize the Branch Davidian disaster at Waco. He was a crony of Krendler's and considered a climber.

"Agent Starling, you've seen the coverage in the papers and on television, you've been widely identified as the shooter in the death of Evelda Drumgo. Unfortunately, you've been sort of demonized."

Starling did not reply.

"Agent Starling?"

"I have nothing to do with the news, Mr. Sneed."

"The woman had the baby in her arms, you can see the problem that creates."

"Not in her arms, in a sling across her chest and her arms and hands were beneath it, under a blanket, where she had her MAC 10."

"Have you seen the autopsy protocol?" Sneed asked.

"No."

"But you've never denied being the shooter."

"Do you think I'd deny it because you haven't recovered the slug?" She turned to her bureau chief. "Mr. Pearsall, this is a friendly meeting, right?"

"Absolutely."

"Then why is Mr. Sneed wearing a wire? Engineering Division quit

making those tiepin microphones years ago. He's got an F-Bird in
his breast pocket just recording away. Are we wearing wires to one
another's offices now?"

Pearsall's face turned red. If Sneed was wired, it was the worst kind
of treachery, but nobody wanted to be heard on tape telling Sneed to
turn it off.

"We don't need any attitude from you or accusations," Sneed said,
pale with anger. "We're all here to help you."

"To help me do what? Your agency called this office and got me
assigned to help *you* on this raid. I gave Evelda Drumgo two chances
to surrender. She was holding a MAC 10 under the baby blanket. She
had already shot John Brigham. I wish she had given up. She didn't.
She shot me. I shot her. She's dead. You might want to check your
tape counter right there, Mr. Sneed."

"You had *foreknowledge* Evelda Drumgo would be there?" Eldredge
wanted to know.

"Foreknowledge? Agent Brigham told me in the van going over
that Evelda Drumgo was cooking in a guarded meth lab. He assigned
me to deal with her."

"Remember, Brigham is dead," Krendler said, "and so is Burke,
damn fine agents, both of them. They're not here to confirm or deny
anything."

It turned Starling's stomach to hear Krendler say John Brigham's
name.

"I'm not likely to forget John Brigham is dead, Mr. Krendler, and
he *was* a good agent, and a good friend of mine. The fact is he asked
me to deal with Evelda."

"Brigham gave you that assignment even though you and Evelda
Drumgo had had a run-in before," Krendler said.

"Come on, Paul," Clint Pearsall said.

"What run-in?" Starling said. "A peaceful arrest. She had fought
other officers before at arrests. She didn't fight me when I arrested

her before, and we talked a little—she was smart. We were civil to each other. I hoped I could do it again."

"Did you make the verbal statement that you would 'deal with her?'" Sneed said.

"I acknowledged my instructions."

Holcomb from the mayor's office and Sneed put their heads together.

Sneed shot his cuffs. "Ms Starling, we have information from Officer Bolton of the Washington PD that you made inflammatory statements about Ms Drumgo in the van on the way to the confrontation. Want to comment on that?"

"On Agent Brigham's instructions I explained to the other officers that Evelda had a history of violence, she was usually armed and she was HIV positive. I said we would give her a chance to surrender peacefully. I asked for physical help in subduing her if it came to that. There weren't many volunteers for the job, I can tell you."

Clint Pearsall made an effort. "After the Crip shooters' car crashed and one perp fled, you could see the car rocking and you could hear the baby crying inside the car?"

"Screaming," Starling said. "I raised my hand for everybody to stop shooting and I came out of cover."

"That's against procedure right there," Eldredge said.

Starling ignored him. "I approached the car in the ready position, weapon out, muzzle depressed. Marquez Burke was dying on the ground between us. Somebody ran out and got a compress on him. Evelda got out with the baby. I asked her to show me her hands, I said something like 'Evelda, don't do this.'"

"She shot, you shot. Did she go right down?"

Starling nodded. "Her legs collapsed and she sat down in the road, leaning over the baby. She was dead."

"You grabbed up the baby and ran to the water. Exhibited concern," Pearsall said.

"I don't know what I exhibited. He had blood all over him. I didn't know if the baby was HIV positive or not, I knew she was."

"And you thought your bullet might have hit the baby," Krendler said.

"No. I knew where the bullet went. Can I speak freely, Mr Pearsall?"

When he did not meet her eyes, she went on.

"This raid was an ugly mess. It put me in a position where I had a choice of dying or shooting a woman holding a child. I chose, and what I had to do burns me. I shot a female carrying an infant. The lower *animals* don't even do that. Mr. Sneed, you might want to check your tape counter again, right there where I admit it. I resent the hell out of being put in that position. I resent the way I feel now." She flashed on Brigham lying facedown in the road and she went too far. "Watching you all run from it makes me sick at my stomach."

"Starling—" Pearsall, anguished, looked her in the face for the first time.

"I know you haven't had a chance to write your 302 yet," Larkin Wainwright said. "When we review—"

"Yes, sir, I have," Starling said. "A copy's on the way to the Office of Professional Responsibility. I have a copy with me if you don't want to wait. I have everything I did and saw in there. See, Mr. Sneed, you had it all the time."

Starling's vision was a little too clear, a danger sign she recognized, and she consciously lowered her voice.

"This raid went wrong for a couple of reasons. BATF's snitch lied about the baby's location because the snitch was desperate for the raid to go down—before his federal grand jury date in Illinois. And Evelda Drumgo knew we were coming. She came out with the money in one bag and the meth in another. Her beeper still showed the number for WFUL-TV. She got the beep five minutes before we got there. WFUL's helicopter got there with us. Subpoena WFUL's phone tapes and see who leaked. It's somebody whose interests are local, gentlemen. If BATF had leaked, like they did in Waco, or DEA had leaked, they'd have done it to national media, not the local TV."

Benny Holcomb spoke for the city. "There's no evidence anybody in city government or the Washington police department leaked anything."

"Subpoena and see," Starling said.

"Do you have Drumgo's beeper?" Pearsall asked.

"It's under seal in the property room at Quantico."

Assistant Director Noonan's own beeper went off. He frowned at the number and excused himself from the room. In a moment, he summoned Pearsall to join him outside.

Wainwright, Eldredge and Holcomb looked out the window at Fort McNair, hands in their pockets. They might have been waiting in an intensive care unit. Paul Krendler caught Sneed's eye and urged him toward Starling.

Sneed put his hand on the back of Starling's chair and leaned over her. "If your testimony at a hearing is that, while you were on TDY assignment from the FBI, your weapon killed Evelda Drumgo, BATF is prepared to sign off on a statement that Brigham asked you to pay . . . special attention to Evelda in order to take her into custody peacefully. Your weapon killed her, that's where your service has to carry the can. There will be no interagency pissing contest over rules of engagement and we won't have to bring in any inflammatory or hostile statements you made in the van about what sort of person she was."

Starling saw Evelda Drumgo for an instant, coming out of the doorway, coming out of the car, saw the carriage of her head and, despite the foolishness and waste of Evelda's life, saw her decision to take her child and front her tormenters and not run from it.

Starling leaned close to the microphone on Sneed's tie and said clearly, "I'm perfectly happy to acknowledge the sort of person she was, Mr. Sneed: She was better than you."

Pearsall came back into the office without Noonan and closed the door. "Assistant Director Noonan has gone back to his office. Gentlemen, I'm going to call a halt to this meeting, and I'll get back to you individually by telephone," Pearsall said.

Krendler's head came up. He was suddenly alert at the scent of politics.

"We've got to decide some things," Sneed began.

"No, we don't."

"But—"

"Bob, believe me, we don't have to decide anything. I'll get back to you. And, Bob?"

"Yeah?"

Pearsall grabbed the wire behind Sneed's tie and pulled down hard, popping buttons off Sneed's shirt and snatching tape loose from his skin. "You come to me with a wire again and I'll put my foot in your ass."

None of them looked at Starling as they left, except Krendler.

Moving toward the door, sliding his feet so he would not have to look where he was going, he used the extreme articulation of his long neck to turn his face to her, as a hyena would shuffle at the fringe of a herd, peering in at a candidate. Mixed hungers crossed his face; it was Krendler's nature to both appreciate Starling's leg and look for the hamstring.

8

BEHAVIORAL SCIENCE is the FBI section that deals with serial murder. Down in its basement offices, the air is cool and still. Decorators with their color wheels have tried in recent years to brighten the subterranean space. The result is no more successful than funeral home cosmetics.

The section chief's office remains in the original brown and tan with the checked café curtains on its high windows. There, surrounded by his hellish files, Jack Crawford sat writing at his desk.

A knock, and Crawford looked up to a sight that pleased him— Clarice Starling stood in his doorway.

Crawford smiled and rose from his chair. He and Starling often talked while standing; it was one of the tacit formalities they had come to impose on their relationship. They did not need to shake hands.

"I heard you came to the hospital," Starling said. "Sorry I missed you."

"I was just glad they let you go so fast," he said. "Tell me about your ear, is it okay?"

"It's fine if you like cauliflower. They tell me it'll go down, most of it." Her ear was covered by her hair. She did not offer to show him.

A little silence.

"They had me taking the fall for the raid, Mr. Crawford. For Evelda Drumgo's death, all of it. They were like hyenas and then suddenly it stopped and they slunk away. Something drove them off."

"Maybe you have an angel, Starling."

"Maybe I do. What did it cost you, Mr. Crawford?"

Crawford shook his head. "Close the door, please, Starling." Crawford found a wadded Kleenex in his pocket and polished his spectacles. "I would have done it if I could. I didn't have the juice by myself. If Senator Martin was still in office, you'd have had some cover . . . They wasted John Brigham on that raid—just threw him away. It would have been a shame if they wasted you like they wasted John. It felt like I was stacking you and John across a Jeep."

Crawford's cheeks colored and she remembered his face in the sharp wind above John Brigham's grave. Crawford had never talked to her about his war.

"You did *something*, Mr. Crawford."

He nodded. "I did something. I don't know how glad you'll be. It's a job."

A job. *Job* was a good word in their private lexicon. It meant a specific and immediate task and it cleared the air. They never spoke if they could help it about the troubled central bureaucracy of the Federal Bureau of Investigation. Crawford and Starling were like medical missionaries, with little patience for theology, each concentrating hard on the one baby before them, knowing and not saying that God wouldn't do a goddamned thing to help. That for fifty thousand Ibo infant lives, He would not bother to send rain.

"Indirectly, Starling, your benefactor is your recent correspondent."

"Dr. Lecter." She had long noted Crawford's distaste for the spoken name.

"Yes, the very same. For all this time he'd eluded us—he was away clean—and he writes you a letter. Why?"

It had been seven years since Dr. Hannibal Lecter, known murderer of ten, escaped from custody in Memphis, taking five more lives in the process.

It was as though Lecter had dropped off the earth. The case remained open at the FBI and would remain open forever, or until he was caught. The same was true in Tennessee and other jurisdictions, but there was no task force assigned to pursue him anymore, though relatives of his victims had wept angry tears before the Tennessee state legislature and demanded action.

Whole tomes of scholarly conjecture on his mentality were available, most of it authored by psychologists who had never been exposed to the doctor in person. A few works appeared by psychiatrists he had skewered in the professional journals, who apparently felt that it was safe to come out now. Some of them said his aberrations would inevitably drive him to suicide and that it was likely he was already dead.

In cyberspace at least, interest in Dr. Lecter remained very much alive. The damp floor of the Internet sprouted Lecter theories like toadstools and sightings of the doctor rivaled those of Elvis in number. Impostors plagued the chat rooms and in the phosphorescent swamp of the Web's dark side, police photographs of his outrages were bootlegged to collectors of hideous arcana. They were second in popularity only to the execution of Fou-Tchou-Li.

One trace of the doctor after seven years—his letter to Clarice Starling when she was being crucified by the tabloids.

The letter bore no fingerprints, but the FBI felt reasonably sure it was genuine. Clarice Starling was certain of it.

"Why did he do it, Starling?" Crawford seemed almost angry at her. "I've never pretended to understand him any more than these psychiatric jackasses do. You tell me."

"He thought what happened to me would . . . destroy, would *disillusion* me about the Bureau, and he enjoys seeing the destruction of faith, it's his favorite thing. It's like the church collapses he used to collect. The pile of rubble in Italy when the church collapsed on all the grandmothers at that special Mass and somebody stuck a Christmas tree in the top of the pile, he loved that. I amuse him, he toys with me. When I was interviewing him he liked to point out holes in my education, he thinks I'm pretty naïve."

Crawford spoke from his own age and isolation when he said, "Have you ever thought that he might like you, Starling?"

"I think I amuse him. Things either amuse him or they don't. If they don't . . ."

"Ever *felt* that he liked you?" Crawford insisted on the distinction between thought and feeling like a Baptist insists on total immersion.

"On really short acquaintance he told me some things about myself that were true. I think it's easy to mistake understanding for empathy— we want empathy so badly. Maybe learning to make that distinction is part of growing up. It's hard and ugly to know somebody can understand you without even liking you. When you see understanding just used as a predator's tool, that's the worst. I . . . I have no idea how Dr. Lecter feels about me."

"What sort of thing did he tell you, if you don't mind?"

"He said I was an ambitious, hustling little rube and my eyes shined like cheap birthstones. He told me I wore cheap shoes, but I had some taste, a little taste."

"That struck you as true?"

"Yep. Maybe it still is. I've improved my shoes."

"Do you think, Starling, he might have been interested to see if you'd rat him out when he sent you a letter of encouragement?"

"He knew I'd rat him out, he'd better know it."

"He killed six after the court committed him," Crawford said. "He killed Miggs in the asylum for throwing semen in your face, and five in his escape. In the present political climate, if the doctor's caught he'll get the needle." Crawford smiled at the thought. He had pioneered the study of serial murder. Now he was facing mandatory retirement and the monster who had tried him the most remained free. The prospect of death for Dr. Lecter pleased him mightily.

Starling knew Crawford mentioned Miggs's act to goose her attention, to put her back in those terrible days when she was trying to interrogate Hannibal the Cannibal in the dungeon at the Baltimore State Hospital for the Criminally Insane. When Lecter toyed with her while a girl crouched in Jame Gumb's pit, waiting to die. Usually Crawford heightened your attention when he was coming to the point, as he did now.

"Did you know, Starling, that one of Dr. Lecter's early victims is still alive?"

"The rich one. The family offered a reward."

"Yes, Mason Verger. He's on a respirator in Maryland. His father died this year and left him the meatpacking fortune. Old Verger also left Mason a U.S. congressman and a member of the House Judiciary Oversight Committee who just couldn't make ends meet without him. Mason says he's got something that might help us find the doctor. He wants to speak with you."

"With *me*."

"You. That's what Mason wants and suddenly everyone agrees it's a really good idea."

"That's what Mason wants after you suggested it to him?"

"They were going to throw you away, Starling, clean up with you like you were a rag. You would have been wasted just like John Brigham. Just to save some bureaucrats at BATF. Fear. Pressure. That's all they understand anymore. I had somebody drop a dime to Mason and tell him how much it would hurt the hunt for Lecter if you got canned. Whatever else happened, who Mason might have called after that, I don't want to know, probably Representative Vollmer."

A year ago, Crawford would not have played this way. Starling

searched his face for any of the short-timer craziness that sometimes comes over imminent retirees. She didn't see any, but he did
look weary.

"Mason's not pretty, Starling, and I don't just mean his face. Find
out what he's got. Bring it here, we'll work with it. At last."

Starling knew that for years, ever since she graduated from the
FBI Academy, Crawford had tried to get her assigned to Behavioral
Science.

Now that she was a veteran of the Bureau, veteran of many
lateral assignments, she could see that her early triumph in catching
the serial murderer Jame Gumb was part of her undoing in the
Bureau. She was a rising star that stuck on the way up. In the
process of catching Gumb, she had made at least one powerful enemy
and excited the jealousy of a number of her male contemporaries.
That, and a certain cross-grainedness, had led to years of jump-
out squads, and reactive squads rolling on bank robberies and years
of serving warrants, seeing Newark over a shotgun barrel. Finally,
deemed too irascible to work with groups, she was a tech agent,
bugging the telephones and cars of gangsters and child pornographers,
keeping lonesome vigils over Title Three wiretaps. And she was
forever on loan, when a sister agency needed a reliable hand in
a raid. She had wiry strength and she was fast and careful with
the gun.

Crawford saw this as a chance for her. He assumed she had always
wanted to chase Lecter. The truth was more complicated than that.

Crawford was studying her now. "You never got that gunpowder
out of your cheek."

Grains of burnt powder from the revolver of the late Jame Gumb
marked her cheekbone with a black spot.

"Never had time," Starling said.

"Do you know what the French call a beauty spot, a *mouche*
like that, high on the cheek? Do you know what it stands for?"

Crawford owned a sizeable library on tattoos, body symbology, ritual mutilation.

Starling shook her head.

"They call that one 'courage,'" Crawford said. "You can wear that one. I'd keep it if I were you."

9

THERE IS a witchy beauty about Muskrat Farm, the Verger family's mansion near the Susquehanna River in northern Maryland. The Verger meatpacking dynasty bought it in the 1930s when they moved east from Chicago to be closer to Washington, and they could well afford it. Business and political acumen has enabled the Vergers to batten on U.S. Army meat contracts since the Civil War.

The "embalmed beef" scandal in the Spanish-American War hardly touched the Vergers. When Upton Sinclair and the muckrakers invest-igated dangerous packing-plant conditions in Chicago, they found that several Verger employees had been rendered into lard inadvertently, canned and sold as Durham's Pure Leaf Lard, a favorite of bakers. The blame did not stick to the Vergers. The matter cost them not a single government contract.

The Vergers avoided these potential embarrassments and many others by giving money to politicians—their single setback being passage of the Meat Inspection Act of 1906.

Today the Vergers slaughter 86,000 cattle a day, and approximately 36,000 pigs, a number that varies slightly with the season.

The new-mown lawns of Muskrat Farm, the riot of its lilacs in the wind, smell nothing at all like the stockyard. The only animals are ponies for the visiting children and amusing flocks of geese grazing on the lawns, their behinds wagging, heads low to the grass. There are no dogs. The house and barn and grounds are near the center of six square miles of national forest, and will remain there in perpetuity under a special exemption granted by the Department of the Interior.

Like many enclaves of the very rich, Muskrat Farm is not easy to find the first time you go. Clarice Starling went one exit too far on the expressway. Coming back along the service road, she first encountered the trade entrance, a big gate secured with chain and padlock in the high fence enclosing the forest. Beyond the gate, a fire road disappeared into the overarching trees. There was no call box. Two miles farther along she found the gatehouse, set back a hundred yards along a handsome drive. The uniformed guard had her name on his clipboard.

An additional two miles of manicured roadway brought her to the farm.

Starling stopped her rumbling Mustang to let a flock of geese cross the drive. She could see a file of children on fat Shetlands leaving a handsome barn a quarter-mile from the house. The main building before her was a Stanford White-designed mansion handsomely set among low hills. The place looked solid and fecund, the province of pleasant dreams. It tugged at Starling.

The Vergers had had sense enough to leave the house as it was, with the exception of a single addition, which Starling could not yet see, a modern wing that sticks out from the eastern elevation like an extra limb attached in a grotesque medical experiment.

Starling parked beneath the central portico. When the engine was off she could hear her own breathing. In the mirror she saw someone coming on a horse. Now hooves clopped on the pavement beside the car as Starling got out.

A broad-shouldered person with short blond hair swung down from the saddle, handed the reins to a valet without looking at him. "Walk him back," the rider said in a deep scratchy voice. "I'm Margot Verger." At close inspection she was a woman, holding out her hand, arm extended straight from the shoulder. Clearly Margot Verger was a bodybuilder. Beneath her corded neck, her massive shoulders and arms stretched the mesh of her tennis shirt. Her eyes had a dry glitter and looked irritated, as though she suffered from a shortage of tears. She wore twill riding breeches and boots with no spurs.

"What's that you're driving?" she said. "An old Mustang?"

"It's an '88."

"Five-liter? It sort of hunkers down over its wheels."

"Yes. It's a Roush Mustang."

"You like it?"

"A lot."

"What'll it do?"

"I don't know. Enough, I think."

"Scared of it?"

"Respectful of it. I'd say I use it respectfully," Starling said.

"Do you know about it, or did you just buy it?"

"I knew enough about it to buy it at a dope auction when I saw what it was. I learned more later."

"You think it would beat my Porsche?"

"Depends on which Porsche. Ms Verger, I need to speak with your brother."

"They'll have him cleaned up in about five minutes. We can start up there." The twill riding breeches whistled on Margot Verger's big thighs as she climbed the stairs. Her cornsilk hair had receded enough to make Starling wonder if she took steroids and had to tape her clitoris down.

To Starling, who spent most of her childhood in a Lutheran orphanage, the house felt like a museum, with its vast spaces and painted beams above her, and walls hung with portraits of important-looking dead people. Chinese cloisonné stood on the landings and long Moroccan runners lined the halls.

There is an abrupt shear in style at the new wing of the Verger mansion. The modern functional structure is reached through frosted glass double doors, incongruous in the vaulted hall.

Margot Verger paused outside the doors. She looked at Starling with her glittery, irritated gaze.

"Some people have trouble talking with Mason," she said. "If it bothers you, or you can't take it, I can fill you in later on whatever you forget to ask him."

There is a common emotion we all recognize and have not yet named—the happy anticipation of being able to feel contempt. Starling saw it in Margot Verger's face. All Starling said was "Thank you."

To Starling's surprise, the first room in the wing was a large and well-equipped playroom. Two African-American children played among oversized stuffed animals, one riding a Big Wheel and the other pushing a truck along the floor. A variety of tricycles and wagons were parked in the corners and in the center was a large jungle gym with the floor heavily padded beneath it.

In a corner of the playroom, a tall man in a nurse's uniform sat on a love seat reading *Vogue*. A number of video cameras were mounted on the walls, some high, others at eye level. One camera high in the corner tracked Starling and Margot Verger, its lens rotating to focus.

Starling was past the point where the sight of a brown child pierced her, but she was keenly aware of these children. Their cheerful industry with the toys was pleasant to see as she and Margot Verger passed through the room.

"Mason likes to watch the kids," Margot Verger said. "It scares them to see him, all but the littlest ones, so he does it this way. They ride ponies after. They're day-care kids out of child welfare in Baltimore."

Mason Verger's chamber is approached only through his bathroom, a facility worthy of a spa that takes up the entire width of the wing. It is institutional-looking, all steel and chrome and industrial carpet, with wide-doored showers, stainless-steel tubs with lifting devices over them, coiled orange hoses, steam rooms and vast glass cabinets of unguents from the Farmacia of Santa Maria Novella in Florence. The air in the bathroom was still steamy from recent use and the scents of balsam and wintergreen hung in the air.

Starling could see light under the door to Mason Verger's chamber. It went out as his sister touched the doorknob.

A seating area in the corner of Mason Verger's chamber was severely lit from above. A passable print of William Blake's *The Ancient of Days* hung above the couch—God measuring with his calipers. The picture was draped with black to commemorate the recent passing of the Verger patriarch. The rest of the room was dark.

From the darkness came the sound of a machine working rhythmically, sighing at each stroke.

"Good afternoon, Agent Starling." A resonant voice mechanically amplified, the fricative *f* lost out of *afternoon*.

"Good afternoon, Mr. Verger," Starling said into the darkness, the overhead light hot on the top of her head. Afternoon was someplace else. Afternoon did not enter here.

"Have a seat."

Going to have to do this. Now is good. Now is called for.

"Mr. Verger, the discussion we'll have is in the nature of a deposition and I'll need to tape-record it. Is that all right with you?"

"Sure." The voice came between the sighs of the machine, the sibilant *s* lost from the word. "Margot, I think you can leave us now."

Without a look at Starling, Margot Verger left in a whistle of riding pants.

"Mr. Verger, I'd like to attach this microphone to your—clothing or your pillow if you're comfortable with that, or I'll call a nurse to do it if you prefer."

"By all means," he said, minus the *b* and the *m*. He waited for power from the next mechanical exhalation. "You can do it yourself, Agent Starling. I'm right over here."

There were no light switches Starling could find at once. She thought she might see better with the glare out of her eyes and she went into the darkness, one hand before her, toward the smell of wintergreen and balsam.

She was closer to the bed than she thought when he turned on the light.

Starling's face did not change. Her hand holding the clip-on microphone jerked backward, perhaps an inch.

Her first thought was separate from the feelings in her chest and stomach; it was the observation that his speech anomalies resulted from his total lack of lips. Her second thought was the recognition that he was not blind. His single blue eye was looking at her through a sort of monocle with a tube attached that kept the eye damp, as it lacked a lid. For the rest, surgeons years ago had done what they could with expanded skin grafts over bone.

Mason Verger, noseless and lipless, with no soft tissue on his face, was all teeth, like a creature of the deep, deep ocean. Inured as we are to masks, the shock in seeing him is delayed. Shock comes with the recognition that this is a human face with a mind behind it. It churns you with its movement, the articulation of the jaw, the turning of the eye to see you. To see your normal face.

Mason Verger's hair is handsome and, oddly, the hardest thing to look at. Black flecked with gray, it is plaited in a ponytail long enough to reach the floor if it is brought back over his pillow. Today his plaited hair is in a big coil on his chest above the turtle-shell respirator. Human hair beneath the blue-john ruin, the plaits shining like lapping scales.

Under the sheet, Mason Verger's long-paralyzed body tapered away to nothing on the elevated hospital bed.

Before his face was the control that looked like panpipes or a harmonica in clear plastic. He curled his tongue tubelike around a pipe end and puffed with the next stroke of his respirator. His bed responded with a hum, turned him slightly to face Starling and increased the elevation of his head.

"I thank God for what happened," Verger said. "It was my salvation. Have you accepted Jesus, Miss Starling? Do you have faith?"

"I was raised in a close religious atmosphere, Mr. Verger. I have whatever that leaves you with," Starling said. "Now, if you don't mind, I'm just going to clip this to the pillowcase. It won't be in the way here, will it?" Her voice sounded too brisk and nursey to suit her.

Her hand beside his head, seeing their two fleshes together, did not aid Starling, nor did his pulse in the vessels grafted over the bones of his face to feed it blood; their regular dilation was like worms swallowing.

Gratefully, she paid out cord and backed to the table and her tape recorder and separate microphone.

"This is Special Agent Clarice M. Starling, FBI number 5143690, deposing Mason R. Verger, Social Security number 475989823, at his home on the date stamped above, sworn and attested. Mr. Verger understands that he has been granted immunity from prosecution by the U.S. Attorney for District Thirty-six, and by local authorities in a combined memorandum attached, sworn and attested.

"Now, Mr. Verger—"

"I want to tell you about camp," he interrupted with his next exhalation. "It was a wonderful childhood experience that I've come back to, in essence."

"We can get to that, Mr. Verger, but I thought we'd—"

"Oh, we can get to it *now*, Miss Starling. You see, it all comes to bear. It was how I met Jesus, and I'll never tell you anything more important than that." He paused for the machine to sigh. "It was a Christian camp my father paid for. He paid for the whole thing, all one hundred twenty-five campers on Lake Michigan. Some of them were unfortunates and they would do anything for a candy bar. Maybe I took advantage of it, maybe I was rough with them if they wouldn't take the chocolate and do what I wanted—I'm not holding anything back, because it's all okay now."

"Mr. Verger, let's look at some material with the same—"

He was not listening to her, he was only waiting for the machine to give him breath. "I have immunity, Miss Starling, and it's all okay now. I've got a grant of immunity from Jesus, I've got immunity from the U.S. Attorney, I've got immunity from the DA in Owings Mills, Hallelujah. I'm free, Miss Starling, and it's all okay now. I'm right with Him and it's all okay now. He's the Risen Jesus, and at camp we called him The Riz. Nobody beats The Riz. We made it contemporary, you know, The Riz. I served him in Africa, Hallelujah, I served him in Chicago, praise His name, and I serve Him now and He will raise me up from this bed and He will smite mine enemies and drive them before me and I will hear the lamentations of their women, and it's all okay now." He choked on saliva and stopped, the vessels on the front of his head dark and pulsing.

Starling rose to get a nurse, but his voice stopped her before she reached the door.

"I'm fine, it's all okay now."

Maybe a direct question would be better than trying to lead him. "Mr. Verger, had you ever seen Dr. Lecter before the court assigned you to him for therapy? Did you know him socially?"

"No."

"You were both on the board of the Baltimore Philharmonic."

"No, my seat was just because we contribute. I sent my lawyer when there was a vote."

"You never gave a statement in the course of Dr. Lecter's trial." She was learning to time her questions so he would have breath to answer.

"They said they had enough to convict him six times, nine times. And he beat it all on an insanity plea."

"The court found him insane. Dr. Lecter did not plead."

"Do you find that distinction important?" Mason asked.

With the question, she first felt his mind, prehensile and deep-sleeved, different from the vocabulary he used with her.

The big eel, now accustomed to the light, rose from the rocks in his aquarium and began the tireless circle, a rippling ribbon of brown beautifully patterned with irregular cream spots.

Starling was ever aware of it, moving in the corner of her vision.

"It's a *Muraena Kidako*," Mason said. "There's an even bigger one in captivity in Tokyo. This one is second biggest.

"Its common name is the Brutal Moray, would you like to see why?"

"No," Starling said, and turned a page in her notes. "So in the course of your court-ordered therapy, Mr. Verger, you invited Dr. Lecter to your home."

"I'm not ashamed anymore. I'll tell you about anything. It's all okay now. I got a walk on those trumped-up molestation counts if I did five hundred hours of community service, worked at the dog pound and got therapy from Dr. Lecter. I thought if I got the doctor involved in something, he'd have to cut me some slack on the therapy and wouldn't violate my parole if I didn't show up all the time, or if I was a little stoned at my appointments."

"This was when you had the house in Owings Mills."

"Yes. I had told Dr. Lecter everything, about Africa and Idi and all, and I said I'd show him some of my stuff."

"You'd show him . . . ?"

"Paraphernalia. Toys. In the corner there, that's the little portable guillotine I used for Idi Amin. You can throw it in the back of a Jeep, go anywhere, the most remote village. Set up in fifteen minutes. Takes the condemned about ten minutes to cock it with a windlass, little longer if it's a woman or a kid. I'm not ashamed of any of that, because I'm cleansed."

"Dr. Lecter came to your house."

"Yes. I answered the door in some leather, you know. Watched for some reaction, didn't see any. I was concerned he'd be afraid of me, but he didn't seem to be. *Afraid* of me—that's funny now. I invited him upstairs. I showed him, I had adopted some dogs from the shelter, two dogs that were friends, and I had them in a cage together with plenty of fresh water, but no food. I was curious about what would eventually happen.

"I showed him my noose setup, you know, autoerotic asphyxsia, you sort of hang yourself but not really, feels good while you—you follow?"

"I follow."

"Well, he didn't seem to follow. He asked me how it worked and I said, you're an odd psychiatrist not to know that, and he said, and I'll never forget his smile, he said, 'Show me.' I thought, *I've got you now!*"

"And you showed him."

"I am not ashamed of that. We grow by our mistakes. I'm cleansed."

"Please go on, Mr. Verger."

"So I pulled down the noose in front of my big mirror and put it on and had the release in my hand, and I was beating off with the other hand watching for his reaction, but I couldn't tell anything. Usually I can read people. He was sitting in a chair over in the corner of the room. His legs were crossed and he had his fingers locked over his knee. Then he stood up and reached in his jacket pocket, all elegant, like James Mason reaching for his lighter, and he said, 'Would you like an amyl popper?' I thought, *Wow!*—he gives me one now and he's got to give them to me forever to keep his license. Prescription city. Well, if you read the report, you know it was a lot more than amyl nitrite."

"Angel Dust and some other methamphetamines and some acid," Starling said.

"I mean, *whoa*! He went over to the mirror I looked at myself in, and kicked the bottom of it and took out a shard. I was flying. He came over and gave me the piece of glass and looked me in the eyes and suggested I might like to peel off my face with it. He let the dogs out. I fed them my face. It took a long time to get it all off, they say. I don't remember. Dr. Lecter broke my neck with the noose. They got my nose back when they pumped the dogs' stomachs at the animal shelter, but the graft didn't take."

Starling took longer than she needed to in rearranging the papers on the table.

"Mr. Verger, your family posted the reward after Dr. Lecter escaped from custody in Memphis."

"Yes, a million dollars. One million. We advertised worldwide."

"And you also offered to pay for any kind of relevant information, not just the usual apprehension and conviction. You were supposed to share that information with us. Have you always done that?"

"Not exactly, but there was never anything good to share."

"How do you know that? Did you follow up on some leads yourself?"

"Just far enough to know they were worthless. And why shouldn't we—you people never told us anything. We had a tip from Crete that was nothing and one from Uruguay that we could never confirm. I want you to understand, this is not a revenge thing, Miss Starling. I have forgiven Dr. Lecter just as Our Savior forgave the Roman soldiers."

"Mr. Verger, you indicated to my office that you might have something now."

"Look in the drawer of the end table."

Starling took the white cotton gloves out of her purse and put them on. In the drawer was a large manila envelope. It was stiff and heavy.

She pulled out an X ray and held it to the bright overhead light. The X ray was of a left hand that appeared to be injured. She counted the fingers. Four plus the thumb.

"Look at the metacarpals, do you know what I'm talking about?"

"Yes."

"Count the knuckles."

Five knuckles. "Counting the thumb, this person had six fingers on his left hand. Like Dr. Lecter."

"Like Dr. Lecter."

The corner where the X ray's case number and origin should be was clipped off.

"Where did it come from, Mr. Verger?"

"Rio de Janeiro. To find out more, I have to pay. A lot. Can you tell me if it's Dr. Lecter? I need to know if I should pay."

"I'll try, Mr. Verger. We'll do our best. Do you have the package the X ray came in?"

"Margot has it in a plastic bag, she'll give it to you. If you don't mind, Miss Starling, I'm rather tired and I need some attention."

"You'll hear from my office, Mr. Verger."

Starling had not been out of the room long when Mason Verger tooted the endmost pipe and said, "Cordell?" The male nurse from the playroom came in and read to him from a folder marked DEPARTMENT OF CHILD WELFARE, CITY OF BALTIMORE.

"*Franklin*, is it? Send *Franklin* in," Mason said, and turned out his light.

The little boy stood alone under the bright overhead light of the seating area, squinting into the gasping darkness.

Came the resonant voice, "Are you *Franklin*?"

"Franklin," the little boy said.

"Where do you stay, *Franklin*?"

"With Mama and Shirley and Stringbean."

"Does Stringbean stay there all the time?

"He in and out."

"Did you say 'He in and out'?"

"Yeah."

"'Mama' is not your real mama, is she, *Franklin?*"

"She my foster."

"She's not the first foster you've had, is she?"

"Nome."

"Do you like it at your house, *Franklin?*"

He brightened. "We got Kitty Cat. Mama make patty-cake in the stove."

"How long have you been there, at Mama's house?"

"I don't know."

"Have you had a birthday there?"

"One time I did. Shirley make Kool-Aid."

"Do you like Kool-Aid?"

"Strawberry."

"Do you love Mama and Shirley?"

"I love, um hum, and Kitty Cat."

"Do you want to live there? Do you feel safe when you go to bed?"

"Um hum. I sleep in the room with Shirley. Shirley, she a big girl."

"*Franklin*, you can't live there anymore with Mama and Shirley and the Kitty Cat. You have to go away."

"Who say?"

"The government say. Mama has lost her job and her approval as a foster home. The police found a marijuana cigarette in your house. You can't see Mama anymore after this week. You can't see Shirley anymore or Kitty Cat after this week."

"No," Franklin said.

"Or maybe they just don't want you anymore, *Franklin*. Is there something wrong with you? Do you have a sore on you or something nasty? Do you think your skin is too dark for them to love you?"

Franklin pulled up his shirt and looked at his small brown stomach. He shook his head. He was crying.

"Do you know what will happen to Kitty Cat? What is Kitty Cat's name?"

"She call Kitty Cat, that her name."

"Do you know what will happen to Kitty Cat? The policemen will take Kitty Cat to the pound and a doctor there will give her a shot. Did you get a shot at day care? Did the nurse give you a shot? With a shiny needle? They'll give Kitty Cat a shot. She'll be so scared when she sees the needle. They'll stick it in and Kitty Cat will hurt and die."

Franklin caught the tail of his shirt and held it up beside his face. He put his thumb in his mouth, something he had not done for a year after Mama asked him not to.

"Come here," said the voice from the dark. "Come here and I'll tell you how you can keep Kitty Cat from getting a shot. Do you want Kitty Cat to have the shot, *Franklin*? No? Then come here, *Franklin*."

Franklin, eyes streaming, sucking his thumb, walked slowly forward into the dark. When he was within six feet of the bed, Mason blew into his harmonica and the lights came on.

From innate courage, or his wish to help Kitty Cat, or his wretched knowledge that he had no place to run to anymore, Franklin did not flinch. He did not run. He held his ground and looked at Mason's face.

Mason's brow would have furrowed if he had a brow, at this disappointing result.

"You can save Kitty Cat from getting the shot if you give Kitty Cat some rat poison yourself," Mason said. The plosive *p* was lost, but Franklin understood.

Franklin took his thumb out of his mouth.

"You a mean old doo-doo," Franklin said. "An you ugly too." He turned around and walked out of the chamber, through the hall of coiled hoses, back to the playroom.

Mason watched him on video.

The nurse looked at the boy, watched him closely while pretending to read his *Vogue*.

Franklin did not care about the toys anymore. He went over and sat under the giraffe, facing the wall. It was all he could do not to suck his thumb.

Cordell watched him carefully for tears. When he saw the child's shoulders shaking, the nurse went to him and wiped the tears away gently with sterile swatches. He put the wet swatches in Mason's martini glass, chilling in the playroom's refrigerator beside the orange juice and the Cokes.

10

FINDING MEDICAL information about Dr. Hannibal Lecter was not easy. When you consider his utter contempt for the medical establishment and for most medical practitioners, it is not surprising that he never had a personal physician.

The Baltimore State Hospital for the Criminally Insane, where Dr. Lecter was kept until his disastrous transfer to Memphis, was now defunct, a derelict building awaiting demolition.

The Tennessee State Police were the last custodians of Dr. Lecter before his escape, but they claimed they never received his medical records. The officers who brought him from Baltimore to Memphis, now deceased, had signed for the prisoner, not for any medical records.

Starling spent a day on the telephone and the computer, then physically searched the evidence storage rooms at Quantico and the J. Edgar Hoover Building. She climbed around the dusty and malodorous bulky evidence room of the Baltimore Police Department for an entire morning, and spent a maddening afternoon dealing with the uncatalogued Hannibal Lecter Collection at the Fitzhugh Memorial Law Library, where time stands still while the custodians try to locate the keys.

At the end, she was left with a single sheet of paper—the cursory physical examination Dr. Lecter received when he was first arrested by the Maryland State Police. No medical history was attached.

Inelle Corey had survived the demise of the Baltimore State Hospital for the Criminally Insane and gone on to better things at the Maryland State Board of Hospitals. She did not want to be interviewed by Starling in the office, so they met in a ground-floor cafeteria.

Starling's practice was to arrive early for meetings and observe the specific meeting point from a distance. Corey was punctual to the minute. She was about thirty-five years old, heavy and pale, without makeup or jewelry. Her hair was almost to her waist, as she had worn it in high school, and she wore white sandals with Supp-Hose.

Starling collected sugar packets at the condiment stand and watched Corey seat herself at the agreed table.

You may labor under the misconception that all Protestants look alike. Not so. Just as one Caribbean person can often tell the specific island of another, Starling, raised by the Lutherans, looked at this woman and said to herself, *Church of Christ, maybe a Nazarene at the outside.*

Starling took off her jewelry, a plain bracelet and a gold stud in her good ear, and put them in her bag. Her watch was plastic, okay. She couldn't do much about the rest of her appearance.

"Inelle Corey? Want some coffee?" Starling was carrying two cups.

"It's pronounced *Eyenelle.* I don't drink coffee."

"I'll drink both of them, want something else? I'm Clarice Starling."

"I don't care for anything. You want to show me some picture ID?"

"Absolutely," Starling said. "Ms. Corey—may I call you Inelle?"

The woman shrugged.

"Inelle, I need some help on a matter that really doesn't involve you personally at all. I just need guidance in finding some records from the Baltimore State Hospital."

Inelle Corey speaks with exaggerated precision to express righteousness or anger.

"We went through this with the state board at the time of closure, Miss—"

"Starling."

"Miss Starling. You will find that not a patient went out of that hospital without a folder. You will find that not a folder went out of that hospital that was not approved by a supervisor. As far as the deceased go, the Health Department did not need their folders, the Bureau of Vital Statistics did not want their folders, and as far as I know, the dead folders, that is the folders of the deceased, remained at the Baltimore State Hospital past my separation date and I was about the last one out. The elopements went to the city police and the sheriff's department."

"Elopements?"

"That's when somebody runs off. Trusties took off sometimes."

"Would Dr. Hannibal Lecter be carried as an elopement? Do you think his records might have gone to law enforcement?"

"He was *not* an elopement. He was never carried as *our* elopement. He was not in our custody when he took off. I went down there to the bottom and looked at Dr. Lecter one time, showed him to my sister when she was here with the boys. I feel sort of nasty and cold when I think about it. He stirred up one of those other ones to throw some"— she lowered her voice—"*jism* on us. Do you know what that is?"

"I've heard the term," Starling said. "Was it Mr. Miggs, by any chance? He had a good arm."

"I've shut it out of my mind. I remember *you*. You came to the hospital and talked to Fred—Dr. Chilton—and went down there in that basement with Lecter, didn't you?"

"Yes."

Dr. Frederick Chilton was the director of the Baltimore State Hospital for the Criminally Insane who went missing while on vacation after Dr. Lecter's escape.

"You know Fred disappeared."

"Yes, I heard that."

Ms Corey developed quick, bright tears. "He was my fiancé," she said. "He was gone, and then the hospital closed, it was just like the roof had fell in on me. If I hadn't had my church I could not have got by."

"I'm sorry," Starling said. "You have a good job now."

"But I don't have Fred. He was a fine, fine man. We shared a love, a love you don't find everday. He was voted Boy of the Year in Canton when he was in high school."

"Well, I'll be. Let me ask you this, Inelle, did he keep the records in his office, or were they out in reception where your desk—"

"They were in the wall cabinets in his office and then they got so many we got big filing cabinets out in the reception area. They was always locked, of course. When we moved out, they moved in the methadone clinic on a temporary basis and a lot of stuff was moved around."

"Did you ever see and handle Dr. Lecter's file?"

"Sure."

"Do you remember any X rays in it? Were X rays filed with the medical reports or separate?"

"With. Filed with. They were bigger than the files and that made it clumsy. We had an X ray but no full-time radiologist to keep a separate file. I honestly don't remember if it was one with his or not. There was an electrocardiogram tape Fred used to show to people, Dr. Lecter—I don't even want to call him a *doctor*—was all wired up to the electrocardiograph when he got the poor nurse. See, it was freakish— his pulse rate didn't even go up much when he attacked her. He got a separated shoulder when all the orderlies, you know, grabbed aholt of him and pulled him off of her. They'd of had to X-ray him for that. They'd have give him plenty more than a separated shoulder if I'd had something to say about it."

"If anything occurs to you, any place the file might be, would you call me?"

"We'll do what we call a global search," Ms Corey said, savoring the term, "but I don't think we'll find anything. A lot of stuff just got abandoned, not by us, but by the methadone people."

The coffee mugs had the thick rims that dribble down the sides. Starling watched Inelle Corey walk heavily away like hell's own option and drank half a cup with her napkin tucked under her chin.

Starling was coming back to herself a little. She knew she was weary of something. Maybe it was tackiness, worse than tackiness, stylelessness maybe. An indifference to things that please the eye. Maybe she was hungry for some style. Even snuff-queen style was better than nothing, it was a statement, whether you wanted to hear it or not.

Starling examined herself for snobbism and decided she had damn little to be snobbish about. Then, thinking of style, she thought of Evelda Drumgo, who had plenty of it. With the thought, Starling wanted badly to get outside herself again.

11

AND SO, Starling returned to the place where it all began for her, the Baltimore State Hospital for the Criminally Insane, now defunct. The old brown building, house of pain, is chained and barred, marked with graffiti and awaiting the wrecking ball.

It had been going downhill for years before the disappearance on vacation of its director, Dr. Frederick Chilton. Subsequent revelations of waste and mismanagement and the decrepitude of the building itself soon caused the legislature to choke off its funds. Some patients were moved to other state institutions, some were dead and a few wandered the streets of Baltimore as Thorazine zombies in an ill-conceived outpatient program that got more than one of them frozen to death.

Waiting in front of the old building, Clarice Starling realized she had exhausted the other possibilities first because she did not want to go in this place again.

The caretaker was forty-five minutes late. He was a stocky older man with a built-up shoe that clopped, and an eastern European haircut that may have been done at home. He wheezed as he led her to a side door, a few steps down from the sidewalk. The lock had been punched out by scavengers and the door secured with a chain and two padlocks. There were fuzzy webs in the links of the chain. Grass growing in the cracks of the steps tickled Starling's ankles as the caretaker fumbled with his keys. The late afternoon was overcast, the light grainy and without shadows.

"I am not knowing this building well, I just check the fire alarums," the man said.

"Do you know if any papers are stored here? Any filing cabinets, any records?"

He shrugged. "After the hospital, they had the methadone clinic here, a few months. They put everything in the basement, some bads, some linens, I don't know what it was. It's bed in there for my asthma, the mold, very bed mold. The mattresses on the bads were moldy, bed mold on the bads. I kint breed in dere. The stairs are hal on my leck. I would show you, but—?"

Starling would have been glad of some company, even his, but he would slow her down. "No, go on. Where's your office?"

"Down the block there where the driver's license bureau was before."

"If I'm not back in an hour—"

He looked at his watch. "I'm supposed to be off in a half hour."

That's just about E goddamned nuff. "What you're going to do for me, sir, is wait for your keys in your office. If I'm not back in an hour, call this number here on the card and show them where I went. If you aren't there when I come out—if you have closed up and gone home, I will personally go to see your supervisor in the morning to report you. In addition—in addition you will be audited by the Internal Revenue Service and your situation reviewed by the Bureau of Immigration and . . . and Naturalization. Do you understand? I'd appreciate a reply, sir."

"I would have waited for you, of course. You don't have to say these things."

"Thank you very much, sir," Starling said.

The caretaker put his big hands on the railing to pull himself up to sidewalk level and Starling heard his uneven gait trail off to silence. She pushed open the door and went in to a landing on the fire stairs. High, barred windows in the stairwell admitted the gray light. She debated whether to lock the door behind her and settled on tying the chain in a knot inside the door so she could open it if she lost the key.

On Starling's previous trips to the asylum, to interview Dr. Hannibal Lecter, she came through the front entrance and now it took her a moment to orient herself.

She climbed the fire stairs to the main floor. The frosted windows further cut the failing daylight and the room was in semidarkness. With her heavy flashlight, Starling found a switch and turned on the overhead light, three bulbs still burning in a broken fixture. The raw ends of the telephone wires lay on top of the receptionist's desk.

Vandals with spray cans of paint had been in the building. An eight-foot phallus and testicles decorated the reception room wall, along with the inscription FARON MAMA JERK ME OF.

The door to the director's office was open. Starling stood in the doorway. It was here she came on her first FBI assignment, when she was still a trainee, still believed everything, still thought that if you could do the job, if you could cut it, you would be accepted, regardless of race, creed, color, national origin or whether or not you were a good old boy. Of all this, there remained to her one article of faith. She believed that she could cut it.

Here Hospital Director Chilton had offered his greasy hand, and come on to her. Here he had traded secrets and eavesdropped and, believing he was as smart as Hannibal Lecter, had made the decisions that allowed Lecter to escape with so much bloodshed.

Chilton's desk remained in the office, but there was no chair, it being small enough to steal. The drawers were empty except for a crushed Alka-Seltzer. Two filing cabinets remained in the office. They had simple locks and former technical agent Starling had them open in less than a minute. A desiccated sandwich in a paper bag and some office forms for the methadone clinic were in a bottom drawer, along with breath freshener and a tube of hair tonic, a comb and some condoms.

Starling thought about the dungeonlike basement level of the asylum where Dr. Lecter had lived for eight years. She didn't want to go down there. She could use her cell phone and ask for a city police unit to go down there with her. She could ask the Baltimore field office to send another FBI agent with her. It was late on the gray afternoon and there was no way, even now, she could avoid the rush-hour traffic in Washington. If she waited, it would be worse.

She leaned on Chilton's desk in spite of the dust and tried to decide. Did she really think there might be files in the basement, or was she drawn back to the first place she ever saw Hannibal Lecter?

If Starling's career in law enforcement had taught her anything about herself, it was this: She was not a thrill seeker, and she would be happy never to feel fear again. But there *might* be files in the basement. She could find out in five minutes.

She could remember the clang of the high-security doors behind her when she went down there years ago. In case one should close behind her this time, she called the Baltimore field office and told them where she was and made an arrangement to call back in an hour to say she was out.

The lights worked in the inside staircase, where Chilton had walked her to the basement level years ago. Here he had explained the safety procedures used in dealing with Hannibal Lecter, and here he had stopped, beneath this light, to show her his wallet photograph of the nurse whose tongue Dr. Lecter had eaten during an attempted physical examination. If Dr. Lecter's shoulder had been dislocated as he was subdued, surely there must be an X ray.

A draft of air on the stairs touched her neck, as though there were a window open somewhere.

A McDonald's hamburger box was on the landing, and scattered napkins. A stained cup that had held beans. Dumpster food. Some ropey turds and napkins in the corner. The light ended at the bottom floor landing, before the great steel door to the violent ward, now standing open and hooked back against the wall. Starling's flashlight held five D-cells and cast a good wide beam.

She shined it down the long corridor of the former maximum security unit. There was something bulky at the far end. Eerie to see the cell doors standing open. The floor was littered with bread wrappers and cups. A soda can, blackened from use as a crack pipe, lay on the former orderly's desk.

Starling flipped the light switches behind the orderly station. Nothing. She took out her cell phone. The red light seemed very bright in the gloom. The phone was useless underground, but she spoke into it loudly. "Barry, back the truck up to the side entrance. Bring a floodlight. You'll need some dollies to move this stuff up the stairs . . . yeah, come on down."

Then Starling called into the dark, "Attention in there. I'm a federal officer. If you are living here illegally, you are free to leave. I will not arrest you. I am not interested in you. If you return after I complete my business, it's of no interest to me. You can come out now. If you attempt to interfere with me you will suffer severe personal injury when I bust a cap in your ass. Thank you."

Her voice echoed down the corridor where so many had ranted their voices down to croaks and gummed the bars when their teeth were gone.

Starling remembered the reassuring presence of the big orderly, Barney, when she had come to interview Dr. Lecter. The curious courtesy with which Barney and Dr. Lecter treated each other. No Barney now. Something from school bumped at her mind and, as a discipline, she made herself recall it:

Footfalls echo in the memory
Down the passage which we did not take
Towards the door we never opened
Into the rose garden.

Rose Garden, right. This was damn sure not the rose garden.

Starling, who had been encouraged in recent editorials to hate her gun as well as herself, found the touch of the weapon not at all hateful when she was uneasy. She held the .45 against her leg and started down the hall behind her flashlight. It is hard to watch both flanks at once, and imperative not to leave anyone behind you. Water dripped somewhere.

Bed frames disassembled and stacked in the cells. In others, mattresses. The water stood in the center of the corridor floor and Starling, ever mindful of her shoes, stepped from one side of the narrow puddle to the other as she proceeded. She remembered Barney's advice from years ago when all the cells were occupied. *Stay in the middle as you go down.*

Filing cabinets, all right. In the center of the corridor all the way down, dull olive in her flashlight beam.

Here was the cell that had been occupied by Multiple Miggs, the one she had hated most to pass. Miggs, who whispered filth to her and threw body fluids. Miggs, whom Dr. Lecter killed by instructing him to swallow his vile tongue. And when Miggs was dead, Sammie lived in the cell. Sammie, whose poetry Dr. Lecter encouraged with startling effect on the poet. Even now she could hear Sammie howling his verse:

I WAN TO GO TO JESA
I WAN TO GO WIV CRIEZ
I CAN GO WIV JESA
EF I AC RELL NIZE.

She still had the labored crayon text, somewhere.

The cell was stacked with mattresses now, and bales of bed linens tied up in sheets.

And at last, Dr. Lecter's cell.

The sturdy table where he read was still bolted to the floor in the middle of the room. The boards were gone from the shelves that had held his books, but the brackets still stuck out of the walls.

Starling should turn to the cabinets, but she was fixed on the cell. Here she had had the most remarkable encounter of her life. Here she had been startled, shocked, surprised.

Here she had heard things about herself so terribly true her heart resounded like a great deep bell.

She wanted to go inside. She wanted to go in, wanting it as we want to jump from balconies, as the glint of the rails tempts us when we hear the approaching train.

Starling shined her light around her, looked on the back side of the row of filing cabinets, swept her light through the nearby cells.

Curiosity carried her across the threshold. She stood in the middle of the cell where Dr. Hannibal Lecter had spent eight years. She occupied his space, where she had seen him standing, and expected to tingle, but she did not. Put her pistol and her flashlight on his table, careful that the flashlight didn't roll, and put her hands flat on his table, and beneath her hands felt only crumbs.

Overall, the effect was disappointing. The cell was as empty of its former occupant as a snake's shed skin. Starling thought then that she came to understand something: Death and danger do not have to come with trappings. They can come to you in the sweet breath of your beloved. Or on a sunny afternoon in a fish market with "La Macarena" playing on a boom box.

To business. There were about eight feet of filing cabinets, four cabinets in all, chin-high. Each had five drawers, secured by a single four-pin lock beside the top drawer. None of them was locked. All were full of files, some of them fat, all of them in folders. Old marbleized paper folders gone limp with time, and newer ones in manila folders. The files on the health of dead men, dating back to the hospital's opening in 1932. They were roughly alphabetical, with some material piled flat behind the folders in the long drawers. Starling skipped quickly along, holding her heavy flashlight on her shoulder, walking the fingers of her free hand through the files, wishing she had brought a small light she could hold in her teeth. As soon as she had some sense of the files she could skip whole drawers, through the *J*'s, very few *K*'s, on to the *L*'s and bam: Lecter, Hannibal.

Starling pulled out the long manila folder, felt it at once for the stiffness of an X ray negative, laid the folder on top of the other files and opened it to find the health history of the late I. J. Miggs. Goddammit. Miggs was going to plague her from the grave. She put the file on top of the cabinet and raced ahead into the *M*'s. Miggs's own manila folder was there, in alphabetical order. It was empty. Filing error? Did someone accidentally put Miggs's records in Hannibal Lecter's jacket? She went through all the *M*'s looking for a file without a jacket. She went back to the *J*'s. Aware of an increasing annoyance. The smell of the place was bothering her more. The caretaker was right, it was hard to breathe in this place. She was halfway through the *J*'s when she realized the stench was . . . increasing rapidly.

A small splash behind her and she spun, flashlight cocked for a blow, hand fast beneath her blazer to the gun butt. A tall man in filthy rags stood in the beam of her light, one of his outsize swollen feet in the water. One of his hands was spread from his side. The other hand held a piece of a broken plate. One of his legs and both of his feet were bound with strips of sheet.

"Hello," he said, his tongue thick with thrush. From five feet Starling could smell his breath. Beneath her jacket, her hand moved from the pistol to the Mace.

"Hello," Starling said. "Would you please stand over there against the bars?"

The man did not move. "Are you Jesa?" he asked.

"No," Starling said. "I'm not Jesus." The voice. Starling remembered the voice.

"Are you Jesa!" His face was working.

That voice. Come on, think. "Hello, Sammie," she said. "How are you? I was just thinking about you."

What about Sammie? The information, served up fast, was not exactly in order. *Put his mother's head in the collection plate while the congregation was singing "Give of Your Best to the Master." Said it was the nicest thing he had. Highway Baptist Church somewhere. Angry, Dr. Lecter said, because Jesus is so late.*

"Are you Jesa?" he said, plaintive this time. He reached in his pocket and came out with a cigarette butt, a good one more than two inches long. He put it on his shard of plate and held it out in offering.

"Sammie, I'm sorry, I'm not. I'm—"

Sammie, suddenly livid, furious that she is not Jesus, his voice booming in the wet corridor:

I WAN TO GO WIV JESA
I WAN TO GO WIV CRIEZ!

He raised the plate shard, its sharp edge like a hoe, and took a step toward Starling, both his feet in the water now and his face contorted, his free hand clutching the air between them.

She felt the cabinets hard at her back.

"YOU CAN GO WITH JESUS . . . IF YOU ACT REAL NICE," Starling recited, clear and loud as though she called to him in a far place.

"Uh huh," Sammie said calmly and stopped.

Starling fished in her purse, found her candy bar. "Sammie, I have a Snickers. Do you like Snickers?"

He said nothing.

She put the Snickers on a manila folder and held it out to him as he had held out the plate.

He took the first bite before he removed the wrapper, spit out the paper and bit again, eating half the candy bar.

"Sammie, has anybody else been down here?"

He ignored her question, put the remainder of the candy bar on his plate and disappeared behind a pile of mattresses in his old cell.

"What the hell is this?" A woman's voice. "Thank you, Sammie."

"Who are you?" Starling called.

"None of your damn business."

"Do you live here with Sammie?"

"Of course not. I'm here on a date. Do you think you could leave us alone?"

"Yes. Answer my question. How long have you been here?"

"Two weeks."

"Has anybody else been here?"

"Some bums Sammie run out."

"Sammie protects you?"

"Mess with me and find out. I can walk good. I get stuff to eat, he's got a safe place to eat it. Lot of people have deals like that."

"Is either one of you in a program someplace? Do you want to be? I can help you there."

"He done all that. You go out in the world and do all that shit and come back to what you know. What are you looking for? What do you want?"

"Some files."

"If it ain't here, somebody stole it, how smart do you have to be to figure that out?"

"Sammie?" Starling said. "Sammie?"

826   T H O M A S   H A R R I S

Sammie did not answer. "He's asleep," his friend said.

"If I leave some money out here, will you buy some food?" Starling said.

"No, I'll buy liquor. You can *find* food. You can't find liquor. Don't let the doorknob catch you in the butt on the way out."

"I'll put the money on the desk," Starling said. She felt like running, remembered leaving Dr. Lecter, remembered holding on to herself as she walked toward what was then the calm island of Barney's orderly station.

In the light of the stairwell, Starling took a twenty-dollar bill out of her wallet. She put the money on Barney's scarred, abandoned desk, and weighted it with an empty wine bottle. She unfolded a plastic shopping bag and put in it the Lecter file jacket containing Miggs's records and the empty Miggs jacket.

"Good-bye. 'Bye, Sammie," she called to the man who had circled in the world and come back to the hell he knew. She wanted to tell him she hoped Jesus would come soon, but it sounded too silly to say.

Starling climbed back into the light, to continue her circle in the world.

12

IF THERE are depots on the way to Hell, they must resemble the ambulance entrance to Maryland-Misericordia General Hospital. Over the sirens' dying wail, wails of the dying, clatter of the dripping gurneys, cries and screams, the columns of manhole steam, dyed red by a great neon EMERGENCY sign, rise like Moses' own pillar of fire in the darkness and change to cloud in the day.

Barney came out of the steam, shrugging his powerful shoulders into his jacket, his cropped round head bent forward as he covered the broken pavement in long strides east toward the morning.

He was twenty-five minutes late getting off work—the police had brought in a stoned pimp with a gunshot wound who liked to fight women, and the head nurse had asked him to stay. They always asked Barney to stay when they took in a violent patient.

Clarice Starling peered out at Barney from the deep hood of her jacket and let him get a half-block lead on the other side of the street before she hitched her tote bag on her shoulder and followed. When he passed both the parking lot and the bus stop, she was relieved. Barney would be easier to follow on foot. She wasn't sure where he lived and she needed to know before he saw her.

The neighborhood behind the hospital was quiet, blue-collar and mixed racially. A neighborhood where you put a Chapman lock on your car but you don't have to take the battery in with you at night, and the kids can play outside.

After three blocks, Barney waited for a van to clear the crosswalk and turned north onto a street of narrow houses, some with marble steps and neat front gardens. The few empty storefronts were intact with the windows soaped. Stores were beginning to open and a few people were out. Trucks parked overnight on both sides of the street blocked Starling's view for half a minute and she walked up on Barney before she realized that he had stopped. She was directly across the street when she saw him. Maybe he saw her too, she wasn't sure.

He was standing with his hands in his jacket pockets, head forward, looking from under his brows at something moving in the center of the street. A dead dove lay in the road, one wing flapped by the breeze of passing cars. The dead bird's mate paced around and around the body, cocking an eye at it, small head jerking with each step of its pink feet. Round and round, muttering the soft dove mutter. Several cars and a van passed, the surviving bird barely dodging the traffic with short last-minute flights.

Maybe Barney glanced up at her, Starling couldn't be positive. She had to keep going or be spotted. When she looked over her shoulder, Barney was squatting in the middle of the road, arm raised to the traffic.

She turned the corner out of sight, pulled off her hooded jacket, took a sweater, a baseball cap and a gym bag out of her tote bag, and changed quickly, stuffing her jacket and the tote into the gym bag, and her hair into the cap. She fell in with some homeward-bound cleaning women and turned the corner back onto Barney's street.

He had the dead dove in his cupped hands. Its mate flew with whistling wings up to the overhead wires and watched him. Barney laid the dead bird in the grass of a lawn and smoothed down its feathers.

He turned his broad face up to the bird on the wire and said something. When he continued on his way, the survivor of the pair dropped down to the grass and continued circling the body, pacing through the grass. Barney didn't look back. When he climbed the steps of an apartment house a hundred yards farther on and reached for keys, Starling sprinted a half-block to catch up before he opened the door.

"Barney. Hi."

He turned on the stairs in no great haste and looked down at her. Starling had forgotten that Barney's eyes were unnaturally far apart. She saw the intelligence in them and felt the little electronic pop of connection.

She took her cap off and let her hair fall. "I'm Clarice Starling. Remember me? I'm—"

"The G," Barney said, expressionless.

Starling put her palms together and nodded. "Well, yes, I *am* the G. Barney, I need to talk with you. It's just informal, I need to ask you some stuff."

Barney came down the steps. When he was standing on the sidewalk in front of Starling, she still had to look up at his face. She was not threatened by his size, as a man would be.

"Would you agree for the record, Officer Starling, that I have not been read my rights?" His voice was high and rough like the voice of Johnny Weismuller's Tarzan.

"Absolutely. I have not Mirandized you. I acknowledge that."

"How about saying it into your bag?"

Starling opened her bag and spoke down into it in a loud voice as though it contained a troll. "I have not Mirandized Barney, he is unaware of his rights."

"There's some pretty good coffee down the street," Barney said. "How many hats have you got in that bag?" he asked as they walked.

"Three," she said.

When the van with handicap plates passed by, Starling was aware that the occupants were looking at her, but the afflicted are often horny, as they have every right to be. The young male occupants of a car at the next crossing looked at her too, but said nothing because of Barney. Anything extended from the windows would have caught Starling's instant attention—she was wary of Crip revenge—but silent ogling is to be endured.

When she and Barney entered the coffee shop, the van backed into an alley to turn around and went back the way it came.

They had to wait for a booth in the crowded ham and egg place while the waiter yelled in Hindi to the cook, who handled meat with long tongs and a guilty expression.

"Let's eat," Starling said when they were seated. "It's on Uncle Sam. How's it going, Barney?"

"The job's okay."

"What is it?"

"Orderly, LPN."

"I figured you for an RN by now, or maybe medical school."

Barney shrugged and reached for the creamer. He looked up at Starling. "They jam you up for shooting Evelda?"

"We'll have to see. Did you know her?"

"I saw her once, when they brought in her husband, Dijon. He was dead, he bled out on them before they ever got him in the ambulance. He was leaking clear IV when he got to us. She wouldn't let him go and tried to fight the nurses. I had to . . . you know . . . Handsome woman, strong too. They didn't bring her in after—"

"No, she was pronounced at the scene."

"I would think so."

"Barney, after you turned over Dr. Lecter to the Tennessee people—"

"They weren't civil to him."

"After you—"

"And they're all dead now."

"Yes. His keepers managed to stay alive for three days. You lasted eight years keeping Dr. Lecter."

"It was six years—he was there before I came."

"How'd you do it, Barney? If you don't mind my asking, how'd you manage to last with him? It wasn't just being civil."

Barney looked at his reflection in his spoon, first convex and then concave, and thought a moment. "Dr. Lecter had perfect manners, not stiff, but easy and elegant. I was working on some correspondence courses and he shared his mind with me. That didn't mean he wouldn't *kill* me any second if he got the chance—one quality in a person doesn't rule out any other quality. They can exist side by side, good and terrible. Socrates said it a lot better. In maximum lock-down you can't afford to forget that, ever. If you keep it in mind, you're all right. Dr. Lecter may have been sorry he showed me Socrates." To Barney, lacking the disadvantage of formal schooling, Socrates was a fresh experience, with the quality of an encounter.

"Security was separate from conversation, a whole other thing," he said. "Security was never personal, even when I had to shut off his mail or put him in restraints."

"Did you talk with Dr. Lecter a lot?"

"Sometimes he went months without saying anything, and sometimes we'd talk, late at night when the crying died down. In fact—I was taking these courses by mail and I knew diddly—and he showed me a whole world, literally, of stuff—Suetonius, Gibbon, all that." Barney picked up his cup. He had a streak of orange Betadine on a fresh scratch across the back of his hand.

"Did you ever think when he escaped that he might come after you?"

Barney shook his huge head. "He told me once that, whenever it was 'feasible,' he preferred to eat the rude. 'Free-range rude,' he called them." Barney laughed, a rare sight. He has little baby teeth and his amusement seems a touch maniacal, like a baby's glee when he blows his pablum in a goo-goo uncle's face.

Starling wondered if he had stayed underground with the loonies too long.

"What about you, did you ever feel . . . creepy after he got away? Did you think he might come after you?" Barney asked.

"No."

"Why?"

"He said he wouldn't."

This answer seemed oddly satisfactory to them both.

The eggs arrived. Barney and Starling were hungry and they ate steadily for a few minutes. Then . . .

"Barney, when Dr. Lecter was transferred to Memphis, I asked you for his drawings out of his cell and you brought them to me. What happened to the rest of the stuff—books, papers? The hospital doesn't even have his medical records."

"There was this big upheaval." Barney paused, tapping the salt shaker against his palm. "There was a big upheaval, you know, at the hospital. I got laid off, a lot of people got laid off, and stuff just got scattered. There's no telling—"

"*Excuse* me?" Starling said. "I couldn't hear what you said for the racket in here. I found out last night that Dr. Lecter's annotated and signed copy of Alexandre Dumas' *Dictionary of Cuisine* came up at a private auction in New York two years ago. It went to a private collector for sixteen thousand dollars. The seller's affidavit of ownership was signed 'Cary Phlox.' You know 'Cary Phlox,' Barney? I hope you do because he did the handwriting on your employment application at the hospital where you're working but he signed it 'Barney.' Made out your tax return too. Sorry I missed what you were saying before. Want to start over? What did you get for the book, Barney?"

"Around ten," Barney said, looking straight at her.

Starling nodded. "The receipt says ten-five. What did you get for that interview with the *Tattler* after Dr. Lecter escaped?"

"Fifteen G's."

"Cool. Good for you. You made up all that bull you told those people."

"I knew Dr. Lecter wouldn't mind. He'd be disappointed if I didn't jerk them around."

"He attacked the nurse before you got to Baltimore State?"

"Yes."

"His shoulder was dislocated."

"That's what I understand."

"Was there an X ray taken?"

"Most likely."

"I want the X ray."

"Ummmm."

"I found out Lecter autographs are divided into two groups, the ones written in ink, or preincarceration, and crayon or felt-tip writing from the asylum. Crayon's worth more, but I expect you know that. Barney, I think you have all that stuff and you figure on parceling it out over the years to the autograph trade."

Barney shrugged and said nothing.

"I think you're waiting for him to be a hot topic again. What do you *want*, Barney?"

"I want to see every Vermeer in the world before I die."

"Do I need to ask who got you started on Vermeer?"

"We talked about a lot of things in the middle of the night."

"Did you talk about what he'd like to do if he was free?"

"No. Dr. Lecter has no interest in hypothesis. He doesn't believe in syllogism, or synthesis, or any absolute."

"What does he believe in?"

"Chaos. And you don't even have to believe in it. It's self-evident."

Starling wanted to indulge Barney for the moment.

"You say that like you believe it," she said, "but your whole job at Baltimore State was maintaining order. You were the chief *orderly*. You and I are both in the order business. Dr. Lecter never got away from you."

"I explained that to you."

"Because you never let your guard down. Even though in a sense you fraternized—"

"I did not *fraternize*," Barney said. "He's nobody's brother. We discussed matters of mutual interest. At least the stuff was interesting to me when I found out about it."

"Did Dr. Lecter ever make fun of you for not knowing something?"

"No. Did he make fun of you?"

"No," she said to save Barney's feelings, as she recognized for the first time the compliment implied in the monster's ridicule. "He could have made fun of me if he'd wanted to. Do you know where the stuff is, Barney?"

"Is there a reward for finding it?"

Starling folded her paper napkin and put it under the edge of her plate. "The reward is my not charging you with obstruction of justice. I gave you a walk before when you bugged my desk at the hospital."

"That bug belonged to the late Dr. Chilton."

"*Late?* How do you know he's the *late* Dr. Chilton?"

"Well, he's seven years late anyway," Barney said. "I'm not expecting him anytime soon. Let me ask you, what would satisfy *you*, Special Agent Starling?"

"I want to see the X ray. I want the X ray. If there are books of Dr. Lecter's, I want to see them."

"Say we came upon the stuff, what would happen to it afterward?"

"Well, the truth is I can't be sure. The U.S. Attorney might seize all the material as evidence in the investigation of the escape. Then it'll molder in his Bulky Evidence Room. If I examine the stuff and find nothing useful in the books, and I say so, you could claim that Dr. Lecter gave them to you. He's been *in absentia* seven years, so you might exercise a civil claim. He has no known relatives. I would recommend that any innocuous material be handed over to you. You should know my recommendation is at the low end of the totem pole. You wouldn't ever get the X ray back probably or the medical report, since they weren't his to give."

"And if I explain to you that I don't have the stuff?"

"Lecter material will become really hard to sell because we'll put out a bulletin on it and advise the market that we'll seize and prosecute for receiving and possession. I'll exercise a search and seizure warrant on your premises."

"Now that you know where my premises is. Or is it premises *are*?"

"I'm not sure. I *can* tell you, if you turn the material over, you won't get any grief for having taken it, considering what would have happened to it if you'd left it in place. As far as promising you'd get it back, I can't promise for sure." Starling rooted in her purse for punctuation. "You know, Barney, I have the feeling you haven't gotten an advanced medical degree because maybe you can't get bonded. Maybe you've got a prior somewhere. See? Now look at that—I never pulled a rap sheet on you, I never checked."

"No, you just looked at my tax return and my job application is all. I'm touched."

"If you've got a prior, maybe the USDA in that jurisdiction could drop a word, get you expunged."

Barney mopped his plate with a piece of toast. "You about finished? Let's walk a little."

"I saw Sammie, remember he took over Miggs's cell? He's still living in it," Starling said when they were outside.

"I thought the place was condemned."

"It is."

"Is Sammie in a program?"

"No, he just lives there in the dark."

"I think you ought to blow the whistle on him. He's a brittle diabetic, he'll die. Do you know why Dr. Lecter made Miggs swallow his tongue?"

"I think so."

"He killed him for offending you. That was just the specific thing. Don't feel bad—he might have done it anyway."

They continued past Barney's apartment house to the lawn where the dove still circled the body of its dead mate. Barney shooed it with his hands. "Go on," he said to the bird. "That's long enough to grieve. You'll walk around until the cat gets you." The dove flew away whistling. They could not see where it lit.

Barney picked up the dead bird. The smooth-feathered body slid easily into his pocket.

"You know, Dr. Lecter talked about you a little, once. Maybe the last time I talked to him, one of the last times. The bird reminds me. You want to know what he said?"

"Sure," Starling said. Her breakfast crawled a little, and she was determined not to flinch.

"We were talking about inherited, hardwired behavior. He was using genetics in roller pigeons as an example. They go way up in the air and roll over and over backwards in a display, falling toward the ground. There are shallow rollers and deep rollers. You can't breed two deep rollers or the offspring will roll all the way down, crash and die. What he said was 'Officer Starling is a deep roller, Barney. We'll hope one of her parents was not.'"

Starling had to chew on that. "What'll you do with the bird?" she asked.

"Pluck it and eat it," Barney said. "Come on to the house and I'll give you the X ray and the books."

Carrying the long package back toward the hospital and her car, Starling heard the surviving mourning dove call once from the trees.

13

THANKS TO the consideration of one madman and the obsession of another, Starling now had for the moment what she always wanted, an office on the storied subterranean corridor at Behavioral Science. It was bitter to get the office this way.

Starling never expected to go straight to the elite Behavioral Science Section when she graduated from the FBI Academy, but she had believed that she could earn a place there. She knew she would spend several years in field offices first.

Starling was good at the job, but not good at office politics, and it took her years to see that she would never go to Behavioral Science, despite the wishes of its chief, Jack Crawford.

A major reason was invisible to her until, like an astronomer locating a black hole, she found Deputy Assistant Inspector General Paul Krendler by his influence on the bodies around him. He had never forgiven her for finding the serial killer Jame Gumb ahead of him, and he could not bear the press attention it brought her.

Once Krendler called her at home on a rainy winter night. She answered the telephone in a robe and bunny slippers with her hair up in a towel. She would always remember the date exactly because it was the first week of Desert Storm. Starling was a tech agent then and she had just returned from New York, where she had replaced the radio in the Iraqi U.N. Mission's limousine. The new radio was just like the old one, except it broadcast conversations in the car to a Defense Department satellite overhead. It had been a dicey maneuver in a private garage and she was still edgy.

For a wild second, she thought Krendler had called to say she'd done a good job.

She remembered the rain against the windows and Krendler's voice on the phone, speech a little slurred, bar noises in the background.

He asked her out. He said he could come by in half an hour. He was married.

"I think not, Mr. Krendler," she said and pushed the record button on her answering machine, it making the requisite legal beep, and the line went dead.

Now, years later in the office she had wanted to earn, Starling penciled her name on a piece of scrap paper and Scotch-taped it to the door. That wasn't funny and she tore it off again and threw it in the trash.

There was one piece of mail in her in-tray. It was a questionnaire from *The Guinness Book of World Records*, which prepared to list her as having killed more criminals than any other female law enforcement officer in United States history. The term *criminals* was being used advisedly, the publisher explained, as all of the deceased had multiple felony convictions and three had outstanding warrants. The questionnaire went into the trash along with her name.

She was in her second hour of pecking away at the computer workstation, blowing stray strands of hair out of her face, when Crawford knocked on the door and stuck his head inside.

"Brian called from the lab, Starling. Mason's X ray and the one you got from Barney are a match. It's Lecter's arm. They'll digitize the images and compare them, but he says there's no question. We'll post everything to the secure Lecter VICAP folder."

"What about Mason Verger?"

"We tell him the truth," Crawford said. "You and I both know he won't share, Starling, unless he gets something he can't move on himself. But if we try to take over his lead in Brazil at this point, it'll evaporate."

"You told me to leave it alone and I did."

"You were doing *something* in here."

"Mason's X ray came by DHL Express. DHL took the bar code and label information and pinpointed the pickup location. It's in the Hotel Ibarra in Rio." Starling raised her hand to forestall interruption. "This is all New York sources, now. No inquiries at all in Brazil.

"Mason does his phone business, a lot of it, through the switchboard of a sports book in Las Vegas. You can imagine the volume of calls they take."

"Do I want to know how you found that out?"

"Strictly legit," Starling said. "Well, pretty much legit—I didn't leave anything in his house. I've got the codes to look at his phone bill, that's all. All the tech agents have them. Let's say he obstructs justice. With his influence, how long would we have to beg for a warrant to tap and trace? What could you do to him anyway if he was convicted? But he's using a *sports* book."

"I see it," Crawford said. "The Nevada Gaming Commission could either tap the phone or squeeze the sports book for what we need to know, which is where the calls go."

She nodded. "I left Mason alone just like you said."

"I can see that," Crawford said. "You can tell Mason we expect to help through Interpol and the embassy. Tell him we need to move people down there and start the framework for extradition. Lecter's probably committed crimes in South America, so we better extradite before the Rio police start looking in their files under *Cannibalismo*. If he's in South America at all. Starling, does it make you sick to talk to Mason?"

"I have to get in the mode. You walked me through it when we did that floater in West Virginia. What am I saying, 'floater.' She was a *person* named Fredrica Bimmel, and, yes, Mason makes me sick. A lot of stuff makes me sick lately, Jack."

Starling surprised herself into silence. She had never before addressed Section Chief Jack Crawford by his first name, she had never planned to call him "Jack" and it shocked her. She studied his face, a face famously hard to read.

He nodded, his smile wry and sad. "Me too, Starling. Want a couple of these Pepto-Bismol tablets to chew before you talk to Mason?"

Mason Verger did not bother to take Starling's call. A secretary thanked her for the message and said he'd return her call. But he didn't get back to her personally. To Mason, several places higher on the notification list than Starling, the X ray match was old news.

14

MASON KNEW that his X ray was truly of Dr. Lecter's arm well before Starling was told, because Mason's sources within the Justice Department were better than hers.

Mason was told in an E-mail message signed with the screen name Token287. That is the second screen name of U.S. Representative Parton Vellmore's assistant on the House Judiciary Committee. Vellmore's office had been E-mailed by Cassius199, the second screen name of the Justice Department's own Paul Krendler.

Mason was excited. He did not think Dr. Lecter was in Brazil, but the X ray proved that the doctor now had the normal number of fingers on his left hand. That information meshed with a new lead from Europe on the doctor's whereabouts. Mason believed the tip came from within Italian law enforcement and it was the strongest whiff of Lecter he had had in years.

Mason had no intention of sharing his lead with the FBI. Owing to seven years of relentless effort, access to confidential federal files, extensive leafleting, no international restrictions and large expenditures of money, Mason was ahead of the FBI in the pursuit of Lecter. He only shared information with the Bureau when he needed to suck its resources.

To keep up appearances, he instructed his secretary to pester Starling for developments anyway. Mason's tickler file prompted the secretary to call her at least three times a day.

Mason immediately wired five thousand dollars to his informant in Brazil to pursue the source of the X ray. The contingency fund he wired to Switzerland was much larger and he was prepared to send more when he had hard information in hand.

He believed that his source in Europe had found Dr. Lecter, but Mason had been cheated on information many times and he had learned to be careful. Soon proof would come. Until it did, to relieve the agony of waiting Mason concerned himself with what would happen after the doctor was in his hands. These arrangements had also been long in the making, for Mason was a student of suffering . . .

God's choices in inflicting suffering are not satisfactory to us, nor are they understandable, unless innocence offends Him. Clearly He needs some help in directing the blind fury with which He flogs the earth.

Mason came to understand his role in all of this in the twelfth year of his paralysis, when he was no longer sizeable beneath his sheet and knew that he would never rise again. His quarters at the Muskrat Farm mansion were completed and he had means, but not unlimited means, because the Verger patriarch, Molson, still ruled.

It was Christmas in the year of Dr. Lecter's escape. Subject to the quality of feelings that commonly attend Christmas, Mason was wishing bitterly that he had arranged for Dr. Lecter to be murdered in the asylum; Mason knew that somewhere Dr. Lecter was going to and fro in the earth and walking up and down in it, and very likely having a good time.

Mason himself lay under his respirator, a soft blanket covering all, a nurse standing by, shifting on her feet, wishing she could sit down. Some poor children had been bussed to Muskrat Farm to carol. With the doctor's permission, Mason's windows were opened briefly to the crisp air and, beneath the windows, holding candles in their cupped hands, the children sang.

The lights were out in Mason's room and in the black air above the farm the stars hung close.

"O little town of Bethlehem, how still we see thee lie!"

How still we see thee lie.
How still we see thee lie.

The mockery of the line pressed down on him. *How still we see thee lie, Mason!*

The Christmas stars outside his window maintained their stifling silence. The stars said nothing to him when he looked up to them with his pleading, goggled eye, gestured to them with the fingers he could move. Mason did not think that he could breathe. If he were suffocating in space, he thought, the last thing he would see would be the beautiful silent airless stars. He was suffocating now, he thought, his respirator could not keep up, he had to *wait for breath* the lines of his vital signs Christmas-green on the scopes and spiking, little evergreens in the black forest night of the scopes. Spike of his heartbeat, systolic spike, diastolic spike.

The nurse, frightened, about to push the alarm button, about to reach for the adrenaline.

Mockery of the lines, *how still we see thee lie, Mason.*

An Epiphany then at Christmas. Before the nurse could ring, or reach for medication, the first coarse bristles of Mason's revenge brushed his pale and seeking, ghost crab of a hand, and began to calm him.

At Christmas communions around the earth, the devout believe that, through the miracle of transubstantiation, they eat the actual body and blood of Christ. Mason began the preparations for an even more impressive ceremony with no transubstantiation necessary. He began his arrangements for Dr. Hannibal Lecter to be eaten alive.

15

MASON'S EDUCATION was an odd one, but perfectly fitted to the life his father envisioned for him and to the task before him now.

As a child he attended a boarding school, to which his father contributed heavily, where Mason's frequent absences were excused. For weeks at a time the elder Verger conducted Mason's real education, taking the boy with him to the stockyards and slaughterhouses that were the basis of his fortune.

Molson Verger was a pioneer in many areas of livestock production, particularly in the area of economy. His early experiments with cheap feed rank with those of Batterham fifty years before. Molson Verger adulterated the pigs' diet with hog hair meal, mealed chicken feathers and manure to an extent considered daring at the time. He was regarded as a reckless visionary in the 1940s when he first took away the pigs' fresh drinking water and had them drink ditch liquor, made of fermented animal waste, to hasten weight gain. The laughter stopped when his profits rolled in, and his competitors hurried to copy him.

Molson Verger's leadership in the meatpacking industry did not stop there. He fought bravely and with his own funds against the Humane Slaughter Act, strictly from the standpoint of economy, and managed to keep face branding legal though it cost him dearly in legislative compensation. With Mason at his side, he supervised large-scale experiments in the problems of lairage, determining how long you could deprive animals of food and water before slaughter without significant weight losses.

It was Verger-sponsored genetic research that finally achieved the heavy double-muscling of the Belgian swine breeds without the concomitant drip losses that plagued the Belgians. Molson Verger bought breeding stock worldwide and sponsored a number of foreign breeding programs.

But slaughterhouses are at base a people business and nobody understood that better than Molson Verger. He managed to cow the leadership of the unions when they tried to encroach on his profits with wage and safety demands. In this area his solid relationships with organized crime served him well for thirty years.

Mason bore a strong resemblance to his father then, with dark shiny eyebrows above pale blue butcher's eyes, and a low hairline that slanted across his forehead, descending from his right to his left. Often, affectionately, Molson Verger liked to take his son's head in his hands and just feel it, as though he were confirming the son's paternity through physiognomy, just as he could feel the face of a pig and tell by the bone structure its genetic makeup.

Mason learned well and, even after his injuries confined him to his bed, he was able to make sound business decisions to be implemented by his minions. It was son Mason's idea to have the U.S. government and the United Nations slaughter all the native pigs in Haiti, citing the danger from them of African swine flu. He was then able to sell the government great white American pigs to replace the native swine. The great sleek swine, when faced with Haitian conditions, died as soon as possible and had to be replaced again and again from Mason's stock until the Haitians replaced their own pigs with hardy little rooters from the Dominican Republic.

Now, with a lifetime of knowledge and experience, Mason felt like Stradivarius approaching the worktable as he built the engines of his revenge.

What a wealth of information and resources Mason had in his faceless skull! Lying in his bed, composing in his mind like the deaf Beethoven, he remembered walking the swine fairs with his father, checking out the competition, Molson's little silver knife ever ready to slip out of his waistcoat and into a pig's back to check the depth of back fat, walking away from the outraged squeal, too dignified to be challenged, his hand back in his pocket, thumb marking the place on the blade.

Mason would have smiled if he had lips, remembering his father sticking a 4-H contestant pig who thought everyone was his friend, the child who owned it crying. The child's father coming over furious, and Molson's thugs taking him outside the tent. Oh, there were some good, funny times.

At the swine fairs Mason had seen exotic pigs from all over the world. For his new purpose, he brought together the best of all that he had seen.

Mason began his breeding program immediately after his Christmas Epiphany and centered it in a small pig-breeding facility the Vergers owned in Sardinia, off the coast of Italy. He chose the place for its remoteness and its convenience to Europe.

Mason believed—correctly—that Dr. Lecter's first stop outside the United States after his escape was in South America. But he had ever been convinced that Europe was where a man of Dr. Lecter's tastes would settle—and he had watchers yearly at the Salzburg Music Festival and other cultural events.

This is what Mason sent to his breeders in Sardinia to prepare the theater of Dr. Lecter's death:

The giant forest pig, *Hylochoerus meinertzhageni*, six teats and thirty-eight chromosomes, a resourceful feeder, an opportunistic omnivore, like man. Two meters in length in the highland families, it weighs about two hundred seventy-five kilograms. The giant forest pig is Mason's ground note.

The classic European wild boar, *S. scrofa scrofa*, thirty-six chromosomes in its purest form, no facial warts, all bristles and great ripping tusks, a big fast and fierce animal that will kill a viper with its sharp hooves and eat the snake like it was a Slim Jim. When aroused or rutting, or protecting its piglets, it will charge anything that threatens. Sows have twelve teats and are good mothers. In *S. scrofa scrofa*, Mason found his theme and the facial appearance appropriate to provide Dr. Lecter a last, hellish vision of himself consumed. (See *Harris on the Pig, 1881*.)

He bought the Ossabaw Island pig for its aggressiveness, and the Jiaxing Black for high estradiol levels.

A false note when he introduced a Babirusa, *Babyrousa babyrussa*, from Eastern Indonesia, known as the hog-deer for the exaggerated length of its tusks. It was a slow breeder with only two teats, and at one hundred kilograms it cost him too much in size. No time was lost, as there were other, parallel litters that did not include the Babirusa.

In dentition, Mason had little variety to choose from. Almost every species had teeth adequate to the task, three pairs of sharp incisors, one pair of elongated canines, four pairs of premolars, and three crushing pairs of molars, upper and lower, for a total of forty-four teeth.

Any pig will eat a dead man, but to get him to eat a live one some education is required. Mason's Sardinians were up to the task.

Now, after an effort of seven years and many litters, the results were . . . remarkable.

16

WITH ALL the actors except Dr. Lecter in place in the Gennargentu Mountains of Sardinia, Mason turned his attention toward recording the doctor's death for posterity and his own viewing pleasure. His arrangements had long been made, but now the alert must be given.

He conducted this sensitive business on the telephone through his legitimate sports book switchboard near the Castaways in Las Vegas. His calls were tiny lost threads in the great volume of weekend action there.

Mason's radio quality voice, minus plosives and fricatives, bounced from the National Forest near the Chesapeake shore to the desert and back across the Atlantic, first to Rome:

In an apartment on the seventh floor of a building on the Via Archimede, behind the hotel of the same name, the telephone is ringing, the hoarse double-rumpf of a telephone ringing in Italian. In the darkness, sleepy voices.

"*Cosa? Cosa c'è?*"

"*Accendi la luce, idiòta.*"

The bedside lamp comes on. Three people are in the bed. The young man nearest the phone picks up the receiver and hands it to a portly older man in the middle. On the other side is a blonde girl in her twenties. She raises a sleepy face to the light, then subsides again.

"Pronto, chi? Chi parla?"

"Oreste, my friend. It's Mason."

The heavy man gets himself together, signals to the younger man for a glass of mineral water.

"Ah, Mason my friend, excuse me, I was asleep, what time is it there?"

"It's late everywhere, Oreste. Do you remember what I said I would do for you and what you must do for me?"

"Well, .of course."

"The time has come, my friend. You know what I want. I want a two-camera setup, I want better quality sound than your sex films have, and you have to make your own electricity, so I want the generator a long way from the set. I want some nice nature footage too for when we edit, and birdcalls. I want you to check out the location tomorrow and set it up. You can leave the stuff there, I'll provide security and you can come back to Rome until the shoot. But be ready to roll on two hours' notice. Do you understand that, Oreste? A draft is waiting for you in Citibank at the EUR, got it?"

"Mason, in this moment, I am making—"

"Do you want to do this, Oreste? You *said* you were tired of making hump movies and snuff movies and historical crap for the RAI. Do you seriously want to make a feature, Oreste?"

"Yes, Mason."

"Then go today. The cash is at Citibank. I want you to go."

"Where, Mason?"

"Sardinia. Fly to Cagliari, you'll be met."

The next call went to Porto Torres on the east coast of Sardinia. The call was brief. There was not a lot to say because the machinery there was long established and as efficient as Mason's portable guillotine. It was sounder too, ecologically, but not as quick.

II

FLORENCE

17

Night in the heart of Florence, the old city artfully lighted.

The Palazzo Vecchio rising from the dark piazza, floodlit, intensely medieval with its arched windows and battlements like jack-o'-lantern teeth, bell tower soaring into the black sky.

Bats will chase mosquitoes across the clock's glowing face until dawn, when the swallows rise on air shivered by the bells.

Chief Investigator Rinaldo Pazzi of the Questura, raincoat black against the marble statues fixed in acts of rape and murder, came out of the shadows of the Loggia and crossed the piazza, his pale face turning like a sunflower to the palace light. He stood on the spot where the reformer Savonarola was burned and looked up at the windows where his own forebear came to grief.

There, from that high window, Francesco de' Pazzi was thrown naked with a noose around his neck, to die writhing and spinning against the rough wall. The archbishop hanged beside Pazzi in all his holy vestments provided no spiritual comfort; eyes bulging, wild as he choked, the archbishop locked his teeth in Pazzi's flesh.

The Pazzi family were all brought low on that Sunday, 26 April,

1478, for killing Giuliano de' Medici and trying to kill Lorenzo the Magnificent in the cathedral at Mass.

Now Rinaldo Pazzi, a Pazzi of the Pazzi, hating the government as much as his ancestor ever did, disgraced and out of fortune, listening for the whisper of the axe, came to this place to decide how best to use a singular piece of luck:

Chief Investigator Pazzi believed that he had found Hannibal Lecter living in Florence. He had a chance to regain his reputation and enjoy the honors of his trade by capturing the fiend. Pazzi also had a chance to sell Hannibal Lecter to Mason Verger for more money than he could imagine—if the suspect was indeed Lecter. Of course, Pazzi would be selling his own ragged honor as well.

Pazzi did not head the Questura investigation division for nothing— he was gifted and in his time he had been driven by a wolfish hunger to succeed in his profession. He also carried the scars of a man who, in the haste and heat of his ambition, once seized his gift by the blade.

He chose this place to cast his lot because he once experienced a moment of Epiphany here that made him famous and then ruined him.

The Italian sense of irony was strong in Pazzi: How fitting that his fateful revelation came beneath this window, where the furious spirit of his forebear might still spin against the wall. In this same place, he could forever change the Pazzi luck.

It was the hunt for another serial killer, *Il Mostro*, that made Pazzi famous and then let the crows peck at his heart. That experience made possible his new discovery. But ending of the *Il Mostro* case was bitter ashes in Pazzi's mouth and inclined him now toward a dangerous game outside the law.

Il Mostro, the Monster of Florence, preyed on lovers in Tuscany for seventeen years in the 1980s and 1990s. The Monster crept up on couples as they embraced in the many Tuscan lovers' lanes. It was his custom to kill the lovers with a small-caliber pistol, arrange them in a careful tableau with flowers and expose the woman's left breast. His tableaux had an odd familiarity about them, they left a sense of déjà vu.

The Monster also excised anatomical trophies, except in the single instance when he slew a long-haired German homosexual couple, apparently by mistake.

The public pressure on the Questura to catch *Il Mostro* was intense, and drove Rinaldo Pazzi's predecessor out of office. When Pazzi took over as chief investigator, he was like a man fighting bees, with the press swarming through his office whenever they were allowed, and photographers lurking in the Via Zara behind Questura headquarters, where he had to drive out.

Tourists to Florence during the period will remember plastered everywhere the posters with the single watching eye that warned couples against the Monster.

Pazzi worked like a man possessed.

He called on the American FBI's Behavioral Science Section for help in profiling the killer and read everything he could find on FBI profiling methods.

He used proactive measures: Some lovers' lanes and cemetery trysting places had more police than lovers sitting in pairs in the cars. There were not enough women officers to go around. During hot weather male couples took turns wearing a wig and many mustaches were sacrificed. Pazzi set an example by shaving off his own mustache.

The Monster was careful. He struck, but his needs did not force him to strike often.

Pazzi noticed that in years past there were long periods when the Monster did not strike at all—one gap of eight years. Pazzi seized on this. Painstakingly, laboriously, dragooning clerical help from every agency he could threaten, confiscating his nephew's computer to use along with the Questura's single machine, Pazzi listed every criminal in northern Italy whose periods of imprisonment coincided with the time gaps in *Il Mostro*'s series of murders. The number was ninety-seven.

Pazzi took over an imprisoned bank robber's fast, comfortable old Alfa-Romeo GTV and, putting more than five thousand kilometers on the car in a month, he personally looked at ninety-four of the convicts and had them interrogated. The others were disabled or dead.

There was almost no evidence at the scenes of the crimes to help him narrow down the list. No body fluids of the perpetrator, no fingerprints.

A single shell casing was recovered from a murder scene at Impruneta. It was a .22 Winchester-Western rimfire with extractor marks consistent with a Colt semiautomatic pistol, possibly a Woodsman. The bullets in all the crimes were .22s from the same gun. There were no wipe marks on the bullets from a silencer, but a silencer could not be ruled out.

Pazzi was a Pazzi and above all things ambitious, and he had a young and lovely wife with an ever-open beak. His efforts ground twelve pounds off his lean frame. Younger members of the Questura privately remarked on his resemblance to the cartoon character Wile E. Coyote.

When some young smart alecks put a morph program in the Questura computer that changed the Three Tenors' faces into those of a jackass, a pig and a goat, Pazzi stared at the morph for minutes and felt his own face changing back and forth into the countenance of the jackass.

The window of the Questura laboratory is garlanded with garlic to keep out evil spirits. With the last of his suspects visited and grilled to no effect, Pazzi stood at this window looking out on the dusty courtyard and despaired.

He thought of his new wife, and her good hard ankles and the patch of down in the small of her back. He thought of how her breasts quivered and bounced when she brushed her teeth and how she laughed when she saw him watching. He thought of the things he wanted to give her. He imagined her opening the gifts. He thought of his wife in visual terms; she was fragrant and wonderful to touch as well, but the visual was first in his memory.

He considered the way he wanted to appear in her eyes. Certainly not in his present role as butt of the press—Questura headquarters in Florence is located in a former mental hospital, and the cartoonists were taking full advantage of that fact.

Pazzi imagined that success came as a result of inspiration. His visual memory was excellent and, like many people whose primary sense is sight, he thought of revelation as the development of an image, first blurred and then coming clear. He ruminated the way most of us look for a lost object: We review its image in our minds and compare that image to what we see, mentally refreshing the image many times a minute and turning it in space.

Then a political bombing behind the Uffizi museum took the public's attention, and Pazzi's time, away from the case of *Il Mostro* for a short while.

Even as he worked the important museum bomb case, *Il Mostro*'s created images stayed in Pazzi's mind. He saw the Monster's tableaux peripherally, as we look beside an object to see it in the dark. Particularly he dwelt on the couple found slain in the bed of a pickup truck in Impruneta, the bodies carefully arranged by the Monster, strewn and garlanded with flowers, the woman's left breast exposed.

Pazzi had left the Uffizi museum one early afternoon and was crossing the nearby Piazza Signoria, when an image jumped at him from the display of a postcard vendor.

Not sure where the image came from, he stopped just at the spot where Savonarola was burned. He turned and looked around him. Tourists were thronging the piazza. Pazzi felt cold up his back. Maybe it was all in his head, the image, the pluck at his attention. He retraced his steps and came again.

There it was: a small, fly-specked, rain-warped poster of Botticelli's painting *Primavera.* The original painting was behind him in the Uffizi museum. *Primavera.* The garlanded nymph on the right, her left breast exposed, flowers streaming from her mouth as the pale Zephyrus reached for her from the forest.

There. The image of the couple dead in the bed of the pickup, garlanded with flowers, flowers in the girl's mouth. Match. Match.

Here, where his ancestor spun choking against the wall, came the idea, the master image Pazzi sought, and it was an image created five hundred years ago by Sandro Botticelli—the same artist who had for forty florins painted the hanged Francesco de' Pazzi's image on the wall of the Bargello prison, noose and all. How could Pazzi resist this inspiration, with its origin so delicious?

He had to sit down. All the benches were full. He was reduced to showing his badge and commandeering a place on a bench from an old man whose crutches he honestly did not see until the old veteran was up on his single foot and very loud and rude about it too.

Pazzi was excited for two reasons. To find the image *Il Mostro* used was a triumph, but much more important, Pazzi had seen a copy of *Primavera* in his rounds of the criminal suspects.

He knew better than to flog his memory; he leaned and loafed and invited it. He returned to the Uffizi and stood before the original "Primavera," but not too long. He walked to the straw market and touched the snout of the bronze boar *Il Porcellino,* drove out to the Ippocampo and, leaning against the hood of his dusty car, the smell of hot oil in his nose, watched the children playing soccer . . .

He saw the staircase first in his mind, and the landing above, the top of the *Primavera* poster appearing first as he climbed the stairs; he could go back and see the entrance doorframe for a second, but nothing of the street, and no faces.

Wise in the ways of interrogation, he questioned himself, going to the secondary senses:

When you saw the poster, what did you hear? . . . *Pots rattling in a ground-floor kitchen. When you went up on the landing and stood before the poster, what did you* hear? *The television. A television in a sitting room. Robert Stack playing Eliot Ness in* Gli intoccabili. *Did you* smell *cooking? Yes, cooking. Did you* smell *anything else? I saw the poster—NO, not what you saw. Did you* smell *anything else? I could still smell the Alfa, hot inside, it was still in my nose, hot oil smell, hot from . . . the Raccordo, going fast on the Raccordo Autostrada to where? San Casciano. I heard a dog barking too, in San Casciano, a burglar and rapist named Girolamo something.*

In that moment when the connection is made, in that synaptic spasm of completion when the thought drives through the red fuse, is our keenest pleasure. Rinaldo Pazzi had had the best moment of his life.

In an hour and a half, Pazzi had Girolamo Tocca in custody. Tocca's wife threw rocks after the little convoy that took her husband away.

CHAPTER

18

TOCCA WAS a dream suspect. As a young man, he had served nine years in prison for the murder of a man he caught embracing his fiancée in a lovers' lane. He had also faced charges of sexually molesting his daughters and other domestic abuse, and had served a prison sentence for rape.

The Questura nearly destroyed Tocca's house trying to find evidence. In the end Pazzi himself, searching Tocca's grounds, came up with a cartridge case that was one of the few pieces of physical evidence the prosecution submitted.

The trial was a sensation. It was held in a high-security building called the Bunker where terrorist trials were held in the seventies, across from the Florence offices of the newspaper *La Nazione*. The sworn and besashed jurors, five men and five women, convicted Tocca on almost no evidence except his character. Most of the public believed him innocent, but many said Tocca was a jerk and well jailed. At the age of sixty-five, he received a sentence of forty years at Volterra.

The next months were golden. A Pazzi had not been so celebrated in Florence for the last five hundred years, since Pazzo de' Pazzi returned from the First Crusade with flints from the Holy Sepulchre.

Rinaldo Pazzi and his beautiful wife stood beside the archbishop in the Duomo when, at the traditional Easter rite, these same holy flints were used to ignite the rocket-powered model dove, which flew out of the church along its wire to explode a cart of fireworks for a cheering crowd.

The papers hung on every word Pazzi said as he dispensed credit, within reason, to his subordinates for the drudgery they had performed. Signora Pazzi was sought for fashion advice, and she did look wonderful in the garments designers encouraged her to wear. They were invited to stuffy teas in the homes of the powerful, and had dinner with a count in his castle with suits of armor standing all around.

Pazzi was mentioned for political office, praised over the general noise in the Italian parliament and given the brief to head Italy's co-operative effort with the American FBI against the Mafia.

That brief, and a fellowship to study and take part in criminology seminars at Georgetown University, brought the Pazzis to Washington, D.C. The chief inspector spent much time at Behavioral Science in Quantico and dreamed of creating a Behavioral Science division in Rome.

Then, after two years, disaster: In a calmer atmosphere, an appellate court not under public pressure agreed to review Tocca's conviction. Pazzi was brought home to face the investigation. Among the former colleagues he had left behind, the knives were out for Pazzi.

An appellate panel overthrew Tocca's conviction and reprimanded Pazzi, saying the court believed he had planted evidence.

His former supporters in high places fled him as they would a bad smell. He was still an important official of the Questura, but he was a lame duck and everyone knew it. The Italian government moves slowly, but soon the axe would fall.

It was in the awful searing time while Pazzi waited for the axe that he first saw the man known among scholars in Florence as Dr. Fell . . .

Rinaldo Pazzi, climbing the stairs in the Palazzo Vecchio on a menial errand, one of many found for him by his former subordinates at the Questura as they enjoyed his fall from grace. Pazzi saw only the toes of his own shoes on the cupped stone and not the wonders of art around him as he climbed beside the frescoed wall. Five hundred years ago, his forebear had been dragged bleeding up these stairs.

At a landing, he squared his shoulders like the man he was, and forced himself to meet the eyes of the people in the frescoes, some of them kin to him. He could already hear the wrangling from the Salon of Lilies above him where the directors of the Uffizi Gallery and the Belle Arti Commission were meeting in joint session.

Pazzi's business today was this: The longtime curator of the Palazzo Capponi was missing. It was widely believed the old fellow had eloped with a woman or someone's money or both. He had failed to meet with his governing body here in the Palazzo Vecchio for the last four monthly meetings.

Pazzi was sent to continue the investigation. Chief Inspector Pazzi, who had sternly lectured these same gray-faced directors of the Uffizi and members of the rival Belle Arti Commission on security following the museum bombing, must now appear before them in reduced circumstances to ask questions about a curator's love life. He did not look forward to it.

The two committees were a contentious and prickly assembly— for years they could not even agree on a venue, neither side willing to meet in the other's offices. They met instead in the magnificent Salon of Lilies in the Palazzo Vecchio, each member believing the beautiful room suitable to his own eminence and distinction. Once established there, they refused to meet anywhere else, even though the Palazzo Vecchio was undergoing one of its thousand restorations, with scaffolding and drop cloths and machinery underfoot.

Professor Ricci, an old schoolmate of Rinaldo Pazzi, was in the hall outside the salon with a sneezing fit from the plaster dust. When he had recovered sufficiently, he rolled his streaming eyes at Pazzi.

"*La solita arringa*," Ricci said, "they are arguing as usual. You've come about the missing Capponi curator? They're fighting over his job right now. Sogliato wants the job for his nephew. The scholars are impressed with the temporary one they appointed months ago, Dr. Fell. They want to keep him."

Pazzi left his friend patting his pockets for tissues, and went into the historic chamber with its ceiling of gold lilies. Hanging drop cloths on two of the walls helped to soften the din.

The nepotist, Sogliato, had the floor, and was holding it by dint of volume:

"The Capponi correspondence goes back to the thirteenth century. Dr. Fell might hold in his hand, in his *non-Italian* hand, a note from Dante Alighieri himself. Would he recognize it? I think *not*. You have examined him in medieval Italian, and I will not deny his language is admirable. For a *straniero*. But is he familiar with the personalities of pre-Renaissance Florence? I think *not*. What if he came upon a note in the Capponi library from—from Guido de' Cavalcanti for instance? Would he recognize it? I think *not*. Would you care to address that, Dr. Fell?"

Rinaldo Pazzi scanned the room and did not see anyone he recognized as Dr. Fell, even though he had examined a photograph of the man not an hour before. He did not see Dr. Fell because the doctor was not seated with the others. Pazzi heard his voice first, then located him.

Dr. Fell stood very still beside the great bronze statue of Judith and Holofernes, giving his back to the speaker and the crowd. He spoke without turning around and it was hard to know which figure the voice came from—Judith, her sword forever raised to strike the drunken king, or Holofernes, gripped by the hair, or Dr. Fell, slender and still beside Donatello's bronze figures. His voice cut through the din like a laser through smoke and the squabbling men fell silent.

"Cavalcanti replied publicly to Dante's first sonnet in *La Vita Nuova*, where Dante describes his strange dream of Beatrice Portinari," Dr. Fell said. "Perhaps Cavalcanti commented privately as well. If he wrote to a Capponi, it would be to Andrea, he was more literary than his brothers." Dr. Fell turned to face the group in his own time, after an interval uncomfortable to everyone but him. "Do you know Dante's first sonnet, Professor Sogliato? *Do* you? It fascinated Cavalcanti and it's worth your time. In part it says:

> *"The first three hours of night were almost spent*
> *The time that every star shines down on us*
> *When Love appeared to me so suddenly*
> *That I still shudder at the memory.*
> *Joyous Love seemed to me, the while he held*
> *My heart within his hands, and in his arms*
> *My lady lay asleep wrapped in a veil.*

He woke her then and trembling and obedient
She ate that burning heart out of his hand;
Weeping I saw him then depart from me.

"Listen to the way he makes an instrument of the Italian vernacular, what he called the *vulgari eloquentia* of the people:

'Allegro mi sembrava Amor tenendo
Meo core in mano, e ne le braccia avea
Madonna involta in un drappo dormendo.
Poi la svegliava, e d'esto core ardendo
Lei paventosa umilmente pascea
Appreso gir lo ne vedea piangendo.'"

Even the most contentious Florentines could not resist the verse of Dante ringing off these frescoed walls in Dr. Fell's clear Tuscan. First applause, and then by wet-eyed acclamation, the memberships affirmed Dr. Fell as master of the Palazzo Capponi, leaving Sogliato to fume. If the victory pleased the doctor, Pazzi could not tell, for he turned his back again. But Sogliato was not quite through.

"If he is such an expert on Dante, let him lecture on Dante, *to the Studiolo.*" Sogliato hissed the name as though it were the Inquisition. "Let him face them *extempore*, next Friday if he can." The Studiolo, named for an ornate private study, was a small, fierce group of scholars who had ruined a number of academic reputations and met often in the Palazzo Vecchio. Preparing for them was regarded as a considerable chore, appearing before them a peril. Sogliato's uncle seconded his motion and Sogliato's brother-in-law called for a vote, which his sister recorded in the minutes. It passed. The appointment stood, but Dr. Fell must satisfy the Studiolo to keep it.

The committees had a new curator for the Palazzo Capponi, they did not miss the old curator, and they gave the disgraced Pazzi's questions about the missing man short shrift. Pazzi held up admirably.

Like any good investigator, he had sifted the circumstances for profit. Who would benefit from the old curator's disappearance? The missing curator was a bachelor, a well-respected quiet scholar with an orderly life. He had some savings, nothing much. All he had was his job and with it the privilege of living in the attic of the Palazzo Capponi.

Here was the new appointee, confirmed by the board after close questioning on Florentine history and archaic Italian. Pazzi had examined Dr. Fell's application forms and his National Health affidavits.

Pazzi approached him as the board members were packing their briefcases to go home.

"Dr. Fell."

"Yes, *Commendatore?*"

The new curator was small and sleek. His glasses were smoked in the top half of the lenses and his dark clothing beautifully cut, even for Italy.

"I was wondering if you ever met your predecessor?" An experienced policeman's antennae are tuned to the bandwidth of fear. Watching Dr. Fell carefully, Pazzi registered absolute calm.

"I never met him. I read several of his monographs in the *Nuova Antologia.*" The doctor's conversational Tuscan was as clear as his recitation. If there was a trace of an accent, Pazzi could not place it.

"I know that the officers who first investigated checked the Palazzo Capponi for any sort of note, a farewell note, a suicide note, and found nothing. If you come upon anything in the papers, anything personal, even if it's trivial, would you call me?"

"Of course, *Commendator* Pazzi."

"Are his personal effects still at the Palazzo?"

"Packed in two suitcases, with an inventory."

"I'll send—I'll come by and pick them up."

"Would you call me first, *Commendatore*? I can disarm the security system before you arrive, and save you time."

The man is too calm. Properly, he should fear me a little. He asks me to call him before coming by.

The committee had ruffled Pazzi's feathers. He could do nothing about that. Now he was piqued by this man's presumption. He piqued back.

"Dr. Fell, may I ask you a personal question?"

"If your duty requires it, *Commendatore*."

"You have a relatively new scar on the back of your left hand."

"And you have a new wedding ring on yours: *La Vita Nuova?*" Dr. Fell smiled. He has small teeth, very white. In Pazzi's instant of surprise, before he could decide to be offended, Dr. Fell held up his scarred hand and went on: "Carpal tunnel syndrome, *Commendatore*. History is a hazardous profession."

"Why didn't you declare carpal tunnel syndrome on your National Health forms when you came to work here?"

"My impression was, *Commendatore*, that injuries are relevant only if one is receiving disability payments; I am not. Nor am I disabled."

"The surgery was in Brazil, then, your country of origin."

"It was not in Italy, I received nothing from the Italian government," Dr. Fell said, as though he believed he had answered completely.

They were the last to leave the council room. Pazzi had reached the door when Dr. Fell called to him.

"*Commendator* Pazzi?"

Dr. Fell was a black silhouette against the tall windows. Behind him in the distance rose the Duomo.

"Yes?"

"I think you are a Pazzi of the Pazzi, am I correct?"

"Yes. How did you know that?" Pazzi would consider a reference to recent newspaper coverage rude in the extreme.

"You resemble a figure from the Della Robbia rondels in your family's chapel at Santa Croce."

"Ah, that was Andrea de' Pazzi depicted as John the Baptist," Pazzi said, a small slick of pleasure on his acid heart.

When Rinaldo Pazzi left the slender figure standing in the council room, his lasting impression was of Dr. Fell's extraordinary stillness.

He would add to that impression very soon.

20

NOW THAT ceaseless exposure has calloused us to the lewd and the vulgar, it is instructive to see what still seems wicked to us. What still slaps the clammy flab of our submissive consciousness hard enough to get our attention?

In Florence it was the exposition called Atrocious Torture Instruments, and it was here that Rinaldo Pazzi next encountered Dr. Fell.

The exhibit, featuring more than twenty classic instruments of torture with extensive documentation, was mounted in the forbidding Forte di Belvedere, a sixteenth-century Medici stronghold that guards the city's south wall. The expo opened to enormous, unexpected crowds; excitement leaped like a trout in the public trousers.

The scheduled run was a month; Atrocious Torture Instruments ran for six months, equaling the draw of the Uffizi Gallery and outdrawing the Pitti Palace Museum.

The promoters, two failed taxidermists who formerly got along by eating offal from the trophies they mounted, became millionaires and made a triumphal tour of Europe with their show, wearing their new tuxedos.

The visitors came in couples, mostly, from all over Europe, taking advantage of the extended hours to file among the engines of pain, and read carefully in any of four languages the provenance of the devices and how to use them. Illustrations by Dürer and others, along with contemporary diaries, enlightened the crowds on matters such as the finer points of wheeling.

The English from one placard:

> *The Italian princes preferred to have their victims broken on the ground with the use of the iron-tired wheel as the striking agent and blocks beneath the limbs as shown, while in northern Europe the popular method was to lash the victim to the wheel, break him or her with an iron bar, and then lace the limbs through the spokes around the periphery of the wheel, compound fractures providing the requisite flexibility, with the still-noisy head and trunk in the center. The latter method was a more satisfactory spectacle, but the recreation might be cut short if a piece of marrow went to the heart.*

The exposition of Atrocious Torture Instruments could not fail to appeal to a connoisseur of the worst in mankind. But the essence of the worst, the true asafoetida of the human spirit, is not found in the Iron Maiden or the whetted edge; Elemental Ugliness is found in the faces of the crowd.

In the semidarkness of this great stone room, beneath the lit, hanging cages of the damned, stood Dr. Fell, connoisseur of facial cheeses, holding his spectacles in his scarred hand, the tip of an ear-piece against his lips, his face rapt as he watched the people file through.

Rinaldo Pazzi saw him there.

Pazzi was on his second menial errand of the day. Instead of having dinner with his wife, he was pushing through the crowd to post new warnings to couples about the Monster of Florence, whom he had failed to catch. Such a warning poster was prominent over his own desk, placed there by his new superiors, along with other wanted posters from around the world.

The taxidermists, watching the box office together, were happy to add a bit of contemporary horror to their show, but asked Pazzi to put up the poster himself, as neither seemed willing to leave the other alone with the cash. A few locals recognized Pazzi and hissed him from the anonymity of the crowd.

Pazzi pushed pins through the corners of the blue poster, with its single staring eye, on a bulletin board near the exit where it would attract the most attention, and turned on a picture light above it. Watching the couples leaving, Pazzi could see that many were in estrus, rubbing against each other in the crowd at the exit. He did not want to see another tableau, no more blood and flowers.

Pazzi did want to speak to Dr. Fell—it would be convenient to pick up the missing curator's effects while he was this near the Palazzo Capponi. But when Pazzi turned from the bulletin board, the doctor was gone. He was not in the crowd at the exit. There was only the stone wall where he had stood, beneath the hanging starvation cage with its skeleton in a fetal curve still pleading to be fed.

Pazzi was annoyed. He pushed through the crowd until he was outside, but did not find the doctor.

The guard at the exit recognized Pazzi and said nothing when he stepped over the rope and walked off the path, onto the dark grounds of the Forte di Belvedere. He went to the parapet, looking north across the Arno. Old Florence was at his feet, the great hump of the Duomo, the tower of the Palazzo Vecchio rising in light.

Pazzi was a very old soul, writhing on a spike of ridiculous circumstance. His city mocked him.

The American FBI had given the knife a final twist in Pazzi's back, saying in the press that the FBI profile of *Il Mostro* had been nothing like the man Pazzi arrested. *La Nazione* added that Pazzi had "rail-roaded Tocca off to prison."

The last time Pazzi had put up the blue *Il Mostro* poster was in America; it was a proud trophy he hung on the wall of Behavioral Science, and he had signed it at the request of the American FBI agents. They knew all about him, admired him, invited him. He and his wife had been guests on the Maryland shore.

Standing at the dark parapet, looking over his ancient city, he smelled the salt air off the Chesapeake, saw his wife on the shore in her new white sneakers.

There was a picture of Florence in Behavioral Science at Quantico, shown him as a curiosity. It was the same view he was seeing now, old Florence from the Belvedere, the best view there is. But not in color. No, a pencil drawing, shaded with charcoal. The drawing was in a photograph, in the background of a photograph. It was a photograph of the American serial murderer, Dr. Hannibal Lecter. Hannibal the Cannibal. Lecter had drawn Florence from memory and the drawing was hanging in his cell in the asylum, a place as grim as this.

When did it fall on Pazzi, the ripening idea? Two images, the real Florence lying before him, and the drawing he recalled. Placing the poster of *Il Mostro* minutes ago. Mason Verger's poster of Hannibal Lecter on his own office wall with its huge reward and its advisories:

DR LECTER WILL HAVE TO CONCEAL HIS LEFT HAND AND MAY ATTEMPT TO HAVE IT SURGICALLY ALTERED, AS HIS TYPE OF POLYDACTYLY, THE APPEARANCE OF PERFECT EXTRA FINGERS, IS EXTREMELY RARE AND INSTANTLY IDENTIFIABLE.

Dr. Fell holding his glasses to his lips with his scarred hand.

A detailed sketch of this view on the wall of Hannibal Lecter's cell.

Did the idea come to Pazzi while he was looking at the city of Florence beneath him, or out of the swarming dark above the lights? And why was its harbinger a scent of the salt breeze off the Chesapeake?

Oddly for a visual man, the connection arrived with a sound, the sound a drop would make as it lands in a thickening pool.

Hannibal Lecter had fled to Florence.

plop

Hannibal Lecter was Dr. Fell.

Rinaldo Pazzi's inner voice told him he might have gone mad in the cage of his plight; his frenzied mind might be breaking its teeth on the bars like the skeleton in the starvation cage.

With no memory of moving, he found himself at the Renaissance gate leading from the Belvedere into the steep Costa di San Giorgio, a narrow street that winds and plunges down to the heart of Old Florence in less than half a mile. His steps seemed to carry him down the steep cobbles without his volition, he was going faster than he wished, looking always ahead for the man called Dr. Fell, for this was the way home for him—halfway down Pazzi turned into the Costa Scarpuccia, always descending until he came out on the Via de' Bardi, near the river. Near the Palazzo Capponi, home of Dr. Fell.

Pazzi, puffing from his descent, found a place shadowed from the streetlight, an apartment entrance across from the palazzo. If someone came along he could turn and pretend to press a bell.

The palazzo was dark. Pazzi could make out above the great double doors the red light of a surveillance camera. He could not be sure if it worked full-time, or served only when someone rang the bell. It was well within the covered entrance. Pazzi did not think it could see along the façade.

He waited a half-hour, listening to his own breath, and the doctor did not come. Perhaps he was inside with no lights on.

The street was empty. Pazzi crossed quickly and stood close against the wall.

Faintly, faintly a thin sound from within. Pazzi leaned his head against the cold window bars to listen. A clavier, Bach's *Goldberg Variations* well played.

Pazzi must wait, and lurk and think. This was too soon to flush his quarry. He must decide what to do. He did not want to be a fool again. As he backed into the shadow across the street, his nose was last to disappear.

21

THE CHRISTIAN martyr San Miniato picked up his severed head from the sand of the Roman amphitheater in Florence and carried it beneath his arm to the mountainside across the river where he lies in his splendid church, tradition says.

Certainly San Miniato's body, erect or not, passed en route along the ancient street where we now stand, the Via de' Bardi. The evening gathers now and the street is empty, the fan pattern of the cobbles shining in a winter drizzle not cold enough to kill the smell of cats. We are among the palaces built six hundred years ago by the merchant princes, the kingmakers and connivers of Renaissance Florence. Within bow-shot across the Arno River are the cruel spikes of the Signoria, where the monk Savonarola was hanged and burned, and that great meat house of hanging Christs, the Uffizi museum.

These family palaces, pressed together in an ancient street, frozen in the modern Italian bureaucracy, are prison architecture on the outside, but they contain great and graceful spaces, high silent halls no one ever sees, draped with rotting, rain-streaked silk where lesser works of the great Renaissance masters hang in the dark for years, and are illuminated by the lightning after the draperies collapse.

Here beside you is the palazzo of the Capponi, a family distinguished for a thousand years, who tore up a French king's ultimatum in his face and produced a pope.

The windows of the Palazzo Capponi are dark now, behind their iron grates. The torch rings are empty. In that pane of crazed old glass is a bullet hole from the 1940s. Go closer. Rest your head against the cold iron as the policeman did and listen. Faintly you can hear a clavier. Bach's *Goldberg Variations* played, not perfectly, but exceedingly well, with an engaging understanding of the music. Played not perfectly, but exceedingly well; there is perhaps a slight stiffness in the left hand.

If you believe you are beyond harm, will you go inside? Will you enter this palace so prominent in blood and glory, follow your face through the web-spanned dark, toward the exquisite chiming of the clavier? The alarms cannot see us. The wet policeman lurking in the doorway cannot see us. Come . . .

Inside the foyer the darkness is almost absolute. A long stone staircase, the stair rail cold beneath our sliding hand, the steps scooped by the hundreds of years of footfalls, uneven beneath our feet as we climb toward the music.

The tall double doors of the main salon would squeak and howl if we had to open them. For you, they are open. The music comes from the far, far corner, and from the corner comes the only light, light of many candles pouring reddish through the small door of a chapel off the corner of the room.

Cross to the music. We are dimly aware of passing large groups of draped furniture, vague shapes not quite still in the candlelight, like a sleeping herd. Above us the height of the room disappears into darkness.

The light glows redly on an ornate clavier and on the man known to Renaissance scholars as Dr. Fell, the doctor elegant, straight-backed as he leans into the music, the light reflecting off his hair and the back of his quilted silk dressing gown with a sheen like pelt.

The raised cover of the clavier is decorated with an intricate scene of banquetry, and the little figures seem to swarm in the candlelight above the strings. He plays with his eyes closed. He has no need of the sheet music. Before him on the lyre-shaped music rack of the clavier is a copy of the American trash tabloid the *National Tattler.* It is folded to show only the face on the front page, the face of Clarice Starling.

Our musician smiles, ends the piece, repeats the saraband once for his own pleasure and as the last quill-plucked string vibrates to silence in the great room, he opens his eyes, each pupil centered with a red pinpoint of light. He tilts his head to the side and looks at the paper before him.

He rises without sound and carries the American tabloid into the tiny, ornate chapel, built before the discovery of America. As he holds it up to the light of the candles and unfolds it, the religious icons above the altar seem to read the tabloid over his shoulder, as they would in a grocery line. The type is seventy-two-point Railroad Gothic. It says *"DEATH ANGEL: CLARICE STARLING, THE FBI'S KILLING MACHINE."*

Faces painted in agony and beatitude around the altar fade as he snuffs the candles. Crossing the great hall he has no need of light. A puff of air as Dr. Hannibal Lecter passes us. The great door creaks, closes with a thud we can feel in the floor. Silence.

Footsteps entering another room. In the resonances of this place, the walls feel closer, the ceiling still high—sharp sounds echo late from above—and the still air holds the smell of vellum and parchment and extinguished candlewicks.

The rustle of paper in the dark, the squeak and scrape of a chair. Dr. Lecter sits in a great armchair in the fabled Capponi Library. His eyes reflect light redly, but they do not glow red in the dark, as some of his keepers have sworn they do. The darkness is complete. He is considering . . .

It is true that Dr. Lecter created the vacancy at the Palazzo Capponi by removing the former curator—a simple process requiring a few seconds' work on the old man and a modest outlay for two bags of cement—but once the way was clear he won the job fairly, demonstrating to the Belle Arti Committee an extraordinary linguistic capability, sight-translating medieval Italian and Latin from the densest Gothic black-letter manuscripts.

He has found a peace here that he would preserve—he has killed hardly anybody, except his predecessor, during his residence in Florence.

His appointment as translator and curator of the Capponi Library is a considerable prize to him for several reasons:

The spaces, the height of the palace rooms, are important to Dr. Lecter after his years of cramped confinement. More important, he feels a resonance with the palace; it is the only private building he has ever seen that approaches in dimension and detail the memory palace he has maintained since youth.

In the library, this unique collection of manuscripts and correspondence going back to the early thirteenth century, he can indulge a certain curiosity about himself.

Dr. Lecter believed, from fragmentary family records, that he was descended from a certain Giuliano Bevisangue, a fearsome twelfth-century figure in Tuscany, and from the Machiavelli as well as the Visconti. This was the ideal place for research. While he had a certain abstract curiosity about the matter, it was not ego-related. Dr. Lecter does not require conventional reinforcement. His ego, like his intelligence quota, and the degree of his rationality, is not measurable by conventional means.

In fact, there is no consensus in the psychiatric community that Dr. Lecter should be termed a man. He has long been regarded by his professional peers in psychiatry, many of whom fear his acid pen in the professional journals, as something entirely Other. For convenience they term him "monster."

The monster sits in the black library, his mind painting colors on the dark and a medieval air running in his head. He is considering the policeman.

Click of a switch and a low lamp comes on.

Now we can see Dr. Lecter seated at a sixteenth-century refectory table in the Capponi Library. Behind him is a wall of pigeonholed manuscripts and great canvas-covered ledgers going back eight hundred years. A fourteenth-century correspondence with a minister of the Republic of Venice is stacked before him, weighted with a small casting Michelangelo did as a study for his horned Moses, and in front of the inkstand, a laptop computer with on-line research capability through the University of Milan.

Bright red and blue among the dun and yellow piles of parchment and vellum is a copy of the *National Tattler*. And beside it, the Florence edition of *La Nazione*.

Dr. Lecter selects the Italian newspaper and reads its latest attack on Rinaldo Pazzi, prompted by an FBI disclaimer in the case of *Il Mostro*. "Our profile never matched Tocca," an FBI spokesman said.

La Nazione cited Pazzi's background and training in America, at the famous Quantico academy, and said he should have known better.

The case of *Il Mostro* did not interest Dr. Lecter at all, but Pazzi's background did. How unfortunate that he should encounter a policeman trained at Quantico, where Hannibal Lecter was a textbook case.

When Dr. Lecter looked into Rinaldo Pazzi's face at the Palazzo Vecchio, and stood close enough to smell him, he knew for certain that Pazzi suspected nothing, even though he had asked about the scar on Dr. Lecter's hand. Pazzi did not even have any serious interest in him regarding the curator's disappearance.

The policeman saw him at the exposition of torture instruments. Better to have encountered him at an orchid show.

Dr. Lecter was well aware that all the elements of epiphany were present in the policeman's head, bouncing at random with the million other things he knew.

Should Rinaldo Pazzi join the late curator of the Palazzo Vecchio down in the damp? Should Pazzi's body be found after an apparent sui-cide? *La Nazione* would be pleased to have hounded him to death.

Not now, the monster reflected, and turned to his great rolls of vellum and parchment manuscripts.

Dr. Lecter does not worry. He delighted in the writing style of Neri Capponi, banker and emissary to Venice in the fifteenth century, and read his letters, aloud from time to time, for his own pleasure late into the night.

22

BEFORE DAYLIGHT Pazzi had in his hands the photographs taken for Dr. Fell's state work permit, attached with the negatives to his *permesso di soggiorno* in the files of the Carabinieri. Pazzi also had the excellent mug shots reproduced on Mason Verger's poster. The faces were similar in shape, but if Dr. Fell was Dr. Hannibal Lecter, some work had been done on the nose and cheeks, maybe collagen injections.

The ears looked promising. Like Alphonse Bertillon a hundred years before, Pazzi pored over the ears with his magnifying glass. They seemed to be the same.

On the Questura's outdated computer, he punched in his Interpol access code to the American FBI's Violent Criminal Apprehension Program and called up the voluminous Lecter file. He cursed his slow modem and tried to read the fuzzy text off the screen until the letters jumped in his vision. He knew most of the case. Two things made him catch his breath. One old and one new. The most recent update cited an X ray indicating Lecter probably had had surgery on his hand. The old item, a scan of a hand-printed Tennessee police report, noted that while he killed his guards in Memphis, Hannibal Lecter played a tape of the *Goldberg Variations*.

The poster circulated by the rich American victim, Mason Verger, dutifully encouraged an informant to call the FBI number provided. It gave the standard warning about Dr. Lecter being armed and dangerous. A private telephone number was provided as well—just below the paragraph about the huge reward.

Airfare from Florence to Paris is ridiculously expensive and Pazzi had to pay it out of his own pocket. He did not trust the French police to give him a phone patch without meddling, and he knew no other way to get one. From an American Express phone cabin near the Opera, he telephoned the private number on Mason's poster. He assumed the call would be traced. Pazzi spoke English well enough, but he knew his accent would betray him as Italian.

The voice was male, American, very calm.

"Would you state your business please?"

"I may have information about Hannibal Lecter."

"Yes, well, thank you for calling. Do you know where he is now?"

"I believe so. Is the reward in effect?"

"Yes, it is. What hard evidence do you have that it's him? You have to understand we get a lot of crank calls."

"I'll tell you he's undergone plastic surgery on his face and had an operation on his left hand. He can still play the *Goldberg Variations*. He has Brazilian papers."

A pause. Then, "Why haven't you called the police? I'm required to encourage you to do that."

"Is the reward in effect in all circumstances?"

"The reward is for information leading to the arrest and conviction."

"Would the reward be payable in . . . special circumstances?"

"Do you mean a bounty on Dr. Lecter? Say, in the case of someone who might not ordinarily be eligible to accept a reward?"

"Yes."

"We are both working toward the same goal. So stay on the telephone please, while I make a suggestion. It is against international convention and U.S. law to offer a bounty for someone's death, sir. Stay on the telephone please. May I ask if you're calling from Europe?"

"Yes, I am, and that's all I'm telling you."

"Good, hear me out—I suggest you contact an attorney to discuss legality of bounties and not to undertake any illegal action against Dr. Lecter. May I recommend an attorney? There's one in Geneva who is excellent in these matters. May I give you the toll-free number? I encourage you strongly to call him and to be frank with him."

Pazzi bought a prepaid telephone card and made his next call from a booth in the Bon Marché department store. He spoke to a person with a dry Swiss voice. It took less than five minutes.

Mason would pay one million United States dollars for Dr. Hannibal Lecter's head and hands. He would pay the same amount for information leading to arrest. He would privately pay three million dollars for the doctor alive, no questions asked, discretion guaranteed. The terms included one hundred thousand dollars in advance. To qualify for the advance, Pazzi would have to provide a positively identifiable fingerprint from Dr. Lecter, the print *in situ* on an object. If he did that, he could see the rest of the cash in an escrowed safe deposit locker in Switzerland at his convenience.

Before he left Bon Marché for the airport, Pazzi bought a peignoir for his wife in peach silk moiré.

How do you behave when you know the conventional honors are dross? When you have come to believe with Marcus Aurelius that the opinion of future generations will be worth no more than the opinion of the current one? Is it possible to behave well then? Desirable to behave well then?

Now Rinaldo Pazzi, a Pazzi of the Pazzi, chief inspector of the Florentine Questura, had to decide what his honor was worth, or if there is a wisdom longer than considerations of honor.

He returned from Paris by dinnertime, and slept a little while. He wanted to ask his wife, but he could not, though he did take comfort in her. He lay awake for a long time afterward, after her breathing was quiet. Late in the night he gave up on sleep and went out to walk and think.

Avarice is not unknown in Italy, and Rinaldo Pazzi had imbibed plenty with his native air. But his natural acquisitiveness and ambition had been whetted in America, where every influence is felt more quickly, including the death of Jehovah and the incumbency of Mammon.

When Pazzi came out of the shadows of the Loggia and stood in the spot where Savonarola was burned in the Piazza Signoria, when he looked up at the window in the floodlit Palazzo Vecchio where his ancestor died, he believed that he was deliberating. He was not. He had already decided piecemeal.

We assign a moment to decision, to dignify the process as a timely result of rational and conscious thought. But decisions are made of kneaded feelings; they are more often a lump than a sum.

Pazzi had decided when he got on the plane to Paris. And he had decided an hour ago, after his wife in her new peignoir had been only dutifully receptive. And minutes later when, lying in the dark, he reached over to cup her cheek and give her a tender good night kiss, and he felt a tear beneath his palm. Then, unaware, she ate his heart.

Honors again? Another chance to endure the archbishop's breath while the holy flints were struck to the rocket in the cloth dove's ass? More praise from the politicians whose private lives he knew too well? What was it worth to be known as the policeman who caught Dr. Hannibal Lecter? For a policeman, credit has a short half-life. Better to SELL HIM.

The thought pierced and pounded Rinaldo, left him pale and determined, and when the visual Rinaldo cast his lot he had two scents mixed in his mind, his wife and the Chesapeake shore.

SELL HIM. SELL HIM. SELL HIM. SELL HIM. SELL HIM. SELL HIM.

Francesco de' Pazzi did not stab harder in 1478 when he had Giuliano on the cathedral floor, when in his frenzy he stabbed himself through the thigh.

CHAPTER

24

DR. HANNIBAL LECTER's fingerprint card is a curiosity and something of a cult object. The original is framed on the wall of the FBI's Identification Section. Following the FBI custom in printing people with more than five fingers, it has the thumb and four adjacent fingers on the front side of the card, and the sixth finger on the reverse.

Copies of the fingerprint card went around the earth when the doctor first escaped, and his thumbprint appears enlarged on Mason Verger's wanted poster with enough points marked on it for a minimally trained examiner to make a hit.

Simple fingerprinting is not a difficult skill and Pazzi could do a workmanlike job of lifting prints, and could make a coarse comparison to reassure himself. But Mason Verger required a fresh fingerprint, *in situ* and unlifted, for his experts to examine independently; Mason had been cheated before with old fingerprints lifted years ago at the scenes of Dr. Lecter's early crimes.

But how to get Dr. Fell's fingerprints without alerting him? Above all, he must not alarm the doctor. The man could disappear too well, and Pazzi would be left with nothing.

The doctor did not often leave the Palazzo Capponi, and it would be a month before the next meeting of the Belle Arti. Too long to wait to plant a water glass at his place, at all the places, as the committee never furnished such amenities.

Once he had decided to sell Hannibal Lecter to Mason Verger, Pazzi had to work alone. He could not afford to bring the attention of the Questura to Dr. Fell by getting a warrant to enter the Palazzo, and the building was too well defended with alarms for him to break in and take fingerprints.

Dr. Fell's refuse can was much cleaner and newer than the others on the block. Pazzi bought a new can and in the dead of night switched lids with the Palazzo Capponi can. The galvanized surface was not ideal and, in an all-night effort, Pazzi came out with a pointillist's nightmare of prints that he could never decipher.

The next morning he appeared red-eyed at the Ponte Vecchio. In a jewelry shop on the old bridge he bought a wide, highly polished silver bracelet and the velvet-covered stand that held it for display. In the artisan sector south of the Arno, in the narrow streets across from the Pitti Palace, he had another jeweler grind the maker's name off the bracelet. The jeweler offered to apply an antitarnish coating to the silver, but Pazzi said no.

Dread Sollicciano, the Florentine jail on the road to Prato.

On the second floor of the women's division, Romula Cjesku, leaning over a deep laundry sink, soaped her breasts, washing and drying carefully before she put on a clean, loose cotton shirt. Another Gypsy, returning from the visiting room, spoke in the Romany language to Romula in passing. A tiny line appeared between Romula's eyes. Her handsome face kept its usual solemn set.

She was allowed off the tier at the customary 8:30 A.M., but when she approached the visitor's room, a turnkey intercepted her and steered her aside to a private interview room on the prison's ground floor. Inside, instead of the usual nurse, Rinaldo Pazzi was holding her infant boy.

"Hello, Romula," he said.

She went straight up to the tall policeman and there was no question that he would hand over the child at once. The baby wanted to nurse and began to nuzzle at her.

Pazzi pointed with his chin at a screen in the corner of the room. "There's a chair back there. We can talk while you feed him."

"Talk about what, *Dottore*?" Romula's Italian was passable, as was her French, English, Spanish, and Romany. She spoke without affect— her best theatrics had not prevented this three-month term for picking pockets.

She went behind the screen. In a plastic bag concealed in the baby's swaddling clothes were forty cigarettes and sixty-five thousand lire, a little more than forty-one dollars, in ragged notes. She had a choice to make here. If the policeman had frisked the baby, he could charge her when she took out the contraband and have all her privileges revoked. She deliberated a moment, looking up at the ceiling while the baby suckled. Why would he bother? He had the advantage anyway. She took out the bag and concealed it in her underwear. His voice came over the screen.

"You are a nuisance in here, Romula. Nursing mothers in jail are a waste of time. There are legitimately sick people in here for the nurses to take care of. Don't you hate to hand over your baby when the visiting time is up?"

What could he want? She knew who he was, all right—a chief, a *Pezzo da novanta*, bastard .90 caliber.

Romula's business was reading the street for a living, and pick-pocketing was a subset of that. She was a weathered thirty-five and she had antennae like the great luna moth. *This policeman*—she studied him over the screen—*look how neat, the wedding ring, the shined shoes, lived with his wife but had a good maid—his collar stays were put in after the collar was ironed. Wallet in the jacket pocket, keys in the right front trouser, money in the left front trouser folded flat probably with a rubber band around. His dick between. He was flat and masculine, a little cauliflower in the ear and a scar at the hairline from a blow. He wasn't going to ask her for sex—if that was the idea, he wouldn't have brought the baby. He was no prize, but she didn't think he would have to take sex from women in jail. Better not to look into his bitter black eyes while the baby was suckling. Why did he bring the baby? Because he wants her to see his power, suggest he could have it taken from her. What does he want? Information? She would tell him anything he wants to hear about fifteen Gypsies who never existed. All right, what can I get out of this? We'll see. Let's show him a bit of the brown.*

She watched his face as she came out from behind the screen, a crescent of aureole showing beside the baby's face.

"It's hot back there," she said. "Could you open a window?"

"I could do better than that, Romula. I could open the *door,* and you know it."

Quiet in the room. Outside the noise of Sollicciano like a constant, dull headache.

"Tell me what you want. I would do something gladly, but not anything." Her instinct told her, correctly, he would respect her for the caveat.

"It's only *la tua solita cosa,* the usual thing you do," Pazzi said, "but I want you to botch it."

25

DURING THE day, they watched the front of the Palazzo Capponi from the high shuttered window of an apartment across the street—Romula, and an older Gypsy woman who helped with the baby and may have been Romula's cousin, and Pazzi, who stole as much time as possible from his office.

The wooden arm that Romula used in her trade waited on a chair in the bedroom.

Pazzi had obtained the daytime use of the apartment from a teacher at the nearby Dante Alighieri School. Romula insisted on a shelf for herself and the baby in the small refrigerator.

They did not have to wait long.

At 9:30 A.M. on the second day, Romula's helper hissed from the window seat. A black void appeared across the street as one of the massive palazzo doors swung inward.

There he was, the man known in Florence as Dr. Fell, small and slender in his dark clothing, sleek as a mink as he tested the air on the stoop and regarded the street in both directions. He clicked a remote control to set the alarms and pulled the door shut with its great wrought-iron handle, pitted with rust and impossible to print. He carried a shopping bag.

Seeing Dr. Fell for the first time through the crack in the shutters, the older Gypsy gripped Romula's hand as though to stop her, looked Romula in the face and gave her head a quick sharp shake while the policeman was not looking.

Pazzi knew at once where he was going.

In Dr. Fell's garbage, Pazzi had seen the distinctive wrapping papers from the fine food store, Vera dal 1926, on the Via San Jacopo near the Santa Trinità Bridge. The doctor headed in that direction now as Romula shrugged into her costume and Pazzi watched out the window.

"*Dunque*, it's groceries," Pazzi said. He could not help repeating Romula's instructions for the fifth time. "Follow along, Romula. Wait this side of the Ponte Vecchio. You'll catch him coming back, carrying the full bag in his hand. I'll be half a block ahead of him, you'll see me first. I'll stay close by. If there's a problem, if you get arrested, I'll take care of it. If he goes someplace else, come back to the apartment. I'll call you. Put this pass in a taxi windshield and come to me."

"*Eminenza*," Romula said, elevating the honorifics in the Italian ironic style, "if there is a problem and someone else helps me, don't hurt him, my friend won't take anything, let him run."

Pazzi did not wait for the elevator, he raced down the stairs in a greasy boilersuit, wearing a cap. It is hard to tail somebody in Florence because the sidewalks are narrow and your life is worth nothing in the street. Pazzi had a battered *motorino* at the curb with a bundle of a dozen brooms tied to it. The scooter started on the first kick and in a puff of blue smoke the chief investigator started down the cobbles, the little motorbike bouncing over the cobbles like a small burro trotting beneath him.

Pazzi dawdled, was honked at by the ferocious traffic, bought cigarettes, killed time to stay behind, until he was sure where Dr. Fell was going. At the end of the Via de' Bardi, the Borgo San Jacopo was one-way coming toward him. Pazzi abandoned the bike on the sidewalk and followed on foot, turning his flat body sideways to slide through the crowd of tourists at the south end of the Ponte Vecchio.

Florentines say Vera dal 1926, with its wealth of cheeses and truffles, smells like the feet of God.

The doctor certainly took his time in there. He was making a selection from the first white truffles of the season. Pazzi could see his back through the windows, past the marvelous display of hams and pastas.

Pazzi went around the corner and came back, he washed his face in the fountain spewing water from its own mustachioed, lion-eared face. "You'd have to shave that to work for me," he said to the fountain over the cold ball of his stomach.

The doctor coming out now, a few light parcels in his bag. He started back down the Borgo San Jacopo toward home. Pazzi moved ahead on the other side of the street. The crowds on the narrow sidewalk forced Pazzi into the street, and the mirror of a passing Carabinieri patrol car banged painfully against his wristwatch. "*Stronzo! Analfabeta!*" the driver yelled out the window, and Pazzi vowed revenge. By the time he reached the Ponte Vecchio he had a forty-meter lead.

Romula was in a doorway, the baby cradled in her wooden arm, her other hand extended to the crowds, her free arm ready beneath her loose clothing to lift another wallet to add to the more than two hundred she had taken in her lifetime. On her concealed arm was the wide and well-polished silver bracelet.

In a moment the victim would pass through the throng coming off the old bridge. Just as he came out of the crowd onto the Via de' Bardi, Romula would meet him, do her business and slip into the stream of tourists crossing the bridge.

In the crowd, Romula had a friend she could depend on. She knew nothing of the victim and she did not trust the policeman to protect her. Giles Prevert, known on some police dossiers as Giles Dumain, or Roger LeDuc, but locally known as Gnocco, waited in the crowd at the south end of the Ponte Vecchio for Romula to make the dip. Gnocco was diminished by his habits and his face beginning to show the skull beneath, but he was still wiry and strong and well able to help Romula if the dip went sour.

In clerk's clothing, he was able to blend with the crowd, popping up from time to time as though the crowd were a prairie dog town. If the intended victim seized Romula and held her, Gnocco could trip, fall all over the victim and remain entangled with him, apologizing profusely until she was well away. He had done it before.

Pazzi passed her, stopped in a line of customers at a juice bar, where he could see.

Romula came out of the doorway. She judged with a practiced eye the sidewalk traffic between her and the slender figure coming toward her. She could move wonderfully well through a crowd with the baby in front of her, supported in her false arm of wood and canvas. All right. As usual she would kiss the fingers of her visible hand and reach for his face to put the kiss there. With her free hand, she would fumble at his ribs near his wallet until he caught her wrist. Then she would pull away from him.

Pazzi had promised that this man could not afford to hold her for the police, that he would want to get away from her. In all her attempts to pick a pocket, no one had ever offered violence to a woman holding a baby. The victim often thought it was someone else beside him fumbling in his jacket. Romula herself had denounced several innocent bystanders as pickpockets to avoid being caught.

Romula moved with the crowd on the sidewalk, freed her concealed arm, but kept it under the false arm cradling the baby. She could see the mark coming through the field of bobbing heads, ten meters and closing.

Madonna! Dr. Fell was veering off in the thick of the crowd, going with the stream of tourists *over* the Ponte Vecchio. He was not going home. She pressed into the crowd, but could not get to him. Gnocco's face, still ahead of the doctor, looking to her, questioning. She shook her head and Gnocco let him pass. It would do no good if Gnocco picked his pocket.

Pazzi snarling beside her as though it were her fault. "Go to the apartment. I'll call you. You have the taxi pass for the old town? Go. *Go!*"

Pazzi retrieved his motorbike and pushed it across the Ponte Vecchio, over the Arno opaque as jade. He thought he had lost the doctor, but there he was, on the other side of the river under the arcade beside the Lungarno, peering for a moment over a sketch artist's shoulder, moving on with quick light strides. Pazzi guessed Dr. Fell was going to the Church of Santa Croce, and followed at a distance through the hellish traffic.

26

THE CHURCH of Santa Croce, seat of the Franciscans, its vast interior ringing with eight languages as the hordes of tourists shuffle
through, following the bright umbrellas of their guides, fumbling
for two-hundred-lire pieces in the gloom so they can pay to light,
for a precious minute in their lives, the great frescoes in the chapels.

Romula came in from the bright morning and had to pause near
the tomb of Michelangelo while her dazzled eyes adjusted. When she
could see that she was standing on a grave in the floor, she whispered,
"*Mi dispiace!*" and moved quickly off the slab; to Romula the throng
of dead beneath the floor was as real as the people above it, and perhaps
more influential. She was daughter and granddaughter of spirit readers
and palmists, and she saw the people above the floor, and the people
below, as two crowds with the mortal plane between. The ones below,
being smarter and older, had the advantage in her opinion.

She looked around for the sexton, a man deeply prejudiced against
Gypsies, and took refuge at the first pillar under the protection of
Rossellino's *Madonna del Latte,* while the baby nuzzled at her breast.
Pazzi, lurking near Galileo's grave, found her there.

He pointed with his chin toward the back of the church where, across the transept, floodlights and forbidden cameras flashed like lightning through the vast high gloom as the clicking timers ate two-hundred-lire pieces and the occasional slug or Australian quarter.

Again and again Christ was born, betrayed, and the nails driven as the great frescoes appeared in brilliant light, and plunged again into a darkness close and crowded, the milling pilgrims holding guidebooks they cannot see, body odor and incense rising to cook in the heat of the lamps.

In the left transept, Dr. Fell was at work in the Capponi Chapel. The glorious Capponi Chapel is in Santa Felicità. This one, redone in the nineteenth century, interested Dr. Fell because he could look through the restoration into the past. He was making a charcoal rubbing of an inscription in stone so worn that even oblique lighting would not bring it up.

Watching through his little monocular, Pazzi discovered why the doctor had left his house with only his shopping bag—he kept his art supplies behind the chapel altar. For a moment, Pazzi considered calling off Romula and letting her go. Perhaps he could fingerprint the art materials. No, the doctor was wearing cotton gloves to keep the charcoal off his hands.

It would be awkward at best. Romula's technique was designed for the open street. But she was obvious, and the furthest thing from what a criminal would fear. She was the person least likely to make the doctor flee. No. If the doctor seized her, he would give her to the sexton and Pazzi could intervene later.

The man was insane. What if he killed her? What if he killed the baby? Pazzi asked himself two questions. Would he fight the doctor if the situation looked lethal? Yes. Was he willing to risk lesser injury to Romula and her child to get his money? Yes.

They would simply have to wait until Dr. Fell took off the gloves to go to lunch. Drifting back and forth along the transept there was time for Pazzi and Romula to whisper. Pazzi spotted a face in the crowd.

"Who's following you, Romula? Better tell me. I've seen his face in the jail."

"My friend, just to block the way if I have to run. He doesn't know anything. Nothing. It's better for you. You don't have to get dirty."

To pass the time, they prayed in several chapels, Romula whispering in a language Rinaldo did not understand, and Pazzi with an extensive list to pray for, particularly the house on the Chesapeake shore and something else he shouldn't think about in church.

Sweet voices from the practicing choir, soaring over the general noise.

A bell, and it was time for the midday closing. Sextons came out, rattling their keys, ready to empty the coin boxes.

Dr. Fell rose from his labors and came out from behind Andreotti's *Pietà* in the chapel, removed his gloves and put on his jacket. A large group of Japanese, crowded in the front of the sanctuary, their supply of coins exhausted, stood puzzled in the dark, not yet understanding that they had to leave.

Pazzi poked Romula quite unnecessarily. She knew the time had come. She kissed the top of the baby's head as it rested in her wooden arm.

The doctor was coming. The crowd would force him to pass close to her, and with three long strides she went to meet him, squared in front of him, held her hand up in his vision to attract his eye, kissed her fingers and got ready to put the kiss on his cheek, her concealed arm ready to make the dip.

Lights on as someone in the crowd found a two-hundred-lire piece and at the moment of touching Dr. Fell she looked into his face, felt sucked to the red centers of his eyes, felt the huge cold vacuum pull her heart against her ribs and her hand flew away from his face to cover the baby's face and she heard her voice say *"Perdonami, perdonami, signore,"* turning and fleeing as the doctor looked after her for a long moment, until the light went out and he was a silhouette again against candles in a chapel, and with quick, light strides he went on his way.

Pazzi, pale with anger, found Romula supporting herself on the font, bathing the baby's head repeatedly with holy water, bathing its eyes in case it had looked at Dr. Fell. Bitter curses stopped in his mouth when he looked at her stricken face.

Her eyes were enormous in the gloom. "That is the Devil," she said. "Shaitan, Son of the Morning, I've seen him now."

"I'll drive you back to jail," Pazzi said.

Romula looked in the baby's face and sighed, a slaughterhouse sigh, so deep and resigned it was terrible to hear. She took off the wide silver cuff and washed it in the holy water.

"Not yet," she said.

IF RINALDO Pazzi had decided to do his duty as an officer of the law, he could have detained Dr. Fell and determined very quickly if the man was Hannibal Lecter. Within a half hour he could have obtained a warrant to take Dr. Fell out of the Palazzo Capponi and all the palazzo's alarm systems would not have prevented him. On his own authority he could have held Dr. Fell without charging him for long enough to determine his identity.

Fingerprinting at Questura headquarters would have revealed within ten minutes if Fell was Dr. Lecter. PFLP DNA testing would confirm the identification.

All those resources were denied to Pazzi now. Once he decided to sell Dr. Lecter, the policeman became a bounty hunter, outside the law and alone. Even the police snitches under his thumb were useless to him, because they would hasten to snitch on Pazzi himself.

The delays frustrated Pazzi, but he was determined. He would make do with these damned Gypsies . . .

"Would Gnocco do it for you, Romula? Can you find him?" They were in the parlor of the borrowed apartment on the Via de' Bardi, across from the Palazzo Capponi, twelve hours after the debacle in the

Church of Santa Croce. A low table lamp lit the room to waist height. Above the light, Pazzi's black eyes glittered in the semi-dark.

"I'll do it myself, but not with the baby," Romula said. "But you have to give me—"

"No. I can't let him see you twice. Would Gnocco do it for you?"

Romula sat bent over in her long bright dress, her full breasts touching her thighs, with her head almost to her knees. The wooden arm lay empty on a chair. In the corner sat the older woman, possibly Romula's cousin, holding the baby. The drapes were drawn. Peering around them through the smallest crack, Pazzi could see a faint light, high in the Palazzo Capponi.

"I can do this, I can change my look until he would not know me. I can—"

"No."

"Then Esmeralda can do it."

"No." This voice from the corner, the older woman speaking for the first time. "I'll care for your baby, Romula, until I die. I will never touch Shaitan." Her Italian was barely intelligible to Pazzi.

"Sit up, Romula," Pazzi said. "*Look* at me. Would Gnocco do it for you? Romula, you're going back to Sollicciano tonight. You have three more months to serve. It's possible that the next time you get your money and cigarettes out of the baby's clothes you'll be caught . . . I could get you six months additional for that last time you did it. I could easily have you declared an unfit mother. The state would take the baby. But if I get the fingerprints, you get released, you get two million lire and your record disappears, and I help you with Australian visas. Would Gnocco do it for you?"

She did not answer.

"Could you find Gnocco?" Pazzi snorted air through his nose. "*Senti*, get your things together, you can pick up your fake arm at the property room in three months, or sometime next year. The baby will have to go to the foundling hospital. The old woman can call on it there."

"*IT?* Call on *IT, Commendatore?* His name is—" She shook her head, not wanting to say the child's name to this man. Romula covered her face with her hands, feeling the two pulses in her face and hands beat against each other, and then she spoke from behind her hands. "I can find him."

"Where?"

"Piazza Santo Spirito, near the fountain. They build a fire and somebody will have wine."

"I'll come with you."

"Better not," she said. "You'd ruin his reputation. You'll have Esmeralda and the baby here—you know I'll come back."

The Piazza Santo Spirito, an attractive square on the left bank of the Arno gone seedy at night, the church dark and locked at that late hour, noise and steamy food smells from Casalinga, the popular trattoria.

Near the fountain, the flicker of a small fire and the sound of a Gypsy guitar, played with more enthusiasm than talent. There is one good *fado* singer in the crowd. Once the singer is discovered, he is shoved forward and lubricated with wine from several bottles. He begins with a song about fate, but is interrupted with demands for a livelier tune.

Roger LeDuc, also known as Gnocco, sits on the edge of the fountain. He has smoked something. His eyes are hazed, but he spots Romula at once, at the back of the crowd across the firelight. He buys two oranges from a vendor and follows her away from the singing. They stop beneath a streetlamp away from the fire. Here the light is colder than firelight and dappled by the leaves left on a struggling maple. The light is greenish on Gnocco's pallor, the shadows of the leaves like moving bruises on his face as Romula looks at him, her hand on his arm.

A blade flicks out of his fist like a bright little tongue and he peels the oranges, the rind hanging down in one long piece. He gives her the first one and she puts a section in his mouth as he peels the second.

They spoke briefly in Romany. Once he shrugged. She gave him a cell phone and showed him the buttons. Then Pazzi's voice was in Gnocco's ear. After a moment, Gnocco folded the telephone and put it in his pocket.

Romula took something on a chain off her neck, kissed the little amulet and hung it around the neck of the small, scruffy man. He looked down at it, danced a little, pretending that the holy image burned him, and got a small smile from Romula. She took off the wide bracelet and put it on his arm. It fit easily. Gnocco's arm was no bigger than hers.

"Can you be with me an hour?" Gnocco asked her.

"Yes," she said.

28

NIGHT AGAIN and Dr. Fell in the vast stone room of the Atrocious Torture Instruments show at Forte di Belvedere, the doctor leaning at ease against the wall beneath the hanging cages of the damned.

He is registering aspects of damnation from the avid faces of the voyeurs as they press around the torture instruments and press against each other in steamy, goggle-eyed *frottage*, hair rising on their forearms, breath hot on one another's neck and cheeks. Sometimes the doctor presses a scented handkerchief to his face against an overdose of cologne and rut.

Those who pursue the doctor wait outside.

Hours pass. Dr. Fell, who has never paid more than passing attention to the exhibits themselves, cannot seem to get enough of the crowd. A few feel his attention, and become uncomfortable. Often women in the crowd look at him with particular interest before the shuffling movement of the line through the exhibit forces them to move on. A pittance paid to the two taxidermists operating the show enables the doctor to lounge at his ease, untouchable behind the ropes, very still against the stone.

Outside the exit, waiting on the parapet in a steady drizzle, Rinaldo Pazzi kept his vigil. He was used to waiting.

Pazzi knew the doctor would not be walking home. Down the hill behind the fort, in a small piazza, Dr. Fell's automobile awaited him. It was a black Jaguar Saloon, an elegant thirty-year-old Mark II glistening in the drizzle, the best one that Pazzi had ever seen, and it carried Swiss plates. Clearly Dr. Fell did not need to work for a salary. Pazzi noted the plate numbers, but could not risk running them through Interpol.

On the steep cobbled Via San Leonardo between the Forte di Belvedere and the car, Gnocco waited. The ill-lit street was bounded on both sides by high stone walls protecting the villas behind them. Gnocco had found a dark niche in front of a barred gateway where he could stand out of the stream of tourists coming down from the fort. Every ten minutes the cell phone in his pocket vibrated against his thigh and he had to affirm he was in position.

Some of the tourists held maps and programs over their heads against the fine rain as they came by, the narrow sidewalk full, and people spilling over into the street, slowing the few taxis coming down from the fort.

In the vaulted chamber of torture instruments, Dr. Fell at last stood away from the wall where he had leaned, rolled his eyes up at the skeleton in the starvation cage above him as though they shared a secret and made his way through the crowd toward the exit.

Pazzi saw him framed in the doorway, and again under a floodlight on the grounds. He followed at a distance. When he was sure the doctor was walking down to his car, he flipped open his cell phone and alerted Gnocco.

The Gypsy's head came up out of his collar like that of a tortoise, eyes sunken, showing, as a tortoise shows, the skull beneath the skin. He rolled his sleeve above the elbow and spit on the bracelet, wiping it dry with a rag. Now that the silver was polished with spit and holy water, he held his arm behind him under his coat to keep it dry as he peered up the hill. A column of bobbing heads was coming. Gnocco pushed through the stream of people out into the street, where he could go against the current and could see better. With no assistant, he would have to do both the bump and the dip himself—not a problem since he wanted to fail at making the dip. There the slight man came—near the curb, thank God. Pazzi was thirty meters behind the doctor, coming down.

Gnocco made a nifty move from the middle of the street. Taking advantage of a coming taxi, skipping as though to get out of the traffic, he looked back to curse the driver and bumped bellies with Dr. Fell, his fingers scrambling inside the doctor's coat, and felt his arm seized in a terrific grip, felt a blow, and twisted away, free of the mark, Dr. Fell hardly pausing in his stride and gone in the stream of tourists, Gnocco free and away.

Pazzi was with him almost instantly, beside him in the niche before the iron gate, Gnocco bent over briefly, straightening up, breathing hard.

"I got it. He grabbed me right. *Cornuto* tried to hit me in the balls, but he missed," Gnocco said.

Pazzi on one knee carefully working the bracelet off Gnocco's arm, when Gnocco felt hot and wet down his leg and, as he shifted his body, a hot stream of arterial blood shot out of a rent in the front of his trousers, onto Pazzi's face and hands as he tried to remove the bracelet holding it only by the edges. Blood spraying everywhere, into Gnocco's own face as he bent to look at himself, his legs caving in. He collapsed against the gate, clung to it with one hand and jammed his rag against the juncture of his leg and body trying to stop the gouting blood from his split femoral artery.

Pazzi, with the freezing feeling he always had in action, got his arm around Gnocco and kept him turned away from the crowd, kept him spraying through the bars of the gate, eased him to the ground on his side.

Pazzi took his cell phone from his pocket and spoke into it as though calling an ambulance, but did not turn the telephone on. He unbuttoned his coat and spread it like a hawk mantling its prey. The crowd was moving, incurious behind him. Pazzi got the bracelet off Gnocco and slipped it into the small box he carried. He put Gnocco's cell phone in his pocket.

Gnocco's lips moved. "Madonna, *che freddo.*"

With an effort of will, Pazzi moved Gnocco's failing hand from the wound, held it as though to comfort him, and let him bleed out. When he was sure Gnocco was dead, Pazzi left him lying beside the gate, his head resting on his arm as though he slept, and stepped into the moving crowd.

In the piazza, Pazzi stared at the empty parking place, the rain just beginning to wet the cobbles where Dr. Lecter's Jaguar had stood.

Dr. Lecter—Pazzi no longer thought of him as Dr. Fell. He was Dr. Hannibal Lecter.

Proof enough for Mason could be in the pocket of Pazzi's raincoat. Proof enough for Pazzi dripped off his raincoat onto his shoes.

29

THE MORNING star over Genoa was dimmed by the lightening east when Rinaldo Pazzi's old Alfa purred down to the dock. A chilly wind riffled the harbor. On a freighter at an outer mooring someone was welding, orange sparks showering into the black water.

Romula stayed in the car out of the wind with the baby in her lap. Esmeralda was scrunched in the small backseat of the *berlinetta* coupe with her legs sideways. She had not spoken again since she refused to touch Shaitan.

They had thick black coffee in paper cups and *pasticcini*.

Rinaldo Pazzi went into the shipping office. By the time he came out again the sun was well risen, glowing orange on the rust-streaked hull of the freighter *Astra Philogenes*, completing its loading at dockside. He beckoned to the women in the car.

The *Astra Philogenes*, twenty-seven thousand tons, Greek registry, could legally carry twelve passengers without a ship's doctor on its route to Rio. There, Pazzi explained to Romula, they would transship to Sydney, Australia, the transshipment supervised by the *Astra* purser. Passage was fully paid and emphatically nonrefundable. In Italy, Australia is considered an attractive alternative where jobs can be found, and it has a large Gypsy population.

Pazzi had promised Romula two million lire, about twelve hundred and fifty dollars at the current rate of exchange, and he gave it to her in a fat envelope.

The Gypsies' baggage amounted to very little, a small valise and Romula's wooden arm packed in a French horn case.

The Gypsies would be at sea and incommunicado for most of the next month.

Gnocco is coming, Pazzi told Romula for the tenth time, but he could not come today. Gnocco would leave word for them general delivery at the Sydney main post office. "I'll keep my promise to him, just as I did to you," he told them as they stood together at the foot of the gangway, the early sun sending their long shadows down the rough surface of the dock.

At the moment of parting, with Romula and the baby already climbing the gangway, the old woman spoke for the second and last time in Pazzi's experience.

With eyes as black as Kalamata olives she looked into his face. "You gave Gnocco to Shaitan," she said quietly. "Gnocco is dead." Bending stiffly, as she would bend to a chicken on the block, Esmeralda spit carefully on Pazzi's shadow, and hurried up the gangway after Romula and the child.

THE DHL Express delivery box was well made. The fingerprint technician, sitting at a table under hot lights in the seating area of Mason's room, carefully backed out the screws with an electric screwdriver.

The broad silver bracelet was held on a velvet jeweler's stand braced within the box so the outer surfaces of the bracelet touched nothing.

"Bring it over here," Mason said.

Fingerprinting the bracelet would have been much easier at Baltimore Police Department's Identification Section, where the technician worked during the day, but Mason was paying a very high and private fee in cash, and he insisted the work be done before his eyes. Or before his eye, the technician reflected sourly as he placed the bracelet, stand and all, on a china plate held by a male attendant.

The attendant held the plate in front of Mason's goggle. He could not set it down on the coil of hair over Mason's heart, because the respirator moved his chest constantly, up and down.

The heavy bracelet was streaked and crusted with blood, and flecks of dried blood fell from it onto the china plate. Mason regarded it with his goggled eye. Lacking any facial flesh, he had no expression, but his eye was bright.

"Dust it," he said.

The technician had a copy of the prints off the front of Dr. Lecter's FBI fingerprint card. The sixth print on the back and the identification were not reproduced.

He dusted between the crusts of blood. The Dragon's Blood fingerprint powder he preferred was too close in color to the dried blood on the bracelet, so he went to black, dusting carefully.

"We got prints," he said, stopping to mop his head under the hot lights of the seating area. The light was good for photography and he took pictures of the prints *in situ* before he lifted them for microscopic comparison. "Middle finger and thumb of the left hand, sixteen-point match—it would hold up in court," he said at last. "No question, it's the same guy."

Mason was not interested in court. His pale hand was already crawling across the counterpane to the telephone.

CHAPTER

31

SUNNY MORNING in a mountain pasture deep in the Gennargentu Mountains of central Sardinia.

Six men, four Sardinians and two Romans, work beneath an airy shed built of timbers cut from the surrounding forest. Small sounds they make seem magnified in the vast silence of the mountains.

Beneath the shed, hanging from rafters with their bark still peeling, is a huge mirror in a gilt rococo frame. The mirror is suspended over a sturdy livestock pen with two gates, one opening into the pasture. The other gate is built like a Dutch door, so the top and bottom halves can be opened separately. The area beneath the Dutch gate is paved with cement, but the rest of the pen is strewn with clean straw in the manner of an executioner's scaffold.

The mirror, its frame carved with cherubs, can be tilted to provide an overhead view of the pen, as a cooking-school mirror provides the pupils with an overhead view of the stove.

The filmmaker, Oreste Pini, and Mason's Sardinian foreman, a professional kidnapper named Carlo, disliked each other from the beginning.

Carlo Deogracias was a stocky, florid man in an alpine hat with a boar bristle in the band. He had the habit of chewing the gristle off a pair of stag's teeth he kept in the pocket of his vest.

Carlo was a leading practitioner of the ancient Sardinian profession of kidnapping, and a professional revenger as well.

If you have to be kidnapped for ransom, wealthy Italians will tell you, it's better to fall into the hands of the Sards. At least they are professional and won't kill you by accident or in a panic. If your relatives pay, you might be returned unharmed, unraped and unmutilated. If they don't pay, your relatives can expect to receive you piecemeal in the mail.

Carlo was not pleased with Mason's elaborate arrangements. He was experienced in this field and had actually fed a man to the pigs in Tuscany twenty years before—a retired Nazi and bogus count who imposed sexual relations on Tuscan village children, girls and boys alike. Carlo was engaged for the job and took the man out of his own garden within three miles of the Badia di Passignano and fed him to five large domestic swine on a farm below the Poggio alle Corti, though he had to withhold rations from the pigs for three days, the Nazi struggling against his bonds, pleading and sweating with his feet in the pen, and still the swine were shy about starting on his writhing toes until Carlo, with a guilty twinge at violating the letter of his agreement, fed the Nazi a tasty salad of the pigs' favorite greens and then cut his throat to accommodate them.

Carlo was cheerful and energetic in nature, but the presence of the filmmaker annoyed him—Carlo had taken the mirror from a brothel he owned in Cagliari, on Mason Verger's orders, just to accommodate this pornographer, Oreste Pini.

The mirror was a boon to Oreste, who had used mirrors as a favorite device in his pornographic films and in the single genuine snuff movie he made in Mauritania. Inspired by the admonition printed on his auto mirror, he pioneered the use of warped reflections to make some objects seem larger than they appear to the unaided eye.

Oreste must use a two-camera setup with good sound, as Mason dictated, and he must get it right the first time. Mason wanted a run-ning, uninterrupted close-up of the face, aside from everything else.

To Carlo, he seemed to fiddle endlessly.

"You can stand there jabbering at me like a woman, or you can watch the practice and ask me whatever you can't understand," Carlo told him.

"I want to *film* the practice."

"*Va bene*. Get your shit set up and let's get on with it."

While Oreste placed his cameras, Carlo and the three silent Sardinians with him made their preparations.

Oreste, who loved money, was ever amazed at what money will buy.

At a long trestle table at one side of the shed, Carlo's brother, Matteo, unpacked a bundle of used clothing. He selected from the pile a shirt and trousers, while the other two Sardinians, the brothers Piero and Tommaso Falcione, rolled an ambulance gurney into the shed, pushing it slowly over the grass. The gurney was stained and battered.

Matteo had ready several buckets of ground meat, a number of dead chickens still in their feathers and some spoiled fruit, already attracting flies, and a bucket of beef tripe and intestines.

Matteo laid out a pair of worn khaki trousers on the gurney and began to stuff them with a couple of chickens and some meat and fruit. Then he took a pair of cotton gloves and filled them with ground meat and acorns, stuffing each finger carefully, and placed them at the ends of the trouser legs. He selected a shirt for his ensemble and spread it on the gurney, filling it with tripe and intestines, and improving the contours with bread, before he buttoned the shirt and tucked the tail neatly into the trousers. A pair of stuffed gloves went at the ends of the sleeves. The melon he used for a head was covered with a hairnet, stuffed with ground meat where the face would be along with two boiled eggs for eyes. When he had finished, the result looked like a lumpy mannequin, looked better on the gurney than some jumpers look when they are rolled away. As a final touch, Matteo sprayed some extremely expensive aftershave on the front of the melon and on the gloves at the ends of the sleeves.

Carlo pointed with his chin at Oreste's slender assistant leaning over the fence, extending the boom mike over the pen, measuring its reach.

"Tell your fuckboy, if he falls in, I'm not going in after him."

At last all was ready. Piero and Tommaso dropped the gurney to its low position with the legs folded and rolled it to the gate of the pen.

Carlo brought a tape recorder from the house and a separate amplifier. He had a number of tapes, some of which he had made himself while cutting the ears off kidnap victims to mail to the relatives. Carlo always played the tapes for the animals while they ate. He would not need the tapes when he had an actual victim to provide the screams.

Two weathered outdoor speakers were nailed to the posts beneath the shed. The sun was bright on the pleasant meadow sloping down to the woods. The sturdy fence around the meadow continued into the forest. In the midday hush Oreste could hear a carpenter bee buzzing under the shed roof.

"Are you ready?" Carlo said.

Oreste turned on the fixed camera himself. "*Giriamo*," he called to his cameraman.

"*Pronti!*" came the reply.

"*Motore!*" The cameras were rolling.

"*Partito!*" Sound was rolling with the film.

"*Azione!*" Oreste poked Carlo.

The Sard pushed the play button on his tape machine and a hellish screaming started, sobbing, pleading. The cameraman jerked at the sound, then steadied himself. The screaming was awful to hear, but a fitting overture for the faces that came out of the woods, drawn to the screams announcing dinner.

ROUND-TRIP to Geneva in a day, to see the money.

The commuter plane to Milan, a whistling Aerospatiale prop jet, climbed out of Florence in the early morning, swinging over the vineyards with their rows wide apart like a developer's coarse model of Tuscany. Something was wrong in the colors of the landscape—the new swimming pools beside the villas of the wealthy foreigners were the wrong blue. To Pazzi, looking out the window of the airplane, the pools were the milky blue of an aged English eye, a blue out of place among the dark cypresses and the silver olive trees.

Rinaldo Pazzi's spirits climbed with the airplane, knowing in his heart that he would not grow old here, dependent on the whim of his police superiors, trying to last in order to get his pension.

He had been terribly afraid that Dr. Lecter would disappear after killing Gnocco. When Pazzi spotted Lecter's work lamp again in Santa Croce, he felt something like salvation; the doctor believed that he was safe.

The death of the Gypsy caused no ripple at all in the calm of the Questura and was believed drug-related—fortunately there were discarded syringes on the ground around him, a common sight in

Florence, where syringes were available for free.

Going to see the money. Pazzi had insisted on it.

The visual Rinaldo Pazzi remembered sights completely: the first time he ever saw his penis erect, the first time he saw his own blood, the first woman he ever saw naked, the blur of the first fist coming to strike him. He remembered wandering casually into a side chapel of a Sienese church and looking into the face of St. Catherine of Siena unexpectedly, her mummified head in its immaculate white wimple resting in a reliquary shaped like a church.

Seeing three million U.S. dollars had the same impact on him.

Three hundred banded blocks of hundred-dollar bills in non-sequential serial numbers.

In a severe little room, like a chapel, in the Geneva Crédit Suisse, Mason Verger's lawyer showed Rinaldo Pazzi the money. It was wheeled in from the vault in four deep lock boxes with brass number plates. The Crédit Suisse also provided a counting machine, a scale and a clerk to operate them. Pazzi dismissed the clerk. He put his hands on top of the money once.

Rinaldo Pazzi was a very competent investigator. He had spotted and arrested scam artists for twenty years. Standing in the presence of this money, listening to the arrangements, he detected no false note; if he gave them Hannibal Lecter, Mason would give him the money.

In a hot sweet rush Pazzi realized that these people were not fooling around—Mason Verger would actually pay him. And he had no illusions about Lecter's fate. He was selling the man into torture and death. To Pazzi's credit, he acknowledged to himself what he was doing.

Our freedom is worth more than the monster's life. Our happiness is more important than his suffering, he thought with the cold egoism of the damned. Whether the "our" was magisterial or stood for Rinaldo and his wife is a difficult question, and there may not be a single answer.

In this room, scrubbed and Swiss, neat as a wimple, Pazzi took the final vow. He turned from the money and nodded to the lawyer, Mr. Konie. From the first box, the lawyer counted out one hundred thousand dollars and handed it to Pazzi.

Mr. Konie spoke briefly into a telephone and handed the receiver to Pazzi. "This is a land line, encrypted," he said.

The American voice Pazzi heard had a peculiar rhythm, words rushed into a single breath with a pause between, and the plosives were lost. The sound of it made Pazzi slightly dizzy, as though he were straining for breath along with the speaker.

Without preamble, the question: "Where is Dr. Lecter?"

Pazzi, the money in one hand and the phone in the other, did not hesitate. "He is the one who studies the Palazzo Capponi in Florence. He is the . . . curator."

"Would you please show your identification to Mr. Konie and hand him the telephone. He won't say your name into the telephone."

Mr. Konie consulted a list from his pocket and said some prearranged code words to Mason, then he handed the phone back to Pazzi.

"You get the rest of the money when he is alive in our hands," Mason said. "You don't have to seize the doctor yourself, but you've got to identify him to us and put him in our hands. I want your documentation as well, everything you've got on him. You'll be back in Florence tonight? You'll get instructions tonight for a meeting near Florence. The meeting will be no later than tomorrow night. There you'll get instructions from the man who will take Dr. Lecter. He'll ask you if you know a florist. Tell him all florists are thieves. Do you understand me? I want you to cooperate with him."

"I don't want Dr. Lecter in my . . . I don't want him near Florence when . . ."

"I understand your concern. Don't worry, he won't be."

The line went dead.

In a few minutes' paperwork, two million dollars was placed in escrow. Mason Verger could not get it back, but he could release it for Pazzi to claim. A Crédit Suisse official summoned to the meeting room informed Pazzi the bank would charge him a negative interest to facilitate a deposit there if he converted to Swiss francs, and pay three percent compound interest only on the first hundred thousand francs. The official presented Pazzi with a copy of Article 47 of the *Bundesgesetz über Banken und Sparkassen* governing bank secrecy and agreed to perform a wire transfer to the Royal Bank of Nova Scotia or to the Cayman Islands immediately after the release of the funds, if that was Pazzi's wish.

With a notary present, Pazzi granted alternate signature power over the account to his wife in the event of his death. The business concluded, only the Swiss bank official offered to shake hands. Pazzi and Mr. Konie did not look at each other directly, though Mr. Konie offered a good-bye from the door.

The last leg home, the commuter plane from Milan dodging through a thunderstorm, the propeller on Pazzi's side of the aircraft a dark circle against the dark gray sky. Lightning and thunder as they swung over the old city, the campanile and dome of the cathedral beneath them now, lights coming on in the early dusk, a flash and boom like the ones Pazzi remembered from his childhood when the Germans blew up the bridges over the Arno, sparing only the Ponte Vecchio. And for a flash as short as lightning he remembered seeing as a little boy a captured sniper chained to the Madonna of Chains to pray before he was shot.

Descending through the ozone smell of lightning, feeling the booms of thunder in the fabric of the plane, Pazzi of the ancient Pazzi returned to his ancient city with his aims as old as time.

33

RINALDO PAZZI would have preferred to maintain constant surveillance on his prize in the Palazzo Capponi, but he could not.

Instead Pazzi, still rapt from the sight of the money, had to leap into his dinner clothes and meet his wife at a long-anticipated concert of the Florence Chamber Orchestra.

The Teatro Piccolomini, a nineteenth-century half-scale copy of Venice's glorious Teatro La Fenice, is a baroque jewel box of gilt and plush, with cherubs flouting the laws of aerodynamics across its splendid ceiling.

A good thing, too, that the theater is beautiful because the performers often need all the help they can get.

It is unfair but inevitable that music in Florence should be judged by the hopelessly high standards of the city's art. The Florentines are a large and knowledgeable group of music lovers, typical of Italy, but they are sometimes starved for musical artists.

Pazzi slipped into the seat beside his wife in the applause following the overture.

She gave him her fragrant cheek. He felt his heart grow big inside him looking at her in her evening gown, sufficiently décolleté to emit a warm fragrance from her cleavage, her musical score in the chic Gucci cover Pazzi had given her.

"They sound a hundred percent better with the new viola player," she breathed into Pazzi's ear. This excellent *viola da gamba* player had been brought in to replace an infuriatingly inept one, a cousin of Sogliato's, who had gone oddly missing some weeks before.

Dr. Hannibal Lecter looked down from a high box, alone, immaculate in white tie, his face and shirtfront seeming to float in the dark box framed by gilt baroque carving.

Pazzi spotted him when the lights went up briefly after the first movement, and in the moment before Pazzi could look away, the doctor's head came round like that of an owl and their eyes met. Pazzi involuntarily squeezed his wife's hand hard enough for her to look round at him. After that Pazzi kept his eyes resolutely on the stage, the back of his hand warm against his wife's thigh as she held his hand in hers.

At intermission, when Pazzi turned from the bar to hand her a drink, Dr. Lecter was standing beside her.

"Good evening, Dr. Fell," Pazzi said.

"Good evening, *Commendatore*," the doctor said. He waited with a slight inclination of the head, until Pazzi had to make the introduction.

"Laura, allow me to present Dr. Fell. Doctor, this is Signora Pazzi, my wife."

Signora Pazzi, accustomed to being praised for her beauty, found what followed curiously charming, though her husband did not.

"Thank you for this privilege, *Commendatore*," the doctor said. His red and pointed tongue appeared for an instant before he bent over Signora Pazzi's hand, his lips perhaps closer to the skin than is customary in Florence, certainly close enough for her to feel his breath on her skin.

His eyes rose to her before his sleek head lifted.

"I think you particularly enjoy Scarlatti, Signora Pazzi."

"Yes, I do."

"It was pleasant to see you following the score. Hardly anyone does it anymore. I hoped that this might interest you." He took a portfolio from under his arm. It was an antique score on parchment, hand-copied. "This is from the Teatro Capranica in Rome, from 1688, the year the piece was written."

"*Meraviglioso!* Look at this, Rinaldo!"

"I marked in overlay some of the differences from the modern score as the first movement went along," Dr. Lecter said. "It might amuse you to follow along in the second. Please, take it. I can always retrieve it from Signor Pazzi—is that permissible, *Commendatore?*"

The doctor looking deeply, deeply as Pazzi replied.

"If it would please you, Laura," Pazzi said. A beat of thought. "Will you be addressing the Studiolo, Doctor?"

"Yes, Friday night in fact. Soglioto can't wait to see me discredited."

"I have to be in the old city," Pazzi said. "I'll return the score then. Laura, Dr. Fell has to sing for his supper before the dragons at the Studiolo."

"I'm sure you'll sing *very* well, Doctor," she said, giving him her great dark eyes—within the bounds of propriety, but just.

Dr. Lecter smiled, with his small white teeth. "Madame, if I manufactured Fleur du Ciel, I would offer you the Cape Diamond to wear it. Until Friday night, *Commendatore.*"

Pazzi made sure the doctor returned to his box, and did not look at him again until they waved good night at a distance on the theater steps.

"I gave you that Fleur du Ciel for your birthday," Pazzi said.

"Yes, and I love it, Rinaldo," Signora Pazzi said. "You have the most marvellous taste."

34

IMPRUNETA IS an ancient Tuscan town where the roof tiles of the Duomo were made. Its cemetery is visible at night from the hilltop villas for miles around because of the lamps forever burning at the graves. The ambient light is low, but enough for visitors to make their way among the dead, though a flashlight is needed to read the epitaphs.

Rinaldo Pazzi arrived at five minutes to nine with a small bouquet of flowers he planned to place on a grave at random. He walked slowly along a gravel path between the tombs.

He felt Carlo's presence, though he did not see him.

Carlo spoke from the other side of a mausoleum more than head high. "Do you know a good florist in the town?"

The man sounded like a Sard. Good, maybe he knew what he was doing.

"Florists are all thieves," Pazzi replied.

Carlo came briskly around the marble structure without peeking.

He looked feral to Pazzi, short and round and powerful, nimble in his extremities. His vest was leather and he had a boar bristle in his hat. Pazzi guessed he had three inches' reach advantage on Carlo and four inches of height. They weighed about the same, he guessed. Carlo was missing a thumb. Pazzi figured he could find him in the Questura's records with about five minutes' work. Both men were lit from beneath by the grave lamps.

"His house has good alarms," Pazzi said.

"I looked at it. You have to point him out to me."

"He has to speak at a meeting tomorrow night, Friday night. Can you do it that soon?"

"It's good." Carlo wanted to bully the policeman a little, establish his control. "Will you walk with him, or are you afraid of him? You'll do what you're paid to do. You'll point him out to me."

"Watch your mouth. I'll do what I'm paid to do and so will you. Or you can pass your retirement as a fuckboy at Volterra, suit yourself."

Carlo at work was as impervious to insult as he was to cries of pain. He saw that he had misjudged the policeman. He spread his hands. "Tell me what I need to know." Carlo moved to stand beside Pazzi as though they mourned together at the small mausoleum. A couple passed on the path holding hands. Carlo removed his hat and the two men stood with bowed heads. Pazzi put his flowers at the door of the tomb. A smell came from Carlo's warm hat, a rank smell, like sausage from an animal improperly gelded.

Pazzi raised his face from the odor. "He's fast with his knife. Goes low with it."

"Has he got a gun?"

"I don't know. He's never used one, that I know of."

"I don't want to have to take him out of a car. I want him on the open street with not many people around."

"How will you take him down?"

"That's my business." Carlo put a stag's tooth in his mouth and chewed at the gristle, protruding the tooth between his lips from time to time.

"It's my business too," Pazzi said. "How will you do it?"

"Stun him with a beanbag gun, net him, then I can give him a shot. I need to check his teeth fast in case he's got poison under a tooth cap."

"He has to lecture at a meeting. It starts at seven in the Palazzo Vecchio. If he works in the Capponi Chapel at Santa Croce on Friday, he'll walk from there to the Palazzo Vecchio. Do you know Florence?"

"I know it well. Can you get me a vehicle pass for the old city?"

"Yes."

"I won't take him out of the church," Carlo said.

Pazzi nodded. "Better he shows up for the meeting, then he probably won't be missed for two weeks. I have a reason to walk with him to the Palazzo Capponi after the meeting—"

"I don't want to take him in his house. That's his ground. He knows it and I don't. He'll be alert, he'll look around him at the door. I want him on the open sidewalk."

"Listen to me, then—we'll come out the front entrance of the Palazzo Vecchio, the Via dei Leoni side will be closed. We'll go along the Via Neri and come across the river on the Ponte alle Grazie. There are trees in front of the Museo Bardini on the other side that block the streetlights. It's quiet at that hour when school is out."

"We'll say in front of the Museo Bardini then, but I may do it sooner if I see a chance, closer to the palazzo, or earlier in the day if he spooks and tries to run. We may be in an ambulance. Stay with him until the beanbag hits him and then get away from him fast."

"I want him out of Tuscany before anything happens to him."

"Believe me, he'll be gone from the face of the earth, *feet first*," Carlo said, smiling at his private joke, sticking the stag's tooth out through the smile.

FRIDAY MORNING. A small room in the attic of the Palazzo Capponi. Three of the whitewashed walls are bare. On the fourth wall hangs a large thirteenth-century Madonna of the Cimabue school, enormous in the little room, her head bent at the signature angle like that of a curious bird, and her almond eyes regarding a small figure asleep beneath the painting.

Dr. Hannibal Lecter, veteran of prison and asylum cots, lies still on this narrow bed, his hands on his chest.

His eyes open and he is suddenly, completely awake, his dream of his sister Mischa, long dead and digested, running seamlessly into this present waking: danger then, danger now.

Knowing he is in danger did not disturb his sleep any more than killing the pickpocket did.

Dressed for his day now, lean and perfectly groomed in his dark silk suit, he turns off the motion sensors at the top of the servants' stairs and comes down into the great spaces of the palazzo.

Now he is free to move through the vast silence of the palace's many rooms, always a heady freedom to him after so many years of confinement in a basement cell.

Just as the frescoed walls of Santa Croce or the Palazzo Vecchio are suffused with mind, so the air of the Capponi Library thrums with presence for Dr. Lecter as he works at the great wall of pigeonholed manuscripts. He selects rolled parchments, blows dust away, the motes of dust swarming in a ray of sun as though the dead, who now are dust, vie to tell him their fate and his. He works efficiently, but without undue haste, putting a few things in his own portfolio, gathering books and illustrations for his lecture tonight to the Studiolo. There are so many things he would have liked to read.

Dr. Lecter opens his laptop computer and, dialing through the University of Milan's criminology department, checks the FBI's home page on the World Wide Web at www.fbi.gov, as any private citizen can do. The Judiciary Subcommittee hearing on Clarice Starling's abortive drug raid has not been scheduled, he learns. He does not have the access codes he would need to look into his own case file at the FBI. On the Most Wanted page, his own former countenance looks at him, flanked by a bomber and an arsonist.

Dr. Lecter takes up the bright tabloid from a pile of parchment and looks at the picture of Clarice Starling on the cover, touches her face with his finger. The bright blade appears in his hand as though he had sprouted it to replace his sixth finger. The knife is called a Harpy and it has a serrated blade shaped like a talon. It slices as easily through the *National Tattler* as it sliced through the Gypsy's femoral artery—the blade was in the Gypsy and gone so quickly Dr. Lecter did not even need to wipe it.

Dr. Lecter cuts out the image of Clarice Starling's face and glues it on a piece of blank parchment.

He picks up a pen and, with a fluid ease, draws on the parchment the body of a winged lioness, a griffon with Starling's face. Beneath it, he writes in his distinctive copperplate, *Did you ever think, Clarice, why the philistines don't understand you? It's because you're the answer to Samson's riddle: You are the honey in the lion.*

★   ★   ★

Fifteen kilometers away, parked for privacy behind a high stone wall in Impruneta, Carlo Deogracias went over his equipment, while his brother Matteo practiced a series of judo takedowns on the soft grass with the other two Sardinians, Piero and Tommaso Falcione. Both Falciones were quick and very strong—Piero played briefly with the Cagliari professional soccer team. Tommaso had once studied to be a priest, and he spoke fair English. He prayed with their victims, sometimes.

Carlo's white Fiat van with Roman license plates was legally rented. Ready to attach to its sides were signs reading OSPEDALE DELLA MISERICORDIA. The walls and floor were covered with mover's pads in case the subject struggled inside the van.

Carlo intended to carry out this project exactly as Mason wished, but if the plan went wrong and he had to kill Dr. Lecter in Italy and abort the filming in Sardinia, all was not lost. Carlo knew he could butcher Dr. Lecter and have his head and hands off in less than a minute.

If he didn't have that much time, he could take the penis and a finger, which with DNA testing would do for proof. Sealed in plastic and packed in ice, they would be in Mason's hands in less than twenty-four hours, entitling Carlo to a reward in addition to his fees.

Neatly stored behind the seats were a small chain saw, long-handled metal shears, a surgical saw, sharp knives, plastic zip-lock bags, a Black & Decker Work Buddy to hold the doctor's arms still, and a DHL Air Express crate with prepaid delivery fee, estimating the weight of Dr. Lecter's head at six kilos and his hands at a kilo apiece.

If Carlo had a chance to record an emergency butchery on videotape, he felt confident Mason would pay extra to see Dr. Lecter butchered alive, even after he had coughed up the one million dollars for the doctor's head and hands. For that purpose Carlo had provided himself with a good video camera, light source and tripod, and taught Matteo the rudiments of operating it.

His capture equipment got just as much attention. Piero and Tommaso were expert with the net, now folded as carefully as a parachute. Carlo had both a hypodermic and a dart gun loaded with enough of the animal tranquilizer acepromazine to drop an animal of Dr. Lecter's size in seconds. Carlo had told Rinaldo Pazzi he would commence with the beanbag gun, which was charged and ready, but if he got a chance to put the hypodermic anywhere in Dr. Lecter's buttocks or legs, the beanbag would not be needed.

The abductors only had to be on the Italian mainland with their captive for about forty minutes, the length of time it took to drive to the jetport at Pisa where an ambulance plane would be waiting. The Florence airstrip was closer, but the air traffic there was light, and a private flight more noticeable.

In less than an hour and a half, they would be in Sardinia, where the doctor's reception committee was growing ravenous.

Carlo had weighed it all in his intelligent, malodorous head. Mason was no fool. The payments were weighted so no harm must come to Rinaldo Pazzi—it would cost Carlo money to kill Pazzi and try to claim all the reward. Mason did not want the heat from a dead policeman. Better to do it Mason's way. But it made Carlo itch all over to think what he might have accomplished with a few strokes of the saw if he had found Dr. Lecter himself.

He tried his chain saw. It started on the first pull.

Carlo conferred briefly with the others, and left on a small *motorino* for town, armed only with a knife and a gun and a hypodermic.

Dr. Hannibal Lecter came in early from the noisome street to the Farmacia di Santa Maria Novella, one of the best-smelling places on Earth. He stood for some minutes with his head back and eyes closed, taking in the aromas of the great soaps and lotions and creams, and of the ingredients in the workrooms. The porter was accustomed to him, and the clerks, normally given to a certain amount of hauteur, had great respect for him. The purchases of the courteous Dr. Fell over his months in Florence would not have totaled more than one hundred thousand lire, but the fragrances and essences were chosen and combined with a sensibility startling and gratifying to these scent merchants, who live by the nose.

It was to preserve this pleasure that Dr. Lecter had not altered his own nose with any rhinoplasty other than external collagen injections. For him the air was painted with scents as distinct and vivid as colors, and he could layer and feather them as though painting wet-on-wet. Here there was nothing of jail. Here the air was music. Here were pale tears of frankincense awaiting extraction, yellow bergamot, sandalwood, cinnamon and mimosa in concert, over the sustaining ground notes of genuine ambergris, civet, castor from the beaver, and essence of the musk deer.

Dr. Lecter sometimes entertained the illusion that he could smell with his hands, his arms and cheeks, that odor suffused him. That he could smell with his face and his heart.

For good, anatomic reasons, scent fosters memory more readily than any other sense.

Here Dr. Lecter had fragments and flashes of memory as he stood beneath the soft light of the Farmacia's great Art Deco lamps, breathing, breathing. Here there was nothing from jail. Except—what was that? Clarice Starling, why? Not the l'Air du Temps he caught when she opened her handbag close to the bars of his cage in the asylum. That was not it. Such perfumes were not sold here in the Farmacia. Nor was it her skin lotion. Ah. *Sapone di mandorle.* The Farmacia's famous almond soap. Where had he smelled it? Memphis, when she stood outside his cell, when he briefly touched her finger shortly before his escape. Starling, then. Clean, and rich in textures. Cotton sun-dried and ironed. Clarice Starling, then. Engaging and toothsome. Tedious in her earnestness and absurd in her principles. Quick in her mother wit. Ummmm.

On the other hand, bad memories for Dr. Lecter were associated with unpleasant odors, and here in the Farmacia he was perhaps as far as he ever got from the rank black oubliettes beneath his memory palace.

Contrary to his usual practice, Dr. Lecter bought quite a lot of soaps and lotions and bath oils on this gray Friday. A few he took with him, and he had the Farmacia ship the rest, making out the shipping labels himself in his distinctive copperplate hand.

"Would the *Dottore* like to include a note?" the clerk asked.

"Why not?" Dr. Lecter replied, and slipped the folded drawing of the griffon into the box.

The Farmacia di Santa Maria Novella is attached to a convent in the Via Scala and Carlo, ever devout, removed his hat to lurk beneath an image of the Virgin near the entrance. He had noticed that air pressure from the foyer's inner doors made the exterior doors puff ajar seconds before anyone comes out. This gave him time to conceal himself and peep from hiding each time a customer left.

When Dr. Lecter came out with his slim portfolio, Carlo was well concealed behind a card vendor's stall. The doctor started on his way. As he passed the image of the Virgin, his head came up, his nostrils flared as he looked up at the statue and tested the air.

Carlo thought it might be a gesture of devotion. He wondered if Dr. Lecter was religious, as crazy men often are. Perhaps he could make the doctor curse God at the end—that might please Mason. He'd have to send the pious Tommaso out of earshot first, of course.

Rinaldo Pazzi in the late afternoon wrote a letter to his wife including his effort at a sonnet, composed early in their courtship, which he had been too shy to give her at the time. He enclosed the codes required to claim the escrowed money in Switzerland, along with a letter for her to mail to Mason if he tried to renege. He put the letter where she would only find it if she were gathering his effects.

At six o'clock, he rode his little *motorino* to the Museo Bardini and chained it to an iron railing where the last students of the day were claiming their bicycles. He saw the white van with ambulance markings parked near the museum and guessed it might be Carlo's. Two men were sitting in the van. When Pazzi turned his back, he felt their eyes on him.

He had plenty of time. The streetlights were already on and he walked slowly toward the river through the black useful shadows under the museum's trees. Crossing over the Ponte alle Grazie, he stared down for a time at the slow-moving Arno and thought the last long thoughts he would have time to entertain. The night would be dark. Good. Low clouds rushed eastward over Florence, just brushing the cruel spike on the Palazzo Vecchio, and the rising breeze swirled the grit and powdered pigeon droppings in the piazza before Santa Croce, where Pazzi now made his way, his pockets heavy with a .380 Beretta, a flat leather sap and a knife to plant on Dr. Lecter in case it was necessary to kill him at once.

The church of Santa Croce closes at six P.M., but a sexton let Pazzi in a small door near the front of the church. He did not want to ask the man if "Dr. Fell" was working, so he went carefully to see. Candles burning at the altars along the walls gave him enough light. He walked the great length of the church until he could see down the right arm of the cruciform church. It was hard to see, past the votive candles, if Dr. Fell was in the Capponi Chapel. Walking quietly down the right transept now. Looking. A great shadow reared up the chapel wall, and for a second Pazzi's breathing stopped. It was Dr. Lecter, bent over his lamp on the floor where he worked at his rubbings. The doctor stood up, peered into the dark like an owl, head turning, body still, lit from beneath by his work light, shadow immense behind him. Then the shadow shrank down the chapel wall as he bent to his task again.

Pazzi felt sweat trickle down his back beneath his shirt, but his face was cold.

There was yet an hour before the meeting at the Palazzo Vecchio began and Pazzi wanted to arrive at the lecture late.

In its severe beauty, the chapel which Brunelleschi built for the Pazzi family at Santa Croce is one of the glories of Renaissance architecture. Here the circle and the square are reconciled. It is a separate structure outside the sanctuary of Santa Croce, reached only through an arched cloister.

Pazzi prayed in the Pazzi chapel, kneeling on the stone, watched by his likeness in the Della Robbia rondel high above him. He felt his prayers constricted by the circle of apostles on the ceiling, and thought perhaps the prayers might have escaped into the dark cloister behind him and flown from there to the open sky and God.

With an effort he pictured in his mind some good things he could do with the money he got in exchange for Dr. Lecter. He saw himself and his wife handing out coins to some urchins, and some sort of medical machine they would give to a hospital. He saw the waves of Galilee, which looked to him much like the Chesapeake. He saw his wife's shapely rosy hand around his dick, squeezing it to further swell the head.

He looked about him, and seeing no one, said aloud to God, "Thank you, Father, for allowing me to remove this monster, monster of monsters, from your Earth. Thank you on behalf of the souls We will spare of pain." Whether this was the magisterial "We" or a reference to the partnership of Pazzi and God is not clear, and there may not be a single answer.

The part of him that was not his friend said to Pazzi that he and Dr. Lecter had killed together, that Gnocco was their victim, since

Pazzi did nothing to save him, and was relieved when death stopped his mouth.

There was some comfort in prayer, Pazzi reflected, leaving the chapel—he had the distinct feeling, walking out through the dark cloister, that he was not alone.

Carlo was waiting under the overhang of the Palazzo Piccolomini, and he fell into step with Pazzi. They said very little.

They walked behind the Palazzo Vecchio and confirmed the rear exit into the Via dei Leone was locked, the windows above it shuttered.

The only open door was the main entrance to the Palazzo.

"We'll come out here, down the steps and around the side to the Via Neri," Pazzi said.

"My brother and I will be on the Loggia side of the piazza. We'll fall in a good distance behind you. The others are at the Museo Bardini."

"I saw them."

"They saw you too," Carlo said.

"Does the beanbag make much noise?"

"Not a lot, not like a gun, but you'll hear it and he'll go down fast." Carlo did not tell him Piero would shoot the beanbag from the shadows in front of the museum while Pazzi and Dr. Lecter were still in the light. Carlo did not want Pazzi to flinch away from the doctor and warn him before the shot.

"You have to confirm to Mason that you have him. You have to do that tonight," Pazzi said.

"Don't worry. This prick will spend tonight begging Mason on the telephone," Carlo said, glancing sideways at Pazzi, hoping to see him uncomfortable. "At first he'll beg for Mason to spare him, and after a while he'll beg to die."

NIGHT CAME and the last tourists were shooed out of the Palazzo Vecchio. Many, feeling the loom of the medieval castle on their backs as they scattered across the piazza, had to turn and look up a last time at the jack-o'-lantern teeth of its parapets, high over them.

Floodlights came on, washing the sheer rough stone, sharpening the shadows under the high battlements. As the swallows went to their nests, the first bats appeared, disturbed in their hunting more by the high-frequency squeals of the restorers' power tools than by the light.

Inside the palazzo the endless job of conservation and maintenance would go on for another hour, except in the Salon of Lilies, where Dr. Lecter conferred with the foreman of the maintenance crew.

The foreman, accustomed to the penury and sour demands of the Belle Arti Committee, found the doctor both courteous and extremely generous.

In minutes his workers were stowing their equipment, moving the great floor polishers and compressors out of the way against the walls and rolling up their lines and electrical cords. Quickly they set up the folding chairs for the meeting of the Studiolo—only a dozen chairs were needed—and threw open the windows to clear out the smell of their paint and polish and gilding materials.

The doctor insisted on a proper lectern, and one as big as a pulpit was found in the former office of Niccolò Machiavelli adjacent to the salon and brought on a tall hand truck, along with the palazzo's overhead projector.

The small screen that came with the projector did not suit Dr. Lecter and he sent it away. Instead he tried showing his images life-sized against one of the hanging canvas drop cloths protecting a refurbished wall. After he had adjusted its fastenings and smoothed out the folds, he found the cloth would serve him very well.

He marked his place in several of the weighty tomes piled on the lectern, and then stood at the window with his back to the room as the members of the Studiolo in their dusty dark suits arrived and seated themselves, the tacit skepticism of the scholars evident as they rearranged their chairs from a semicircle into more of a jury-box configuration.

Looking out the tall windows, Dr. Lecter could see the Duomo and Giotto's campanile, black against the west, but not Dante's beloved Baptistry below them. The upturned floodlights prevented him from seeing down into the dark piazza where the assassins awaited him.

As these, the most renowned medieval and Renaissance scholars in the world, settled in their chairs, Dr. Lecter composed in his mind his lecture to them. It took him a little more than three minutes to organize the lecture. Its subject was Dante's *Inferno* and Judas Iscariot.

Much in accord with the Studiolo's taste for the pre-Renaissance, Dr. Lecter began with the case of Pier della Vigna, Logothete of the Kingdom of Sicily, whose avarice earned him a place in Dante's Hell. For the first half-hour the doctor fascinated them with the real-life medieval intrigues behind della Vigna's fall.

"Della Vigna was disgraced and blinded for his betrayal of the emperor's trust through his avarice," Dr. Lecter said, approaching his principal topic. "Dante's pilgrim found him in the seventh level of the Inferno, reserved for suicides. Like Judas Iscariot, he died by hanging.

"Judas and Pier della Vigna and Ahithophel, the ambitious counsellor of Absalom, are linked in Dante by the avarice he saw in them and by their subsequent deaths by hanging.

"Avarice and hanging are linked in the ancient and the medieval mind: St Jerome writes that Judas' very surname, Iscariot, means 'money' or 'price,' while Father Origen says Iscariot is derived from the Hebrew 'from suffocation' and that his name means 'Judas the Suffocated.'"

Dr. Lecter glanced up from his podium, looking over his spectacles at the door.

"Ah, *Commendator* Pazzi, welcome. Since you are nearest to the door, would you be kind enough to dim the lights? You will be interested in this, *Commendatore*, as there are two Pazzis already in Dante's *Inferno* . . ." The professors of the Studiolo cackled dryly. "There is Camicion de' Pazzi, who murdered a kinsman, and he is expecting the arrival of a second Pazzi—but it's not you—it's Carlino, who will be placed even farther down in Hell for treachery and betrayal of the White Guelphs, the party of Dante himself."

A little bat flew in through one of the open windows and circled the room over the heads of the professors for a few laps, a common event in Tuscany and ignored by everyone.

Dr. Lecter resumed his podium voice. "Avarice and hanging, then, linked since antiquity, the image appearing again and again in art." Dr. Lecter pressed the switch in his palm and the projector came to life, throwing an image on the drop cloth covering the wall. In quick succession further images followed as he spoke:

"Here is the earliest known depiction of the Crucifixion, carved on an ivory box in Gaul about A.D. four hundred. It includes the death by hanging of Judas, his face upturned to the branch that suspends him. And here on a reliquary casket of Milan, fourth century, and an ivory diptych of the ninth century, Judas hanging. He's *still* looking up."

The little bat flickered across the screen, hunting bugs.

"In this plate from the doors of the Benevento Cathedral, we see Judas hanging with his bowels falling out as St. Luke, the physician, described him in the Acts of the Apostles. Here he hangs beset by Harpies, above him in the sky is the face of Cain-in-the-Moon; and here he's depicted by your own Giotto, again with pendant viscera.

"And finally, here, from a fifteenth-century edition of the *Inferno*, is Pier della Vigna's body hanging from a bleeding tree. I will not belabor the obvious parallel with Judas Iscariot.

"But Dante needed no drawn illustration: It is the genius of Dante Alighieri to make Pier della Vigna, now in Hell, speak in strained hisses and coughing sibilants as though he is hanging still. Listen to him as he tells of dragging, with the other damned, his own dead body to hang upon a thorn tree:

'*Surge in vermena e in pianta silvestra:*
  l'Arpie, pascendo poi de le sue foglie,
  fanno dolore, e al dolor fenestra.'"

Dr. Lecter's normally white face flushes as he creates for the Studiolo the gargling, choking words of the agonal Pier della Vigna, and as he thumbs his remote control, the images of della Vigna and Judas with his bowels out alternate on the large field of the hanging drop cloth.

"'*Come l'altre verrem per nostre spoglie,*
  ma non però ch'alcuna sen rivesta,
  ché non è giusto aver ciò ch'om si toglie.

'Qui le strascineremo, e per la mesta
  selva saranno i nostri corpi appesi,
  ciascuno al prun de l'ombra sua molesta.

"So Dante recalls, in sound, the death of Judas in the death of Pier della Vigna for the same crimes of avarice and treachery.

"Ahithophel, Judas, your own Pier della Vigna. Avarice, hanging, self-destruction, with avarice counting as self-destruction as much as hanging. And what does the anonymous Florentine suicide say in his torment at the end of the canto?

'Io fei gibetto a me de le mie case.

"And I—I made my own house be my gallows.

"On the next occasion you might like to discuss Dante's son Pietro. Incredibly, he was the only one of the early writers on the thirteenth canto who links Pier della Vigna and Judas. I think, too, it would be interesting to take up the matter of chewing in Dante. Count Ugolino chewing on the back of the archbishop's head, Satan with his three faces chewing Judas, Brutus and Cassius, all betrayers like Pier della Vigna.

"Thank you for your kind attention."

The scholars applauded him enthusiastically, in their soft and dusty way, and Dr. Lecter left the lights down as he said good-bye to them, each by name, holding books in his arms so he would not have to shake their hands. Going out of the soft light of the Salon of Lilies, they seemed to carry the spell of the lecture with them.

Dr. Lecter and Rinaldo Pazzi, alone now in the great chamber, could hear wrangling over the lecture break out among the scholars as they descended the stairs.

"Would you say that I saved my job, *Commendatore?*"

"I'm not a scholar, Dr. Fell, but anyone can see that you impressed them. Doctor, if it's convenient for you, I'll walk home with you and collect your predecessor's effects."

"They fill two suitcases, *Commendatore*, and you already have your briefcase. Do you want to carry them?"

"I'll have a patrol car come for me at the Palazzo Capponi." Pazzi would insist if necessary.

"Fine," Dr. Lecter said. "I'll be a minute, putting things away."

Pazzi nodded and went to the tall windows with his cell phone, never taking his eyes off Lecter.

Pazzi could see that the doctor was perfectly calm. From the floors below came the sounds of power tools.

Pazzi dialed a number and when Carlo Deogracias answered, Pazzi said, "Laura, *amore*, I'll be home very shortly."

Dr. Lecter took his books off the podium and packed them in a bag. He turned to the projector, its fan still humming, dust swimming in its beam.

"I should have shown them this one, I can't imagine how I missed it." Dr. Lecter projected another drawing, a man naked hanging beneath the battlements of the palace. "This one will interest you, *Commendator* Pazzi, let me see if I can improve the focus."

Dr. Lecter fiddled with the machine, and then he approached the image on the wall, his silhouette black on the cloth the same size as the hanged man.

"Can you make this out? It won't enlarge any more. Here's where the archbishop bit him. And beneath him is written his name."

Pazzi did not get close to Dr. Lecter, but as he approached the wall he smelled a chemical, and thought for an instant it was something the restorers used.

"Can you make out the characters? It says 'Pazzi' along with a rude poem. This is your ancestor, Francesco, hanging outside the Palazzo

Vecchio, beneath these windows," Dr. Lecter said. He held Pazzi's eyes across the beam of light between them.

"On a related subject, Signore Pazzi, I must confess to you: I'm giving serious thought to eating your wife."

Dr. Lecter flipped the big drop cloth down over Pazzi, Pazzi flailing at the canvas, trying to uncover his head as his heart flailed in his chest, and Dr. Lecter behind him fast, seizing him around the neck with terrible strength and clapping an ether-soaked sponge over the canvas covering Pazzi's face.

Rinaldo Pazzi strong and thrashing, feet and arms tangled in the canvas, feet tangled in the cloth, he was still able to get his hand on his pistol as they fell to the floor together, tried to point the Beretta behind him under the smothering canvas, pulled the trigger and shot himself through the thigh as he sank into spinning black . . .

The little .380 going off beneath the canvas did not make much more noise than the banging and grinding on the floors below. No one came up the staircase. Dr. Lecter swung the great doors to the Salon of Lilies closed and bolted them . . .

A certain amount of nausea and gagging as Pazzi came back to consciousness, the taste of ether in his throat and a heaviness in his chest.

He found that he was still in the Salon of Lilies and discovered that he could not move. Rinaldo Pazzi was bound upright with the drop cloth canvas and rope, stiff as a grandfather clock, strapped to the tall hand truck the workers had used to move the podium. His mouth was taped. A pressure bandage stopped the bleeding of the gunshot wound in his thigh.

Watching him, leaning against the pulpit, Dr. Lecter was reminded of himself, similarly bound when they moved him around the asylum on a hand truck.

"Can you hear me, Signor Pazzi? Take some deep breaths while you can, and clear your head."

Dr. Lecter's hands were busy as he talked. He had rolled a big floor polisher into the room and he was working with its thick orange power cord, tying a hangman's noose in the plug end of the cord. The rubber-covered cord squeaked as he made the traditional thirteen wraps.

He completed the hangman's noose with a tug and put it down on the pulpit. The plug protruded from the coils at the noose end.

Pazzi's gun, his plastic handcuff strips, the contents of his pockets and briefcase were on top of the podium.

Dr. Lecter poked among the papers. He slipped into his shirtfront the Carabinieri's file containing his *permesso di soggiorno*, his work permit, the photos and negatives of his new face.

And here was the musical score Dr. Lecter loaned Signora Pazzi. He picked up the score now and tapped his teeth with it. His nostrils flared and he breathed in deeply, his face close to Pazzi's. "Laura, if I may call her Laura, must use a wonderful hand cream at night, Signore. Slick. Cold at first and then warm," he said. "The scent of orange blossoms. Laura, *l'orange*. Ummmm. I haven't had a bite all day. Actually, the liver and kidneys would be suitable for dinner right away—tonight—but the rest of the meat should hang a week in the current cool conditions. I did not see the forecast, did you? I gather that means 'no.'

"If you tell me what I need to know, *Commendatore*, it would be convenient for me to leave without my meal; Signora Pazzi will remain unscathed. I'll ask you the questions and then we'll see. You can trust me, you know, though I expect you find trust difficult, knowing yourself.

"I saw at the theater that you had identified me, *Commendatore*. Did you wet yourself when I bent over the Signora's hand? When the police didn't come, it was clear that you had sold me. Was it Mason Verger you sold me to? Blink twice for yes.

"Thank you, I thought so. I called the number on his ubiquitous poster once, far from here, just for fun. Are his men waiting outside? Umm hmmm. And one of them smells like tainted boar sausage? I see. Have you told anyone in the Questura about me? Was that a single blink? I thought so. Now, I want you to think a minute, and tell me your access code for the VICAP computer at Quantico."

Dr. Lecter opened his Harpy knife. "I'm going to take your tape off and you can tell me." Dr. Lecter held up his knife. "Don't try to scream. Do you think you can keep from screaming?"

Pazzi was hoarse from the ether. "I swear to God I don't know the code. I can't think of the whole thing. We can go to my car, I have papers—"

Dr. Lecter wheeled Pazzi around to face the screen and flipped back and forth between his images of Pier della Vigna hanging, and Judas hanging with his bowels out.

"Which do you think, *Commendatore*? Bowels in or out?"

"The code's in my notebook."

Dr. Lecter held the book in front of Pazzi's face until he found the notation, listed among telephone numbers.

"And you can log on remotely, as a guest?"

"Yes," Pazzi croaked.

"Thank you, *Commendatore*." Dr. Lecter tilted back the hand truck and rolled Pazzi to the great windows.

"*Listen to me!* I have *money*, man! You'll have to have *money* to run. Mason Verger will never quit. He'll never quit. You can't go home for *money*, they're watching your house."

Dr. Lecter put two boards from the scaffolding as a ramp over the low windowsill and rolled Pazzi on the hand truck out onto the balcony outside.

The breeze was cold on Pazzi's wet face. Talking quickly now, "You'll never get away from this building alive. I have *money*. I have *one hundred and sixty million lire* in cash, U.S. dollars *one hundred thousand*! Let me telephone my wife. I'll tell her to get the money and put it in my car, and leave the car right in front of the palazzo."

Dr. Lecter retrieved his noose from the pulpit and carried it outside, trailing the orange cord behind him. The other end was tight in a series of hitches around the heavy floor polisher.

Pazzi was still talking. "She'll call me on the cell phone when she's outside, and then she'll leave it for you. I have the police pass, she can drive right across the piazza to the entrance. She'll do what I tell her. The car *smokes*, man, you can look down and see it's running, the keys will be in it."

Dr. Lecter tilted Pazzi forward against the balcony railing. The railing came to his thighs.

Pazzi could look down at the piazza and make out through the floodlights the spot where Savonarola was burned, where he had sworn to sell Dr. Lecter to Mason Verger. He looked up at the clouds scudding low, colored by the floodlights, and hoped, so much, that God could see.

Down is the awful direction and he could not help staring there, toward death, hoping against reason that the beams of the floodlights gave some substance to the air, that they would somehow press on him, that he might snag on the light beams.

The orange rubber cover of the wire noose cold around his neck, Dr. Lecter standing so close to him.

"*Arrivederci, Commendatore.*"

Flash of the Harpy up Pazzi's front, another swipe severed his attachment to the dolly and he was tilting, tipped over the railing trailing the orange cord, ground coming up in a rush, mouth free to scream, and inside the salon, the floor polisher rushed across the floor and slammed to a stop against the railing, Pazzi jerked head-up, his neck broke and his bowels fell out.

Pazzi and his appendage swinging and spinning before the rough wall of the floodlit palace, jerking in posthumous spasms but not choking, dead, his shadow thrown huge on the wall by the floodlights, swinging with his bowels swinging below him in a shorter, quicker arc, his manhood pointing out of his rent trousers in a death erection.

Carlo charging out of a doorway, Matteo beside him, across the piazza toward the entrance to the palazzo, knocking tourists aside, two of whom had video cameras trained on the castle.

"It's a trick," someone said in English as he ran by.

"Matteo, cover the back door. If he comes out just kill him and cut him," Carlo said, fumbling with his cell phone as he ran. Into the palazzo now, up the stairs to the first level, then the second.

The great doors of the salon stood ajar. Inside, Carlo swung his gun on the projected figure on the wall, ran out onto the balcony, searched Machiavelli's office in seconds.

With his cell phone he reached Piero and Tommaso, waiting with the van in front of the museum. "Get to his house, cover it front and back. Just kill him and cut him."

Carlo dialed again. "Matteo?"

Matteo's phone buzzed in his breast pocket as he stood, breathing hard, in front of the locked rear exit of the palazzo. He had scanned the roof, and the dark windows, tested the door, his hand under his coat, on the pistol in his waistband.

He flipped open the phone. "*Pronto!*"

"What do you see?"

"Door's locked."

"The roof?"

Matteo looked up again, but not in time to see the shutters open on the window above him.

Carlo heard a rustle and a cry in his telephone, and Carlo was running, down the stairs, falling on a landing, up again and running, past the guard before the palace entrance, who now stood outside, past the statues flanking the entrance, around the corner and pounding now toward the rear of the palace, scattering a few couples. Dark back here now, running, the cell phone squeaking like a small creature in his hand as he ran. A figure ran across the street in front of him shrouded in white, ran blindly in the path of a *motorino*, and the scooter knocked it down, the figure up again and crashing into the front of a shop across the narrow street of the palace, ran into the plate glass, turned and ran blindly, an apparition in white, screaming, "Carlo! Carlo," great stains spreading on the ripped canvas covering him, and Carlo caught his brother in his arms, cut the plastic handcuff strip around his neck binding the canvas tight over his head, the canvas a mask of blood. Uncovered Matteo and found him ripped badly, across the face, across the abdomen, deeply enough across the chest for the wound to suck. Carlo left him long enough to run to the corner and look both ways, then he came back to his brother.

With sirens approaching, flashing lights filling the Piazza Signoria, Dr. Hannibal Lecter shot his cuffs and strolled up to a *gelateria* in the nearby Piazza de Giudici. Motorcycles and *motorinos* were lined up at the curb.

He approached a young man in racing leathers starting a big Ducati.

"Young man, I am desperate," he said with a rueful smile. "If I am not at the Piazza Bellosguardo in ten minutes, my wife will kill me," he said, showing the young man a fifty-thousand-lire note. "This is what my life is worth to me."

"That's all you want? A ride?" the young man said.

Dr. Lecter showed him his open hands. "A ride."

The fast motorcycle split the lines of traffic on the Lungarno, Dr. Lecter hunched behind the young rider, a spare helmet that smelled like hairspray and perfume on his head. The rider knew where he was going, peeling off the Via de' Serragli toward the Piazza Tasso, and out the Via Villani, hitting the tiny gap beside the Church of San Francesco di Paola that leads into the winding road up to Bellosguardo, the fine residential district on the hill overlooking Florence from the south.

The big Ducati engine echoed off the stone walls lining the road with a sound like ripping canvas, pleasing to Dr. Lecter as he leaned into the curves and coped with the smell of hairspray and inexpensive perfume in his helmet. He had the young man drop him off at the entrance to the Piazza Bellosguardo, not far from the home of Count Montauto, where Nathaniel Hawthorne had lived. The rider tucked his wages in the breast pocket of his leathers and the taillight of the motorcycle receded fast down the winding road.

Dr. Lecter, exhilarated by his ride, walked another forty meters to the black Jaguar, retrieved the keys from behind the bumper and started the engine. He had a slight fabric burn on the heel of his hand where his glove had ridden up as he flung the canvas drop cloth over Matteo and leaped down on him from the first-floor palazzo window. He put a dab of the Italian antibacterial unguent Cicatrine on it and it felt better at once.

Dr. Lecter searched among his music tapes as the engine warmed. He decided on Scarlatti.

37

THE TURBOPROP air ambulance lifted over the red tile roofs and banked southwest toward Sardinia, the Leaning Tower of Pisa poking above the wing in a turn steeper than the pilot would have made if he carried a living patient.

The stretcher intended for Dr. Hannibal Lecter held instead the cooling body of Matteo Deogracias. Older brother Carlo sat beside the corpse, his clothing stiff with blood.

Carlo Deogracias made the medical attendant put on earphones and turn up the music while he spoke on his cell phone to Las Vegas, where a blind encryption repeater relayed his call to the Maryland shore . . .

For Mason Verger, night and day are much the same. He happened to be sleeping. Even the aquarium lights were off. Mason's head was turned on the pillow, his single eye ever open like the eyes of the great eel, which was sleeping too. The only sounds were the regular hiss and sigh of the respirator, the soft bubbling of the aerator in the aquarium.

Above these constant noises came another sound, soft and urgent. The buzzing of Mason's most private telephone. His pale hand walked on its fingers like a crab to push the telephone button. The speaker was under his pillow, the microphone near the ruin of his face.

First Mason heard the airplane in the background and then a cloying tune, "*Gli Innamorati.*"

"I'm here. Tell me."

"It's a bloody *casino*," Carlo said.

"Tell me."

"My brother Matteo is dead. I have my hand on him now. Pazzi's dead too. Dr. Fell killed them and got away."

Mason did not reply at once.

"You owe two hundred thousand dollars for Matteo," Carlo said. "For his family." Sardinian contracts always call for death benefits.

"I understand that."

"The shit will fly about Pazzi."

"Better to get it out that Pazzi was dirty," Mason said. "They'll take it better if he's dirty. Was he dirty?"

"Except for this, I don't know. What if they trace from Pazzi back to you?"

"I can take care of that."

"I have to take care of *myself*," Carlo said. "This is too much. A chief inspector of the Questura dead, I can't buy out of that."

"You didn't do anything, did you?"

"We did nothing, but if the Questura put my name in this—*dirty Madonna*! They'll watch me for the rest of my life. Nobody will take fees from me, I won't be able to break wind on the street. What about Oreste? Did he know who he was supposed to film?"

"I don't think so."

"The Questura will have Dr. Fell identified by tomorrow or the next day. Oreste will put it together as soon as he sees the news, just from the timing."

"Oreste is well paid. Oreste is harmless to us."

"Maybe to you, but Oreste is facing a judge in a pornography case in Rome next month. Now he has a thing to trade. If you don't know that already you should kick some ass. You got to have Oreste?"

"I'll talk with Oreste," Mason said carefully, the rich tones of a radio announcer coming from his ravaged face. "Carlo, are you still game? You *want* to find Dr. Fell now, don't you? You *have* to find him for Matteo."

"Yes, but at your expense."

"Then keep the farm going. Get certified swine flu and cholera inoculations for the pigs. Get shipping crates for them. You have a good passport?"

"Yes."

"I mean a *good* one, Carlo, not some upstairs Trastevere crap."

"I have a good one."

"You'll hear from me."

Ending his connection in the droning airplane, Carlo inadvertently pushed the auto dial on his cell phone. Matteo's telephone beeped loudly in his dead hand, still held in the steely grip of cadaveric spasm. For an instant Carlo thought his brother would raise the telephone to his ear. Dully, seeing that Matteo could not answer, Carlo pushed his hang-up button. His face contorted and the medical attendant could not look at him.

38

THE DEVIL'S Armor with its horned helmet is a splendid suit of fifteenth-century Italian armor that has hung high on the wall in the village church of Santa Reparata south of Florence since 1501. In addition to the graceful horns, shaped like those of the chamois, the pointed gauntlet cuffs are stuck where shoes should be, at the ends of the greaves, suggesting the cloven hooves of Satan.

According to the local legend, a young man wearing the armor took the name of the Virgin in vain as he passed the church, and found that afterward he could not take his armor off until he beseeched the Virgin for forgiveness. He gave the armor to the church as a gift of thanksgiving. It is an impressive presence and it honored its proof marks when an artillery shell burst in the church in 1942.

The armor, its upper surfaces covered with a feltlike coating of dust, looks down on the small sanctuary now as Mass is being completed. Incense rises, passes through the empty visor.

Only three people are in attendance, two elderly women, both dressed in black, and Dr. Hannibal Lecter. All three take Communion, though Dr. Lecter touches his lips to the cup with some reluctance.

The priest completes the benediction and withdraws. The women depart. Dr. Lecter continues his devotions until he is alone in the sanctuary.

From the organ loft, Dr. Lecter can just reach over the railing and, leaning between the horns, raise the dusty visor on the helmet of the Devil's Armor. Inside, a fishhook over the lip of the gorget suspends a string and a package hanging inside the cuirass where the heart would be. Carefully, Dr. Lecter draws it out.

A package: passports of the best Brazilian manufacture, identification, cash, bankbooks, keys. He puts it under his arm beneath his coat.

Dr. Lecter does not indulge much in regret, but he was sorry to be leaving Italy. There were things in the Palazzo Capponi that he would have liked to find and read. He would have liked to play the clavier and perhaps compose; he might have cooked for the Widow Pazzi, when she overcame her grief.

WHILE BLOOD still fell from the hanging body of Rinaldo Pazzi to fry and smoke on the hot floodlights beneath Palazzo Vecchio, the police summoned the fire department to get him down.

The *pompieri* used an extension on their ladder truck. Ever practical, and certain the hanged man was dead, they took their time retrieving Pazzi. It was a delicate process requiring them to boost the dangling viscera up to the body and wrap netting around the whole mass, before attaching a line to lower him to the ground.

As the body reached the upstretched arms of those on the ground, *La Nazione* got an excellent picture that reminded many readers of the great Deposition paintings.

The police left the noose in place until it could be fingerprinted, and then cut the stout electrical cord in the center of the noose to preserve the integrity of the knot.

Many Florentines were determined that the death be a spectacular suicide, deciding that Rinaldo Pazzi bound his own hands in the manner of a jail suicide, and ignoring the fact that the feet were also bound. In the first hour, local radio reported Pazzi had committed hara-kiri with a knife in addition to hanging himself.

The police knew better at once—the severed bonds on the balcony and the hand truck, Pazzi's missing gun, eyewitness accounts of Carlo running into the Palazzo and the bloody shrouded figure running blindly behind the Palazzo Vecchio told them Pazzi was murdered.

Then the Italian public decided *Il Mostro* had killed Pazzi.

The Questura began with the wretched Girolamo Tocca, once convicted of being *Il Mostro*. They seized him at home and drove away with his wife once again howling in the road. His alibi was solid. He was drinking a Ramazzotti at a café in sight of a priest at the time. Tocca was released in Florence and had to return to San Casciano by bus, paying his own fare.

The staff at Palazzo Vecchio were questioned in the first hours, and the questioning spread through the membership of the Studiolo.

The police could not locate Dr. Fell. By noon on Saturday close attention was brought to bear on him. The Questura recalled that Pazzi had been assigned to investigate the disappearance of Fell's predecessor.

A clerk at the Carabinieri reported Pazzi in recent days had examined a *permesso di soggiorno*. Fell's records, including his photographs, attached negatives and fingerprints, were signed out to a false name in what appeared to be Pazzi's handwriting. Italy has not yet computerized its records nationwide and the *permessos* are still held at the local level.

Immigration records yielded Fell's passport number, which rang the lemons in Brazil.

Still, the police did not beep to Dr. Fell's true identity. They took fingerprints from the coils of the hangman's noose and fingerprints from the podium, the hand truck and from the kitchen at the Palazzo Capponi. With plenty of artists available, a sketch of Dr. Fell was prepared in minutes.

By Sunday morning, Italian time, a fingerprint examiner in Florence had laboriously, point by point, determined that the same fingerprints were on the podium, the noose, and Dr. Fell's kitchen utensils at the Palazzo Capponi.

The thumbprint of Hannibal Lecter, on the poster hanging in Questura headquarters, was not examined.

The fingerprints from the crime scene went to Interpol on Sunday night, and arrived as a matter of course at FBI headquarters in Washington, D.C., along with seven thousand other sets of crime scene prints. Submitted to the automated fingerprint classification system, the fingerprints from Florence registered a hit of such magnitude that an audible alarm sounded in the office of the assistant director in charge of the Identification Section. The night duty officer watched the face and fingers of Hannibal Lecter crawl out of the printer, and called the assistant director at home, who called the director first, and then Krendler at Justice.

Mason's telephone rang at 1:30 A.M. He acted surprised and interested.

Jack Crawford's telephone rang at 1:35. He grunted several times and rolled over to the empty, haunted side of his marriage bed where his late wife, Bella, used to be. It was cool there and he seemed to think better.

Clarice Starling was the last to know that Dr. Lecter had killed again. After she hung up the phone, she lay still for many minutes in the dark and her eyes stung for some reason she did not understand, but she did not cry. From her pillow looking up, she could see his face on the swarming dark. It was Dr. Lecter's old face, of course.

40

THE PILOT of the air ambulance would not go into the short, uncontrolled airfield at Arbatax in darkness. They landed at Cagliari, refueled and waited until daylight, and flew up the coast in a spectacular sunrise that gave a false pink cast to Matteo's dead face.

A truck with a coffin was waiting at the Arbatax airstrip. The pilot argued about money and Tommaso stepped in before Carlo slapped his face.

Three hours into the mountains and they were home.

Carlo wandered alone to the rough timber shed he had built with Matteo. All was ready there, the cameras in place to film Lecter's death. Carlo stood beneath the work of Matteo's hands and looked at himself in the great rococo mirror above the animal pen. He looked around at the timbers they had sawn together, he thought of Matteo's great square hands on the saw and a great cry escaped him, a cry from his anguished heart loud enough to ring off the trees. Tusked faces appeared from the brush of the mountain pasture.

Piero and Tommaso, brothers themselves, left him alone.

Birds sang in the mountain pasture.

Came Oreste Pini from the house buttoning his fly with one hand

and waving his cell phone with the other. "So you missed Lecter. Bad luck."

Carlo appeared not to hear him.

"Listen, everything is not lost. This can still work out," Oreste Pini said. "I have Mason here. He'll take a *simulado*. Something he can show Lecter when he does catch him. Since we're all set up. We've got a body—Mason says it was just a thug you hired. Mason says we could just, ah, just jerk it around under the fence when the pigs come and just play the canned sound. Here, talk to Mason."

Carlo turned and looked at Oreste as though he had arrived from the moon. Finally he took the cell phone. As he spoke with Mason, his face cleared and a certain peace seemed to settle on him.

Carlo snapped the cell phone shut. "Get ready," he said.

Carlo spoke with Piero and Tommaso, and with the cameraman's help they carried the coffin to the shed.

"You don't want that close enough to get in the frame," Oreste said. "Let's get some footage of the animals milling and then we'll go from there."

Seeing the activity in the shed, the first pigs broke cover.

"*Giriamo!*" Oreste called.

They came running, the wild swine, brown and silver, tall, hip-high to a man, deep in the chest, long-bristled, moving with the speed of a wolf on their little hooves, intelligent little eyes in their hellish faces, massive neck muscles beneath the ridge of standing bristles on their backs capable of lifting a man on their great ripping tusks.

"*Pronti!*" the cameraman called.

They had not eaten in three days, others coming now in an advancing line unfazed by the men behind the fence.

"*Motore!*" Oreste called.

"*Partito!*" the cameraman yelled.

The pigs stopped ten yards short of the shed in a milling, pawing line, a thicket of hooves and tusks, the pregnant sow in the center.

They surged forward and back like linemen, and Oreste framed them with his hands.

"*Azione!*" he yelled at the Sards, and Carlo coming up behind him cut him up the crease of his buttocks and made him scream, gripped him around the hips and hoisted him headfirst into the pen, and the pigs charged. Oreste tried to get to his feet, got to one knee and the sow hit him in the ribs and knocked him sprawling. And they were on him, snarling and squealing, two boars pulling at his face got his jaw off and divided it like a wishbone. And still Oreste nearly made his feet and then he was on his back again with his belly exposed and open, his arms and legs waving above the milling backs, Oreste screaming with his jaw gone, not able to make any words.

Carlo heard a shot and turned. The cameraman had deserted his running camera and tried to flee, but not fast enough to escape Piero's shotgun.

The pigs were settling in now, dragging things away.

"*Azione* my ass," Carlo said, and spit on the ground.

III

TO THE NEW
WORLD

41

A CAREFUL SILENCE surrounded Mason Verger. His staff treated him as though he had lost a baby. Asked how he was feeling, he said, "I feel like I just paid a lot of money for a dead dago."

After a sleep of several hours, Mason wanted children brought into the playroom outside his chamber, and to have a talk with one or two of the most troubled ones, but there were no troubled children to be had immediately, and no time for his supplier in the Baltimore slums to trouble some for him.

That failing, he had his attendant Cordell cripple ornamental carp and drop them to the eel until the eel could eat no more and retreated into its rock, the water clouded pink and gray and full of iridescent golden shreds.

He tried to torment his sister Margot, but she retired to the workout room and for hours ignored his pages. She was the only person at Muskrat Farm who dared to ignore Mason.

A short, much-edited piece of tourist's videotape showing the death of Rinaldo Pazzi was on the television evening news Saturday night, before Dr. Lecter was identified as the killer. Blurred areas of the image spared viewers the anatomical details.

Mason's secretary was on the telephone immediately to get the unedited tape. It arrived by helicopter four hours later.

The videotape had a curious provenance:

Of the two tourists who were videotaping the Palazzo Vecchio at the moment of Rinaldo Pazzi's death, one panicked and the camera swung away at the moment of the fall. The other tourist was Swiss and held steady through the entire episode, even panning back up the jerking, swinging cord.

The amateur cameraman, a patent clerk named Viggert, was fearful that the police would seize the videotape and the RAI Italian television would get it free. He called his lawyer in Lausanne at once, made arrangements to copyright the images and sold the rights on a per-broadcast basis to ABC television news after a bidding war. First North American serial rights for print went to the *New York Post*, followed by the *National Tattler*.

The tape instantly took its place among the classic horrific spectacles—Zapruder, the assassination of Lee Harvey Oswald and the suicide of Edgar Bolger—but Viggert would bitterly regret selling so soon, before Dr. Lecter was accused of the crime.

This copy of the Viggerts' vacation videotape was complete. We see Swiss family Viggert dutifully orbiting the balls of the David at the Accademia hours before the events at Palazzo Vecchio.

Mason, watching the video with his single goggled eye, had little interest in the expensive piece of meat twitching at the end of the electrical cord. The little history lesson *La Nazione* and *Corriere della Sera* provided on the two Pazzis hanged from the same window five hundred twenty years apart did not interest him either. What held him, what he ran over and over and over, was the pan up the jerking cord to the balcony where a slender figure stood in fuzzy silhouette against the dim light within, waving. Waving to Mason. Dr. Lecter waved to Mason from the wrist the way you would wave bye-bye to a child.

"Bye-bye," Mason replied from his darkness. "Bye-bye," the deep radio voice shaking with rage.

42

THE IDENTIFICATION of Dr. Hannibal Lecter as the murderer of Rinaldo Pazzi gave Clarice Starling something serious to do, thank God. She became the de facto low-level liaison between the FBI and the Italian authorities. It was good to make a sustained effort at one task.

Starling's world had changed since the drug raid shoot-out. She and the other survivors of the Feliciana Fish Market were kept in a kind of administrative purgatory pending a Department of Justice report to a minor House Judiciary Subcommittee.

After finding the Lecter X ray, Starling had marked time as a highly qualified temporary, filling in at the National Police Academy, Quantico, for instructors who were ill or on vacation.

Through the fall and winter, Washington was obsessed with a scandal in the White House. The frothing reformers used more saliva than did the sad little sin, and the President of the United States publicly ate more than his portion of ordure trying to avoid impeachment.

In this circus, the small matter of the Feliciana Fish Market Massacre was pushed aside.

Each day, inside Starling a grim knowledge grew: The federal service would never be the same for her again. She was marked. Her coworkers had caution in their faces when they dealt with her, as though she had something contagious. Starling was young enough for this behavior to surprise and disappoint her.

It was good to be busy—requests from the Italians for information about Hannibal Lecter were pouring into Behavioral Science, usually in duplicate—one copy being forwarded by the State Department. And Starling replied with a will, stoking the fax lines and E-mailing Lecter files. She was surprised at how much the peripheral material had scattered over the seven years since the doctor's escape.

Her small cubicle in the basement at Behavioral Science was overflowing with paper, inky faxes from Italy, copies of the Italian papers.

What could she send the Italians that would be of value? The item they seized on was the single Questura computer query to the Lecter VICAP file at Quantico a few days before Pazzi's death. The Italian press resurrected Pazzi's reputation with it, claiming he was working in secret to capture Dr. Lecter and reclaim his honor.

On the other hand, Starling wondered, what information from the Pazzi crime could be useful here, in case the doctor returned to the United States?

Jack Crawford was not in the office much to advise her. He was in court a lot, and as his retirement approached he was deposed in a lot of open cases. He took more and more sick days, and when he was in the office he seemed increasingly distant.

The thought of not having his counsel gave Starling flashes of panic.

In her years at the FBI, Starling had seen a great deal. She knew that if Dr. Lecter killed again in the United States, the trumpets of flatulence would sound in Congress, an enormous roar of second-guessing would go up from Justice, and the Catch-Me-Fuck-Me would begin in earnest. Customs and Border Patrol would catch it first for letting him in.

The local jurisdiction where the crime occurred would demand everything relating to Lecter and the FBI effort would center around the local line bureau. Then, when the doctor did it again someplace else, everything would move.

If he were caught, the authorities would fight for credit like bears around a bloody seal.

Starling's business was to prepare for the eventuality of his coming, whether he ever came or not, putting aside all the weary knowledge of what would happen around the investigation.

She asked herself a simple question that would have sounded corny to the career climbers inside the Beltway: How could she do exactly what she was sworn to do? How could she protect the citizens and catch him if he came?

Dr. Lecter obviously had good papers and money. He was brilliant at concealing himself. Take the elegant simplicity of his first hideout after his escape from Memphis—he checked into a four-star hotel next door to a great plastic surgery facility in St Louis. Half the guests had their faces bandaged. He bandaged his own face and lived high on a dead man's money.

Among her hundreds of scraps of paper, she had his room service receipts from St Louis. Astronomical. A bottle of Bâtard-Montrachet one hundred twenty-five dollars. How good it must have tasted after all those years of jail food.

She had asked for copies of everything from Florence and the Italians obliged. From the quality of the print, she thought they must copy with some kind of soot blower.

There was no order anywhere. Here were Dr. Lecter's personal papers from the Palazzo Capponi. A few notes on Dante in his familiar handwriting, a note to the cleaning lady, a receipt from the Florentine fine grocer Vera dal 1926 for two bottles of Bâtard-Montrachet and some *tartufi bianchi*. Same wine again, and what was the other thing?

Starling's *Bantam New College Italian & English Dictionary* told her *tartufi bianchi* were white truffles. She called the chef at a good Washington Italian restaurant and asked him about them. She had to beg off the phone after five minutes as he raved about their taste.

Taste. The wine, the truffles. Taste in all things was a constant between Dr. Lecter's lives in America and Europe, between his life as a successful medical practitioner and fugitive monster. His face may have changed but his tastes did not, and he was not a man who denied himself.

Taste was a sensitive area to Starling, because it was in the area of taste that Dr. Lecter first touched her in the quick, complimenting her on her pocketbook and making fun of her cheap shoes. What had he called her? A well-scrubbed hustling rube with a little taste.

It was taste that itched at her in the daily round of her institutional life with its purely functional equipment in utilitarian settings.

At the same time her faith in *technique* was dying and leaving room for something else.

Starling was weary of technique. Faith in technique is the religion of the dangerous trades. To go up against an armed felon in a gunfight or to fight him in the dirt you have to believe perfect technique, hard training, will guarantee that you are invincible. This is not true, particularly in firefights. You can stack the odds in your favor, but if you get into enough gunfights, you will be killed in one.

Starling had seen it.

Having come to doubt the religion of technique, where could Starling turn?

In her tribulation, in the gnawing sameness of her days, she began to look at the shapes of things. She began to credit her own visceral reactions to things, without quantifying them or restricting them to words. At about this time she noticed a change in her reading habits. Before, she would have read a caption before she looked at a picture. Not now. Sometimes she did not read captions at all.

For years she had read couture publications on the sly, guiltily as though they were pornography. Now she began to admit to herself that there was something in those pictures that made her hungry. Within the framework of her mind, galvanized by the Lutherans against corrupting rust, she felt as though she were giving in to a delicious perversion.

She would have arrived at her tactic anyway, in time, but she was aided by the sea change inside her: It sped her toward the idea that Dr. Lecter's taste for rarified things, things in a small market, might be the monster's dorsal fin, cutting the surface and making him visible.

Using and comparing computerized customer lists, Starling might be able to crack one of his alternate identities. To do this, she had to know his preferences. She needed to know him better than anyone in the world knew him.

What are the things I know he likes? He likes music, wine, books, food. And he likes me.

The first step in the development of taste is to be willing to credit your own opinion. In the areas of food and wine and music, Starling would have to follow the doctor's precedents, looking at what he used in the past, but in one area she was at least his equal. Automobiles. Starling was a car buff, as anyone who saw her car could tell.

Dr. Lecter had owned a supercharged Bentley before his disgrace. Supercharged, not turbocharged. Custom supercharged with a Rootes-type positive displacement blower, so it had no turbo lag. She quickly realized that the custom Bentley market is so small, he would entail some risk going back to it.

What would he buy now? She understood the feeling he liked. A blown, big displacement V8, with power down low, and not peaky. What would she buy in the current market?

No question, an XJR Jaguar supercharged sedan. She faxed the East and West Coast Jaguar distributors asking for weekly sales reports.

What else did Dr. Lecter have a taste for, that Starling knew a lot about?

He likes me, she thought.

How quickly he had responded to her plight. Even considering the delay from using a remailing service to write to her. Too bad the postage meter lead fizzled—the meter was in such a public place any thief could use it.

How quickly did the *National Tattler* get to Italy? That's one place he saw Starling's trouble, a copy was found in the Palazzo Capponi. Did the scandal sheet have a Web site? Also, if he had a computer in Italy, he might have read a summary of the gunfight on the FBI's public Web site. What might be learned from Dr. Lecter's computer?

No computer was listed among the personal effects at Palazzo Capponi.

Still, she had seen *something*. She got out the photos of the library at the Palazzo Capponi. Here was a picture of the beautiful desk where he wrote to her. Here on the desk was a computer. A Phillips laptop. In subsequent pictures it was gone.

With her dictionary, Starling painfully composed a fax to the Questura in Florence:

Fra le cose personali del dottor Lecter, c'è un computer portatile?

And so, with small steps, Clarice Starling began to pursue Dr. Lecter down the corridors of his taste, with more confidence in her footing than was entirely justified.

43

MASON VERGER'S assistant Cordell, with an example posted in a frame on his desk, recognized the distinctive handwriting at once. The stationery was from the Excelsior Hotel in Florence, Italy.

Like an increasing number of wealthy people in the era of the Unabomber, Mason had his own mail fluoroscope, similar to the one at the U.S. Post Office.

Cordell pulled on some gloves and checked the letter. The fluoroscope showed no wires or batteries. In accordance with Mason's strict instructions, he copied the letter and the envelope on the copying machine, handling it with tweezers, and changed gloves before picking up the copy and delivering it to Mason.

In Dr. Lecter's familiar copperplate:

Dear Mason,

Thank you for posting such a huge bounty on me. I wish you would increase it. As an early-warning system, the bounty is better than radar. It inclines authorities everywhere to forsake their duty and scramble after me privately, with the results you see.

Actually, I'm writing to refresh your memory on the subject of your former nose. In your inspirational antidrug interview the other day in the Ladies' Home Journal *you claim that you fed your nose, along with the rest of your face, to the pooches, Skippy and Spot, all waggy at your feet. Not so: You ate it yourself, for refreshment. From the crunchy sound when you chewed it up, I would say it had a consistency similar to that of a chicken gizzard— "Tastes just like chicken!" was your comment at the time. I was reminded of the sound in a bistro when a French person tucks into a gésier salad.*

You don't remember that, Mason?

Speaking of chicken, you told me in therapy that, while you were subverting the underprivileged children at your summer camp, you learned that chocolate irritates your urethra. You don't remember that either, do you?

Don't you think it likely you told me all sorts of things you don't remember now?

There is an inescapable parallel between you and Jezebel, Mason. Keen Bible student that you are, you will recall the dogs ate Jezebel's face, along with the rest of her, after the eunuchs threw her out the window.

Your people might have assassinated me in the street. But you wanted me alive, didn't you? From the aroma of your henchmen, it's obvious how you planned to entertain me. Mason, Mason. Since you want to see me so badly, let me give you some words of comfort, and you know I never lie.

Before you die you will see my face.

Sincerely,

Hannibal Lecter, MD

P.S. I worry, though, that you won't live that long, Mason. You must avoid the new strains of pneumonia. You're very susceptible, prone as you are (and will remain). I would recommend vaccination immediately, along with immunization shots for hepatitis A and B. Don't want to lose you prematurely.

Mason seemed somewhat out of breath when he finished reading. He waited, waited and in his own good time said something to Cordell, which Cordell could not hear.

Cordell leaned close and was rewarded with a spray of spit when Mason spoke again:

"Get me Paul Krendler on the phone. And get me the Pigmaster."

44

THE SAME helicopter that brought the foreign newspapers daily to Mason Verger also brought Deputy Assistant Inspector General Paul Krendler to Muskrat Farm.

Mason's malign presence and his darkened chamber with its hissing and sighing machinery and its ever-moving eel would have made Krendler uneasy enough, but he also had to sit through the video of Pazzi's death again and again.

Seven times Krendler watched the Viggerts orbit the David, saw Pazzi plunge and his bowels fall out. By the seventh time, Krendler expected David's bowels to fall out too.

Finally the bright overhead lights came on in the seating area of Mason's room, hot on top of Krendler's head and shining off his scalp through the thinning brush cut.

The Vergers have an unparalleled understanding of piggishness, so Mason began with what Krendler wanted for himself. Mason spoke out of the dark, his sentences measured by the stroke of his respirator.

"I don't need to hear . . . your whole platform . . . how much money will it take?"

Krendler wanted to talk privately with Mason, but they were not alone in the room. A broad-shouldered figure, terrifically muscled, loomed in black outline against the glowing aquarium. The idea of a bodyguard hearing them made Krendler nervous.

"I'd rather it was just us talking, do you mind asking him to leave?"

"This is my sister, Margot," Mason said. "She can stay."

Margot came out of the darkness, her bicycle pants whistling.

"Oh, I'm sorry," Krendler said, half-rising from his chair.

"Hello," she said, but instead of taking Krendler's outstretched hand, Margot picked up two walnuts from the bowl on the table and, squeezing them together in her fist until they cracked loudly, returned to the gloom in front of the aquarium where presumably she ate them. Krendler could hear the hulls dropping to the floor.

"Oookay, let's hear it," Mason said.

"For me to unseat Lowenstein in the twenty-seventh district, ten million dollars minimum." Krendler crossed his legs and looked off somewhere into the dark. He didn't know if Mason could see him. "I'd need that much just for media. But I guarantee you he's vulnerable. I'm in a position to know."

"What's his thing?"

"We'll just say his conduct has—"

"Well, is it money or snatch?"

Krendler didn't feel comfortable saying "snatch" in front of Margot, though it didn't seem to bother Mason. "He's married and he's had a longtime affair with a state court of appeals judge. The judge has ruled in favor of some of his contributors. The rulings are probably coincidence, but when TV convicts him that's all I'll need."

"The judge a woman?" Margot asked.

Krendler nodded. Not sure Mason could see him, he added, "Yes. A woman."

"Too bad," Mason said. "It would be better if he was a *queer,* wouldn't it, Margot? Still, you can't sling that crap yourself, Krendler. It can't come from you."

"We've put together a plan that offers the voters . . ."

"You can't sling the crap yourself," Mason said again.

"I'll just make sure the Judicial Review Board knows where to look, so it'll stick to Lowenstein when it hits him. Are you saying you can help me?"

"I can help you with half of it."

"Five?"

"Let's not just toss it off like 'five.' Let's say it with the respect it deserves—*five million dollars*. The Lord has blessed me with this money. And with it I will do His will: You get it only if Hannibal Lecter falls cleanly into my hands." Mason breathed for a few beats. "If that happens, you'll be Mr. Congressman Krendler of the twenty-seventh district, free and clear, and all I'll ever ask you to do is oppose the Humane Slaughter Act. If the FBI gets Lecter, the cops grab him someplace and he gets off with lethal injection, it's been nice to know you."

"I can't help it if a local jurisdiction gets him. Or Crawford's outfit lucks up and catches him, I can't control that."

"How many states with death penalties could Dr. Lecter be charged in?" Margot asked. Her voice was scratchy but deep like Mason's from the hormones she had taken.

"Three states, multiple Murder One in each."

"If he's arrested I want him prosecuted at the state level," Mason said. "No kidnapping rap, no civil rights violations, no interstate. I want him to get off with life, I want him in a state prison, not a maximum federal pen."

"Do I have to ask why?"

"Not unless you want me to tell you. It doesn't fall under the Humane Slaughter Act," Mason said, and giggled. Talking had exhausted him. He gestured to Margot.

She carried a clipboard into the light and read from her notes. "We want everything you get and we want it before Behavioral Science sees it, we want Behavioral Science reports as soon as they're filed and we want the VICAP and National Crime Information Center access codes."

"You'd have to use a public phone every time you access VICAP," Krendler said, still talking out into the dark as though the woman wasn't there. "How can you do that?"

"*I* can do it," Margot said.

"She can do it," Mason whispered from the dark. "She writes workout programs for exercise machines in gyms. It's her little business so she doesn't have to live off of *Brother*."

"The FBI has a closed system and some of it's encrypted. You'll have to sign on from a guest location exactly as I tell you and download to a laptop programmed at the Justice Department," Krendler said. "Then if VICAP hides a tracer cookie on you, it will just come back to Justice. Buy a fast laptop with a fast modem for cash over-the-counter at a volume dealer and don't mail any warranties. Get a zip drive too. Stay off the Net with it. I'll need it overnight and I want it back when you're through. You'll hear from me. Okay, that's it." Krendler stood and gathered his papers.

"That's not *quite* it, Mr. Krendler . . ." Mason said. "Lecter doesn't have to come out. He's got the money to hide forever."

"How does he have money?" Margot said.

"He had some very rich old people in his psychiatric practice," Krendler said. "He got them to sign over a lot of money and stocks to him and he hid it good. The IRS hasn't been able to find it. They exhumed the bodies of a couple of his benefactors to see if he'd killed them, but they couldn't find anything. Toxin scans negative."

"So he won't get caught in a stickup, he has cash," Mason said. "We've got to lure him out. Be thinking of ways."

"He'll know where the hit came from in Florence," Krendler said.

"Sure he will."

"So he'll want you."

"I don't know," Mason said. "He likes me like I am. Be thinking, Krendler." Mason began to hum.

All Deputy Assistant Inspector General Krendler heard was humming as he went out the door. Mason often hummed hymns while he was scheming: *You've got the prime bait, Krendler, but we'll discuss it after you've made an incriminating bank deposit—when you belong to me.*

ONLY FAMILY remains in Mason's room, brother and sister.

Soft light and music. North African music, an oud and drums. Margot sits on the couch, head down, elbows on her knees. She might have been a hammer thrower resting, or a weight lifter resting in a gym after a workout. She breathes a little faster than Mason's respirator.

The song ends and she rises, goes to his bedside. The eel pokes his head out of the hole in the artificial rock to see if his wavy silver sky might rain carp again tonight. Margot's raspy voice at its softest. "Are you awake?"

In a moment Mason was present behind his ever-open eye. "Is it time to talk about—a hiss of breath—what *Margot* wants? Sit here on Santa's knee."

"You know what I want."

"Tell me."

"Judy and I want to have a baby. We want to have a Verger baby, our own baby."

"Why don't you buy a Chinese baby? They're cheaper than shoats."

"It's a good thing to do. We might do that too."

"What does Papa's will say . . . *To an heir, confirmed as my descendent in the Cellmark Laboratory or its equivalent by DNA testing, my estate entire upon the passing of my beloved son, Mason.* Beloved son, Mason, that's me. *In the absence of an heir, the sole beneficiary shall be the Southern Baptist Convention with specific clauses concerning Baylor University at Waco, Texas.* You really pissed Papa off with that muff-diving, Margot."

"You may not believe this, Mason, but it's not the money—well, it is a little bit, but don't you want an heir? It would be your heir too, Mason."

"Why don't you find a nice fellow and give him a little nooky, Margot? It's not like you don't know how."

The Moroccan music is building again, the obsessive repetitions of the oud in her ear like anger.

"I've messed myself up, Mason. I shriveled my ovaries with all the stuff I took. And I want Judy to be part of it. She wants to be the birth mother. Mason, you said if I helped you—you promised me some sperm."

Mason's spidery fingers gestured. "Help yourself. If it's still there."

"Mason, there's every chance that you still have viable sperm, and we could arrange to harvest it painlessly—"

"*Harvesting* my *viable sperm?* Sounds like you've been talking to somebody."

"Just the fertility clinic, it's confidential." Margot's face softened, even in the cold light of the aquarium. "We could be really good to a child, Mason, we've been to parenting classes, Judy comes from a big, tolerant family and there's a support group of women parents."

"You used to be able to make me come when we were kids, Margot. Made me shoot like a belt-fed mortar. And pretty damn fast too."

"You *hurt* me when I was little, Mason. You hurt me and you dislocated my elbow making me do the other—I still can't curl more than eighty pounds with my left arm."

"Well, you wouldn't take the chocolate. I said we'll talk about it, Little Sister, when this job is done."

"Let's just test you now," Margot said. "The doctor can take a painless sample—"

"What *painless*, I can't feel anything down there anyway. You could suck it till you're blue in the face, and it wouldn't be like it was the first time. But I've made people do that already and nothing happens."

"The doctor can take a painless sample, just to see if you've got motile sperm. Judy's taking Clomid already. We're getting her cycle charted, there's a lot of stuff to do."

"I haven't had the pleasure of meeting Judy in all this time. Cordell says she's bowlegged. How long have you two been an *item*, Margot?"

"Five years."

"Why don't you bring her by? We might . . . *work something out*, so to speak."

The North African drums end with a final slap and leave a ringing silence in Margot's ear.

"Why don't you manage your little hookup with the Justice Department by yourself?" she said close to his ear hole. "Why don't you try to get in a phone booth with your fucking laptop. Why don't you pay some more fucking guineas to catch the guy that made dog food out of your face? *You said you'd help me, Mason*."

"I will. I just have to think about the timing."

Margot crushed two walnuts together and let the shells fall on Mason's sheet. "Don't think too goddamned long, Smiley." Her cycle pants whistled like building steam as she walked out of the room.

ARDELIA MAPP cooked when she felt like it, and when she cooked the result was extremely good. Her heritage was a combination of Jamaican and Gullah, and at the moment she was making jerk chicken, seeding a Scotch bonnet pepper she held carefully by the stem. She refused to pay the premium for cut-up chickens and had Starling busy with the cleaver and the cutting board.

"If you leave the pieces whole, Starling, they won't take the seasoning like they will if you cut them up," she explained, not for the first time. "Here," she said, taking the cleaver and splitting a back with such force bone splinters stuck to her apron. "Like that. What are you doing throwing those necks out? Put that handsome thing back in there."

And a minute later, "I was at the post office today. Mailing the shoes to my mom," Mapp said.

"I was in the post office too, I could have taken them."

"Did you *hear* anything at the post office?"

"Nope."

Mapp nodded, not surprised. "The drum says they're covering your mail."

"Who is?"

"Confidential directive from the Postal Inspector. You didn't know that, did you?"

"No."

"So discover it some other way, we need to cover my post office buddy."

"Okay." Starling put down her cleaver for a moment. "Jesus, Ardelia."

Starling had stood at the post office counter and bought her stamps, reading nothing in the closed faces of the busy postal clerks, most of them African-American, and several of whom she knew. Clearly someone wanted to help her, but it was a big chance to take with criminal penalties and your pension on the line. Clearly that someone trusted Ardelia more than Starling. Along with her anxiety, Starling felt a happy flash at having a favor from the African-American hot line. Maybe it expressed a tacit judgment of self-defense in the shooting of Evelda Drumgo.

"Now, take those green onions and mash them with the knife handle and give them here. Mash the green and all," Ardelia said.

When she had finished the prep work, Starling washed her hands and went into the absolute order of Ardelia's living room and sat down. Ardelia came in in a minute, drying her hands on a dish towel.

"Hell kind of bullshit is this?" Ardelia said.

It was their practice to curse heartily before taking up anything truly ominous, a late-century form of whistling in the dark.

"Be Got Dam if I know," Starling said. "*Who's* the sumbitch looking at my mail, that's the thing."

"PI's office is as far back as my folks can go."

"It's not the shooting, it's not Evelda," Starling said. "If they're looking at my mail, it's got to be about Dr. Lecter."

"You turned in every damn thing he ever sent you. You down with Crawford on that."

"Damn straight. If it's the Bureau OPR checking up on me I can find that out, I think. If it's Justice OPR, I don't know."

The Justice Department and its subsidiary, the FBI, have separate Offices of Professional Responsibility, which theoretically cooperate and sometimes collide. Such conflicts are known in-house as pissing contests, and agents caught in the middle sometimes get drowned. In addition, the Inspector General at Justice, a political appointee, can jump in anytime and take over a sensitive case.

"If they know something Hannibal Lecter's up to, if they think he's close, they got to let you know it to protect yourself. Starling, do you ever . . . feel him around you?"

Starling shook her head. "I don't worry about him much. Not that way. I used to go a long time and not even think about it. You know that lead feeling, that heavy gray feeling when you dread something? I don't ever have that. I just think I'd know if I had a problem."

"What would you *do*, Starling? What would you do if you saw him in front of you? All of a sudden? Have you got it set in your mind? Would you throw down on him?"

"Fast as I could grab it out of my *britches*, I'd throw down on his ass."

Ardelia laughed. "And then what?"

Starling's smile went away. "That would be up to him."

"Could you shoot him?"

"To keep my own chitterlings in place, are you kidding me? My *God*, I hope that never happens, Ardelia. I'd be glad if he got back in custody without anybody else getting hurt—including him. I'll tell you though, sometimes I think, if he's ever cornered, I'd want to take the point going in for him."

"Don't even say that."

"With me he'd have a better chance to come out alive. I wouldn't shoot him because I'm scared of him. He's not the wolf man. It would just be up to him."

"Are you scared of him? You better be scared *enough*."

"You know what's scary, Ardelia? It's scary when somebody tells you the truth. I'd like to see him beat the needle. If he can do that, and he's put in an institution, there's enough academic interest in him to keep his treatment pretty good. And he won't have any problem with roommates. If he was in the slams I'd thank him for his note. Can't waste a man that's crazy enough to tell the truth."

"There's a reason somebody's monitoring your mail. They got a court order and it's someplace under seal. We're not staked out yet— we'd have spotted it," Ardelia said. "I wouldn't put it past those sons of bitches to know he's coming and not tell you. You watch out tomorrow."

"Mr. Crawford would have told us. They can't mount much against Lecter without bringing Mr. Crawford in on it."

"Jack Crawford is *history*, Starling. You've got a blind spot there. What if they mount something against *you*? For having a wise mouth, for not letting Krendler get in your pants? What if somebody wants to trash you? Hey, I'm serious about covering my source now."

"Is there something we can do for your post office buddy? Do we need to do something?"

"Who do you think is coming to dinner?"

"*All right, Ardelia!* . . . Wait a minute, I thought *I* was coming to dinner."

"You can take some home with you."

"I 'preciate it."

"No trouble, girl. My pleasure, in fact."

47

WHEN STARLING was a child she moved from a clapboard house that groaned in the wind to the solid redbrick of the Lutheran Orphanage.

The most ramshackle family dwelling of her early childhood had had a warm kitchen where she could share an orange with her father. But death knows where the little houses are, where people live who do dangerous work for not much money. Her father rode away from this house in his old pickup truck on the night patrol that killed him.

Starling rode away from her foster home on a slaughter horse while they were killing the lambs, and she found a kind of refuge in the Lutheran Orphanage. Institutional structures, big and solid, made her feel safe ever since. The Lutherans might have been short on warmth and oranges and long on Jesus, but the rules were the rules and if you understood them you were okay.

As long as impersonal competitive testing was the challenge, or doing the job on the street, she knew she could make her place secure. But Starling had no gift for institutional politics.

Now, as she got out of her old Mustang at the beginning of the day, the high façades of Quantico were no more the great brick bosom of her refuge. Through the crazed air over the parking lot, the very entrances looked crooked.

She wanted to see Jack Crawford, but there was no time. Filming at Hogan's Alley began as soon as the sun was well up.

The investigation of the Feliciana Fish Market Massacre required filmed reenactments made on the Hogan's Alley shooting range at Quantico, with every shot, every trajectory, accounted for.

Starling had to perform her part. The undercover van they used was the original one with body putty, unpainted, plugging the latest bullet holes. Again and again they piled out of the old van, over and over the agent playing John Brigham went down on his face and the one playing Burke writhed on the ground. The process, using noisy blank ammunition, left her wrung out.

They finished in midafternoon.

Starling hung up her SWAT gear and found Jack Crawford in his office.

She was back to addressing him as Mr. Crawford now, and he seemed increasingly vague and distant from everyone.

"Want an Alka-Seltzer, Starling?" he said when he saw her in his office door. Crawford took a number of patent medicines in the course of the day. He was also taking Ginkgo Biloba, Saw Palmetto, St. John's Wort and baby aspirin. He took them in a certain order from his palm, his head going back as though he were taking a shot of liquor.

In recent weeks, he had started hanging up his suit coat in the office and putting on a sweater his late wife, Bella, had knitted for him. He looked much older now than any memory she had of her own father.

"Mr. Crawford, some of my mail is being opened. They're not very good at it. Looks like they're steaming the glue with a teapot."

"You've had mail surveillance since Lecter wrote to you."

"They just fluoroscoped packages. That was fine, but I can read my own personal mail. Nobody's said anything to me."

"It's not our OPR doing it."

"It's not Deputy Dawg either, Mr. Crawford—it's somebody big enough to get a Title Three intercept warrant under seal."

"But it looks like amateurs doing the opening?" She was quiet long enough for him to add, "Better if you noticed it that way, is it, Starling?"

"Yes, sir."

He pursed his lips and nodded. "I'll look into it." He arranged his patent medicine bottles in the top drawer of his desk. "I'll speak to Carl Schirmer at Justice, we'll straighten that out."

Schirmer was a lame duck. The grapevine said he'd be retiring at the end of the year—all Crawford's cronies were retiring.

"Thank you, sir."

"Anybody in your cop classes show much promise? Anybody recruiting ought to talk to?"

"In the forensics, I can't tell yet—they're shy with me in sex crimes. There's a couple of pretty good shooters."

"We've got all we need of those." He looked at her quickly. "I didn't mean you."

At the end of this day of playing out his death, she went to John Brigham's grave in Arlington National Cemetery.

Starling put her hand on his stone, still gritty from the chisel. Suddenly she had on her lips the distinct sensation of kissing his forehead, cold as marble and gritty with powder, when she came to his bier the last time and put in his hand, beneath the white glove, her own last medal as Open Combat Pistol Champion.

Now leaves were falling in Arlington, strewing the crowded ground. Starling, with her hand on John Brigham's stone, looking over the acres of graves, wondered how many like him had been wasted by stupidity and selfishness and the bargaining of tired old men.

Whether you believe in God or not, if you are a warrior Arlington is a sacred place, and the tragedy is not to die, but to be wasted.

She felt a bond with Brigham that was no less strong because they were never lovers. On one knee beside his stone she remembered: He asked her something gently and she said no, and then he asked her if they could be friends, and meant it, and she said yes, and meant it.

Kneeling in Arlington, she thought about her father's grave far away. She had not visited it since she graduated first in her college class and went to his grave to tell him. She wondered if it was time to go back.

The sunset through Arlington's black branches was as orange as the orange she shared with her father; the distant bugle shivered her, the tombstone cold beneath her hand.

WE CAN see it through the vapor of our breath—in the clear night over Newfoundland a brilliant point of light hanging in Orion, then passing slowly overhead, a Boeing 747 bucking a hundred-mile-per-hour head wind westward.

Back in steerage where the package tours go, the fifty-two members of Old World Fantasy, a tour of eleven countries in seventeen days, are returning to Detroit and Windsor, Canada. Shoulder room is twenty inches. Hip room between armrests is twenty inches. This is two inches more space than a slave had on the Middle Passage.

The passengers are being slopped with freezing-cold sandwiches of slippery meat and processed cheese food, and are rebreathing the farts and exhalations of others in economically reprocessed air, a variation on the ditch-liquor principle established by cattle and pig merchants in the 1950s.

Dr. Hannibal Lecter is in the center of the middle row in steerage with children on both sides of him and a woman holding an infant at the end of the row. After so many years in cells and restraints, Dr. Lecter does not like to be confined. A computer game in the lap of the small boy beside him beeps incessantly.

Like many others scattered throughout the cheapest seats, Dr. Lecter wears a bright yellow smiley-face badge with CAN-AM TOURS on it in big red letters, and like the tourists he wears faux athletic warm-ups. His warm-ups bear the insignia of the Toronto Maple Leafs, a hockey team. Beneath his clothing, a considerable amount of cash is strapped to his body.

Dr. Lecter has been with the tour three days, having bought his place from a Paris broker of last-minute illness cancellations. The man who should have been in this seat went home to Canada in a box after his heart gave out climbing the dome of St. Peter's.

When he reaches Detroit, Dr. Lecter must face passport control and customs. He can be sure security and immigration officers at every major airport in the western world have been alerted to watch for him. Where his picture is not taped to the wall of passport control, it is waiting under the hot button of every customs and immigration computer.

In all of this, he thinks that he may enjoy one piece of luck: The pictures the authorities are using could be of his old face. The false passport he used to enter Italy has no corresponding home-country file to provide a current likeness: In Italy, Rinaldo Pazzi had tried to simplify his own life and satisfy Mason Verger by taking the Carabinieri's file, including the photograph and negative used on "Dr. Fell's" *permesso di soggiorno* and work permit. Dr. Lecter found them in Pazzi's briefcase and destroyed them.

Unless Pazzi took photos of "Dr. Fell" from hiding, there is a good chance that no current likeness of Dr. Lecter's new face exists in the world. It is not so different from his old face—a little collagen added around the nose and cheeks, changed hair, spectacles—but it is different enough if attention is not called to him. For the scar on the back of his hand, he has found a durable cosmetic and a tanning agent.

He expects that at Detroit Metropolitan Airport the Immigration Service will divide the arrivees into two lines, U.S. Passports and

Other. He has chosen a border city so the Other line will be full. This airplane is loaded with Canadians. Dr. Lecter thinks he can be swept through with the herd, as long as the herd accepts him. He has toured some historic sites and galleries with these tourists, he has flown in the stews of the airplane with them, but there are limits: He cannot eat this airline swill with them.

Tired and footsore, weary of their clothes and their companions, the tourists root in their supper bags, and from their sandwiches remove the lettuce, black with cold.

Dr. Lecter, not wishing to call attention to himself, waits until the other passengers have picked through this sorry fare, waits until they have gone to the bathroom and most have fallen asleep. Far at the front, a stale movie plays. Still he waits with the patience of a python. Beside him the small boy has fallen asleep over his computer game. Up and down the broad airplane, the reading lights wink out.

Then and only then, with a furtive glance around, Dr. Lecter takes from beneath the seat in front of him his own lunch in an elegant yellow box trimmed with brown from Fauchon, the Paris caterer. It is tied with two ribbons of silk gauze in complementary colors. Dr. Lecter has pro-visioned himself with wonderfully aromatic truffled pâté de foie gras, and Anatolian figs still weeping from their severed stems. He has a half-bottle of a St Estephe he favors. The silk bow yields with a whisper.

Dr. Lecter is about to savor a fig, holds it before his lips, his nostrils flared to its aroma, deciding whether to take all the fig in one glorious bite or just half, when the computer game beside him beeps. It beeps again. Without turning his head, the doctor palms the fig and looks down at the child beside him. The scents of truffle, foie gras and cognac climb from the open box.

The small boy sniffs the air. His narrow eyes, shiny as those of a rodent, slide sideways to Dr. Lecter's lunch. He speaks with the piercing voice of a competitive sibling:

"Hey, Mister. Hey, Mister." He's not going to stop.

"What is it?"

"Is that one of those special meals?"

"It is not."

"What've you got in there, then?" The child turned his face up to Dr. Lecter in a full wheedle. *"Gimme a bite?"*

"I'd very much like to," Dr. Lecter replied, noting that beneath the child's big head, his neck was only as big around as a pork tenderloin, "but you wouldn't like it. It's *liver*."

"Liverwurst! Awesome! Mom won't care, Mooaaaahm!" Unnatural child, who loves liverwurst and either whines or screams.

The woman holding the baby at the end of the row started awake.

Travelers in the row ahead, their chairs cranked back until Dr. Lecter can smell their hair, look back through the crack between seats. "We're trying to sleep up here."

"Mooooaaaahm, can I have some of his samwich?"

The baby in Mother's lap awoke and began to cry. Mother dipped a finger into the back of its diaper, came up negative, and gave the baby a pacifier.

"What is it you're trying to *give* him, sir?"

"It's liver, Madame," Dr. Lecter said as quietly as possible. "I haven't given—"

"Liverwurst, my favorite, I want it, he said *I could have some of it . . ."* The child stretched the last word into a piercing whine.

"Sir, if you're giving something to my *child*, could I see it?"

The stewardess, her face puffed from an interrupted nap, stopped by the woman's seat as the baby howled. "Everything all right here? Could I bring you something? Warm a bottle?"

The woman took out a capped baby bottle and gave it to the stewardess. She turned on her reading light, and while she searched for a nipple, she called to Dr. Lecter. "Would you pass it down to me? If you're offering it to my *child*, I want to see it. No offense, but he's got a tricky tummy."

We routinely leave our small children in day care among strangers. At the same time, in our guilt we evince paranoia about strangers and foster fear in children. In times like these, a genuine monster has to watch it, even a monster as indifferent to children as Dr. Lecter.

He passed his Fauchon box down to Mother.

"Hey, nice bread," she said, poking it with her diaper finger.

"Madame, you may *have* it."

"I don't want the *liquor*," she said, and looked around for a laugh. "I didn't know they'd let you bring your own. Is this *whiskey*? Do they *allow* you to drink this on the plane? I think I'll keep this ribbon if you don't want it."

"*Sir*, you can't open this alcoholic beverage on the aircraft," the stewardess said. "I'll hold it for you, you can claim it at the gate."

"Of course. Thank you so much," Dr. Lecter said.

Dr. Lecter could overcome his surroundings. He could make it all go away. The beeping of the computer game, the snores and farts, were nothing compared to the hellish screaming he'd known in the violent wards. The seat was no tighter than restraints. As he had done in his cell so many times, Dr. Lecter put his head back, closed his eyes and retired for relief into the quiet of his memory palace, a place that is quite beautiful for the most part.

For this little time, the metal cylinder howling eastward against the wind contains a palace of a thousand rooms.

As once we visited Dr. Lecter in the Palazzo of the Capponi, so we will go with him now into the palace of his mind . . .

The foyer is the Norman Chapel in Palermo, severe and beautiful and timeless, with a single reminder of mortality in the skull graven in the floor. Unless he is in a great hurry to retrieve information from the palace, Dr. Lecter often pauses here as he does now, to admire the chapel. Beyond it, far and complex, light and dark, is the vast structure of Dr. Lecter's making.

The memory palace was a mnemonic system well known to ancient scholars and much information was preserved in them through the Dark Ages while Vandals burned the books. Like scholars before him, Dr. Lecter stores an enormous amount of information keyed to objects in his thousand rooms, but unlike the ancients, Dr. Lecter has a second purpose for his palace; sometimes he lives there. He has passed years among its exquisite collections, while his body lay bound on a violent ward with screams buzzing the steel bars like hell's own harp.

Hannibal Lecter's palace is vast, even by medieval standards. Translated to the tangible world it would rival the Topkapi Palace in Istanbul for size and complexity.

We catch up to him as the swift slippers of his mind pass from the foyer into the Great Hall of the Seasons. The palace is built according to the rules discovered by Simonides of Ceos and elaborated by Cicero four hundred years later; it is airy, high-ceilinged, furnished with objects and tableaux that are vivid, striking, sometimes shocking and absurd, and often beautiful. The displays are well spaced and well lighted like those of a great museum. But the walls are not the neutral colors of museum walls. Like Giotto, Dr. Lecter has frescoed the walls of his mind.

He has decided to pick up Clarice Starling's home address while he is in the palace, but he is in no hurry for it, so he stops at the foot of a great staircase where the Riace bronzes stand. These great bronze warriors attributed to Phidias, raised from the seafloor in our own time, are the centerpiece of a frescoed space that could unspool all of Homer and Sophocles.

Dr. Lecter could have the bronze faces speak Meleager if he wished, but today he only wants to look at them.

A thousand rooms, miles of corridors, hundreds of facts attached to each object furnishing each room, a pleasant respite awaiting Dr. Lecter whenever he chooses to retire there.

But this we share with the doctor: In the vaults of our hearts and brains, danger waits. All the chambers are not lovely, light and

high. There are holes in the floor of the mind, like those in a
medieval dungeon floor—the stinking oubliettes, named for forgetting,
bottle-shaped cells in solid rock with the trapdoor in the top. Nothing
escapes from them quietly to ease us. A quake, some betrayal by our
safeguards, and sparks of memory fire the noxious gases—things trapped
for years fly free, ready to explode in pain and drive us to dangerous
behavior . . .

Fearfully and wonderfully made, we follow as he moves with a swift
light stride along the corridor of his own making, through a scent of
gardenias, the presence of great sculpture pressing on us, and the light
of pictures.

His way leads around to the right past a bust of Pliny and up the
staircase to the Hall of Addresses, a room lined with statuary and
paintings in a fixed order, spaced wide apart and well lit, as Cicero
recommends.

Ah . . . The third alcove from the door on the right is dominated
by a painting of St. Francis feeding a moth to a starling. On the floor
before the painting is this tableau, life-sized in painted marble:

A parade in Arlington National Cemetery led by Jesus, thirty-three,
driving a '27 Model-T Ford truck, a "tin lizzie," with J. Edgar Hoover
standing in the truck bed wearing a tutu and waving to an unseen
crowd. Marching behind him is Clarice Starling carrying a .308 Enfield
rifle at shoulder arms.

Dr. Lecter appears pleased to see Starling. Long ago he obtained
Starling's home address from the University of Virginia Alumni Association. He stores the address in this tableau, and now, for his own
pleasure, he summons the numbers and the name of the street where
Starling lives:

3327 Tindal

Arlington, VA 22308

Dr. Lecter can move down the vast halls of his memory palace with
unnatural speed. With his reflexes and strength, apprehension and speed

of mind, Dr. Lecter is well armed against the physical world. But there are places within himself that he may not safely go, where Cicero's rules of logic, of ordered space and light do not apply . . .

He has decided to visit his collection of ancient textiles. For a letter he is writing to Mason Verger, he wants to review a text of Ovid on the subject of flavored facial oils which is attached to the weavings.

He proceeds down an interesting flat-weave kilim runner toward the hall of looms and textiles.

In the world of the 747, Dr. Lecter's head is pressed back against the seat, his eyes are closed. His head bobs gently as turbulence bumps the airplane.

At the end of the row, the baby has finished its bottle and is not yet asleep. Its face reddens. Mother feels the little body tense within the blanket, then relax. There is no question what has happened. She does not need to dip her finger in the diaper. In the row ahead someone says "Jeeeezus."

To the stale gymnasium reek of the airplane is added another layer of smell. The small boy, seated beside Dr. Lecter, inured to the baby's habits, continues to eat the lunch from Fauchon.

Beneath the memory palace, the traps fly up, the oubliettes yawn their ghastly stench . . .

A few animals had managed to survive the artillery and machine-gun fire in the fighting that left Hannibal Lecter's parents dead and the vast forest on their estate scarred and blasted.

The mixed bag of deserters who used the remote hunting lodge ate what they could find. Once they found a miserable little deer, scrawny, with an arrow in it, that had managed to forage beneath the snow and survive. They led it back into the camp to keep from carrying it.

Hannibal Lecter, six, watched through a crack in the barn as they brought it in, pulling and twisting its head against the plowline twisted around its neck. They did not wish to fire a shot and managed to knock it off its spindly legs and hack at its throat with an axe, cursing at one another in several languages to bring a bowl before the blood was wasted.

There was not much meat on the runty deer and in two days, perhaps three, in their long overcoats, their breaths stinking and steaming, the deserters came through the snow from the hunting lodge to unlock the barn and choose again from among the children huddled in the straw. None had frozen, so they took a live one.

They felt Hannibal Lecter's thigh and his upper arm and chest, and instead of him, they chose his sister, Mischa, and led her away. To play, they said. No one who was led away to play ever returned.

Hannibal held on to Mischa so hard, held to Mischa with his wiry grip until they slammed the heavy barn door on him, stunning him and cracking the bone in his upper arm.

They led her away through snow still stained bloody from the deer.

He prayed so hard that he would see Mischa again, the prayer consumed his six-year-old mind, but it did not drown out the sound of the axe. His prayer to see her again did not go entirely unanswered—he did see a few of Mischa's milk teeth in the reeking stool pit his captors used between the lodge where they slept and the barn where they kept the captive children who were their sustenance in 1944 after the Eastern Front collapsed.

Since this partial answer to his prayer, Hannibal Lecter had not been bothered by any considerations of deity, other than to recognize how his own modest predations paled beside those of God, who is in irony matchless, and in wanton malice beyond measure.

In this hurtling aircraft, his head bouncing gently against the headrest, Dr. Lecter is suspended between his last view of Mischa crossing the bloody snow and the sound of the axe. He is held there and he cannot stand it. In the world of the airplane comes a short scream from his sweating face, thin and high, piercing.

Passengers ahead of him turn, some wake from sleep. Some in the row ahead of him are snarling. "Kid, Jesus Christ, what is the *matter* with you? My God!"

Dr. Lecter's eyes open, they look straight ahead, a hand is on him. It is the small boy's hand.

"You had a bad dream, huh?" The child is not frightened, nor does he care about the complaints from the forward rows.

"Yes."

"I have bad dreams a lot of times too. I'm not laughing at you."

Dr. Lecter took several breaths, his head pressed back against the seat. Then his composure returned as though calm rolled down from his hairline to cover his face. He bent his head to the child and said in a confidential tone, "You're right not to eat this swill, you know. Don't ever eat it."

Airlines no longer provide stationery. Dr. Lecter, in perfect command of himself, took some hotel stationery from his breast pocket and began a letter to Clarice Starling. First, he sketched her face. The sketch is now in a private holding at the University of Chicago and available to scholars. In it Starling looks like a child and her hair, like Mischa's, is stuck to her cheek with tears . . .

We can see the airplane through the vapor of our breath, a brilliant point of light in the clear night sky. See it cross the Pole star, well past the point of no return, committed now to a great arc down to tomorrow in the New World.

49

THE STACKS of paper and files and diskettes in Starling's cubicle reached critical mass. Her request for more space went unanswered. *Enough.* With the recklessness of the damned she commandeered a spacious room in the basement at Quantico. The room was supposed to become Behavioral Science's private darkroom as soon as Congress appropriated some money. It had no windows, but plenty of shelves and, being built for a darkroom, it had double blackout curtains instead of a door.

Some anonymous office neighbor printed a sign in Gothic letters that read HANNIBAL'S HOUSE and pinned it on her curtained entrance. Fearful of losing the room, Starling moved the sign inside.

Almost at once she found a trove of useful personal material at the Columbia College of Criminal Justice Library, where they maintained a Hannibal Lecter Room. The college had original papers from his medical and psychiatric practices and transcripts of his trial and the civil actions against him. On her first visit to the library Starling waited forty-five minutes while custodians hunted for the keys to the Lecter room without success. On the second occasion, she found an indifferent graduate student in charge, and the material uncatalogued.

Starling's patience was not improving in her fourth decade. With

Section Chief Jack Crawford backing her at the U.S. Attorney's office, she got a court order to move the entire college collection to her basement room at Quantico. Federal marshals accomplished the move in a single van.

The court order created waves, as she feared it would. Eventually, the waves brought Krendler . . .

At the end of a long two weeks, Starling had most of the library material organized in her makeshift Lecter center. Late on a Friday afternoon she washed her face and hands of the bookdust and grime, turned down the lights and sat on the floor in the corner, looking at the many shelf-feet of books and papers. It is possible that she nodded off for a moment . . .

A smell awakened her, and she was aware that she was not alone. It was the smell of shoe polish.

The room was semidark, and Deputy Assistant Inspector General Paul Krendler moved along the shelves slowly, peering at the books and pictures. He hadn't bothered to knock—there was no place to knock on the curtains and Krendler was not inclined to knocking anyway, especially at subordinate agencies. Here, in this basement at Quantico, he was definitely slumming.

One wall of the room was devoted to Dr. Lecter in Italy, with a large photograph posted of Rinaldo Pazzi hanging with his bowels out from the window at Palazzo Vecchio. The opposite wall was concerned with crimes in the United States, and was dominated by a police photograph of the bow hunter Dr. Lecter had killed years ago. The body was hanging on a peg board and bore all the wounds of the medieval Wound Man illustrations. Many case files were stacked on the shelves along with civil records of wrongful death lawsuits filed against Dr. Lecter by families of the victims.

Dr. Lecter's personal books from his medical practice were here in an order identical to their arrangement in his old psychiatric office.

Starling had arranged them by examining police photos of the office with a magnifying glass.

Much of the light in the dim room came through an X ray of the doctor's head and neck which glowed on a light box on the wall. The other light came from a computer workstation at a corner desk. The screen theme was "Dangerous Creatures." Now and then the computer growled.

Piled beside the machine were the results of Starling's gleaning. The painfully gathered scraps of paper, receipts, itemized bills that revealed how Dr. Lecter had lived his private life in Italy, and in America before he was sent to the asylum. It was a makeshift catalog of his tastes.

Using a flatbed scanner for a table, Starling had laid a single place setting that survived from his home in Baltimore—china, silver, crystal, napery radiant white, a candlestick—four square feet of elegance against the grotesque hangings of the room.

Krendler picked up the large wineglass and pinged it with his fingernail.

Krendler had never felt the flesh of a criminal, never fought one on the ground, and he thought of Dr. Lecter as a sort of media bogeyman and an opportunity. He could see his own photograph in association with a display like this in the FBI museum once Lecter was dead. He could see its enormous campaign value. Krendler had his nose close to the X-ray profile of the doctor's capacious skull, and when Starling spoke to him, he jumped enough to smudge the X ray with nose grease.

"Can I help you, Mr. Krendler?"

"Why're you sitting there in the dark?"

"I'm thinking, Mr. Krendler."

"People on the Hill want to know what we're doing about Lecter."

"This is what we're doing."

"Brief me, Starling. Bring me up to speed."

"Wouldn't you prefer Mr. Crawford—"

"Where *is* Crawford?"

"Mr. Crawford's in court."

"I think he's losing it, do you ever feel that way?"

"No, sir, I don't."

"What are you doing here? We got a beef from the college when you seized all this stuff out of their library. It could have been handled better."

"We've gathered everything we can find regarding Dr. Lecter here in this place, both objects and records. His weapons are in Firearms and Toolmarks, but we have duplicates. We have what's left of his personal papers."

"What's the point? You catching a crook, or writing a book?" Krendler paused to store this catchy rhyme in his verbal magazine. "If, say, a ranking Republican on Judiciary Oversight should ask me what *you*, Special Agent Starling, are doing to catch Hannibal Lecter, what could I tell him?"

Starling turned on all the lights. She could see that Krendler was still buying expensive suits while saving money on his shirts and ties. The knobs of his hairy wrists poked out of his cuffs.

Starling looked for a moment through the wall, past the wall, out to forever and composed herself. She made herself see Krendler as a police academy class.

"We know Dr. Lecter has very good ID," she began. "He must have at least one extra solid identity, maybe more. He's careful that way. He won't make a dumb mistake."

"Get to it."

"He's a man of very cultivated tastes, some of them exotic tastes, in food, in wine, music. If he comes here, he'll want those things. He'll have to get them. He won't deny himself.

"Mr. Crawford and I went over the receipts and papers left from Dr. Lecter's life in Baltimore before he was first arrested, and what receipts the Italian police were able to furnish, lawsuits from creditors after his arrest. We made a list of some things he likes. You can see here: In the month that Dr. Lecter served the flautist Benjamin Raspail's sweetbreads to other members of the Baltimore Philharmonic Orchestra board, he bought two cases of Château Pétrus bordeaux at thirty-six hundred dollars a case. He bought five cases of Bâtard-Montrachet at eleven hundred dollars a case, and a variety of lesser wines.

"He ordered the same wine from room service in St Louis after he escaped, and he ordered it from Vera dal 1926 in Florence. This stuff is pretty rarified. We're checking importers and dealers for case sales.

"From the Iron Gate in New York, he ordered Grade A foie gras at two hundred dollars a kilo, and through the Grand Central Oyster Bar he got green oysters from the Gironde. The meal for the Philharmonic board began with these oysters, followed by sweetbreads, a sorbet, and then, you can read here in *Town & Country* what they had"— she read aloud quickly—"*a notable dark and glossy ragout, the constituents never determined, on saffron rice. Its taste was darkly thrilling with great bass tones that only the vast and careful reduction of the* fond *can give.* No victim's ever been identified as being in the ragout. Da da, it goes on—here it describes his distinctive tableware and stuff in detail. We're cross-checking credit card purchases at the china and crystal suppliers."

Krendler snorted through his nose.

"See, here in this civil suit, he still owes for a Steuben chandelier, and Galeazzo Motor Company of Baltimore sued to get back his Bentley. We're tracking sales of Bentleys, new and used. There aren't that many. And the sales of supercharged Jaguars. We've faxed the restaurant game suppliers asking about purchases of wild boar and we'll do a bulletin the week before the red-legged partridges come in from Scotland." She pecked at her keyboard and consulted a list, then stepped away from the machine when she felt Krendler's breath too close behind her.

"I've put in for funds to buy cooperation from some of the premier scalpers of cultural tickets, the culture vultures, in New York and

San Francisco—there are a couple of orchestras and string quartets he particularly likes, he favors the six or seventh row and always sits on the aisle. I've distributed the best likenesses we have to Lincoln Center and Kennedy Center, and most of the philharmonic halls. Maybe you could help us with that out of the DOJ budget, Mr. Krendler." When he didn't reply, she went on. "We're cross-checking new subscriptions to some cultural journals he's subscribed to in the past—anthropology, linguistics, *Physical Review*, mathematics, music."

"Does he hire S and M whores, that kind of thing? Male prostitutes?"

Starling could feel Krendler's relish in the question. "Not to our knowledge, Mr. Krendler. He was seen at concerts in Baltimore years ago with several attractive women, a couple of them were prominent in Baltimore charity work and stuff. We have their birthdays flagged for gift purchases. None of them was ever harmed to our knowledge, and none has ever agreed to speak about him. We don't know anything about his sexual preferences."

"I've always figured he was a homosexual."

"Why would you say that, Mr. Krendler?"

"All this artsy-fartsy stuff. Chamber music and tea-party food. I don't mean anything personal, if you've got a lot of sympathy for those people, or friends like that. The main thing, what I'm impressing on you, Starling: I *better* see cooperation here. There are no little fiefdoms. I want to be copied on every 302, I want every time card, I want every lead. Do you understand me, Starling?"

"Yes, sir."

At the door he said, "Be sure you do. You might have a chance to improve your situation here. Your so-called career could use all the help it can get."

The future darkroom was already equipped with vent fans. Looking him in the face, Starling flipped them on, sucking out the smell of his aftershave and his shoe polish. Krendler pushed through the blackout curtains without saying good-bye.

The air danced in front of Starling like heat shimmer on the gunnery range.

In the hall Krendler heard Starling's voice behind him.

"I'll walk outside with you, Mr. Krendler."

Krendler had a car and driver waiting. He was still at the level of executive transport where he made do with a Mercury Grand Marquis sedan.

Before he could get to his car, out in the clear air, she said, "Hold it, Mr. Krendler."

Krendler turned to her, wondering. Might be a glimmer of something here. Angry surrender? His antenna went up.

"We're here in the great out-of-doors," Starling said. "No listening devices around, unless you're wearing one." An urge hit her that she could not resist. To work with the dusty books she was wearing a loose denim shirt over a snug tank top.

Shouldn't do this. *Fuck it.*

She popped the snaps on her shirt and pulled it open. "See, I'm not wearing a wire." She wasn't wearing a bra either. "This is maybe the only time we'll ever talk in private, and I want to ask you. For years I've been doing the job and every time you could you've stuck the knife in me. What is it with you, Mr. Krendler?"

"You're welcome to come talk about it . . . I'll make time for you, if you want to review . . ."

"We're talking about it now."

"You figure it out, Starling."

"Is it because I wouldn't see you on the side? Was it when I told you to go home to your wife?"

He looked at her again. She really wasn't wearing a wire.

"Don't flatter yourself, Starling . . . this town is full of cornpone country pussy."

He got in beside his driver and tapped on the dash, and the big car moved away. His lips moved, as he wished he had framed it: "Cornpone cunts like you." There was a lot of political speaking in Krendler's future, he believed, and he wanted to sharpen his verbal karate, and get the knack of the sound bite.

50

"IT COULD work, I'm telling you," Krendler said into the wheezing dark where Mason lay. "Ten years ago, you couldn't have done it, but she can move customer lists through that computer like shit through a goose." He shifted on the couch under the bright lights of the seating area.

Krendler could see Margot silhouetted against the aquarium. He was used to cursing in front of her now, and rather enjoyed it. He bet Margot wished she had a dick. He felt like saying *dick* in front of Margot, and thought of a way: "It's how she's got the fields set up, and paired Lecter's preferences. She could probably tell you which way he carries his dick."

"On that note, Margot, bring in Dr. Doemling," Mason said.

Dr. Doemling had been waiting out in the playroom among the giant stuffed animals. Mason could see him on video examining the plush scrotum of the big giraffe, much as the Viggerts had orbited the David. On the screen he looked much smaller than the toys, as though he had compressed himself, the better to worm his way into some childhood other than his own.

Seen under the lights of Mason's seating area, the psychologist was a dry person, extremely clean but flaking, with a dry comb-over on his spotted scalp and a Phi Beta Kappa key on his watch chain. He sat down on the opposite side of the coffee table from Krendler and seemed familiar with the room.

There was a worm hole in the apple on his side of the bowl of fruits and nuts. Dr. Doemling turned the hole to face the other way. Behind his glasses, his eyes followed Margot with a degree of wonderment bordering on the oafish as she got another pair of walnuts and returned to her place by the aquarium.

"Dr. Doemling's head of the psychology department at Baylor University. He holds the Verger Chair," Mason told Krendler. "I've asked him what kind of bond there might be between Dr. Lecter and the FBI agent Clarice Starling. Doctor . . ."

Doemling faced forward in his seat as though it were a witness stand and turned his head to Mason as he would to a jury. Krendler could see in him the practiced manner, the careful partisanship of the two-thousand-dollar-a-day expert witness.

"Mr. Verger obviously knows my qualifications, would you like to hear them?" Doemling asked.

"No," Krendler said.

"I've reviewed the Starling woman's notes on her interviews with Hannibal Lecter, his letters to her, and the material you provided me on their backgrounds," Doemling began.

Krendler winced at this, and Mason said, "Dr. Doemling has signed a confidentiality agreement."

"Cordell will put your slides up on the elmo when you want them, Doctor," Margot said.

"A little background first." Doemling consulted his notes. "We *knooowww* Hannibal Lecter was born in Lithuania. His father was a count, title dating from the tenth century, his mother high-born Italian, a Visconti. During the German retreat from Russia some passing Nazi panzers shelled their estate near Vilnius from the high road and killed both parents and most of the servants. The children disappeared after that. There were two of them, Hannibal and his sister. We don't know what happened to the sister. The point is, Lecter was an orphan, like Clarice Starling."

"Which I told *you*," Mason said impatiently.

"But what did you conclude from it?" Dr. Doemling asked. "I'm not proposing a kind of sympathy between two orphans, Mr. Verger. This is not about sympathy. Sympathy does not enter here. And mercy is left bleeding in the dust. Listen to me. What a common experience of being an orphan gives Dr. Lecter is simply a better ability to understand her, and ultimately control her. This is all about *control*.

"The Starling woman spent her childhood in institutions, and from what you tell me she does not evidence any stable personal relationship with a man. She lives with a former classmate, a young African-American woman."

"That's very likely a sex thing," Krendler said.

The psychiatrist did not even spare Krendler a look—Krendler was automatically overruled. "You can never say to a certainty why someone lives with someone else."

"It is one of the things that is hid, as the Bible says," Mason said.

"Starling looks pretty tasty, if you like whole wheat," Margot offered.

"I think the attraction's from Lecter's end, not hers," Krendler said. "You've seen her—she's a pretty cold fish."

"*Is* she a cold fish, Mr. Krendler?" Margot sounded amused.

"You think she's queer, Margot?" Mason asked.

"How the hell would I know? Whatever she is, she treats it as her own damn business—that was my impression. I think she's tough, and she had on her game face, but I wouldn't say she's a cold fish. We didn't talk much, but that's what I took from it. That was before you *needed* me to *help* you, Mason—you ran me out, remember? I'm not going to say she's a cold fish. Girl who looks like Starling has to keep a certain distance in her face because *assholes* are hitting on her all the time."

Here Krendler felt that Margot looked at him a beat too long, though he could only see her in outline.

How curious, the voices in this room. Krendler's careful bureauese, Doemling's pedantic bray, Mason's deep and resonant tones with his badly pruned plosives and leaking sibilants and Margot, her voice rough and low, tough-mouthed as a livery pony and resentful of the bit. Under it all, the gasping machinery that finds Mason breath.

"I have an idea about her private life, regarding her apparent father fixation," Doemling went on. "I'll get into it shortly. Now, we have three documents of Dr. Lecter's concerning Clarice Starling. Two letters and a drawing. The drawing is of the Crucifixion Clock he designed while he was in the asylum." Dr. Doemling looked up at the screen. "The slide, please."

From somewhere outside the room, Cordell put up the extraordinary sketch on the elevated monitor. The original is charcoal on butcher paper. Mason's copy was made on a blueprint copier and the lines are the blue of a bruise.

"He tried to patent this," Dr. Doemling said. "As you can see, here is Christ crucified on a clock face and His arms revolve to tell the time, just like the Mickey Mouse watches. It's interesting because the face, the head hanging forward, is that of Clarice Starling. He drew it at the time of their interviews. Here's a photograph of the woman, you can see. *Cordell*, is it? Cordell, put up the photo please."

There was no question, the Jesus head was Starling.

"Another anomaly is that the figure is nailed to the cross through the wrists rather than the palms."

"That's accurate," Mason said. "You've *got* to nail them through the wrists and use big wooden washers, otherwise they get loose and start flapping. Idi Amin and I found that out the hard way when we reenacted the whole thing in Uganda at Easter. Our Saviour was actually nailed through the wrists. All the Crucifixion paintings are wrong. It's a mistranslation between the Hebrew and Latin Bibles."

"Thank you," Dr. Doemling said without sincerity. "The Crucifixion clearly represents a destroyed object of veneration. Note that the arm that forms the minute hand is at six, modestly covering the pudenda. The hour hand is at nine, or slightly past. Nine is a clear reference to the traditional hour when Jesus was crucified."

"And when you put six and nine together, note that you get sixty-nine, a figure popular in social intercourse," Margot could not help saying. In response to Doemling's sharp glance, she cracked her walnuts and shells rattled to the floor.

"Now let's take up Dr. Lecter's letters to Clarice Starling. Cordell, if you'd put them up." Dr. Doemling took a laser pointer from his pocket. "You can see that the writing, a fluent copperplate executed with a square-nibbed fountain pen, is machinelike in its regularity. You see that sort of handwriting in medieval papal bulls. It's quite beautiful, but freakishly regular. There is nothing spontaneous here. He's planning. He wrote this first one soon after he had escaped, killing five people in the process. Let's read from the text:

Well, Clarice, have the lambs stopped screaming?

You owe me a piece of information, you know, and that's what I'd like.

An ad in the national edition of the Times *and in the* International Herald-Tribune *on the first of any month will be fine. Better put it in the* China Mail *as well.*

I won't be surprised if the answer is yes and no. The lambs will stop for now. But, Clarice, you judge yourself with all the mercy of the dungeon scales at Threave; you'll have to earn it again and again, the blessed silence. Because it's the plight that drives you, seeing the plight, and the plight will not end, ever.

I have no plans to call on you, Clarice, the world being more interesting with you in it. Be sure you extend me the same courtesy . . .

Dr. Doemling pushed his rimless glasses up on his nose and cleared his throat. "This is a classic example of what I have termed in my published work *avunculism*—it's beginning to be referred to broadly in the professional literature as *Doemling's avunculism.* Possibly it will be included in the next *Diagnostic and Statistical Manual.* It may be defined for laymen as the act of posturing as a wise and caring patron to further a private agenda.

"I gather from the case notes that the question about the lambs screaming refers to a childhood experience of Clarice Starling's, the slaughter of the lambs on the ranch in Montana, her foster home," Dr. Doemling went on in his dry voice.

"She was trading information with Lecter," Krendler said. "He knew something about the serial killer Buffalo Bill."

"The second letter, seven years later, is on the face of it a letter of condolence and support," Doemling said. "He taunts her with references to her parents, whom she apparently venerates. He calls her father 'the dead night watchman' and her mother 'the chambermaid.' And then he invests them with excellent qualities she can imagine that they had, and further enlists these qualities to excuse her own failings in her career. This is about ingratiation, this is about control.

"I think the woman Starling may have a lasting attachment to her father, an *imago*, that prevents her from easily forming sexual relationships and may incline her to Dr. Lecter in some kind of transference, which in his perversity he would seize on at once. In this second letter he again encourages her to contact him with a personal ad, and he provides a code name."

My Christ, the man went on! Restlessness and boredom were torture for Mason because he couldn't fidget. "Right, fine, good, Doctor," Mason interrupted. "Margot, open the window a little. I've got a new source on Lecter, Dr. Doemling. Someone who knows both Starling and Lecter and saw them together, and he's been around Lecter more than anyone. I want you to talk to him."

Krendler squirmed on the couch, his bowels beginning to stir as he saw where this was going.

51

MASON SPOKE into his intercom and a tall figure came into the room. He was as muscular as Margot and dressed in whites.

"This is Barney," Mason said. "He was in charge of the violent ward at the Baltimore State Hospital for the Criminally Insane for six years when Lecter was there. Now he works for me."

Barney preferred to stand in front of the aquarium with Margot, but Dr. Doemling wanted him in the light. He took a place beside Krendler.

"*Barney*, is it? Now, *Barney*, what is your professional training?"

"I have an LPN."

"You're a *licensed practical nurse*? Good for you. Is that all?"

"I have a bachelor's degree in the humanities from the United States Correspondence College," Barney said, expressionless. "And a certificate of attendance from the Cummins School of Mortuary Science. I'm qualified as a diener. I did that at night during nursing school."

"You worked your way through LPN school as a morgue attendant?"

"Yes, removing bodies from crime scenes and assisting at autopsies."

"Before that."

"Marine Corps."

"I see. And while you were working at the state hospital you saw Clarice Starling and Hannibal Lecter interacting—what I mean is, you saw them talking together?"

"It seemed to me they—"

"Let's start with just exactly *what* you saw, not what you *thought* about what you saw, can we do that?"

Mason interrupted. "He's smart enough to give his opinion. Barney, you know Clarice Starling."

"Yes."

"You knew Hannibal Lecter for six years."

"Yes."

"What was it between them?"

At first Krendler had trouble understanding Barney's high, rough voice, but it was Krendler who asked the pertinent question. "Did Lecter act differently in the Starling interviews, Barney?"

"Yes. Most of the time he didn't respond at all to visitors," Barney said. "Sometimes he would open his eyes long enough to insult some academic who was trying to pick his brain. He made one visiting professor cry. He was tough with Starling, but he answered her more than most. He was interested in her. She intrigued him."

"How?"

Barney shrugged. "He hardly ever got to see women. She's really good-looking—"

"I don't need your opinion on that," Krendler said. "Is that all you know?"

Barney did not reply. He looked at Krendler as though the left and right hemispheres of Krendler's brain were two dogs stuck together.

Margot cracked another walnut.

"Go on, Barney," Mason said.

"They were frank with one another. He's disarming that way. You have the feeling that he wouldn't deign to lie."

"Wouldn't do *what* to lie?" Krendler said.

"*Deign*," Barney said.

"D-E-I-G-N," Margot Verger said out of the dark. "To condescend. Or to *stoop*, Mr. Krendler."

Barney went on. "Dr. Lecter told her some unpleasant things about herself, and then some pleasant ones. She could face the bad things, and then enjoy the good more, knowing it wasn't bullshit. He thought she was charming and amusing."

"*You* can judge what Hannibal Lecter found 'amusing'?" Dr. Doemling said. "Just how do you go about that, *Nurse* Barney?"

"By listening to him laugh, Dr. *Dumling*. They taught us that in LPN school, a lecture called 'Healing and the Cheerful Outlook.'"

Either Margot snorted or the aquarium behind her made the noise.

"Cool it, Barney. Tell us the rest," Mason said.

"Yes, sir. Sometimes Dr. Lecter and I would talk late at night, when it got quiet enough. We talked about courses I was taking, and other things. He—"

"Were you taking some kind of mail-order course in *psychology*, by any chance?" Doemling had to say.

"No, sir, I don't consider psychology a science. Neither did Dr. Lecter." Barney went on quickly, before Mason's respirator permitted him to utter a rebuke. "I can just repeat what he told me—he could see what she was *becoming*, she was charming the way a cub is charming, a small cub that will grow up to be—like one of the big cats. One you can't play with later. She had the cublike earnestness, he said. She had all the weapons, in miniature and growing, and all she knew so far was how to wrestle with other cubs. That amused him.

"The way it began between them will tell you something. At the beginning he was courteous but he pretty much dismissed her—then as she was leaving another inmate threw some semen in her face. That disturbed Dr. Lecter, embarrassed him. It was the only time I ever saw him upset. She saw it too and tried to use it on him. He admired her moxie, I think."

"What was his attitude toward the other inmate—who threw the semen? Did they have any kind of relationship?"

"Not exactly," Barney said. "Dr. Lecter just killed him that night."

"They were in separate cells?" Doemling asked. "How did he do it?"

"Three cells apart on opposite sides of the corridor," Barney said. "In the middle of the night Dr. Lecter talked to him awhile and then told him to swallow his tongue."

"So Clarice Starling and Hannibal Lecter became . . . friendly?" Mason said.

"Inside a kind of formal structure," Barney said. "They exchanged information. Dr. Lecter gave her insight on the serial killer she was hunting, and she paid for it with personal information. Dr. Lecter told me he thought Starling might have too much nerve for her own good, an 'excess of zeal,' he called it. He thought she might work too close to the edge if she thought her assignment required it. And he said once that she was 'cursed with taste.' I don't know what that means."

"Dr. Doemling, does he want to fuck her or kill her, or eat her, or what?" Mason asked, exhausting the possibilities he could see.

"Probably all three," Dr. Doemling said. "I wouldn't want to predict the order in which he wants to perform those acts. That's the burden of what I can tell you. No matter how the tabloids—and tabloid mentalities—might want to romanticize it, and try to make it *Beauty and the Beast*, his object is her degradation, her suffering, and her death. He has responded to her twice: when she was insulted with the semen in her face and when she was torn apart in the newspapers after she shot those people. He comes in the guise of a mentor, but it's the *distress* that excites him. When the history of Hannibal Lecter is written, and it will be, this will be recorded as a case of *Doemling's avunculism*. To draw him she needs to be distressed."

A furrow has appeared in the broad rubbery space between Barney's eyes. "May I put something in here, Mr. Verger, since you asked me?" He did not wait for permission. "In the asylum, Dr. Lecter responded to her when she held on to herself, stood there wiping come off her face and did her job. In the letters he calls her a warrior, and points out that she saved that child in the shoot-out. He admires and respects her courage and her discipline. He says himself he's got no plans to come around. One thing he does *not* do is lie."

"That's exactly the kind of tabloid thinking I was talking about," Doemling said. "Hannibal Lecter does not have emotions like admiration or respect. He feels no warmth or affection. That's a romantic delusion, and it shows the dangers of a little education."

"Dr. Doemling, you don't remember me, do you?" Barney said. "I was in charge of the ward when *you* tried to talk to Dr. Lecter, a lot of people tried it, but you're the one who left crying as I recall. Then he reviewed your book in the *American Journal of Psychiatry*. I couldn't blame you if the review made you cry."

"That'll do, Barney," Mason said. "See about my lunch."

"A half-baked autodidact, there's nothing worse," Doemling said when Barney was out of the room.

"You didn't tell me you'd interviewed Lecter, Doctor," Mason said.

"He was catatonic at the time, there was nothing to get."

"And that made you cry?"

"That's not true."

"And you discount what Barney says."

"He's as deceived as the girl."

"Barney's probably hot for Starling himself," Krendler said.

Margot laughed to herself, but loudly enough for Krendler to hear.

"If you want to make Clarice Starling attractive to Dr. Lecter, let him see her *distressed*," Doemling said. "Let the damage he *sees* suggest the damage he could *do*. Seeing her wounded in any symbolic way will incite him like seeing her play with herself. When the fox hears a rabbit scream, he comes running, but not to help."

"I CAN'T deliver Clarice Starling," Krendler said when Doemling was gone. "I can pretty much tell you where she is and what she's doing, but I can't control Bureau assignments. And if the Bureau puts her out there for bait, they'll cover her, believe me."

Krendler pointed his finger into Mason's darkness to make his point. "You can't move in on that action. You couldn't get outside that coverage and intercept Lecter. The stakeout would spot your people in no time. Second, the Bureau won't initiate proactive unless he contacts her again or there's evidence he's close—he wrote to her before and he never came around. It would take twelve people minimum to stake her out, it's expensive. You'd be better off if you hadn't gotten her off the hot seat in the shooting. It'll be messy, reversing your field and trying to hang her with that again."

"Shoulda, woulda, coulda," Mason said, doing a fair job with the *s*, all things considered. "Margot, look in the Milan paper, *Corriere della Sera*, for Saturday, the day after Pazzi was killed, check the first item in the agony column. Read it to us."

Margot held the dense print up to the light. "It's in English, addressed to A. A. Aaron. Says: *Turn yourself in to the nearest authorities, enemies are close. Hannah.* Who's Hannah?"

"That's the name of the horse Starling had as a kid," Mason said. "It's a warning to Lecter from Starling. He told her in his letter how to contact him."

Krendler was on his feet. "God*dammit*. She couldn't have known about Florence. If she knows about that, she must know I've been showing you the stuff."

Mason sighed and wondered if Krendler was smart enough to be a useful politician. "*She* didn't know anything. I placed the ad, in *La Nazione* and *Corriere della Sera* and in the *International Herald-Tribune*, to run the day *after* we moved on Lecter. That way if we missed, he'd think Starling tried to help him. We'd still have a tie to him through Starling."

"Nobody picked it up."

"No. Except maybe Hannibal Lecter. He may thank her for it— by mail, in person, who knows? Now, listen to me: You've still got her mail covered?"

Krendler nodded. "Absolutely. If he sends her anything, you'll see it before she does."

"Listen carefully to this, Krendler: The way this ad was ordered and paid for, Clarice Starling can never prove she *didn't* place it on her own, and that's a felony. That's crossing the bright line. You can break her with it, Krendler. You know how much the FBI gives a shit about you when you're out. You could be dog meat. She won't even be able to get a concealed weapon permit. Nobody will watch her but me. And Lecter will know she's out there by herself. We'll try some other things first." Mason paused to breathe and then went on. "If they don't work, we'll do like Doemling says and 'distress' her with this ad—*distress* her, hell, you can break her in two with it. Save the half with the pussy, is my advice. The other end is too goddamned earnest. Ouch—I didn't mean to blaspheme."

CLARICE STARLING running through falling leaves in a Virginia state park an hour from her house, a favorite place, no sign of any other person in the park on this fall weekday, a much-needed day off. She ran a familiar path in the forested hills beside the Shenandoah River. The air was warmed by the early sun on the hilltops, and in the hollows suddenly cool, sometimes the air was warm on her face and cool on her legs at the same time.

The earth these days was not quite still beneath Starling as she walked; it seemed steadier when she ran.

Starling running through the bright day, bright and dancing flares of light through the leaves, the path dappled and in other places striped with the shadows of tree trunks in the low early sun. Ahead of her three deer started, two does and a spike buck clearing the path in a single heart-lifting bound, their raised white flags shining in the gloom of the deep forest as they bounded away. Gladdened, Starling leaped herself.

Still as a figure in a medieval tapestry, Hannibal Lecter sat among the fallen leaves on the hillside above the river. He could see one hundred fifty yards of the running path, his field glasses proofed against reflection by a homemade cardboard shroud. First he saw the deer start, and bound past him up the hill and then, for the first time in seven years, he saw Clarice Starling whole.

Below the glasses his face did not change expression, but his nostrils flared with a deep intake of breath as though he could catch her scent at this distance.

The breath brought him the smell of dry leaves with a hint of cinnamon in them, the molding leaves beneath, and the gently decaying forest mast, a whiff of rabbit pellets from yards away, the deep wild musk of a shredded squirrel skin beneath the leaves, but not the scent of Starling, which he could have identified anywhere. He saw the deer start ahead of her, saw them bounding long after they had left her sight.

She was in his view for less than a minute, running easily, not fighting the ground. A minimal day pack high on her shoulders with a bottle of water. Backlit, the early light behind her blurring her outline as though she had been dusted with pollen on her skin. Tracking with her, Dr. Lecter's binoculars picked up a sun flare off the water beyond her that left him seeing spots for minutes. She disappeared as the path sloped down and away, the back of her head the last thing he saw, the ponytail bouncing like the flag of a white-tail deer.

Dr. Lecter remained still, made no attempt to follow her. He had her image running clearly in his head. She would run in his mind for as long as he chose for her to. His first real sight of her in seven years, not counting tabloid pictures, not counting distant glimpses of a head in a car. He lay back in the leaves with his hands behind his head, watching the thinning foliage of a maple above him quiver against the sky, so dark the sky that it was almost purple. Purple, purple, the bunch of wild muscadines he had picked climbing to this spot were purple, beginning to shrivel from the full, dusty grape, and he ate several, and squeezed some in his palm and licked the juice as a child will lick its hand spread wide. Purple, purple.

Purple the eggplant in the garden.

There was no hot water at the high hunting lodge during the middle of the day and Mischa's nurse carried the beaten copper tub into the kitchen garden for the sun to warm the two-year-old's bathwater. Mischa sat in the gleaming tub among the vegetables in the warm sun, white cabbage butterflies around her. The water was only deep enough to cover her chubby legs, but her solemn brother Hannibal and the big dog were strictly set to watch her while the nurse went inside to get a receiving blanket.

Hannibal Lecter was to some of the servants a frightening child, frighteningly intense, preternaturally knowing, but he did not frighten the old nurse, who knew her business, and he did not frighten Mischa, who put her star-shaped baby hands flat on his cheeks and laughed into his face. Mischa reached past him and held out her arms to the eggplant, which she loved to stare at in the sun. Her eyes were not maroon like her brother Hannibal's, but blue, and as she stared at the eggplant, her eyes seemed to draw color from it, to darken with it. Hannibal Lecter knew that the color was her passion. After she was carried back inside and the cook's helper came grumbling to dump the tub in the garden, Hannibal knelt beside the row of eggplants, the skin of the bath-soap bubbles swarming with reflections, purple and green, until they burst on the tilled soil. He took out his little penknife and cut the stem of an eggplant, polished it with his handkerchief, the vegetable warm from the sun in his arms as he carried it, warm like an animal, to Mischa's nursery and put it where she could see it. Mischa loved dark purple, loved the color aubergine, as long as she lived.

Hannibal Lecter closed his eyes to see again the deer bounding ahead of Starling, to see her come bounding down the path, limned golden with the sun behind her, but this was the wrong deer, it was the little deer with the arrow in it pulling, pulling against the rope around its neck as they led it to the axe, the little deer they ate before they ate Mischa, and he could not be still anymore and he got up, his hands and mouth stained with the purple muscadines, his mouth turned down like a Greek mask. He looked after Starling down the path. He took a deep breath through his nose, and took in the cleansing scent of the forest. He stared at the spot where Starling disappeared. Her path seemed lighter than the surrounding woods, as though she had left a bright place behind her.

He climbed quickly to the ridge and headed downhill on the other side toward the parking area of a nearby campsite where he had left his truck. He wanted to be out of the park before Starling returned to her automobile, parked two miles away in the main lot near the ranger booth, now closed for the season.

It would be at least fifteen minutes before she could run back to her car.

Dr. Lecter parked beside the Mustang and left his motor running. He had had several opportunities to examine her car in the parking lot of a grocery near her house. It was the state park's annual discount admittance sticker on the window of Starling's old Mustang that first alerted Hannibal Lecter to this place, and he had bought maps of the park at once and explored it at his leisure.

The car was locked, hunkered down over its wide wheels as though it were asleep. Her car amused him. It was at once whimsical and terribly efficient. On the chrome door handle, even bending close, he could smell nothing. He unfolded his flat steel slim jim and slid it down into the door above the lock. Alarm? Yes? No? *Click.* No.

Dr. Lecter got into the car, into air that was intensely Clarice Starling. The steering wheel was thick and covered with leather. It had the word MOMO on the hub. He looked at the word with his head tilted like that of a parrot and his lips formed the words "MO MO." He sat back in the seat, his eyes closed, breathing, his eyebrows raised, as though he were listening to a concert.

Then, as though it had a mind of its own, the pointed pink tip of his tongue appeared, like a small snake finding its way out of his face. Never altering expression, as though he were unaware of his movements, he leaned forward, found the leather steering wheel by scent, and put around it his curled tongue, cupping with his tongue the finger indentations on the underside of the wheel. He tasted with his mouth the polished two o'clock spot on the wheel where her palm would rest. Then he leaned back in the seat, his tongue back where it lived, and his closed mouth moved as though he savored wine. He took a deep breath and held it while he got out and locked Clarice Starling's Mustang. He did not exhale, he held her in his mouth and lungs until his old truck was out of the park.

IT IS an axiom of behavioral science that vampires are territorial, while cannibals range widely across the country.

The nomadic existence held little appeal for Dr. Lecter. His success in avoiding the authorities owed much to the quality of his long-term false identities and the care he took to maintain them, and his ready access to money. Random and frequent movement had nothing to do with it.

With two alternate identities long established, each with excellent credit, plus a third for the management of vehicles, he had no trouble feathering for himself a comfortable nest in the United States within a week of his arrival.

He had chosen Maryland, about an hour's drive south from Mason Verger's Muskrat Farm, and reasonably convenient to the music and theater in Washington and New York.

Nothing about Dr. Lecter's visible business attracted attention, and either of his principal identities would have had a good chance of surviving a standard audit. After visiting one of his lockboxes in Miami, he rented from a German lobbyist for one year a pleasant, isolated house on the Chesapeake shore.

With distinct-ring call forwarding from two telephones in a cheap apartment in Philadelphia, he was able to provide himself with glowing references whenever they were required without leaving the comfort of his new home.

Always paying cash, he quickly obtained from scalpers premium tickets for the symphony, and those ballet and opera performances that interested him.

Among his new home's desirable features was a generous double garage with a workshop, and good overhead doors. There Dr. Lecter parked his two vehicles, a six-year-old Chevrolet pickup truck with a pipe frame over the bed and a vise attached, which he bought from a plumber and a housepainter, and a supercharged Jaguar sedan leased through a holding company in Delaware. His truck offered a different appearance from day to day. The equipment he could put into the back or onto the pipe frame included a housepainter's ladder, pipe, PVC, a barbecue kettle, and a butane tank.

With his domestic arrangements well in hand, he treated himself to a week of music and museums in New York, and sent catalogs of the most interesting art shows to his cousin, the great painter Balthus, in France.

At Sotheby's in New York, he purchased two excellent musical instruments, rare finds both of them. The first was a late eighteenth-century Flemish harpsichord nearly identical to the Smithsonian's 1745 Dulkin, with an upper manual to accommodate Bach—the instrument was a worthy successor to the *gravicembalo* he had in Florence. His other purchase was an early electronic instrument, a theremin, built in the 1930s by Professor Theremin himself. The theremin had long fascinated Dr. Lecter. He had built one as a child. It is played with gestures of the empty hands in an electronic field. By gesture you evoke its voice.

Now he was all settled in and he could entertain himself. . . .

★   ★   ★

Dr. Lecter drove home to this pleasant refuge on the Maryland shore after his morning in the woods. The sight of Clarice Starling running through the falling leaves on the forest path was well established now in the memory palace of his mind. It is a source of pleasure to him, reachable in less than a second starting from the foyer. He sees Starling run and, such is the quality of his visual memory, he can search the scene for new details, he can hear the big, healthy whitetails bounding past him up the slope, see the calluses on their elbows, a grass burr on the belly fur of the nearest. He has stored this memory in a sunny palace room as far as possible from the little wounded deer . . .

Home again, home again, the garage door dropping with a quiet hum behind his pickup truck.

When the door rose again at noon the black Jaguar came out, bearing the doctor dressed for the city.

Dr. Lecter very much liked to shop. He drove directly to Hammacher Schlemmer, the purveyor of fine home and sporting accessories and culinary equipment, and there he took his time. Still in his woodsy mood, with a pocket tape measure he checked the dimensions of three major picnic hampers, all of them lacquered wicker with sewn leather straps and solid brass fittings. Finally, he settled on the medium-sized hamper, as it only had to accommodate a place setting for one.

The wicker case had in it a thermos, serviceable tumblers, sturdy china, and stainless-steel cutlery. The case came only with the accessories. You were obliged to buy them.

In successive stops at Tiffany and Christofle, the doctor was able to replace the heavy picnic plates with Gien French china in one of the *chasse* patterns of leaves and upland birds. At Christofle he obtained a place setting of the nineteenth-century silverware he preferred, in a Cardinal pattern, the maker's mark stamped in the bowl of the spoons, the Paris rat tail on the underside of the handles. The forks were deeply curved, the tines widely spaced, and the knives had a pleasing heft far back in the palm. The pieces hang in the hand like a good dueling pistol. In crystal, the doctor was torn between sizes in his aperitif glasses, and chose a chimney *ballon* for brandy, but in wineglasses there was no question. The doctor chose Riedel, which he bought in two sizes with plenty of room for the nose within the rim.

At Christofle he also found place mats in creamy white linen, and some beautiful damask napkins with a tiny damask rose, like a drop of blood, embroidered in the corner. Dr. Lecter thought the play on damask droll and bought six napkins, so that he would always be equipped, allowing for laundry turnaround time.

He bought two good 35,000 BTU portable gas burners, of the kind restaurants use to cook at tableside, and an exquisite copper sauté pan and a copper *fait-tout* to make sauces, both made for Dehillerin in Paris, and two whisks. He was not able to find carbon-steel kitchen knives, which he much preferred to stainless steel, nor could he find some of the special-purpose knives he had been forced to leave in Italy.

His last stop was a medical supply company not far from Mercy General Hospital, where he found a bargain in a nearly brand-new Stryker autopsy saw, which strapped down neatly in his picnic hamper where the thermos used to go. It was still under warranty, and came with general-purpose and cranial blades, as well as a skull key, to nearly complete his *batterie de cuisine*.

Dr. Lecter's French doors are open to the crisp evening air. The bay lies soot-and-silver under the moon and moving shadows of the clouds. He has poured himself a glass of wine in his new crystal and set it on a candle stand beside the harpsichord. The wine's bouquet mixes with the salt air and Dr. Lecter can enjoy it without ever taking his hands from the keyboard.

He has in his time owned clavichords, virginals, and other early keyboard instruments. He prefers the sound and feel of the harpsichord; because it is not possible to control the volume of the quill-plucked strings, the music arrives like experience, sudden and entire.

Dr. Lecter looks at the instrument, opening and closing his hands.

He approaches his newly acquired harpsichord as he might approach an attractive stranger via an interesting light remark—he plays an air written by Henry VIII, "Green Grows the Holly."

Encouraged, he essays upon Mozart's "Sonata in B Flat Major." He and the harpsichord are not yet intimate, but its responses to his hands tell him they will come together soon. The breeze rises and the candles flare, but Dr. Lecter's eyes are closed to the light, his face is lifted and he is playing. Bubbles fly from Mischa's star-shaped hands as she waves them in the breeze above the tub and, as he attacks the third movement, through the forest lightly flying, Clarice Starling is running, running, rustle of the leaves beneath her feet, rustle of the wind high in the turning trees, and the deer start ahead of her, a spike buck and two does, leaping across the path like the heart leaps. The ground is suddenly colder and the ragged men lead the little deer out of the woods, an arrow in it, the deer pulling against the rope twisted around its neck, men pulling it wounded so they will not have to carry it to the axe, and the music clangs to a stop above the bloody snow, Dr. Lecter clutching the edges of the piano stool. He breathes deep, breathes deep, puts his hands on the keyboard, forces a phrase, then two that clang to silence.

We hear from him a thin and rising scream that stops as abruptly as the music. He sits for a long time with his head bent above the keyboard. He rises without sound and leaves the room. It is not possible to tell where he is in the dark house. The wind off the Chesapeake gains strength, whips the candle flames until they gutter out, sings through the strings of the harpsichord in the dark—now an accidental tune, now a thin scream from long ago.

THE MID-ATLANTIC Regional Gun and Knife Show in War Memorial Auditorium. Acres of tables, a plain of guns, mostly pistols and assault-style shotguns. The red beams of laser sights flicker on the ceiling.

Few genuine outdoorsmen come to gun shows, as a matter of taste. Guns are black now, and gun shows are bleak, colorless, as joyless as the inner landscape of many who attend them.

Look at this crowd: scruffy, squinty, angry, egg-bound, truly of the resinous heart. They are the main danger to the right of a private citizen to own a firearm.

The guns they fancy are assault weapons designed for mass production, cheaply made of stampings to provide high firepower to ignorant and untrained troops.

Among the beer bellies, the flab and pasty white of the indoor gunmen moved Dr. Hannibal Lecter, imperially slim. The guns did not interest him. He went directly to the display of the foremost knife merchant of the show circuit.

The merchant's name is Buck and he weighs three hundred twenty-five pounds. Buck has a lot of fantasy swords, and copies of medieval and barbarian items, but he has the best real knives and blackjacks too, and Dr. Lecter quickly spotted most of the items on his list, things he'd had to leave in Italy.

"Can I hep you?" Buck has friendly cheeks and a friendly mouth, and baleful eyes.

"Yes. I'll have that Harpy, please, and a straight, serrated Spyderco with a four-inch blade, and that drop-point skinner at the back."

Buck gathered the items.

"I want the good game saw. Not that one, the good one. Let me feel that flat leather sap, the black one . . ." Dr. Lecter considered the spring in the handle. "I'll take it."

"Anything else?"

"Yes. I'd like a Spyderco Civilian, I don't see it."

"Not a whole lot of folks know about that. I never stock but one."

"I only require one."

"It's regular two hundred and twenty dollars, I could let you have it for one ninety with the case."

"Fine. Do you have carbon-steel kitchen knives?"

Buck shook his massive head. "You'll have to find old ones at a flea market. That's where I get mine at. You can put an edge on one with the bottom of a saucer."

"Make a parcel and I'll be back for it in a few minutes."

Buck had not often been told to make a parcel, and he did it with his eyebrows raised.

Typically, this gun show was not a show at all, it was a bazaar. There were a few tables of dusty World War Two memorabilia, beginning to look ancient. You could buy M-1 rifles, gas masks with the glass crazing in the goggles, canteens. There were the usual Nazi memorabilia booths. You could buy an actual Zyklon B gas canister, if that is to your taste.

There was almost nothing from the Korean or Vietnam wars and nothing at all from Desert Storm.

Many of the shoppers wore camouflage as if they were only briefly back from the front lines to attend the gun show, and more camouflage clothing was for sale, including the complete ghillie suit for total concealment of a sniper or a bow hunter—a major subdivision of the show was archery equipment for bow hunting.

Dr. Lecter was examining the ghillie suit when he became aware of uniforms close beside him. He picked up an archery glove. Turning to hold the maker's mark to the light, he could see that the two officers beside him were from the Virginia Department of Game and Inland Fisheries, which maintained a conservation booth at the show.

"Donnie Barber," said the older of the two wardens, pointing with his chin. "If you ever git him in court, let me know. I'd love to git that son of a bitch out of the woods for good." They were watching a man of about thirty at the other end of the archery exhibit. He was facing them, watching a video. Donnie Barber wore camouflage, his blouse tied around his waist by the sleeves. He had on a khaki-colored sleeveless T-shirt to show off his tattoos and a baseball cap reversed on his head.

Dr. Lecter moved slowly away from the officers, looking at various items as he went. He paused at a display of laser pistol sights an aisle away and, through a trellis hung with holsters, the doctor watched the flickering video that held Donnie Barber's attention.

It was a video about hunting mule deer with bow and arrow.

Apparently someone off camera was hazing a deer along a fence through a wooded lot, while the hunter drew his bow. The hunter was wired for sound. His breathing grew faster. He whispered into the microphone, "It don't git any better than this."

The deer humped when the arrow hit it and ran into the fence twice before leaping the wire and running away.

Watching, Donnie Barber jerked and grunted at the arrow strike.

Now the video huntsman was about to field-dress the deer. He began at what he called the ANN-us.

Donnie Barber stopped the video and ran it back to the arrow strike again and again, until the concessionaire spoke to him.

"Fuck yourself, asshole," Donnie Barber said. "I wouldn't buy shit from you."

At the next booth, he bought some yellow arrows, broad-heads with a razor fin crosswise in the head. There was a box for a prize drawing and, with his purchase, Donnie Barber received an entry slip. The prize was a two-day deer lease.

Donnie Barber filled out his entry and dropped it through the slot, and kept the merchant's pen as he disappeared with his long parcel into the crowd of young men in camouflage.

As a frog's eyes pick up movement, so the merchant's eyes noted any pause in the passing crowd. The man before him now was utterly still.

"Is that your best crossbow?" Dr. Lecter asked the merchant.

"No." The man took a case from under the counter. "This is the best one. I like the recurve better than the compound if you got to tote it. It's got the windlass you can drive off a 'lectric drill or use it manual. You know you can't use a crossbow on deer in Virginia unless you're handicapped?" the man said.

"My brother's lost one arm and he's anxious to kill something with the other one," Dr. Lecter said.

"Oh, I gotcha."

In the course of five minutes, the doctor purchased an excellent crossbow and two dozen quarrels, the short, thick arrows used with a crossbow.

"Tie up a parcel," Dr. Lecter said.

"Fill out this slip and you might win you a deer hunt. Two days on a good lease," the merchant said.

Dr. Lecter filled out his slip for the drawing and dropped it through the slot in the box.

As soon as the merchant was engaged with another customer, Dr. Lecter turned back to him.

"Bother!" he said. "I forgot to put my telephone number on my drawing slip. May I?"

"Sure, go ahead."

Dr. Lecter took the top off the box and took out the top two slips. He added to the false information on his own, and took a long look at the slip beneath, blinking once, like a camera clicking.

56

THE GYM at Muskrat Farm is high-tech black and chrome, with the complete Nautilus cycle of machines, free weights, aerobic equipment and a juice bar.

Barney was nearly through with his workout, cooling down on a bike, when he realized he was not alone in the room. Margot Verger was taking off her warm-ups in the corner. She wore elastic shorts and a tank top over a sports bra and now she added a weight-lifting belt. Barney heard weights clank in the corner. He heard her breathing as she did a warm-up set.

Barney was pedaling the bicycle against no resistance, toweling his head, when she came over to him between sets.

She looked at his arms, looked at hers. They were about the same. "How much can you bench-press?" she said.

"I don't know."

"I expect you know, all right."

"Maybe three eighty-five, like that."

"*Three eighty-five?* I don't think so, big boy. I don't think you can press three eighty-five."

"Maybe you're right."

"I got a hundred dollars that says you can't bench-press three eighty-five."

"Against?"

"Against a hundred dollars, the hell you think? And I'll spot you."

Barney looked at her and wrinkled his rubbery forehead. "Okay."

They loaded on the plates. Margot counted the ones on the end of the bar Barney had loaded as though he might cheat her. He responded by counting with elaborate care the ones on Margot's end.

Flat on the bench now, Margot standing above him at his head in her spandex shorts. The juncture of her thighs and abdomen was knurled like a baroque frame and her massive torso seemed to reach almost to the ceiling.

Barney settled himself, feeling the bench against his back. Margot's legs smelled like cool liniment. Her hands were lightly on the bar, nails painted coral, shapely hands to be so strong.

"Ready?"

"Yes." He pushed the weight up toward her face, bent over him.

It wasn't much trouble for Barney. He set the weight back on its bracket ahead of Margot's spot. She got the money from her gym bag.

"Thank you," Barney said.

"I do more squats than you" is all she said.

"I know."

"How do you know that?"

"I can pee standing up."

Her massive neck flushed. "So can I."

"Hundred bucks?" Barney said.

"Make me a smoothie," she said.

There was a bowl of fruit and nuts on the juice bar. While Barney made fruit smoothies in the blender, Margot took two walnuts in her fist and cracked them.

"Can you do just one nut, with nothing to squeeze it against?"

Barney said. He cracked two eggs on the rim of the blender and dropped them in.

"Can you?" Margot said, and handed him a walnut.

The nut lay in Barney's open palm. "I don't know." He cleared the space in front of him on the bar and an orange rolled off on Margot's side. "Oops, sorry," Barney said.

She picked it up from the floor and put it back in the bowl.

Barney's big fist clenched. Margot's eyes went from his fist to his face, then back and forth as his neck corded with strain, his face flushed. He began to tremble, from his fist a faint cracking sound, Margot's face falling, he moved his trembling fist over the blender and the cracking came louder. An egg yolk and white plopped into the blender. Barney turned the machine on and licked the tips of his fingers. Margot laughed in spite of herself.

Barney poured the smoothies into glasses. From across the room they might have been wrestlers or power lifters in two weight divisions.

"You feel like you *have* to do everything guys do?" he said.

"Not some of the dumb stuff."

"You want to try male bonding?"

Margot's smile went away. "Don't set me up for a dick joke, Barney."

He shook his massive head. "Try me," he said.

IN HANNIBAL'S House the gleanings grew as day by day Clarice Starling felt her way along the corridors of Dr. Lecter's taste:

Rachel DuBerry had been somewhat older than Dr. Lecter when she was an active patron of the Baltimore Symphony and she was very beautiful, as Starling could see in the *Vogue* pictures from the time. That was two rich husbands ago. She was now Mrs. Franz Rosencranz of the textile Rosencranzes. Her social secretary put her on the line:

"Now I just send the orchestra money, dear. We're away far too much for me to be actively involved," Mrs. Rosencranz nee DuBerry told Starling. "If it's some sort of tax question, I can give you the number of our accountants."

"Mrs. Rosencranz, when you were active on the boards of the Philharmonic and the Westover School you knew Dr. Hannibal Lecter."

A considerable silence.

"Mrs. Rosencranz?"

"I think I'd better take your number and call you back through the FBI switchboard."

"Certainly."

When the conversation resumed:

"Yes, I knew Hannibal Lecter socially years ago and the press has camped on my doorstep ever since about it. He was an extraordinarily charming man, absolutely singular. Sort of made a girl's *fur crackle*, if you know what I mean. It took me years to believe the other side of him."

"Did he ever give you any gifts, Mrs. Rosencranz?"

"I received a note from him on my birthdays usually, even after he was in custody. Sometimes a gift, before he was committed. He gives the *most* exquisite gifts."

"And Dr. Lecter gave the famous birthday dinner for you. With the wine vintages keyed to your birth date."

"Yes," she said. "Suzy called it the most remarkable party since Capote's Black and White Ball."

"Mrs. Rosencranz, if you should hear from him, would you please call the FBI at the number I'll give you? Another thing I'd like to ask you if I may, do you have any special anniversaries with Dr. Lecter? And Mrs. Rosencranz, I need to ask you your birth date."

A distinct chill on the phone. "I would think that information was easily available to you."

"Yes, ma'am, but there are some inconsistencies among the dates on your social security, your birth certificate and your driver's license. In fact, none of them are the same. I apologize, but we're keying custom orders on high-end items to the birthdays of Dr. Lecter's known acquaintances."

"'Known acquaintances.' I'm a *known acquaintance* now, what an awful term." Mrs. Rosencranz chuckled. She was of a cocktail and cigarette generation and her voice was deep. "Agent Starling, how old are you?"

"I'm thirty-two, Mrs. Rosencranz. I'll be thirty-three two days before Christmas."

"I'll just say, in all kindness, I hope you'll have a couple of 'known acquaintances' in your life. They do help pass the time."

"Yes, ma'am, and your birth date?"

Mrs. Rosencranz at last parted with the correct information, characterizing it as "the date Dr. Lecter is familiar with."

"If I may ask, ma'am, I can understand changing the birth year, but why the month and day?"

"I wanted to be a Virgo, it matches better with Mr. Rosencranz, we were dating then."

The people Dr. Lecter had met while he was living in a cage viewed him somewhat differently:

Starling rescued former U.S. Senator Ruth Martin's daughter, Catherine, from the hellish basement of the serial killer Jame Gumb and, had Senator Martin not been defeated in the next election, she might have done Starling much good. She was warm to Starling on the telephone, gave her news of Catherine, and wanted her news.

"You never asked me for anything, Starling. If you ever want a job—"

"Thank you, Senator Martin."

"About that goddamned Lecter, no, I'd have notified the Bureau of course if I heard from him, and I'll put your number here by the phone. Charlsie knows how to handle mail. I don't expect to hear from him. The last thing that prick said to me in Memphis was '*Love* your suit.' He did the single cruelest thing anybody's ever done to me, do you know what it was?"

"I know he taunted you."

"When Catherine was missing, when we were desperate and he said he had information on Jame Gumb, and I was pleading with him, he asked me, he looked into my face with those snake eyes and asked me if I had nursed Catherine. He wanted to know if I *breast-fed* her. I told him yes. And then he said, 'Thirsty work, isn't it?' It just brought it all back suddenly, holding her as a baby, thirsty, waiting for her to get full, it pierced me like nothing I ever felt, and he *just sucked down my pain.*"

"What kind was it, Senator Martin?"

"What kind—I'm sorry?"

"What kind of suit did you have on, that Dr. Lecter liked?"

"Let me think—a navy Givenchy, very tailored," Senator Martin said, a little piqued at Starling's priorities. "When you've got him back in the slammer, come see me, Starling, we'll ride some horses."

"Thank you, Senator, I'll remember that."

Two phone calls, one on each side of Dr. Lecter, one showed his charm, the other his scales. Starling wrote down:

Vintage keyed to birthdays, which was already covered in her little program. She made a note to add *Givenchy* to her list of high-end goods. As an afterthought she wrote down *breast-fed*, for no reason she could say, and there was no time to think about it because her red phone was ringing.

"This is Behavioral Science? I'm trying to get through to Jack Crawford, this is Sheriff Dumas in Clarendon Country, Virginia."

"Sheriff, I'm Jack Crawford's assistant. He's in court today. I can help you. I'm Special Agent Starling."

"I needed to speak to Jack Crawford. We got a fella in the morgue that's been trimmed up for *meat*, have I got the right department?"

"Yes, sir, this is the mea—yes, sir, you certainly do. If you'll tell me exactly where you are, I'm on the way, and I'll alert Mr. Crawford as soon as he's through testifying."

Starling's Mustang got enough second-gear rubber out of Quantico to make the Marine guard frown at her, and wag his finger, and keep himself from smiling.

THE CLARENDON County Morgue in northern Virginia is attached to the county hospital by a short air lock with an exhaust fan in the ceiling and wide double doors at each end to facilitate access by the dead. A sheriff's deputy stood before these doors to keep out the five reporters and cameramen who crowded around him.

From behind the reporters, Starling stood on her tiptoes and held her badge high. When the deputy spotted it and nodded, she plunged through. Strobe lights flashed and a sun gun flared behind her.

Quiet in the autopsy room, only the clink of instruments put down in a metal tray.

The county morgue has four stainless-steel autopsy tables, each with its scales and sink. Two of the tables were draped, the sheets oddly tented by the remains they covered. A routine hospital postmortem was in progress at the table nearest the windows. The pathologist and his assistant were doing something delicate and did not look up when Starling came in.

The thin shriek of an electric saw filled the room, and in a moment the pathologist carefully set aside the cap of a skull and lifted in his cupped hands a brain, which he placed on the scales. He whispered the weight into the microphone he wore, examined the organ in the scale pan, poked it with a gloved finger. When he spotted Starling over the shoulder of his assistant, he dumped the brain into the open chest cavity of the corpse, shot his rubber gloves into a bin like a boy shooting rubber bands and came around the table to her.

Starling found shaking his hand a bit crawly.

"Clarice Starling, Special Agent, FBI."

"I'm Dr. Hollingsworth—medical examiner, hospital pathologist, chief cook and bottle washer." Hollingsworth has bright blue eyes, shiny as well-peeled eggs. He spoke to his assistant without looking away from Starling. "Marlene, page the sheriff in cardiac ICU, and undrape those remains, please, ma'am."

In Starling's experience medical examiners were usually intelligent but often silly and incautious in casual conversation, and they liked to show off. Hollingsworth followed Starling's eyes. "You're wondering about that brain?"

She nodded and showed him her open hands.

"We're not careless here, Special Agent Starling. It's a favor I do the undertaker, not putting the brain back in the skull. In this case they'll have an open coffin and a lengthy wake, and you can't prevent brain material leaking onto the pillow, so we stuff the skull with Huggies or whatever we have and close it back up, and I put a notch in the skull cap over both ears, so it won't slide. Family gets the whole body back, everybody's happy."

"I understand."

"Tell me if you understand *that*," he said. Behind Starling, Dr. Hollingsworth's assistant had removed the covering sheets from the autopsy tables.

Starling turned and saw it all in a single image that would last as long as she lived. Side by side on their stainless-steel tables lay a deer and a man. From the deer projected a yellow arrow. The arrow shaft and the antlers had held up the covering sheet like tent poles.

The man had a shorter, thicker yellow arrow through his head transversely at the tips of his ears. He still wore one garment, a reversed baseball cap, pinned to his head by the arrow.

Looking at him, Starling suffered an absurd burp of laughter, suppressed so fast it might have sounded like dismay. The similar positions of the two bodies, on their sides instead of in the anatomical position, revealed that they had been butchered almost identically, the sirloin and loin removed with neatness and economy along with the small filets that lie beneath the spine.

A deer's fur on stainless steel. Its head elevated by the antlers on the metal pillow block, the head turned and the eye white as though it tried to look back at the bright shaft that killed it—the creature, lying on its side in its own reflection in this place of obsessive order, seemed wilder, more alien to man than a deer ever seemed in the woods.

The man's eyes were open, some blood came from his lachrymal ducts like tears.

"Odd to see them together," Dr. Hollingsworth said. "Their hearts weighed exactly the same." He looked at Starling and saw that she was all right. "One difference on the man, you can see here where the short ribs were separated from the spine and the lungs pulled out the back. They almost look like wings, don't they?"

"Bloody Eagle," Starling muttered, after a moment's thought.

"I never saw it before."

"Me either," Starling said.

"There's a term for that? What did you call it?"

"The Bloody Eagle. The literature at Quantico has it. It's a Norse sacrificial custom. Chop through the short ribs and pull the lungs out the back, flatten them out like that to make wings. There was a neo-Viking doing it in Minnesota in the thirties."

"You see a lot of this, I don't mean *this*, but this kind of stuff."

"Sometimes I do, yes."

"It's out of my line a little. We get mostly straightforward murders—people shot and knifed, but do you want to know what I think?"

"I'd like very much to know, Doctor."

"I think the man, his ID says Donnie Barber, killed the deer illegally yesterday, the day before the season started—I know that's when it died. That arrow's consistent with the rest of his archery equipment. He was butchering it in a hurry. I haven't done the antigens on that blood on his hands, but it's deer blood. He was just going to take what deer hunters call the backstrap, and he started a sloppy job, this short ragged cut here. Then he got a big surprise, like this arrow through his head. Same color, but a different kind of arrow. No notch in the butt. Do you recognize it?"

"It looks like a crossbow quarrel," Starling said.

"A second person, maybe the one with the crossbow, finished dressing the deer, doing a much better job, and then, by God, he did the man too. Look how precisely the hide is reflected here, how *decisive* the incisions are. Nothing spoiled or wasted. Michael DeBakey couldn't do it better. There's no sign of any kind of sexual interference with either of them. They were simply butchered for meat."

Starling touched her lips with her knuckle. For a second the pathologist thought she was kissing an amulet.

"Dr. Hollingsworth, were the livers missing?"

A beat of time before he replied, peering at her over his glasses. "The *deer's* liver is missing. Mr. Barber's liver apparently wasn't up to standard. It was partly excised and examined, there's an incision just along the portal vein. His liver is cirrhotic and discolored. It remains in the body, would you like to see?"

"No, thank you. What about the thymus?"

"The sweetbreads, yes, missing in both cases. Agent Starling, nobody's said the name yet, have they?"

"No," Starling said. "Not yet."

A puff from the air lock and a lean, weathered man in a tweed sports jacket and khaki pants stood in the doorway.

"Sheriff, how's Carleton?" Hollingsworth said. "Agent Starling, this is Sheriff Dumas. The sheriff's brother is upstairs in cardiac ICU."

"He's holding his own. They say he's stable, he's 'guarded,' whatever that means," the sheriff said. He called outside, "Come on in here, Wilburn."

The sheriff shook Starling's hand and introduced the other man. "This is Officer Wilburn Moody, he's a game warden."

"Sheriff. If you want to stay close to your brother we could go back upstairs," Starling said.

Sheriff Dumas shook his head. "They won't let me in to see him again for another hour and a half. No offense, Miss, but I called for Jack Crawford. Is he coming?"

"He's stuck in court—he was on the stand when your call came. I expect we'll hear from him very shortly. We really appreciate you calling us so fast."

"Old Crawford taught my National Police Academy Class at Quantico umpteen years ago. Damndest fellow. If he sent you, you must know what you're doing—want to go ahead?"

"Please, Sheriff."

The sheriff took a notebook out of his coat pocket. "The individual here with the arrow through his head is Donnie Leo Barber, WM thirty-two, resides in a trailer at Trail's End Park at Cameron. No employment I can find. General discharge with prejudice from the Air Force four years ago. He's got an airframe and power plant ticket from the FAA. Sometime airplane mechanic. Paid a misdemeanor fine for discharging a firearm in the city limits, paid a fine for criminal trespass last hunting season. Pled guilty to poaching deer in Summit County, when was that, Wilburn?"

"Two seasons ago, he just got his license back. He's known to the department. He don't bother to track nothing after he shoots it. If it don't fall, just wait on another'n . . . one time—"

"Tell what you found today, Wilburn."

"Well, I was coming along on county road forty-seven, about a mile west of the bridge there around seven o'clock this morning when Old Man Peckman flagged me down. He was breathing hard and holding his chest. All he could do was open and shut his mouth and point off in the woods there. I went maybe, oh, not more than a hunderd and fifty yards in the thick woods and there was this Barber here sprawled up against a tree with a arrow through his head and that deer there with a arrow in it. They was stiff from yesterday at least."

"Yesterday morning early, I'd say, cool as it was," Dr. Hollingsworth said.

"Now the season just opened *this* morning," the game warden said. "This Donnie Barber had a climbing tree stand with him that he hadn't set up yet. Looked like he went out there yesterday to get ready for today, or else he went to poach. I don't know why else he'd take his bow, if he was just setting up the stand. Here come this nice deer and he just couldn't help himself—I've saw people do this a lots. This kinda behavior's got common as pig tracks. And then this other 'un come up on him while he was butchering. I couldn't tell nothing from the tracks, a rain come down out there so hard, the bottom just fell out right then—"

"That's why we took a couple of pictures and pulled out the bodies," Sheriff Dumas said. "Old Man Peckman owns the woods. This Donnie had on him a legitimate two-day lease to hunt starting today, with Peckman's signature on it. Peckman always sold one lease a year, and he advertised it and had it farmed out with some brokers. Donnie also had a letter in his back pocket saying *Congratulations you have won a deer lease.* The papers are wet, Miss Starling. Nothing against our fellows, but I'm wondering if you ought to do the fingerprinting at your lab. The arrows too, the whole thing was wet when we got there. We tried not to touch them."

"You want to take these arrows with you, Agent Starling? How would you like me to take 'em out?" Dr. Hollingsworth asked.

"If you'd hold them with retractors and saw them in two at the skin line on the feather side and push the rest through, I'll wire them to my board with some twist ties," Starling said, opening her case.

"I don't think he was in a fight, but do you want fingernail scrapings?"

"I'd rather clip them to do DNA. I don't need them ID'd by finger, but separate them hand from hand, if you would, Doctor."

"Can you run PCR-STR?"

"They can in the main lab. We'll have something for you, Sheriff, in three to four days."

"Can you do that deer blood yourself?" Warden Moody asked.

"No, we can just tell it's animal blood," Starling said.

"What if you was to just find the deer meat in somebody's Frigidaire?" Warden Moody offered. "You'd want to know whether it come out of that deer, wouldn't you? Sometimes *we* have to be able to tell deer from deer by blood to make a poaching case. Every individual deer is different. You wouldn't think that, would you? We have to send blood off to Portland, Oregon, to the Oregon Game and Fish, they can tell you if you wait long enough. They come back with 'This is Deer No. One,' they'll say, or just call it 'Deer A,' with a long case number since, you know, a deer don't have any name. That *we* know of."

Starling liked Moody's old weather-beaten face. "We'll call this one 'John Doe,' Warden Moody. That's useful to know about Oregon, we might have to do some business with them, thank you," she said and smiled at him until he blushed and fumbled with his cap.

As she bent her head to rummage in her bag, Dr. Hollingsworth considered her for the pleasure it gave him. Her face had lit up for a moment, talking with old Moody. That beauty spot in her cheek looked very much like burnt gunpowder. He wanted to ask, but thought better of it.

"What did you put the papers in, not plastic?" she asked the sheriff.

"Brown paper sacks. A brown paper sack never hurt much of anything." The sheriff rubbed the back of his neck with his hand, and looked up at Starling. "You know why I called your outfit, why I wanted Jack Crawford over here. I'm glad you came, now that I recollect who you are. Nobody's said 'cannibal' outside this room because the press will tromp the woods flat as soon as it's out. All they know is it could be a hunting accident. They heard maybe a body was mutilated. They don't know Donnie Barber was cut for meat. There's not that many cannibals, Agent Starling."

"No, Sheriff. Not that many."

"It's awful neat work."

"Yessir, it is."

"I may be thinking about him because he's been in the paper so much—does this look like that Hannibal Lecter to you?"

Starling watched a daddy longlegs hide in the drain of the vacant autopsy table. "Dr. Lecter's sixth victim was a bow hunter," Starling said.

"Did he eat him?"

"That one, no. He left him hanging from a peg board wall with all sorts of wounds in him. He left him looking like a medieval medical illustration called Wound Man. He's interested in medieval things."

The pathologist pointed to the lungs spread across Donnie Barber's back. "You were saying this was an old ritual."

"I think so," Starling said. "I don't know if Dr. Lecter did this. If he did it, the mutilation's not a fetish—this arrangement's not a compulsive thing with him."

"What is it, then?"

"It's whimsy," she said, looking to see if she put them off with the exact word. "It's *whimsy*, and it's what got him caught last time."

THE DNA lab was new, smelled new, and the personnel were younger than Starling. It was something she'd have to get used to, she thought with a twinge—she'd be a year older very soon.

A young woman with A. BENNING on her name tag signed for the two arrows Starling brought.

A. Benning had had some bad experiences receiving evidence, judging from her evident relief when she saw the two missiles wired carefully to Starling's evidence board with twist ties.

"You don't want to know what I see sometimes when I open these things," A. Benning said. "You have to understand that I can't tell you anything, like in five minutes—"

"No," Starling said. "There's no reference RFLP on Dr. Lecter, he escaped too long ago and the artifacts have been polluted, handled by a hundred people."

"Lab time is too valuable to run every sample, like fourteen hairs, say, from a motel room. If you bring me—"

"Listen to me," Starling said, "then you talk. I've asked the Questura in Italy to send me the toothbrush they think belonged to Dr. Lecter. You can get some epithelial cheek cells off it. Do both RFLP and short tandem repeats on them. This crossbow quarrel has been in the rain, I doubt you'll get much off it, but look here—"

"I'm sorry, I didn't think you'd understand—"

Starling managed a smile. "Don't worry, A. Benning, we'll get along fine. See, the arrows are both yellow. The crossbow quarrel is yellow because it's been painted by hand, not a bad job, but a little streaky. Look here, what does that look like under the paint?"

"Maybe a hair off the brush?"

"Maybe. But look how it's curved toward one end and has a little bulb at the end. What if it's an eyelash?"

"If it's got the follicle—"

"Right."

"Look, I can run PCR-STR—three colors at once—in the same line in the gel and get you three DNA sites at a time. It'll take thirteen sites for court, but a couple of days will be enough to know pretty well if it's him."

"A. Benning, I knew you could help me."

"You're Starling. I mean Special Agent Starling. I didn't mean to get off on the wrong foot—I see a lot of real bad evidence the cops send in—it has nothing to do with you."

"I know."

"I thought you'd be older. All the girls—the women know about you, I mean everybody does, but you're kind of"—A. Benning looked away—"kind of special to us." A. Benning held up her chubby little thumb. "Good luck with the Other. If you don't mind my saying so."

MASON VERGER's major domo, Cordell, was a large man with exaggerated features who might have been handsome with more animation
in his face. He was thirty-seven years old and he could never work
in the health industry in Switzerland again, or have any employment
there that put him in close contact with children.

Mason paid him a large salary to be in charge of his wing, with
responsibility for his care and feeding. He had found Cordell to be
absolutely reliable and capable of anything. Cordell had witnessed acts
of cruelty on video as Mason interviewed little children that would
have moved anyone else to rage or tears.

Today Cordell was a little concerned about the only matter holy
to him, money.

He gave his familiar double knock on the door and went into Mason's
room. It was completely dark except for the glowing aquarium. The eel
knew he was there and rose from his hole, hoping.

"Mr. Verger?"

A moment while Mason came awake.

"I need to mention something to you, I have to make an extra
payment in Baltimore this week to the same person we spoke about

before. It's not any kind of emergency basis, but it would be prudent. That Negro child Franklin ate some rat poison and was in *cridical* condition earlier this week. He's telling his foster mother it was your suggestion he should poison his cat to keep the police from torturing it. So, he gave the cat to a neighbor and took the rat poison himself."

"That's absurd," Mason said. "I had nothing to do with it."

"Of course it's absurd, Mr. Verger."

"Who's complaining, the woman you get the kids from?"

"She's the one that has to be paid at once."

"Cordell, you didn't interfere with the little bastard? They didn't find anything in him at the hospital, did they? I'll find out, you know."

"No, sir. In your home? Never, I swear it. You know I'm not a fool. I love my job."

"Where is *Franklin?*"

"Maryland-Misericordia Hospital. When he gets out he'll go to a group home. You know the woman he lived with got kicked off the foster home list for smoking marijuana. She's the one complaining about you. We may have to deal with her."

"Coon doper, shouldn't be much problem."

"She doesn't know anybody to go to with it. I think she needs some careful handling. Kit gloves. The welfare worker wants her to shut up."

"I'll think about that. Go ahead and pay the welfare clerk."

"A thousand dollars?"

"Just make sure she knows that's all she gets."

Lying on Mason's couch in the dark, her cheeks stiff with dried tears, Margot Verger listened to Cordell and Mason talking. She had been trying to reason with Mason when he fell asleep. Obviously Mason thought she had left. She opened her mouth to breathe quietly, trying to time her breaths to the hiss of his respirator. A pulse of gray light in the room as Cordell left. Margot lay flat on the couch. She waited almost twenty minutes, until the pump settled into Mason's sleep rhythm, before she left the room. The eel saw her go, but Mason did not.

61

MARGOT VERGER and Barney had been hanging out together. They did not talk a great deal, but they watched football in the recreation room, and *The Simpsons*, and concerts sometimes on educational TV, and together they followed *I, Claudius*. When Barney's shift made him miss some episodes, they ordered the tape.

Margot liked Barney, she liked the way she was one of the guys with him. He was the only person she'd known who was cool like that. Barney was very smart, and there was something a little other-worldly about him. She liked that too.

Margot had a good liberal arts education as well as her computer science. Barney, self-taught, had opinions that ranged from childish to penetrating. She could provide context for him. Margot's education was a broad and open plain defined by reason. But the plain rested on top of her mentality like the Flat Earther's world rests on a turtle.

Margot Verger made Barney pay for his joke about squatting to pee. She believed that her legs were stronger than his, and time proved her right. By feigning difficulty at lower weights she lured him into a bet on leg presses and won back her hundred dollars. In addition, using the advantage of her lighter weight, she beat him in one-armed pull-ups, but she would only bet on the right arm, her left being weaker from a childhood injury sustained in a struggle with Mason.

Sometimes at night, after Barney's shift with Mason was over, they worked out together, spotting one another on the bench. It was a serious workout, largely silent except for their breathing. Sometimes they only said good night as she packed her gym bag and disappeared toward the family quarters, off-limits to the staff.

This night she came into the black and chrome gymnasium directly from Mason's room with tears in her eyes.

"Hey, hey," Barney said. "You all right?"

"Just family crap, what can I tell you? I'm all right," Margot said.

She worked out like a fiend, too much weight, too many reps.

Once Barney came and took a barbell from her and shook his head. "You're gonna tear something," he said.

She was still grinding on an exercise bike when he called it quits, and stood under the gym's steaming shower, letting the hot water take the long day down the drain. It was a communal gym shower with four overhead nozzles and some extra nozzles at waist and thigh level. Barney liked to turn on two showers and converge their streams on his big body.

Soon Barney was enveloped in a thick fog that shut out everything but the pounding of the water on his head. Barney liked to reflect in the shower: Clouds of steam. *The Clouds.* Aristophanes. Dr. Lecter explaining about the lizard pissing on Socrates. It occurred to him that, before he was peened under the relentless hammer of Dr. Lecter's logic, somebody like Doemling could have pushed him around.

When he heard another shower go on, he paid little attention and continued scrubbing himself. Other personnel used the gym, but mostly in the early morning and late afternoon. It is male etiquette to pay little attention to other bathers in a communal athletic shower, but Barney wondered who it was. He hoped it wasn't Cordell, who gave him the creeps. It was rare for anyone else to use this facility at night. Who in the hell *was* that? Barney turned to let the water pound on the back of his neck. Clouds of steam, fragments of the person next to him appear between the billows like fragments of fresco on a plastered wall. Here a massive shoulder, there a leg. A shapely hand scrubbing a muscular neck and shoulder, coral fingernails, that was Margot's hand. Those were painted toes. That was Margot's leg.

Barney put his head back against the pulsing shower stream and took a deep breath. Next door the figure turning, scrubbing in a businesslike way. Washing her hair now. That was Margot's flat ribbed belly, her small breasts standing up on her big pecs, nipples raised to the jetting water, that was Margot's groin, knurled at the juncture of body and thigh, and that's got to be Margot's pussy, framed in a blond trimmed mohawk.

Barney took as deep a breath as he could and held it . . . he could feel himself developing a problem. She was shining like a horse, pumped to the limit from the hard workout. As Barney's interest grew more apparent, he turned his back to her. Maybe he could just ignore her until she left.

The water went off next door. But now her voice came. "Hey, Barney, what's the spread on the Patriots?"

"With . . . with my guy, you can get Miami and five and a half." He looked over his shoulder.

She was drying herself just beyond the range of Barney's spray. Her hair was plastered down. Her face looked fresh now and the tears were gone. Margot had excellent skin.

"So you gonna take the points?" she said. "The pick 'em pool at Judy's office has got . . . ."

Barney couldn't pay attention to the rest. Margot's mohawk, jeweled with droplets, framed pink. Barney's face felt hot and he had a major cockstand. He was puzzled and disturbed. That freezing feeling came over him. He had never felt any attraction to men. But Margot for all her muscles was clearly not a man, and he liked her.

What is this shit of coming in the shower with him anyway?

He turned off his water and faced her wet. Without thinking about it, he put his big hand on her cheek. "For God's sake, Margot," he said, his breath thick in his throat.

She looked down at him. "God*dammit*, Barney. Don't . . ."

Barney stretched his neck and leaned forward, trying to kiss her gently anywhere on her face without touching her with his member, but touched her anyway, she pulling away, looked down at the catenary strand of crystal fluid that stretched between him and her flat stomach, and she caught him across his broad chest with a forearm worthy of a middle guard, his feet went out from under him and he sat hard on the shower floor.

"You fucking bastard," she hissed, "I might have known it. Faggot! Take that thing and stick it up . . ."

Barney rolled to his feet and was out of the shower, pulling on his clothes wet, and he left the gym without a word.

Barney's quarters were in a building separate from the house, slate-roofed former stables that were garages now with apartments in the gables. Late at night he sat pecking on his laptop, working on a correspondence course on the Internet. He felt the floor tremble as someone solid came up the stairs.

A light knock at the door. When he opened it, Margot stood there, muffled in heavy sweats and a stocking cap.

"Can I come in a minute?"

Barney looked at his feet for a few seconds before he stood back from the door.

"Barney. Hey, I'm sorry about in there," she said. "I kind of panicked. I mean, I screwed up and then I panicked. I liked being friends."

"Me too."

"I thought we could be like, you know, regular buddies."

"Margot, come *on*. I said we'd be friends but I'm not a damn eunuch. You came in the fucking shower with me. You looked good to me, I can't help that. You come in the shower naked and I see two things together I really *like*."

"Me and a pussy," Margot said.

They were surprised to laugh together.

She came and grabbed him in a hug that might have injured a less powerful man. "Listen, if it was gonna be a guy it would have to be you. But that's not my thing. It really is not. Not now, never will be."

Barney nodded. "I know that. It just got away from me."

They stood quiet a minute with their arms around each other.

"You want to try to be friends?" she said.

He thought about it a minute. "Yeah. But you've got to help me a little bit. Here's the deal: I'm going to make this major effort to forget what I saw in the shower, and you don't show it to me anymore. And don't show me any boobs either, while you're at it. How's that?"

"I can be a good friend, Barney. Come to the house tomorrow. Judy cooks, I cook."

"Yeah, but you may not cook any better than I do."

"Try me," Margot said.

DR. LECTER held a bottle of Château Pétrus up to the light. He had raised it to the upright position and set it on its bottom a day ago, in case it might have sediment. He looked at his watch and decided it was time to open the wine.

This was what Dr. Lecter considered a serious risk, more of a chance than he liked to take. He did not want to be rash. He wanted to enjoy the wine's color in a crystal decanter. What if, after drawing the cork too early, he decided there was none of its holy breath to be lost in decanting? The light revealed a bit of sediment.

He removed the cork as carefully as he might trepan a skull, and placed the wine in his pouring device, which was driven by a crank and screw to tilt the bottle by minute increments. Let the salt air do a bit of work and then he would decide.

He lit a fire of shaggy chunk charcoal and made himself a drink, Lillet and a slice of orange over ice, while he considered the *fond* he had been working on for days. Dr. Lecter followed the inspired lead of Alexandre Dumas in fashioning his stock. Only three days ago, upon his return from the deer-lease woods, he had added to the stockpot a fat crow which had been stuffing itself with juniper berries. Small black feathers swam on the calm waters of the bay. The primary feathers he saved to make plectra for his harpsichord.

Now Dr. Lecter crushed juniper berries of his own and began to sweat shallots in a copper saucepan. With a neat surgical knot, he tied a piece of cotton string around a fresh bouquet garni and ladled stock over it in the saucepan.

The tenderloin Dr. Lecter lifted from his ceramic crock was dark from the marinade, dripping. He patted it dry and turned the pointed end back on itself and tied it to make the diameter constant for the length of the meat.

In time the fire was right, banked with one very hot area and a step in the coals. The tenderloin hissed on the iron and blue smoke whirled across the garden, moving as though to the music on Dr. Lecter's speakers. He was playing Henry VIII's moving composition "If True Love Reigned."

Late in the night, his lips stained by the red Château Pétrus, a small crystal glass of honey-colored Château d'Yquem on his candle stand, Dr. Lecter plays Bach. In his mind Starling runs through the leaves. The deer start ahead of her, and run up the slope past Dr. Lecter, sitting still on the hillside. Running, running, he is into "Variation Two" of the *Goldberg Variations*, the candlelight playing on his moving hands—a stitch in the music, a flash of bloody snow and dirty teeth, this time no more than a flash that disappears with a distinct sound, a solid *thock*, a crossbow bolt driving through a skull—and we have the pleasant woods again, and flowing music and Starling, limned in polleny light, runs out of sight, her ponytail bobbing like the flag of a deer, and without further interruption, he plays the movement through to the end and the sweet silence after was as rich as Château d'Yquem.

Dr. Lecter held his glass up to the candle. The candle flared behind it as the sun flared on water, and the wine itself was the color of the winter sun on Clarice Starling's skin. Her birthday was coming soon, the doctor reflected. He wondered if there was extant a bottle of Château d'Yquem from her birth year. Perhaps a present was in order for Clarice Starling, who in three weeks would have lived as long as Christ.

63

AT THE moment Dr. Lecter raised his wine to the candle, A. Benning, staying late at the DNA lab, raised her latest gel to the light and looked at the electrophoresis lines dotted with red, blue, and yellow. The sample was epithelial cells from the toothbrush brought over from the Palazzo Capponi in the Italian diplomatic pouch.

"Ummmm umm umm umm," she said and called Starling's number at Quantico.

Eric Pickford answered.

"Hi, may I speak to Clarice Starling please?"

"She's gone for the day and I'm in charge, how can I help you?"

"Do you have a beeper number for her?"

"She's on the other phone. What have you got?"

"Would you please tell her it's Benning from the DNA lab. Please tell her the toothbrush and the eyelash off the arrow are a match. It's Dr. Lecter. And ask her to call me."

"Give me your extension number. Sure, I'll tell her right now. Thanks."

Starling was not on the other line. Pickford called Paul Krendler at home.

When Starling did not call A. Benning at the lab, the technician was a little disappointed. A. Benning had put in a lot of extra time. She went home long before Pickford ever called Starling at home.

Mason knew an hour before Starling.

He talked briefly to Paul Krendler, taking his time, letting the breaths come. His mind was very clear.

"It's time to get Starling out, before they start thinking proactive and put her out for bait. It's Friday, you've got the weekend. Get things started, Krendler. Tip the Wops about the ad and get her out of there, it's time for her to go. And Krendler?"

"I wish we could just—"

"Just do it, and when you get that next picture postcard from the Caymans, it'll have a whole new number written under the stamp."

"All right, I'll—" Krendler said, and heard the dial tone.

The short talk was uncommonly tiring for Mason.

Last, before sinking into a broken sleep, he summoned Cordell and said to him, "Send for the pigs."

IT IS more trouble physically to move a semiwild pig against its will than to kidnap a man. Pigs are harder to get hold of than men and big ones are stronger than a man and they cannot be intimidated with a gun. There are the tusks to consider if you want to maintain the integrity of your abdomen and legs.

Tusked pigs instinctively disembowel when fighting the upright species, men and bears. They do not naturally hamstring, but can quickly learn the behavior.

If you need to maintain the animal alive, you cannot haze it with electrical shock, as pigs are prone to fatal coronary fibrillation.

Carlo Deogracias, master of the pigs, had the patience of a crocodile. He had experimented with animal sedation, using the same acepromazine he planned to use on Dr. Lecter. Now he knew exactly how much was required to quiet a hundred-kilo wild boar and the intervals of dosage that would keep him quiet for as long as fourteen hours without any lasting aftereffects.

Since the Verger firm was a large-scale importer and exporter of animals and an established partner of the Department of Agriculture in experimental breeding programs, the way was made smooth for

Mason's pigs. The Veterinary Service Form 17–129 was faxed to the Animal and Plant Health Inspection Service at Riverdale, Maryland, as required, along with veterinary affidavits from Sardinia and a $39.50 user's fee for fifty straws of frozen semen Carlo wanted to bring.

The permits for swine and semen came by return fax, along with a waiver of the usual Key West quarantine for swine, and a confirmation that an on-board inspector would clear the animals at Baltimore-Washington International Airport.

Carlo and his helpers, the brothers Piero and Tommaso Falcione, put the crates together. They were excellent crates with sliding doors at each end, sanded inside and padded. At the last minute, they remembered to crate the bordello mirror too. Something about its rococo frame around reflected pigs delighted Mason in photographs.

Carefully, Carlo doped sixteen swine—five boars raised in the same pen and eleven sows, one of them pregnant, none in estrus. When they were unconscious he gave them a close physical examination. He tested their sharp teeth and the tips of their great tusks with his fingers. He held their terrible faces in his hands, looked into the tiny glazed eyes and listened to make sure their airways were clear, and he hobbled their elegant little ankles. Then he dragged them on canvas into the crates and slid the end doors in place.

The trucks groaned down from the Gennargentu Mountains into Cagliari. At the airport waited an airbus jet freighter operated by Count Fleet Airlines, specialists in transporting racehorses. This airplane usually carried American horses back and forth to race meets in Dubai. It carried one horse now, picked up in Rome. The horse would not be still when it scented the wild-smelling pigs, and whinnied and kicked in its close padded stall until the crew had to unload it and leave it behind, causing much expense later for Mason, who had to ship the horse home to its owner and pay compensation to avoid a lawsuit.

Carlo and his helpers rode with the hogs in the pressurized cargo hold. Every half-hour out over the heaving sea, Carlo visited each pig individually, put his hand on its bristled side and felt the thump of its wild heart.

Even if they were good and hungry, sixteen pigs could not be expected to consume Dr. Lecter in his entirety at one seating. It had taken them a day to completely consume the filmmaker.

The first day, Mason wanted Dr. Lecter to watch them eat his feet. Lecter would be sustained on a saline drip overnight, awaiting the next course.

Mason had promised Carlo an hour with him in the interval.

In the second course, the pigs could eat him all hollow and consume the ventral-side flesh and the face within an hour, as the first shift of the biggest pigs and the pregnant female fell back sated and the second wave came on. By then the fun would be over anyway.

BARNEY HAD never been in the barn before. He came in a side door under the tiers of seats that surrounded an old showring on three sides. Empty and silent except for the muttering of the pigeons in the rafters, the showring still held an air of expectation. Behind the auctioneer's stand stretched the open barn. Big double doors opened into the stable wing and the tack room.

Barney heard voices and called, "Hello."

"In the tack room, Barney, come on in." Margot's deep voice.

The tack room was a cheerful place, hung with harnesses and the graceful shapes of saddlery. Smell of leather. Warm sunlight streaming in through dusty windows just beneath the eaves raised the smell of leather and hay. An open loft along one side opened into the hayloft of the barn.

Margot was putting up the currycombs and some hackamores. Her hair was paler than the hay, her eyes as blue as the inspection stamp on meat.

"Hi," Barney said from the door. He thought the room was a little stagy, set up for the sake of visiting children. In its height and the slant of light from the high windows it was like a church.

"Hi, Barney. Hang on and we'll eat in about twenty minutes."

Judy Ingram's voice came from the loft above. "Barneeeeeey. Good morning. Wait till you see what we've got for lunch! Margot, you want to try to eat outside?"

Each Saturday it was Margot and Judy's habit to curry the motley assortment of fat Shetlands kept for the visiting children to ride. They always brought a picnic lunch.

"Let's try on the south side of the barn, in the sun," Margot said.

Everyone seemed a little too chirpy. A person with Barney's hospital experience knows excessive chirpiness does not bode well for the chirpee.

The tack room was dominated by a horse's skull, mounted a little above head height on the wall, with its bridle and blinkers on, and draped with the racing colors of the Vergers.

"That's Fleet Shadow, won the Lodgepole Stakes in '52, the only winner my father ever had," Margot said. "He was too cheap to get him stuffed." She looked up at the skull. "Bears a strong resemblence to Mason, doesn't it?"

There was a forced-draft furnace and bellows in the corner. Margot had built a small coal fire there against the chill. On the fire was a pot of something that smelled like soup.

A complete set of farrier's tools was on a workbench. She picked up a farrier's hammer, this one with a short handle and a heavy head. With her great arms and chest, Margot might have been a farrier herself, or a blacksmith with particularly pointed pectorals.

"You want to throw me the blankets?" Judy called down.

Margot picked up a bundle of freshly washed saddle blankets and with one scooping move of her great arm, sent it arching up to the loft.

"Okay, I'm gonna wash up and get the stuff out of the Jeep. We'll eat in fifteen, okay?" Judy said, coming down the ladder.

Barney, feeling Margot's scrutiny, did not check out Judy's behind. There were some bales of hay with horse blankets folded on them for seats. Margot and Barney sat.

"You missed the ponies. They're gone to the stable in Lester," Margot said.

"I heard the trucks this morning. How come?"

"Mason's business." A little silence. They had always been easy with silence, but not this one. "Well, Barney. You get to a point where you can't talk anymore, unless you're going to do something. Is that where we are?"

"Like an affair or something," Barney said. The unhappy analogy hung in the air.

"*Affair*," Margot said, "I've got something for you a hell of a lot better than that. You know what we're talking about."

"Pretty much," Barney said.

"But if you decided you *didn't* want to do something, and later it happened anyway, do you understand you could never come back on me about it?" She tapped her palm with the farrier's hammer, absently perhaps, watching him with her blue butcher's eyes.

Barney had seen some countenances in his time and stayed alive by reading them. He saw she was telling the truth.

"I know that."

"Same if we did something. I'll be extremely generous one time, and one time only. But it would be enough. You want to know how much?"

"Margot, nothing's gonna happen on my watch. Not while I'm taking his money to take care of him."

"*Why*, Barney?"

Sitting on the bale, he shrugged his big shoulders. "Deal's a deal."

"You call that a *deal*? This is a *deal*," Margot said. "*Five million dollars, Barney*. The same five Krendler's supposed to get for selling out the FBI, if you want to know."

"We're talking about getting enough semen from Mason to get Judy pregnant."

"We're talking about something else too. You know if you take Mason's jism from him and leave him alive, he'd get you, Barney. You couldn't run far enough. You'd go to the fucking pigs."

"I'd do what?"

"What is it, Barney, *Semper Fi*, like it says on your arm?"

"When I took his money I said I'd take care of him. While I work for him, I won't do him any harm."

"You don't have to . . . *do* anything to him except the medical, after he's dead. I can't touch him there. Not one more time. You might have to help me with Cordell."

"You kill Mason, you only get one batch," Barney said.

"We get five cc's, even a low-normal sperm count, put extenders in it, we could try five times with insemination, we could do it in vitro—Judy's family's real fertile."

"Did you think about buying Cordell?"

"No. He'd never keep the deal. His word would be crap. Sooner or later he'd come back on me. He'd have to go."

"You've thought about it a lot."

"Yes. Barney, you have to control the nurse station. There's tape backup on the monitors, there's a record of every second. There's live TV, but no videotape running. We—I put my hand down inside the shell of the respirator and immobilize his chest. Monitor shows the respirator still working. By the time his heart rate and blood pressure show a change, you rush in and he's unconscious, you can try to revive him all you want. The only thing is, you don't happen to notice me. I just press on his chest until he's dead. You've worked enough autopsies, Barney. What do they look for when they suspect smothering?"

"Hemorrhages behind the eyelids."

"Mason doesn't have any eyelids."

She had read up, and she was used to buying anything, anybody.

Barney looked her in the face but he fixed the hammer in his peripheral vision as he gave his answer: "No, Margot."

"If I had let you fuck me would you do it?"

"No."

"If I had fucked *you* would you do it?"

"No."

"If you didn't work here, if you didn't have any medical responsibility to him would you do it?"

"Probably not."

"Is it ethics or chickenshit?"

"I don't know."

"Let's find out. You're fired, Barney."

He nodded, not particularly surprised.

"And, Barney?" She raised a finger to her lips. "Shhhh. Give me your word? Do I have to say I could kill you with that prior in California? I don't need to say that, do I?"

"You don't have to worry," Barney said. "*I've* got to worry. I don't know how Mason lets people go. Maybe they just disappear."

"You don't have to worry either, I'll tell Mason you've had hepatitis. You don't know a lot about his business except that he's trying to help the law—and he knows we got the prior on you, he'll let you go."

Barney wondered which Dr. Lecter had found more interesting in therapy, Mason Verger or his sister.

IT WAS night when the long silver transport pulled up to the barn at Muskrat Farm. They were late and tempers were short.

The arrangements at Baltimore-Washington International Airport had gone well at first, the on-board inspector from the Department of Agriculture rubber-stamped the shipment of sixteen swine. The inspector had an expert's knowledge of swine and he had never seen anything like them.

Then Carlo Deogracias looked inside the truck. It was a livestock transporter and smelled like one, with traces in the cracks of many former occupants. Carlo would not let his pigs be unloaded. The airplane waited while the angry driver, Carlo and Piero Falcione found another livestock truck more suitable to moving crates, located a truck wash with a steam hose and steam-cleaned the cargo area.

Once at the main gate of Muskrat Farm, a last annoyance. The guard checked the tonnage of the truck and refused them entrance, citing a load limit on an ornamental bridge. He redirected them to the service road through the national forest. Tree branches scraped the tall truck as it crept the last two miles.

Carlo liked the big clean barn at Muskrat Farm. He liked the little forklift that gently carried the cages into the pony stalls.

When the driver of the livestock truck brought an electric cattle prod to the cages and offered to zap a pig to see how deeply drugged it was, Carlo snatched the instrument away from him and frightened him so badly he was afraid to ask for it back.

Carlo would let the great rough swine recover from their sedation in the semidarkness, not letting them out of the cages until they were on their feet and alert. He was afraid that those awakening first might take a bite out of a drugged sleeper. Any prone figure attracted them when the herd was not napping together.

Piero and Tommaso had to be doubly careful since the herd ate the filmmaker Oreste, and later his frozen assistant. The men could not be in the pen or the pasture with the pigs. The swine did not threaten, they did not gnash their teeth as wild pigs will, they simply kept watching the men with the terrible single-mindedness of a swine and sidled nearer until they were close enough to charge.

Carlo, equally single-minded, did not rest until he had walked by flashlight the fence enclosing Mason's wooded pasture which adjoined the great national forest.

Carlo dug in the ground with his pocketknife and examined the forest mast under the pasture trees and found acorns. He had heard jays in the last light driving in and thought it likely there would be acorns. Sure enough, white oaks grew here in the enclosed field, but not too many of them. He did not want the pigs to find their meals on the ground, as they could easily do in the great forest.

Mason had built across the open end of the barn a stout barrier with a Dutch gate in it, like Carlo's own gate in Sardinia.

From behind the safety of this barrier, Carlo could feed them, sailing clothing stuffed with dead chickens, legs of lamb and vegetables over the fence into their midst.

They were not tame, but they were not afraid of men or noise. Even Carlo could not go into the pen with them. A pig is not like other animals. There is a spark of intelligence and a terrible practicality in pigs. These were not at all hostile. They just liked to eat men. They were light of foot like a Miura bull and could cut like a sheep-dog, and their movements around their keepers had the sinister quality of premeditation. Piero had a near moment retrieving from a feeding a shirt that they thought they could use again.

There had never been such pigs before, bigger than the European wild boar and just as savage. Carlo felt he had created them. He knew that the thing they would do, the evil they would destroy, would be all the credit he would ever need in the hereafter.

By midnight, all were asleep in the barn: Carlo, Piero and Tommaso slept without dreaming in the tack room loft, the swine snored in their cages where their elegant little feet were beginning to trot in their dreams and one or two stirred on the clean canvas. The skull of the trotting horse, Fleet Shadow, faintly lit by the coal fire in the farrier's furnace, watched over all.

C H A P T E R

67

To ATTACK an agent of the Federal Bureau of Investigation with
Mason's false evidence was a big leap for Krendler. It left him a little
breathless. If the Attorney General caught him, she would crush him
like a roach.

Except for his own personal risk, the matter of ruining Clarice
Starling did not weigh with Krendler as would breaking a man. A
man had a family to support—Krendler supported his own family, as
greedy and ungrateful as they were.

And Starling definitely had to go. Left alone, following the threads
with the picky, petty homemaking skills of a woman, Clarice Starling
would find Hannibal Lecter. If that happened, Mason Verger would
not give Krendler anything.

The sooner she was stripped of her resources and put out there as
bait, the better.

Krendler had broken careers before, in his own rise to power, first
as a state prosecuting attorney active in politics, and later at Justice. He
knew from experience that crippling a woman's career is easier than
damaging a man. If a woman gets a promotion that women shouldn't
have, the most efficient way is to say she won it on her back.

It would be impossible to make that charge stick to Clarice Starling, Krendler thought. In fact, he couldn't think of anyone more in *need* of a grudge-fucking up the dirt road. He sometimes thought of that abrasive act as he twisted his finger in his nose.

Krendler could not have explained his animosity to Starling. It was visceral and it belonged to a place in himself where he could not go. A place with seat covers and a dome light, door handles and window cranks and a girl with Starling's coloring but not her sense and her pants around one ankle asking him what in the hell was the matter with him, and why didn't he come on and do it, was he *some kind of queer? some kind of queer? some kind of queer?*

If you didn't know what a cunt Starling was, Krendler reflected, her performance in black and white was much better than her few promotions would indicate—he had to admit that. Her rewards had been satisfyingly few: By adding the odd drop of poison to her record over the years, Krendler had been able to influence the FBI career board enough to block a number of plum assignments she should have gotten, and her independent attitude and smart mouth had helped his cause.

Mason wouldn't wait for the disposition of Feliciana Fish Market. And there was no guarantee any shit would stick to Starling in a hearing. The shooting of Evelda Drumgo and the others was the result of a security failure, obviously. It was a miracle Starling was able to save that little bastard of a baby. One more for the public to have to feed. Tearing the scab off that ugly event would be easy, but it was an unwieldy way to get at Starling.

Better Mason's way. It would be quick and she would be out of there. The timing was propitious:

One Washington axiom, proved more times than the Pythagorean theorem, states that in the presence of oxygen, one loud fart with an obvious culprit will cover many small emissions in the same room, provided they are nearly simultaneous.

Ergo, the impeachment trial was distracting the Justice Department enough for him to railroad Starling.

Mason wanted some press coverage for Dr. Lecter to see. But Krendler must make the coverage seem an unhappy accident. Fortunately an occasion was coming that would serve him well: the very birthday of the FBI.

Krendler maintained a tame conscience with which to shrive himself.

It consoled him now: If Starling lost her job, at worst some goddamned dyke den where Starling lived would have to do without the big TV dish for sports. At worst he was giving a loose cannon a way to roll over the side and threaten nobody anymore.

A "loose cannon" over the side would "stop rocking the boat," he thought, pleased and comforted as though two naval metaphors made a logical equation. That the rocking boat moves the cannon bothered him not at all.

Krendler had the most active fantasy life his imagination would permit. Now, for his pleasure, he pictured Starling as old, tripping over those tits, those trim legs turned blue-veined and lumpy, trudging up and down the stairs carrying laundry, turning her face away from the stains on the sheets, working for her board at a bed-and-breakfast owned by a couple of goddamned hairy old dykes.

He imagined the next thing he would say to her, coming on the heels of his triumph with "cornpone country pussy."

Armed with Dr. Doemling's insights, he wanted to stand close to her after she was disarmed and say without moving his mouth, "You're old to still be fucking your daddy, even for Southern white trash." He repeated the line in his mind, and considered putting it in his notebook.

Krendler had the tool and the time and the venom he needed to smash Starling's career, and as he set about it, he was vastly aided by chance and the Italian mail.

68

THE BATTLE Creek Cemetery outside Hubbard, Texas, is a small scar on the lion-colored hide of central Texas in December. The wind is whistling there at this moment, and it will always whistle there. You cannot wait it out.

The new section of the cemetery has flat markers so it's easy to mow the grass. Today a silver heart balloon dances there over the grave of a birthday girl. In the older part of the cemetery they mow along the paths every time and get between the tombstones with a mower as often as they can. Bits of ribbon, the stalks of dried flowers, are mixed in the soil. At the very back of the cemetery is a compost heap where the old flowers go. Between the dancing heart balloon and the compost heap, a backhoe is idling, a young black man at the controls, another on the ground, cupping a match against the wind as he lights a cigarette . . .

"Mr. Closter, I wanted you to be here when we did this so you could see what we're up against. I'm sure you will discourage the loved ones from any viewing," said Mr. Greenlea, director of the Hubbard Funeral Home. "That casket—and I want to compliment you again on your taste—that casket will make a proud presentation, and that's as far as they need to see. I'm happy to give you the professional discount on it. My own father, who is dead at the present time, rests in one just like it."

He nodded to the backhoe operator and the machine's claw took a bite out of the weedy, sunken grave.

"You're positive about the stone, Mr. Closter?"

"Yes," Dr. Lecter said. "The children are having one stone made for both the mother and the father."

They stood without talking, the wind snapping their trouser cuffs, until the backhoe stopped about two feet down.

"We'd better go with shovels from here," Mr. Greenlea said. The two workers dropped into the hole and started moving dirt with an easy, practiced swing.

"Careful," Mr. Greenlea said. "That wasn't much of a coffin to start with. Nothing like what he's getting now."

The cheap pressboard coffin had indeed collapsed on its occupant. Greenlea had his diggers clear the dirt around it and slide a canvas under the bottom of the box, which was still intact. The coffin was raised in this canvas sling and swung into the back of a truck.

On a trestle table in the Hubbard Funeral Home garage, the pieces of the sunken lid were lifted away to reveal a sizeable skeleton.

Dr. Lecter examined it quickly. A bullet had notched the short rib over the liver and there was a depressed fracture and bullet hole high on the left forehead. The skull, mossy and clogged and only partly exposed, had good, high cheekbones he had seen before.

"The ground don't leave much," Mr. Greenlea said.

The rotted remains of trousers and the rags of a cowboy shirt draped the bones. The pearl snaps from the shirt had fallen through the ribs. A cowboy hat, a triple-X beaver with a Fort Worth crease, rested over the chest. There was a notch in the brim and a hole in the crown.

"Did you know the deceased?" Dr. Lecter asked.

"We just bought this mortuary and took over this cemetery as an addition to our group in 1989," Mr. Greenlea said. "I live locally now, but our firm's headquarters is in St Louis. Do you want to try to preserve the clothing? Or I could let you have a suit, but I don't think—"

"No," Dr. Lecter said. "Brush the bones, no clothing except the hat and the buckle and the boots, bag the small bones of the hands and feet, and bundle them in your best silk shroud with the skull and the long bones. You don't have to lay them out, just get them all. Will keeping the stone compensate you for reclosing?"

"Yes, if you'll just sign here, and I'll give you copies of those others," Mr. Greenlea said, vastly pleased at the coffin he had sold. Most funeral directors coming for a body would have shipped the bones in a carton and sold the family a coffin of his own.

Dr. Lecter's disinterment papers were in perfect accord with the Texas Health and Safety Code Sec. 711.004, as he knew they would be, having made them himself, downloading the requirements and fac-simile forms from the Texas Association of Counties Quick Reference Law Library.

The two workmen, grateful for the power tailgate on Dr. Lecter's rental truck, rolled the new coffin into place and lashed it down on its dolly beside the only other item in the truck, a cardboard hanging wardrobe.

"That's such a good idea, carrying your own closet. Saves wrinkling your ceremonial attire in a suitcase, doesn't it?" Mr. Greenlea said.

In Dallas, the doctor removed from the wardrobe a viola case and put in it his silk-bound bundle of bones, the hat fitting nicely into the lower section, the skull cushioned in it.

He shoved the coffin out the back at the Fish Trap Cemetery and turned in his rental at Dallas—Fort Worth Airport, where he checked the viola case straight through to Philadelphia.

IV

NOTABLE OCCASIONS ON THE CALENDAR OF DREAD

ON MONDAY, Clarice Starling had the weekend exotic purchases to check, and there were glitches in her system that required the help of her computer technician from Engineering. Even with severely pruned lists of two or three of the most special vintages from five vintners, the reduction to two sources for American foie gras, and five specialty grocers, the numbers of purchases were formidable. Call-ins from individual liquor stores using the telephone number on the bulletin had to be entered by hand.

Based on the identification of Dr. Lecter in the murder of the deer hunter in Virginia, Starling cut the list to East Coast purchases except for Sonoma foie gras. Fauchon in Paris refused to cooperate. Starling could make no sense of what Vera dal 1926 in Florence said on the telephone, and faxed the Questura for help in case Dr. Lecter ordered white truffles.

At the end of the workday on Monday, December 17, Starling had twelve possibilities to follow up. They were combinations of purchases on credit cards. One man had bought a case of Pétrus and a supercharged Jaguar, both on the same American Express.

Another placed an order for a case of Bâtard-Montrachet and a case of green Gironde oysters.

Starling passed each possibility along to the local line bureau for follow-up.

Starling and Eric Pickford worked separate but overlapping shifts in order to have the office manned during store retail hours.

It was Pickford's fourth day on the job and he spent part of it programming his auto-dial telephone. He did not label the buttons.

When he went out for coffee, Starling pushed the top button on his telephone, Paul Krendler himself answered.

She hung up and sat in silence. It was time to go home. Swiveling her chair slowly around and around, she regarded all the objects in Hannibal's House. The X rays, the books, the table set for one. Then she pushed out through the curtains.

Crawford's office was open and empty. The sweater his late wife knitted for him hung on a coat tree in the corner. Starling put her hand out to the sweater, did not quite touch it, slung her coat over her shoulder and started the long walk to her car.

She would never see Quantico again.

ON THE evening of December 17, Clarice Starling's doorbell rang. She could see a federal marshal's car behind the Mustang in her driveway.

The marshal was Bobby, who drove her home from the hospital after the Feliciana shoot-out.

"Hi, Starling."

"Hi, Bobby. Come in."

"I'd like to, but I oughta tell you first. I've got a notice here I've got to serve you."

"Well, hell. Serve me in the house where it's warm," Starling said, numb in the middle.

The notice, on the letterhead of the Inspector General of the Department of Justice, required her to appear at a hearing the next morning, December 18, at nine A.M. in the J. Edgar Hoover Building.

"You want a ride tomorrow?" the marshal asked.

Starling shook her head. "Thanks, Bobby, I'll take my car. Want some coffee?"

"No, thanks. I'm sorry, Starling." The marshal clearly wanted to go. There was an awkward silence. "Your ear's looking good," he said at last.

She waved to him as he backed out of the drive.

The letter simply told her to report. No reason was given.

Ardelia Mapp, veteran of the Bureau's internecine wars and thorn in the side of the good-old-boy network, immediately brewed her grandmother's strongest medicinal tea, renowned for enhancing the mentality. Starling always dreaded the tea, but there was no way around it.

Mapp tapped the letterhead with her finger. "The Inspector General doesn't *have* to tell you a damn thing," Mapp said between sips. "If our Office of Professional Responsibility had charges, or the OPR-DOJ had something on you, they'd have to tell you, they'd have to serve you with papers. They'd have to give you a damn 645 or a 644 with the charges right there on it, and if it was criminal you'd have a lawyer, full disclosure, everything the crooks get, right?"

"Damn straight."

"Well, this way you get diddly-squat in advance. Inspector General's political, he can take over any case."

"He took over this one."

"With Krendler blowing smoke up his butt. Whatever it is, if you decide you want to go with an Equal Opportunity case, I've got all the numbers. Now, listen to me, Starling, you've got to tell them you want to tape. IG doesn't use signed depositions. Lonnie Gains got into that mess with them over that. They keep a record of what you say, and sometimes it changes after you say it. You don't ever see a transcript."

When Starling called Jack Crawford, he sounded as though he'd been asleep.

"I don't know what it is, Starling," he said. "I'll call around. One thing I do know, I'll be there tomorrow."

MORNING, AND the armored concrete cage of the Hoover Building brooding under a milky overcast.

In this era of the car bomb, the front entrance and the courtyard are closed most days, and the building is ringed by old Bureau automobiles as an improvised crash barrier.

The D.C. police follow a mindless policy, writing tickets on some of the barrier cars day after day, the sheaf building up under the wipers and tearing off in the wind to blow down the street.

A derelict warming himself over a grate in the sidewalk called to Starling and raised his hand as she passed. One side of his face was orange from some emergency room's Betadine. He held out a Styrofoam cup, worn down at the edges. Starling fished in her purse for a dollar, gave him two, leaning in to the warm stale air and the steam.

"Bless your heart," he said.

"I need it," said Starling. "Every little bit helps."

Starling got a large coffee at Au Bon Pain on the Tenth Street side of the Hoover Building as she had done so many times over the years. She wanted the coffee after a ragged sleep, but she didn't want to need to pee during the hearing. She decided to drink half of it.

She spotted Crawford through the window and caught up with him on the sidewalk. "You want to split this big coffee, Mr. Crawford? They'll give me another cup."

"Is it decaf?"

"No."

"I better not, I'll jump out of my skin." He looked peaked and old. A clear drop hung at the end of his nose. They stood out of the foot traffic streaming toward the side entrance of the FBI headquarters.

"I don't know what this meeting is, Starling. Nobody else from the Feliciana shoot-out has been called, that I can find out. I'll be with you." Starling passed him a Kleenex and they entered the steady stream of the arriving day shift.

Starling thought the clerical personnel looked unusually spiffy.

"Ninetieth anniversary of the FBI. Bush is coming to speak today," Crawford reminded her.

There were four TV satellite uplink trucks on the side street.

A camera crew from WFUL-TV was set up on the sidewalk filming a young man with a razor haircut talking into a hand microphone. A production assistant stationed on top of the van saw Starling and Crawford coming in the crowd.

"That's her, that's her in the navy raincoat," he called down.

"Here we go," said Razor Cut. "Rolling."

The crew made a swell in the stream of people to get the camera in Starling's face.

"Special Agent Starling, can you comment on the investigation of the Feliciana Fish Market Massacre? Has the report been submitted? Are you the subject of charges in killing the five—" Crawford took off his rain hat and, pretending to shield his eyes from the lights, managed to block the camera lens for a moment. Only the security door stopped the TV crew.

Sumbitches were tipped.

Once inside Security, they stopped in the hall. The mist outside had covered Starling and Crawford with tiny droplets. Crawford popped a Ginkgo Biloba tablet dry.

"Starling, I think they may have picked today because there's all the stir over the impeachment and the anniversary. Whatever they want to do could slide by in the rush."

"Why tip the press then?"

"Because not everybody in this hearing is singing off the same page. You've got ten minutes, want to powder your nose?"

72

STARLING HAD rarely been up to seven, the executive floor of the J. Edgar Hoover Building. She and the other members of her graduating class gathered there seven years ago to see the director congratulate Ardelia Mapp as valedictorian, and once an assistant director had summoned her to accept her medal as Combat Pistol Champion.

The carpet in Assistant Director Noonan's office was deep beyond her experience. In the clubby atmosphere of leather chairs in his meeting room there was the distinct smell of cigarettes. She wondered if they had flushed the butts and fanned the air before she got there.

Three men stood up when she and Crawford came into the room and one did not. The standees were Starling's former boss, Clint Pearsall of the Washington Field Office, Buzzard's Point; A/DIC Noonan of the FBI, and a tall red-haired man in a raw silk suit. Keeping his seat was Paul Krendler of the Inspector General's Office. Krendler turned his head to her on his long neck as though he were locating her by scent. When he faced her she could see both his round ears at the same time. Oddly, a federal marshal she didn't know stood in the corner of the room.

FBI and Justice personnel customarily are neat in their appearance, but these men were groomed for TV. Starling realized they must be appearing in the ceremonies downstairs with former President Bush later in the day. Otherwise she would have been summoned to the Justice Department rather than the Hoover Building.

Krendler frowned at the sight of Jack Crawford at Starling's side.

"Mr. Crawford, I don't think your attendance is required for this procedure."

"I'm Special Agent Starling's immediate supervisor. My place is here."

"I don't think so," Krendler said. He turned to Noonan. "Clint Pearsall is her boss of record, she's just TDY with Crawford. I think Agent Starling should be questioned privately," he said. "If we need additional information, we can ask Section Chief Crawford to stand by where we can reach him."

Noonan nodded. "We certainly would welcome your input, Jack, after we've heard independent testimony by the—by Special Agent Starling. Jack, I want you to stand by. If you want to make it the reading room of the library, make yourself comfortable, I'll call you."

Crawford got to his feet. "Director Noonan, may I say—"

"You *may* leave, is what you *may* do," Krendler said.

Noonan got to his feet. "Hold it please, it's my meeting, Mr. Krendler, until I turn it over to you. Jack, you and I go way back. The gentleman from Justice is too recently appointed to understand that. You'll get to say your piece. Now leave us and let Starling talk for herself," Noonan said. He leaned to Krendler and said something in his ear that made his face turn red.

Crawford looked at Starling. All he could do was bitch himself up.

"Thank you for coming, sir," she said.

The marshal let Crawford out.

Hearing the door click shut behind her, Starling straightened her spine and faced the men alone.

From there the proceeding went forward with the dispatch of an eighteenth-century amputation.

Noonan was the highest FBI authority in the room, but the Inspector General could overrule him, and the inspector apparently had sent Krendler as his plenipotentiary.

Noonan picked up the file before him. "Would you identify yourself, please, for the record?"

"Special Agent Clarice Starling. *Is* there a record, Director Noonan? I'd be glad if there was."

When he did not answer, she said, "Do you mind if I tape the proceedings?" She took a tough little Nagra tape recorder from her purse.

Krendler spoke up. "Ordinarily this sort of preliminary meeting would be in the Inspector General's office at Justice. We're doing it here because it's to everybody's convenience with the ceremony today, but the IG rules apply. This is a matter of some diplomatic sensitivity. No tape."

"Tell her the charges, Mr. Krendler," Noonan said.

"Agent Starling, you stand accused of unlawful disclosure of sensitive material to a fugitive felon," Krendler said, his face under careful control. "Specifically you are accused of placing this advertisement in two Italian newspapers warning the fugitive Hannibal Lecter that he was in danger of being captured."

The marshal brought Starling a page of smudged newsprint from *La Nazione*. She turned it to the window to read the circled material:

A. A. Aaron—Turn yourself in to the nearest authorities, enemies are close. Hannah.

"How do you respond?"

"I didn't do it. I never saw this before."

"How do you account for the fact that the letter uses a code name 'Hannah' known only to Dr. Hannibal Lecter and this Bureau? The code name Lecter asked you to use?"

"I don't know. Who found this?"

"The Document Service at Langley happened to see it in the course of translating *La Nazione*'s coverage on Lecter."

"If the code is a secret within the Bureau, how did Document Service at Langley recognize it in the paper? CIA runs Document Service. Let's ask them who brought 'Hannah' to their attention."

"I'm sure the translator was familiar with the case file."

"*That* familiar? I doubt it. Let's ask him who suggested he watch out for it. How would I have known Dr. Lecter was in Florence?"

"You're the one who found the computer query from the Questura in Florence to the Lecter VICAP file," Krendler said. "The query came several days prior to the Pazzi murder. We don't know when you discovered it. Why else would the Questura in Florence be asking about Lecter?"

"What possible reason would I have to warn him? Director Noonan, why is this a matter for the IG? I'm prepared to take a polygraph examination anytime. Wheel it in here."

"The Italians registered a diplomatic protest over the attempted warning of a known felon in their country," Noonan said. He indicated the red-haired man beside him. "This is Mr. Montenegro from the Italian Embassy."

"Good morning, sir. And the *Italians* found out how?" Starling said. "Not from Langley."

"The diplomatic beef puts the ball in our court," Krendler said before Montenegro could open his mouth. "We want this cleaned up to the satisfaction of the Italian authorities, and to my satisfaction and that of the IG, and we want it PDQ. It's better for everybody if we look at all the facts together. What is it with you and Dr. Lecter, Ms. Starling?"

"I interrogated Dr. Lecter several times on the orders of Section Chief Crawford. Since Dr. Lecter's escape I've had two letters from him in seven years. You have both of them," Starling said.

"Actually, we have more," Krendler said. "We got this yesterday.

What else you might have received, we don't know." He reached behind him to get a cardboard box, much stamped and much battered by the mails.

Krendler pretended to enjoy the fragrances coming from the box. He indicated the shipping label with his finger, not bothering to show Starling. "Addressed to you at your home in Arlington, Special Agent Starling. Mr. Montenegro, would you tell us what these items are?"

The Italian diplomat poked through the tissue-wrapped items, his cufflinks winking.

"Yes, this are lotions, *sapone di mandorle*, the famous almond soap of Santa Maria Novella in Florence, from the Farmacia there, and some perfumes. The sort of thing people are giving when they felt in love."

"These have been scanned for toxins and irritants, right, Clint?" Noonan asked Starling's former supervisor.

Pearsall looked ashamed. "Yes," he said. "There's nothing wrong with them."

"A gift of love," Krendler said with some satisfaction. "Now we have the mash note." He unfolded the sheet of parchment from the box and held it up, revealing the tabloid picture of Starling's face with the winged body of a lioness. He turned the sheet to read Dr. Lecter's copperplate script: "*Did you ever think, Clarice, why the Philistines don't understand you? It's because you're the answer to Samson's riddle: You are the honey in the lion.*"

"*Il miele dentro la leonessa*, that's nice," Montenegro said, filing it away for his own use at a later time.

"It's *what?*" Krendler said.

The Italian waved the question away, seeing that Krendler would never hear the music in Dr. Lecter's metaphor, nor feel its tactile evocations anywhere else.

"The Inspector General wants to take it from here, because of the international ramifications," Krendler said. "Which way it will go, administrative charges or criminal, depends on what we find out in our ongoing probe. If it goes criminal, Special Agent Starling, it'll be turned over to the Public Integrity Section of the Justice Department, and PIS will take it to trial. You'll be informed in plenty of time to prepare. Director Noonan . . ."

Noonan took a deep breath and swung the axe. "Clarice Starling, I'm placing you on administrative leave until such time as this matter is adjudicated. You will surrender weapons and FBI identification. Your access is revoked to all but public federal facilities. You will be escorted from the building. Please surrender your sidearms and ID now to Special Agent Pearsall. Come."

Walking to the table, Starling saw the men for a second as bowling pins at a shooting contest. She could kill the four of them before one could clear his weapon. The moment passed. She took out her .45, looked steadily at Krendler as she dropped the clip into her hand, put the clip on the table and shucked the round out of the pistol's chamber. Krendler caught it in the air and squeezed it until his knuckles turned white.

Badge and ID went next.

"You have a backup sidearm?" Krendler said. "And a shotgun?"

"Starling?" Noonan prompted.

"Locked in my car."

"Other tactical equipment?"

"A helmet and a vest."

"Mr. Marshal, you will retrieve those when you escort Miss Starling to her vehicle," Krendler said. "Do you have an encryption cell phone?"

"Yes."

Krendler raised his eyebrows to Noonan.

"Turn it in," Noonan said.

"I want to say something, I think I'm entitled to that."

Noonan looked at his watch. "Go ahead."

"This is a frame. I think Mason Verger is trying to capture Dr. Lecter himself for purposes of personal revenge. I think he just missed him in Florence. I think Mr. Krendler may be in collusion with Verger and wants the FBI's effort against Dr. Lecter to work for Verger. I think Paul Krendler of the Department of Justice is making money out of this and I think he is willing to destroy me to do it. Mr. Krendler has behaved toward me before in an inappropriate manner and is acting now out of spite as well as financial self-interest. Only this week he called me a 'cornpone country pussy.' I would challenge Mr. Krendler before this body to take a lie detector test with me on these matters. I'm at your convenience. We could do it now."

"Special Agent Starling, it's a good thing you're not sworn here today—" Krendler began.

"*Swear* me. You swear too."

"I want to assure you, if the evidence is lacking you're entitled to full reinstatement without prejudice," Krendler said in his kindliest voice. "In the meantime you'll receive pay and remain eligible for insurance and medical benefits. The administrative leave is not itself punitive, Agent Starling, use it to your advantage," Krendler said, adopting a confidential tone. "In fact, if you wanted to take this hiatus to have that dirt taken out of your cheek, I'm sure the medical—"

"It's not dirt," Starling said. "It's gunpowder. No wonder you didn't recognize it."

The marshal was waiting, his hand outstretched to her.

"I'm sorry, Starling," Clint Pearsall said, his hands full of her equipment.

She looked at him and looked away. Paul Krendler drifted toward her as the other men waited to let the diplomat, Montenegro, leave the room first. Krendler started to say something between his teeth, he had it ready: "Starling, you're old to still be—"

"Excuse me." It was Montenegro. The tall diplomat had turned away from the door and come to her.

"Excuse me," Montenegro said again, looking into Krendler's face until he went away, his face twisted.

"I am sorry this has happen to you," he said. "I hope you are innocent. I promise I will press the Questura in Florence to find out how the *inserzione*, the ad, was paid for at *La Nazione*. If you think of something in . . . in my sphere of Italy to follow up, please tell me and I will insist on it." Montenegro handed her a card, small and stiff and bumpy with engraving and seemed not to notice Krendler's outstretched hand as he left the room.

Reporters, cleared through the main entrance for the coming anniversary ceremony, thronged in the courtyard. A few seemed to know whom to watch for.

"Do you have to hold my elbow?" Starling asked the marshal.

"No, ma'am, I don't," he said, and made a way for her through the boom microphones and the shouted questions.

This time Razor Cut seemed to know the issue. The questions he shouted were "Is it true that you've been suspended from the Hannibal Lecter case? Do you anticipate criminal charges being brought against you? What do you say to the Italian charges?"

In the garage, Starling handed over her protective vest, her helmet, her shotgun and her backup revolver. The marshal waited while she unloaded the little pistol and wiped it down with an oily cloth.

"I saw you shoot at Quantico, Agent Starling," he said. "I got to the quarterfinals myself for the marshal's service. I'll wipe down your .45 before we put it up."

"Thank you, Marshal."

He lingered after she was in the car. He said something over the boom of the Mustang. She rolled down the window and he said it again.

"I hate this happening to you."

"Thank you, sir. I appreciate you saying it."

A press chase car was waiting outside the garage exit. Starling pushed the Mustang to lose him and got a speeding ticket three blocks from the J. Edgar Hoover Building. Photographers took pictures while the D.C. patrolman wrote it out.

Assistant Director Noonan sat at his desk after the meeting was over, rubbing the spots his glasses left on the sides of his nose.

Getting rid of Starling didn't bother him so much—he believed there was an emotional element in women that often didn't fit in with the Bureau. But it hurt him to see Jack Crawford cut down. Jack had been very much one of the boys. Maybe Jack had a blind spot for the Starling girl, but that happens—Jack's wife was dead and all. Noonan had a week once when he couldn't keep from looking at an attractive stenographer and he had to get rid of her before she caused some trouble.

Noonan put on his glasses and took the elevator down to the library. He found Jack Crawford in the reading area, in a chair with his head back against the wall. Noonan thought he was asleep. Crawford's face was gray and he was sweating. He opened his eyes and gasped.

"Jack?" Noonan patted his shoulder, then touched his clammy face. Noonan's voice then, loud in the library. "You, librarian, call the medics!"

Crawford went to the FBI infirmary, and then to the Jefferson Memorial Intensive Care Cardiac Unit.

KRENDLER COULD not have asked for better coverage.

The ninetieth birthday of the FBI was combined with a tour for newsmen of the new crisis management center. Television news took full advantage of this unaccustomed access to the J. Edgar Hoover Building, C-SPAN carrying former President Bush's remarks in full, along with those of the Director, in live programming. CNN excerpted the speeches in running coverage and the networks covered for the evening news. It was as the dignitaries filed off the dais that Krendler had his moment. Young Razor Cut, standing near the stage, posed the question: "Mr. Krendler, is it true that Special Agent Clarice Starling has been suspended in the Hannibal Lecter investigation?"

"I think it would be premature, and unfair to the agent, to comment on that, at the moment. I'll just say that the Inspector General's office is looking into the Lecter matter. No charges have been filed against anyone."

CNN caught a whiff too. "Mr. Krendler, Italian news sources are saying Dr. Lecter may have received information improperly from a government source warning him to flee. Is that the basis of

Special Agent Starling's suspension? Is that why the Inspector General's office is involved rather than the internal Office of Professional Responsibility?"

"I can't comment on foreign news reports, Jeff. I *can* say the IG's office is investigating allegations that so far have not been proven. We have as much responsibility toward our own officers as we do our friends overseas," Krendler said, poking his finger into the air like a Kennedy. "The Hannibal Lecter matter is in good hands, not just the hands of Paul Krendler, but experts drawn from all the disciplines of the FBI and the Justice Department. We have a project under way that we can reveal in due time when it has borne fruit."

The German lobbyist who was Dr. Lecter's landlord furnished his house with an enormous Grundig television set, and tried to blend it into the décor by putting one of his smaller bronzes of Leda and the Swan on top of the ultramodern cabinet.

Dr. Lecter was watching a film called *A Brief History of Time*, about the great astrophysicist Stephen Hawking and his work. He had watched it many times before. This was his favorite part, where the teacup falls off the table and smashes on the floor.

Hawking, twisted in his wheelchair, speaks in his computer-generated voice:

"Where does the difference between the past and the future come from? The laws of science do not distinguish between the past and the future. Yet there is a big difference between the past and future in ordinary life.

"You may see a cup of tea fall off of a table and break into pieces on the floor. But you will never see the cup gather itself back together and jump back on the table."

The film, run backward, shows the cup reassembling itself on the table. Hawking continues:

"The increase of disorder or entropy is what distinguishes the past from the future, giving a direction to time."

Dr. Lecter admired Hawking's work very much and followed it as closely as he could in the mathematical journals. He knew that Hawking had once believed the universe would stop expanding and would shrink again, and entropy might reverse itself. Later Hawking said he was mistaken.

Lecter was quite capable in the area of higher mathematics, but Stephen Hawking is on another plane entirely from the rest of us. For years Lecter had teased the problem, wanting very much for Hawking to be right the first time, for the expanding universe to stop, for entropy to mend itself, for Mischa, eaten, to be whole again.

Time. Dr. Lecter stopped his videotape and turned to the news.

Television and news events involving the FBI are listed daily on the FBI's public Web site. Dr. Lecter visited the Web site every day to make sure they were still using his old photograph among the Ten Most Wanted. So he learned of the FBI birthday in plenty of time to tune in. He sat in a great armchair in his smoking jacket and ascot and watched Krendler lie. He watched Krendler with his eyes half closed, holding his brandy snifter close under his nose and swirling the contents gently. He had not seen that pale face since Krendler stood outside his cage in Memphis seven years ago, just before his escape.

On the local news from Washington, he saw Starling receive a traffic ticket with microphones stuck in the window of her Mustang. By now the television news had Starling "accused of breaching U.S. security" in the Lecter case.

Dr. Lecter's maroon eyes opened wide at the sight of her and in the depths of his pupils sparks flew around his image of her face. He held her countenance whole and perfect in his mind long after she was gone from the screen, and pressed her with another image, Mischa, pressed them together until, from the red plasma core of their fusion, the sparks flew upward, carrying their single image to the east, into the night sky to wheel with the stars above the sea.

Now, should the universe contract, should time reverse and teacups come together, a place could be made for Mischa in the world. The worthiest place that Dr. Lecter knew: Starling's place. Mischa could have Starling's place in the world. If it came to that, if that time came round again, Starling's demise would leave a place for Mischa as sparkling and clean as the copper bathtub in the garden.

CHAPTER
74

DR. LECTER parked his pickup a block from Maryland-Misericordia Hospital and wiped his quarters before he put them in the meter. Wearing the quilted jumpsuit workmen wear against the cold, and a long-billed cap against the security cameras, he went in the main entrance.

It had been more than fifteen years since Dr. Lecter was in Maryland-Misericordia Hospital, but the basic layout appeared unchanged. Seeing this place where he began his medical practice meant nothing to him. The secure areas upstairs had undergone cosmetic renovation, but should be almost the same as when he practiced here, according to the blueprints at the Department of Buildings.

A visitor's pass from the front desk got him onto the patient floors. He walked along the hall reading the names of patients and doctors on the doors of the rooms. This was the postoperative convalescent unit, where patients came when released from Intensive Care after cardiac or cranial surgery.

Watching Dr. Lecter proceed down the hall, you might have thought he read very slowly, as his lips moved soundlessly, and he scratched his head from time to time like a bumpkin. Then he took a seat in the waiting room where he could see the hallway. He waited an hour and a half among old women recounting family tragedies, and endured *The Price Is Right* on television. At last he saw what he was waiting for, a surgeon still in surgical greens making rounds alone. This would be . . . the surgeon was going in to see a patient of . . . Dr. Silverman. Dr. Lecter rose and scratched. He picked up a blowzy newspaper from an end table and walked out of the waiting room. Another room with a Silverman patient was two doors down. Dr. Lecter slipped inside. The room was semidark, the patient satisfactorily asleep, his head and the side of his face heavily bandaged. On the monitor screen, a worm of light humped steadily.

Dr. Lecter quickly stripped off his insulated coveralls to reveal surgical greens. He pulled on shoe covers and a cap and mask and gloves. He took out of his pocket a white trash bag and unfolded it.

Dr. Silverman came in speaking over his shoulder to someone in the hall. *Was a nurse coming with him? No.*

Dr. Lecter picked up the wastebasket and began to tip the contents into his trash bag, his back to the door.

"Excuse me, Doctor, I'll get out of your way," Dr. Lecter said.

"That's all right," Dr. Silverman said, picking up the clipboard at the end of the bed. "Do what you need to do."

"Thank you," Dr. Lecter said, and swung the leather sap against the base of the surgeon's skull, just a flip of the wrist, really, and caught him around the chest as he sagged. It is always surprising to watch Dr. Lecter lift a body; size for size he is as strong as an ant. Dr. Lecter carried Dr. Silverman into the patient's bathroom and pulled down his pants. He set Dr. Silverman on the toilet.

The surgeon rested there with his head hanging forward over his knees. Dr. Lecter raised him up long enough to peer into his pupils and remove the several ID tags clipped to the front of his surgical greens.

He replaced the doctor's credentials with his own visitor's pass, inverted. He put the surgeon's stethoscope around his own neck in the fashionable boa drape and the doctor's elaborate magnifying surgical glasses went on top of his head. The leather sap went up his sleeve.

Now he was ready to penetrate to the heart of Maryland-Misericordia.

The hospital adheres to strict federal guidelines in handling narcotic drugs. On the patient floors, the drug cabinets on each nurse's station are locked. Two keys, held by the duty nurse and her first assistant, are required to get in. A strict log is kept.

In the operating suites, the most secure area of the hospital, each suite is furnished with drugs for the next procedure a few minutes before the patient is brought in. The drugs for the anesthesiologist are placed near the operating table in a cabinet that has one area refrigerated and one at room temperature.

The stock of drugs is kept in a separate surgical dispensary near the scrub room. It contains a number of preparations that would not be found in the general dispensary downstairs, the powerful sedatives and exotic sedative-hypnotics that make possible open-heart surgery and brain surgery on an aware and responsive patient.

The dispensary is always manned during the working day, and the cabinets are not locked while the pharmacist is in the room. In a heart surgery emergency there is no time to fumble for a key. Dr. Lecter, wearing his mask, pushed through the swinging doors to the surgical suites.

In an effort at cheer, the surgery had been painted in several bright color combinations even the dying would find aggravating. Several doctors ahead of Dr. Lecter signed in at the desk and proceeded to the scrub room. Dr. Lecter picked up the sign-in clipboard and moved a pen over it, signing nothing.

The posted schedule showed a brain tumor removal in Suite B scheduled to start in twenty minutes, the first of the day. In the scrub room, he pulled off his gloves and put them in his pockets, washed up thoroughly, working up to his elbows, dried his hands and powdered them and regloved. Out into the hall now. The dispensary should be the next door on the right. No. A door painted apricot with the sign EMERGENCY GENERATORS and ahead the double doors of Suite B. A nurse paused at his elbow.

"Good morning, Doctor."

Dr. Lecter coughed behind his mask and muttered good morning. He turned back toward the scrub room with a mutter as though he had forgotten something. The nurse looked after him for a moment and went on into the operating theater. Dr. Lecter stripped off his gloves and shot them into the waste bin. Nobody was paying attention. He got another pair. His body was in the scrub room, but in fact he raced through the foyer of his memory palace, past the bust of Pliny and up the stairs to the Hall of Architecture. In a well-lit area dominated by Christopher Wren's model of St Paul's, the hospital blueprints were waiting on a drawing table. The Maryland-Misericordia surgical suites blueprints line for line from the Baltimore Department of Buildings. He was here. The dispensary was there. No. The drawings were wrong. Plans must have been changed after the blueprints were filed. The generators were shown on the other side in mirror-image space off the corridor to Suite A. Perhaps the labels were reversed. Had to be. He could not afford to poke around.

Dr. Lecter came out of the scrub room and started down the corridor to Suite A. Door on the left. The sign said MRI. Keep going. The next door was Dispensary. They had split the space on the plan into a lab for magnetic resonance imaging and a separate drug storage area.

The heavy dispensary door was open, wedged with a doorstop. Dr. Lecter ducked quickly into the room and pulled the door closed behind him.

A pudgy male pharmacist was squatting, putting something on a low shelf.

"Can I help you, Doctor?"

"Yes, please."

The young man started to stand, but never made it. Thump of the sap, and the pharmacist broke wind as he folded on the floor.

Dr. Lecter raised the tail of his surgical blouse and tucked it behind the gardener's apron he wore beneath.

Up and down the shelves fast, reading labels at lightning speed; *Ambien, amobarbital, Amytal, chloral hydrate, Dalmane, flurazepam, Halcion,* and raking dozens of vials into his pockets. Then he was in the refrigerator, reading and raking, *midazolam, Noctec, scopolamine, Pentothal, quazepam, solzidem.* In less than forty seconds, Dr. Lecter was back in the hall, closing the dispensary door behind him.

He passed back through the scrub room and checked himself for lumps in the mirrors. Without haste, back through the swinging doors, his ID tag deliberately twisted upside down, mask on and the glasses down over his eyes, binocular lenses raised, pulse seventy-two, exchanging gruff greetings with other doctors. Down in the elevator, down and down, mask still on, looking at a clipboard he had picked up at random.

Visitors coming in might have thought it odd that he wore his surgical mask until he was well down the steps and away from the security cameras. Idlers on the street might have wondered why a doctor would drive such a ratty old truck.

Back in the surgical suite an anesthesiologist, after pecking impatiently on the door of the dispensary, found the pharmacist still unconscious and it was another fifteen minutes before the drugs were missed.

When Dr. Silverman came to, he had slumped to the floor beside the toilet with his pants down. He had no memory of coming into the room and had no idea where he was. He thought he might have had a cerebral event, possibly a strokelet occasioned by the strain of a bowel movement. He was very leery of moving for fear of dislodging a clot. He eased himself along the floor until he could put his hand out into the hall. Examination revealed a mild concussion.

Dr. Lecter made two more stops before he went home. He paused at a mail drop in suburban Baltimore long enough to pick up a package he had ordered on the Internet from a funeral supply company. It was a tuxedo with the shirt and tie already installed, and the whole split up the back.

All he needed now was the wine, something truly, truly festive. For that he had to go to Annapolis. It would have been nice to have had the Jaguar for the drive.

KRENDLER WAS dressed for jogging in the cold and had to unzip his running suit to keep from overheating when Eric Pickford called him at his Georgetown home.

"Eric, go to the cafeteria and call me on a pay phone."

"Excuse me, Mr. Krendler?"

"Just do what I tell you."

Krendler pulled off his headband and gloves and dropped them on the piano in his living room. With one finger he pecked out the theme from *Dragnet* until the conversation resumed: "Starling was a techie, Eric. We don't know how she might have rigged her phones. We'll keep the government's business secure."

"Yes, sir."

"Starling called me, Mr. Krendler. She wanted her plant and stuff— that stupid weather bird that drinks out of the glass. But she told me something that worked. She said to discount the last digit on the zip codes for the suspect magazine subscriptions if the difference is three or less. She said Dr. Lecter might use several mail drops that were conveniently close to each other."

"And?"

"I got a hit that way. The *Journal of Neurophysiology*'s going to one zip code and *Physica Scripta* and *ICARUS* are going to another. They're about ten miles apart. The subscriptions are in different names, paid with money orders."

"What's *ICARUS*?"

"It's the international journal of solar system studies. He was a charter subscriber twenty years ago. The mail drops are in Baltimore. They usually deliver the journals about the tenth of the month. Got one more thing, a minute ago, a sale on a bottle of Château, what is it, *Yuckum?*"

"Yeah, it's pronounced like EEE-Kim. What about it?"

"High-end wine store in Annapolis. I entered the purchase and it hit on the sensitive dates list Starling put in. The program hit on Starling's birth year. That's the year they made this wine, her birth year. Subject paid three hundred twenty-five dollars cash for it and—"

"This was before or after you talked with Starling?"

"Just after, just a minute ago—"

"So she doesn't know it."

"No. I should call—"

"Are you saying the merchant called you on a single-bottle purchase?"

"Yes, sir. She's got notes here, there are only three bottles like that on the East Coast. She'd notified all three. You've got to admire it."

"Who bought it—what did he look like?"

"White male, medium height with a beard. He was bundled up."

"Has the wine store got a security camera?"

"Yes, sir, that's the first thing I asked. I said we'd send somebody for the tape. I haven't done it yet. The wine store clerk hadn't read the bulletin, but he told the owner because it was such an unusual purchase. Owner ran outside in time to see the subject—he thinks it was the subject—driving away in an old pickup truck. Gray with a vise on the back. If it's Lecter, you think he'll try to deliver it to Starling? We better alert her."

"No," Krendler said. "Don't tell her."

"Can I post the VICAP bulletin board and the Lecter file?"

"*No*," Krendler said, thinking fast. "Have you got a reply from the Questura about Lecter's computer?"

"No, sir."

"Then you can't post VICAP until we can be sure Lecter's not reading it himself. He could have Pazzi's access code. Or Starling could be reading it and tipping him some way like she did in Florence."

"Oh, *right*, I see. Annapolis FO can get the tape."

"Leave it all strictly to me."

Pickford dictated the address of the wine store.

"Keep going on the subscriptions," Krendler instructed. "You can tell Crawford about the subscriptions when he comes back to work. He'll organize coverage on the mail drops after the tenth."

Krendler called Mason's number, and started out running from his Georgetown town house, trotting easily toward Rock Creek Park.

In the gathering gloom only his white Nike headband and his white Nike shoes, and the white stripe down the side of his dark Nike running suit were visible, as though there were no man at all among the trademarks.

It was a brisk half-hour run. He heard the blat of helicopter blades just as he came in sight of the landing pad near the zoo. He was able to duck under the turning propeller blades and reach the step without ever breaking stride. The lift of the jet helicopter thrilled him, the city, the lighted monuments falling away as the aircraft took him to the heights he deserved, to Annapolis for the tape and to Mason.

"WILL YOU focus the fucking thing, Cordell?" In Mason's deep radio voice, with its lipless consonants, "focus" and "fucking" sounded more like "hocus" and "hucking."

Krendler stood beside Mason in the dark part of the room, the better to see the elevated monitor. In the heat of Mason's room he had his yuppie running suit pulled down to his waist and the sleeves tied around him, exposing his Princeton T-shirt. His headband and shoes gleamed in the light from the aquarium.

In Margot's opinion Krendler had the shoulders of a chicken. They had barely acknowledged one another when he arrived.

There was no tape or time counter on the liquor store security camera and Christmas business was brisk. Cordell was pushing fast-forward from customer to customer through a lot of purchases. Mason passed the time by being unpleasant.

"What did you say when you went in the liquor store in your running suit and flashed the tin, Krendler? You say you were in the Special Olympics?" Mason was much less respectful since Krendler had been depositing the checks.

Krendler could not be insulted when his interests were at stake.

"I said I was undercover. What kind of coverage have you got on Starling now?"

"Margot, tell him." Mason seemed to want to save his own scarce breath for insults.

"We brought in twelve men from our security in Chicago. They're in Washington. Three teams, one member of each is deputized in the state of Illinois. If the police catch them grabbing Dr. Lecter, they say they recognized him and it's a citizen's arrest and blah blah. The team that catches turns him over to Carlo. They go back to Chicago and that's all they know."

The tape was running.

"Wait a minute—Cordell, back it up thirty seconds," Mason said. "Look at this."

The liquor store camera covered the area from the front door to the cash register.

In the silent videotape's fuzzy image, a man came in wearing a billed cap, a lumber jacket and mittens. He had full whiskers and wore sunglasses. He turned his back to the camera and carefully closed the door behind him.

It took a moment for the shopper to explain to the clerk what he wanted and he followed the man out of sight into the wine racks.

Three minutes dragged by. At last they came back into camera range. The clerk wiped dust off the bottle and wrapped padding around it before he put it in a bag. The customer pulled off only his right mitten and paid in cash. The clerk's mouth moved as he said "thank you" to the man's back as he was leaving.

A pause of a few seconds, and the clerk called to someone off camera. A heavyset man came into the picture and hurried out the door.

"That's the owner, guy who saw the truck," Krendler said.

"Cordell, can you copy off this tape and enlarge the customer's head?"

"Take a second, Mr. Verger. It'll be fuzzy."

"Do it."

"He kept the left mitten on," Mason said. "I may have gotten screwed on that X ray I bought."

"Pazzi said he got his hand fixed, didn't he? Had the extra finger off," Krendler said.

"Pazzi might have had his finger up his butt, I don't know who to believe. You've seen him, Margot, what do you think? Was that Lecter?"

"It's been eighteen years," Margot said. "I just had three sessions with him and he always just stood up behind his desk when I came in, he didn't walk around. He was really still. I remember his voice more than anything else."

Cordell's voice on the intercom. "Mr. Verger, Carlo is here."

Carlo smelled of the pigs and more. He came into the room holding his hat over his chest and the rank boar-sausage smell of his head made Krendler blow air out his nose. As a mark of respect, the Sardinian kidnapper withdrew all the way into his mouth the stag's tooth he was chewing.

"Carlo, look at this. Cordell, roll it back and walk him in from the door again."

"That's the *stronzo* son of bitch," Carlo said before the subject on the screen had walked four paces. "The beard is new, but that's the way he moves."

"You saw his hands in *Firenze*, Carlo."

"*Sì.*"

"Five fingers or six on the left?"

". . . Five."

"You hesitated."

"Only to think of *cinque* in English. It's five, I'm sure."

Mason parted his exposed teeth in all he had for a smile. "I love it. He's wearing the mitten trying to keep the six fingers in his description," he said.

Perhaps Carlo's scent had entered the aquarium via the aeration pump. The eel came out to see, and remained out, turning, turning in his infinite Möbius eight, showing his teeth as he breathed.

"Carlo, I think we may finish this soon," Mason said. "You and Piero and Tommaso are my first team. I've got confidence in you, even though he did beat you in Florence. I want you to keep Clarice Starling under surveillance for the day before her birthday, the day itself, and the day after. You'll be relieved while she's asleep in her house. I'll give you a driver and the van."

"*Padrone*," Carlo said.

"Yes."

"I want some private time with the *dottore*, for the sake of my brother, Matteo. You said I could have it." Carlo crossed himself as he mentioned the dead man's name.

"I understand your feelings completely, Carlo. You have my deepest sympathy. Carlo, I want Dr. Lecter consumed in two sittings. The first evening, I want the pigs to gnaw off his feet, with him watching through the bars. I want him in good shape for that. You bring him to me in good shape. No blows to the head, no broken bones, no eye damage. Then he can wait overnight without his feet, for the pigs to finish him the next day. I'll talk to him for a while, and then you can have him for an hour before the final sitting. I'll ask you to leave him an eye and leave him conscious so he can see them coming. I want him to see their faces when they eat his face. If you, say, should decide to unman him, it's entirely up to you, but I want Cordell there to manage the bleeding. I want film."

"What if he bleeds to death the first time in the pen?"

"He won't. Nor will he die overnight. What he'll do overnight is wait with his feet eaten off. Cordell will see to that and replace his body fluids, I expect he'll be on an IV drip all night, maybe two drips."

"Or four drips if we have to," said Cordell's disembodied voice on the speakers. "I can do cut-downs on his legs."

"You can spit and piss in his IV at the last, before you roll him into the pen," Mason told Carlo in his most sympathetic voice. "Or you can come in it if you like."

Carlo's face brightened at the thought, then he remembered the muscular *signorina* with a guilty sideways glance. "*Grazie mille, Padrone.* Can you come to see him die?"

"I don't know, Carlo. The dust in the barn disturbs me. I may watch on video. Can you bring a pig to me? I want to put my hand on one."

"To this room, *Padrone*?"

"No, they can bring me downstairs briefly, on the power pack."

"I would have to put one to sleep, *Padrone*," Carlo said doubtfully.

"Do one of the sows. Bring her on the lawn outside the elevator. You can run the forklift over the grass."

"You figure on doing this with one van, or a van and a crash car?" Krendler asked.

"Carlo?"

"The van is plenty. Give me a deputy to drive."

"I've got something else for you," Krendler said. "Can we have some light?"

Margot moved the rheostat and Krendler put his backpack on the table beside the bowl of fruit. He put on cotton gloves and took out what appeared to be a small monitor with an antenna and a mounting bracket, along with an external hard drive and a rechargeable battery pack.

"It's awkward covering Starling because she lives in a cul-de-sac with no place to lurk. But she has to come out—Starling's an exercise freak," Krendler said. "She's had to join a private gym since she can't use the FBI stuff anymore. We caught her parked at the gym Thursday and put a beacon under her car. It's Ni-Cad and recharges when the motor's running so she won't find it from a battery drain. The software covers these five contiguous states. Who's going to work this thing?"

"Cordell, come in here," Mason said.

Cordell and Margot knelt beside Krendler and Carlo stood over them, his hat held at the height of their nostrils.

"Look here." Krendler switched his monitor on. "It's like a car navigation system except it shows where Starling's car is." An overview of metropolitan Washington appeared on the screen. "Zoom here, move the area with the arrows, got it? Okay, it's not showing any acquisition. A signal from Starling's beacon will light this, and you'll hear a beep. Then you can pick up the source on overview and zoom in. The beep gets faster as you get closer. Here's Starling's neighborhood in street-map scale. You're not getting any blip from her car because we're out of range. Anywhere in metro Washington or Arlington you would. I picked it up from the helicopter coming out. Here's the converter for the AC plug in your van. One thing. You have to guarantee me this thing never gets in the wrong hands. I could get heat from this, it's not in the spy shops yet. Either it's back in my hands or it's in the bottom of the Potomac. You got it?"

"You understand that, Margot?" Mason said. "You, Cordell? Get Mogli to drive and brief him."

V

A POUND OF FLESH

THE BEAUTY of the pneumatic rifle was that it could be fired with the muzzle inside the van without deafening everyone around it—there was no need to stick the muzzle out the window where the public could see it.

The mirrored window would open a few inches and the small hypodermic projectile would fly, carrying a major load of acepromazine into the muscle mass of Dr. Lecter's back or buttocks.

There would be only the crack of the gun's muzzle signature, like a green branch breaking, no bang and no ballistic report from the subsonic missile to draw attention.

The way they had rehearsed it, when Dr. Lecter started to collapse, Piero and Tommaso, dressed in white, would "assist" him into the van, assuring any bystanders they were taking him to the hospital. Tommaso's English was best, as he had studied it in seminary, but the *h* in hospital was giving him a fit.

Mason was right in giving the Italians the prime dates for catching Dr. Lecter. Despite their failure in Florence, they were by far the most capable at physical man-catching and the most likely to take Dr. Lecter alive.

Mason allowed only one gun on the mission other than the tranquilizer rifle—that of the driver, Deputy Johnny Mogli, an off-duty sheriff's deputy from Illinois and long a creature of the Vergers. Mogli grew up speaking Italian at home. He was a person who agreed with everything his victim said before he killed him.

Carlo and the brothers Piero and Tommaso had their net, beanbag gun, Mace, and a variety of restraints. It would be plenty.

They were in position at daylight, five blocks from Starling's house in Arlington, parked in a handicap spot on a commercial street.

The van today was marked with adhesive signs, SENIOR CITIZEN MEDICAL TRANSPORT. It had a handicap tag hanging from the mirror and a false handicap license plate on the bumper. In the glove compartment was a receipt from a body shop for recent replacement of the bumper—they could claim a mix-up at the garage and confuse the issue for the time being if the tag number were questioned. The vehicle identification numbers and registration was legitimate. So were the hundred-dollar bills folded inside them for a bribe.

The monitor, Velcroed to the dashboard and running off the cigarette lighter socket, glowed with a street map of Starling's neighborhood. The same Global Positioning Satellite that now plotted the position of the van also showed Starling's vehicle, a bright dot in front of her house.

At 9:00 A.M., Carlo allowed Piero to eat something. At 10:30 Tommaso could eat. He did not want them both full at the same time, in the event of a long chase on foot. Afternoon meals were staggered too. Tommaso was rummaging in the cooler for a sandwich at midafternoon when they heard the beep.

Carlo's malodorous head swung to the monitor.

"She's moving," Mogli said. He started the van.

Tommaso put the lid back on the cooler.

"Here we go. Here we go . . . Here she goes up Tindal toward the main road." Mogli swung into traffic. He had the great luxury of lying back three blocks where Starling could not possibly see him.

Nor could Mogli see the old gray pickup pull into traffic a block behind Starling, a Christmas tree hanging over the tailgate.

Driving the Mustang was one of the few pleasures Starling could count on. The powerful car, with no ABS and no traction control, was a handful on slick streets for much of the winter. While the roads were clear it was pleasant to wind the V8 out a little in second gear and listen to the pipes.

Mapp, a world-class couponeer, had sent with Starling a thick sheaf of her discount coupons pinned to the grocery list. She and Starling were doing a ham, a pot roast and two casseroles. Others were bringing the turkey.

A holiday dinner on her birthday was the last thing Starling cared about. She had to go along with it because Mapp and a surprising number of female agents, some of whom she only knew slightly and didn't particularly like, were turning out to support her in her misery.

Jack Crawford weighed on her mind. She couldn't visit him in intensive care, nor could she call him. She left notes for him at the nursing station, funny dog pictures with the lightest messages she could compose.

Starling distracted herself in her misery by playing with the Mustang, double-clutching and downshifting, using engine compression to slow for the turn into the Safeway supermarket parking lot, touching her brakes only to flash the brake lights for the drivers behind her.

She had to make four laps of the parking lot before she found a parking place, empty because it was blocked by an abandoned grocery cart. She got out and moved the cart. By the time she parked, another shopper had taken the basket.

She found a grocery cart near the door and rolled it toward the grocery store.

Mogli could see her turn in and stop on the screen of his monitor and in the distance he could see the big Safeway coming up on his right.

"She's going in the grocery store." He turned into the parking lot. It took a few seconds to spot her car. He could see a young woman pushing a cart toward the entrance.

Carlo put the glasses on her. "That's Starling. She looks like her pictures." He handed the glasses to Piero.

"I'd like to take her picture," Piero said. "I got my zoom right here."

There was a handicap parking space across the parking lane from her car. Mogli pulled into it, ahead of a big Lincoln with handicap plates. The driver honked angrily.

Now they were looking out the back window of the van at the tail of Starling's car.

Perhaps because he was used to looking at American cars, Mogli spotted the old truck first, parked at a distant parking place near the edge of the lot. He could only see the gray tailgate of the pickup.

He pointed the truck out to Carlo. "Has he got a vise on the tailgate? That what the liquor store guy said? Put the glasses on it, I can't see for the fucking tree. *Carlo, c'è una morsa sul camione?*"

"*Sì.* Yes, it's there, the vise. Nobody inside."

"Should we cover her in the store?" Tommaso did not often question Carlo.

"No, if he does it, he'll do it here," Carlo said.

The dairy items were first. Starling, consulting her coupons, selected cheese for a casserole and some heat 'em and eat 'em rolls. *Damn making scratch rolls for this crowd.* She had reached the meat counter when she realized she had forgotten butter. She left her cart and went back for it.

When she returned to the meat department, her cart was gone. Someone had removed her few purchases and put them on a shelf nearby. They had kept the coupons, and the list.

"God damn it," Starling said, loudly enough for nearby shoppers to hear. She looked around her. Nobody had a thick sheaf of coupons in sight. She took a couple of deep breaths. She could lurk near the cash registers and try to recognize her list, if they still had it clipped to the coupons. What the hell, couple of bucks. Don't let it ruin your day.

There were no free grocery carts near the registers. Starling went outside to find another one in the parking lot.

"*Ecco!*" Carlo saw him coming between the vehicles with his quick, light stride, Dr. Hannibal Lecter in a camel's hair overcoat and a fedora, carrying a gift in an act of utter whimsy. "*Madonna!* He's coming to her car." Then the hunter in Carlo took over and he began to control his breathing, getting ready for the shot. The stag's tooth he was chewing appeared briefly through his lips.

The back window of the van did not roll down.

"*Metti in moto!* Back around with your side to him," Carlo said.

Dr. Lecter stopped by the passenger side of the Mustang, then changed his mind and went to the driver's side, possibly intending to give the steering wheel a sniff.

He looked around him and slid the slim-jim out of his sleeve.

The van was broadside now. Carlo ready with the rifle. He touched the electric window button. Nothing happened.

Carlo's voice, unnaturally calm now in action. "*Mogli, il finestrino!*"

Had to be the child safety lock, Mogli fumbled for it.

Dr. Lecter plunged the slim-jim into the crack beside the window and unlocked the door of Starling's car. He started to get in.

With an oath Carlo slid the side door open a crack and raised the rifle, Piero moving out of his way, the van rocking as the rifle cracked.

The dart flashed in the sunlight and with a small *thock* went through Dr. Lecter's starched collar and into his neck. The drug worked fast, a big dose in a critical place. He tried to straighten up, but his knees were going. The package dropped from his hands and rolled under the car. He managed to get a knife out of his pocket and open it as he slumped between the door and the car, the tranquilizer turning his limbs to water. "Mischa," he said as his vision failed.

Piero and Tommaso were on him like big cats, pinning him down between the cars until they were sure he was weak.

Starling, trundling her second grocery cart of the day across the lot, heard the slap of the air rifle and recognized it instantly as a muzzle signature—she ducked by reflex as the people around her shuffled along, oblivious. Hard to tell where it came from. She looked in the direction of her car, saw a man's legs disappearing into a van and thought it was a mugging.

She slapped her side where the gun no longer lived and began to run, dodging through the cars toward the van.

The Lincoln with the elderly driver was back, honking to get in the handicapped spot blocked by the van, drowning out Starling yelling.

"Hold it! Stop! FBI! Stop or I'll shoot!" Maybe she could get a look at the plate.

Piero saw her coming and, moving fast, cut the valve stem off Starling's front tire on the driver's side with Dr. Lecter's knife and dived into the van. The van bumped over a parking median and away toward the exit. She could see the plate. She wrote the number in dirt on the hood of a car with her finger.

Starling had her keys out. She heard the hissing of air rushing out the valve stem as she got to her car. She could see the top of the van moving toward the exit.

She tapped on the window of the Lincoln, honking at her now. "Do you have a cell phone? FBI, please, do you have a cell phone?"

"Go on, Noel," the woman in the car said, poking the driver's leg and pinching. "This is just trouble, it's some kind of trick. Don't get involved." The Lincoln pulled away.

Starling ran for a pay phone and called 911.

Deputy Mogli drove the speed limit for fifteen blocks.

Carlo pulled the dart from Dr. Lecter's neck, relieved when the hole didn't spurt. There was a hematoma about the size of a quarter under his skin. The injection was supposed to be diffused by a major muscle mass. The son of a bitch might die yet, before the pigs could kill him.

There was no talking in the van, only the heavy breathing of the men and the quacking of the police scanner under the dash. Dr. Lecter lay on the floor of the van in his fine overcoat, his hat rolled off his sleek head, one spot of bright blood on his collar, elegant as a pheasant in a butcher's case.

Mogli pulled into a parking garage and drove up to the third level, only pausing long enough to peel the signs off the sides of the van and change the plates.

He needn't have bothered. He laughed to himself when the police scanner picked up the bulletin. The 911 operator, apparently misunderstanding Starling's description of a "gray van or minibus," issued an all-points bulletin for a Greyhound bus. It must be said that 911 got all but one digit of the false license plate right.

"Just like Illinois," Mogli said.

"I saw the knife, I was afraid he'd kill himself to get out of what's coming," Carlo told Piero and Tommaso. "He'll wish he had cut his throat."

When Starling checked her other tires, she saw the package on the ground beneath her car.

A three-hundred-dollar bottle of Château d'Yquem, and the note, written in that familiar hand: *Happy Birthday, Clarice.*

It was then that she understood what she had seen.

78

STARLING HAD the numbers that she needed in her mind. Drive ten blocks home to her own phone? No, back to the pay phone, taking the sticky receiver from a young woman, apologizing, putting in quarters, the woman summoning a grocery store guard.

Starling called the reactive squad at Washington Field Office, Buzzard's Point.

They knew all about Starling on the squad where she had served so long, and transferred her to Clint Pearsall's office, she digging for more quarters and dealing with the grocery store security guard at the same time, the guard asking again and again for ID.

At last Pearsall's familiar voice on the phone.

"Mr. Pearsall, I saw three men, maybe four, kidnap Hannibal Lecter in the Safeway parking lot about five minutes ago. They cut my tire, I couldn't pursue."

"Is this the bus business, the police APB?"

"I don't know about any bus. This was a gray van, handicap plate." Starling gave the number.

"How do you know it was Lecter?"

"He . . . left a gift for me, it was under my car."

"I see . . ." Pearsall paused and Starling jumped into the silence.

"Mr. Pearsall, you know Mason Verger's behind it. It has to be. Nobody else would do it. He's a sadist, he'll torture Dr. Lecter to death and he'll want to watch. We need to put out a BOLO on all Verger's vehicles and get the U.S. Attorney in Baltimore started on a warrant to search his place."

"Starling . . . Jesus, Starling. Look, I'll ask you one time. Are you sure about what you saw? Think about it a second. Think about every good thing you ever did here. Think about what you swore. There's no going back from here. What did you see?"

What should I say—I'm not a hysteric? That's the first thing hysterics say. She saw in the instant how far she had fallen in Pearsall's trust, and of what cheap material his trust was made.

"I saw three men, maybe four, kidnap a man on the parking lot at Safeway. At the scene I found a gift from Dr. Hannibal Lecter, a bottle of Château d'Yquem wine from my birth year with a note in his handwriting. I have described the vehicle. I am reporting it to you, Clint Pearsall, SAC Buzzard's Point."

"I'm going forward with it as kidnapping, Starling."

"I'm coming over there. I could be deputized and go with the reactive squad."

"Don't come, I couldn't let you in."

Too bad Starling didn't get away before the Arlington police arrived in the parking lot. It took fifteen minutes to correct the all-points bulletin on the vehicle. A thick woman officer in heavy patent-leather shoes took Starling's statement. The woman's ticket book and radio, Mace and gun and handcuffs, stood out at angles from her big behind and the vents of her jacket gaped. The officer could not decide whether to enter Starling's place of employment as the FBI, or to put "None." When Starling angered her by anticipating her questions, the officer slowed down. When Starling pointed out the tracks of mud and snow tires where the van bumped over the divider, nobody responding had a camera. She showed the officers how to use hers.

Over and over in her head as she repeated her answers, Starling told herself, *I should have pursued, I should have pursued. I should have snatched his ass out of that Lincoln and pursued.*

CHAPTER

79

KRENDLER CAUGHT the first squeal on the kidnapping. He called around to his sources and then he got Mason on a secure phone.

"Starling saw the snatch, we hadn't counted on that. She's making a flap at the Washington Field Office. Recommending a warrant to search your place."

"Krendler . . ." Mason waited for breath, or perhaps he was exasperated, Krendler couldn't tell. "I've already registered complaints with the local authorities, the sheriff and the U.S. Attorney's office that Starling was harassing me, calling late at night with incoherent threats."

"Has she?"

"Of course not, but she can't prove she didn't and it muddies the water. Now, I can head off a warrant in this county and in this state. But I want you to call the U.S. Attorney over here and remind him this hysterical bitch is after me. I can take care of the locals myself, believe me."

80

FREE AT last from the police, Starling changed her tire and drove home to her own phones and computer. She sorely missed her FBI cell phone and had not yet replaced it.

There was a message from Mapp on the answering machine: "Starling, season the pot roast and put it in the slow cooker. Do *not* put the vegetables in yet. Remember what happened last time. I'll be in a damn exclusion hearing until about five."

Starling fired up her laptop and tried to call up the Violent Criminal Apprehension Program file on Lecter, but was denied admission not only to VICAP, but the entire FBI computer net. She did not have as much access as the most rural constable in America.

The telephone rang.

It was Clint Pearsall. "Starling, have you harassed Mason Verger on the phone?"

"Never, I swear."

"He claims you have. He's invited the sheriff up there to tour his property, actually requested him to come do it, and they're on the way to look around now. So there's no warrant and no warrant forthcoming. We haven't been able to find any other witnesses to the kidnapping. Only you."

"There was a white Lincoln with an old couple in it. Mr. Pearsall, how about checking the credit card purchases at Safeway just before it happened? Those sales have a time stamp."

"We'll get to that, but it'll . . ."

". . . it'll take time," Starling finished.

"Starling?"

"Yes, sir?"

"Between us, I'll keep you posted on the big stuff. But you stay out of it. You're not a law officer while you're on suspension, and you're not supposed to have information. You're Joe Blow."

"Yes, sir, I know."

What do you look at while you're making up your mind? Ours is not a reflective culture, we do not raise our eyes up to the hills. Most of the time we decide the critical things while looking at the linoleum floor of an institutional corridor, or whispering hurriedly in a waiting room with a television blatting nonsense.

Starling, seeking something, anything, walked through the kitchen into the quiet and order of Mapp's side of the duplex. She looked at the photograph of Mapp's fierce little grandmother, brewer of the tea. She looked at Grandmother Mapp's insurance policy framed on the wall. Mapp's side looked like Mapp lived there.

Starling went back to her side. It looked to her like nobody lived there. What did she have framed? Her diploma from the FBI Academy. No photograph of her parents survived. She had been without them for a long time and she had them only in her mind. Sometimes, in the flavors of breakfast or in a scent, a scrap of conversation, a homely expression overheard, she felt their hands on her: She felt it strongest in her sense of right and wrong.

Who the hell was she? Who had ever recognized her?

You are a warrior, Clarice. You can be as strong as you wish to be.

Starling could understand Mason wanting to kill Hannibal Lecter. If he had done it himself or had hired it done, she could have stood it; Mason had a grievance.

But she could not abide the thought of Dr. Lecter tortured to death; she shied from it as she had from the slaughter of the lambs and the horses so long ago.

You are a warrior, Clarice.

Almost as ugly as the act itself was the fact that Mason would do this with the tacit agreement of men sworn to uphold the law. It is the way of the world.

With this thought, she made a simple decision:

The world will not be this way within the reach of my arm.

She found herself in her closet, on a stool, reaching high.

She brought down the box John Brigham's attorney had delivered to her in the fall. It seemed forever ago.

There is much tradition and mystique in the bequest of personal weapons to a surviving comrade in arms. It has to do with a continuation of values past individual mortality.

People living in a time made safe for them by others may find this difficult to understand.

The box John Brigham's guns came in was a gift in itself. He must have bought it in the Orient when he was a Marine. A mahogany box with the lid inlaid in mother of pearl. The weapons were pure Brigham, well worn, well maintained and immaculately clean. An M1911A1 Colt .45 pistol, and a Safari Arms cut-down version of the .45 for concealed carry, a boot dagger with one serrated edge. Starling had her own leather. John Brigham's old FBI badge was mounted on a mahogany plaque. His DEA badge was in the box loose.

Starling pried the FBI badge off the plaque and put it in her pocket. The .45 went in her Yaqui slide behind her hip, covered by her jacket.

The short .45 went on one ankle, the knife on the other, inside her boots. She took her diploma out of the frame and folded it for her pocket. In the dark somebody might mistake it for a warrant. As she creased the heavy paper, she knew she was not quite herself, and she was glad.

Another three minutes at her laptop. From the Mapquest Web site she printed out a large-scale map of the Muskrat Farm and the national forest around it. For a moment she looked at Mason's meat kingdom, traced its boundaries with her finger.

The Mustang's big pipes blew the dead grass flat as she pulled out of her driveway to call on Mason Verger.

A HUSH over Muskrat Farm like the quiet of the old Sabbath. Mason excited, terribly proud that he could bring this off. Privately, he compared his accomplishment to the discovery of radium.

Mason's illustrated science text was the best-remembered of his schoolbooks; it was the only book tall enough to allow him to masturbate in class. He often looked at an illustration of Madame Curie while doing this, and he thought of her now and the tons of pitchblende she boiled to get the radium. Her efforts were very much like his, he thought.

Mason imagined Dr. Lecter, the product of all his searching and expenditure, glowing in the dark like the vial in Madame Curie's laboratory. He imagined the pigs that would eat him going to sleep afterward in the woods, their bellies glowing like lightbulbs.

It was Friday evening, nearly dark. The maintenance crews were gone. None of the workers had seen the van arrive, as it did not come by the main gate, but by the fire road through the national forest that served as Mason's service road. The sheriff and his crew had completed their cursory search and were well away before the van arrived at the barn. Now the main gate was manned and only a trusted skeleton crew remained at Muskrat:

Cordell was at his station in the playroom—overnight relief for Cordell would drive in at midnight. Margot and Deputy Mogli, still wearing his badge from cozening the sheriff, were with Mason, and the crew of professional kidnappers were busy in the barn.

By the end of Sunday it would all be done, the evidence burnt or roiling in the bowels of the sixteen swine. Mason thought he might feed the eel some delicacy from Dr. Lecter, his nose perhaps. Then for years to come Mason could watch the ferocious ribbon, ever circling in its figure eight, and know that the infinity sign it made stood for Lecter dead forever, dead forever.

At the same time, Mason knew that it is dangerous to get exactly what you want. What would he do after he had killed Dr. Lecter? He could wreck some foster homes, and torment some children. He could drink martinis made with tears. But where was the hard-core fun coming from?

What a fool he would be to dilute this ecstatic time with fears about the future. He waited for the tiny spray against his eye, waited for his goggle to clear, then puffed his breath into a tube switch: Anytime he liked he could turn on his video monitor and see his prize . . .

THE SMELL of a coal fire in the tack room of Mason's barn and the resident smells of animals and men. Firelight on the trotting horse Fleet Shadow's long skull, empty as Providence, watching it all in blinkers.

Red coals in the farrier's furnace flare and brighten with the hiss of the bellows as Carlo heats a strap of iron, already cherry-red.

Dr. Hannibal Lecter hangs on the wall beneath the horse skull like a terrible altarpiece. His arms are outstretched straight from his shoulders on either side, well bound with rope to a singletree, a thick oak crosspiece from the pony cart harness. The singletree runs across the doctor's back like a yoke and is fastened to the wall with a shackle of Carlo's manufacture. His legs do not reach the floor. His legs are bound over his trousers like roasts rolled and tied, with many spaced coils, each coil knotted. No chain or handcuffs are used—nothing metal that would damage the teeth of the pigs and discourage them.

When the iron in the furnace reaches white heat, Carlo brings it to the anvil with his tongs and swings his hammer, beating the bright strap into a shackle, red sparks flying in the semidark, bouncing off his chest, bouncing on the hanging figure of Dr. Hannibal Lecter.

Mason's TV camera, odd among the ancient tools, peers at Dr. Lecter from its spidery metal tripod. On the workbench is a monitor, dark now.

Carlo heats the shackle again, and hurries with it outside to attach it to the forklift while it is glowing and pliable. His hammer echoes in the vast height of the barn, the blow and its echo, *BANG-bang, BANG-bang.*

A scratchy chirping from the loft as Piero finds a rebroadcast of the soccer game on shortwave. His Cagliari team is playing hated Juventus in Rome.

Tommaso sits in a cane chair, the tranquilizer rifle propped against the wall beside him. His dark priest's eyes never leave Dr. Lecter's face.

Tommaso detects a change in the stillness of the bound man. It is a subtle change, from unconsciousness to unnatural self-control, perhaps no more than a difference in the sound of his breathing.

Tommaso gets up from his chair and calls out into the barn.

"Si sta svegliando."

Carlo returns to the tack room, the stag's tooth flicking in and out of his mouth. He is carrying a pair of trouser legs stuffed with fruit and greens and chickens. He rubs the trousers against Dr. Lecter's body and under his arms.

Keeping his hand carefully away from the face, he seizes Lecter's hair and raises his head.

"Buona sera, Dottore."

A crackle from the speaker on the TV monitor. The monitor lights and Mason's face appears . . .

"Turn on the light over the camera," Mason said. "Good evening, Dr. Lecter."

The doctor opened his eyes for the first time.

Carlo thought sparks flew behind the fiend's eyes, but it might have been a reflection of the fire. He crossed himself against the Evil Eye.

"Mason," the doctor said to the camera. Behind Mason, Lecter could see Margot's silhouette, black against the aquarium. "Good evening, Margot," his tone courteous now. "I'm glad to see you again." From the clarity of his speech, Dr. Lecter may have been awake for some time.

"Dr. Lecter," came Margot's hoarse voice.

Tommaso found the sun gun over the camera and turned it on.

The harsh light blinded them all for a second.

Mason in his rich radio tones: "Doctor, in about twenty minutes we're going to give the pigs their first course, which will be your feet. After that we'll have a little pajama party, you and I. You can wear shorties by then. Cordell's going to keep you alive for a long time—"

Mason was saying something further, Margot leaning forward to see the scene in the barn.

Dr. Lecter looked into the monitor to be sure Margot was watching him. Then he whispered to Carlo, his metallic voice urgent in the kidnapper's ear:

"Your brother, Matteo, must smell worse than you by now. He shit when I cut him."

Carlo reached to his back pocket and came out with the electric cattle prod. In the bright light of the TV camera, he whipped it across the side of Lecter's head. Holding the doctor's hair with one hand, he pressed the button on the handle, holding the prod close in front of Lecter's face as the high-voltage current arced in a wicked line between the electrodes on the end.

"Fuck your mother," he said and plunged it arcing into Dr. Lecter's eye.

Dr. Lecter made no sound—the sound came from the speaker, Mason roaring as his breath permitted him, and Tommaso strained to pull Carlo away. Piero came down from the loft to help. They sat Carlo down in the cane chair. And held him.

"Blind him and there's no money!" they screamed in both his ears at once.

Dr. Lecter adjusted the shades in his memory palace to relieve the terrible glare. Ahhhhh. He leaned his face against the cool marble flank of Venus.

Dr. Lecter turned his face full to the camera and said clearly: "I'm not taking the chocolate, Mason."

"Sumbitch is crazy. Well, we knew he was crazy," said Deputy Sheriff Mogli. "But Carlo is too."

"Go down there and get between them," Mason said.

"You sure they got no guns?" Mogli said.

"You hired out to be tough, didn't you? No. Just the tranquilizer gun."

"Let me do it," Margot said. "Keep from starting some macho crap between them. The Italians respect their mamas. And Carlo knows I handle the money."

"Walk the camera out and show me the pigs," Mason said. "Dinner's at eight!"

"I don't have to stay for that," Margot said.

"Oh, yes you do," Mason said.

MARGOT TOOK a deep breath outside the barn. If she was willing to kill him, she ought to be willing to look at him. She could smell Carlo before she opened the door to the tack room. Piero and Tommaso stood on either side of Lecter. They faced Carlo, seated in the chair.

"*Buona sera, signori,*" Margot said. "Your friends are right, Carlo. You ruin him now, no money. And you've come so far and done so well."

Carlo's eyes never left Dr. Lecter's face.

Margot took a cell phone from her pocket. She punched numbers on its lighted face and held it out to Carlo. "Take it." She held it in his line of vision. "Read it."

The automatic dialer read BANCO STEUBEN.

"That's your bank in Cagliari, Signor Deogracias. Tomorrow morning, when this is done, when you've made him pay for your brave brother, then I'll call this number and tell your banker my code and say, 'Give Signor Deogracias the rest of the money you hold for him.' Your banker will confirm it to you on the phone. Tomorrow evening you'll be in the air, on your way home, a rich man. Matteo's family will be rich too. You can take them the doctor's *cojones* in a zip-lock bag to comfort them. But if Dr. Lecter can't see his own death, if he can't see the pigs coming to eat his face, you get nothing. Be a man, Carlo. Go get your pigs. I'll sit with the son of a bitch. In half an hour you can hear him scream while they eat his feet."

Carlo threw his head back and took a deep breath. *"Piero, andiamo! Tu, Tommaso, rimani."*

Tommaso took his seat in the cane chair beside the door.

"I've got it under control, Mason," Margot said to the camera.

"I'll want to bring his nose with me back to the house. Tell Carlo," Mason said. The screen went dark. Moving out of his room was a major effort for Mason and the people around him, requiring reconnection of his tubes to containers on his traveling gurney and switching over his hard-shell respirator to an AC power pack.

Margot looked into Dr. Lecter's face.

His injured eye was swollen shut between the black burn marks the electrodes had left at each end of his eyebrow.

Dr. Lecter opened his good eye. He was able to keep the cool feeling of Venus' marble flank on his face.

"I like the smell of that liniment, it smells cool and lemony," Dr. Lecter said. "Thank you for coming, Margot."

"That's exactly what you said to me when the matron brought me into your office the first day. When they were doing presentencing on Mason the first time."

"Is that what I said?" Having just returned from the memory palace where he read over his interviews with Margot, he knew it to be so.

"Yes. I was crying, dreading to tell you about Mason and me. I was dreading having to sit down too. But you never asked me to sit—you knew I had stitches, didn't you? We walked in the garden. Do you remember what you told me?"

"You were no more at fault for what happened to you—"

"'—than if I had been bitten on the behind by a mad dog' was what you said. You made it easy for me then, and the other visits too, and I appreciated it for a while."

"What else did I tell you?"

"You said you were much weirder than I would ever be," she said. "You said it was all right to be weird."

"If you try, you can remember everything we ever said. Remember—"

"Please don't beg me now." It jumped out of her, she didn't mean to say it that way.

Dr. Lecter shifted slightly and the ropes creaked.

Tommaso got up and came to check his bonds. "*Attenzione alla bocca, Signorina.* Be careful of the mouth."

She didn't know if Tommaso meant Dr. Lecter's mouth or his words.

"Margot, it's been a long time since I treated you, but I want to talk to you about your medical history, just for a moment, privately." He cut his good eye toward Tommaso.

Margot thought for a moment. "Tommaso, could you leave us for a moment."

"No, I'm sorry, Signorina, but I stand outside with the door open." Tommaso went with the rifle out into the barn and watched Dr. Lecter from a distance.

"I'd never make you uncomfortable by begging, Margot. I would be interested to know *why* you're doing this. Would you tell me that? Have you started taking the chocolate, as Mason likes to say, after you fought him so long? We don't need to pretend you're revenging Mason's face."

She did tell him. About Judy, about wanting the baby. It took her less than three minutes; she was surprised at how easily her troubles summarized.

A distant noise, a screech and half a scream. Outside in the barn, against the fence he had erected across the open end of the barn, Carlo was fiddling with his tape recorder, preparing to summon the pigs from the wooded pasture with recorded cries of anguish from victims long dead or ransomed.

If Dr. Lecter heard, he did not show it. "Margot, do you think Mason will just *give* you what he promised? You're begging Mason. Did begging help you when he tore you? It's the same thing as taking his chocolate and letting him have his way. But he'll make Judy eat the cheese. And she's not used to it."

She did not answer, but her jaw set.

"Do you know what would happen if, instead of crawling to Mason, you just stimulated his prostate gland with Carlo's cattle prod? See it there by the workbench?"

Margot started to get up.

"*Listen to me,*" the doctor hissed. "Mason will deny you. You know you'll have to kill him, you've known it for twenty years. You've known it since he told you to bite the pillow and not make so much noise."

"Are you saying you'd do it *for* me? I could never trust you."

"No, of course not. But you could trust me *never to deny that I did it*. It would actually be more therapeutic for you to kill him yourself. You'll remember I recommended that when you were a child."

"'Wait until you can get away with it,' you said. I took some comfort from that."

"Professionally, that's the sort of catharsis I had to recommend. You're old enough now. And what difference would one more murder charge make to me? You know you'll have to kill him. And when you do, the law will follow the money—right to you and the new baby. Margot, I'm the only other suspect you've got. *If I'm dead before Mason, who would the suspect be?* You can do it when it suits you and I'll write you a letter gloating about how I enjoyed killing him myself."

"No, Dr. Lecter, I'm sorry. It's too late. I've got my arrangements made." She looked into his face with her bright butcher's blue eyes. "I can do this and sleep afterward, and you know I can."

"Yes, I know you can. I always liked that in you. You are much more interesting, more . . . capable than your brother."

She got up to go. "I'm sorry, Dr. Lecter, for what that's worth."

Before she reached the door, he said, "Margot, when does Judy ovulate again?"

"What? In two days, I think."

"Do you have everything else you need? Extenders, equipment to fast-freeze?"

"I've got all the facilities of a fertilization clinic."

"Do one thing for me."

"Yes?"

"Curse at me and snatch out a piece of my hair, back from the hairline if you don't mind. Get a little skin. Hold it in your hand walking back to the house. Think about putting it in Mason's hand. After he's dead.

"When you get to the house, ask Mason for what you want. See what he says. You've delivered me, your part of the bargain is complete. Hold the hair in your hand and ask him for what you want. See what he says. When he laughs in your face, come back here. All you have to do is take the tranquilizer rifle and shoot the one behind you. Or hit him with the hammer. He has a pocketknife. Just cut the ropes on one arm and give me the knife. And leave. I can do the rest."

"No."

"Margot?"

She put her hand on the door, braced against a plea.

"Can you still crack a walnut?"

She reached in her pocket and brought out two. The muscles of her forearm bunched and the nuts cracked.

The doctor chuckled. "Excellent. With all that strength, walnuts. You can offer Judy walnuts to help her get past the taste of Mason."

Margot walked back to him, her face set. She spat in his face and jerked out a lock of his hair near the top of his head. It was hard to know how she meant it.

She heard him humming as she left the room.

As Margot walked toward the lighted house, the little divot of scalp stuck to the palm of her hand with blood, the hair hanging from her hand and she did not even need to close her fingers around it.

Cordell passed her in a golf cart loaded with medical equipment to prepare the patient.

84

FROM THE expressway overpass northbound at Exit 30, Starling could see a half-mile away the lighted gatehouse, far outpost of Muskrat Farm. Starling had made up her mind on the drive to Maryland: she would go in the back way. If she went to the front gate with no credentials and no warrant she'd get a sheriff's escort out of the county, or to the county jail. By the time she was free again, it would all be done.

Never mind permission. She drove up to Exit 29, well beyond Muskrat Farm, and came back along the service road. The blacktop road seemed very dark after the expressway lights. It was bounded by the expressway on her right, on the left a ditch and a high chain-link fence separated the roadway from the looming black of the national forest. Starling's map showed a gravel fire road intersecting this blacktop a mile farther along and well out of sight of the gatehouse. It was where she had mistakenly stopped on her first visit. According to her map, the fire road ran through the national forest to Muskrat Farm. She was measuring by her odometer. The Mustang seemed louder than usual, running just above idle, booming off the trees.

There it was in her headlights, a heavy gate welded of metal pipe and topped with barbed wire. The SERVICE ENTRANCE sign she had seen on her first visit was gone now. Weeds had grown up in front of the gate and over the ditch-crossing with its culvert.

She could see in her headlights that the weeds had recently been pressed down. Where the fine grit and sand had washed off the pavement and made a little sandbar, she could see the tracks of mud-and-snow tires. Were they the same as the van tracks she saw in the parking median at Safeway? She didn't know if they were exactly the same, but they could have been.

A chrome padlock and chain secured the gate. No sweat there. Starling looked up and down the road. Nobody coming. *A little illegal entry here.* It felt like a crime. She checked the gateposts for sensor wires. None. Working with two picks and holding her little flashlight in her teeth, it took her less than fifteen seconds to open the padlock. She drove through the entrance and continued well into the trees before she walked back to close the gate. She draped the chain back on the gate with the padlock on the outside. From a little distance it looked normal. She left the loose ends inside so she could butt it open more easily with the car if she had to.

Measuring on the map with her thumb, it was about two miles through the forest to the farm. She drove through the dark tunnel of the fire road, the night sky sometimes visible overhead, sometimes not, as the branches closed overhead. She eased along in second gear at little over an idle, with just the parking lights, trying to keep the Mustang as quiet as possible, dead weeds brushing the undercarriage. When the odometer said a mile and eight-tenths, she stopped. With the engine off, she could hear a crow calling in the dark. *The crow was pissed at something.* She hoped to God it was a crow.

85

CORDELL CAME into the tack room brisk as a hangman, intravenous bottles under his arms, tubes dangling from them. "*The* Dr. Hannibal Lecter!" he said. "I wanted that mask of yours so badly for our club in Baltimore. My girlfriend and I have a *dungeony* sort of thing, sort of Jay-O and leather."

He put his things down on the anvil stand and put a poker in the fire to heat.

"Good news and bad news," Cordell said in his cheerful nursey voice and faint Swiss accent. "Did Mason tell you the drill? The drill is, in a little while I'll bring Mason down here and the pigs will get to eat your feet. Then you'll wait overnight and tomorrow Carlo and his brothers will feed you through the bars head first, so the pigs can eat your face, just like the dogs ate Mason's. I'll keep you going with IVs and tourniquets until the last. You really *are* done, you know. That's the bad news."

Cordell glanced at the TV camera to be sure it was off. "The *good* news is, it doesn't *have* to be much worse than a trip to the dentist. Check this out, *Doctor*." Cordell held a hypodermic syringe with a long needle in front of Dr. Lecter's face. "Let's talk like two medical people. I could get behind you and give you a spinal that would keep you from feeling *anything* down there. You could just close your eyes and try not to listen. You'd just feel some jerking and pulling. And once Mason's got his jollies for the evening and gone to the house I could give you something that would just stop your heart. Want to see it?" Cordell palmed a vial of Pavulon and held it close enough to Dr. Lecter's open eye, but not close enough to get bitten.

The firelight played on the side of Cordell's avid face, his eyes were hot and happy. "You've got lots of money, Dr. Lecter. Everybody says so. *I* know how this stuff works—I put money around in places too. Take it out, move it, *fuss* with it. I can move mine on the phone and I bet you can too."

Cordell took a cell phone from his pocket. "We'll call your banker, you say him a code, he'll confirm to me and I'll fix you right up." He held up the spinal syringe. "Squirt, squirt. Talk to me."

Dr. Lecter mumbled, his head down. "Suitcase" and "locker" were all Cordell could hear.

"Come on, Doctor, and then you can just sleep. Come on."

"Unmarked hundreds," Dr. Lecter said, and his voice trailed away.

Cordell leaned closer and Dr. Lecter struck to the length of his neck, caught Cordell's eyebrow in his small sharp teeth and ripped a sizeable piece of it out as Cordell leaped backward. Dr. Lecter spit the eyebrow like a grape skin into Cordell's face.

Cordell mopped the wound and put a tape butterfly on it that gave him a quizzical expression.

He packed up his syringe. "All that relief, wasted," he said. "You'll look at it differently before daylight. You know I have stimulants to take you quite the other way. And I'll make you wait."

He took the poker from the fire.

"I'm going to hook you up now," Cordell said. "Whenever you resist me I'll burn you. This is what it feels like."

He touched the glowing end of the poker to Dr. Lecter's chest and crisped his nipple through his shirt. He had to smother the widening circle of fire on the doctor's shirtfront.

Dr. Lecter did not make a sound.

Carlo backed the forklift into the tack room. With Piero and Carlo lifting together, Tommaso ever ready with the tranquilizer rifle, they moved Dr. Lecter to the fork and shackled his singletree to the front of the machine. He was seated on the fork, his arms bound to the singletree, with his legs extended, each leg fastened to one tine of the fork.

Cordell inserted an IV needle with a butterfly into the back of each of Dr. Lecter's hands. He had to stand on a bale of hay to hang the plasma bottles on the machine on each side of him. Cordell stood back and admired his work. Odd to see the doctor splayed there with an IV in each hand, like a parody of something Cordell couldn't quite remember. Cordell rigged slip-knot tourniquets just above each knee with cords that could be pulled behind the fence to keep the doctor from bleeding to death. They could not be tightened now. Mason would be furious if Lecter's feet were numb.

Time to get Mason downstairs and put him in the van. The vehicle, parked behind the barn, was cold. The Sards had left their lunch in it. Cordell cursed and threw their cooler out on the ground. He'd have to vacuum the fucking thing at the house. He'd have to air it out too. The fucking Sards had been smoking in here too, after he forbade it. They'd replaced the cigarette lighter and left the power cord of the car beacon monitor still swinging from the dash.

86

STARLING SWITCHED off the Mustang's interior light and pulled the trunk release before she opened the door.

If Dr. Lecter was here, if she could get him, maybe she could put him cuffed hand and foot in the trunk and get as far as the county jail. She had four sets of cuffs and enough line to hog-tie him and keep him from kicking. Better not to think about how strong he was.

There was some frost on the gravel when she put her feet out. The old car groaned as her weight came off the springs.

"Got to complain, don't you, you old son of a bitch," she said to the car beneath her breath. Suddenly she remembered talking to Hannah, the horse she rode away into the night from the slaughter of the lambs. She did not close the car door all the way. The keys went into a tight trouser pocket so they would not tinkle.

The night was clear under a quarter moon and she could walk without her flashlight as long as there was some open night sky. She tried the edge of the gravel and found it loose and uneven. Quieter to walk in a packed wheel track in the gravel, looking ahead to judge how the road lay with her peripheral vision, her head slightly turned to the side. It was like wading in soft darkness, she could hear her feet crunch the gravel but she couldn't see the ground.

The hard moment came when she was out of sight of the Mustang, but could still feel its loom behind her. She did not want to leave it.

She was suddenly a thirty-three-year-old woman, alone, with a ruined civil service career and no shotgun, standing in a forest at night. She saw herself clearly, saw the crinkles of age beginning in the corners of her eyes. She wanted desperately to go back to her car. Her next step was slower, she stopped and she could hear herself breathing.

The crow called, a breeze rattled the bare branches above her and then the scream split the night. A cry so horrible and hopeless, peaking, falling, ending in a plea for death in a voice so wracked it could have been anyone. "*Uccidimi!*" And the scream again.

The first one froze Starling, the second one had her moving at a trot, wading fast through the dark, the .45 still holstered, one hand holding the dark flashlight, the other extended into the night before her. *No, you don't, Mason. No, you don't. Hurry. Hurry.* She found she could stay in the packed track by listening to her footfalls, and feeling the loose gravel on either side. The road turned and ran along a fence. Good fence, pipe fence, six feet high.

Came sobs of apprehension and pleas, the scream building, and ahead of Starling, beyond the fence, she heard movement through brush, the movement breaking into a trot, lighter than the hoofbeats of a horse, quicker in rhythm. She heard grunting she recognized.

Closer the agonized sounds, clearly human, but distorted, with a single squeal over the cries for a second, and Starling knew she was hearing either a recording or a voice amplified with feedback in the microphone. Light through the trees and the barn looming. Starling pressed her head on the cold iron to look through the fence. Dark shapes rushing, long and hip-high. Across forty yards of clear ground the open end of a barn with the great doors open wide, a barrier across the end of the barn with a Dutch gate in it, and an ornate mirror suspended above the gate, the mirror reflecting the light of the barn in a bright patch on the ground. Standing in the clear pasture outside the barn, a stocky man in a hat with a boom box radio/tape player. He covered one ear with his hand as a series of howls and sobs came from the machine.

Out of the brush now they came, the wild swine with their savage faces, wolflike in their speed, long-legged and deep-chested, shaggy, spiky gray bristles.

Carlo dashed back through the Dutch gate and closed it when they were still thirty yards from him. They stopped in a semicircle waiting, their great curved tusks holding their lips in a permanent snarl. Like linemen anticipating the snap of the ball, they surged forward, stopped, jostled, grunting, clicking their teeth.

Starling had seen livestock in her time, but nothing like these hogs. There was a terrible beauty in them, grace and speed. They watched the doorway, jostling and rushing forward, then backing, always facing the barrier across the open end of the barn.

Carlo said something over his shoulder and disappeared back into the barn.

The van backed into view inside the barn. Starling recognized the gray vehicle at once. It stopped at an angle near the barrier. Cordell got out and opened the sliding side door. Before he turned off the dome light, Starling could see Mason inside in his hard-shell respirator, propped on pillows, his hair coiled on his chest. A ringside seat. Floodlights came on over the doorway.

From the ground beside him, Carlo picked up an object Starling did not recognize at first. It looked like someone's legs, or the lower half of a body. If it was half a body, Carlo was very strong. For a second Starling feared it was the remains of Dr. Lecter, but the legs bent wrong, bent in ways the joints would not permit.

They could only be Lecter's legs if he had been wheeled and braided, she thought for a bad moment. Carlo called into the barn behind him. Starling heard a motor start.

The forklift came into Starling's view, Piero driving, Dr. Lecter raised high with the fork, his arms spread on the singletree and the IV bottles swaying above his hands with the movement of the vehicle. Held high so that he could see the ravening swine, could see what was coming.

The forklift came at an awful processional speed, Carlo walking beside it and on the other side Johnny Mogli, armed.

Starling fixed on Mogli's deputy badge for an instant. A star, not like the locals' badges. White hair, white shirt, like the driver of the kidnap van.

From the van came Mason's deep voice. He hummed "Pomp and Circumstance" and giggled.

The pigs, raised with noise, were not afraid of the machine, they seemed to welcome it.

The forklift stopped near the barrier. Mason said something to Dr. Lecter that Starling could not hear. Dr. Lecter did not move his head or give any sign that he had heard. He was higher even than Piero at the controls. Did he look in Starling's direction? She never knew because she was moving fast along the fence line, along the side of the barn, finding the double doors where the van had backed in.

Carlo sailed the stuffed trousers into the pigpen. The hogs leaped forward as one, room for two on each leg, shouldering the others aside. Tearing, snarling, pulling and ripping, dead chickens in the trouser legs coming to pieces, pigs shaking their heads from side to side with chicken guts flailing. A field of tossing bristled backs.

Carlo had only provided the lightest of appetizers, just three chickens and a little salad. In moments the trousers were rags and the slavering pigs turned their avid little eyes back to the barrier.

Piero lowered the fork to just the height above ground level. The upper part of the Dutch gate would keep the pigs away from Dr.

Lecter's vitals for the time being. Carlo removed the doctor's shoes and socks.

"This little piggy went EEE EEE EEE all the way home," Mason called from the van.

Starling was coming up behind them. All were facing the other way, facing the pigs. She passed the tack room door, moved out into the center of the barn.

"Now, don't let him bleed out," Cordell said from the van. "Be ready when I tell you to tighten the tourniquets." He was clearing Mason's goggle with a cloth.

"Anything to say, Dr. Lecter?" came Mason's deep voice.

The .45 boomed in the enclosure of the barn and Starling's voice: *"Hands up and freeze. Turn off the motor."*

Piero seemed not to understand.

"Fermate il motore," Dr. Lecter said helpfully.

Only the impatient squealing of the pigs now.

She could see one gun, on the hip of the white-haired man wearing the star. Holster with a thumb break. *Put the men on the ground first.*

Cordell slid behind the wheel fast, the van moving. Mason yelling at him. Starling swung with the van, caught the white-haired man's movement in the corner of her eye, swung back to him as he pulled his gun to kill her, him yelling *"Police,"* and she shot him twice in the chest, a fast double tap.

His .357 shot two feet of fire toward the ground, he went back a half step and to his knees, looking down at himself, his badge tuliped by the fat .45 slug that had passed through it and tumbled sideways through his heart.

Mogli went over backward and lay still.

In the tack room, Tommaso heard the shots. He grabbed the air rifle and climbed to the hayloft, dropped to his knees in the loose hay and crawled toward the side of the hayloft that overlooked the barn.

"Next," Starling said in a voice she did not know. Do this fast while

Mogli's death still had them. "On the ground, *you*, head toward the wall. *You*, on the ground, head this way. *This way*."

"*Girati dall' altra parte*," Dr. Lecter explained from the forklift.

Carlo looked up at Starling, saw that she would kill him and lay still. She cuffed them fast with one hand, their heads in opposite directions, Carlo's wrist to Piero's ankle and Piero's ankle to Carlo's wrist. All the time the cocked .45 behind one of their ears.

She pulled her boot knife and went around the forklift to the doctor.

"Good evening, Clarice," he said when he could see her.

"Can you walk, are your legs working?"

"Yes."

"Can you see all right?"

"Yes."

"I'm going to cut you loose. With all due respect, Doctor, if you fuck with me I'll shoot you dead, here and now. Do you understand that?"

"Perfectly."

"Do right and you'll live through this."

"Spoken like a Protestant."

She was working all the time. The boot knife was sharp. She found the serrated edge worked fastest on the slick new rope.

His right arm was free.

"I can do the rest if you give me the knife."

She hesitated. Backed to the length of his arm and gave him the short dagger. "My car's a couple of hundred yards down the fire road." She had to watch him and the men on the ground.

He had a leg free. He was working on the other, having to cut each coil separately. Dr. Lecter could not see behind him where Carlo and Piero were lying facedown.

"When you're loose, don't try to run. You'll never make the door. I'll give you two pairs of cuffs," Starling said. "There's two guys cuffed on the ground behind you. Make 'em crawl to the forklift and cuff them to it so they can't get a phone. Then cuff yourself."

"Two?" he said. *"Watch it, there ought to be three."*

As he spoke the dart from Tommaso's rifle flew, a silver streak under the floodlights, and quivered in the center of Starling's back. She spun, instantly dizzy, vision going dark, trying to spot a target, saw the barrel at the edge of the loft and fired, fired, fired, fired. Tommaso rolling back from the edge, splinters stinging him, blue gun smoke rolling up into the lights. She fired once more as her vision failed, reached behind her hip for a magazine even as her knees gave way.

The noise seemed to further animate the pigs and seeing the men in their inviting position on the ground, they squealed and grunted, pressing against the barrier.

Starling pitched forward on her face, the empty pistol bouncing away the breech locked open. Carlo and Piero raised their heads to look and they were scrambling, crawling awkwardly together as a bat crawls, toward Mogli's body and his pistol and handcuff keys. Sound of Tommaso pumping the tranquilizer rifle in the loft. He had a dart left. He rose now and came to the edge, looking over the barrel, seeking Dr. Lecter on the other side of the forklift.

Here came Tommaso walking along the edge of the loft, there would be no place to hide.

Dr. Lecter lifted Starling in his arms and backed fast toward the Dutch gate, trying to keep the forklift between him and Tommaso, advancing carefully, watching his footing at the edge of the loft. Tommaso fired and the dart, aimed at Lecter's chest, hit bone in Starling's shin. Dr. Lecter pulled the bolts on the Dutch gate.

Piero snatched Mogli's key chain, frantic, Carlo scrambling for the gun, and came the pigs in a rush to the meal that was struggling to get up. Carlo managed to fire the .357 once, and a pig collapsed, the others climbing over the dead pig and onto Carlo and Piero, and the body of Mogli. More rushed on through the barn and into the night.

Dr. Lecter, holding Starling, was behind the gate when the pigs rushed through.

Tommaso from the loft could see his brother's face down in the pack and then it was only a bloody dish. He dropped the rifle in the hay. Dr. Lecter, erect as a dancer and carrying Starling in his arms, came out from behind the gate, walked barefoot out of the barn, through the pigs. Dr. Lecter walked through the sea of tossing backs and blood spray in the barn. A couple of the great swine, one of them the pregnant sow, squared their feet to him, lowered their heads to charge.

When he faced them and they smelled no fear, they trotted back to the easy pickings on the ground.

Dr. Lecter saw no reinforcements coming from the house. Once under the trees of the fire road, he stopped to pull the darts out of Starling and suck the wounds. The needle in her shin had bent on the bone.

Pigs crashed through the brush nearby.

He pulled off Starling's boots and put them on his own bare feet. They were a little tight. He left the .45 on her ankle so that, carrying her, he could reach it.

Ten minutes later, the guard at the main gatehouse looked up from his newspaper toward a distant sound, a ripping noise like a piston-engined fighter on a strafing run. It was a 5.0-liter Mustang turning 5800 rpm across the interstate overpass.

MASON WHINING and crying to get back in his room, crying as he had when some of the smaller boys and girls fought him at camp and managed to get in a few licks before he could crush them under his weight.

Margot and Cordell took him up in the elevator on his wing and secured him in his bed, hooked up to his permanent sources of power.

Mason was as angry as Margot had ever seen him, the blood vessels pulsing over the exposed bones of his face.

"I better give him something," Cordell said when they were out in the playroom.

"Not yet. He's got to think for a little while. Give me the keys to your Honda."

"Why?"

"Somebody's got to go down there and see if anybody's alive. Do you want to go?"

"No, but—"

"I can drive your car into the tack room, the van won't go through the door, now give me the fucking keys."

Downstairs now, out in the drive. Tommaso coming across the field from the woods, trotting, looking behind him. *Think, Margot.* She looked at her watch. 8:20. *At midnight, Cordell's relief would come. There was time to bring men from Washington in the helicopter to clean up.* She drove to Tommaso across the grass.

"I try to catch up them, a pig knock me. He"—Tommaso pantomimed Dr. Lecter carrying Starling—"the woman. They go in the loud car. She have *due*"—he held up two fingers—"*freccette*." He pointed to his back and leg. *Freccette. Dardi.* Stick 'em. Bam. *"Due freccette."* He pantomimed shooting.

"Darts," Margot said.

"Darts, maybe too much *narcotico*. She's maybe dead."

"Get in," Margot said. "We've got to go see."

Margot drove into the double side doors, where Starling had entered the barn. Squeals and grunts and tossing bristled backs. Margot drove forward honking and drove the pigs back enough to see there were three human remains, none recognizable anymore.

They drove into the tack room and closed the doors behind them.

Margot considered that Tommaso was the only one left alive who had ever seen her at the barn, not counting Cordell.

This may have occurred to Tommaso too. He stood a cautious distance from her, his dark intelligent eyes on her face. There were tears on his cheeks.

Think, Margot. You don't want any shit from the Sards. They know on their end that you handle the money. They'll dime you out in a second.

Tommaso's eyes followed her hand as it went into her pocket.

The cell phone. She punched up Sardinia, the Steuben banker at home at two-thirty in the morning. She spoke to him briefly and passed the telephone to Tommaso. He nodded, replied, nodded again and gave her back the phone. The money was his. He scrambled to the loft and got his satchel, along with Dr. Lecter's overcoat and hat. While he was getting his things, Margot picked up the cattle prod, tested the current and slid it up her sleeve. She took the farrier's hammer too.

TOMMASO, DRIVING Cordell's car, dropped Margot off at the house. He would leave the Honda in long-term parking at Dulles International Airport. Margot promised him she would bury what was left of Piero and Carlo as well as she could.

There was something he felt he should say to her and he gathered himself and got his English together. "Signorina, the pigs, you must know, the pigs help the *Dottore*. They stand back from him, circle him. They kill my brother, kill Carlo, but they stand back from Dr. Lecter. I think they worship him." Tommaso crossed himself. "You should not chase him anymore."

And throughout his long life in Sardinia, Tommaso would tell it that way. By the time Tommaso was in his sixties, he was saying that Dr. Lecter, carrying the woman, had left the barn borne on a drift of pigs.

After the car was gone down the fire road, Margot stood for minutes looking up at Mason's lighted windows. She saw the shadow of Cordell moving on the walls as he fussed around Mason, replacing the monitors on her brother's breath and pulse.

She slipped the handle of the farrier's hammer down the back of her pants and settled the tail of her jacket over the head.

Cordell was coming out of Mason's room with some pillows when Margot got off the elevator.

"Cordell, fix him a martini."

"I don't know—"

"*I* know. Fix him a martini."

Cordell put the pillows on the love seat and knelt in front of the bar refrigerator.

"Is there any juice in there?" said Margot, coming close behind him. She swung the farrier's hammer hard against the base of his skull and heard a popping sound. His head smashed into the refrigerator, rebounded, and he fell over backward off his haunches looking at the ceiling with his eyes open, one pupil dilating, the other not. She turned his head sideways against the floor and came down with the hammer, depressing his temple an inch, and thick blood came out his ears.

She did not feel anything.

Mason heard the door of his room open and he rolled his goggled eye. He had been asleep for a few moments, the lights soft. The eel was also asleep beneath its rock.

Margot's great frame filled the doorway. She closed the door behind her.

"Hi, Mason."

"What happened down there? What took you so fucking long?"

"They're all dead down there, Mason." Margot came to his bedside and unclipped the telephone line from Mason's phone and dropped it on the floor.

"Piero and Carlo and Johnny Mogli are all dead. Dr. Lecter got away and he carried the Starling woman with him."

Froth appeared between Mason's teeth as he cursed.

"I sent Tommaso home with his money."

"You *what*???? You fucking idiot bitch, now listen, we're going to clean this up and start over. We've got the weekend. We don't have to worry about what Starling saw. If Lecter's got her, she's good as dead."

Margot shrugged. "She never saw *me*."

"Get on the horn to Washington and get four of those bastards up here. Send the helicopter. Show them the backhoe—show them—Cordell! Get in here." Mason whistled into his panpipes. Margot pushed the pipes aside and leaned over him, so that she could see his face.

"Cordell's not coming, Mason. Cordell's dead."

"What?"

"I killed him in the playroom. Now. Mason, you're going to give me what you owe me." She put up the side rails on his bed and, lifting the great coil of his plaited hair, she stripped the cover off his body. His little legs were no bigger around than rolls of cookie dough. His hand, the only extremity he could move, fluttered at the phone. His hard-shell respirator puffed up and down in its regular rhythm.

From her pocket Margot took a nonspermicidal condom and held it up for him to see. From her sleeve she took the cattle prod.

"Remember, Mason, how you used to spit on your cock for lubrication? Think you could work up some spit? No? Maybe I can."

Mason bellowed when his breath permitted, a series of donkeylike brays, but it was over in half a minute, and very successfully too.

"You're dead, Margot." It sounded more like "Nargot."

"Oh, Mason, we all are. Didn't you know? But these aren't," she said, securing her blouse over her warm container. "They're wiggling. I'll show you how. I'll show you how they wiggle—show-and-tell."

Margot picked up the spiky fish-handling gloves beside the aquarium.

"I could adopt Judy," Mason said. "She could be my heir, and we could do a trust."

"We certainly could," Margot said, lifting a carp out of the holding tank. She brought a chair from the seating area, and standing on it, took the lid off the big aquarium. "But we won't."

She bent over the aquarium with her great arms down in the water. She held the carp by the tail down close to the grotto and when the eel came out she grabbed it behind the head with her powerful hand and lifted it clear out of the water, over her head. The mighty eel thrashing, as long as Margot and thick, its festive skin flashing. She gripped the eel with the other hand too and when it flexed it was all she could do to hold on with the spiky gloves imbedded in its hide.

Careful down off the chair and she came to Mason carrying the flexing eel, its head shaped like a bolt cutter, teeth clicking together with a sound like a telegraph key, the back-curved teeth no fish ever escaped. She flopped the eel on top of his chest, on the respirator and holding it with one hand, she lashed his pigtail around and around and around it.

"Wiggle, wiggle, Mason," she said.

She held the eel behind the head with one hand and with the other she forced down Mason's jaw, forced it down, putting her weight on his chin, him straining with what strength he had, and with a creaking, cracking sound his mouth opened.

"You should have taken the chocolate," Margot said, and stuffed the eel's maw into Mason's mouth, it seizing his tongue with its razor-sharp teeth as it would a fish and not letting go, never letting go, its body thrashing tangled in Mason's pigtail. Blood blew out Mason's nose hole and he was drowning.

Margot left them together, Mason and the eel, the carp circling alone in the aquarium. She composed herself at Cordell's desk and watched the monitors until Mason flat-lined.

The eel was still moving when she went back into Mason's room. The respirator went up and down, inflating the eel's air bladder as it pumped bloody froth out of Mason's lungs. Margot rinsed the cattle prod in the aquarium and put it in her pocket.

Margot took from a baggie in her pocket the bit of Dr. Lecter's scalp and the lock of his hair. She scraped blood from the scalp with Mason's fingernails, unsteady work with the eel still moving, and entwined the hair in his fingers. Last, she stuffed a single hair into one of the fish gloves.

Margot walked out without looking at the dead Cordell and went home to Judy with her warm prize, tucked where it would stay warm.

VI

A LONG SPOON

Therefore bihoveth hire a ful long spoon
That shal ete with a feend.

—*Geoffrey Chaucer,*
FROM *THE CANTERBURY TALES,*
"THE MERCHANT'S TALE"

89

CLARICE STARLING lies unconscious in a large bed beneath a linen sheet and a comforter. Her arms, covered by the sleeves of silk pajamas, are on top of the covers and they are restrained with silk scarves, only enough to keep her hands away from her face and to protect the IV butterfly in the back of her hand.

There are three points of light in the room, the low shaded lamp and the red pinpoints in the center of Dr. Lecter's pupils as he watches her.

He is sitting in an armchair, his fingers steepled under his chin. After a time he rises and takes her blood pressure. With a small flashlight he examines her pupils. He reaches beneath the covers and finds her foot, brings it out from under the covers and, watching her closely, stimulates the sole with the tip of a key. He stands for a moment, apparently lost in thought, holding her foot gently as though it were a small animal in his hand.

From the manufacturer of the tranquilizer dart, he has learned its content. Because the second dart that struck Starling hit bone in her shin, he believes she did not get a full double dose. He is administering stimulant countermeasures with infinite care.

Between ministrations to Starling, he sits in his armchair with a big pad of butcher paper doing calculations. The pages are filled with the symbols both of astrophysics and particle physics. There are repeated efforts with the symbols of string theory. The few mathematicians who could follow him might say his equations begin brilliantly and then decline, doomed by wishful thinking: Dr. Lecter wants time to reverse—no longer should increasing entropy mark the direction of time. He wants increasing order to point the way. He wants Mischa's baby teeth back out of the stool pit. Behind his fevered calculations is the desperate wish to make a place for Mischa in the world, perhaps the place now occupied by Clarice Starling.

MORNING AND yellow sunlight in the playroom at Muskrat Farm. The great stuffed animals with their button eyes regard the body of Cordell, covered now.

Even in the middle of winter, a bluebottle fly has found the body and is walking over the covering sheet where blood has soaked through.

Had Margot Verger known the raw ablative tension suffered by the principals in a media-ridden homicide, she might never have stuffed the eel down her brother's throat.

Her decision not to try to clean up the mess at Muskrat Farm and to simply duck until the storm was over was a wise one. No one living saw her at Muskrat when Mason and the others were killed.

Her story was that the first frantic call from the midnight relief nurse wakened her in the house she shared with Judy. She came to the scene and arrived shortly after the first sheriff's officers.

The lead investigator for the sheriff's department, Detective Clarence Franks, was a youngish man with eyes a bit too close together, but he was not stupid as Margot had hoped he would be.

"Can't just anybody come up here in that elevator, it takes a key to get in, right?" Franks asked her. The detective and Margot sat awkwardly side by side on the love seat.

"I suppose so, if that's the way they came."

"'They,' Ms. Verger? Do you think there might be more than one?"

"I have no idea, Mr. Franks."

She had seen her brother's body still joined to the eel and covered by a sheet. Someone had unplugged the respirator. The criminalists were taking samples of aquarium water and taking swipes of blood from the floor. She could see in Mason's hand the piece of Dr. Lecter's scalp. They hadn't found it yet. The criminalists looked to Margot like Tweedledum and Tweedledee.

Detective Franks was busy scribbling in his notebook.

"Do they know who those other poor people are?" Margot said. "Did they have families?"

"We're working it out," Franks said. "There were three weapons we can trace."

In fact, the sheriff's department was not sure how many persons had died in the barn, as the pigs had disappeared into the deep woods dragging with them the depleted remains for later.

"In the course of this investigation, we might have to ask you and your—your *longtime companion* to undergo a polygraph examination, that's a lie detector, would you consent to that, Ms. Verger?"

"Mr. Franks, I'll do anything to catch these people. To specifically answer your question, ask me and Judy when you need us. Should I talk to the family lawyer?"

"Not if you don't have anything to hide, Ms. Verger."

"Hide?" Margot managed tears.

"Please, I have to do this, Ms. Verger." Franks started to put his hand on her massive shoulder and thought better of it.

CHAPTER

91

STARLING WOKE in the fresh-smelling semidark, knowing in some primal way that she was near the sea. She moved slightly on the bed. She felt a deep soreness all over, and then she fell away from consciousness again. When next she woke, a voice was talking quietly to her, offering a warm cup. She drank from it, and the taste was similar to the herbal tea Mapp's grandmother sent her.

Day and evening again, the smell of fresh flowers in the house, and once the faint sting of a needle. Like the thud and crackle of distant fireworks, the remnants of fear and pain popped on the horizon, but not close, never close. She was in the garden of the hurricane's eye.

"Waking. Waking, calm. Waking in a pleasant room," a voice said. She heard faint chamber music.

She felt very clean and her skin was scented with mint, some ointment that gave a deep comforting warmth.

Starling opened her eyes wide.

Dr. Lecter stood at a distance from her, very still, as he had stood in his cell when she first saw him. We are accustomed to seeing him unfettered now. It is not shocking to see him in open space with another mortal creature.

"Good evening, Clarice."

"Good evening, Dr. Lecter," she said, responding in kind with no real idea of the time.

"If you feel uncomfortable, it's just bruises you suffered in a fall. You'll be all right. I'd just like to be positive about something though, could you please look into this light?" He approached her with a small flashlight. Dr. Lecter smelled like fresh broadcloth.

She forced herself to keep her eyes open as he examined her pupils, then he stepped away again.

"Thank you. There's a very comfortable bathroom, just in there. Want to try your feet? Slippers are beside your bed, I'm afraid I had to borrow your boots."

She was awake and not awake. The bathroom was indeed comfortable and furnished with every amenity. In the following days she enjoyed long baths there, but she did not bother with her reflection in the mirror, so far was she from herself.

DAYS OF talk, sometimes hearing herself and wondering who was speaking with such intimate knowledge of her thoughts. Days of sleep and strong broth and omelettes.

And one day Dr. Lecter said, "Clarice, you must be tired of your robes and pajamas. There are some things in the closet you might like—only if you want to wear them." And in the same tone, "I put your personal things, your purse and your gun and your wallet, in the top drawer of the chest, if you want any of that."

"Thank you, Dr. Lecter."

In the closet were a variety of clothes, dresses, pants suits, a shimmery long gown with a beaded top. There were cashmere pants and pullovers that appealed to her. She chose tan cashmere, and moccasins.

In the drawer was her belt and Yaqui slide, empty of the lost .45, but her ankle holster was there beside her purse, and in it was the cut-down .45 automatic. The clip was full of fat cartridges, nothing in the chamber, the way she wore it on her leg. And her boot knife was there, in its scabbard. Her car keys were in her purse.

Starling was herself and not herself. When she wondered about events it was as though she saw them from the side, saw herself from a distance.

She was happy to see her car in the garage when Dr. Lecter took her out to it. She looked at the wipers and decided to replace them.

"Clarice, how do you think Mason's men followed us to the grocery store?"

She looked up at the garage ceiling for a moment, thinking.

It took her less than two minutes to find the antenna running crosswise between the backseat and the package shelf, and she followed the antenna wire to the hidden beacon.

She turned it off and carried it into the house by the antenna as she might carry a rat by the tail.

"Very nice," she said. "Very new. Decent installation too. I'm sure it's got Mr. Krendler's prints on it. May I have a plastic bag?"

"Could they search for it with aircraft?"

"It's off now. They couldn't search with aircraft unless Krendler admitted he used it. You know he didn't do that. Mason could sweep with his helicopter."

"Mason is dead."

"Ummmm," Starling said. "Would you play for me?"

93

PAUL KRENDLER swung between tedium and rising fear in the first days after the murders. He arranged for direct reports from the FBI local field office in Maryland.

He felt reasonably safe from any audit of Mason's books because the passage of money from Mason to his own numbered account had a fairly foolproof cutout in the Cayman Islands. But with Mason gone, he had big plans and no patron. Margot Verger knew about his money, and she knew he had compromised the security of the FBI files on Lecter. Margot had to keep her mouth shut.

The monitor for the auto beacon worried him. He had taken it from the Engineering building at Quantico without signing it out, but he was on the entry log at Engineering for that day.

Dr. Doemling and the big nurse, Barney, had seen him at Muskrat, but only in a legitimate role, talking with Mason Verger about how to catch Hannibal Lecter.

General relief came to everyone on the fourth afternoon after the murders when Margot Verger was able to play for the sheriff's investigators a newly taped message on her answering machine.

The policemen stood rapt in the bedroom, staring at the bed she shared with Judy and listening to the voice of the fiend. Dr. Lecter gloated over the death of Mason and assured Margot that it was extremely painful and prolonged. She sobbed into her hand, and Judy held her. Finally Franks led her from the room, saying "No need for you to hear it again."

With the prodding of Krendler, the answering machine tape was brought to Washington and a voiceprint confirmed the caller was Dr. Lecter.

But the greatest relief for Krendler came in a telephone call on the evening of the fourth day.

The caller was none other than U.S. Representative Parton Vellmore of Illinois.

Krendler had only spoken to the congressman on a few occasions, but his voice was familiar from television. Just the fact of the call was a reassurance; Vellmore was on the House Judiciary Subcommittee and a notable shitepoke; he would fly from Krendler in an instant if Krendler was hot.

"Mr. Krendler, I know you were well acquainted with Mason Verger."

"Yes, sir."

"Well, it's just a goddamned shame. That sadistic son of a bitch ruined Mason's life, mutilated him and then came back and killed him. I don't know if you're aware of it, but one of my constituents also died in that tragedy. Johnny Mogli, served the people of Illinois for years in law enforcement."

"No, sir, I wasn't aware of that. I'm sorry."

"The point is, Krendler, we have to go on. The Vergers' legacy of philanthropy and their keen interest in public policy will continue. It's bigger than the death of one man. I've been talking to several people in the twenty-seventh district and to the Verger people. Margot Verger has made me aware of your interest in public service. Extraordinary woman. Has a real practical side. We're getting together very soon, real informal and quiet, and talk about what we can do next November. We want you on board. Think you could make the meeting?"

"Yes, Congressman. Definitely."

"Margot will call you with the details, it'll be in the next few days."

Krendler put the phone down, relief washing over him.

The discovery in the barn of the .45 Colt registered to the late John Brigham, now known to be the property of Clarice Starling, was a considerable embarrassment to the Bureau.

Starling was listed as missing, but the case was not carried as a kidnapping, as no living person saw her abducted. She was not even an agent missing from active duty. Starling was an agent on suspension, whose whereabouts were unknown. A bulletin was issued for her vehicle with the VIN number and the license plate, but with no special emphasis on the owner's identity.

Kidnapping commands much more effort from law enforcement than a missing persons case. The classification made Ardelia Mapp so angry she wrote her letter of resignation to the Bureau, then thought it better to wait and work from within. Again and again Mapp found herself going to Starling's side of the duplex to look for her.

Mapp found the Lecter VICAP file and National Crime Information Center files maddeningly static, with only trivial additions: The Italian police had managed to find Dr. Lecter's computer at last— the Carabinieri were playing Super Mario on it in their recreation room. The machine had purged itself the moment investigators hit the first key.

Mapp badgered everyone of influence she could reach in the Bureau since Starling disappeared.

Her repeated calls to Jack Crawford's home were unanswered.

She called Behavioral Science and was told Crawford remained in Jefferson Memorial Hospital with chest pains.

She did not call him there. In the Bureau, he was Starling's last angel.

STARLING HAD no sense of time. Over the days and nights there were the conversations. She heard herself speaking for minutes on end, and she listened.

Sometimes she laughed at herself, hearing artless revelations that normally would have mortified her. The things she told Dr. Lecter were often surprising to her, sometimes distasteful to a normal sensibility, but what she said was always true. And Dr. Lecter spoke as well. In a low, even voice. He expressed interest and encouragement, but never surprise or censure.

He told her about his childhood, about Mischa.

Sometimes they looked at a single bright object together to begin their talks, almost always there was but a single light source in the room. From day to day the bright object changed.

Today, they began with the single highlight on the side of a teapot, but as their talk progressed, Dr. Lecter seemed to sense their arrival at an unexplored gallery in her mind. Perhaps he heard trolls fighting on the other side of a wall. He replaced the teapot with a silver belt buckle.

"That's my daddy's," Starling said. She clapped her hands together like a child.

"Yes," Dr. Lecter said. "Clarice, would you like to talk with your father? Your father is here. Would you like to talk with him?"

"My daddy's here! Hey! All right!"

Dr. Lecter put his hands on the sides of Starling's head, over her temporal lobes, which could supply her with all of her father she would ever need. He looked deep, deep into her eyes.

"I know you'll want to talk privately. I'll go now. You can watch the buckle, and in a few minutes, you'll hear him knock. All right?"

"Yes! Super!"

"Good. You'll just have to wait a few minutes."

Tiny sting of the finest needle—Starling did not even look down—and Dr. Lecter left the room.

She watched the buckle until the knock came, two firm knocks, and her father came in as she remembered him, tall in the doorway, carrying his hat, his hair slicked down with water the way he came to the supper table.

"Hey, Baby! What time do you eat around here?"

He had not held her in the twenty-five years since his death, but when he gathered her to him, the western snaps on his shirtfront felt the very same, he smelled of strong soap and tobacco, and she sensed against her the great volume of his heart.

"Hey, Baby. Hey, Baby. Did you fall down?" It was the same as when he gathered her up in the yard after she tried to ride a big goat on a dare. "You was doing pretty good 'til she swapped ends so fast. Come on in the kitchen and let's see what we can find."

Two things on the table in the spare kitchen of her childhood home, a cellophane package of SNO BALLS, and a bag of oranges.

Starling's father opened his Barlow knife with the blade broken off square and peeled a couple of oranges, the peelings curling on the oilcloth. They sat in ladder-back kitchen chairs and he freed the sections by quarters and alternately he ate one, and he gave one to

Starling. She spit the seeds in her hand and held them in her lap. He was long in a chair, like John Brigham.

Her father chewed more on one side than the other and one of his lateral incisors was capped with white metal in the fashion of forties army dentistry. It gleamed when he laughed. They ate two oranges and a SNO BALL apiece and told a few knock-knock jokes. Starling had forgotten that wonderful squirmy feeling of springy icing under the coconut. The kitchen dissolved and they were talking as grown people.

"How you doin', Baby?" It was a serious question.

"They're pretty down on me at work."

"I know about that. That's that courthouse crowd, Sugar. Sorrier bunch never—never drew breath. You never shot nobody you didn't have to."

"I believe that. There's other stuff."

"You never told a lie about it."

"No, sir."

"You saved that little baby."

"He came out all right."

"I was real proud of that."

"Thank you, sir."

"Sugar, I got to take off. We'll talk."

"You can't stay."

He put his hand on her head. "We can't never stay, Baby. Can't nobody stay like they want to."

He kissed her forehead and walked out of the room. She could see the bullet hole in his hat as he waved to her, tall in the doorway.

C H A P T E R

95

CLEARLY STARLING loved her father as much as we love anybody, and she would have fought in an instant over a slur on his memory. Yet, in conversation with Dr. Lecter, under the influence of a major hypnotic drug and deep hypnosis, this is what she said:

"I'm really mad at him, though. I mean, come on, how come he had to be behind a goddamned drugstore in the middle of the night going up against those two pissants that killed him? He short-shucked that old pump shotgun and they had him. They were nothing and they had him. He didn't know what he was doing. He never learned anything."

She would have slapped the face of anybody else saying that.

The monster settled back a micron in his chair. *Ahh, at last we've come to it. These schoolgirl recollections were becoming tedious.*

Starling tried to swing her legs beneath the chair like a child, but her legs were too long. "See, he had that job, he went and did what they told him, went around with that damned watchman's clock and then he was dead. And Mama was washing the blood out of his hat to bury it with him. Who came home to *us*? Nobody. Damn few SNO BALLS after that, I can tell you. Mama and me, cleaning up motel rooms. People leaving wet Trojans on the nightstand. He got killed and left us because he was too goddamned stupid. He should have told those town jackasses to stuff the job."

Things she would never have said, things banned from her higher brain.

From the beginning of their acquaintance, Dr. Lecter had needled her about her father, calling him a night watchman. Now he became Lecter the Protector of her father's memory.

"Clarice, he never wished for anything but your happiness and well-being."

"Wish in one hand and shit in the other one and see which one gets full the first," said Starling. This adage of the orphans' home should have been particularly distasteful coming from that attractive face, but Dr. Lecter seemed pleased, even encouraged.

"Clarice, I'm going to ask you to come with me to another room," Dr. Lecter said. "Your father visited you, as best you could manage. You saw that, despite your intense wish to keep him with you, he couldn't stay. He visited you. Now it's time for you to visit him."

Down a hall to a guest bedroom. The door was closed.

"Wait a moment, Clarice." He went inside.

She stood in the hall with her hand on the knob and heard a match struck.

Dr. Lecter opened the door.

"Clarice, you know your father is dead. You know that better than anyone."

"Yes."

"Come in and see him."

Her father's bones were composed on a twin bed, the long bones and rib cage covered by a sheet. The remains were in low relief beneath the white cover, like a child's snow angel.

Her father's skull, cleaned by the tiny ocean scavengers off Dr. Lecter's beach, dried and bleached, rested on the pillow.

"Where was his star, Clarice?"

"The village took it back. They said it cost seven dollars."

"This is what he is, this is all of him now. This is what time has reduced him to."

Starling looked at the bones. She turned and quickly left the room. It was not a retreat and Lecter did not follow her. He waited in the semidark. He was not afraid, but he heard her coming back with ears as keen as those of a staked-out goat. Something bright metal in her hand. A badge, John Brigham's shield. She put it on the sheet.

"What could a badge mean to you, Clarice? You shot a hole through one in the barn."

"It meant everything to him. That's how much he knewww." The last word distorted and her mouth turned down. She picked up her father's skull and sat on the other bed, hot tears springing in her eyes and pouring down her cheeks.

Like a toddler she caught up the tail of her pullover and held it to her cheek and sobbed, bitter tears falling with a hollow *tap tap* on the dome of her father's skull resting in her lap, its capped tooth gleaming. "I *love* my daddy, he was as good to me as he knew how to be. It was the best time I ever had." And it was true, and no less true than before she let the anger out.

When Dr. Lecter gave her a tissue she simply gripped it in her fist and he cleaned her face himself.

"Clarice, I'm going to leave you here with these remains. Remains, Clarice. Scream your plight into his eyeholes and no reply will come." He put his hands on the sides of her head. "What you need of your father is here, in your head, and subject to your judgment, not his. I'll leave you now. Do you want the candles?"

"Yes, please."

"When you come out, bring only what you need."

He waited in the drawing room, before the fire. He passed the time playing his theremin, moving his empty hands in its electronic field to create the music, moving the hands he had placed on Clarice Starling's head as though he now directed the music. He was aware of Starling standing behind him for some time before he finished his piece.

When he turned to her, her smile was soft and sad and her hands were empty.

Ever, Dr. Lecter sought pattern.

He knew that, like every sentient being, Starling formed from her early experience matrices, frameworks by which later perceptions were understood.

Speaking to her through the asylum bars so many years ago, he had found an important one for Starling, the slaughter of lambs and horses on the ranch that was her foster home. She was imprinted by their plight.

Her obsessive and successful hunt for Jame Gumb was driven by the plight of his captive.

She had saved him from torture for the same reason.

Fine. Patterned behavior.

Ever looking for situational sets, Dr. Lecter believed that Starling saw in John Brigham her father's good qualities—and with her father's virtues the unfortunate Brigham was also assigned the incestual taboo. Brigham, and probably Crawford, had her father's good qualities. Where were the bad?

Dr. Lecter searched for the rest of this split matrix. Using hypnotic drugs and hypnotic techniques much modified from cameral therapy, he was finding in Clarice Starling's personality hard and stubborn nodes, like knots in wood, and old resentments still flammable as resin.

He came upon tableaux of pitiless brightness, years old but well tended and detailed, that sent limbic anger flashing through Starling's brain like lightning in a thunderhead.

Most of them involved Paul Krendler. Her resentment of the very real injustices she had suffered at Krendler's hands was charged with the anger at her father that she could never, never acknowledge. She could not forgive her father for dying. He had left the family, he had stopped peeling oranges in the kitchen. He had doomed her mother to the commode brush and the pail. He had stopped holding Starling close, his great heart booming like Hannah's heart as they rode into the night.

Krendler was the icon of failure and frustration. He could be blamed. But could he be defied? Or was Krendler, and every other authority and taboo, empowered to box Starling into what was, in Dr. Lecter's view, her little low-ceiling life?

To him one hopeful sign: Though she was imprinted with the badge, she could still shoot a hole through one and kill the wearer. Why? Because she had committed to action, identified the wearer as a criminal and made the judgment ahead of time, overruling the imprinted icon of the star. Potential flexibility. The cerebral cortex rules. Did that mean room for Mischa *within* Starling? Or was it simply another good quality of the place Starling must vacate?

96

BARNEY, BACK in his apartment in Baltimore, back in the round of working at Misericordia, had the three to eleven shift. He stopped for a bowl of soup at the coffee shop on his way home and it was nearly midnight when he let himself into his apartment and turned on the light.

Ardelia Mapp sat at his kitchen table. She was pointing a black semiautomatic pistol at the center of his face. From the size of the hole in the muzzle, Barney judged it was a .40 caliber.

"Sit down, Nursey," Mapp said. Her voice was hoarse and around her dark pupils her eyes were orange. "Pull your chair over there and tip back against the wall."

What scared him more than the big stopper in her hand was the other pistol on the place mat before her. It was a Colt Woodsman .22 with a plastic pop bottle taped to the muzzle as a silencer.

The chair groaned under Barney's weight. "If the chair legs break don't shoot me, I can't help it," he said.

"Do you know anything about Clarice Starling?"

"No."

Mapp picked up the small-caliber gun. "I'm not fucking around with you, Barney. The second I think you're lying, Nursey, I'm gonna darken your stool, do you believe me?"

"Yes." Barney knew it was true.

"I'm going to ask you again. Do you know anything that would help me find Clarice Starling? The post office says you had your mail forwarded to Mason Verger's place for a month. *What the fuck, Barney?*"

"I worked up there. I was taking care of Mason Verger, and he asked me all about Lecter. I didn't like it up there and I quit. Mason was pretty much of a bastard."

"Starling's gone away."

"I know."

"Maybe Lecter took her, maybe the pigs got her. If he took her what would he do with her?"

"I'm being honest with you—I don't know. I'd help Starling if I could. Why wouldn't I? I kind of liked her and she was getting me expunged. Look in her reports or notes or—"

"I have. I want you to understand something, Barney. This is a one-time-only offer. If you know anything you better tell me now. If I *ever* find out, no matter how long from now, that you held out something that might have helped, I will come back here and this gun will be the last thing you ever see. I will kill your big ugly ass. Do you believe me?"

"Yes."

"Do you know anything?"

"No." The longest silence he could ever remember.

"Just sit still there until I'm gone."

It took Barney an hour and a half to go to sleep. He lay in his bed looking at the ceiling, his brow, broad as a dolphin's, now sweaty, now dry. Barney thought about callers to come. Just before he turned out his light, he went into his bathroom and took from his DOP kit a stainless-steel shaving mirror, Marine Corps issue.

He padded into the kitchen, opened an electrical switch box in the wall and taped the mirror inside the switch box door.

It was all he could do. He twitched in his sleep like a dog.

After his next shift, he brought a rape kit home from the hospital.

97

THERE WAS only so much Dr. Lecter could do to the German's house while retaining the furnishings. Flowers and screens helped. Color was interesting to see against the massive furniture and high darkness; it was an ancient, compelling contrast, like a butterfly lit on an armored fist.

His absentee landlord apparently had a fixation on Leda and the Swan. The interspecies coupling was represented in no less than four bronzes of varying quality, the best a reproduction of Donatello, and eight paintings. One painting delighted Dr. Lecter, an Anne Shingleton with its genius anatomical articulation and some real heat in the fucking. The others he draped. The landlord's ghastly collection of hunting bronzes was draped as well.

Early in the morning the doctor laid his table carefully for three, studying it from different angles with the tip of his finger beside his nose, changed candlesticks twice and went from his damask place mats to a gathered tablecloth to reduce to more manageable size the oval dining table.

The dark and forbidding sideboard looked less like an aircraft carrier when high service pieces and bright copper warmers stood on it. In fact, Dr. Lecter pulled out several of the drawers and put flowers in them, in a kind of hanging gardens effect.

He could see that he had too many flowers in the room, and must add more to make it come back right again. Too many was too many, but way too many was just right. He settled on two flower arrangements for the table: a low mound of peonies in a silver dish, white as SNO BALLS, and a large, high arrangement of massed Bells of Ireland, Dutch iris, orchids and parrot tulips that screened away much of the table's expanse and created an intimate space.

A small ice storm of crystal stood before the service plates, but the flat silver was in a warmer to be laid at the last moment.

The first course would be prepared at table, and accordingly he organized his alcohol burners, with his copper *fait-tout*, his saucepan and sauté pan, his condiments and his autopsy saw.

He could get more flowers when he went out. Clarice Starling was not disturbed when he told her he was going. He suggested she might like to sleep.

98

IN THE afternoon of the fifth day after the murders, Barney had finished shaving and was patting alcohol on his cheeks when he heard the footsteps on the stairs. It was almost time for him to go to work.

A firm knock. Margot Verger stood at his door. She carried a big purse and a small satchel.

"Hi, Barney." She looked tired.

"Hi, Margot. Come in."

He offered her a seat at the kitchen table. "Want a Coke?" Then he remembered that Cordell's head was driven into a refrigerator and he regretted the offer.

"No thanks," she said.

He sat down across the table from her. She looked over his arms as a rival bodybuilder, then back to his face.

"You okay, Margot?"

"I think so," she said.

"Looks like you don't have any worries, I mean from what I read."

"Sometimes I think about the talks we had, Barney. I kind of thought I might hear from you sometime."

He wondered if she had the hammer in the purse or the satchel.

"Only way you hear from me, maybe I'd like to see how you're doing sometime, if that was okay. Never asking for anything. Margot, you're cool with me."

"It's just, you know, you worry about loose ends. Not that I've got anything to hide."

He knew then she had the semen. It was when the pregnancy was announced, if they managed one, that she'd be worried about Barney.

"I mean, it was a godsend, his death, I'm not going to lie about that."

The speed of her talk told Barney she was building momentum.

"Maybe I would like a Coke," she said.

"Before I get it for you, let me show you something I've got for you. Believe me, I can put your mind at rest and it'll cost you nothing. Take a second. Hold on."

He picked a screwdriver out of a canister of tools on the counter. He could do that with his side to Margot.

In the kitchen wall were what appeared to be two circuit breaker boxes. Actually one box had replaced the other in the old building, and only the one on the right was in service.

At the electrical boxes, Barney had to turn his back to Margot. Quickly he opened the one on the left. Now he could watch her in the mirror taped inside the switchbox door. She put her hand inside the big purse. Put it in, didn't take it out.

By removing four screws, he was able to lift out of the box the disconnected panel of circuit breakers. Behind the panel was the space within the hollow wall.

Reaching carefully inside, Barney removed a plastic bag.

He heard a hitch in Margot's breathing when he took out the object the bag contained. It was a famous brutish visage—the mask Dr. Lecter had been forced to wear in the Baltimore State Hospital for the Criminally Insane to prevent him from biting. This was the last and most valuable item in Barney's cache of Lecter memorabilia.

"Whoa!" Margot said.

Barney placed the mask facedown on the table on a piece of waxed paper under the bright kitchen light. He knew Dr. Lecter had never been allowed to clean his mask. Dried saliva was crusted inside the mouth opening. Where the straps attached to the mask were three hairs, caught in the fastenings and pulled out by their roots.

A glance at Margot told him she was okay for the moment.

Barney took from his kitchen cabinet the rape kit. The small plastic box contained Q-tips, sterile water, swatches and clean pill bottles.

With infinite care he swabbed up the saliva flakes with a moistened Q-tip. He put the Q-tip into a pill bottle. The hairs he pulled loose from the mask and put them in a second bottle.

He touched his thumb to the sticky sides of two pieces of scotch tape, leaving a clear fingerprint each time, and taped the lids on the bottles. He gave the two containers to Margot in a baggie.

"Let's say I got in some trouble and I lost my mind and I tried to roll over on you—say I tried to tell the police some story on you to beat some charges of my own. You have proof there that I was at least an accomplice in the death of Mason Verger and maybe did the whole thing myself. At the least I supplied you with the DNA."

"You'd get immunity before you ratted."

"For conspiring maybe, but not for physically taking part in a big-publicity murder. They'd promise me use-immunity on conspiracy and then fuck me when they figured I helped. I'd be screwed forever. It's right there in your hands."

Barney was not positive of this, but he thought it sounded pretty good.

She could also plant the Lecter DNA on Barney's still form anytime she needed to, and they both knew it.

She looked at him for what seemed like a very long time with her bright blue butcher's eyes.

She put the satchel on the table. "Lot of money in there," she said. "Enough to see every Vermeer in the world. Once." She seemed a little giddy, and oddly happy. "I've got Franklin's cat in the car, I've got to go. Franklin and his stepmother and his sister Shirley and some guy named Stringbean and God knows who else are coming out to Muskrat when Franklin gets out of the hospital. Cost me fifty dollars to get that fucking cat. It was living next door to Franklin's old house under an alias."

She did not put the plastic bag in her purse. She carried it in her free hand. Barney guessed she didn't want him to see her other option in the purse.

At the door he said, "Think I could have a kiss?"

She stood on tiptoe and gave him a quick kiss on the lips.

"That will have to do," she said primly. The stairs creaked under her weight going down.

Barney locked his door and stood for minutes with his forehead against the cool refrigerator.

CHAPTER

99

STARLING WOKE to distant chamber music, and the tangy aromas of cooking. She felt wonderfully refreshed and very hungry. A tap at her door and Dr. Lecter came in wearing dark trousers, a white shirt and an ascot. He carried a long suit bag and a hot cappuccino for her.

"Did you sleep well?"

"Great, thank you."

"The chef tells me we'll dine in an hour and a half. Cocktails in an hour, is that all right? I thought you might like this—see if it suits you." He hung the bag in the closet and left without another sound.

She did not look in her closet until after a long bath, and when she did look she was pleased. She found a long dinner gown in cream silk, narrowly but deeply décolleté beneath an exquisite beaded jacket.

On the dresser were a pair of earrings with pendant cabochon emeralds. The stones had a lot of fire for an unfaceted cut.

Her hair was always easy for her. Physically, she felt very comfortable in the clothes. Even unaccustomed as she was to this level of dress, she did not examine herself long in the mirror, only looking to see if everything was in place.

The German landlord built his fireplaces oversized. In the drawing room, Starling found a good-sized log blazing. She approached the warm hearth in a whisper of silk.

Music from the harpsichord in the corner. Seated at the instrument, Dr. Lecter in white tie.

He looked up and saw her and his breath stopped in his throat. His hands stopped too, still spread above the keyboard. Harpsichord notes do not carry, and in the sudden quiet of the drawing room, they both heard him take his next breath.

Two drinks waited before the fire. He occupied himself with them. Lillet with a slice of orange. Dr. Lecter handed one to Clarice Starling.

"If I saw you every day, forever, I'd remember this time." His dark eyes held her whole.

"How many times have you seen me? That I don't know about?"

"Only three."

"But here—"

"Is outside of time, and what I may see taking care of you does not compromise your privacy. That's kept in its own place with your medical records. I'll confess it *is* pleasant to look at you asleep. You're quite beautiful, Clarice."

"Looks are an accident, Dr. Lecter."

"If comeliness were earned, you'd still be beautiful."

"Thanks."

"Do not say '*Thanks.*'" A fractional turn of his head was enough to dash his annoyance like a glass thrown in the fireplace.

"I say what I mean," Starling said. "Would you like it better if I said 'I'm glad you find me so?' That would be a little fancier, and equally true."

She raised her glass beneath her level prairie gaze, taking back nothing.

It occurred to Dr. Lecter in the moment that with all his knowledge and intrusion, he could never entirely predict her, or own her at all.

He could feed the caterpillar, he could whisper through the chrysalis; what hatched out followed its own nature and was beyond him. He wondered if she had the .45 on her leg beneath the gown.

Clarice Starling smiled at him then, the cabochons caught the firelight and the monster was lost in self-congratulation at his own exquisite taste and cunning.

"Clarice, dinner appeals to taste and smell, the oldest senses and the closest to the center of the mind. Taste and smell are housed in parts of the mind that precede pity, and pity has no place at my table. At the same time, playing in the dome of the cortex like miracles illumined on the ceiling of a church are the ceremonies and sights and exchanges of dinner. It can be far more engaging than theater." He brought his face close to hers, taking some reading in her eyes. "I want you to understand what riches you bring to it, Clarice, and what your *entitlements* are. Clarice, have you studied your reflection lately? I think not. I doubt that you ever do. Come into the hall, stand in front of the pier glass."

Dr. Lecter brought a candelabrum from the mantel.

The tall mirror was one of the good eighteenth-century antiques, but slightly smoky and crazed. It was out of Château Vaux-le-Vicomte and God knows what it has seen.

"Look, Clarice. That delicious vision is what you are. This evening you will see yourself from a distance for a while. You will see what is just, you will say what is true. You've never lacked the courage to say what you think, but you've been hampered by constraints. I will tell you again, pity has no place at this table.

"If remarks are passed that are unpleasant in the instant, you will see that context can make them something between droll and riotously funny. If things are said that are painfully true, then it is only passing truth and will change." He took a sip of his drink. "If you feel pain bloom inside you, it will soon blossom into relief. Do you understand me?"

"No, Dr. Lecter, but I remember what you said. Damn a bunch of self-improvement. I want a pleasant dinner."

"That I promise you." He smiled, a sight that frightens some.

Neither looked at her reflection now in the clouded glass; they watched each other through the burning tapers of the candelabrum and the mirror watched them both.

"Look, Clarice."

She watched the red sparks pinwheel deep in his eyes and felt the excitement of a child approaching a distant fair.

From his jacket pocket Dr. Lecter took a syringe, the needle fine as a hair and, never looking, only feeling, he slipped the needle into her arm. When he withdrew it, the tiny wound did not even bleed.

"What were you playing when I came in?" she asked.

"'If Love Now Reigned.'"

"It's very old?"

"Henry the Eighth composed it about 1510."

"Would you play for me?" she said. "Would you finish it now?"

THE BREEZE of their entry into the dining room stirred the flames of the candles and the warmers. Starling had only seen the dining room in passage and it was wonderful to see the room transformed. Bright, inviting. Tall crystal repeating the candle flames above the creamy napery at their places and the space reduced to intimate size with a screen of flowers shutting off the rest of the table.

Dr. Lecter had brought his flat silver from the warmer at the last minute and when Starling explored her place setting, she felt in the handle of her knife an almost feverish heat.

Dr. Lecter poured wine and gave her only a tiny *amuse-gueule* to eat for starters, a single Belon oyster and a morsel of sausage, as he had to sit over half a glass of wine and admire her in the context of his table.

The height of his candlesticks was exactly right. The flames lit the deeps of her décolleté and he did not have to be vigilant about her sleeves.

"What are we having?"

He raised his finger to his lips. "You never ask, it spoils the surprise."

They talked about the trimming of crow quills and their effect on the voice of a harpsichord, and only for a moment did she recall a crow robbing her mother's service cart on a motel balcony long ago. From a distance she judged the memory irrelevant to this pleasant time and she deliberately set it aside.

"Hungry?"

"Yes!"

"Then we'll have our first course."

Dr. Lecter moved a single tray from the sideboard to a space beside his place at the table and rolled a service cart to tableside. Here were his pans, his burners, and his condiments in little crystal bowls.

He fired up his burners and began with a goodly knob of Charante butter in his copper *fait-tout* saucepan, swirling the melting butter and browning the butterfat to make *beurre-noisette*. When it was the brown of a hazelnut, he set the butter aside on a trivet.

He smiled at Starling, his teeth very white.

"Clarice, do you recall what we said about pleasant and unpleasant remarks, and things being very funny in context?"

"That butter smells wonderful. Yes, I remember."

"And do you remember who you saw in the mirror, how splendid she was?"

"Dr. Lecter, if you don't mind my saying so this is getting a little *Dick and Jane*. I remember perfectly."

"Good. Mr. Krendler is joining us for our first course."

Dr. Lecter moved the large flower arrangement from the table to the sideboard.

Deputy Assistant Inspector General Paul Krendler, in the flesh, sat at the table in a stout oak armchair. Krendler opened his eyes wide and looked about. He wore his runner's headband and a very nice funeral tuxedo, with integral shirt and tie. The garment being split up the back, Dr. Lecter had been able to sort of tuck it around him, covering the yards of duct tape that held him to the chair.

Starling's eyelids might have lowered a fraction and her lips slightly pursed as they sometimes did on the firing range.

Now Dr. Lecter took a pair of silver tongs from the sideboard and peeled off the tape covering Krendler's mouth.

"Good evening, again, Mr. Krendler."

"Good evening." Krendler did not seem to be quite himself. His place was set with a small tureen.

"Would you like to say good evening to Ms. Starling?"

"Hello, Starling." He seemed to brighten. "I always wanted to watch you eat."

Starling took him in from a distance, as though she were the wise old pier glass watching. "Hello, Mr. Krendler." She raised her face to Dr. Lecter, busy with his pans. "How did you ever catch him?"

"Mr. Krendler is on his way to an important conference about his future in politics," Dr. Lecter said. "Margot Verger invited him as a favor to me. Sort of a quid pro quo. Mr. Krendler jogged up to the pad in Rock Creek Park to meet the Verger helicopter. But he caught a ride with me instead. Would you like to say grace before our meal, Mr. Krendler? Mr. *Krendler*?"

"Grace? Yes." Krendler closed his eyes. "Father, we thank thee for the blessings we are about to receive and we dedicate them to Thy service. Starling is a big girl to be fucking her daddy even if she is southern. Please forgive her for that and bring her to my service. In Jesus' name, amen."

Starling noted that Dr. Lecter kept his eyes piously closed throughout the prayer.

She felt quick and calm. "*Paul*, I have to tell you, the Apostle *Paul*, couldn't have done better. He hated women too. He should have been named *Appall*."

"You really blew it this time, Starling. You'll never be reinstated."

"Was that a *job* offer you worked into the blessing? I never saw such tact."

"I'm going to Congress." Krendler smiled unpleasantly. "Come around the campaign headquarters, I might find something for you to do. You could be an office girl. Can you type and file?"

"Certainly."

"Can you take dictation?"

"I use voice-recognition software," Starling said. She continued in a judicious tone. "If you'll excuse me for talking shop at the table, you aren't fast enough to steal in Congress. You can't make up for a second-rate intelligence just by playing dirty. You'd last longer as a big crook's gofer."

"Don't wait on us, Mr. Krendler," Dr. Lecter urged. "Have some of your broth while it's hot." He raised the covered *potager* and straw to Krendler's lips.

Krendler made a face. "That soup's not very good."

"Actually, it's more of a parsley and thyme infusion," the doctor said, "and more for our sake than yours. Have another few swallows, and let it circulate."

Starling apparently was weighing an issue, using her palms like the Scales of Justice. "You know, Mr. Krendler, every time you ever leered at me, I had the nagging feeling I had done something to deserve it." She moved her palms up and down judiciously, a motion similar to passing a Slinky back and forth. "I *didn't* deserve it. Every time you wrote something negative in my personnel folder, I resented it, but still I searched myself. I doubted myself for a moment, and tried to scratch this tiny itch that said Daddy knows best.

"You *don't* know best, Mr. Krendler. In fact, you don't know anything." Starling had a sip of her splendid white Burgundy and said to Dr. Lecter, "I *love* this. But I think we should take it off the ice." She turned again, attentive hostess, to her guest. "You are forever an . . . an *oaf*, and beneath notice," she said in a pleasant tone. "And that's enough about you at this lovely table. Since you are Dr. Lecter's guest, I hope you enjoy the meal."

"*Who are you anyway?*" Krendler said. "You're not Starling. You've got the spot on your face, but you're not Starling."

Dr. Lecter added shallots to his hot browned butter and at the instant their perfume rose, he put in minced caper berries. He set the saucepan off the fire, and set his sauté pan on the heat. From the sideboard he took a large crystal bowl of ice cold water and a silver salver and put them beside Paul Krendler.

"I had some plans for that smart mouth," Krendler said, "but I'd *never* hire you now. Who gave you an appointment anyway?"

"I don't expect you to change your attitude entirely as the other Paul did, Mr. Krendler," Dr. Lecter said. "You are not on the road to Damascus, or even on the road to the Verger helicopter."

Dr. Lecter took off Krendler's runner's headband as you would remove the rubber band from a tin of caviar.

"All we ask is that you keep an open mind." Carefully, using both hands, Dr. Lecter lifted off the top of Krendler's head, put it on the salver and removed it to the sideboard. Hardly a drop of blood fell from the clean incision, the major blood vessels having been tied and the others neatly sealed under a local anesthetic, and the skull sawn around in the kitchen a half-hour before the meal.

Dr. Lecter's method in removing the top of Krendler's skull was as old as Egyptian medicine, except that he had the advantage of an autopsy saw with cranial blade, a skull key and better anesthetics. The brain itself feels no pain.

The pinky-gray dome of Krendler's brain was visible above his truncated skull.

Standing over Krendler with an instrument resembling a tonsil spoon, Dr. Lecter removed a slice of Krendler's prefrontal lobe, then another, until he had four. Krendler's eyes looked up as though he were following what was going on. Dr. Lecter placed the slices in the bowl of ice water, the water acidulated with the juice of a lemon, in order to firm them.

"Would you like to swing on a star," Krendler sang abruptly. *"Carry moonbeams home in a jar."*

In classic cuisine, brains are soaked and then pressed and chilled overnight to firm them. In dealing with the item absolutely fresh, the challenge is to prevent the material from simply disintegrating into a handful of lumpy gelatin.

With splendid dexterity, the doctor brought the firmed slices to a plate, dredged them lightly in seasoned flour, and then in fresh brioche crumbs.

He grated a fresh black truffle into his sauce and finished it with a squeeze of lemon juice.

Quickly he sautéed the slices until they were just brown on each side.

"Smells great!" Krendler said.

Dr. Lecter placed the browned brains on broad croutons on the warmed plates, and dressed them with the sauce and truffle slices. A garnish of parsley and whole caper berries with their stems, and a single nasturtium blossom on watercress to achieve a little height, completed his presentation.

"How is it?" Krendler asked, once again behind the flowers and speaking immoderately loud, as persons with lobotomies are prone to do.

"Really excellent," Starling said. "I've never had caper berries before."

Dr. Lecter found the shine of butter sauce on her lip intensely moving.

Krendler sang behind the greens, mostly day-care songs, and he invited requests.

Oblivious to him, Dr. Lecter and Starling discussed Mischa. Starling knew of the doctor's sister's fate from their conversations about loss, but now the doctor spoke in a hopeful way about her possible return. It did not seem unreasonable to Starling on this evening that Mischa might return.

She expressed the hope that she might meet Mischa.

"You could never answer the phone in my office. You sound like a cornbread country cunt," Krendler yelled through the flowers.

"See if I sound like Oliver Twist when I ask for *MORE*," Starling replied, releasing in Dr. Lecter glee he could scarcely contain.

A second helping consumed most of the frontal lobe, back nearly to the premotor cortex. Krendler was reduced to irrelevant observations about things in his immediate vision and the tuneless recitation behind the flowers of a lengthy lewd verse called "Shine."

Absorbed in their talk, Starling and Lecter were no more disturbed than they would have been by the singing of happy birthday at another table in a restaurant, but when Krendler's volume became intrusive, Dr. Lecter retrieved his crossbow from a corner.

"I want you to listen to the sound of this stringed instrument, Clarice."

He waited for a moment of silence from Krendler and shot a bolt across the table through the tall flowers.

"That particular frequency of the crossbow string, should you hear it again in any context, means only your complete freedom and peace and self-sufficiency," Dr. Lecter said.

The feathers and part of the shaft remained on the visible side of the flower arrangement and moved at more or less the pace of a baton directing a heart. Krendler's voice stopped at once and in a few beats the baton stopped too.

"It's about a D below middle C?" Starling said.

"Exactly."

A moment later Krendler made a gargling sound behind the flowers. It was only a spasm in his voice box caused by the increasing acidity of his blood, he being newly dead.

"Let's have our next course," the doctor said, "a little sorbet to refresh our palates before the quail. No, no, don't get up. Mr. Krendler will help me clear, if you'll excuse him."

It was all quickly done. Behind the screen of the flowers, Dr. Lecter simply scraped the plates into Krendler's skull and stacked them in his lap. He replaced the top of Krendler's head and, picking up the rope attached to a dolly beneath his chair, towed him away to the kitchen.

There Dr. Lecter rewound his crossbow. Conveniently it used the same battery pack as his autopsy saw.

The quails' skins were crisp and they were stuffed with foie gras. Dr. Lecter talked about Henry VIII as composer and Starling told him about computer-aided design in engine sounds, the replication of pleasing frequencies.

Dessert would be in the drawing room, Dr. Lecter announced.

A SOUFFLÉ and glasses of Château d'Yquem before the fire in the drawing room, coffee ready on a side table at Starling's elbow.

Fire dancing in the golden wine, its perfume over the deep tones of the burning log.

They talked about teacups and time, and the rule of disorder.

"And so I came to believe," Dr. Lecter was saying, "that there had to be a place in the world for Mischa, a prime place vacated for her, and I came to think, Clarice, that the best place in the world was yours."

The firelight did not plumb the depths of her bodice as satisfactorily as the candlelight had done, but it was wonderful playing on the bones of her face.

She considered a moment. "Let me ask you this, Dr. Lecter. If a prime place in the world is required for Mischa, and I'm not saying it isn't, what's the matter with *your* place? It's well occupied and I know you would never deny her. She and I could be like sisters. And if, as you say, there's room in me for my father, why is there not room in you for Mischa?"

Dr. Lecter seemed pleased, whether with the idea, or with Starling's resource is impossible to say. Perhaps he felt a vague concern that he had built better than he knew.

When she replaced her glass on the table beside her, she pushed off her coffee cup and it shattered on the hearth. She did not look down at it.

Dr. Lecter watched the shards, and they were still.

"I don't think you have to make up your mind right this minute," Starling said. Her eyes and the cabochons shone in the firelight. A sigh from the fire, the warmth of the fire through her gown, and there came to Starling a passing memory—*Dr. Lecter, so long ago, asking Senator Martin if she breast-fed her daughter.* A jeweled movement turning in Starling's unnatural calm: For an instant many windows in her mind aligned and she saw far across her own experience. She said, "Hannibal Lecter, did your mother feed you at her breast?"

"Yes."

"Did you ever feel that you had to relinquish the breast to Mischa? Did you ever feel you were required to give it up for her?"

A beat. "I don't recall that, Clarice. If I gave it up, I did it gladly."

Clarice Starling reached her cupped hand into the deep neckline of her gown and freed her breast, quickly peaky in the open air. "You don't have to give up this one," she said. Looking always into his eyes, with her trigger finger she took warm Château d'Yquem from her mouth and a thick sweet drop suspended from her nipple like a golden cabochon and trembled with her breathing.

He came swiftly from his chair to her, went on a knee before her chair, and bent to her coral and cream in the firelight his dark sleek head.

Buenos Aires, Argentina, three years later:

Barney and Lillian Hersh walked near the Obelisk on the Avenida 9 de Julio in the early evening. Ms. Hersh is a lecturer at London University, on sabbatical. She and Barney met in the anthropology museum in Mexico City. They like each other and have been traveling together two weeks, trying it a day at a time, and it is getting to be more and more fun. They are not getting tired of one another.

They had arrived in Buenos Aires too late in the afternoon to go to the Museo Nacional, where a Vermeer was on loan. Barney's mission to see every Vermeer in the world amused Lillian Hersh and it did not get in the way of a good time. He had seen a quarter of the Vermeers already, and there were plenty to go.

They were looking for a pleasant café where they could eat outside.

Limousines were backed up at the Teatro Colón, Buenos Aires' spectacular opera house. They stopped to watch the opera lovers go in.

Tamerlane was playing with an excellent cast, and a Buenos Aires opening night crowd is worth seeing.

"Barney, you up for the opera? I think you'd like it. I'll spring."

It amused him when she used American slang. "If you'll walk me through it, *I'll* spring," Barney said. "You think they'll let us in?"

At that moment a Mercedes Maybach, deep blue and silver, whispered up to the curb. A doorman hurried to open the car.

A man, slender and elegant in white tie, got out and handed out a woman. The sight of her raised an admiring murmur in the crowd around the entrance. Her hair was a shapely platinum helmet and she wore a soft sheath of coral frosted with an overlayer of tulle. Emeralds flashed green at her throat. Barney saw her only briefly, through the heads of the crowd, and she and her gentleman were swept inside.

Barney saw the man better. His head was sleek as an otter and his nose had an imperial arch like that of Perón. His carriage made him seem taller than he was.

"Barney? Oh, Barney," Lillian was saying, "when you come back to yourself, if you ever do, tell me if you'd like to go to the opera. If they'll let us in *in mufti*. There, I said it, even if it's not precisely apt—I've always wanted to say I was *in mufti*."

When Barney did not ask what mufti was, she glanced at him sidelong. He always asked everything.

"Yes," Barney said absently. "*I'll* spring." Barney had plenty of money. He was careful with it, but not cheap. Still, the only tickets available were in the rafters among the students.

Anticipating the altitude of his seats, he rented field glasses in the lobby.

The enormous theater is a mix of Italian Renaissance, Greek and French styles, lavish with brass and gilt and red plush. Jewels winked in the crowd like flashbulbs at a ball game.

Lillian explained the plot before the overture began, talking in his ear quietly.

Just before the houselights went down, sweeping the house from the cheap seats, Barney found them, the platinum blonde lady and her escort. They had just come through the gold curtains into their ornate box beside the stage. The emeralds at her throat glittered in the brilliant houselights as she took her seat.

Barney had only glimpsed her right profile as she entered the opera. He could see the left one now.

The students around them, veterans of the high-altitude seats, had brought all manner of viewing aids. One student had a powerful spotting scope so long that it disturbed the hair of the person in front of him. Barney traded glasses with him to look at the distant box. It was hard to find the box again in the long tube's limited field of vision, but when he found it, the couple was startlingly close.

The woman's cheek had a beauty spot on it, in the position the French call "Courage." Her eyes swept over the house, swept over his section and moved on. She seemed animated and in expert control of her coral mouth. She leaned to her escort and said something, and they laughed together. She put her hand on his hand and held his thumb.

"*Starling*," Barney said under his breath.

"What?" Lillian whispered.

Barney had a lot of trouble following the first act of the opera. As soon as the lights came up for the first intermission, he raised his glass to the box again. The gentleman took a champagne flute from a waiter's tray and handed it to the lady, and took a glass himself. Barney zoomed in on his profile, the shape of his ears.

He traced the length of the woman's exposed arms. They were bare and unmarked and had muscle tone, in his experienced eye.

As Barney watched, the gentleman's head turned as though to catch a distant sound, turned in Barney's direction. The gentleman raised opera glasses to his eyes. Barney could have sworn the glasses were aimed at him. He held his program in front of his face and hunkered down in his seat to try to be about average height.

"Lillian," he said. "I want you to do me a great big favor."

"Um," she said. "If it's like some of the others, I'd better hear it first."

"We're leaving when the lights go down. Fly with me to Rio tonight. No questions asked."

The Vermeer in Buenos Aires is the only one Barney never saw.

FOLLOW THIS handsome couple from the opera? All right, but very carefully . . .

At the millennium, Buenos Aires is possessed by the tango and the night has a pulse. The Mercedes, windows down to let in the music from the dance clubs, purrs through the Recoleta district to the Avenida Alvear and disappears into the courtyard of an exquisite Beaux Arts building near the French Embassy.

The air is soft and a late supper is laid on the terrace of the top floor, but the servants are gone.

Morale is high among the servants in this house, but there is an iron discipline among them. They are forbidden to enter the top floor of the mansion before noon. Or after service of the first course at dinner.

Dr. Lecter and Clarice Starling often talk at dinner in languages other than Starling's native English. She had college French and Spanish to build on, and she has found she has a good ear. They speak Italian a lot at mealtimes; she finds a curious freedom in the visual nuances of the language.

Sometimes our couple dances at dinnertime. Sometimes they do not finish dinner.

Their relationship has a great deal to do with the penetration of Clarice Starling, which she avidly welcomes and encourages. It has much to do with the envelopment of Hannibal Lecter, far beyond the bounds of his experience. It is possible that Clarice Starling could frighten him. Sex is a splendid structure they add to every day.

Clarice Starling's memory palace is building as well. It shares some rooms with Dr. Lecter's own memory palace—he has discovered her in there several times—but her own palace grows on its own. It is full of new things. She can visit her father there. Hannah is at pasture there. Jack Crawford is there, when she chooses to see him bent over his desk—after Crawford was home for a month from the hospital, the chest pains came again in the night. Instead of calling an ambulance and going through it all again, he chose simply to roll over to the solace of his late wife's side of the bed.

Starling learned of Crawford's death during one of Dr. Lecter's regular visits to the FBI public Web site to admire his likeness among the Ten Most Wanted. The picture the Bureau is using of Dr. Lecter remains a comfortable two faces behind.

After Starling read Jack Crawford's obituary, she walked by herself for most of a day, and she was glad to come home at evening.

A year ago she had one of her own emeralds set in a ring. It is engraved inside with AM-CS. Ardelia Mapp received it in an untraceable wrapper with a note. *Dear Ardelia, I'm fine and better than fine. Don't look for me. I love you. I'm sorry I scared you. Burn this. Starling.*

Mapp took the ring to the Shenandoah River where Starling used to run. She walked a long way with it clutched in her hand, angry, hot-eyed, ready to throw the ring in the water, imagining it flashing in the air and the small plop. In the end she put it on her finger and shoved her fist in her pocket. Mapp doesn't cry much. She walked a long way, until she could be quiet. It was dark when she got back to her car.

It is hard to know what Starling remembers of the old life, what she chooses to keep. The drugs that held her in the first days have had no part in their lives for a long time. Nor the long talks with a single light source in the room.

Occasionally, on purpose, Dr. Lecter drops a teacup to shatter on the floor. He is satisfied when it does not gather itself together. For many months now, he has not seen Mischa in his dreams.

Someday perhaps a cup will come together. Or somewhere Starling may hear a crossbow string and come to some unwilled awakening, if indeed she even sleeps.

We'll withdraw now, while they are dancing on the terrace—the wise Barney has already left town and we must follow his example. For either of them to discover us would be fatal.

We can only learn so much and live.

ACKNOWLEDGMENTS

In trying to understand the structure of Dr. Lecter's memory palace, I was aided by Frances A. Yates's remarkable book *The Art of Memory*, as well as Jonathan D. Spence's *The Memory Palace of Matteo Ricci*.

Robert Pinsky's translation of *Dante's Inferno* was a boon and a pleasure to use, as were the annotations of Nicole Pinsky. The term "festive skin" is Pinsky's translation of Dante.

"In the garden of the hurricane's eye" is John Ciardi's phrase and the title of one of his poems.

The first lines of poetry Clarice Starling recalls in the asylum are from T.S. Eliot's "Burnt Norton," *Four Quartets*.

My thanks to Pace Barnes for her encouragement, support and wise counsel.

Carole Baron, my publisher, editor and friend, helped me make this a better book.

Athena Varounis and Bill Trible in the United States and Ruggero Perugini in Italy showed me the best and brightest in law enforcement. None of them is a character in this book, nor is any other living person. The wickedness herein I took from my own stock.

Niccolo Capponi shared with me his deep knowledge of Florence and its art and allowed Dr. Lecter to use his family palazzo. My thanks also to Robert Held for his scholarship and to Caroline Michahelles for much Florentine insight.

The staff of Carnegie Public Library in Coahoma County, Mississippi, looked up things for years. Thank you.

I owe a lot to Marguerite Schmitt: With one white truffle and the magic in her heart and hands, she introduced us to the wonders of Florence. It is too late to thank Marguerite; in this moment of completion I want to say her name.